THE WOMEN'S ROOM

'Compulsory reading' Fay Weldon

'Her dialogue, her characterizations, her knowledge of the changing relationships, sexual and otherwise, between men and women in a complex world of shifting values are all extraordinary' *Publishers Weekly*

'It's fierceness, its relentless refusal to compromise are as stirring as a marching song' *Washington Post*

'A courageous, powerful, honest novel' *Chicago Tribune*

'An experience not to be missed' *San Francisco Chronicle*

'A real page-turner' *Philadelphia Inquirer*

The Women's Room

MARILYN FRENCH

SPHERE BOOKS LIMITED
30/32 Gray's Inn Road, London WC1X 8JL

First published in Great Britain by André Deutsch Ltd 1978
Copyright © Marilyn French 1977
First published by Sphere Books Ltd 1978

Set in Intertype Times

Printed in Great Britain by
Hazell Watson & Viney Ltd
Aylesbury, Bucks

To Isabel, to Janet ——
sisters, friends

CHAPTER ONE

1

Mira was hiding in the ladies' room. She called it that, even though someone had scratched out the word *ladies'* in the sign on the door, and written *women's* underneath. She called it that out of thirty-eight years of habit, and until she saw the cross-out on the door, had never thought about it. 'Ladies' room' was an euphemism, she supposed, and she disliked euphemisms on principle. However, she also detested what she called vulgarity, and had never in her life, even when handling it, uttered the word *shit*. But here she was at the age of thirty-eight huddled for safety in a toilet booth in the basement of Sever Hall, gazing at, no, studying that word and others of the same genre, scrawled on the gray enameled door and walls.

She was perched, fully clothed, on the edge of the open toilet seat, feeling stupid and helpless, and constantly looking at her watch. It would all have been redeemed, even translated into excitement, had there been some grim-faced Walter Matthau in a trench coat, his hand in a gun-swollen pocket, or some wild-eyed Anthony Perkins in a turtleneck, his itching strangler's hands clenching and unclenching – someone glamorous and terrifying at any rate – waiting for her outside in the hall, if she had been sitting in panic searching for another way out. But of course if that were the case, there would also be a cool and desperate Cary Grant or Burt Lancaster sliding along the walls of another hallway, waiting for Walter to show himself. And that by itself, she thought mournfully, feeling somehow terribly put upon, would have been enough. If she had one of them, anyone at all, waiting for her at home, she would not be hiding in a toilet booth in the basement of Sever Hall. She would have been upstairs in a corridor with the other students, leaning against a wall with her books at her feet, or strolling past the unseeing faces. She could have transcended, knowing she had one of them at home, and could therefore move alone in a crowd. She puzzled over that paradox, but only briefly. The graffiti were too interesting.

'Down with capitalism and the fucking military-industrial complex. KILL ALL FASCIST PIGS!'

This had been answered. 'You simplify too much. New ways must be found to kill pigs: out of their death new pigs spring as armed men sprouted from the bulls' teeth planted by that mcp Jason. Pigs batten on pig blood. The way is slow and hard. We must cleanse our minds of all the old shit, we must work in silence, exile, and cunning like that mcp Joyce. We must have a revolution of sensibility.'

A third party entered the argument in purple ink:

'Stay in your cocoon. Who needs you? Those who are not with us are against us. Anyone who supports the status quo is part of the problem. THERE IS NO TIME. THE REVOLUTION IS HERE! KILL PIGS!'

Writer No. 2 was apparently fond of this booth and had returned, for the next entry was in her handwriting and in the same pen:

'Those who live by the sword die by the sword.'

Wild printing in the purple felt-tip followed this in great sprawling letters:

'FUCKING CHRISTIAN IDIOT! TAKE YOUR MAXIMS AND STUFF THEM! THERE IS ONLY POWER! POWER TO THE PEOPLE! POWER TO THE POOR! WE ARE DYING BY THE SWORD NOW!'

The last outburst ended that symposium, but there were others like it scrawled on the side walls. Almost all of them were political. There were pasted-on notices of SDS meetings, meetings of Bread and Roses, and Daughters of Bilitris. Mira withdrew her eyes from a crude drawing of female genitalia with 'Cunt is Beautiful' scratched beneath it. She presumed, at least, that it was a drawing of female genitalia, although it looked

8

remarkably like a wide-petaled flower. She wasn't sure because she had never seen her own, that being part of the anatomy that did not present itself directly to the vision.

She looked at her watch again: she could leave now. She stood and from force of habit turned to flush the unused toilet. On the wall behind it someone had printed great jagged letters in what looked like nail polish. The red enamel had dripped and each stroke had a thick pearl at its base. It looked as if it had been written in blood. SOME DEATHS TAKE FOREVER, it read. She drew her breath in sharply and left the booth.

It was 1968.

2

She washed her hands vigorously, also from force of habit, and combed her hair, which was arranged in careful curls. She stood back, examining it in the glaring light of the lavatory. It looked a strange color. Since she had stopped dyeing it last year, it had grown out not just grayer, but with a mousy brown tinge, so she had been tinting it, and this time it had come out perhaps a bit too orange. She moved closer to the mirror and checked her eyebrows and the blue eye shadow she had applied only an hour before. Both were still okay.

She stepped back again and tried to see her whole self. She couldn't do it. Ever since she had changed her style of dress – that is, ever since she had been at Harvard – her self refused to coalesce in the mirror. She could see bits and pieces – hair, eyes, legs – but the pieces wouldn't come together. The hair and eyes went together, but the mouth was wrong; it had changed during the past years. The legs were all right, but didn't go with the bulky shoes and the pleated skirt. They looked too thin under the thicker body – yet she was the same weight now she'd been for the past ten years. She began to feel something rising in her chest, and hastily looked away from the mirror. This was no time to get upset. Then she turned back jerkily, looking at nothing,

9

pulled out her lipstick and applied a line of it to her lower lip, her eyes careful to look at nothing but the mouth. In spite of herself, however, her eyes caught her whole face, and in a moment her head was full of tears. She leaned her hot forehead against the cool tile wall, then remembered that this was a public place full of other people's germs, and straightened up hurriedly and left the room.

She climbed up the three flights of ancient, creaky stairs, reflecting that the ladies' room was in an inconvenient location because it had been added long after the building was erected. The school had been planned for men, and there were places, she had been told, where women were simply not permitted to go. It was odd. Why? she wondered. Women were so unimportant anyway, why would anyone bother to keep them out? She arrived in the corridor a little late. No one was left in the hallway, lingering, loitering outside classroom doors. The blank eyes, the empty faces, the young bodies that ten minutes earlier had paced its length, were gone. It was these that, passing her without seeing her, seeing her without looking at her, had driven her into hiding. For they had made her feel invisible. And when all you have is a visible surface, invisibility is death. Some deaths take forever, she found herself repeating as she walked into the classroom.

3

Perhaps you find Mira a little ridiculous. I do myself. But I also have some sympathy for her, more than you, probably. You think she was vain and shallow. I suppose those are words that could have been applied to her, but they are not the first ones that spring to my mind. I think she was ridiculous for hiding in the toilet, but I like her better for that than for the meanness of her mouth, which she herself perceived, and tried to cover up with lipstick. Her meanness was of the tut-tut variety; she slammed genteel doors in her head, closing out charity. But I also feel a little sorry for her, at least I did then. Not anymore.

Because in a way it doesn't matter whether you open doors or close them, you still end up in a box. I have failed to ascertain an objective difference between one way of living and another. The only difference I can see is between varying levels of happiness, and I cringe when I say that. If old Schopenhauer is right, happiness is not a human possibility, since it means the absence of pain, which, as an uncle of mine used to say, only occurs when you're dead or dead drunk. There's Mira with all her closed doors, and here's me with all my open ones, and we're both miserable.

I spend a lot of time alone here, walking along the beach in any weather, and I think over and over about Mira and the others, Val, Isolde, Kyla, Clarissa, Grete, back at Harvard in 1968. That year itself was an open door, but a magical one; once you went through it, you could never return. You stand just beyond it, gazing back at what you have left, and it looks like a country in a fairy-tale book, all little patches and squares of color, fields and farms and castles with turrets and pennons and crenellated parapets. The houses are all cozy, thatched-roof cottages, slowly burnishing in the afternoon sun, and the people who live in castle or cottage have the same simple outlines and offer themselves for immediate recognition. A good prince or princess or fairy has blond hair and blue eyes, and bad queens and stepmothers have black hair. I think there was one girl who had black hair and was still good, but she's the exception that proves the rule. Good fairies wear pale blue gauzy tutus and carry golden wands; bad ones wear black and are humpbacked and have big chins and long noses. There are no bad kings in fairyland, although there are a few giants of unsavory reputation. There are lots of wicked stepmothers and old witches and crones, though. When I was a child, fairyland as it appeared in the books was the place I wanted to live, and I judged my surroundings according to how well they matched it: beauty was fairyland, not truth. I used to try to concentrate hard

11

enough to make fairyland come true in my head. If I had been able to do it, I would gladly have deserted the real world to go there, willing abandoning my parents. Perhaps you call that incipient schizophrenia, but it seems to me that that's what I did in the end, lived in fairyland where there are only five basic colors, clear lines, and no beer cans cluttering up the grass.

One reason I like the Maine coast so much is that it allows so little room for such fantasies. The wind is hard and cold and raw; my face is a little chapped all winter. The sea pounds in and no matter how many times I see it it excites me the same way the skyline of New York does, no matter how many times I see that. The words are trite – grand, powerful, overwhelming – oh, it doesn't matter what one calls it. The thing is as close as I can come to a notion of God. The sheer naked power of those great waves constantly rolling up with such an ominous rumble, hitting against the rocks and sending up skyfuls of white froth. It is so powerful and so beautiful and so terrifying at the same time that for me it is a symbol of what life is all about. And there's the sand and the rocks and all the life they foster – snails, mussels. I often smile to myself, calling the rocks snail tenements, shellfish ghettos. They are, you know: the snails are more crowded together there than the people in Hong Kong. The sand wasn't designed for easy walking, and the gray Maine sky seems to open out into the void itself. This sky has no notion of – it can never have been in – brilliant lands where olives grow and tomatoes turn blood red and oranges shine among the green leaves of trees in front yards behind white stucco walls dusty under the sun, and the sky is nearly as blue as the sea. Here, everything is gray: sea, sky, rocks. This sky looks only to the north, to icy poles; you can almost see the color fading and fading as the sky arches northward, until there is no color at all. The white world of the Snow Queen.

Well, I said I was going to try to avoid fairy-tale fantasies, but I seem to be incorrigible. So I'm feeling alone and a little superior standing in this doorway looking

12

back at fairy-tale land and almost enjoying my pain. Maybe I should turn around. But I can't, I can't see ahead yet, only backward. Anyway all of this is ridiculous. Because I was on my way to saying that Mira had lived all her life in fairy-tale land and when she went through the doorway, her head was still full of fairyland images, she had no notion of reality. But obviously she did, fairyland was her reality. So if you want to stand in judgment on her you have to determine whether her reality was the same as other people's, i.e., was she crazy? In ther economy, the wicked queen was known by her face and body shape, and the good fairy by hers. The good fairy showed up whenever she was needed, never took a dime for all her wand-waving, and then conveniently disappeared. I leave it to you to decide on Mira's sanity.

4

I no longer try to label things. Here, where everything seems so arid and austere, the place teems with life: in the sea, in the sky, on the rocks. I come here to get away from a greater emptiness. Inland a couple of miles stands the third-rate community college where I teach courses like 'Fairy Tale and Folklore' (can't get away from it!) and 'Grammar 12,' mostly to female students who aim to do well enough here to get into the state college and acquire teacher certification and the joys of the ten-month year. Wait, I think, just wait and see how much joy it holds.

Look at those snail clusters on that rock. There are thousands of snails, and mussels too, among the heaped boulders, clustering together like inhabitants of an ancient city. They are gorgeous, they shimmer with colors they've had for thousands of years: red and gold and blue and white and orange. They all live together. I find that extraordinary. Each one occupies its own tiny space, no one seems to push around for more room. Do you suppose there are snails with too little room who just die? It is clear that their life must be mainly interior. I like to come here and stare at them. I never touch them. But as I look, I keep thinking that they don't have to create their order, they don't have to create their lives, those things are just programmed into them. All they have to do is live. Is that an illusion, do you suppose?

I feel terribly alone. I have enough room, but it's empty. Or maybe I don't, maybe room means more than space. Clarissa once said that isolation was insanity. She never says anything carelessly, her words come out of her mouth like fruit that is perfectly ripened. Unripe fruit she doesn't deal in: that's why she is silent so often. So I guess isolation is insanity. But what can I do? At the one or two parties a year I'm invited to, I have to listen to academic gossip, snarling retorts (never made in fact) to the president, nasty cracks about the mediocrity of the dean. In a place like Harvard, academic gossip is pretentious and hollow, full of name dropping and craven awe, or else it oozes complacency, the invulnerability of the elect. In a place like this, where everyone feels a loser, the gossip is mean-minded and full of that kind of hate and contempt that is really disgust at one's own failure in life. There aren't many single people here except for a few very young male instructors. There are damned few women, none single, except for one sixty-year-old widow who does needlepoint at faculty meetings. I mean, not everything is in your head, is it? Do I have to accept total responsibility for my fate? I don't think it's my fault that I'm lonely. People say – well, Iso wrote (she would!) – that I should drive down to Boston on weekends and go to the singles bars. You know, she could do it and she'd find someone interesting. But not me. I know it. I'd meet some middle-aged swinger with a deep tan and sideburns (not quite a beard) and a mod suit (pink jacket, maroon pants) and a belly kept in by three hours a week at the gym or the tennis club, and I'd die of his emptiness even more than I'm dying of my own.

So I walk the beach. I've been coming out here all year, since last September, with a kerchief tied around my head, blue jeans splashed with the paint I used to try to make my apartment a bit more livable, an embroidered poncho Kyla brought me from Mexico, and in the winter months, a heavy, lined nylon jacket over that. I know I am already pointed to, whispered about as a madwoman. It is so easy for a woman to seem mad if she once deserts The Image, as Mira did when she ridiculously went out and bought short pleated skirts because she was back in college. But on the other hand, maybe they are right, maybe I am mad. There aren't too many people here – a few surfcasters, some women with children, people like me who just come down to walk. But they all look at me strangely.

So they look at me strangely: I have other problems. Because the school year ended last week and in the flurry of papers and exams I didn't have to think about it, and then suddenly it was there – two and a half whole months with nothing to do. The joys of the ten-month year. To me it looked like the Sahara Desert, stretching on and on under the crazy sun, and empty, empty. Well, I thought I'll plan my courses for next year; I'll read some more fairy tales (Fairy Tales and Folklore), try to understand Chomsky better (Grammar 12), try to find a better writing handbook (Composition 1–2).

Oh God.

It comes to me that this is the first time in years, maybe in my life, that I am completely alone with nothing to do. Maybe that is why everything comes crowding in on me now. These things that jar their way into my mind make me think that my loneliness may not be entirely the fault of the place, that somehow or other – although I can't understand it – I have chosen it.

I have bad dreams, dreams full of blood. I am pursued, night after night, and night after night I turn and strike out at my pursuer, I smash, I stab. That sounds like anger. It sounds like hate. But hate is an emotion I have never permitted myself. Where could it come from?

As I walk along the beach, my memory keeps going back to Mira those first weeks in Cambridge, tottering

15

around on her high heels (she always walked shakily in high heels, but she always wore them) in a three-piece wool knit suit, with her hair set and sprayed, looking almost in panic at the faces that passed her, desperate for a sharp glance, an appraisng smile that would assure her she existed. When I think of her, my belly twists a little with contempt. But how do I dare to feel that for her, for that woman so much like me, so much like my mother?

Do you? You know her: she's that blonded made-up matron, a little tipsy with her second manhattan, playing bridge at the country club. In the Moslem countries, they make their women wear jubbah and yashmak. This makes them invisible, white wraiths drifting through streets buying a bit of fish or some vegetables, turning into dark narrow alleys and entering doors that slam shut loudly, reverberating among the ancient stones. People don't see them, they are less differentiated than the dogs that run among the fruit carts. Only the forms are different here. You don't really see the woman standing at the glove or stocking counter, poking among cereal boxes, loading six steaks into her shopping cart. You see her clothes, her sprayed helmet of hair, and you stop taking her seriously. Her appearance proclaims her respectability, which is to say she's just like all other women who aren't whores. But maybe she is, you know. Distinction by dress isn't what it used to be. Women are capable of anything. It doesn't really matter. Wife or whore, women are the most scorned class in America. You may hate niggers and PRs and geeks, but you're a little frightened of them. Women don't get even the respect of fear.

What's to fear, after all, in a silly woman always running for her mirror to see who she is? Mira lived by her mirror as much as the Queen in *Snow White*. A lot of us did: we absorbed and believed the things people said about us. I always took the psychological quizzes in the magazines: are you a good wife? a good mother? Are you keeping the romance in your marriage? I believed Philip Wylie when he said mothers were a generation of

16

vipers, and I swore never, never to act that way. I believed Sigmund's 'anatomy is destiny' and tried to develop a sympathetic, responsive nature. I remember Martha saying that she hadn't had a real mother; her mother did nothing in the way women were supposed to — she collected old newspapers and pieces of string and never dusted and took Martha to a cheap cafeteria to eat every night. So when Martha got married and tried to make friends with other couples, she didn't know how. She didn't know you were supposed to serve drinks and food. She just sat there with George, talking to them. People always left early, they never came back, they never invited her. 'So I went out and bought *The Ladies' Home Journal* and *Good Housekeeping*. I did it for years religiously. I read them like the Bible, trying to find out how to be a woman.'

I hear Martha's voice often as I walk along the beach. And others' too – Lily, Val, Kyla. I sometimes think I've swallowed every woman I ever knew. My head is full of voices. They blend with the wind and the sea as I walk the beach, as if they were disembodied forces of nature, a tornado whirling around me. I feel as if I were a medium and a whole host of departed spirits has descended on me clamoring to be let out.

So this morning (shades of the past!) I decided on a project to fill this vacant stretching summer. I will write it all down, go back as far as I have to, and try to make some sense out of it. But I'm not a writer. I teach grammar (and I hate it) and composition, but as anyone who's ever taken a comp course knows, you don't have to know anything about writing to teach it. In fact, the less you know the better, because then you can go by rules, whereas if you really know how to write, rules about leading sentences and paragraphs and so forth don't exist. Writing is hard for me. The best I can do is put down bits and pieces, fragments of time, fragments of lives.

I am going to try to let the voices out. Maybe they will help me understand how they ended as they did, how I ended here feeling engulfed and isolated at the same

17

time. Somehow it all starts with Mira. How did she manage to get herself, at the age of thirty-eight, to hide in that toilet?

Mira was an independent baby, fond of removing her clothes and taking a stroll of a summer's day to the local candy store. The second time she was returned home by a policeman she had directed, Mrs. Ward began to tie her up. She did not mean to be unkind: Mira had been crossing a busy boulevard. She used a long rope, so Mira could still move around, and tied it to the handle of the front door. Mira continued in her disconcerting habit of removing all her clothes, however. Mrs. Ward did not believe in corporal punishment and used stern reproach and withdrawal of affection instead. It worked. Mira had trouble removing all her clothes on her wedding night. In time, Mira's fury and tears at being tied up abated, and she learned to operate within a small space, digging into things since she was not permitted to range outward. The leash was then removed, and Mira showed herself to be a docile and even timid child, only somewhat given to sullenness.

She was a bright child: she finished all the textbooks on the first day of school and, bored, spent the rest of the term enlivening her classmates. The solution decided upon was to move her ahead, into a class 'more on her level,' as the teacher put it. She was moved ahead several times, but never found such a class. What she did find was classmates years older, inches taller, pounds heavier, and with a world of sophistication greater than hers. She could not talk to them, and retreated into novels she kept hidden in her desk. She even read walking to and from school.

Mrs. Ward, convinced that Mira was headed for great things, which meant a good marriage, to that good woman, scraped together money to send her for lessons. She had two years of elocution, two years of dancing school, two years of piano, and two years of water-color painting. (Mrs. Ward had loved the novels of Jane Austen in her youth.) At home, Mrs. Ward taught her not to cross her legs at the knee, not to climb trees with boys, not to play tag in the alley, not to speak in a raised voice, not to wear more than three pieces of jewelry at a time, and never to mix gold and silver. When these lessons had been learned, she considered Mira 'finished.'

But Mira had a private life. Being so much younger than her classmates, she had no friends, but she did not seem to care. She spent all her time reading, drawing, daydreaming. She especially loved fairy tales and myths. Then she was sent for two years of religious instruction, and her concerns changed.

At twelve, her preoccupation was determining the precise relation of God, heaven, hell, and earth. She would lie in bed at night looking out at the moon and clouds. Her bed stood beside a window, and she could lie comfortably on her pillow and gaze up and out. She tried to imagine all the people who had died, standing around up there in the sky. She tried to make them out; surely they must be peering down, longing for a friendly face? But she never caught a glimpse of one, and after reading a little history and considering how many millions of people had in fact inhabited the earth, she began to worry about the population problems of the afterworld. She imagined searching for her grandmother, dead three years now, and wandering forever through mobs of people and never finding her. Then she realized that all those people would be very heavy, that it was impossible that they should all be up there without the heavens falling down. Perhaps then there were only a few up there and all the rest were in hell.

But Mira's social studies texts implied that the poor – whom Mira already knew to be the wicked – were not really wicked at heart but only environmentally deprived. God, Mira felt sure, if He was worth anything at all, would be able to see through such injustices to the good heart, and would not consign to hell all the juvenile delinquents who appeared in the pages of the *New York Daily News* which her father brought back from the city

19

each night. This was a knotty problem, and gave her several weeks of heavy brainwork.

To solve it, she found it necessary to look into herself, not just to feel her feelings, but to examine them. She believed she really wanted to love and be loved, really wanted to be good and have the approval of her parents and her teachers. But somehow she could never do it. She was always making nasty cracks to her mother, resenting her father's fussiness; she resented that they treated her like a child. They lied to her and she knew it. She asked her mother about an ad in magazines, and her mother said she did not know what sanitary napkins were. She asked her mother what *fuck* meant; she had heard it at the schoolyard. Her mother said she did not know, but later Mira heard her whisper to Mrs. Marsh, 'How can you tell a child a thing like that?' And there were other things, things she could not put her finger on, that told her her parents' idea of being good and her own were not the same. She could not have said why, but her parents' idea of what she should do felt like someone strangling her, stifling her.

She remembered one night when she had been very fresh to her mother about something, had been fresh because she was right and her mother refused to admit it. Her mother scolded her severely, and she went into the dark porch of the house and sat on the floor sulking, feeling very wronged. She refused to go in to dinner. Her mother came out to the porch and said, 'Come on, now, Mira, don't be silly.' Her mother had never done a thing like that before. She even reached out her hand to Mira, to pull her up. But Mira sat sulking and wouldn't take the hand. Her mother went back to the dining room. Mira was near to tears. 'Why do I have to be so sullen, so stubborn?' she cried to herself, wishing she had taken the hand, wishing her mother would come back. She didn't. Mira sat on and a phrase came into her head: 'They ask too much. It costs too much.' What the cost was, she was not sure; she labeled it 'myself.' She adored her mother, and she knew that by being sullen and fresh she lost her mother's love; sometimes Mrs. Ward would

20

not speak to her for days. But she went on being bad. She was spoiled, selfish, and fresh. Her mother told her all the time.

She was bad, but she didn't want to be bad. Surely God must know that. She would be good if it didn't cost so much. And in her badness, she was not really bad. She only wanted to do what she wanted to do: was that so terrible? Surely God would understand. He did understand because they said He saw the heart. And if He understood her, then He understood everyone. And no one really wanted to be bad, everyone wanted to be loved and approved. So there was no one in hell. But if there was no one there, why have it? There was no hell.

When Mira was fourteen, she had finished all the interesting books they would allow her to take from the library – they did not permit her into the adult section. So she leafed through the unappetizing family bookcase. The family itself had no notion what was in it: their books had collected themselves, being leavings from the attics of dead relatives. Mira found Paine's *Common Sense* and Nietzsche's *Beyond Good and Evil*, as well as Radclyffe Hall's *Well of Loneliness*, a book she read with complete incomprehension.

She became convinced of the nonexistence not only of hell but also of heaven. However, without heaven a new problem arose. For if there were neither hell nor heaven, there was no final reward or punishment, and this world was all there was. But this world – even by fourteen one knows this – is a terrible place. Mira did not need to read the newspapers, to see pictures of exploding ships and burning cities, to read rumors of places called concentration camps, to realize how terrible it was. She needed only to look around her. There was brutality and cruelty everywhere: in the classroom, in the schoolyard, in the block she lived on. One day, as she walked to the grocery store on an errand, she heard a boy screaming, and the thwack of a strap in the end house. Having been brought up with gentleness, Mira was horrified and wondered why a parent would do such a thing to a child.

Had her parents done that to her, she would have been worse than she was, she knew that. She would have tried to defy them in any way she could. She would have hated them. But the terribleness of life existed even in her own home. It was a tight, silent place; there was little conversation at the dinner table. There were always tensions between her mother and father that she did not understand, and often tensions between her mother and her, as well. She felt as if she were in the middle of a war in which the weapons were like light beams, darting across the room, wounding everybody, but unable to be grasped. Mira wondered if the insides of everybody were as tumultuous and explosive as hers. She looked at her mother and saw bitter misery and resentment in her face; she saw sadness and disappointment in her father's. She herself felt wild clamorous emotions toward them both – love, hate, resentment, fury, and a crying ache for physical affection – but she never moved, never threw herself at either of them in either love or hate. The rules of the household forbade such behaviour. She wondered if anyone at all was happy. She had more reason to be than most : she was treated well, fed well, clothed well, safe. But she was a screaming battlefield. So what were other people?? If this were the only world there was, there could not be a God. No benevolent mind could have created this earth. Finally, she disposed of the problem by dispensing with the deity.

Next, she set about planning a world where unjust and cruel things could not happen. It was based on gentleness toward and freedom for children, and moved upward using intelligence as the distinguishing characteristic. The rulers of the world – for she could not conceive of a world without rulers – were its most intelligent and wisest members. Everyone had enough to eat, and no one had too much, like gross Mr. Mittlow. Although she was as yet innocent of Plato, she came up with a structure remarkably similar to his. But in a few months, she disposed of that also. It was simply that once she had the whole thing perfectly organized, it bored her. It was the same as when she used to imagine stories about her-

22

self, stories in which she was adopted, and one day a wonderful handsome man, one with a real face, not like Daddy Warbucks', but possessed of equal resources, would drive up to the Wards' front door in his long black car, and claim her. He would take her to wonderful foreign places and would love her forever. Or stories about how there really were fairies, only they didn't appear anymore because people had stopped believing in them, but she still did, so one would come to her and offer her three wishes, and she had to think a long time about those, and kept changing her mind, but finally she decided the best wishes would be that her parents could be happy and healthy and rich and if they were then they would love her and they would all live happily ever after. The trouble was the endings of these stories were always boring, and you could never go beyond the end. She tried to imagine what life would be like once everything was perfect, but she could never do it.

Later, much later, she would remember these years, and realize with astonishment that she had, by fifteen, decided on most of the assumptions she would carry for the rest of her life: that people were essentially not evil, that perfection was death, that life was better than order, and a little chaos good for the soul. Most important, this life was all. Unfortunately, she forgot these things, and had to remember them the hard way.

6

Because at the same time that she was making all these decisions, she was being undermined. The problem was sex. Couldn't you have guessed that? That Garden of Eden story hasn't hung on all these years for nothing. Even though Genesis suggests and Milton insists that it wasn't sex itself that caused the Fall, but was only the first place the reverberations were felt, we go on equating sex with fall because that's the way it happens to us. The main problem with sex, I'm convinced (and now I'm beginning to sound like Val), is that it comes on us when we are already formed. Maybe if we were fondled and

23

petted all our lives, it wouldn't be such a shock, but we aren't, at least I wasn't and Mira wasn't, and so the strong desire for bodily contact comes upon us as a violation.

At the end of her fourteenth year, Mira began to menstruate and was finally let in on the secret of sanitary napkins. Soon afterward, she began to experience strange fluidities in her body, and her mind, she was convinced, had begun to rot. She could feel the increasing corruption, but couldn't seem to do anything to counter it. The first sign was that when she lay in bed at night, trying to move ahead from her disposal of both God and Perfect Order to something more usable, she could not concentrate. Her mind wandered vaguely. She stared at the moon and thought about songs, not God. She smelled the air of the summer night and a tremendous sensation of pleasure encompassed her whole body. She was restless, could not sleep or think, and would get up and kneel on her bed, lean on the windowsill, peer out at the gently waving branches, and smell the sweet night air. She had sudden overwhelming desires to put her hand under her pajamas and rub the skin of her shoulder, her sides, the insides of her thighs. And when she did that, strange spurts would happen inside her. She would lie back and try to think, but only images rampaged through her head. These images were always, horrifyingly, of the same things. She had a code word for her decaying condition: she called it *boys*.

Now, in the past fifteen years she had lived on earth, Mira had been quite alone, had lived mostly in her head. She had despised the children she saw jumping rope or playing tag in the streets: she found their occupations stupid. She despised the empty boredom of adults' lives, gathered mainly from occasions when the Wards entertained friends, and found their conversation stupid. She respected only two people: her English teacher, Mrs. Sherman, and Friedrich Nietzsche. But of all the stupid creatures that lumbered around on earth, the most stupid were boys. They were loud, truculent, sloppy, dirty, silly, boisterous, and dumb at school. Everyone knew that.

24

Whereas she was smart and clean and neat and precise and able and got A's even without studying. All the girls had been smarter than the boys until the last few years when the girls had started to get silly, too. One by one, they had started to lick their lips all the time to make them shiny, only to end up with chappedness around their mouth. They would pinch their cheeks to make them pink. And smoke in the girls' room, even though you got expelled from school for that. Girls who had been smart in sixth grade acted stupid in class in seventh and eighth. They walked in groups and talked in whispers and giggled. She couldn't even find anyone to walk to school with. But now she discovered that if she didn't want to act like them, she really wanted to know what it was they were whispering and giggling about. That her easy disdain for them should turn into a vulnerable curiosity outraged her.

And the boys! She would eye them furtively, having finished writing out her Latin declensions ten minutes before the rest of the class. She saw skinny necks, wetly plastered hair, pimply faces. They threw spitballs and made paper airplanes and never knew the answer when the teacher called on them. They giggled over nothing. And the girls would watch them, smiling and tittering, as if they were doing something clever. It was inexplicable, but no more so than the fact that if one of them looked right at her, she felt her heart start to pound and her face get red.

But there was another problem, even deeper because she understood it even less than he understood what was happening to her. It had to do with the transformation of boys to men. Because everybody despised boys, everyone looked down on them, the teachers, her mother, even her father. 'Boys!' they would exclaim in disgust. But everyone admired men. When the principal came into the classroom, the teachers (all women) got all fluttery and nervous and smiled a lot. It was like when the priest came into the room when she was taking religious instruction: the nuns bowed all the way down to the floor, as if he were a king, and they made the children stand up and say 'Good afternoon, Father,' as if he were really their father. And when Mr. Ward came home from work, even though he was the gentlest man in the world, all Mrs. Ward's friends would scurry home and their cup of coffee still half full.

Boys were ridiculous, troublesome, always fighting and showing off and making noise, but men strode purposefully to the center of every stage and took up the whole surface of every scene. Why was that? She began to realize that something was awry in the world. Her mother was dominant at home; in school, the authorities had all been women except for the principal. But it was not so in the outside world. The stories in the newspaper were always about men, except once in a while when a woman got murdered, and there was Eleanor Roosevelt, but everyone made fun of her. Only the page that gave recipes and dress patterns was for women. When she listened to the radio, the programs were all about men, or else about boys like Jack Armstrong, and she hated all of those and would not eat Wheaties when her mother bought them. Jack, Doc, and Reggie did the exciting things, and the women were always faithful secretaries in love with their bosses, or they were beautiful heiresses needing to be rescued. It was all like Perseus and Andromeda, or Cinderella and the Prince. Of course it was true that there were also in the newspapers pictures of ladies in bathing suits being handed bunches of roses, and down at the Sunoco station there was a full-size cardboard poster of a lady in a bathing suit holding up a thing called a spark plug. The connection between these two puzzled her, and she pondered it long and often. Worst of all, so bad that she did not think much about it, she realized that her childhood notions, when she had read about and adored Bach and Mozart and Beethoven and Shakespeare and Thomas E. Dewey and thought that she would be like them, were somehow inappropriate.

She did not know how to deal with any of this, and her fear and her resentment brought out all her stubborn pride. *She* would never be anybody's secretary, she

26

would have her own adventures. She would never let anybody rescue her. She would never read the recipes and dress patterns, but only the news and the funnies. And no matter what went on in her head about boys, she would never let them know it. She would never lick her lips and pinch her cheeks and giggle and whisper like the other girls. She would never let a boy know she even looked at him. She would not let drop her suspicion that men were only grown-up boys who had learned some manners and were not to be trusted, being also members of the inferior gender. She would never marry, having seen enough in her parents' friends to warn her off that state. And she would never, never look like those women she had seen walking around with their bodies all popping out and deformed. Never.

7

She turned to literature. She looked for books about adolescents, books she could find herself and her problems in. There were none. She read every thin, saccharine 'girl's book' she could find, and gave up. She began to read trashy novels, anything she could find in the library that looked as if it were about women. She swallowed them whole. She read, without making distinctions among them, Jane Austen and Fanny Burney and George Eliot and Gothic novels of all sorts, Daphne du Maurier and Somerset Maugham and Frank Yerby and John O'Hara, along with hundreds of nameless mystery tales, love stories, and adventures. But nothing helped. Like the person who gets fat because they eat unnourishing foods and so is always hungry and so is always eating, she drowned in words that could not teach her to swim. She had a perpetual headache; sometimes she felt she was reading to escape from life, for the escape, at least, occurred. Her head always felt the way it would, years later, when she had smoked three packs of cigarettes in a day. She begrudged going to school, and often claimed illness; she begrudged sitting at the dinner table without a book. She read on the toilet and in the bath;

she read late into the night; and when her mother insisted she turn out the light, she read under the covers with a flashlight. She had begun to do baby-sitting, and would sneak around the houses she sat in, searching for books, books she might not be allowed to take from the library. She struck pay dirt one night, finding *Forever Amber*, and reading it in Saturday-night installments, always careful to slide it back into the closed china closet when she heard the Evanses' car come up the driveway. Finally, a friend at school lent her *The Fountainhead*. That was it. She nearly swooned with it. She read it twice, and when the girl asked her to return the book, Mira asked her mother to give it to her for Christmas.

Nevertheless, this reading she was so immersed in and that filled her entire mind for over a year was, in her own view, *low*. It felt like a kind of insanity to her, something she couldn't help, but something that was not good. It swam in pinkish purple waters in the lower part of her brain, and she kept trying to lift herself out of it, to use the other part. Bored as she was doing the reading demanded in school – *Silas Marner, Julius Caesar, The Autobiography of Lincoln Steffens* – she realized that this reading was higher, whatever that meant. Good literature, what her teachers would call good literature, was not involved with the world. To be involved with the world is lower than not to be. The world is a cesspool, flesh was base, spirit and mind are exalted. A descent into the world of matter was like bathing a clean body in a muddy pool. It might perhaps be forgiven in the name of experience, but only if one learned from it and returned to the higher world. And it was clear that women never did this. Only the inferior sex did it. Oh, a few bad women did it too, but they never returned to the world of spirit and mind. Women were always pure and true and clean, like Cordelia and Marina and Jane Eyre. And they were always virgins, too, at least until they got married. What could sex be like, that having it was enough to damn you forever to the cesspool? She wanted to be good and pure and true like them, but she didn't want to have the bad things happen to her that happened

28

to them. She would try not to descend to the cesspool, but on the other hand, she was sinking in it day by day. She had found some girlfriends; she even found herself whispering and giggling with them. She did not know how it happened. For a while, she resisted the magazines they read but eventually borrowed and finally even bought them. *Seventeen* was full of advice to girls about clothes, hairdos, makeup, and boys.

They read *The Taming of the Shrew* in English class; she got *The Fountainhead* for Christmas, and read it again. She tried to read Nietzsche again and found that he said women were liers, calculating, out to dominate the male. He said you should take a whip when you go to woman. What did he mean? Her mother did dominate her father, but her mother was not a liar. Mira lied, but only to get out of going to school. Still, it was impossible not to respect Nietzsche; he was smarter than even the men teachers, much smarter than Mr. Woodie-field, her father's boss, who had come with his fat wife to dinner one night and Mira's mother had said afterward how smart he was. But why should Nietzsche say carry a whip? Mira's father liked her mother to dominate him. He liked her. Whenever he grumbled and grouched, it was at Mira, not at her mother. Kate was his dog, his horse, Petruchio said; the teacher said that was the way it used to be. But when they were at the Mittlows' for dinner, fat gross Mr. Mittlow would bark 'Milk!' at his wife, and even though she was just as tall as he and pretty fat herself, she would jump up from the table and run for a pitcher of milk. And sometimes they would hear screaming at night and Mrs. Ward whispered to Mira that Mr. Willis beat his wife. She also told her that the German butcher who lived across the street with only his daughter, would chain her to the bed when he wanted to go out drinking at night, and when he came back, he would beat her. Mira didn't ask how her mother knew this.

And since she had begun to buy magazines, she let her eyes wander among them on the rack and she saw, even though she immediately averted her eyes, that a lot of them had pictures of women in black underwear on them, or women chained up and naked and a man standing over them with a whip. In the movies too, these things happened. Not just the ones at the Emporium, the theater she and her friends were not allowed to go to, although there were pictures like that in the cases outside, but even in regular movies, sometimes the hero would spank the heroine, who before that was fresh and talked back, like Mira herself. He would come bursting through a door and pull her over his knee and she would yell, but after that she would adore him, she would follow him with her eyes and obey him submissively, and you knew she loved him forever. It was called conquest and surrender, and a man did one and a woman did the other, and everybody knew it.

8

These things crept into her imagination as her hands crept about her body as she lay in bed: it was perhaps inevitable that there would be a meeting of elements. Her first experiments with what she did not know until years later was called masturbation were inept, but incredibly titilating. She was drawn to continue bravely in them, terrified about what she might be doing to her body, but charging boldly onward. And invariably her mind, as she probed and rubbed, was drawn to what she did not know until years later were called masochistic fantasies. She grasped at any material, and there was never a dearth. History lessons about the treatment of women in China, the laws of England before the twentieth century, or the customs of Moslem countries would provide her with weeks of new fantasties. Shakespeare's *Comedy of Errors*, and plays by Romans, Greeks, and Englishmen offered visions of worlds where such things were permitted. And there were lots of movies like *Gone With the Wind*, or movies with Nazis invading a little town in the Netherlands and taking over the big house in which lived the daughter of the man who owned it, or with mean men, like James Mason, threatening beautiful women. Even lesser scenes could serve to trigger the alert imagination.

She would choose a culture, a time and place, and embroider all the surroundings. At the center, there had to be a power struggle. Years later, when she finally encountered pornographia, she found it tedious and dull compared to her own brilliant fantasies with their stage sets, costumes, and the intense power struggle. She realized, after hundreds of hours of mind-wandering down the corridors of male cruelty toward women, that the essential ingredient of her titilation was humiliation, and for that, a power struggle was necessary. Her female characters might be noble and brave, spunky, tough, or helpless and passive but resentful, but they had to put up a fight. Her male characters were always the same, though: arrogant, convinced of male supremacy, and cruel, but always intensely involved with the female. Her submission is the most important thing in the world to them, and worth any effort. Since he holds all the power, the only way she can defy him is to resist. Yet the moment of surrender itself, the instant of orgasm, always seemed to Mira a surrender of both characters. At that moment, all the fear and hate the female character felt turned to love and gratitude; and she knew that the male character must feel the same way. For that brief time, power was annulled and all was harmonized.

But if Mira fantasied masochistically, she did not act so. She recognized that there was a large difference between life and art. In the movies and in her fantasies, the things that were done to the heroine hurt but did not hurt. They left no scars. She felt no hatred for the hero afterward. But that was not so in life. In life such things would hurt and scar and build up incredible hatred. Mr. Willis beat Mrs. Willis, but she was so thin and frail and had teeth missing and hunched-over shoulders and she looked at her husband with blank eyes. Mira could not imagine Mr. Willis who was also rather thin and frail and blank, acting like Rhett Butler. And both Mr. and Mrs. Mittlow were large and bossy. He had glasses and she had a broad stiff bosom and they lived in an immacu-

31

late house and talked about their neighbours and their automobile. Even if she jumped when he spoke, Mira could not imagine him chaining her up and torturing her.

It was sex itself, Mira decided, that was the humiliation. That was why she had such thoughts. Two years ago she had been her own person, her mind was her own, a clear clean space for the working out of clear, clean, and interesting problems. Mathematics had been fun, an elaborate puzzle, and people had been unwelcome distractions from the play of mind. Suddenly her body had been invaded by a disgusting, smelly substance that brought pain to her lower half and anxiety to her mind. Could other people smell her? Her mother said she would have this the rest of her life, until she got old. The rest of her life! The blood caked on the napkin and chafed her. It smelled. She had to wrap it up in toilet paper – she used nearly a quarter of a roll – then carry it to her room and put it in a paper bag and later carry it downstairs and put it in the garbage. Five or six times a day for five or six days a month she had to do this. Her clean white smooth body had this inside it? Mrs. Mittlow had said that women build poisons up in their bodies and they had to be gotten rid of. Women always whispered about it, for men, she understood, were not subject to such things. They did not have the same poisons in them, Mrs. Mittlow said. Mira's mother said, 'Oh, Doris!' but Mrs. Mittlow was insistent. The priest had told her, she said. So men remained in charge of their bodies; they were not invaded by painful and disgusting and bloody events they could not control. That was the great secret, that was what boys knew and laughed at, that's why they were always poking each other and looking at girls and laughing. That was why they were the conquerors. Women were victims by nature.

Bad enough the body, but even her mind was invaded by shadowy longing, yearnings as deep and vague that as she sat on her bed near the window, she thought only death could fill them. She fell in love with Keats. Mathe-

32

matics was no longer fun and she dropped out of calculus. Latin was all about men doing stupid things, so was history. Only English stayed interesting – there were women in it, blood, suffering. Still, she kept her pride. Part of her mind dropped out of the world, but her feelings were kept strictly private. Whatever she felt, she reasoned, at least she didn't have to show it. She had been shy and withdrawn, but she became stiff, aloof, mechanical and rigid. Her posture and walk became stiff – her mother urged her to wear a girdle although she was slender, because her bottom might wiggle when she walked, and boys would see. Her demeanor towards boys was hostile, even furious. She hated them because they knew. She knew they knew and that they were not subject, they were free, and they laughed at her, at all women. The girls who laughed with them knew too but h...l no pride. It was because the boys were free that they ruled the world. They went about on motorcycles, they even had their own cars, they went out alone at night, and their bodies were free and clean and clear and their minds were their own, and she hated them. She whirled to attack if one of them even dared to speak to her. They might, at night, control her imagination, but she was damned if in the daytime they so much as touched it.

9

Gradually, as her body developed mature configurations, and boys began to cluster around her, Mira began to perceive that boys wanted girls as much as girls wanted them. She also heard some whispered stories about things called wet dreams. And if she still did not see males as being like her – but then she did not see females as being like her, either – at least they were not quite the terrifying strangers they had been. They too were subject to nature: that was some consolation. Their bodies too had changed: they were less skinny and pimply, and the smell of male cologne and hair cream reinforced her sense that they, like girls, cared about how they appeared. Perhaps some of their laughter had been out of

33

embarrassment as severe as hers. Perhaps they did not look down on women as much as she thought. Perhaps.

She was attending a small local college, still much alone. She had lost her age handicap, because she had worked as a clerk in a department store for a year after high school in order to save enough money to go at all. The Wards were in hard times. So she was eighteen, or almost eighteen, like the others, except for the veterans who were swarming back from World War II. Girls tried to be friendly with her, but she talked to them only to discover that they were as silly as the girls in high school, interested in nothing but boys and clothes. She retreated, as usual, to her books. In 1948, the Saturday-night date was a necessity for anybody who was anybody: Mira was often nobody. But her mind had returned, and if it was not as clear as it had been, it included more. She loved to sit and read and grapple with Hawthorne's moral philosophy, or figure out alone the political implications of Rousseau's philosophy. She was disappointed if she found her own discoveries in someone else's book, as she almost always did. She would sit in the cafeteria, drinking coffee and reading, and look up to find them – boys – fluttering, clustering around her. She was bewildered, surprised, incomprehending, and flattered. They sat all around her, they told jokes, they teased her. Some asked her out for a Saturday-night date. She would go to a movie with one of them. They wanted to 'neck,' but she despised it. She had slapped the face of the first male who had placed a kiss on her lips, finding it wet and ugly, hating the feel of another flesh against her own. Some accused her (who was so afraid of her own desire that male violence be committed upon her) of committing violence upon them by her attitude. This gave her pause. Nevertheless, she would get out of the car. 'My parents don't allow me to sit in cars in the driveway,' she would explain firmly.

Still, they hovered in the cafeteria. They laughed and joked, sparring for attention. She had the sense of being the only spectator in a circus full of monkeys who would one by one jump on the cafeteria table to perform, scratching their underarms and making faces until they were pushed off by another squeaking member who did somersaults and grunts. If their behavior only mildly entertained her – Mira was very serious – her wonder at why they had selected her kept her in awed silence. She smiled at their jokes, which were mostly scatological but sometimes sexual, having learned enough to pick up what it was they were talking about – most of the time, at least. What she did not know was why they were funny. She hid her ignorance under smiles, and was astonished to learn later that she had gained a reputation for easy virtue by her tolerant acceptance of their foreign language.

She did not learn this, however, until sometime later, and only then was she able to connect it with her difficulties in cars. Still, she would have been all right had she followed her feelings, but she had been doing some reading in psychology. She had learned that her form of orgasm was immature and showed that she had not yet moved into the 'genital' stage of development. Maturity was the great goal: everyone agreed about that. A mature woman relates to males: everyone knows that too. So when they slid their arms around her, or tried to grab her body, she began to sit passively and even to turn her face towards theirs. They would bend their heads toward her, and kiss her. Then they would try to get their slimy tongues inside her mouth. Ugh! But since she had not cut them off entirely, as she had done before, they felt, with what reasoning she never knew, that she owed them something. They would pull her back, they would struggle to get a hand inside her blouse or on her thigh under her skirt. They would begin to breathe hard. It outraged her. She felt invaded, violated. She did not want their slimy mouths, their clumsy hard strange hands, their breath, on her mouth, her clean body, her fine ears. She couldn't stand it. She would pull violently away, grateful that they were parked in her driveway, and uncaring about what they thought or said, leap out of the car and run up to her doorstep. Sometimes they followed and apologized, sometimes they only slammed the door she had left hanging open, and pulled out of the driveway with screeching tires. It didn't matter. She didn't care. She stopped going out on Saturday-night dates.

10

One bright fall day (Mira was nineteen) a tall, gawky boy named Lanny, who was in her course in the Structure of Music, approached her as she was walking across campus, and began to talk. She had noticed him in class: he seemed intelligent, he knew something about music. They talked briefly, and suddenly, gracelessly, he asked her to go out. She was surprised. She looked at his eyes. They were shining at her. She liked his awkwardness, his lack of polish: it was such a change from the hollow suave manner adopted by most of the young men. She agreed to go.

As she was dressing on the evening of their date, she noticed that she was excited, that her heart was pounding, that her eyes had a special shine. Why? Although she had liked his manner, there was nothing extraordinary about him, was there? She felt as if she were falling in love, but couldn't understand why or how. During the evening they spent together, she found herself deferring to him, smiling at all his demands, seeing his face as beautiful. When he brought her home that night, she turned to him and when he kissed her, she kissed him back, and the kiss penetrated her whole body. Terrified, she pulled away; but he knew. He let her go, but two nights later they went out again.

Lanny came to her with a kind of intensity. He had a wild imagination; he was disconnected, gay, unbound. He had been spoiled – totally accepted, totally approved – by his family, and he was a free spirit, full of gaiety and assurance and eccentricities. He told her that when he woke up in the morning, he immediately began to sing, that he would take his guitar with him into the toilet and sit there, singing and playing, while he defecated. She was astounded, being herself one of those people who

36

have to drag themselves up in the morning in a silent house where such behaviour would have been seen as an insane disturbance of the peace. He was like that all the time. He would collect people, call her suddenly, come pick her up, and a whole car load of them would be off to a tavern, someone's house, Greenwich Village. Wherever they were, he was restless, he wanted to be off again, to get a pizza, to play some music, to visit some- one he had just thought of but who was suddenly his best friend. He kept her out all night, and he rarely pressed her sexually. She was enchanted. She felt herself stodgy beside him, bound by obligations like papers due, a job to go to, books to be read – in short, responsibili- ties. He shrugged off such trivia; it was not, he said, what life was all about. Life was about joy. She leaned toward him, yearning; she wanted to be like him, but could not. So she lived his life and her own too. She stayed out all night, night after night, and slept much of the day, but she did her work as well. She grew quite haggard and tired, and she began to feel resentment because it seemed to her that Lanny only wanted an audience. He grew chilly when she tried to participate, when she jumped up into the singing group and stood with her arms around his (and she believed her) friends. For him, she was the smile of approval, the applause, the admiring gleam.

They were rarely alone at night, because when she had to leave, everyone would pile into the car with them and drive her home. Or he would get too drunk to drive, and someone else would drive her home. But on the few occasions when he did take her alone, and would put his arms around her in the driveway, she would turn to him fully, loving to kiss him, loving to hold him and have him hold her. The impulses in her body no longer frightened her; she felt ecstatic. She loved the way he smelled, not like most of the boys, of shaving lotion or cologne, but of himself. She loved his hands on her body, and he never pressed them too far. She thought she was in love. After a time, she began to invite him into the house. He took it as a further invitation, which it probably was, but she would allow herself to get just so passionate before she pulled away.

They talked about it, he all reassurance, she all doubt. But she could not move. She wanted him: her body wanted his, and her mind wanted the experience. But her mother's dire message about sex was engraved on her brain. It had nothing to do with dirt and sin: it was far more potent. Sex, Mrs. Ward said, led to pregnancy; no matter what boys said, there was no sure way to avoid it. And pregnancy led to marriage, to a marriage enforced on both, which meant poverty, resentment, an immediate baby, and 'a life like mine,' Mrs. Ward ended, her face alone testimony to what that was like. Mira had long noticed, and resented her father's adoration of her mother, her mother's disdain of him. The turned cheek when Mr. Ward tried to kiss his wife hello in the evenings, the bitter grimaces at his statement, the arguments fiercely whispered in the dark at night when Mira was supposed to be sleeping, the grinding poverty of their life that was only now beginning to abate: all represented a life no one would choose who had a choice. She told Lanny some of this, told him of her fear of pregnancy. He said he would 'use something'. She told him of her mother's warning that nothing was safe: he said that if she got pregnant, they'd get married. He even offered, finally, to marry her first.

Looking back, Mira could imagine some of what he felt. He had come, it must have seemed to him, more than halfway, and she had not budged. That made her a flirt, a prick tease. He had offered her marriage: what more could any woman want?

But the very qualities Mira loved in Lanny made her dread him as a husband. Mira understood – what young woman does not? – that to choose a husband is to choose a life. She had not needed Jane Austen to teach her that. It is, in a sense, a woman's first, last, and only choice. Marriage and a child make her totally dependent on the man, on whether he is rich or poor, responsible or not, where he chooses to live, what work he chooses to do. I guess this is still true; I don't know, I'm a bit out of touch, but sometimes on my car radio I hear a song that seems to be popular now. It's pretty, but its lyrics go something like this: 'If I were a carpenter, and you were a lady, would you still love me, would you have my baby?' It asks the woman to 'follow' her man, in whatever condition he chooses to live, as if a man alone could be a substitute for a life. Anyway, I understand Mira's hesitations. What she discovered suddenly was that she wanted to pick her own life. It was a breathtaking revelation to her, and it terrified her, for she didn't know how she was going to be able to do that. She recognized it for the shocking, divisive, arrogant rending of the social fabric that it was. Even convincing her parents, for instance, that she would like to live away from home would be a terrible feat. And what would she do then? She had some idea of what kinds of jobs she wanted, but she never heard of women getting them. She knew she wanted to be sexual in a free way: how could she manage that?

Whenever she thought of marriage to Lanny, the picture that presented itself was of herself on her hands and knees scrubbing the kitchen floor, a baby crying in the next room, while Lanny was out carousing with the boys. Life was about joy, he would insist, and if she asked responsibility, she would become the oppressive, demanding wife – the ball and chain, the grim-faced haggard who did not understand that boys would be boys. She saw herself weepily complaining to him, him stalking out of the house to go find solace with his mates. Her film would not run any other way; she could not come up with a sweeter picture. The role he offered her was not the role she coveted. She continued to refuse to sleep with him.

He began to call her less often, and when they did go out together, he would not speak to her. He was always in the center of a group of friends. Sometimes he abandoned her completely, and someone else would have to take her home. But no one made a pass at her. It was clear that she was Lanny's property. She became aware that she had developed a reputation at school.

She never fully understood how this happened. She was outspoken and free-thinking in class and out, and she would talk about anything. She had frequent serious discussions of conventional morality, and even about sex, which she approached dispassionately and abstractly, and with very little knowledge. She freely admitted to atheism; she attacked contemptuously bigotry and any sort of sloppy thinking, and she tolerated dull minds poorly.

Increasingly, people regarded her strangely and made odd remarks. It was, however, not her mind or her manners that they criticized; it was her morals. She was loose, but a bitch, whatever that meant. It was clear that people believed she was sleeping not only with Lanny, but with others as well. She applied for a job in the college bookstore and was told by the manager, a thin-necked, pimply-faced man in his twenties, that he not only wouldn't hire her, but he felt sorry for the man she married. She was astonished by this, since she had never met him before, but he shook his head knowingly at her: he had heard plently about her, he said. She was a castrater, domineering. Some people told her that others thought she was a snob. One day a young man from her history class came up to her on campus, smoking a pipe. He seemed to want to talk, and she was glad. She liked him – he seemed a gentle, intelligent fellow. He asked her a few questions: were her parents divorced? had she ever been taught Christian doctrine? As she grew wary and gazed at him intently, he pointed to her cigarette and told her that she should know she was not supposed to be smoking while walking across campus. It was forbidden to women, he said.

The presumption of these males in telling her what she was supposed to be enraged her, but beneath the anger and contempt was a profound sense of discomfort, wrongness in the world. She felt that people were in league against her, trying to force her to give up what she had gone on calling 'myself'. However, she had some good friends – Lanny, Biff, Tommy, Dan – who were unfailingly kind and respectful, and with whom she felt

40

easy and had fun. She did not care at all what people said behind her back, and although she wished they would not say such things to her face, she dismissed the people and their comments as stupid and insignificant.

Nor did she worry about what people might be saying about her to Lanny. She was sure he knew she loved him, and also that she mistrusted him; she was sure he knew that if she would not sleep with him, she would not sleep with anyone. But their friendship soured. They had several bad fights. When they did not openly fight, they pulled against each other, as if they tugged at different ends of a one-foot rope, neither moving far in any direction. He called her rarely now; he told her that because of her he had been forced to resort to dating Ada, the campus prostitute. For the first time in her life, Mira felt jealous.

Still, she could not give in. She didn't want to be in a power struggle with him, but each of his actions convinced her of the rightness of her original judgment of him as untrustworthy. She was too frightened of sex to risk it without a sense that he was, and would be, there for her. Now, when they were together, he talked only about how much fun he had with his male friends; and he pressured her toward sex. He seemed to have no other interest in her; when she spoke, he barely listened. He never asked her about herself. Eventually, he stopped calling altogether.

She was miserable. She curled in on herself. She felt she had to withdraw, feeling defeated, feeling that it was, after all, the world that she wanted and the world that she was repudiating. But she had no choice. She tried to tell herself that the life she wanted would someday be possible, that someday she would have it all, adventure and excitement and independence. But she also knew that such a life had, for her, to include sex, and there was no way she could reconcile that danger and those aspirations. She saw her choice clearly as being between sex and independence, and she was paralyzed by that. Since she always risked pregnancy, which meant dependence, a sexual woman lived with Damocles' sword always over her head. Sex meant surrender to the male. If Mira wanted the independent life, she would have to give up being sexual. The situation was a terrible incarnation of her masochistic fantasies. Women were indeed victims by nature.

11

Young men like to say that young women want to be raped; no doubt this statement is intended partly to alleviate their guilt about the kinds of pressure they place on women, but there is a germ of truth in it. Young women caught in psychological bonds like Mira's probably, at moments, half welcome a violent solution to the dilemma. But the kind of rape they imagine is like the one in *The Fountainhead*: it springs from passion and love, and it has no consequences more serious than the consequences for Justine's body of all her whippings and torture. No broken bones, scars, destroyed tissue. Act without consequence, arrows with rubber tips, comedy: like the cartoons they make for children in which the cat or bear or whatever gets smashed over and over, but always rises from its own ashes. Revocability is an ideal, it frees us from the grimness of puritanical insistence on the seriousness of all things.

Sex, being what it is, is pretty drab for young people. Val used to say it was wasted on the young. She said they combined the utmost in desire with the utmost in ineptitude. I told her she'd been reading too much Shaw. She didn't even smile. Earnestly, she went on, amending her statement: the males had the utmost in desire. Females, she said, whether it was from fear or physiology, wouldn't reach the utmost in desire until their thirties. It was nature, she thought, that had made humans strangely; it had intended young men to rape and impregnate young women and then go their way, as the gods did in Greek myth. The young women were supposed to have the babies and bring them up alone. Then, in their thirties, the young women became sexually charged – if they hadn't died along the way – at which point they become terrifying to the male of the species. The men sniff the female's revenge, and identify such women with forbidden mothers, or scorpions, witches, and sibyls. By this time, most of the older males were dead from their adventures or dissipations, so the older women tried to seduce young men, although without the violence young men used on women. She said the ideal marriage was between exhausted middle-aged men and young women, or between middle-aged women and young men. The young woman would get pregnant by a young man, and then the older man would take over and take care of her without giving her too hard a time with sexual demands, and when he did make love, would have some idea of what he was about, and would give her at least some pleasure. Then, when she was older and the old geezer had kicked the bucket, she'd send her kids out into the world and take in some struggling young guy who could satisfy her sexually, after she'd taught him all of what she'd learned from her years with the old geezer.

Val amused us with many such evening entertainments, but I thought it made sense, at least as much sense as the way things are presently ordered. I said the major problem was for the young women to bring up the children. It was different when everyone lived on the land, and a woman could grow her crops and kids at the same time. She said if a society wanted children, it would have to pay for them the same as it paid for guns and bombers. She said that if it paid for them, it might value them a little more and spoil them a little less.

At any rate, it does seem true that a young woman may sometimes behave in a way that can be called titillating, and that men take such behaviour as being directed entirely at them. Now there's no doubt that most of us are a little finer, a little more attractive and electric when there's someone in the room who appeals to us sexually. I've often seen blushing young men with shining eyes behave in the same way, but no one says of them that they want to be raped. If, after taking a few steps forward, they then decide to retreat, no one accuses them of being cunt teasers. In fact, the disappointed woman probably thinks it's all her fault. The mating game is as complicated as the dances derived from it – that terrible, wonderful, macho flamenco, for instance. Maybe it was easier back in the old days when it was performed with bodyguards called chaperons: the girls could be as free and gay and thoughtless as the boys without having to worry about consequences. Now we have the pill, but that doesn't work quite the same way. It might have helped poor Mira though. There was just no rational way out of her dilemma; all the alternatives rot. Like being in a burning building, the fire beyond you, two windows in front of you, one looking down on a tiny bunch of firemen holding a canvas that looks no bigger than your thumb, the other looking down on the filthy Hudson River. When you are in situations like that, the only thing you can do is close your eyes and plunge. No amount of ratiocination can help you decide whether the fire is only a corridor deep and you could reach the staircase beyond, whether your chances are better with the water or the net.

12

One evening, after a long silence, Lanny called and asked Mira to go out. Her heart fluttered a little, like a bird long grounded, whose broken wing has healed, and who is tentatively trying it out. Perhaps he would be willing to try it her way – to be friends, to stay close and loving until someday she would be ready to risk. And she knew, as soon as she opened the door to him, that she, or at least her body, loved the gangling awkward figure with the pale disconnected eyes and the smooth long hands. But he was stiff and polite; in the car, he barely spoke.

'You seem angry?' she ventured.

'Why should I be angry?' But there was a sarcastic twang in his voice. It silenced her.

After a long pause, she asked coolly: 'Why did you call me, then?'

He did not answer. She glanced at him. His mouth was working.

'Why?' she pursued.

'I don't know,' he said in a dull voice.

Her mind was in tumult. He had called her, it seemed, against his will. What could that be but love, something beyond simple desire? She wanted to go someplace quiet, where they could talk, but he drove to Kelley's, a college hangout near the campus where they had often gone. It was a saloon: knotty pine paneling and college pennants, a long bar in front, a few tables and a jukebox in back: red-checkered tablecloths, blaring music, and the smell of beer. As usual on Saturday nights, the place was mobbed; they were standing four deep at the bar. She did not like standing at bars, and Lanny took her to the rear, and unusually polite, helped her with her coat. She sat down; he went to the bar to get their drinks. There was a bartender who waited table, but with such a crowd, they would have to wait long for him. Lanny disappeared into the mob at the bar. Mira lighted a cigarette. She sat. She smoked another cigarette. Men paused and gave her the once-over on their way to the toilet. She was humiliated and anxious. He had met some friends, no doubt. She glanced at the crowd, but she could not spot him. She smoked another cigarette.

She was tamping it out when Biff and Tommy came in through the back door and saw her. They came to the table, asked where Lanny was, stood around talking. Tommy went up to the bar and came back in a few minutes with a pitcher of beer, and he and Biff sat down with her. She talked with them, but she was stiff and the corners of her mouth were trembling. After the pitcher was nearly empty, Lanny suddenly appeared, carrying one glass – her Canadian Club. He stared coldly at his friends, then at her, plunked the glass down in front of her, and stalked stiffly back to the bar. Biff and Tommy looked at each other and at her: all three shrugged questioningly. They went on talking.

Mira's innards were quivering. She was angry with Lanny, but much more she was confused, uneasy, and

45

even frightened. Why had he called her in the first place? Had he intended to take her out and ignore her all night? She remembered, miserably, many nights when he had done that, but there had always been a group of friends with them. She felt, above all, humiliated, and that gave her strength. The hell with him. She would act as if she didn't care. She would act as if she were having fun. She would have fun. She grew very animated, and her friends responded with high spirits.

Other people joined them. Biff got another pitcher of beer, and brought her a Canadian. She was touched. Biff was so poor. She smiled at him and he glowed at her. Biff always treated her as if she were fragile and innocent; he hovered, protecting her, but never tried to make a claim on her. His haggard cheeks, his tattered jacket cuffs hurt her. She wanted to give him something. She knew he would never approach her sexually. Because of his limp, probably: he was in college by virtue of a scholarship given to poor children with disabilities. Biff had had polio. So, bright as he was, attractive as he could have been if he'd had enough to eat, he never made the first move with women. And because she felt safe with him, she could afford to love him. She smiled her love at him and he smiled love back. Tommy was gleaming at her too, and Dan. They were all singing together now, over a third or fourth pitcher, she had lost count, being on her third Canadian.

She no longer had to act: she *was* having fun. She was having more fun than she did when Lanny was around. He always made her feel as if she didn't belong, as if she should not be joining in, but should be sitting in a chair against the dining room wall, faintly smiling, watching the men around the table eat and drink. It was sex, she thought, that caused the problem. With these friends, that didn't come up, so they could be just friends, could have fun together. They were her comrades, her brothers, she loved them all. They had crisscrossed arms and were holding hands around the table, singing 'The Whiffenpoof Song.'

Lanny did not return. People were playing the jukebox, and Tommy asked her to dance. She agreed: they were playing an old Glenn Miller record that she liked. They kept playing. They put on 'Sentimental Journey', 'String of Pearls', and 'Baby, It's Cold Outside'. She kept dancing. They kept buying pitchers of beer, and a fourth Canadian sat melting and sweating on the table. Other people arrived, people she didn't know well but who were in her class and knew her name. They were playing Stan Kenton now; the music, like her head, seemed louder, wilder. She noticed while she was dancing that there was no other girl in the back, that she was the only one dancing, that the guys were standing around almost as if they were lined up, waiting. But it seemed all right, because, she reasoned, there was only one guy dancing at a time, too.

The lindy is a man's dance. The male gets to hurl and whirl his partner all around the floor and he can just stand there. It must have been invented for men who didn't know how to dance. Mira was dizzy from all the swinging around, but she was loving it. She was moving and swinging and her head pounded, but the outside world had disappeared, she did not have to think about Lanny. She was music and movement, she was irresponsible, she did not even have to think about her partner, since whoever he was, she didn't care about him. She was whirling in a great ballroom, she was sheer motion.

As a song ended, Biff appeared suddenly at her side and took her elbow in his hand. He whispered in her ear: 'I think you'd better leave.'

She turned on him indignantly. 'Why?'

'Mira.' His voice was urgent. 'Come on.'

'I have to wait for Lanny.'

'Mira.' His voice was low, but almost desperate. She was totally bewildered.

'Trust me,' he said, and since she did, she docilely allowed him to guide her through the crowd and out the back door. They stood there for a moment, then he said quickly, 'Let's go upstairs.'

Upstairs was an apartment shared by Biff and Lanny and two other boys. She had been there at many parties,

47

and Biff had often been the one to drive her home after Lanny collapsed, using Lanny's car. So she felt no nervousness at all. But the fresh air had made her know how drunk she was, three Canadians being more than her system was used to, and when they got upstairs, she fell on the couch.

'No,' Biff said, and pointed toward the bedroom.

She obeyed him easily, let him help her up and lead her gently toward a bedroom she knew was Lanny's. He helped her gently onto the bed, and when she was lying there watching the room swirl, he softly placed a blanket over her, went out, and closed the door. She thought she heard him fuss with the key, but the dizziness made her so wretched that she forced herself to go to sleep.

After a time she awoke, gradually, drifting in and out of puzzlement. She seemed to hear noise, shouting, slamming, arguing. It grew louder. She tried to sit up. The room was still whirling, and she half-sat, resting her body on her arm. She listened, trying to make out what was happening. The noises grew nearer, they seemed to be coming down the hall toward the bedrooms. There was a crash, slams, it sounded like a fight. She leaped up and headed for the door and tried to open it. It was locked. She fell back and sat on the bed, sitting there with her shoes off, huddled in the blanket. The noises subsided. There were door slams, several of them. Then silence. She started to get up again, planning to pound for Biff to let her out, when suddenly the door flew open, light poured in blinding her, and a figure was standing in the doorway.

'I hope you're satisfied, you slut!' Lanny shouted.

She blinked. He slammed the door. She sat there blinking. There were other slams, then again quiet, then the door opened again. Biff came in and switched on a dim lamp on the bureau. She blinked at him. He came over and sat on the bed beside her.

'What happened?'

His voice sounded thin, like someone else's voice. He talked around and around; she did not understand what he was not saying. She asked questions; he tried to parry

48

them. She insisted. At last she understood. The dancing, he said, and Lanny's leaving her alone. It was all Lanny's fault, the bastard. So those guys got the wrong impression. It was not her fault. They didn't know her as Biff knew her, didn't know her innocence, her 'purity' he called it. So . . .

'All of them?' she asked, appalled.

He nodded grimly.

Her mind churned that. How would they manage that? 'In turns?' she asked him.

He shrugged disgustedly.

She put her hand on his arm. 'Biff, you had to fight them all off? Oh, Biff!'

He was frail; he weighed less than she did. 'It was okay. Not real fighting, just some shoving and yelling. No harm done.' He stood up. 'I'll take you home. I've got the keys to Lanny's car.'

He had tried hard enough to spare her the ugliness, as if not knowing were somehow less ugly than knowing. But nothing could spare her that. He drove her home in sympathetic silence, and while she was endlessly grateful to him not only for doing what he had done for her, but for being who he was, she could not speak to him. She thanked him over and over, in a monotone, but could not say anything more. She went up to her room and lay on the bed and fell immediately into a deep sleep and slept for fourteen hours. The next day she did not get up at all. She told her mother she didn't feel well. All Sunday she lay there.

13

She was overwhelmed. This was what it was all about, all the strange things she had been taught. Everything fell into place, everything made sense. And that everything was too big for her. Other girls went to bars, other girls danced. The difference was she had appeared to be alone. That a woman was not marked as the property of some male made her a bitch in heat to be attacked by any male, or even by all of them at once. That a woman could not go out in public and enjoy herself dancing without worrying what every male in the place was thinking or even worse, what they might do, seemed to her an injustice so extreme that she could not swallow it.

She was a woman and that alone was enough to deprive her of freedom no matter how much the history books pretended that women's suffrage had ended inequality, or that women's feet had been bound only in an ancient and outmoded and foreign place like China. She was constitutionally unfree. She could not go out alone at night. She could not in a moment of loneliness go out to a local tavern to have a drink in company. The twice she had taken the train during the daytime, to make excursions to museums in New York, she had been continually approached. She could not even appear to be lacking an escort; if that escort decided to abandon her, she was helpless. And she couldn't defend herself: she had to depend on a male for that. Even frail, limping Biff could handle such a situation better than she. Had those guys gotten to her, all the rage and hauteur and fighting in the world wouldn't have helped her.

And she would never be free, never. Never. It would always be like this. She thought about her mother's friends and suddenly understood them. No matter where she went or what she did, she would always have to worry about what men were thinking, how they looked at her, what they might do. One day some months before, in an elevator on her way to the dentist's office, she had overheard an ugly aged woman with dyed red hair and a crooked back talking to another woman, fiftyish and fat, about rape. Both of them were clucking their tongues, talking about locks on doors and windows, and they looked to her as if to include her in conversation, as if she were one of them. She had looked away, full of contempt for them. Who would want to rape them? It was wishful thinking, she thought. Yet a few nights later there was an item in the newspaper about an eighty-year-old woman, raped and killed in her own apartment.

She thought about what would have happened had Biff not been there and her mind went black with the horror, the blood, the desecration. It was not her virginity she treasured, but her right to herself, to her own mind and body. Horrible, horrible it would have been, and her beloved Lanny would no doubt have called her slut and said she had gotten what she deserved. He would simply have erased her from his list of women one is required to treat with respect. That was the way things were. And no matter how high she held her head, no matter how alone she walked, that is the way things would stay. It was ridiculous to talk about injustice; it was useless to protest. She knew from her few experiences of talking about women and freedom that such protests were always taken by men as invitations to their taking greater freedoms with her.

Mira retreated. She was defeated. Her pride, such as was left her, was spent entirely in not letting the defeat show. She walked alone on campus, head high, an icy look on her face. She sat alone in the cafeteria, or with Biff, or a girl from class. She averted her eyes from any male who passed her, and never smiled at them even when they greeted her. She was never sure which of them had been there that night, there had been so many, such familiar faces, so dizzy and smoky an air. If she happened to see Lanny at a distance, she walked the other way.

At the end of the school year, she met Norm. He was the son of friends of the family, and she met him at a family cookout. He was gentle and intelligent, he treated her with respect, and he never pressed her toward sex. Her dream of choosing and living a life of her own had vanished. Any life in which she was alone would contain the risk of encountering that pack of savages. Bitterly, she thought she was being unkind to those usually called savages, who would probably never behave that way: only civilized men behave that way. Bitterness closed her in. She had lost her life. She would live out a half-life, like the rest of women. She had no choice but to protect herself against a savage world she did not understand and by her gender alone was made unfit to deal with. There was marriage and there was the convent.

51

She retreated into the one as if it were the other, and wept at her wedding. She knew she was renouncing the world, the world that a year before had shimmered with excitement and allure. She had been taught her place. She had learned the limits of her courage. She had failed, she had been vanquished. She would devote herself to Norm, and crept into his arms as into a fortress. It was true what they said: woman's place is in the home. When Biff heard she was getting married, he came up to her in the cafeteria, congratulating her in front of a group of young men. 'I really congratulate Norm,' he said loudly. 'He's getting a virgin, that I know.' It was to justify her in some way, she knew; but also, he meant it as a compliment to her. She closed her mind to him, then. They thought one thing or they thought another: but their thinking was all the same.

14

Some dramatic sense, probably culled from reading plays, or female *Bildungsromane*, which always end with the heroine's marriage, make me want to stop here, make a formal break, like the curtain going down. Marriage should mean a great change, a new life. But it was less a new beginning for Mira than a continuation. Although the external events of her life changed, the internal ones remained much the same.

Oh, Mira was able to leave her parents' tense home, and pick out little things – towels, throw rugs, some curtains – that would turn their furnished rooms into her own 'home,' and she enjoyed that. She and Norm had taken a small furnished place near Coburg, where Norm was in medical school. She had left school, and with few regrets. She did not want to go back there again, to have have to look at those faces again. She did most of her reading on her own anyway, she reasoned, and would learn as much out of school as in it. Norm would finish med school and his internship while she worked to support them, and once he was out, the future would be secure. They had worked it all out.

After a honeymoon spent in Norm's parents' New Hampshire cottage, they returned, he to the books and she to try to find a job. She was hindered in this because she could not drive; she asked Norm to teach her. He was reluctant. In the first place, he needed the car most days, in the second, she was not mechanically apt and would be a poor driver. He took her in his arms. 'I couldn't bear to live if anything happened to you.' Something nagged at her, but she was so encompassed by his love, so grateful for it, that she did not probe to find out what it was. Taking buses, and begging her mother to drive her around, she finally found a job as a clerk-typist for $35 a week. They could live on that, but not well, and she decided to try to get a job in New York, commuting back and forth from New Jersey. Norm was horrified. The city! It was such a dangerous place. Commutation would eat up a third of what she earned. She would have to get up early and arrive home late. And then there would be the men . . .

Mira had never told Norm about the night at Kelley's, but he either had the same fears as she, or he had sensed that she had them, because the unspoken threat contained in the word was one he was to continue to use for the next years – indeed, until it was no longer necessary. If he had not, Mira might have learned to overcome her fears. Armed by the title of *Mrs.*, property of some man, she felt stronger in the world. They would be less likely to attack her if they knew some man had her under his protection.

She gave up the idea of the city, accepted the clerk-typist job; Norm got a part-time job, spending much of his time reading beforehand the texts he would be studying in the fall, and they settled into their life together.

She had enjoyed their honeymoon. It was incredible delight to be able to kiss and hold without fear. Norm was using only condoms, but somehow being married made it less threatening. She was shy about revealing her body. So was Norm for that matter. And the two of them giggled and delighted in their mutual shyness, their mutual pleasure. The only problem was, Mira did not reach orgasm.

After a month, she decided she was frigid. Norm said that was ridiculous, that she was only inexperienced. He had married friends and he knew that it would pass in time. She asked him, timidly, if it would be possible for him to hold back a little, that she felt she was on the verge, but then he would come, and lose all erectness. He said no healthy male could or should try to hold back. She asked, even more timidly, if they could try a second time. He said that would be unhealthy for him, and probably impossible. He was a medical student, and she believed him. She settled back to enjoy what she could, and waited for him to fall asleep to masturbate herself to orgasm. He always fell asleep quickly after sex.

So they went on. They entertained friends on occasion: she learned to cook. He always shared the laundry chores with her and took her grocery shopping on Friday nights, when she got paid. If she teased him enough, he would help her clean the apartment on Saturday. Sometimes she felt very grown up: when offering a drink to a guest, say, or when putting on makeup and jewelry before leaving to go out with her husband. But most of the time she felt like a child who had stumbled, bumbled into the wrong house. Her job was stultifyingly dull; the long bus rides with other gray, tired people made her feel grimy and poor. At night, Norm turned on the TV (the one large purchase they had made with wedding-gift money), and since there was only the kitchen and the bed-living room, she had no choice but to hear it. She tried to read, but her concentration was continually broken. The tube is demanding. Life felt hideously empty. But she told herself that was only because women are educated to think that marriage will be a sudden panacea to all emptiness, and although she'd fought off such notions, she had no doubt been infected by them. She told herself it was her own fault, that if she had wanted to do some real studying and intellectual work, she could. But, she argued, she was so tired after eight hours in an office, two on buses, preparing dinner, washing dishes – a job Norm simply refused to touch. Besides, Norm always had TV on at night. Well, she argued back, it would be better when he started school; then he would have to study at night. Nevertheless, she was approaching her twentieth birthday: look, her other self said, what Keats had done by twenty. And finally her whole self would rise up and wipe it all out. Oh, don't bother me with it! I do the best I can!

Part of her knew that she was simply surviving in the only way she could. Dull day by dull day she paced through her responsibilities, moving toward some goal she could not discern. The word *freedom* had dropped from her vocabulary; the word *maturity* replaced it. And dimly she sensed that maturity was knowing how to survive. She was as lonely as ever; except sometimes at night, she and Norm, cuddled up together, would talk seriously. One night she was discussing what she wanted: to go back to school and eventually get a Ph.D. and teach. Norm was horrified. He mentioned the problems, financial difficulties, her exhaustion – she would have to do all that and still cook and clean, because when he went back to school he would no longer have time to help her. She argued that they could share. He reminded her that after all he was the one responsible for earning the living: he didn't insist, he wasn't peremptory, he didn't demand. He merely stated it and asked if that weren't so. Frowning and puzzled, reluctantly, she agreed. It was what she had wanted: Norm was responsible, not like Lanny. He would never leave her to go out and get drunk with the boys while she listened to a crying baby, down on her hands and knees scrubbing the kitchen floor. Medical school was difficult, demanding, he added. She could do that, she insisted: do what he said he couldn't, go to med school and still help out in the house. He pulled his big gun: there would be guys, they would give her a hard time, male professors insisting she screw her way to a degree. He was too obvious this time. She pondered. 'Sometimes I think you'd like to lock me up in a convent, Norm, where only you could visit me.'

'It's true. I would.' He was serious.

She turned away from him, and he fell asleep. In three months, the protection she had sought had already become oppressive. It was what she had wanted too, wasn't it? If she had been less wretched, she would have laughed.

15

Survival is an art. It requires the dulling of the mind and the senses, and a delicate attunement to waiting, without insisting on precision about just what it is you are waiting for. Vaguely, Mira thought of 'The End' as Norm's finishing both med school and his internship, but that was so far off, and five years of the boredom she was living in seemed so unendurable that she preferred not to think at all.

Norm went back to school, and as she had expected, no longer watched TV. But she found that she could not concentrate even though it was off. She suspected the problem was not just tiredness; when she picked up a serious book, one that made her think, she thought. And that was unbearable, because to think involves thinking about one's own life. She read at night, read voluminously. It was like the beginning of her adolescence. She read junk: mystery novels, light social satirists like O'Hara and Marquand and Maugham. She could not handle anything more true.

She blamed Norm for nothing. She took care of him, worried about him, cooked what he liked, and asked nothing of him. It was not Norm she hated, but her life. But what other life could she have, being the way she was? Although Norm was often ill-tempered, he insisted that he loved her and was happy with her. It was the stupid school he hated, the stupid finicky professors. He was not doing well: he got through his first year with an undistinguished record. He blamed his low grades on being upset about her. For she was pregnant.

It was in May that she missed her period. This made her nervous because she was regular, but also because, after her first disastrous attempts with a diaphragm, Norm had insisted that they continue in the old way. He did not like her fiddling for ten minutes in the bathroom when he was full of ardor. And she suspected that he wanted control of the situation himself. She worried about the risk with condoms, but sometimes, when they were very broke, Norm used nothing at all, and withdrew before orgasm. She felt that was risky; he assured her it was all right.

The way she gave herself over to him in this area seemed strange to her in later years. The fact was she hated using a diaphragm. She had come to dislike sex entirely, for he would get her aroused and leave her dissatisfied; now, when she masturbated, she wept. She realized, looking back, that she had given her life over to him just as she had perforce given her life over to her parents. She had simply transferred her childhood. And Norm, although he was seven years older than she, had been in the army during the war and had a few adventures, was not old enough to have a twenty-year-old child. Perhaps, in some dark hidden place in her mind, she had wanted a child: perhaps what she was waiting for, what she called maturity, involved having one and getting it over with. Perhaps.

At the time, it felt like disaster. How would they live? White and drawn, she went to a gynecologist. She came home with the news on an evening when Norm was studying for an important exam. She was worn out from work, the bus rides, the hour's wait in the doctor's office. She imagined as she walked the two blocks from the bus stop that maybe Norm would have cooked some dinner. But he was studying, eating cheese and crackers when she came in, and he was irritated with her for being out so late, although he knew where she had gone and why. As she entered the apartment, she looked across the room at him: he stared mutely back. For three weeks they had discussed little else: there was no need to speak.

Suddenly he threw the book he had been holding across the room.

'You've just ruined my life, do you realize that?'

She sat down on the edge of a rocking chair. '*I* just ruined *your* life?'

'I'll have to quit school now, how else are we going to live?' He lighted a cigarette with nervous intensity. 'And how am I supposed to study for this exam when you come home with this? If I flunk it, I flunk out. Did you realize that?'

She sat back, half closing her eyes, detached. She wanted to point out to him the illogic of his last sentences. She wanted to point out to him the injustice of his attack. But the fact that he felt right in making it, felt that he had legitimate grounds to treat her like a naughty child, overwhelmed her. It was a force against which she could not struggle, for his legitimacy was supported by the outside world, and she knew that. She tried. She leaned forward:

'Did I chase you around the bed? You said your way was safe. *You* said it, Mr. Medical Student!'

'It is!'

'Yeah. That's why I'm pregnant.'

'It is, I tell you.'

She looked at him. His face was nearly blue at the edges, his mouth a tight cruel accusing line.

Her voice faltered. 'Are you saying you are not the father of this child? Are you suggesting it happened some other way?'

He glared at her with bitter hate. 'How should I know? You tell me you never slept with anybody but me, but how can I tell? There sure was enough talk about you and Lanny. Everybody talked about you. You were free enough in those days, why should it be different now?'

She leaned back again. She had told Norm about her fear of sex, her fear of men, her timidity in a part of the world she did not understand. And he had listened sweetly, caressing her face, holding her close to him. She had thought he understood, thought it even more because he seemed, despite his stories about army adventures, to share it – her shyness and fear and timidity. She thought she had escaped, but all she had done was to let the enemy into her house, let him into her body, he was growing there now. He thought in the same way they did; he, like them, believed he had innate rights over her because he was male and she female; he, like them, believed in things they called virginity and purity, or corruption and whoredom, in women. But he was gentle and respectful; he was among the best of men. If he was like them, there was no hope. It was not worthwhile living in such a world. She leaned back farther and closed her eyes; she began to rock gently in the chair. She went into a quiet darkened place in her mind. There were many ways to die, she did not have to think about that now. All she had to do was find a way out, and she had done that. She would die, and all this would end. It would go away. She would never again have to feel what she was feeling now, which was just like what she had been feeling for years, except stronger. The rockets were exploding all over her body. Her heart ached no more than her stomach or her brain. It was all exploding in fire and tears, and the tears were as hot and hurtful as the fires of rage. There was nothing to be said. He simply would not have understood. It went too deep, and it seemed that she was alone, that she was the only person who felt this way. It must be that, although she felt entirely right, she was wrong. It didn't matter. Nothing mattered.

After a long time, Norm approached her. He knelt down at the side of her chair. 'Honey,' he said sweetly. 'Honey?'

She rocked.

He put his hand on her shoulder and she shuddered away from it.

'Get away from me,' she said dully, her tongue cleaving to the roof of her mouth. 'Just leave me alone.'

He pulled a footstool over and sat close to her, putting his arms around her legs, laying his head in her lap. 'Honey, I'm sorry. It's just that I don't know how I'll finish school. Maybe my folks will help us.'

She knew it was true. She knew that he was just

frightened, as frightened as she. But he felt he had a
right to blame her. Upset as she had been when she
heard the news, it had not occurred to her to blame him.
She had seen it simply as a mess they were in together.
She put her hand on his head. It was not his fault. It was
just that everything was poisoned. It didn't matter. She
would die and be out of it. When she touched him, he
began to cry. He was as frightened as she, more frightened maybe. He clutched her legs tighter, he sobbed, he
apologized. He didn't mean it, he didn't know what had
got into him, it was ridiculous childishness, he was sorry.
He clutched and cried and she began to caress his head.
He cheered up, he looked at her, he caressed her cheek,
he joked, he wiped away the water that was running
down her face, he laid his head against her breast. She
wept fully in great jolting sobs and he held her against
him in astonishment, not having known, saying, 'I'm
sorry, honey, oh, God, I'm sorry,' thinking, she imagined, that she was weeping about his suspicion of her
fidelity, not knowing, never to know, never to understand. Finally he smiled up at her as her sobs came less
often and less strong, and asked her if she weren't hungry. She understood. She rose and made dinner. And in
January, she had the baby, and a year and a half later,
she had another. Norm's parents lent them money on a
note: eight thousand dollars to be repaid when he went
into practice. After that she got another diaphragm. But
by then she was a different person.

16

Virginia Woolf, whom I revere, complained about
Arnold Bennett. In a literary manifesto, she attacked his
way of writing novels. She thought he placed too much
emphasis on facts and figures, grimy dollars – or pounds
– on exterior elements that were irrelevant to the dancing moments that were a person. That essence shone, she
felt, through my accent, through ten-year-old winter
coats and string bags laden with vegetables and spaghetti, shone in the glance of an eye, in a sigh, a heavy if

enduring trudge down the steps of a train and off into the murky light of Liverpool. One doesn't need a person's bank statement to see their character. I don't care much for Bennett, and I love Woolf, but I think his grimy pounds and pence had more to do with her Rhoda and Bernard than she would admit. Oh, she did know. She understood the need for five hundred pounds a year; and a room of one's own. She could envision Shakespeare's sister. But she imagined a violent, an apocalyptic end for Shakespeare's sister, whereas I know that isn't what happened. You see, it isn't necessary. I know that lots of Chinese women, given in marriage to men they abhorred and lives they despised, killed themselves by throwing themselves down the family well. I'm not saying it doesn't happen. I'm only saying that isn't what usually happens. If it were, we wouldn't be having a population problem. And there are so much easier ways to destroy a woman. You don't have to rape or kill her; you don't even have to beat her. You can just marry her. You don't even have to do that. You can just let her work in your office for thirty-five dollars a week. Shakespeare's sister did, as Woolf thought, follow her brother to London, but she never got there. She was raped the first night out, and bleeding and inwardly wounded, she stumbled for shelter into the next village she found. Realizing before too long that she was pregnant, she sought a way to keep herself and her child safe. She found some guy with the hots for her, realized he was credulous, and screwed him. When she announced her pregnancy to him, a couple months later, he dutifully married her. The child, born a bit early, makes him suspicious: they fight, he beats her, but in the end he submits. Because there is something in the situation that pleases him: he has all the comforts of home including something Mother didn't provide, and if he has to put up with a screaming kid he isn't sure is his, he feels now like one of the boys down at the village pub, none of whom is sure they are the children of their fathers or the fathers of their children. But Shakespeare's sister has learned the lesson all women learn: men are the ultimate

61

enemy. At the same time she knows she cannot get along in the world without one. So she uses her genius, the genius she might have used to make plays and poems with, in speaking, not writing. She handles the man with language: she carps, cajoles, teases, seduces, calculates, and controls this creature to whom God saw fit to give power over her, this hulking idiot whom she despises because he is dense and fears because he can do her harm.

So much for the natural relation between the sexes.

But you see, he doesn't have to beat her much, he surely doesn't have to kill her: if he did, he'd lose his maidservant. The pounds and pence by themselves are a great weapon. They matter to men, of course, but they matter more to women, although their labor is generally unpaid. Because women, even unmarried ones, are required to do the same kind of labor regardless of their training or inclinations, and they can't get away from it without those glittering pounds and pence. Years spent scraping shit out of diapers with a kitchen knife, finding places where string beans are two cents less a pound, learning to wake at the sound of a cough, spending one's intelligence in figuring the most efficient, least time-consuming way to iron men's white shirts or to wash and wax the kitchen floor or take care of the house and kids and work at the same time and save money, hiding it from the boozer so the kid can go to college – these not only take energy and courage and mind, but they may constitute the very essence of a life.

They may, you say wearily, but who's interested? Well, you can go read about whales, or stockyards, or rivets if you like, or *One Day in the Life of Ivan Denisovich*. Truthfully, I hate these grimy details as much as you do. I love Dostoevsky, who doesn't harp on them but suggests them. They are always there in the background, like Time's winged chariot. But grimy details are not in the background of the lives of most women; they are the entire surface.

Mira had gone down twice, and she was to go down again. Then she drowned. After all her years of growth

62

and preparation, she reached maturity – for isn't giving birth to a child the realization of maturity? And then began the dwindling down. Woolf saw that, noticed it often – how women shrink after marriage. But Mira's going down, or even drowning, is also called sanity, accepting the inevitable one is not powerful enough to change. Still she was right when she wept walking down the aisle to be married; she was right when she wept in the rocking chair, choosing death.

Our culture believes strong individuals can transcend their circumstances. I myself don't much enjoy books by Hardy or Dreiser or Wharton, where the outside world is so strong, so overwhelming, that the individual hasn't a chance. I get impatient, I keep feeling that somehow the deck is stacked unfairly. That is the point, of course, but my feeling is that if that's true, I don't want to play. I prefer to move to another table where I can retain my illusion, if illusion it be, that I'm working against only probabilities, and have a chance to win. Then if you lose, you can blame it on your own poor playing. That is called a tragic flaw, and like guilt, it's very comforting. You can go on believing that there is really a right way, and you just didn't find it.

People I respect most, like Cassirer, beautiful soul, insist that the inside remains untouched by the exterior. Is this true, do you suppose? All my life I've read that the life of the mind is preeminent, and that it can transcend all bodily degradation. But that's just not my experience. When your body has to deal all day with shit and string beans, your mind does too.

17

Norm's confident sense that somehow this baby was all Mira's doing infected her. Although she was aware that rationally this was ridiculous, Norm's behavior – apologetic towards his parents for his rebellious wife who had gone and done exactly what they had warned her not to do, kindly tolerant of Mira's condition, tossing off his poor grades at the end of the first year as being not *really* her fault – was more potent than any rational argument. And by now, of course, it was all her doing. The thing was growing inside her. She began to feel squeamish, a drop of oil crushed by a boot. The roofing company she worked for did not like pregnant women in their office: pregnancy was somehow obscene and ought to be hidden, like used sanitary napkins. Mira stuffed what was left of her pride into the small box of mementos where it belonged, and went begging. She explained that her husband was a student – a *medical* student. It was a magic word. They allowed her, out of the kindness of their hearts, to work up to her eighth month, only adjuring her always to appear clean, neat, and well-groomed.

She was sick during the entire pregnancy, with constant nausea and stomach pain. It never occurred to her that this might be other than physically caused. Her small body swelled up enormously with the child, and by the seventh month she was miserably uncomfortable. She ate constantly to calm her stomach, and gained thirty-five pounds. During the last two months, after she had stopped working, she was so off balance that even walking was an effort and lying down was not much better. Mostly she sat in the darkened living-bedroom, her great belly propped by cushions on either side of her, her feet propped on a footstool, and read *Remembrance of Things Past*. She shopped, and cleaned the apartment, and cooked, and took the laundry to the laundromat (little dreaming that after the baby was born this would become one of her great pleasures – the chance to get out of the house alone, or at least accompanied only by a great white silent uncrying laundry bag). She ironed sheets and Norm's shirts and paid bills and read the recipe columns of the newspapers searching for an interesting or different way to serve inexpensive foods. The thing she most notably did not do was think.

I don't know what it is like to be pregnant voluntarily. I assume it's a very different experience from that of the women I know. Maybe it's joyful – something shared between the woman and her man. But for the women I know, pregnancy was terrible. Not because it's so painful – it isn't, only uncomfortable. But because it wipes you out, it erases you. You aren't you anymore, you have to forget you. If you see a green lawn in a park and you're hot and you'd love to sit on the grass and roll over in its cool dampness, you can't; you have to toddle over to the nearest bench and let yourself down gently on it. Everything is an effort – getting a can down from a high shelf is a major project. You can't let yourself fall, unbalanced as you are, because you're responsible for another life besides your own. You have been turned, by some tiny pinprick in a condom, into a walking, talking vehicle, and when this has happened against your will, it is appalling.

Pregnancy is a long waiting in which you learn what it means completely to lose control over your life. There are no coffee breaks, no days off in which you regain your normal shape and self, and can return refreshed to your labors. You can't wish away even for an hour the thing that is swelling you up, stretching your stomach until the skin feels as if it will burst, kicking you from the inside until you are black and blue. You can't even hit back without hurting yourself. The condition and you are identical: you are no longer a person, but a pregnancy. You're like a soldier in a trench who is hot and constricted and hates the food, but has to sit there for nine months. He gets to the point where he yearns for the battle, even though he may be killed or maimed in it. You look forward even to the pain of labor because it will end the waiting.

It is this sense of not being a self that makes the eyes of pregnant women so often look vacant. They can't let themselves think about it because it is intolerable and there is nothing they can do about it. Even if they let themselves think about afterward, it is depressing. After all, pregnancy is only the beginning. Once it is over, you have really had it: the baby will be there and it will be yours and it will demand of you for the rest of your life. The rest of your life: your whole life stretches out in front of you in that great belly of yours propped on cushions. From there it looks like an eternal sequence of bottles and diapers and cries and feedings. You have no self but a waiting, no future but pain, and no hope but the tedium of humble taks. Pregnancy is the greatest training, disciplining device in the human experience. Compared to it, army discipline that attempts to humble the individual, get him into the impersonal line that can function like a machine, is soft. The soldier gets time off to get back to his identity; he can, if he is willing to take the risk, retort to his superior, or even bolt. At night, as he lies on his bunk, he can play poker, write letters, remember, look forward to the day he'll get out.

All of this is what Mira did not think about, or at least tried not to think about. It was in these months that she developed her pursed lips and the set frown on her brow. She saw the situation as the end of her personal life. Her life, from pregnancy on, was owned by another creature.

What is wrong with this woman?? you ask. It is Nature, there is no recourse, she must submit and make the best of what she cannot change. But the mind is not easily subdued. Resentment and rebellion grow in it – resentment and rebellion against Nature itself. Some wills are crushed, but those that are not contain within them, for the rest of their days, seeds of hate. All of the women I know feel a little like outlaws.

18

At the end of her pregnancy, Mira could sleep only for brief snatches. Her body was so big and painful that any position hurt after a while. She would get up gently, so as not to wake Norm, put on the cotton wrapper which was the only thing that fit her now, and tiptoe into the kitchen. She would make tea and sit drinking it at the kitchen table, staring blankly at the walls which some-one had papered in yellow oilcloth patterned with little red houses with smoke coming out of their chimneys, and a little green tree next to each.

One night she could not sit. She paced the kitchen for an hour, thoughtless, listening to her body. The pains began and she woke Norm. He examined her and timed her, joking about the good luck that his course in gynecology had occurred the previous semester. He said it was early, but that he would take her to the hospital.

The nurses were cold and brusque. They sat her down and asked for information: father's name, mother's name, address, religion, Blue Cross number. Then they gave her a hospital gown and told her to get undressed in a cold damp room that looked and smelled like the locker room of a gym. She was in some pain now and the very air of the place irritated her as it brushed against her skin. They ordered her to get up on a table, and they shaved her pubic hair. The water was warm but it got cold as soon as they put it on her body, which was already shivering. Then they gave her an enema: it drove her insane, she couldn't believe they were doing this to her. Her belly and abdomen were aching worse and worse, as if part of her insides were pulling away from the rest and wrenching the organs with it and pounding down on her pelvic bones like a steady hammer. There was no let up, no rest, it just kept happening. At the same time, they were pumping warm water into her backside. It pulsed upward in a different rhythm, then bent her double with a different cramp. When it was over, they told her to get up on the table again, and they wheeled her into a different room. It was bare and functional: white walls and four beds, two against each wall, foot to head. They put her feet up into stirrups and laid a cloth over her knees. Every so often a nurse or an orderly would come into the room, lift the cloth and peer in. Out in the hall, beds on wheels were lined up waiting to enter the delivery room. The women on them were moaning, some crying, some silent. One screamed, 'God damn you, Morris, you bastard!' and another kept weeping, 'Oh, God, dear God, Mary, Jesus, Joseph, help me, help me.' The nurses threaded through the corridors unheeding. One woman shrieked, and a nurse turned and snapped at her, 'Stop being such a baby! You'd think you were dying!'

The bed behind Mira was closed off by a pink curtain hanging on iron rings from a bar set in the walls. The

woman in the bed kept expelling air in great gusts:
'Unnh! Unhh!' She called for the nurse, but no one
came. She called several times, and finally gave a piercing shriek. A nurse ran in.

'What is it now, Mrs. Martinelli?' There was irritation
and contempt in her voice. Mira could not see the nurse,
but she imagined her standing there with hands on her
hips and a sneer on her face.

'It's time for the spinal,' the woman wailed in the
irritating whine of the child, the helpless, the victim
known and accepted. 'Tell the doctor to come, it's time.'

The nurse was silent; there was a ruffling of a sheet.
'It's not time yet.'

The woman's voice rose hysterically. 'It is, it is! I
ought to know, I've had five kids. I know when it's
coming. It'll be too late, it happened before, it was too
late and they couldn't give it to me at all. Tell him, tell
the doctor!'

The nurse left, and after a time a gray-faced man in a
rumpled suit entered. He went to Mrs. Martinelli's bed.
'Well, what's this I hear about you stirring up a rumpus,
Mrs. Martinelli? I thought you were a brave girl.'

The woman's voice cringed and whimpered. 'Oh,
Doctor, please give me the spinal. It's time, I know it's
time, I've had five kids . . . you know I told you when I
came to you what happened to me the last time. Please.'

'It's not time yet, Mrs. Martinelli. Quiet down now
and don't bother the nurses. Don't worry. Trust me.
Everything will be fine.'

She was silent, and he trudged out, his mouth pursed,
Mira was sure, with contempt for the troublesome
woman. She firmed her own mouth. She would not do
that, she determined; she would not act whiny and
childish and cry. She would not utter a sound. She would
be good. No matter how bad the pain got, she would
show them that a woman could have courage.

Mrs. Martinelli was stubborn, though. She was silent
only until the doctor left, like a child who has been
warned that another cry will reap another blow, and
waits until the parent has left the room to resume their

68

whimpering. She cried softly, talking to herself, murmuring over and over without pause, 'I ought to know, I've had five kids, it'll be too late, oh, God, I know it'll be too late, I know it, I know it.'

Mira tried not to feel. It was not the labor that was agonizing her: it hurt, but not too much. It was the scene – the coldness and sterility of it, the contempt of the nurses and the doctor, the humiliation of being in stirrups and having people peer at her exposed genitals whenever they chose. She tried to pull away into some inner place where all this did not exist. A phrase kept going through her mind: there is no other way out.

Suddenly Mrs. Martinelli shrieked again. A nurse came in, sighing angrily under her breath. She did not speak; Mrs. Martinelli was simply screaming now. The nurse ran out, then came back with another nurse. Swiftly they pushed back the pink curtain. Mira half sat up. A third nurse came in with the doctor and saw her.

'Sit down, lie down!' she ordered Mira, but Mira rose up and awkwardly turned her upper body to watch. They were beginning to wheel Mrs. Martinelli's bed out of the room. Mira looked: between Mrs. Martinelli's raised knees a small furry brown head was emerging from a pinkish doorway. A nurse glanced at Mira and quickly threw a cloth over Mrs. Martinelli's knees. The woman was just crying out, 'Oh, Jesus, help me, God, help me.' It was too late for the spinal, too late for reproach. They wheeled her into the delivery room.

19

An hour and a half later, they sent Mira home. Her labor had completely stopped. She sat in the apartment, knitting her fingers. Norm went to school, but told her he would be near a phone all day. She sat in the kitchen, staring at the wallpaper. In midafternoon, the pains started again, but she did not move. She did not eat or drink. When Norm came home, earlier than usual, he took one look at her and cried out, 'What are you doing, sweetheart? You should be at the hospital!' He gathered her up and helped her down the stairs. She let herself be manipulated.

They put her back in the same bed, in the same room. The baby was coming, she knew that. It was painful, but the pain was only physical. Her mind held another sort, much worse. She kept thinking: This is one thing that once you're in it, there's no other way out. She rebelled. She refused to have anything to do with it. It had happened against her will, beyond her control; it could end as it chose, against her will, beyond her control. The room, the moaning women, the nurses, faded. There was a clear white space just above the pain, and she stretched her head to breathe in it. She was vaguely aware that someone gave her a shot, that they were wheeling her someplace. She heard her doctor's voice scolding her: 'You have to push! Push! You have to help!'

'Go to hell,' she said, or thought she said. And lost consciousness.

They delivered the baby with instruments. It arrived with two deep cuts in its temples and a pointed head. The doctor came to see her early the next morning.

'Why did you hypnotize yourself?'

She looked at him vaguely. 'I didn't know I did.'

She lay there surrounded by pink curtain in a different room. The light came through the curtains; the world was pink.

They would not let her see the baby. She began to ask about it after a few hours, and they told her it was a boy and that it was fine. But they wouldn't bring it in.

She raised herself up from the bed. 'Nurse!' She called peremptorily, the first time in her life she had acted that way. When the nurse came through the pink curtains, Mira spoke with contained fury: 'I want to see my baby! It's my baby and I have a right to it! Get it!' The nurse, surprised, darted out. About twenty minutes later another nurse appeared, carrying an infant in a receiving blanket. She stood about a foot away from Mira, holding it, but she would not let Mira touch it.

She was wild. 'Get my doctor!' she shouted. Luckily, he was in the hospital, and came racing in about a half hour later. He looked at her with worry in his face; he asked her some questions. Why did she want to see the baby?

'Because it's my baby!' she exploded, then, seeing the concern on his face, she settled back against the pillow. 'The way they won't let me see it makes me think there's something wrong with it,' she said more calmly.

He nodded understandingly at this. 'I'll have them bring it,' he said kindly, and patted her hand.

She began to understand that because of the way she'd acted during delivery, they thought she was crazy and would harm the child. Later in the week, a nurse confirmed that sometimes women do. Sometimes they even kill themselves, or try to. It had a name: post-partum depression. She smiled bitterly. It was insanity, of course. All women were thrilled to get pregnant, over-joyed to go into labor, and worked their mightiest to help the nice doctor. They were all good little girls and when their babies were born, they were just so happy! And cuddled the little darlings and cooed. Of course. And if you didn't do that, you were nuts. It never occurred to anyone to ask why women would kill the babies that had cost them so much pain, or kill themselves after the pain was over. But she had learned her lesson. They had the power. You had to act the way they expected you to act or they could keep the child of your own body and your own pain from you. You had to figure out their expectations and adjust yourself to them, and if you did that you might be able to make it in this world. When the nurse came again with the child, Mira smiled at her. She asked again about the indentations and the pointed head, not trusting what the morning nurse had told her. She understood that those marks were a stigma upon her, not the child: *she had not pushed*. Finally the nurse laid the infant in her arms, and after watching her for a few minutes, left.

It felt funny. The nurse had said not to leave its neck unsupported, because it could not hold up its own head. And not to touch the top of the head because it was still soft, the skull wasn't closed yet. It was terrifying. The

71

baby looked old and wizened like an aged man. It had some fuzz on its head. When she was sure the nurse was gone, she stopped smiling and opened the receiving blanket. She peered in. Two arms, two legs, hands and feet intact. She looked with amazement at the ten tiny nails on hands and feet. They were a little bluer than the rest of the body, which was splotched red and blue. Nervously, peering up to see if the nurse had returned, Mira undid the pins on one side of the diaper. A penis, tiny as a worm, suddenly darted up and pissed right in her eye. She laughed.

She closed the diaper up again, and surveyed the baby. She saw family resemblances, mostly to a dead uncle of hers. It was lying with closed eyes, but its mouth was working and the tiny hands were convulsively clutching. It must be scared, she thought, after all that time in the warm dark. She put her pinky into the tiny palm when it opened, and it grabbed her finger hard and held it fast. The tiny fingers turned blue with the effort, the nails were dead white. Something went through her body as he clenched her pinky. He seemed to be trying to get it to his mouth. She smiled: always, always, from the very beginning: I want, I want. She left her finger in his grasp and helped him guide it to his mouth. He tried to suck at it, although he didn't seem really to know how. She held him close against her breast and lay back resting with him. He settled against her, almost turning toward her, and relaxed. After a while, the nurse came and took him away.

Mira rested against the pillow, her body utterly still. Her arms felt empty. She felt something happening inside her body, a pull that started around her genitals and pierced through her stomach, her chest, her heart, right into her throat. Her breast ached. She wanted to put it in his mouth; she wanted to hold him in her arms. She wanted to put her finger in his hand, and to let him lie against her, warmed by her body, feeling her heartbeat. She wanted to take care of him. What she was feeling, she knew, was love, a love blinder and more irrational than even sexual love. She loved him because he

72

needed her; it was secondary that he happened to be hers, to have come from her body. He was helpless and he would move against her as if her body were his own, as if she were a source of everything he wanted. She knew that her life would from now on be dictated by that tiny creature, that his needs would be the most important thing in her life, that forever and forever she would be trying to fill that convulsive grasp, that rosebud hole of mouth, wiping urine out of her eye. But somehow it was all right because of that love, which was not just love, which was more even than need: it was absolute will and the answer to all ache.

20

She had heard, during the course of the day, voices outside the pink curtains. They were soft, even whispered, and she had not heard what they were saying. But now the nurse, apparently deciding she was sane after all, pulled back the curtains around her bed. She was in a large bright room with three other women; the beds were all placed with the headboards against the walls. The women greeted her like a late guest for whom they had been waiting.

'Oh, you're awake! We tried not to disturb you.'

'How do you feel? Do your stiches hurt?'

'Your baby is beautiful. I saw the nurse bring him in. He's going to be a hoosher! He woke up the whole maternity ward last night.' She laughed, showing several missing teeth.

Mira laughed too. 'I feel fine, thank you. And you?'

They all felt fine. They were in the middle of a conversation. Later, Mira could not remember what it had been about. It didn't matter: their talk was never linear, it did not have a beginning and an end, a point to be made. It went round and round and round. They could talk about anything, because the point was not in what they said. For four days, Mira listened to them; she even joined in. They compared how many stitches they had but never complained about them, except once, when the curtain was drawn and the nurse was bathing Amelia, Mira heard her whisper a little anxiously that she was having considerable pain 'down there'. They compared pounds and ounces of childflesh produced, oohing at tiny Amelia's thirteen-pounder. They compared number and order of children. Grace had seven, Amelia had four, Margaret had two, and this was Mira's first. 'Your first!' they exclaimed, smiling with joy, as if she had accomplished some marvelous feat. She had. She was one of them now.

They talked about their other children. Margaret was worried about her three-year-old: would he accept the new baby? Grace laughed, then caught herself and put her hand on her side with a gasp. She had had a Caesarean. She didn't worry about such things anymore, she resumed. Her children would be confused if they did not find a new baby in the small crib every two years. How old was her eldest? Mira asked. Sixteen, she said. Mira wanted to ask, but did not, how old she herself was. She could have been anywhere between thirty-four or -five and fifty-odd, Mira calculated, but she looked fifty-odd. She was the one with the missing teeth. When Mira saw her husband, who visited that evening, she knew that Grace had to be in her thirties: her husband looked young.

They talked and talked and talked, but had great delicacy. If one of them leaned back against her pillow and closed her eyes, the others lowered their voices and sometimes subsided into complete silence. They talked about babies, children, rashes, colic, formulas, diets, fretting. They talked about the best way to repair a torn carpet, their favorite recipes for hamburger, easy ways to make a sun-suit. They had their children categorized and discussed them that way: one had a temper, another was shy, a third was smart, a fourth didn't get along with his father. But they seemed to make no judgments about these things. They gave her no sense that they were pleased or displeased with temper, shyness, intelligence, or harmoniousness. Their children simply were, they were what they were, and the women loved them no

74

matter what they were. It was their children who occupied them; they rarely mentioned their husbands. When they did, it was in passing, as one might mention the rules of the institution in which one is incarcerated. Husbands were strange, inexplicable creatures to whom one must defer, outer constrictions which must be placated. One would eat no fish, another no vegetables, another refused to eat with children at the dinner table. One bowled three nights a week and had to be fed early. One permitted no vacuuming to be done while he was in the house. Their private relations with their men, their feelings, were hidden, and Mira felt strongly that they were secondary to the great, the engrossing fact of children.

She was drawn to these women because of their warmth and their easy acceptance of her. She realized that had she lived down the block from any of them, they might not be so accepting. The hospital ward, like any artificial collective, makes for easy bedfellows. Their conversation often bored her, although she learned from it: she went home and mended the carpet in the bed-living room as Amelia had suggested, and it worked. But it was not their conversation itself she listened to: she listened to what lay beneath it. As they grew stronger and the pain of the stitches subsided, they laughed more often and more heartily. Husbands, mothers-in-law, children: all were subjects for humor. But they never talked about themselves.

They did not complain, they did not insist, they did not demand, they did not seem to want anything. Mira, used to the egotistic male world with its endless 'I', being in fact part of it herself, was astonished by the selflessness of these women. She had always enjoyed asserting *her* intellect, *her* opinions, *her* knowledge, but as she listened to what a month ago she would have called stupid conversation, she heard what the women were really saying and it shamed her. It was: yes, I am like you. I worry about the same things as you – the everyday, the trivial, the petty economics, and small repairs. And I, like you, know that these mundane events somehow mean more than the large sweeping things, the corporation mergers, invasions, depressions, and decisions of the President's Cabinet. Not that the things I am concerned with are important. Heavens, no, they're just little things, but they matter, you know, they matter most to a life. To my life, my children's life, even my husband's life, although he'd never admit it. My husband threw a tantrum because there was no coffee in the house one morning! Would you believe it? A grown man. Yes, these things matter very much to them. And my own life – well, my life is bounded by small things. When Johnny has had a good day at Little League; when the sun pours through the kitchen window in a certain way on a fall morning; when I am able to transform cheap meat into a delicious stew, or my shoddy room into something almost – not quite – beautiful; those are the times I am happy. When I feel useful, when there is harmony in my world.

She listened and she heard their acceptance, their love, their selflessness, and for the first time in her life, she thought that women were great. Their greatness made all the exploits of warriors and rulers look like pompous self-aggrandizement, made even the poets and painters look like egotistical children jumping up and down shouting, 'Look at me, Ma!' Their pains, their problems, were secondary to the harmony of the whole. The same women who had moaned or cursed downstairs in the labor room had chosen to forget the pain, the bitterness. Brave they were. Brave and good-humored and accepting, they picked up the dropped stitches and finished knitting something warm for someone else, letting their own teeth rot and skimping on clothes to pay Johnny's dentist bill, laying aside their desire like a crushed flower from their first prom stuck in the back of a baby book.

She looked at them with eyes blinded by sunlight and smiled, hearing Margaret worry again about whether her three-year-old was unhappy without her, and Amelia worrying about whether her mother was remembering to put fruit rather than candy in Jimmy's lunchbox, and Grace, silent and lined with her worries, hoping that Johnny had got his bike fixed, and that Stella was coping with the cooking. She smiled with them, laughed with them at the absurdities of the big world. She was unable to be with them with more than her heart, but was that. She felt she had arrived, finally, at womanhood.

21

Valerie, of course, snorted when she heard this. We were sitting around in Val's place one night, Iso and Ava, Clarissa, Kyla, and me, and Mira told us about her experience of childbirth. It was in the late fall of 1968, and we didn't know each other well as a group. We were still skirting around the edges of politeness, not yet sure enough of each other to let it go completely, but getting there.

Although we weren't aware of this then, we had been brought together by our dislike of the same things – values and behavior we saw all around us at Harvard. Our dislike was of a specific kind: all the first-year graduate students were unhappy there. But we were not so much unhappy as outraged, and our dislike, as we would come to realize, was the expression of a profound and positive sense of the way things *ought* to be. On this evening, however, we were still feeling each other out.

We were complimenting Val on the beauty of her apartment. She had little money, but she'd painted it, filled it with plants, and strewn it with odds and ends collected in her travels. It was a delightful place.

And Mira said – in that sort of gushing suburban way she had – how wonderful women were, look at Val's beautiful apartment, no man would have been willing to do it or would have had the imagination, especially with so little money. And Kyla, who had also beautifully fixed up her and Harley's apartment, jumped to agree. Then Mira said she'd suddenly seen how great women were after giving birth to Normie, and she described the experience. And Val snorted.

'You bought it! You bought the whole damned bag!'

Mira blinked.

'How convenient to have a whole class of people who

77

give up their lives for other people! How nice, while you're out doing things that serve your ego, to have somebody home washing the bathroom floor and picking up your dirty underwear! And never, never cooking brussels sprouts because you don't like them.'

Everybody burst in at once.

'It's true, it's true!!' Kyla crowed.

'How come you don't do that for me?' Isolde grinned at Ava.

Clarissa, serious-faced, tried to get a word in – 'I don't think . . .'

But Val was not to be stopped. 'I mean, Mira, don't you hear what you're saying? "Women's greatness lies in their selflessness." You might as well say women's place is in the home.'

'Nonsense!' Mira began to turn a little pink. 'I'm not prescribing, I'm describing. The constrictions exist. No matter what you say about the way things ought to be, they are the way they are. And if the world changed tomorrow, it would be too late for those women . . .'

'Is it too late for you?' Kyla shot in.

Mira leaned back, half laughing. 'Look, all I'm saying is that women are great because they get so little and give so much . . .'

'Exactly!' Val stormed.

Isolde giggled. 'She'll never be allowed to get it out.'

'They have so little room,' Mira went on doggedly, 'but they don't get bitter and mean, they try to make that little room graceful and harmonious.'

'Tell it to the women in the schizophrenic wards. Or the ones who sit in their kitchens drinking themselves to death. Or the ones covered with bruises from the husbands who got drunk last night. Or the ones who burn their children's hands.'

'I'm not saying all women . . .'

'Okay,' Clarrisa began authoritatively, and the room quietened a bit, 'but not all these things spring from the same root. Men have constrictions too.'

'I'm not worried about men,' Val exclaimed. 'Let them worry about themselves. They've taken pretty good

78

care of themselves for the past four thousand years. And women's problems *do* all spring from the same root: that they're women. Everything Mira's told us about her life shows it to be one long training in humiliation, an education in suppressing self.'

'That's as if you're saying women have no individual identity,' Isolde demurred.

'They don't. Not when you talk about women's greatness or women's constrictions: as soon as you say that, you're admitting an identity among all women, which implies lack of individuality. Kyla asked if Mira had been destroyed by her constrictions, and the answer is yes, or nearly so. Look!' she plunked her glass down on the table, 'my real point is that to tell women they're great because they've given themselves up is to tell them to go on doing it.'

Mira held up her hand like a traffic cop ordering *Stop*. 'Wait,' she ordered. 'I want you to keep quiet a minute, Val, because I want to answer you, but I have to figure out what I want to say.'

Val laughed and got up. 'Okay. Who wants more wine?'

When she returned, Mira said, 'Okay,' in that thoughtful way we had all picked up from Clarissa, whose mind clicked points off like a clock measuring precise moments, each one preceded by 'Okay.' 'Yes. I want them to go on doing it.'

Howls.

'I mean it. What will happen to the world if they don't do it? It would be unbearable. Who else would do it? The men go to work to make life possible and the women work to make it bearable.'

'Why are you in graduate school, then?' Kyla was nearly leaping out of her chair. 'Why are you living in – pardon me – that sterile grungy drab apartment of yours? Why aren't you making a nice cozy home for your boys and your husband?'

'I was! I would be!'

'And you loved it.'

'I hated it.'

They all laughed, and Mira too grinned wryly, then began to laugh.

'Okay. You're not saying – tell me if I'm wrong, Mira – but you're not saying that creating felicity is all women should do. You're saying it's part of what they should do. Am I right?' Kyla still perched forward, as if Mira's answer were the most important thing in the world to her.

'No. I'm saying it's what they do do, and it's beautiful.'

'Okay.' It was Clarissa this time. 'But if they want to and can do other things as well, so much the better, right?'

Mira nodded, and everyone leaned back. A kind of peace fell among them. They were glad that their boundaries meshed. But the peace was only momentary.

Val leaned back in her chair and crossed her arms. 'Sure, sure. As long as women do what they're supposed to do, what they've always done, we're told. (But I doubt it: when they were out plowing the fields or hauling in the fishing nets or marching to war, as they did in Scotland and other places, they didn't have much time for interior decoration or gourmet cuisine. This whole shit about what woman's labor is supposed to be is only about a hundred years old – do you realize that? It's no older than the industrial revolution, and probably really began on a wide scale in the Victorian period.) Well, anyway, if women do what is now conceived to be their natural and proper job and have any time or energy left over, they then have permission to do something else. But in fact if you've been brainwashed into selflessness, it wouldn't occur to you to do what you wanted to do, you wouldn't even think in such terms. There isn't enough *you* to want.'

'That's not true!' Kyla exclaimed. 'I do both. I really take care of Harley, I take care of the apartment, I cook – Harley always makes breakfast, of course,' she added quickly. 'And I do what I want to do too.'

Isolde's quiet voice broke in startlingly. 'And look at you.'

Everyone turned to look at Isolde instead, even Kyla,

who almost jumped around in her chair to face her.

'You're a nervous wreck, you have bags under your eyes, you get hysterical every time you have three drinks . . .'

'Wait a minute, I'm not that bad . . .'

'For Superwoman,' Val smiled at Kyla, 'it may be possible if difficult. What about more ordinary mortals?'

It went on like that. It was Clarissa, finally, who came up with a solution, who suggested that the only way to resolve it was to insist that everyone should have some selflessness, that everyone should act in both roles. Everyone agreed.

But you know, it didn't help. It was a rhetorical solution. Because the fact is that everyone doesn't act in both roles and probably can't and not everyone would be willing to accept that and so the whole thing seemed to me as if we'd been talking about the street plan and architecture of heaven. In fact, it didn't make much sense even for us to insist that men and women both should be selfless, because although we were all in graduate school, all of us took the female role at home, especially Kyla and Clarissa, who had husbands, and Val, who had a child, and sometimes a man staying with her. Even Ava, who rarely did domestic tasks, would rush home from work when she and Iso were having guests for dinner because she was convinced that Isolde's cooking would poison everyone. She'd cook chicken tarragon and risotto and worry over it. And we were supposed to be 'liberated'.

I mentioned this, and Isolde sighed. 'I hate discussions of feminism that end up with who does the dishes,' she said. So do I. But at the end, there are always the damned dishes.

CHAPTER TWO

1

After all her elation in the hospital, it was dirty dishes Mira came home to and her life, for several years afterward, seemed an unending mound of them. She and Norm stayed in their two-room apartment for a few months after Normie was born, but it was too crowded, so they moved to a place with a bedroom and living room. When she found herself pregnant a second time, she was distressed only briefly. Might as well have it now, she told herself, not finishing the thought. Now, she meant, when I am nobody already and have no other life anyway.

For months, her day began at 2:00 A.M. with one of the babies waking hungry. She would rise quickly when the baby began to cry, gather him up in blankets, and take him out of the room before he could awaken Norm. She would lay him on the living room floor, gently shutting the bedroom door before his yells got too loud. Clutching her old flannel bathrobe about her – the apartment was always cold at that hour – she would go into the kitchen, turn on the oven, leaving the door open, then heat the bottle. When the baby could hold up its head, she carried him with her, propping him against her as she worked at the stove. She would close the kitchen door and sit with the baby at the table, feeding him in the warm room.

She usually got back to bed again, the baby full and changed, by about 3:00, and could sleep until 6:30 or 7:00, when Normie or Clark would again realize that their stomachs were empty. Norm also got up then, so there was an hour of chaos, with baby screaming. Norm showering, and Mira trying to heat a bottle, make coffee, and cook some eggs for Norm. After Clark was born, the chaos was compounded by little Normie, old enough to move but not yet to walk, crawling restlessly among the kitchen chairs and his mother's feet in search of adventure. After Norm left, Mira could sit down and feed the baby or babies boiled eggs and cereal, bathe them and dress them, and put the little one back in a clean bed, laying him on the floor – you can't fall off the floor – while she changed the urinous sheets. By nine she had baby clothes soaking in the deep sink and soiled diapers boiling in a large pot. She could then make the bed, clean up the bathroom, get the bottles in the sterilizer, dress herself, and clean the apartment, which, because it housed so many people and was so small, was constantly dusty and messy. By eleven thirty she had scrubbed the baby's clothes and the diapers on a washboard and hung them out on the clothesline strung from the apartment window to a pole out in the backyard. This was tricky, especially in cold weather, when her fingers froze. If she dropped something, she had to leave the children alone and run down three flights of stairs, go back into the yard, retrieve it, run back up panting, rewash it, and hope she did not repeat her error. Then she would put the potatoes in the stove-top oven and start baking them, and begin to heat the jars of strained meat. This was also tricky: Normie didn't like liver and lamb and spit them out when she fed them to him. Clark didn't like chicken. But some days they would spit out things they had swallowed the day before.

Babies need fresh air, so after cleaning up the lunch dishes (having swallowed some tea while she was feeding them, and eating the skins from the baked potatoes), she would bundle the baby up, put on warm clothes herself, gather the baby in one arm and the collapsible carriage in the other, and lug both down three flights of stairs. The real problem came at the bottom, when she needed both hands to set up the carriage, but had to find someplace to put the baby. Sometimes a neighbor helped her. Sometimes she simply had to lay the baby on the sidewalk. This problem was aggravated when there were two, neither of whom could walk. After settling them in, she would walk to the grocery store. She had to shop every day for perishables, since she could not carry much at a time. From there, she would walk to the park, where there were other young mothers sitting on benches, airing their children.

She liked these women and was cheered when she saw them. They were often the only people she spoke to all day, since Norm was frequently absent at night, and even when he did come home he had to study. The women talked with passionate interest about stool color and formulas, colic and its causes; they compared notes, offered helpful hints, and admired each other's children. It was as if there existed a secret sisterhood, an underground movement to which anyone could belong who had a baby. Any new women who strolled past with infants in carriages were easily welcomed, were immediate friends. But there was almost never any conversation about anything else. In the year or two Mira knew these women, she never discovered anything about their husbands except their first names, and sometimes, their occupations. This was not because of reticence. The women were simply not interested in anything, but children; they really felt – although they could not have articulated it – like members of a secret cult that was fascinated by children, childbirth, and childrearing. They did not have to try to keep their group secret, they did not need rites, handshakes, rulebooks; no one else was in the least interested. They felt united by their profound and delicate knowledge; tacitly, by a smile or a nod, they told each other that this was the most, no, the only important thing in life. Outsiders seemed to them cut off from the beating heart of things.

Mira would sit there with them as long as she could. When he could walk, Normie would play in the grass – or snow – with other infants. But around three thirty; he began to fuss and cry. Everyone understood. All children had their bad time. If a woman left early, or was too distracted to talk much, no one commented. The babies came first; the babies were everything; no one expected anything else.

Mira would walk home carrying the tired, fretful

Normie in one arm, pushing the carriage with the other. Getting upstairs was a bit of a problem. She did it in shifts, carrying baby, groceries, and purse up first, entering the apartment, laying the baby on the floor and putting the groceries in the kitchen, then returning for the carriage. After Clark was born, she would take only babies and purse, and return for groceries and carriage. She was always anxious, fearing that either baby or babies would hurt themselves or that the carriage and groceries would be stolen while she was upstairs.

When she got back into the apartment, her heart sank. This was the worst time of day. The baby would wake up fussy, wanting to be played with; Normie was cranky and hungry. And she had to start dinner. On nights when Norm came home early, he wanted to eat immediately. She would work in the kitchen, then go and play with them, then return as she smelled something burning or heard something boiling over. (Norm complained much about her cooking in those years.) But each time she returned to the kitchen, one child or the other, sometimes both, screamed. She let them cry, peeled her potatoes or turnips, strung the beans, and then went back to them. Norm did not like to come home to their confusion, so she tried to feed them before he got in, but whichever one she fed first, the other cried and fussed.

Norm sometimes played with them a little, but he had no notion of how to play with a baby except to throw it in air and catch it, and she would not let him do that. They had just eaten, and she wanted them to relax so they could sleep, and not get all excited. Even so, more often than not, while she and Norm sat at the kitchen table trying to talk, they were interrupted several times by fretful children. Mira was always leaping up to go to them, and after a while, Norm brought a book to the table and simply read while he ate.

2

Things changed, of course. Babies grow. By the time she had perfected the art of vacuuming with a child on

85

her hip (screaming at the noise of the vacuum), they were able to walk. And then, there were the evenings.

Norm would go into the living room to study directly after dinner. Mira would wash and dry the dishes, thinking only that in a little while she would be free. She would take her shower then, brush her hair out, and go into the living room with a book. From eight thirty to eleven, she read. By ten she was sleepy, but there was no point in going to bed then, since the baby would wake at eleven for his final bottle. She and Norm rarely talked. Norm finished med school the June after Clark's birth, but then he was interning and he seemed to study even more than before. Often, he was on duty at night, and Mira found herself looking forward to that. For he could not sleep in 'this damned place with all the noise' when he was there in the daytime, so he would drive from the hospital to his mother's house where he could sleep in peace in his old bedroom. Sometimes he ate there too, and Mira did not see him for three or four days. Norm was apologetic about this once he realized Mira was not going to complain. But she found it easier with him gone. She could adjust her schedule completely to the babies and wasn't nearly as anxious when they cried. Norm was often tired and irritable: it was hard, she thought, to be under pressure all day long, and have to come home to a tiny place full of screaming infants. It would be better when they had a little more room; it would be better when the kids were a little older; it would be better when they had a little more money.

They had little sex life. Norm was away, or he was tired. But the pattern that had begun at their marriage had enforced itself now as unbreakable. Coitus was quick and unsatisfying. Mira lay back and permitted it. Norm seemed to realize she did not enjoy it; strangely, this seemed to please him. She could only guess at this: they never discussed it. Once or twice, she tried to talk to him about it, but he adamantly refused. He refused with charm, not hostility, teasing her, calling her a 'sexpot,' or smiling that he was completely happy, and putting his hand on her cheek. But it seemed to her that he felt it was somehow proper for her not to enjoy sex; it made her more worthy of respect. On the rare occasions when he wanted to make love, he apologized to her for it, explaining that for a male body it was necessary.

But there were pleasures in Mira's life: the children themselves. They were a deep pleasure, especially when she was alone with them and wasn't anxious about preparing Norm's dinner, or about their making noise. Holding their tiny bodies, bathing them as they gurgled with pleasure, oiling and powdering them while they poked at her face or at their own, trying to figure out what eyes and noses were, she would smile endlessly, unconciously. She had seen their birth and the birth of her love for them as miraculous, but it was just as miraculous when they first smiled, first sat up, first babbled a sound that resembled, of course, mama. The tedious days were filled with miracles. When a baby first looks at you; when it gets excited at seeing a ray of light and like a dog pawing a gleam, tries to capture it in its hand; or when it laughs that deep, unselfconscious gurgle; or when it cries and you pick it up and it clings sobbing to you, saved from some terrible shadow moving across the room, or a loud clang in the street, or perhaps, already, a bad dream: then you are – happy is not the precise word – filled. Mira still felt as she had the first time she held Normie in the hospital, that the child and her feeling for it were somehow absolute, truer and more binding than any other experience life had to offer: she felt she lived at the blind true core of life.

Suddenly teeth appeared, tiny white shoots in the vulva-soft pink of their gums. They moved, crawled, stood up, took some steps, with the exaltation and delight and terror the first human must have felt when she stood up on her hind legs. Then they were talking, two words, seven, then no more counting. They looked at her seriously, looked in her eyes and asked and spoke. They were complete little people talking to her from a mind she knew nothing about and would have to learn to apprehend; although this person had grown in her body, had torn it emerging, had once shared pulse and food

87

and blood and joy and grief, it was now a separate person whose innards, mind and spirit and emotion, she would never completely comprehend. It was as if one weren't born suddenly, but progressively; as if each birth were also a death, each step they made in development moving them further away from her, from their oneness with her, and in time, far, far away from her, they would merge with others, have children themselves, join and separate, until the final separation, which would also be a birth into a new mode. They would ask questions, make statements and demands: 'Dis blue?' 'Hot. Mats hot.' 'Cookie!' Spoken imperiously. She would answer or agree or negate, but she had no idea where her statements went, into what context of thinking and feeling, what network of colors and tastes and sounds they had already built up.

Not that they didn't have personalities from the beginning. Mira had her own set of old wives' tales and believed in them as much as if she had been an old Irishwoman sitting by a hearth in Galway. Normie, who had lain in a churning anxious unhappy womb, who had had to be dragged out of her by metal tongs, was independent and unfriendly. He did not smile until he was over four months old. He tottered around the apartment as soon as he could walk, resenting any guidance from Mira, furious if he were not permitted to touch something. Yet he was also demanding; he was often fussy, and would not calm even if she held him. He wanted something, but didn't know what. He was very bright; he talked early and was drawing deductions before he could walk. Staring at the coatrack as she held him in her arms after he'd wakened from a daytime sleep one day, he said, 'Daddy bye-bye.' She didn't understand at first, then realized he saw that Norm's raincoat was missing, which had to mean so was Norm. He was a restless, searching child, seeming always to want to be a step ahead of where he was.

Clark, on the other hand, had rested in a still, accepting womb. His birth had been easy – he seemed to just slide out. He smiled at ten days, and Norm said it was gas, but Clark did it every time he saw her and finally Norm had to admit it was a smile. He clung to her, he smiled at her, he pattered to her, he loved her. Yet she could leave him in a jump seat for an hour and he would bounce around and entertain himself. He was, in the early years, what people called an angel of a baby, and sometimes Mira worried that he was too good. She broke her attention away from Normie purposely sometimes to go and play with Clark, fearful that Normie's demanding nature would accustom her to cater to it alone and ignore Clark.

Of course there were worries too. Oh, God, I remember those years! A petulant afternoon convinces you you've turned out a monster; two rainy days of squabbling children and you're sure you have a severe case of sibling rivalry (which is all your fault – you're giving them insufficient attention) on your hands. Every fever is a potential killer, every cough wrenches your own insides. Some dimes taken from a table indicate a potential thief; one well-drawn picture indicates a potential Matisse. Lordy, lordy. Well, I'm glad I know better for my grandchildren, if I ever have any.

Yes, a blind true core. It was what I imagine it is like to live on a huge ocean liner run by engines buried in a base deck, and to tend, feed, and stoke, to hear and see, all day long, every day, the great pounding heart – except you watch it grow and change, watch it take over the ship. And that is magnificent, but it is also obliterating. You do not exist; even they are secondary, the children, to the fact of life itself. Their needs and desires are, must be, subordinate to their survival, to the great pounding heart that must be kept alive. The tender of a child is the priest in a temple; the child is the vessel; what is sacred is the fire within it. Unlike priests, however, tenders of children do not receive privilege and respect; their lives pass unnoticed even by themselves as the washing and feeding, the caring and slapping – 'Hot! Match hot! No, no!' – goes on.

The face and body change; the eyes forget the world; the interests narrow to focus on the energies of one or two or three small bodies presently charging around the room screaming at high pitch on 'horsies' made of broomsticks. Sacred fire may occasionally smoke; sacred life often jars.

· But either obliterates the individual. There were things going on in the world while Mira was caring for her children. Eisenhower had been elected; Joseph McCarthy was having some trouble with the United States Army. But the most striking event in Mira's life apart from the children occurred one day when she was down on her hands and knees scrubbing the kitchen floor, and one of the babies began to cry, and Norm was out – at the hospital, sleeping at his mother's, somewhere. And she sat back on her heels, shaking her head up and down, half smiling, half grimacing, remembering her fears of marrying Lanny. It had all happened anyhow. Oedipus couldn't escape his fate, and neither could she. The scenario had been written before she was even born.

3

Once, when Tad had been listening to Val talk about her former husband, he shook his head slowly and said, 'I used to wish I'd known you when you were young. I used to imagine you riding your bike down the street, with your hair flying, passing me on the sidewalk and waving, and me standing there, a sophisticated twenty, giving you a special eye, marking you out for myself. I don't wish that anymore. You women eat men. You get men to make you pregnant, to take care of you and the kids while they're little, and then you shut the door, you toss them out, you clutch your kids – and they are *your* kids – and go on your merry way. I'm glad I met you now, when you're merry, when you have time for me.'

This statement wasn't really fair to Val, but she was struck by it and repeated it to me. It wasn't at all true to me, but I was struck by it too. Because it sounds – it feels – almost as if men felt like victims too. It sounds as if Tad felt that men were cut off by nature from the blind true core of things, as if they could reach it only through

90

women, as if they had to resent even their own children for coming between their women and them. And there is no contest between a baby and its father – in my book anyway. A baby becomes your life by necessity, not by choice. This arrangement is ancient: it lies curled in the heart of myth. What I do not know is if it is necessary. Can you imagine a world where neither mother nor father required the other for survival, where both mother and father could love and tend the baby, could get in touch with the beating engine that drives life? I can, vaguely. But only vaguely. What I can't do is envision a social structure that could contain such an arrangement without changing what is called human nature – that is, eradicating not only capitalism but greed, tyranny, apathy, dependency – oh, well.

At any rate, Tad was twenty-four to Val's thirty-nine and it seemed to all of us that he adored her, and he did: but still, he saw her as a devourer. It's as though, deep, deep at the heart, the silent heart that rarely erupts, that keeps still because if it didn't the world would be destroyed, deep there underneath, the sexes hate and fear each other. Women see men as oppressors, as tyrants, as an enemy with superior strength to be outwitted. Men see women as underminers, slaves who rattle their chains threateningly, constantly reminding the men that if they wanted to, they could poison his food: just watch out.

I know a lot about what women feel in marriage; what I don't know is what men feel. God knows there is a slew of books on the market reciting the woes there are in marriage from the male point of view. The problem is, they are not honest. Did you ever read a book by a male that showed the hero clinging to his wife because she was such an efficient housekeeper? Or because she understood his sexual problems and didn't make him feel too inadequate about it – something he could not count on another woman to do? Or because she did not much like sex, and so he was off the hook – not liking sex much himself? No, you didn't. Or maybe you did, but if so, it was a comic novel, and the main character got called an antihero.

Anyway, I don't want to write a dishonest account, so I am trying to figure out what Norm felt through these years. One problem I have is that Mira didn't know much about what Norm felt through those years. I suspect he was considerably more involved with getting through medical school than he was with her and the babies. (Absolutely proper, you nod your head.) Although he was grouchy and grumbly often, when she asked him what was wrong, he would stroke her cheek and tell her nothing: he was completely happy with her. (Nevertheless she had to put up with the tantrums and the grumbling.) And although he would watch her with the baby, looking up from his book across the room, and get misty-eyed, he also had begun to order her about peremptorily, something he had never dared to do before the children were born.

I can't even write the next sentence I had intended because Val's hoot comes charging in: 'Hah! After the kids were born, he knew he had her, she was dependent on him and would have to take anything he dished out!' There's probably truth in that, but I was trying to get what Norm felt, and if he felt *that*, he didn't know he felt it, which is almost as good as not feeling it at all. Isn't it? Or no, that's repression, I guess. I'm confused. Subside, Val. I'm trying to get to Norm.

Okay, here he had married his dream girl – and there's no question but that Norm did love Mira. He loved what he saw as her independence, but it was independence of a particular sort, a sort he didn't have: it seemed to him that she always pursued truth and when that pursuit conflicted with the notions of the people in her world, she simply told them to go to hell – not in those words, of course. At the same time, though, she was very dependent – fragile, sensitive, frightened. He felt she needed him to protect her, and being fragile, sensitive, and frightened himself, he could feel strong when he put his arm around her and assured her he could take care of her.

This is all understandable. The thing that bothers me – or if truth be told, the thing that bothers Val, since

92

she won't go away – is that these qualities that appeal to us in each other have nothing to do with reality. Maybe it's our culture, Val, that posits such a relationship as desirable. Please go away, just for a little while.

Because of course, what did Norm actually protect Mira from? Well, other men, I suppose. He used to say to her, often, often, shaking his head wisely, 'You don't know men. I do. They're terrible.' And when Mira said she thought she had some notion about them, he would shake his head no, and tell her about being attacked at the corner candy store when he was a gentle ten, by a bunch of Irish Catholic kids who hung around in wait for public schoolers. Or about how his friends in the army had given the business to the one poor Jew who had unhappily been assigned to their unit. He would unfailingly report to her every story of rape he heard.

But in fact, Norm was not around Mira enough to protect her against men. She did it herself, by locking herself in, by not looking at them or thinking about them. She could do this because she was a married woman.

I'm still trying to come to Norm. He had married his girl. Things weren't bad. She was working to support them while he went to med school. They didn't have the material things he wanted, but he had her pretty body in bed when he wanted it, and she was a fair cook. Med school was hard for him, but being married, he studied more than he would if he had been single. He didn't have money to go carousing with the boys; he didn't even want to. He liked sitting there studying at night and looking up to see Mira mending or ironing or reading, intent on her work, the sweetness of her face slowly hardening into severity. It made him feel content, at home, settled.

Am I getting there?

And if he got irritated with her once in a while for things that were not her fault, well, he was only human, wasn't he? In a way, although he never thought this through, it was nice to have someone you could yell at without worrying about their never speaking to you

93

again. All day at school he had to be polite. With his father, too, he had to be polite. He had yelled at his mother, but she got angry and wouldn't speak to him for days. In the end, of course she always took him back, but he suffered. Mira couldn't manage to stay angry that long, and he could always get around her, get her to caress him again. He was sure Mira was as happy with him as he was with her.

But then the kids came. God, first she swelled up like a balloon, then she gets all anxious and self-involved, and he has to worry about her all the time and she never seems to consider him and then, when it's over, the baby is there, it is there, there, there. Not that he doesn't love it. But it is *always there.* He wasn't blaming her: the kid is always crying or she has to do its laundry or she has to cook its potato. But after all, she was his, totally his, isn't that what women were supposed to be – there for you completely? Suddenly she isn't his at all, she belongs to the kid.

I don't know. I think I'm missing something. I feel as if Val were curling up the edges of the letters even as I type them. If you want to write letters of complaint about my handling of Norm, please address them to her.

4

In 1955, while other people were worried about the Cold War and were building air raid shelters, Mira and Norm were worried about the down payment on a small house they wanted to buy in Meyersville. Norm had finished his internship, and had entered as an assistant in the practice of an old friend of his family. He had wanted to go on with his training, he wanted to specialize, but he couldn't bear living another year in that tiny apartment cooped up with the kids. With the help of their parents, they bought a small house in the suburbs. It had two bedrooms, and a dining room. Mira was thrilled, even though they had no furniture. The relatives swept out their attics, and the young couple were established.

Meyersville was a ghetto of sorts, in a world made up

of small enclaves designed to isolate classes and colors, the aged and infirm, from each other. It contained a large number of identical small houses, each with its own refrigerator and stove and washing machine and fenced yard. And almost all of the people who moved in were young couples with small children who were not welcome in apartments, who needed the yard and the washing machine. People who once would have rented little houses in their hometowns, now that rented houses were nearly extinct, bought houses in Meyersville for a $500 down payment and a $4\frac{1}{2}$ percent VA mortage. The distinctions that existed in Meyersville – race was not even a question – were three: religion, age and education. There were many Catholics, numerous Protestants, a few Jews. There were a very few elderly retired couples who could put up with the noise of streets full of children all day long. But there was a nearly fifty-fifty division between those men who had gone to college and those who had not. A college degree was still a mark of something in 1955. What it marked was not intelligence or culture, but upward mobility, although of all the people Norm and Mira knew in their years there, the two who became really wealthy were noncollege men, one who ran a used-car lot and eventually became a Chevrolet dealer and millionaire, the other a real-estate agent who got in on a couple of good land deals. At any rate, Norm was not too uncomfortable there with his M.D. There were other young doctors, lawyers, accountants, teachers: people Norm considered respectable. And there were their wives who had been nurses, teachers, or private secretaries: people Mira could talk to, or so she thought. They were all in the same condition. They were broke and struggling, they had small children, they aspired. Little by little, block by block, they sorted themselves out. For all of them, without question, there was one real standard: money. Nothing else came near it in value. They were the young people who drove shabby old cars packed with kids and went out into the world longing, longing. They wanted a new couch for the living room, a dining room set, a new car.

They could only dream of things like trips to Europe, fur coats, and sunken swimming pools. Whatever they wanted, the visions that danced in their heads really were of lollipops – of things, that is.

Meantime, and in some cases, for a long time, they had to do without things, and they lived day to day with their longing, not realizing that life was passing, never to be recovered. The men took their aspirations to work, where desire gave a fine competitive edge to their behavior. Most of them had no friends. The women stayed home with the children, watched the sky to see whether to pull the laundry off the line before it rained, or whether they should turn on the lawn spray because it would not rain. Along the main streets of towns like this, the few old buildings were razed. The streets were widened, and on either side of them sprang up shops selling garden furniture and equipment, used-car lots, discount furniture houses, television and appliance stores, carpet outlets. Some people say the uglification of America began then, but lots of main streets were ugly enough before that. Perhaps materials of ugliness changed: chrome, glass, neon, and plastic replaced board and brick. There was more ugliness because there were more people. It seemed almost as if World War II had not killed as many people as it spawned. The world burst out, and people burst out too. Because of the GI Bill, men who would not have otherwise, went to college. Everyone aspired, everyone wanted it, the good life. And the good life was made up, everyone knew, of frost-free refrigerators and hi-fis with two speakers and wall-to-wall carpeting and a clothes dryer.

It's easy enough to sneer at now, from this vantage point. It didn't work, *la dolce vita* did not come packed with the detergent inside the new washing machine. But for women especially, the new washing machine or dryer or freezer really was a little release from slavery. Without them and without the pill, there would not be a woman's revolution now. Facts, ma'am, I just want the facts. Grimy pounds and pence matter. And Woolf did know that, even if she didn't think they belonged in literature. After all, she was the one who asked: Why have women no money? Haven't they, throughout time, worked as hard as men, labored in vineyard and kitchen, in field and house? How is it the men ended up with all the pounds and pence? Why do women not even have a room of their own, when in her day, at least, every gentleman had his study?

Well, the world exploded: few people had rooms of their own. They had to make do with washing machines and a backyard barbecue. The working classes had entered the realm of the human.

5

Mira's life was so much easier after the move that she felt like a lady of leisure. Little by little the 2:00 A.M. feedings had vanished, then the seven feedings a day had shrunk to six, then five, then four, and finally even the bottles were gone. In another year, the diapers also went. It is a great day in a woman's life when the diapers vanish, but few women are assured enough to get rid of them: they pack them away up in the attic – 'just in case'. There was still laundry, of course, but now she had a machine to wash it in, and had to wash only three times a week. There was still cleaning, too. Mira had thought the cleaning would be easier once they had a larger place, but in fact a larger place has more space to clean, a fact she had not considered. Her experience with cleaning was that it grew in direct parallel with wealth, and the only way to avoid it is to be born male or pay another woman to do it. Still, life felt luxurious. The long summer days stretched before her; she hummed in the kitchen, washing the breakfast dishes, the boys tumbling and playing out in the backyard. Maybe she would get a life back. Once a week, on a night when Norm came home early enough, her friend Theresa would drive her to the library and she would get stacks of books, all by one author. She read all the James, Huxley, Faulkner, Woolf, Austen, and Dickens the library possessed, read uncritically, making no distinctions. She took out popular and scholarly books on psychology, sociology, anthropology and only after a time was she able to see the difference among more or less simplistic approaches to a discipline. She forgot most of what she read, having no context to put it in, and she felt, after a time, that it was all somehow useless, that she wasn't really learning anything. But in the first years, she was happy. Her home hummed and sparkled, her children were beautiful and cried only once or twice a day. She was getting her life back.

The children still napped in the afternoon, so she had an hour or two of leisure then. They went to bed by seven, and she was able now to stay up later, so she had some hours of leisure then too. In the evenings, she read, even if Norm had the TV set on; in the afternoons, she had a social life.

It is often noticed that women in suburbia, much like the women in ancient Greece, are locked into the home, and see no one but children all day. The Greek women saw slaves, who might have been interesting people. But suburban women have each other.

The women on the block were all anxious to make friends, and a newcomer was invited to endless kaffee-klatsches. In time, groups formed. Mira had several friends: Bliss, Adele, and Natalie. Each of them had other friends, so there was a kind of cell network. Mira was twenty-five, her friends a year or two older. They all had small children. And they were all married to men who thought of their lives in terms of career, not job.

They spent most of their free time in each other's kitchens and yards. They sat over coffee, hot or iced, and a home-baked, packaged coffee cake, watching the children. When the weather was poor, they sat in the kitchen rather than the living room because it was easier for the woman whose house it was to reach over and get the cookies for whatever child came in crying, or to refill the coffee cups, and when the children came in with mud or chocolate or shit all over them, they would mess up only the kitchen. The houses were close enough together that they could even risk leaving napping children alone: with the windows open, you could hear anything loud that happened in another house.

In summer, they sat in the grass or on homemade patios, sipping iced tea or coffee, watching the children in the sandbox or the plastic pool. They didn't bother much about their clothes: they always had children's sticky hands all over them, or the sour milk of babies' spit-up. Conversation was a physical challenge, words uttered while a baby clung to a neck or sat on a lap tugging Mother's ear, or while leaping up to get to Johnny before he swallowed that stone, to get to Midge before she clobbered Johnny over the head with that shovel, or to pull Deena out from the little space in the fence where she'd wedged herself trying to escape from the yard.

For all its activity, it was a lazy life because it went nowhere. One day was like another: the sun shone or it did not; jackets were needed, or heavy snowsuits and boots. Toilet training proceeded or snagged. Sometimes the sheets froze on the clothesline. The women worked in the mornings, the late afternoons, and sometimes in the evenings, when they would mend or iron or sew a new outfit for Cheryl or Midge while the TV set blared 'Dragnet' or Mike Wallace. It was not a bad life; it was a hell of a lot better than collecting coins at a toll booth all day, or examining cans as they came off the assembly line. The unspoken, unthought-about conditions that made it oppressive had long since been accepted by all of them: that they had not chosen but had been automatically slotted into their lives, and that they were never free to move (the children were much more effective as clogs than confinement on a prison farm would be). Having accepted the shit and string beans, they were content.

6

Their daily conversations drew them very close. Most of them would never again know with such detail and intimacy the elements of others' lives. They never forgot to ask how Johnny's cough was today, whether Mira's period was still so heavy, or if Bill had been able to fix the broken toilet. Indeed, while it was broken, the family had been using your toilet, or your neighbor's, so you knew when it got fixed as well as you knew your own showering habits.

Most often, they talked about the children. Each one looked at her own with shiny eyes, finding beauty and cleverness in all of them. And indeed, they were all beautiful and clever and funny, even if sometimes they broke each other's heads. The women treated with tender pity the sobs of the worst bully, the worst whiner. Once in a while they spoke sharply to the children, sometimes they struck them. But a little later, there the child would be, sobbing sorrowfully on Mother's lap, resting against her breast. This is not to say that sometimes you would not hear in the street a woman calling a child, her harriedness and frustration shrieking out in her voice, or even that there were not, in this neighborhood, parents who punished their children by hitting them with belts. But it was not usual. This generation of children was gently nourished far from the sprawling city and its infected tenements, from impoverished farms and their misery.

The children were endlessly interesting to the women: their colic, their fever, their funny doings and sayings, their grades at school, their stubbornness, whatever. You might find such conversations boring: you may prefer to talk about cars, or football games. But I find them humane, and believe it or not, they were educational too, for we learned a lot about what to do for a child whose fever won't come down, or how to get that stain out of Johnny's sunsuit, and in the process, we learned something about acceptance of many variations. For the children were all different, and although one might be larger and stronger, another smarter, another prettier than the others, there was no ultimate difference among them. They were differentiated only by our love for them: you loved your own most, naturally.

100

But there were other things besides children. The menu for a special dinner (in-laws coming Sunday) could provide several hours of discussion; a new pair of shorts or a blouse could occupy them through two cups of coffee. They sighed and laughed together about house-cleaning, but the houses were each immaculate. Probably because mess is so constant when there are small children about, the women kept their houses cleaner than they did in later years. Husbands were rarely discussed, but were always in the background. They were usually brought up to illustrate some absurdity or some constriction:

'Paul likes his coffee strong, so I make it strong and add water to mine.'

'Norm refuses to eat pork.'

'Hamp will not touch a baby's diaper. Never has. So when they were little, I couldn't leave them with him at all. That's why I toilet-trained them so early.'

No one ever questioned such statements, asked why Natalie or Mira didn't simply insist, or Adele make the coffee the way she liked it and let Paul make his own. Never. Husbands were walls, absolutes, in small things at least. The women often would howl and cackle at them, at their incredible demands and impossible delusions, their inexplicable eating habits and their strange prejudices, but it was as if they were de black folk down to de shanty recounting the absurd pretensions of de white massas up to de big house.

For the men, of course, were experiencing life on a different level. Hamp flew around the country for his company, so he went first class and ate at expensive restaurants and was fawned over by stewardesses and waiters; Bill was a navigator for an airline and flew all over the world, staying at expensive hotels and resorts, eating at fancy restaurants, fawned over by stewardesses and waiters. And even Norm and Paul had a good share of expensive lunches out, 'company' dinners, and fawning over by nurses and secretaries. They brought their demands home; they began to see home and the women in them as provincial, small-minded, shabby. Increasingly, and perhaps inevitably, the equals they had married became servants. So when Bill had a cold one winter, he lay in bed bored and miserable, and called Bliss – she counted – twenty-three times to climb the stairs to bring him some tea, ginger ale, another aspirin, a magazine. Bliss caught his cold, but he had to make a flight, so he insisted she get up and drive him to the airport. She did. Lily told us an absurd, hilarious story about Carl, furious at Lily's cooking, deciding he would make potato pancakes the way his mother did, spilling the batter on the stove, where it stuck, and in a rage, throwing the whole bowl across the kitchen, saying it was her job anyway, and storming out of the house to eat at McDonald's, and leaving her with the mess, the kids to be fed and bathed, both of them crying at the failure of Daddy's boasted dinner and at the shock, the noise, and confusion. Samantha could bubble over for twenty minutes about her poltergeist ice-cube trays that were always somehow banging her on the head (they were, really), and how Simp wouldn't permit her to buy others. Martha ran a continuing saga on the incidence of lethality of any tool in George's hand: he'd just dropped a hammer from a ladder and it had hit Jeff on the head and he'd had to have ten stitches. The Cold War was innocuous compared to Sean's insistence on clean sheets daily and Norm's year-long refusal to teach Mira to drive.

But no one ever suggested that the situation could be changed; no one ever challenged the men's right to demand and control. Only Martha directly put her husband down. 'He's inept, he's a klutz!' she'd laugh. The rest of them only laughed and shook their heads at one's stubborness, the other's thickness. Husbands, like children, had their eccentricities, and women had to put up with them. And if on occasion the clean sheets or the slippery ice-cube trays or the driving lessons were the subjects of real arguments, they happened inside the house, quietly, late at night, and were never mentioned in the open sunlight with the children padding in the grass. The women had intimations, but no one said anything about causes when Samantha developed a rash all over her hands, or

Natalie was seen to start drinking in the afternoon, lugging her rye bottle from house to house since none of the women could afford to buy liquor except for evening entertainment, when men were present. No one seemed to hear the day Bliss went tearing out of her house screaming for Cheryl to get her bike out of the street, and Bliss's voice went out of control and sounded like hysterical shrieking. All of them heard their own voices do the same thing on occasion, days when the washing machine overflowed, the bacon burned, Johnny fell down and cut his head open, and then Norm or Paul or Hamp called and said they were not coming home until late that evening because they were going to a professional dinner, a business conference, a party for someone on the staff.

No one remarked or made connections if they were all sitting in Mira's kitchen and Bliss was in the middle of a funny story about Bill's demandingness and suddenly Bill stuck his head in and asked was Bliss there and she immediately leaped up and left, laughing and rolling her eyes as she went.

There were two cultures – the world, which had men in it, and their own, which had only women and children. Within their own world they were there for each other physically and emotionally. They gave, through good humor and silent understanding, support and affection and legitimacy to each other and to the concerns they shared. Mira thought that they were more important to each other then their husbands were to them. She wondered if they could have survived without each other. She loved them.

7

Within the next few years, the material circumstances of most of them had improved a little, enough that they could afford once or twice a year to buy a dress or the fabric to make one, to buy some liquor and food and give a party. Bliss and Bill bought a cheap coffee table and a lamp for their bare living room; Norm and Mira had a slipcover made for the old couch Norm's mother had given them. Children were older; some were even in school. The women had extra energy, and decided to use it this way. The living rooms were about to be used publicly, and their husbands to be integrated into their community. Up until now, the men had spoken to each other only rarely and briefly over the lawn mower on a Sunday afternoon.

Mira gave the first party. Almost everyone arrived at once. The small living room was immaculate and had been cleared for the party: the clean laundry that had that afternoon been piled on a corner of the couch, the toys that had been scattered on the floor, had been swept into closets for the evening. The few small tables held plates of deviled eggs and olives, cheese and crackers, and baskets of potato chips and pretzels. Although the women saw each other almost every day, the air when they arrived was frenetic. The men looked as they usually looked: a little less formally dressed than when they went to work, but neat and groomed in blazers and sports jackets, shined shoes. But the women! The shabby slacks, the unmade-up faces, the curlers and aprons had vanished. They were done up in low-cut dresses, rhinestone jewelry, high-piled hair, stockings, high-heeled shoes, eye shadow, rouge. They were all attractive, and tonight in their glamorous outfits, they looked gorgeous, and they knew it. They invaded the living room edgily; their voices were higher pitched than usual; they laughed louder and more easily than usual.

The men, sensing something different, shrugged and left the living room to the 'girls,' stood with their highballs in the kitchen discussing football scores, cars, the best buys in tires. The women settled uncertainly in the unfamiliar room in their unfamiliar clothes, and looked at each other. Suddenly they were appraising each other, seeing the curve of a figure or the length of an eyelash as they had never seen it before. They were only half-conscious of what was happening.

These women were never away from their children. Going out cost money for babysitters, dinner, tickets for a play or a movie, money they almost never had. They had all been trained by pregnancy not to think too much about the future: the future was simply more of the present. Their horizons were limited by their lives.

But tonight they had entered the living room all dressed up and fit to kill, as they giggled about it among themselves. They had seen themselves and each other anew. They were still young; they were attractive. Gazing at themselves in the full-length mirrors before they left their houses, they saw that they did not look very different from the creatures on whom they had modeled themselves – those glamorous women in the fashion and movie magazines. They began dimly to realize that they had another self from the one they lived with daily. It was a kind of miracle. It seemed as if they might have another chance, could live out a life different from the one they had. What kind of life it was they didn't know. They didn't pursue the subject. Not one of them would have given up her children, and few would have given up their husbands: and both of these acts seemed necessary for a different life. Yet they all felt somehow stretched.

They refused to admit it was illusion. As they sat there in the living room together, much as they sat in the kitchen most days, drinking highballs instead of coffee, they talked about Amy being unable to come because her youngest had measles, about Tommy's reaction to having crabmeat crepes for dinner, and about the extension the Foxes were planning to put on their house after the new baby was born. But they were all itchy, simmering. At last someone (Natalie?) said, 'Those men!' and all instantly agreed. Someone (Bliss?) got up and said, 'I'll get them in here,' and left for the kitchen, but did not return. The whole point, they all laughingly agreed, of being done up in uncomfortable bras and girdles, high heels, false eyelashes, and hair plastered into shape by hair spray, was *not* to sit around in the living room talking about the same things they talked about every day. Natalie had brought some records and she and Mira put them on the record player. Sinatra and Belafonte, Andy

Williams and Johnny Mathis and Ella Fitzgerald and Peggy Lee: that was what they all liked. Gradually the men drifted in; conversation grew more animated; groups dispersed and reformed; a few people started to get drunk. At last, Paul, Adele's husband, got up and danced with Natalie; Sean danced with Oriane and then with Adele.

By midnight, many couples were dancing, dispersing, re-forming. Almost everyone was flirting mildly with somebody. What else was the point of the rouge, the sequins, the corselets? And everyone agreed the next day that they had had a wonderful time, the best in years. There were no arguments about whether there should be more parties: the husbands were as agreeable as the wives.

This may sound foolish, but in fact, the parties were terribly innocent; terribly because innocence is terrible. A little flirtation was good for them. Both the men and the women had lived for years in worlds bounded by their own genders, and by their own occupations. If the women found it difficult to talk about things in the large, outer world, the men found it difficult to talk about anything but their work. They might move to the neutral zones of cars and games and even politics, but they could not talk personally, humanely, knew nothing of others except gossip and nothing of themselves except the external image. And each group was ignorant of the other.

Was it wrong if at the end of the evening eyes were brilliant and cheeks were pink? Was it sinful if talking to someone else's spouse brought out charm and humor one had not known one possessed? Or if the affection born of finding oneself attractive to someone else began to flow over all of them like icing on a cake? They may have looked like the sophisticates in *Vogue*, but most of them were as innocent as they had been at fourteen. Sex had been tried, children engendered, but still they knew nothing. Sex was for most of the men and all of the women a disappointment they never mentioned. Sex, after all, was THE thing that came naturally, and if it didn't – if it wasn't for them worth anywhere near all the furtiveness and dirty joke and pinup calendars and 'men's' magazines, all the shock and renunciation of hundreds of heroines in hundreds of books – why then it was they who were inadequate. For the men, sex was strangely lacking: it was a physical event that felt good, but when it was over they felt alone, unloving, spent. For the women, it was a tiresome duty. Why then did they so much enjoy the fluidities and poundings that a party aroused?

Probably because most people have an extremely limited sexual experience, it is easy for them, when things are wrong, to place the blame on their partner. It would be different if, instead of graying Theresa with her sagging breasts, her womb hanging low from having held six children, Don were in bed with – Marilyn Monroe, say. Or even Bliss. And Bliss might feel that Sean, since he was experienced with women, would excite her more than Bill did, and would know what to do to keep her excited. Nowadays, there are so many manuals and guidebooks on do-it-yourself sex, maybe things are different. But in those days, we looked outward: the problem was not in our ignorance, but in having the wrong partner. That deduction seems to be borne out: the excitement of a new partner in sex is often great enough to cover flaws in performance, and not until the affair has become custom do the flaws again stand out.

But all the sexual energy and discontent were below the surface for the women. They spoke merely of having parties. They planned them, did the work of giving them. The men came behind their wives like shadows. They had less color, less distinctiveness, less personality. They were like the males in pornographic movies: the film is written, directed, and produced by them, includes male figures, and is intended for them, intended to please men. But the whole film focuses on the female, upon her body, her joy as semen spurts all over her face or she is penetrated through her anus. Twentieth-century pornography, Iso said once, was like Greek tragedy, and situates emotion in the woman. So here.

107

The men did not complain about the parties; they were even willing to add an extra twenty dollars to the household allowance to help pay for them. They allowed the women to plan, shop, cook, clean, make a new dress or buy one. They stood in the kitchen every time, and every time had to be pried out. They came into the living room reluctantly, making jokes about the 'girls.' They allowed the women to ask them to dance and smiled with pleasure at the praise of their dancing style that was invariably offered. They were shy virgins at adultery and the women were the horny ones (or the cavey ones, as Val used to say). They were being wooed. They lapped it up.

8

I have been lumping together the eight or ten couples that made up these parties, but each of them was quite different. Theirs are some of the voices I hear.

Natalie: She was always up early. She had to drive Hamp to the station and get the older kids off to school. After the chaos of early morning, after bathing Deena and putting her into the playpen, she'd make a cup of instant coffee in the stained plastic cup she always used, and sit down at the cluttered kitchen table, planning her day.

Natalie was a large woman, generously built, with great physical energy. She loved to work with her hands: she painted and wallpapered, refinished furniture, and washed and waxed her own floors not out of economic necessity but because her body needed to be used. Her consuming interest was in her house. It was her pride and it always looked almost like a house in one of the home magazines – almost, because Natalie was never finished. She would end one project only to begin another, so the house was always in disarray.

She had married young and her parents had sighed with relief. She had been a wild one. Now she had three children; her husband worked in her father's company, in a highly placed position protected from contact with anything or anybody important. Hamp was a loser, but they both knew that Daddy would never fire him, and the salary checks were so good these days that Nat was thinking of moving to a larger house.

She liked her days. She liked putting her feet up on the table and sipping her coffee and planning what to do with her morning. There was wallpaper to be bought, and while she was there, she would look at Mr. Johnstone's patterns for a new paper for the bathroom, which was starting to look shabby. She would stop at Carver's and see if the new pink glass lampshade had arrived. They needed rye; something for dinner. Then she would come home and start in on the study. She was papering one wall with a velvety red design that would warm up the paneling on the others.

She slipped sandals on her feet, a jacket over her shirt, packed the baby up, and slid her into the car seat. She had perfect body ease, Natalie; no matter how she dressed, she looked as if she were somebody, as if she belonged. She raced from shop to shop, bantering just a little suggestively with all the shopkeepers, was home by ten thirty, and by two had finished the wall, cleaned up the paste, and stood leaning on the cutting table, admiring her work.

She had unending patience and unerring taste: it was very nice. Luxuriously, she stretched, gave the baby some crackers and cheese and put her in for a nap, and poured herself a rye and soda. Then she went into her bathroom for a shower. She was the only one in the neighborhood with two bathrooms: she couldn't understand what was wrong with the others. Who wants to take a shower in a bathroom stinky with diapers? It wasn't that expensive, less than a thousand.

She dressed, cleaned up the kitchen, and checked her watch. It was almost three. The kids – blah! – would be home soon. She phoned Adele. But Adele couldn't come – she could never come.

'What's the matter with you, anyway?' Natalie taunted her, and grimaced as one of Adele's many excuses followed: somebody had to go to the dentist, somebody to Cub Scouts, somebody was sick. 'It's really disgusting that you have so many kids,' Nat concluded, not worried about the sensitivities of others. Money is a great armorer; and Natalie had always been wealthy. She did not have to worry about people's feelings because she give the best parties, and was generous to her friends, giving them something if they admired it.

She dialed Mira, who as usual was reading. Clark was still napping and Normie was not yet back from kindergarten. And it was raining out, they would have to be indoors. Natalie grimaced but she was desperate: 'Sure, bring the kids. Come when Clark wakes up. Sure it's okay.'

So Mira came over at three thirty and Lena and Rena arrived home, had some peanut butter and jelly, and the four children, who did not play together because their ages were too different, sat in front of the TV in the newly papered study. Later, Evelyn stopped in with her two, who swelled the TV crowd. The women sat in the kitchen, drinking rye. The children were whiny; they kept coming in for cookies or ice cream, which were liberally offered, although Mira's brow wrinkled. 'No more, now, Normie, you won't eat dinner.'

'What a worrywart you are,' Nat grinned. 'Who cares if they eat dinner?'

Everyone left by four thirty, and Nat felt let down. Lena came into the kitchen for another peanut butter and jelly sandwich and Nat snapped at her.

'I'm going to do homework, and I need energy,' the child replied coolly, ignoring her mother.

Rena looked out and saw it had stopped raining. She rushed about, ferreted in the kitchen for her skate key, and ran out. Only Deena was left, sitting like a lump in the playpen. Natalie bent over her.

'Did dose bad sisters go away and weave wittoo Deena all alone? Bad sisters. Momma take.' She picked the child up and carried her to the kitchen and set her on the floor to crawl.

Dinner, Nat thought with sinking heart. She hated this time of day, she hated to cook. For herself, she would have been content with a cheese sandwich. She

110

had picked up some pork chops, though and rummaged through the cookbook, looking for an interesting way to serve them. She found a casserole made with lima beans and tomato sauce, and carefully, trying to follow directions precisely, prepared it. Rena came in again, disgusted with the returned rain, and turned on the TV set. Deena was cranky, and was clattering pots on the kitchen floor and whimpering at the same time. At quarter to six, Nat picked up her coat and set Deena in the playpen, cautioning Rena to watch her. She drove to the station to pick up Hamp, who as soon as he got home poured a double shot of rye into a glass, and took a can of beer out of the refrigerator. He settled himself in 'his' chair in the study, before the TV set.

'How do you like the wall?' Natalie asked enthusiastically.

'Nice, hon, really nice.' His voice was lifeless.

Natalie put Deena in the high chair and heated some jars of baby food, and fed her. The casserole was bubbling in the oven, and she thought it smelled good. She poured another rye. The house was chaotic, as always in the evening. Lena and Rena were fighting about something, the baby was cranky, the TV set was blaring – and Hamp was sitting like a lump in his easy chair, drinking and reading the paper or watching some stupid cowboy program.

'Can't you shut those kids up, Nat?' he called in.

'Goddamn!' Nat picked Deena out of the high chair and carried her upstairs. 'You kids shut up, now, you hear me? You're bothering your father!'

Rena came crying into the baby's room as Nat prepared her for bed. 'Lena took my pad! She says it's hers! But it's my pad!'

'Let her use it, she needs it for homework.'

High wailing.

'I'll buy you another one tomorrow.'

Resentment and contentment warred for a moment. Rena wanted the new pad, but she didn't want to give in too easily, or to make it appear that she was not completely sensible of the wrong done her. Sniffling and

111

murmuring about injustice, she went back into the room she shared with her older sister.

'You're mean, Lena, and I don't like you. And Mommy's going to buy me a whole new pad, nyaahhh!'

'Oh, shut up, Rena. She'll buy me one too.'

'She will not! She's just buying one for me.'

'She will too!'

'She will not!'

Lena leaped up and came into the baby's room. 'Aren't you going to buy me a pad too, Mom?' Furious eyes, demanding mouth.

'Will you shut up, Lena? The baby's trying to get to sleep.' Natalie turned out the light, and closed the door.

Lena stood staring at her in the hallway. 'You are going to buy me one, aren't you?'

'If you need one, I'll buy you one.'

'I do.'

Rena was standing just inside the doorway to her bedroom, and as soon as she heard her mother's 'Okay,' she bounded out.

'That's not fair! She takes my pad and she gets a new one! It isn't fair!'

Lena turned swiftly on her sister: '*I* need it to do homework, baby! I don't just scribble on it like you!'

Rena was crying again.

'SHUT UP!' a voice blasted from downstairs. The girls quieted. The baby began to scream.

'Jesus H. Christ,' Nat murmured, and went in to soothe the baby. The girls went into their room and sat glaring at each other.

The casserole was terrible, dry and thick, and no one would eat it. They filled up on cookies and ice cream, and Hamp had a peanut butter sandwich. Natalie shouted the girls into baths and bed, cleaned up the kitchen, and around nine, joined Hamp in the study with a drink.

A show was just going off, and Hamp looked up at her as she came in. She smiled.

'How was your day?'

112

'Okay.' He answered her sleepily: since he'd been home, he'd had four double shots and beers.

'Doesn't the wall really look great?' She was delighted with herself.

'Yeah, hon, I told you. Looks really good.'

'Mira and Evelyn came over this afternoon.'

He perked up a bit. 'Oh, yeah?'

'Evelyn came from the doctor's. Tommy fell down and had to have three stitches in his lip. And Clark whimpered the whole time Mira was here. God, she spoils that kid.'

He stared at the TV.

'I stopped at Carver's, but the shade wasn't in yet.'

'Umm.'

She smiled at him coyly. 'Mr. Carver said every time he looks at me he wishes he were twenty years younger. Isn't he cute?'

'Adorable.'

'Well, you're as interesting as a book with blank pages.'

'Maybe that's what I am.'

'I don't doubt it. Daddy says he pays you to dictate form letters.'

'Really!' He turned to look at her. 'And when did His Eminence say that?'

'When we were out on the yacht. Last month.'

'Why doesn't he say it to me?'

She shrugged.

He turned back to stare at the TV, but he was not watching it. 'Would you like me to quit? Is that the point?'

'Oh, Hampy, I want you to do what you want. You know I think you're really smart.' Her voice was coddling and her smile coy. She moved toward his chair, and settled herself on the floor beside it, smiling up at him. 'Remember you started that course in – oh, whatever it was? You're an engineer, you could get another job.'

'And you'd live on what I earn.'

'Why should I if I'm still on Daddy's payroll?'

'So why should I leave if *I'm* still on Daddy's payroll?'

'Because you're not happy there.'

He got up and turned up the sound of the TV. Gunshots rang out sharply; a cowboy fell. Nat sighed loudly and got up and went into the kitchen for another drink. 'Get me one too, will you?' Hamp called, and she came back, handed him his shots and beers, went back for her own, and returned, settling herself in a chair across the room.

'Bliss called,' Natalie began again. 'She's having a party next weekend.'

'Oh, yeah?' Hamp's head rose again.

'Yeah. That's the one sure way to get your interest, isn't it? Who is it? I know it isn't Evelyn, wonderful as she is. Mira, with her books, or is it Bliss, skinny little Bliss with her ass? Who's the love interest these days? You might as well tell me. I sure know it isn't me.' Her voice was acid, etched with hurt.

He looked at her slowly. 'What do you mean, these days?'

Hampden was a large, heavy man with a round boyish face. He had a pleasant, childlike grin that made him seem somehow unthreatening. His voice was boyish too. Natalie's voice, especially when she was annoyed, was sharp and thin, and no matter what they were saying in an argument, it always sounded as if Nat was jabbing and piercing, and Hamp was parrying and retreating.

'You won't sleep with me but you seem to find everybody else irresistible.'

'Natalie,' he looked directly at her, 'you're the last person in the world to accuse anyone else.'

She colored a little and looked away. Both of them had always maintained the pretense of ignorance about her affairs, and she was not sure how much he knew. But she had not had an affair for a year now, not since her father had stopped sending Hamp out of town on business trip. Hamp had proven a poor salesman and was 'promoted' and was now home every night.

114

She pulled herself together. 'Christ, you're here every night, you see what I do. Nothing!' Her fear turned into anger. 'I sit and watch the stupid boob tube with you sitting there like a lump of lard slowly blotting your mind out! You don't do anything!! You don't help me with the kids, you don't even take out the garbage. You don't lift a finger and I wait on you hand and foot and then you say I'm screwing around!'

'Well, there are always the days,' he said sarcastically.

'Sure, sure!' She was near to tears of self-pity, self-justification, and rage. 'I raced around shopping, papered a wall, took care of *your* bratty kids all day, put up with Mira and Evelyn, and had time for a toss in the hay with Norm!'

He said nothing, watching three cowboys hide behind a rock, guns cocked.

She watched him. 'Or Paul!' she added, prodding him. 'Or Sean! Or – who do you think?'

He turned to her wearily. 'Oh, Natalie, what the hell difference does it make? You're a whore. You've always been one, you always will be one, and it doesn't matter with who.'

Gunshots rang out and three cowboys lay dead. Natalie charged across the room and slapped Hamp hard across the side of the head. 'Bastard, liar! And what the hell are you, I'd like to know! Mr. Superior, you should've been a priest, you don't give a damn about sex, so I'm not supposed to!'

She stood there waiting, yelling. When he did not respond, she hit him again. Her body was aching. She wanted him to leap up, to grab her wrists and force her onto the couch, to take her by force. That was how it had been in the early years. She would attack him, he would fight back, he would rape her, and then she would lie back in his arms content, promising in a baby voice to be a good girl and do what Daddy Hamp wanted.

He sat there, gazing impassively at her. There was a sickly grin on his large gray face.

She cried out and threw herself at him, flailing arms trying, but not too hard, to hit him. He held her wrists;

115

her heart began to pound; he sighed. She was sobbing. He stood up, holding her wrists, then shoved her down into the chair. Then he got his jacket and went out. She sat there sobbing, listening to the car pull out of the driveway.

9

'Oh, I'm not one for fancy cooking. Hamp doesn't care a thing about food, he lives on peanut butter sandwiches. But I really like to clean. When we were first married, Hamp used to come home and run his finger over things – the windowsills, you know, and the moldings. He said it was called the white-glove test when he was in the navy. Heaven help me if he found any dust!'

'Norm's very conservative too. He looks at anything besides beef and chicken as if it were a rattlesnake. Pork he absolutely refuses to eat. I blame it on his mother.'

'I never know what anybody's eating in my house!' Gaily said, belying the twitching forehead. 'Everybody eats at different times. It's impossible! Sometimes Paul doesn't get in until nine or ten, sometimes he eats out. The baby doesn't eat human food yet, and the others! So fussy! And Eric has Cub Scouts and Linda has piano lessons and Billy has the orthodontist, and on Tuesdays I have Women's Guild – it's always a madhouse!' Gaily laughed, belying the twitching hands. 'So I just cook up a big pot of stew or spaghetti or chicken or something, and dole it out as they come in.'

'Have some more wine, Adele.'

'I shouldn't, but I will,' she laughed, gaily.

'I don't know how you do it, really, you're marvelous. I go out of my head with my three brats.'

'Adele has the casual touch,' Bliss laughed softly.

Adele smiled gratefully. 'Well, I try to just take things as they come. I don't get excited. I was raised in a big house full of kids. My mother was wonderful, so calm. "It's not the end of the world, yet," she always said. We had this enormous house, a real old-fashioned monster, you know, ten bedrooms. Well, there were nine kids. She

116

had a girl in from the neighborhood to help her, and we all pitched in, you know. When my kids get older, things will be easier. When Mindy's out of diapers, it will be better.' Her hand twitched in her lap, and she raised it and drank her wine.

10

She climbed the fence that separated her backyard from Bliss's and helped Mike through it. Then Bliss handed Mindy over to her, they said good-bye, and Adele went in through her back door. She took Mindy into the living room and laid her in the playpen, but the baby was fussy and kept up a running complaint just verging on crying.

'Play with Mindy, Mike,' Adele said. Mike toddled over to the playpen and waved things over the baby's head.

Adele went back to the kitchen and checked her schedule. Wednesday afternoon: Eric to Cub Scouts, pick up a case of soda for Cub Scout meeting; get Paul's grey suit from the cleaners; Billy to the DiNapolis' to work on project. MILK, she had scrawled in large letters at the bottom of the page. She looked at the clock: five after three. She picked up the telephone.

'Elizabeth? Hi. How are things? Oh.' She laughed a little. 'Yes, okay. We're surviving.' Again, the gay little laugh. 'I keep thinking I just have to get through today, you know? Like an AA.' Another rich giggle. 'It did? Ooooh, Elizabeth! Oh, I know. Listen, you're welcome to bring the clothes over here and wash them. Mine's been working fine ever since the day it vomited soapsuds all the way into the living room.' Laughter. 'Oh, okay. Sure. Well, if you need it . . . yes, right. No, listen, it's my turn to drive them and it's okay because I have to go out anyway. Can you drive the girls to dancing lessons tomorrow?? God, you're a blessing. I don't know what I'd do without you.' Here Adele's voice got a little tremulous, but she collected herself. 'Yes, I am. Yeah, my house is the drop-off place for old clothes. I've thought

117

of going through them, some of them look pretty good.' Giggle. 'Will you be at the meeting? Father Spinola said he wants to talk to us, thank us, I guess, you know. We're going to have coffee and cake and we need volunteers to bring something. Oh, thanks, Elizabeth. Always ask the busiest person, and she comes through. I'm going to bring my gingerbread, yes, that one, oh, I'm glad. Yes, I don't know how I'm going to get them in the car. I have six feet of old clothes standing in the garage. I had them in the kitchen, but the baby kept running into them.' Giggle. 'Yes, they're soft, but the thing is they sort of ... well ... *smell*. Oh, no, she isn't walking yet, I meant Mike, I guess I'd better stop calling him the baby, hah?' She laughed loudly and her voice edged sharply. 'Sure. We really have to get together one of these days. Maybe some night we can do something. No, not this week – Paul has all these obligations – maybe one night next week. Maybe we can go to a movie together or something. Oh. Oh. Night shift, oh. Will it last long? Well, actually, sometimes it's not so bad. I'm not always so unhappy when Paul works late.' Laughter, more laughter. 'Yeah, and then he screams he can't sleep with all the noise. I know. Well, the poor soul, he must feel strange having to sleep in the daylight. I couldn't do it, I'm sure. Yes. Peace and quiet at night, I know what you mean. Yes.' Laughter.

A sound of children burst into the kitchen.

'Elizabeth? I have to go. The Indians are charging in and it sounds as though the cavalry is just behind them. Right. So long.'

Eric and Linda were both screaming. She gathered them up in her arms and took their coats off, shushing them, trying to find out what was wrong. They sobbed breathlessly. A big boy on the school bus had bullied Eric, Linda had punched him, he had got off the school bus at their stop and had chased them home and promised to come back and get even. She put their coats back on. She was still wearing her jacket.

'Okay, kids, we'll find this big bully,' she said, starting toward the front door, when a crash resounded from the

118

living room, followed by terrified screaming.

She rushed in. The playpen was on its side, Mindy was lying helplessly on the wooden slats, screaming, with Mike lying on top of her, whimpering himself, glancing guiltily toward his mother. Adele picked Mike up roughly and set him down hard on the floor. He began to scream. She bent for the baby and picked her up, holding Mindy against her body, and bounced her gently. With her free hand, she righted the playpen.

'What happened?' she demanded angrily of Mike, who at eighteen months could barely talk. He tried to explain, sobbing and hurt at her roughness, glaring at her reproachfully. He had wanted to play with the baby, had tried to get into the playpen.

'All right, all right,' she said apologetically, ruffling Mike's hair. 'It's okay, Mikey, she isn't hurt.' He calmed a little, but was still sobbing under his breath. 'Come on, we'll get some cookies.'

He trailed behind her into the kitchen. The baby was calming against her shoulder. She reached for the cookie box, which had to be kept up high, and handed him two cookies. The older children clamored. She handed them each two. The baby was quiet. She carried her back inside and placed her back down inside the playpen. The baby howled in protest.

'Oh, God,' Adele sighed. She turned to Mike sharply. 'I have to go out. Now you watch Mindy, you hear, and don't try to get inside the playpen! Just stay here and watch her.' She left.

Mike turned large eyes to watch her, confused, but half-contented with his cookies. He sat down and watched the baby scream herself blue in the face as she saw her mother leave. He put out his hand to pat her face and smeared chocolate all over it. He sat there until his cookies were gone, then put his hands around his knees and rocked himself, talking to Mindy all the while. After ten minutes, she gave up and fell asleep.

Adele had grabbed the collars of the two older children and pulled them out of the door. 'Now where is this boy! Show me!'

Calmed by the safety of home and the comfort of cookies, they were eager to let the whole thing go, but she insisted. She trudged the two of them down the street. Just then the bus from Gardiner School (grades 4–6) arrived, and a group of children got off. A boy who had apparently been standing behind a bush ran to get on. 'There he is!' the children yelled and pointed, and Adele ran toward the bus, but collided with Billy, who leaped aside at their encounter, and sent Adele sprawling across the sidewalk. She looked up as the school bus chugged off. She lay there on the sidewalk, her chin propped on a hand, wondering if she were hurt, wondering if she could have accomplished a broken leg. Oh, well: it would make a good story to tell the girls. She got up, limping; her knee was bruised.

On their return to the house, she lectured Linda and Eric. They were not to speak to that naughty boy, they were to ignore him. If he came around or followed them home again, they were to come straight to her, she would take care of it. They nodded with large-eyed, solemn faces. They had giggled when she fell, and felt guilty.

She looked at the clock. 'Oh, God! Eric, get your uniform on!' She took a bottle from the refrigerator and set it in a pan of water. She went into the living room. Compressing her lips, Adele picked the baby up and carried her to the kitchen and washed the chocolate off her face and hands, jammed her into a jacket, and plunked her on the kitchen floor. The baby whimpered quietly; the others were hushed: they all recognized their mother's danger point. They put their coats on quickly; Adele jammed Mike into his and tested the bottle. It was too hot, so she ran it under cold water briefly, then packed up the baby and her bag and ordered all of them into the car. She strapped the baby into the car seat and put the bottle in the baby's hands and the baby began to suck it and screamed, and Adele snatched it away and tested it again and found it was still too hot and she sat in the front of the car leaning her head on the steering wheel and said, 'Oh, God, oh, God,' over and over, then pulled herself up and jerked the car out of the driveway, the baby screaming with a burned tongue, her own knee burning where she had bruised it, the other kids hushed with anxiety, and she realized she should have washed her knee, and she jerked the car all the way down the street until she had calmed a little.

Ordering everyone to behave, she went into the cut-rate soda place and bought a case of the cheapest canned soda. Then she drove to Elizabeth's and honked. Tom ran out and got into the car. Next she drove to Mrs. Amory's, where the Cub Scout meeting was being held this week. Tom helped Eric carry the case of soda. She drove to the DiNapolis' and dropped Billy off, telling him to call her when he wanted to be picked up. She drove to the tailor at the other side of town, the only one Paul felt did decent work, and picked up his gray suit, ordering the children not to touch it as she hung it on a hook over the rear seat of the car. She stopped at Milkmart for a gallon of milk. By now the bottle had cooled and Mindy was peacefully sucking it. Then Adele drove home. The baby had worn herself out with screaming, and the warm milk had sent her back to sleep. She was heavy as Adele lifted her out of the car seat, her bag dangling on her arm. Linda tried to help, and picked up the milk to carry it indoors, but it was too heavy for her and she dropped it halfway up the driveway. Adele heard the crash, turned and looked. Linda's face was white and terror-stricken as she looked up at her mother. (Oh, my God, my God!) Adele turned around, walked back, put the baby back in the car seat. Linda just stood there. Adele brought her voice into control. 'Get back in the car, Linda.' She drove back to Milkmart and picked up another gallon of milk.

'Take my purse, Linda,' Adele said as they pulled again into the driveway. She lugged the now deeply sleeping baby out of the car seat again, and Linda followed her up the driveway. 'Stay away from the broken glass,' Adele ordered sharply. Linda hopped dangerously among the pieces. Adele carried the baby into the living room and laid her in the playpen. She sighed. Mindy would be awake until late tonight: three naps in one day were too many. She went back out to the car and got the milk and the suit, brought them into the house, put the milk in the refrigerator, and hung the suit on a hook. Then she got a broom and dustpan and told Linda to follow her. She swept up the glass with Linda holding the dustpan. She poured the glass fragments directly into the garbage pail, being sure to jam the cover on tightly – you never know what kids might take it into their heads to pry into. She gave the broom and dustpan to Linda and pulled the hose off the rack and turned on the outside spigot and hosed down the spilled milk.

She went inside and took off her jacket. Linda stood in the hallway staring at her. 'What are you looking at me for!' Adele shrieked. 'Are you just going to stand there looking at me all day?' Linda edged away. 'Take off your coat and hang it up!'

Linda took off her coat slowly, and walked toward the hall closet. Adele went into the living room and removed the baby's jacket. She picked her up and started upstairs, then noticed Linda's small form standing inside the closet door, silently moving. She went back down. Linda was leaning against the closet wall, weeping. Adele reached out her hand and touched the child's head. She cried out loud then, burying her head in the coats.

'I'm sorry, I'm sorry,' Adele said, near tears herself. 'It's all right, honey, I know you didn't mean to do it.' The child turned suddenly and buried her head in her mother's side. Adele stood there, the baby heavy on her arm, fondling Linda's head, murmuring, 'It's okay, it's all right, baby.' Linda stopped crying and Adele stooped down to her. 'I'm going to put Mindy to bed. Do you want to come and help me?'

Linda nodded eagerly, and Adele stood and took the child's hand in hers, and the three of them mounted the stairs together. Adele's heart was full of emotion: the small hand was placed in hers so trustingly, after so many betrayals. Adele changed Mindy's diaper and put her in the crib.

'How come Mindy's sleeping now, Mommy?'

'She's just tired.'

122

'But can I play with my dolls?'

'Of course not! The room has to be dark and quiet.'

'But I want to play with my Barbie doll.' The voice was already rising into hysteria.

'Take it downstairs, then. Hurry, get it, and be quiet.'

Linda got her doll and its paraphernalia, dropping bits of it to Adele's whispered 'Be quiet, I said!'

Linda took her toys into a corner of the living room. Adele went into the kitchen and sat for a moment on a high stool, thinking. Easy night, tonight: Paul was going out. There was some leftover spaghetti for Eric and Linda. Paul wouldn't touch spaghetti, claiming not to like it, but Adele suspected it was worry about his figure. Billy had adopted this dislike. There was a little leftover chicken for Billy. She would heat that. She sat there hunched over. She had not even asked the children about school today, she should find out what had happened to Linda in kindergarten. She sat up, drew in a deep breath, and walked toward the living room. Linda was squatting on the floor, playing with her doll.

'Now you're a bad girl, a bad, bad girl,' she was saying as she slapped the doll on its bottom several times. 'You go straight in your room and don't come out! And don't wake up the baby!' her little voice said angrily. She put the baby doll on its feet and marched it toward the couch.

'Mmmmmm,' she whined, 'I didn't mean it, Mommy,' she said in a tiny high voice.

'You did so and you're bad!' she said in her Mommy voice, and threw the baby doll down on the floor on its face. The baby doll was eighteen inches long; the Mommy doll was small, less than a foot tall. She put an apron on Barbie, and said in a calm, happy voice: 'I wonder what I should make for Daddy's supper tonight. I know, I'll make chocolate cake with raisins, and bacon.' Then she paraded the Barbie doll around in a circle, humming all the while. 'Hello, dear,' she said in an artificial voice. 'How was your day today? Guess what I've made! Chocolate cake with raisins!' There was a silence, in which presumably the father answered.

123

'Oh, yes, it's been one of those days. After you eat, I want you to go in and spank that baby, she was so bad today! Isn't this chocolate cake delicious?'

Adele stood there silently, then turned back into the kitchen. She poured herself a glass of wine and turned on the radio. The gallon jug of cheap California was going fast: Paul would notice. Turning furtively to see where Linda was, she poured some water into the wine. She sat down again on the high stool. The radio was playing some Mantovani-ish music: 'You'd be so nice to come home to, You'd be so nice by the fire.' She and Paul had danced to that song, clinging to each other, way back, years ago, a lifetime ago. She'd been brisk and efficient and independent, a legal secretary, earning good money for a woman, and Paul was still a law student. She had always known that a career was not really what she wanted. She wanted to get married and have kids; she wanted to marry a professional man and have some luxuries, a life less harried than her own mother's. But she had fallen in love with Paul in a hopeless way, like diving off the board without checking first to see if there's water in the pool.

She leaned on her elbow, sipping the wine. The song ended, the radio announced that it was five o'clock. Wearily she rose and got the spaghetti and chicken out of the refrigerator. Eric had gotten a ride home; he came in the door grousing about something. Adele sent him upstairs to change his clothes and start on his homework.

'What's for dinner?' Eric asked, and contented with spaghetti, went upstairs.

But Linda came trailing into the kitchen. 'Do I have to eat spaghetti too?'

Adele's back straightened. 'You like spaghetti!'

'No, I don't. I don't like it, I hate spaghetti!'

'You always liked spaghetti!' Adele argued. 'You liked it when we had it on Monday.'

'No, I didn't. I don't want it! I won't eat it!' The child jumped up and down on the kitchen floor. Adele swiftly reached out and swatted her on the rear, sending the

124

child into screams of agony. She ran into the living room and threw herself on the couch crying.

The front door opened and Paul came in. 'For God's sake,' he said softly, 'can't I ever come home to peace and quiet? All day long I listen to shit.'

Adele turned to him white-faced. 'You have five children,' she said hoarsely. 'What do you expect?'

He turned to her. He was handsome and well-dressed and he had great elegance of movement. 'Did you get my suit?'

She nodded toward the hook.

'For God's sake, Adele, why didn't you hang it in the bedroom? You leave it here where the kids with their grubby paws ...'

'I didn't have *time*!' she snapped. 'Besides,' she added defensively, 'it has a plastic cover. And the kids didn't touch it.'

The door opened and Billy came in. Billy was eight. Adele's eyes shone when she looked at him. 'Mrs. DiNapoli had to go out for milk, so she dropped me off.'

'Oh, that was nice, honey. How did the project go? Are you finished?'

Billy, authoritative and knowledgeable even at his age, began to explain to her the difficulty of the project and the incredible stupidity of Johnny DiNapoli.

Paul still stood idly in the kitchen. 'Can I at least get a drink around here?' he interjected.

'Oh, Paul!' Adele gasped. 'I'm sorry!' She ran to the refrigerator, where she had a small pitcher of martinis cooling.

'Spaghetti!' Paul sniffed. 'Glad I'm going out.'

'Oh, are we having spaghetti, Mom?' Billy protested, his voice rising into a whine. She looked at him grimly. To children, food was everything, she thought. Their whole evening rose or fell according to what they were to have for dinner.

Paul was in the living room with his drink and his paper. Linda had snuggled up beside him on the couch. 'I hate spaghetti!' Linda yelled toward the kitchen.

125

'Well, I have to confess I do too,' Paul said, putting his arm around her and tickling her.

'That's great, that's just great!' Adele stormed in. 'I try to live on our budget and spaghetti is one of the cheapest things we can have, and you undermine me right and left!'

'Oh, for God's sake, Adele, if she doesn't like it, why should she have to eat it?'

'Because,' Adele said, and was surprised herself to hear the level and height of her voice, 'it's all I have, there's only enough chicken for Billy, and I didn't have time to make anything else!'

Paul looked up at her coolly, almost appraisingly. 'Why not? From your color, I'd guess you've had time to booze it up with the girls this afternoon.' He rose, took his suit and his drink, and went upstairs.

She stared at him. Her throat was full of tears. Injustice, injustice.

'Am I having chicken, Mom?' Billy asked eagerly.

'Why can he have chicken and I can't?' Linda leaped up.

'Shut up! Just shut up! You get what you get!' she shouted and ran into the kitchen and poured herself another glass of wine. Then she made the salad and set the table. Paul came down looking beautiful, kissed her lightly on the cheek, and said he probably wouldn't be late, but not to worry.

Adele felt calmer after he was gone. She called the children to dinner. Linda gazed at her spaghetti and refused to eat, her voice edged with hysteria.

'You'll go to bed without dinner, then,' Adele said grimly.

Linda wailed.

Adele sank to a chair. She took Linda's arm and pulled her toward her, trying not to be rough. 'Linda, I didn't know you didn't like spaghetti. You always liked it before. You can look at Billy's plate. There isn't enough chicken for both of you.'

'Why does he get it and I don't? He always gets everything!' Linda wailed.

'He got it because I knew Billy didn't like spaghetti. Listen. I won't make it for you anymore, okay? I didn't know you didn't like it. Okay?'

Linda gazed at her mother, figuring her chances. It looked as if it was spaghetti or nothing for dinner, no matter how she responded, but she was not sure whether she could trust this momentary conciliatory mood. She was not sure she wanted to; she wanted to protest about something. But Adele let go of her and rose wearily. Clearly she was not going to bend any further. Linda ate her spaghetti, expecting some reward afterward. But none came.

Adele ran the bathwater. She bathed Mike, then Linda, then called Eric to take his bath. Each time, she emptied and cleaned the tub and refilled it. She put Mike to bed and came back down.

'Read me a story,' Linda demanded.

Demands, Adele thought bleakly. There was nothing like demands from a child who had done something wrong. She drops the milk and I have to pay: all night. 'I'm too busy,' she said.

Linda pouted.

'Turn on the TV.'

The baby cried. Adele went up and knocked on the bathroom door. 'Hurry up out of that tub.' She changed the baby and carried her downstairs. She took a jar from the refrigerator and placed it in a pan of water. 'Eric!' she yelled up. There was no answer. She marched up the stairs to the bathroom and opened the door swiftly. Eric glanced at her guiltily. There was water all over the floor; he was sitting in the tub, pink with warmth, a toy airplane in his hand. She marched into the bathroom, almost slipping on the water, pulled the plug in the tub, and lifted Eric out by one arm, roughly. Roughly, with a terry towel, she dried him, then said, 'Now, you get in your pajamas and get your homework done.' She got down on the floor and sponged up the spilled water. Well, it's one way to get the bathroom floor cleaned, and thought she would repeat that to the girls tomorrow.

When she got back to the kitchen, the water in the pan

127

was boiling. She took the jar out with pot holders and placed it in the sink. She heated a bottle.

'Time for bed, Linda,' she called. Linda rose, sidled into the kitchen, and looked reproachfully at her mother.

'Bed,' Adele said firmly. Linda turned on her heel, and with a certain erectness of neck and shoulders, let her mother know what she thought of her. She marched solemnly and severely up the stairs.

Adele poured some milk into the cereal bowl and fed the baby cereal and jarred plums. She left the baby in the high chair, giving her rubber toys to play with, and set about cleaning up the kitchen. She realized she had not eaten. She scraped the leftovers from the children's plates into the spaghetti pot, and ate what was left in it.

Eric and Billy were quarreling. She ordered Billy to bring his homework downstairs and Eric to go to bed. Eric was unhappy. He muttered about unfairness, he slammed the bedroom door. She finished cleaning the kitchen, then glanced at the clock.

'Billy?'

'Yes,' came a reluctant sigh.

'Did you finish your homework?'

'Yes.' Almost groaned.

'Okay, bedtime.'

'Oh, Mom, can't I just see the end of this program?'

'All right. But as soon as it's over . . .'

'It's a movie, Mom.'

'What time is it over?'

'Ten o'clock.'

'Well, you can just go up right now, young man.'

'Oh, can't I . . .'

'NO!'

Reluctantly, he turned off the set; reluctantly he kissed her. But she kissed him hard and held him for a minute, and he hugged her then, and laid his cheek against hers. They stayed that way for a few moments, then he went up.

It was after nine. The house was silent. Adele carried the baby upstairs and put her in the crib with her bottle, praying. And Mindy, just as if she hadn't had three naps,

128

fell off to sleep. She'll probably wake up at four, Adele sighed and went into the bathroom. She drew bathwater and poured in bath oil, a luxury at ninety-eight cents a bottle, but one she felt she owed herself. She bathed, put on her nightgown and robe, and went back downstairs. She relished the silence; she felt she was eating it, breathing it in. She poured herself a glass of wine. The hell with him. She sat down in the living room. It was a mess: the doll things were sprawled over one corner, Billy's social studies project was piled on a chair, and some unhung coats were thrown over the other chair. Paul's tie, which he had removed when he was sitting with Linda, dangled over the couch. Adele picked up the tie and hung it over the banister, resolutely turned her eyes away from the rest, and sat down. This is your life, Mrs. O'Neill.

She had looked in the mirror after getting out of the bath, and had seen a broad, handsome face with shiny black hair curling round it. It was a face. It could have been, she thought idly, in a magazine. She'd seen worse. But she didn't want to be in a magazine, that wasn't it. She had never wanted a glamorous life. She thought about Linda's resentment as she drifted off to sleep, and Eric's muttering. She thought about Mikey's terrified face as he looked at her after he overturned the playpen, and Linda's dead white face after she dropped the milk. Tears came into her eyes; she put her head in her hands. 'Oh, God, help me, please help me. I don't want to be bad. I don't want them to be frightened of me, my own babies; oh, God, what's wrong with me? I try not to yell at them. I don't want to be unhappy, I don't want them to be unhappy. I want to be good, oh, Mary, mother of God, help me, show me the way.' She thought about the martyred saints of the Church, about Mary Magdalen, about Christ's sufferings on the cross. She knew that if she were better, she would be able to be good enough, she could be kind, patient, and loving, which is all she had ever wanted to be. She slid onto the floor and knelt by the couch and prayed.

'Give me strength, oh Lord, let me not be cruel to them, I love them so much.'

She rose wearily. It was early, and she thought about watching TV for a while, or reading the newspaper. But she felt exhausted. She went into the kitchen and poured herself another glass of wine, turned off all lights but the front door and front hallway, picked up Paul's tie, and went upstairs.

She switched on the lamp in the bedroom and looked around. It was a shabby room; she always closed the door when she had company. They had never had the money to fix it up. There was a double bed without a headboard and a couple of old, uncomplementary dressers. An orange crate on its side served as a bed table. She always intended to paint it, but never seemed to have time.

I suppose if I didn't sit for an hour with the girls, she started to think, then brushed it away. I need it for my sanity, she concluded.

She lowered herself onto the bed like an invalid, and sat there, hunched over, her hands clasped between her knees. She thought about Paul and how beautiful he had looked going out. Fancy dinner : they probably even had shrimp cocktail. She wondered if the other lawyers had brought their wives; she wondered if all the lawyers were men. Then brushed that away as unworthy: another sign of her evil, miserable, suspicious, jealous nature. Of course . . . but he always came home to her. She could not ask more. She sipped her wine, and then, like a person who had been putting off looking at her bank-book because she knows the last withdrawal probably canceled her account, but who now decides to face facts, she pulled a small book from the stack of papers and paperback mysteries in the orange crate. She opened it to a calendar. She counted days, over and over again. She sat there gazing into space, her face unmoving, her lips stiff. She could hear Paul's voice: 'It's up to you, Adele, I'm not fanatic about it. It *is* getting a bit heavy. I'll use something so you don't have to.' He acted as if it was all her doing. But it wasn't. It wasn't: there was a higher law. She had to obey.

'Please, God, let me learn to be patient. Let me learn

130

to accept Your Will. Behold, I am the handmaiden of the Lord.'

But her face was furrowed and her lips grim; there was no grace on her. She was sure her prayers never mounted to heaven.

11

Natalie's acidity and bluntness upset Adele, who believed in politeness, and although she liked Mira, she always had the feeling that Mira somewhat looked down on her. It was Bliss she felt closest to, and Elizabeth, but Elizabeth lived across town and they rarely got to see each other. It was easy to carry the kids over the fence for a cup of coffee for an hour; it was a project to drag them all the way over to Elizabeth's. Bliss was polite and soft-spoken and very feminine, which Adele admired. There was something almost – mannish – about Natalie's dress and movements, about Mira's speech. Bliss laughed a lot and had that easy casualness that Adele tried to emulate. And even if she was not Catholic, she seemed to understand.

Bliss was having coffee in Adele's kitchen. The women had never, in the three years they'd been friends, criticized each other. When they spoke of each other it was to give news, to analyze feelings at least superficially. But Adele was feeling terribly angular; she had had coffee with Mira the day before and Mira had shown her their new chairs and lamp tables. The house had been clean and orderly and empty: Normie was at school all day now, and Clark was in kindergarten. Mira had been readng philosophy when Adele came in with Mikey and Mindy, and she felt the kids had sloppied up Mira's house. She was uncomfortable, and decided she would not go to Mira's again. She felt better going where there was already a house full of kids.

So she said, 'Sometimes I think Mira's neurotic, you know? I mean, why would she read those fancy books? As if she were trying to show off.'

Bliss laughed that soft laugh of hers, down in her

131

throat, like a laughed sigh. 'Bill says she's overeducated.'

'She's always talking about women's rights.'

'I don't think she's happy staying at home.'

Adele looked shocked. 'What does she expect? She has kids. She is neurotic. Sometimes I pray for her at night.'

'Listen, don't forget me. We can all use a few prayers,' Bliss laughed softly. 'This morning Bill had to get to the airport by eight and you should have seen the madhouse. Then Cheryl decided she had a sore throat and didn't want to go to school, and Midge cried and said she wasn't going if Cheryl wasn't going,' Bliss laughed. 'So everybody stayed home and watched TV.'

'Don't you worry about them missing school so often?' Adele's voice had a brittle edge.

'No,' Bliss shrugged. 'They don't learn anything anyway.' She stirred sugar into her coffee. 'I wouldn't send them at all – they learn more from TV – but I want to get them out of the house.'

All the women bad-mouthed their kids this way. They laughed about telling them to go play in the traffic, or called them 'the brats.' All except Mira, who found this immoral, although she also thought it might be their way of balancing their almost single-minded love for concern about their children. But when Bliss did it, it had such a relaxed, comic feel that you could not believe she meant it at all; when Natalie did it, it sounded real.

'Well,' Adele frowned, 'Billy's doing well in school; he seems to be learning a lot.'

'Oh, I suppose it's different for a boy.'

'Yes.' Adele fiddled with her spoon. 'But you couldn't say that to Mira. She'd get indignant. But what good did all her education do her?'

'Well, I feel my education was worthwhile,' Bliss said smiling, reminding Adele that Mira might have gone to college but only Bliss, of the women in their group, had graduated. 'Someday I'll go back and teach first grade. Meantime, I have to keep the three first-graders I live with in line. It's good experience. The classroom will be a snap after this.' She was laughing as she spoke.

Adele laughed. 'What grade is Cheryl in now? Third?'

'That's what it says on her report card, but I don't believe it.'

'What does it say on Bill's report card?'

'It says he's a navigator, but that's only when he's working. The rest of the time he's a first-grader too.'

Adele envied Bliss her ease with her husband. Bliss teased him that way right to his face and he laughed along with her. Adele would never dare do that. It wasn't that she was afraid of Paul, it was . . . well, she wasn't sure what it was. Bliss lived easily too. She didn't worry about laundry piled in the living room, or whether or not her kids ate. Of course, she had only two, and Bill was home a lot and she could get out by herself to go marketing or shopping. But he didn't help her that much: most of the time he sat upstairs in the little room he'd built in the attic, and made model airplanes.

'Are you going marketing tonight?'

'Yes. Norm's supposed to be home, so I'm dropping my kids at Mira's and driving her. Want to come?'

'I can't. Paul has a meeting tonight. But you could pick up some instant for me. I'm nearly out.'

'Sure. Anything else?'

Adele's brow clouded. 'Well . . . if it's not too much trouble, could you get me some milk? My car's on the blink and we can't afford to get it fixed this week.'

'Sure. A gallon?'

'Yes. Oh, thanks, Bliss. That's a real help. I don't know what I'd do without my friends.' Her throat got thick. 'They're all so great,' she continued, but by now there were tears in her eyes. Bliss sat quiet, watching her.

Adele lifted her head and looked across at her friend.

'What is it?' Bliss finally asked quietly.

'Oh, nothing,' Adele said, regaining the brittle cheerful voice she used, and reaching for a tissue to blow her nose. 'Just,' and her voice broke again, 'I'm pregnant again.'

'Oh, God!'

'Well, what's one more,' cheerfully spoken.

133

But Bliss just sat there, and Adele began to cry. 'It must've been after Natalie's party. Paul and I got a little high and . . . you know . . . and even though it was the wrong time, we took a chance.'

'What does Paul say?'

She shrugged. 'He's really wonderful. I mean he says it's up to me. He doesn't get aggravated. He says he's going to do well in time, and there will be enough money. He doesn't worry. But I . . .'

'You don't want it.'

'It isn't that I don't want it. I love kids. It's just . . . I don't know, it's all so hard, I can't cope . . .' She had stopped crying and had dried her face. She looked blotchy and swollen and dried out. She stared at the wall.

'Adele,' Bliss said slowly, 'I know it's against your religion, but have you thought about an abortion? You know, Mindy's still in diapers, and Mikey isn't two yet. It will be an awful handful.'

'I know.'

'And you're only . . . what are you?'

'I'll be thirty next week.'

'Billy's only eight. It will be years before the kids can help you.'

'I know.'

Bliss was silent then, but so was Adele. Bliss feared she had angered her friend. 'You probably think it's wrong . . .'

'I don't!' Adele burst out. 'I'd love to get one! But if I did it, I'd have to go to confession and say I was sorry, but I wouldn't be sorry so I couldn't say it so I couldn't go to confession and I could never take communion again!' It poured out like a stream of rage.

'Oh, God,' Bliss murmured softly.

Adele rose and reached for the wine bottle. It was nearly empty and it crossed her mind to ask Bliss to pick up some more for her so Paul wouldn't see . . . 'Oh, we'll get by, I guess. By the time the baby's born, Mindy will be walking and if I work hard with her, she may be out of diapers. There's room for another bed in the girls' room. So if it's a girl, we're okay,' she laughed. 'The

134

Women's Guild is talking about starting a nursery school. The church will let us use some of their rooms, and we'd chip in one afternoon a week and have to hire only one full-time person, to direct. And it would be cheap. Mikey will be old enough for that. Money will be tight for another couple of years, until Paul pays off his partnership, but then things should be good. My car's on its last legs, but . . .' She rubbed her forehead.

Bliss gazed at her. She had been shocked to hear that Adele was a year younger than she was. Adele's face was pretty, prettier than her own, but it was already lined, and her dark hair was showing gray. Bliss thought Adele's church was cruel to its women, but did not say so.

'Sure,' she said cheerfully. 'And while it's a baby it won't matter whether it's a girl or a boy, you can put the crib in the girls' room until you get a bigger house. And by the time it's born, Billy will be nine and Eric will be seven and Linda will be six and Mikey will be in nursery school and Mindy will be walking, and you won't have anything to do!'

They both laughed then. 'That's what Paul said when I told him about the nursery school. He says nursery schools are for spoiled women who want to play bridge all afternoon.'

She poured the wine in two glasses, and handed one to Bliss.

'Want me to pick up some more wine for you tonight?' Bliss asked.

'Sure!' Adele said with real cheer, as if she were making a declaration of independence. She sat down smiling. 'And I have all those baby clothes.'

'I'd think they'd be worn out by now.'

'Oh, they were! This is the second batch. Might as well use them up.'

'Sure.' Bliss's face became serious then. 'But after this . . .'

'I don't want to think about it. I just don't want to think about it.'

'Well,' Bliss said, smiling again, 'at least you can feel safe for the next few months.'

Adele laughed, and Bliss added, 'The one compensation for pregnancy.'

12

Bliss had a pale oval face that gleamed white in the mirror of the unlighted room. Her gestures were slow and graceful, her body long and slender. Her eyes gave away intelligence, a careful mind that summed up situations before allowing her to act. She dressed well for her means, in tight pants that showed her ass, and soft loose shirts. She had soft speech and a soft laugh and she revealed little about herself to anyone. She did not trust people.

She took her children to Mira's and picked her friend up and they drove to the supermarket. It was very crowded, as always on Friday nights. They did not talk much in the market; both concentrated intently on getting the best food for the least money. This is quite a skill, even an art. It involves understanding food, knowing how to make a delicious *navarin* from a cheap cut of lamb, or soups from bones – which in those days you could get free – and an inexpensive cut of beef. Funny. I spent years of my life learning how to do it and I am very good at it, but now I don't need to do it at all.

After they got back in the car, Bliss told Mira about Adele.

'Oh, no! Poor soul! She's on the brink of a breakdown as it is.'

'She's too tense. She doesn't know how to take things easy. If I were Adele, I'd just tell Paul he had to be home one night a week so I could go out. She's not demanding enough. I wouldn't let him get away with what he gets away with.'

'Well, that might help, but even so, with five kids . . .'

'Six, soon.'

'Why doesn't she get an abortion?'

Bliss explained. Mira sat there hushed. 'Lordy, lordy,' she sighed finally.

'In the old days, nobody had birth control.'

'In the old days, babies died.'

'So did mothers.'

They fell silent. Bliss dropped Mira off and picked up her children. She put away the groceries, saw that the children were washed up, and put them to bed. She climbed the fence and knocked at Adele's back door, and handed her the food and wine.

'Come in for a while,' Adele said. She looked desolate.

'I can't, the kids are alone,' Bliss said, glad of an excuse. She did not want to have to look too hard at Adele's pain.

She went back and cleaned up the kitchen, then took a shower and washed her hair. She stayed a long time in the bathroom. She put lotion on her body after the shower and stood gazing at herself in the full-length mirror.

She was thirty-one. Her body was smooth and white, and when she let it down, her red hair hung halfway to her waist. She looked like a flame, she thought, white at the center. She put on a wrapper and straightened the bathroom, then padded out in soft terry slippers and poured herself a glass of diet soda. She turned on the TV set and settled down on the couch with the dress she was making. It needed only a few touches, things that had to be done by hand. It would be beautiful, she thought. She was making it for her party.

She liked this time of night when everything was quiet, especially when Bill was gone. She could sit with her thoughts and her quietness. Somehow, when Bill was around, even though he gave no sign of sensitivity, she had the feeling that he could sense her thoughts. And these days, she did not want him to sense them.

Bliss had been brought up in a tight, poor home where there was often not enough food. Her father called himself a rancher, which was, she told people, a fancy word for dirt farmer. In fact, he had not really even been that,

137

and the Texas shack – it was not much more than that – looked as bad as any she'd seen pictures of in Kentucky or Tennessee. There were a lot of children; some died. But Bliss was her mother's pet. The women saw Bliss's quick mind, saw her sizing up situations and finding the best way to survive. The father was often drunk and sometimes brutal, but after a few years, he no longer touched Bliss. She scared him. When she was ten, her brothers in their teens, he abandoned them; they were not much worse off than they had been before. Her brothers were saved by the war: they were drafted and afterward remained in the army. It was a better life than they'd had in Texas. Bliss's mother pinched and hoarded; Bliss worked hard in school. Together they got Bliss into the state teacher's college, and somehow, she got through. She had no illusions about her intelligence. She knew she was smart and quick and clever, but not intellectual. She had known since infancy that life was survival and she had only contempt for people who had yet to discover that. You did what you had to do, because the world was wide and cold and heartless, and you, no matter who or where you were, were alone.

She had met Bill during her first year of teaching. She taught a first-grade class in a little Texas town that paid her a salary of $2000 a year and seemed to expect she would be grateful for it. Actually, she could live on that and send money to her mother – a thing she did until the day her mother died. Bill had been a pilot in the air force during the war, and afterward he got a job piloting a small private plane for a Texas businessman. He was earning $7000 a year. Bliss married him. She was not without affection for him. She thought he was cute and funny and eminently manipulable. She thought the reason her marriage was so much better than those she saw around her was that she had expected so much less than the other women: survival, not happiness.

When Bill had gotten the job with Crossways, they had had to move to the New York area. It was a good job, with a great future: in ten years, Bill would earn over $30,000 a year. But she dreaded the move. She

138

associated New York with Jews and niggers, both of whom she hated. And she was a little worried about her hick edges showing in the big city. She had lain in bed at night in Texas, planning her demeanor. She would be calm and cool, which was her nature anyway; she would not talk about her past; and she would keep a watchful eye out. It was her normal behavior. She did not have to violate herself.

They had been able to avoid New York by buying a little house in the New Jersey suburbs. Bliss drove Bill to Newark when he had a flight. And there were few Jews and no niggers, so Bliss didn't have to deal with that. In the four years she'd been there, she had scraped off any unfinished edges she might have had. She felt she had not had many anyway; the cityfolk had proven to be not very different from Texas folk, and did not live up to their legendary superiority. She suspected that Mira, for instance, looked down on her because she was a Southerner. Just some of Mira's remarks about the South and how it treated 'the colored people,' as she called them. Inside, Bliss curled her lip at such talk. The South, she felt, treated niggers better than the North treated its 'colored folk.' The South understood niggers: they were children, incapable of taking care of themselves. When nigger maids got sick, the white women in Redora took them straight to the doctor and sat there while they were being examined, and paid the bill afterward. The nigger women didn't have sense enough to do that by themselves.

There was much Bliss disapproved of in the North. Welfare, for instance, which was starting to be a big thing. A lot of Puerto Ricans coming up to New York to get a free handout. Bliss knew what she had come from, and she knew she had made it. If she could do it, so could they. She still remembered what it was like. She remembered hunger, a pain you got used to after a while, and always being full of gas. She remembered her parents' faces and was astonished when she considered the ages they must have been. Both had great gaps instead of teeth; both were wrinkled, spare, like very old people.

She remembered wanting to get out. She would lie in bed when she was eight, nine, ten, clenching her teeth, hearing her father batter her mother, or, after he was gone, her brothers arguing violently and her mother trying to shush them, hearing the rage that is poverty, and knowing. She did not have to say anything to herself. She clenched her teeth against the present and knew that she had to get out, that she would get out, that getting out was worth anything it cost. It was worth herself, it was worth her feelings.

And she had done it.

And she was as happy as she'd ever imagined being. They had to be careful about money, it would continue to be tight until Bill made pilot, which would be, they thought, a few years off. But there was always enough food; she had a decent little house, and here she was, with a beautiful peach chiffon dress in her lap, a shade lighter than her hair, bringing out all its highlights. She stitched contentedly.

At eleven, she switched off the TV, checked the locks and lights, and went upstairs to the bedroom. She carried a novel in her hand, a paperback that Amy Fox had lent her. It was a love story set in the Deep South in the Reconstruction era. On its cover was a beautiful red-haired woman in a low-cut white gown with her breasts popping out of it. It showed only her bust, because she was near the bottom of the cover. Behind her, full length, stood a handsome man holding a riding whip, and behind him, in the background, was a white plantation house gleaming against greenness. She didn't usually read such trash. She didn't usually read books. But Amy had gotten her interested, and somehow she felt sort of in the mood for something light and relaxing, a fairy story. She thought she might start it tonight.

She took off her robe and draped it over a chair in the bedroom. She turned toward the bed and caught a glimpse of herself in the mirror over Bill's chest of drawers. Her hair was down, and her shoulders gleamed warm peach against the white nightgown. She stood there, not thinking about herself, just looking at an image. It was beautiful. Unthinking still, she slipped the nightgown off her shoulders and meditated on her body. It was beautiful, white and slender, the breasts round and lifted, the legs slim and unmarred. It would not always be so. Bliss thought about her mother's body, with the skin hanging from the bone on fleshless arms. She ran her hands over her breasts, her sides, her belly, her thighs. Her blood ran to her touch, as if it had been waiting. Since she was grown and had a regular room to take a bath in, no one but Bill had ever seen her body. And no one but Bill had ever touched it. She had never been much concerned about sex, she had not had room for that. Sex was for the wealthy. Suppose she had let herself get attracted to someone? Suppose he was a truck driver or a ditch-digger, or a no-good like her father? And if she had had to get married (if she'd been really attracted to someone, that's most likely what would have happened; she couldn't have held him off until afterward the way she had Bill) then there she would have been, forever and forever.

Bliss understood how women could become prostitutes: if you have to pay the bill, you'd damn well better make them pay the first installments. Otherwise you'd go on paying it by yourself forever and forever – like her mother. Adele and Mira, for God sakes, complaining about money. She said nothing, or she made a joke, but she sat there smirking inwardly. Poverty. What did they know about poverty? Her mother with her creased face, knobbed hands from scrubbing clothes on a washboard, calluses and hunched back from lugging great tin vats of water to wash the clothes in, bathe the children in, scrub the bare floor. Her mother digging roots in the weedy, dry vegetable garden. Yes. She pulled her nightgown back on and turned toward the bed. But something made her turn and look again, catch sight of herself again in the mirror with her hair down. She realized her body was throbbing: it felt as if every pore were a tiny open mouth, hungry, thirsty, dying of thirst. As it would. Shrivel and die. She turned out the light and slid into bed. The cool sheets caressed her. She felt, as she lay there, like a white flower, spread out in the bed throbbing, warm, waiting to be picked.

The women's heads turned with every new arrival, and Mira realized that everyone was waiting for Paul. Over the year or so that they had been giving these parties, Paul's star had risen. Before that, he had been Adele's husband, occasionally glimpsed in the backyard awkwardly plucking weeds. But now he was the center of the parties, although no one admitted that.

There were rumors about him and his affairs which half-titillated the women much as they deplored them. He was handsome, he danced well and liked to dance, and he liked women. He had a line for each of them – they had privately compared notes – which he would repeat, with variations, whenever the mood was right. Mira realized that she felt disappointed after a party in which she had not danced with Paul, or in which the mood was not sufficiently intimate for him to murmur, looking at her intensely, 'You have eyes like a cat, did you know that? Sexy eyes.' Mira had never thought of herself as possessing anything that could be so described, but secretly, she was pleased. And she sensed that the others felt the same way. Bliss said he'd told her she had a beautiful neck and he'd like to get his hands around it; Natalie said he'd told her she smelled of sex. Mira was quietly appalled at that, but Nat seemed to think it a compliment.

Mira was talking with Bliss in the living room, when she noticed a tiny start on Bliss's face and turned around to see that Paul and Adele were standing in the doorway. She turned back to continue the conversation: 'Yes, really beautiful. I envy you your talent. Such a color!' Bliss was wearing a flowing chiffon dress in a pale peach color that brought out the highlights in her red hair.

The party was at Bliss's house, and the usual crowd was there. One new couple had been invited, Samantha and Hugh Simpson, who had recently moved in a few blocks away, and who were friends of Amy and Don Fox. Mira went to Samantha, who was standing alone, and introduced herself. Samantha was very young, no more than twenty-three or four: not much younger, Mira thought, than I was when I moved here. Now I'm the only one left under thirty. Samantha was bubbly; she was talking happily about their new house, and how nice it was to be in a house, and about all the catastrophes that had occurred since she had moved in. 'So Simp – my husband – had to take the lock off the bathroom door, and Fleur was crying hysterically and I was trying to calm her through the door, and we had no tools and Simp had to go up and down the block to find someone home who had tools . . .' So it went. The catastrophes were always comic, even when in fact they were not, even when a child ended up with an injury. The catastrophes were comic, the men were inadequate, and the women functioned against overwhelming odds, defeated before they began. This was the myth, Mira realized, listening to Samantha; it was a myth of heroism and good humor. This was how they made it out. She liked Samantha, in spite of the way she looked.

'You must come over for coffee one day,' she began.

'Oh, I'd love to! Since the moving was done and Simp went back to work, I've been so lonely!'

They talked. The party simmered. People shifted from group to group. The dancing began. Mira went to get herself another drink. Bliss was getting out more ice.

'God, you look gorgeous. Really!' Mira said again.

Bliss turned with a snarky smile. 'Thanks. Paul thinks so too, I guess. He asked me to go to the Bahamas with him. Some lawyers' conference. Think I should go?'

Mira had learned enough sophistication to be able to play the snarky game. 'Why not? It's a long cold winter. But I'm jealous. He didn't ask me.'

'Oh, just wait. He will.'

And in time, he did. It was after midnight and people had begun to undress — the men removing their jackets

143

and ties, the women their shoes and earrings. Paul was dancing in a brown shirt and cream trousers that showed his slimness; his handsome Irish face was pink with heat and wine. He was dancing the cha-cha with Mira with a bottle of Beaujolais in his hand. 'Have some,' he kept saying.

The music changed to a slow dance and he grabbed Mira's always stiff body around the waist with his free arm and held her close. He looked into her face. 'Oh, those cat's eyes,' he murmured. 'I wish I knew what was behind them. Why don't you give me a chance to find out? Come to the Bahamas with me, I'm flying down on Tuesday.'

'I thought you'd never ask,' she grinned.

Norm was dancing with Adele, teasing her all the while, so that their dance was really just a moving conversation. Hamp was sitting on the couch talking to Oriane. Hamp never danced. Sean was dancing with Samantha.

'I'm jealous, can I cut in? I haven't danced with Paul all night, have I, Pauly baby?' Natalie was a little drunk.

'Come to Poppa,' Paul said, opening his arms to enclose both of them, but Mira laughed and slipped out. 'Spoilsport!' he called after her.

Mira went into the bathroom. After a time – she was retouching her makeup – there was a knock. 'Be right out!' Mira called.

'Oh, Mira?' It was Samantha. 'Can I come in?'

'Sure.'

Samantha came in and pulled up her skirt. 'Damned thing,' she muttered. Mira glanced at her. 'Can I help?'

'No, it's this damned corselet. Whenever I have to pee, it's a major production.'

Mira smiled. She did not ask why anyone as slender as Samantha would be wearing a thing like that. She was wearing one herself. Samantha finally got herself adjusted and sat on the toilet. Mira sat on the edge of the tub and lighted a cigarette. This sort of intimacy had shocked her when she first came to Meyersville, but she was used to it now.

'Mira,' Samantha began uneasily, 'I saw you dancing with Paul. Paul – O'Connor?'

'O'Neill. Yes.'

'Well, what sort of person is he? I mean, is he a friend of yours?'

Mira laughed. 'What did he do?'

'Mira!' Samantha leaned forward and nearly whispered. 'He put his hand on my – bottom! I was so embarrassed I nearly died! I didn't know what to say! Luckily, my back was to the wall, so I don't think anyone else saw. And then he said I had a – well, he said a *sexy ass*. Can you imagine?'

'And then he asked you to go to the Bahamas with him.'

'Yes! How did you know? As if I could – I have to take the baby to the doctor on Tuesday. Besides, I never even met him before.'

'He's going to have quite an entourage on this trip. He's asked every woman in the room.'

'Oh.' Samantha looked disappointed.

'Except Theresa and Adele, I warrant.'

'Why not them?'

'Because Theresa's always pregnant, and Adele's his wife.'

Samantha gazed at Mira. Mira felt superior, sophisticated. Her voice took on an 'older-woman-giving-advice' quality. 'Oh, he only does it to attractive women. I'm sure he meant part of what he said. But the rest . . . it's just his game, the way he gets along socially. It is a little shocking at first, I guess, but at least he tries to talk to women. And he's harmless.'

Samantha's face brighened. 'Oh, I like him! I mean, I thought he was fun even if he did . . . I don't know, Mira, these people seem awfully sophisticated to me. Maybe I've been too protected. I went to a junior college in the South and when I came back I lived at home and started dating Simp. Then we got married and lived with my folks. This is the first place of our own we've ever had. I feel like an awful baby.'

Samantha stood and washed her hands and combed

her hair, or rather, ran a comb along the top of it. Her hair was bleached light blond, almost white; it was piled in a high puff and sprayed hard, and there were little rigid curls around her face. She heightened the red on her cheeks. Mira watched her, thinking she looked like a mechanical doll.

'Why do you dye your hair? Surely you're not gray yet.'

'I don't know. I started because I thought it would make me look more sophisticated. And Simp likes it.'

'Do you?'

Samantha turned in surprise. 'Why? I mean, I guess so.' She was a little offended.

'Oh, it's just that it must be an awful lot of trouble.'

'Oh, it is! It takes me all day, on and off, to do it, and I have to touch it up every two weeks or the dark roots show.' She began to explain the process to Mira.

Paul had stopped dancing with Natalie and was now doing a slow fox-trot with Bliss, holding her very close. Hamp was sitting on the couch with Adele. He was telling her about a new book about the Cold War. He hadn't read it, but it had been reviewed well. Adele was bored, but sat there sympathetically, listening with apparent intentness. She was thinking that his eyes never met anyone else's, that he looked at people a little awry. He was a nice guy, though, everyone liked him. He never said an unkind thing. But his color was bad.

Natalie had been talking to Evelyn, but stopped abruptly. 'I need another drink!' she announced. Her face was splotchy. She staggered a little as she entered the kitchen, where a group of men were talking. She poured her glass almost full of straight rye, and stood there for a moment, but no one spoke to her. 'You men make me sick!' she burst out suddenly. 'All you know anything about is football! God, it's disgusting!' Carrying her drink, she stumbled out of the room.

The men glanced at her and went on talking.

She came into the living room, toward the couch where Hamp was sitting. 'God, you're as bad as they are. You sit on the couch all night like a lump of lard talking, talking, talking! About books, I suppose! As if you ever read! Why don't you talk about form letters, or TV? That's all you know anything about!'

The room hushed. Natalie looked around, embarrassed, and enraged with them for her discomfort. 'I'm going home! This party stinks!' And did: not even taking her coat, but still carrying her drink. She walked through the snow in her red satin high heels, slipping all the way down the street and falling twice.

No one said anything. Natalie was known to drink too much on occasion. They shrugged and resumed their conversations. Mira wondered how they were able to write it off that way, as though when people were drunk they were no longer persons, were not to be taken seriously. Of course, Nat would sleep it off; of course, she would probably even forget she'd done it. But meantime there was that anguish in her voice, despair underlying the anger. Where did those come from? Mira glanced at Hamp. He was still talking, unperturbed. He seemed to be a good sort, a bit lethargic, maybe even dull, but most husbands were rather dull, a woman had to find her own interest. And Natalie seemed happy enough during the days.

Paul was whispering in Bliss's ear; Norm came over and appropriated Mira and they danced awkwardly. He held her close, and her heart sank: she knew he would be feeling erotic later.

Then somebody she barely knew asked her to dance. Roger and Doris were comparative newcomers to the crowd; Roger was attractive, dark, intense looking. He put his arm around her with assurance, something none of the other men did. Paul's touch was sexual – he was tentative, delicate, questing. Roger touched her as if he had a right to her body, as if she were his to be handled. She felt this instantly, although she could not articulate it until later. But instantly, she resented him. He was a good dancer, though. She did not know what to say, so she held herself stiff and kept talking. She asked him where they lived, how many children they

147

had, how many bedrooms in their house.

'Don't you know how to be quiet?' he said, pulling her closer. He meant it to be romantic, she knew. And in a way, she felt it so. He had a good body, a good smell. But she could not let herself slide into that, accepting his scolding as a child would, accepting, somehow, his terms.

'I'm quiet when *I* want to be quiet,' she said fiercely, pulling away from him.

He looked at her with astonishment for a moment, then his face changed. 'You know what *you* need,' he said contemptuously, 'a good lay.'

'Yeah, I saw that game. They lost it on the last down.'

'The hell they did,' Simp said. 'It was that pass Smith threw.'

Hamp grinned. 'Well, one way or another, they lost it.'

'Sure, but they were playing better than they are. They should've lost that game by twenty points.'

'I don't know,' Roger argued. 'They always play better at home. All that ass in the stands, cheering for them.'

'Yes, she crawls now. Which is nice because I can let her out of the playpen. But of course, she's into everything.'

'Fleur won't stay in the playpen at all. She screams if I so much as put her in it.'

'She's your first. When you have five, they stay in the playpen.'

'Did I hear that you're pregnant again?'

'Oh, yes! The more the merrier.'

'You certainly don't look it.'

'Oh, it's only the third month. I blow up like a balloon.'

'You've really kept your figure for having had five kids.' Samantha eyes wandered toward Theresa, who was standing near the wall taking to Mira. She was tall, with a hunched-over back. Her belly literally hung, like

148

a stone-filled sack attached to her body. Her breasts sagged, and her hair was limp and full of gray.

Adele followed Samantha's glance. 'Poor Theresa. They're so poor. It makes everything so hard.'

Samantha leaned toward Adele with wide eyes and whispered. 'I heard the milkman feels so sorry for them he leaves them his left-over milk free.'

Adele nodded. 'Don's been out of work for a year now. He gets odd jobs, part-time or temporary things, but that's not enough with six kids. Most of the time he just sits around the house. She was trying to get a job as a substitute teacher – she has a college degree – but now she's pregnant again. I don't know what they'll do.'

Samantha looked at Theresa with loathing and fear. It was terrible that a woman could let herself get to look like that. It was terrible what had happened to her. What could you do if a man didn't work? It was awful. She would never let that happen to her, no way, never. You had to have some control over your life. She turned to Adele. 'Is she Catholic?'

'Yes,' Adele said firmly. 'And so am I.'

Samantha blushed.

'I haven't seen Paul in a while.'

'Oh, he left.'

Mira turned in surprise. 'He left? Adele's still here.'

Bliss laughed. 'He went after Natalie. Said he felt sorry for her, said he thought she was upset. Adele knows he's gone. He'll be back.'

Mira was surprised. She had not thought him that sensitive, that caring about other people. A suspicion curled around the edges of her mind, but she flattened it out. 'That was nice of him,' she said seriously. 'I was concerned about her.'

She wondered at the odd look that Bliss gave her.

Bill was in the kitchen with a small group of laughing people. He had just returned from a flight to California, and he always came back with a packet of obscene funny stories. 'So the stewardess says, "Is there anymore I can get you, Captain?" And he turns around and looks her up and down. And he says, "Yeah, you can get me a little pussy." And she just stands there and looks at him, cool as a cucumber, and she says, "I can't help you there, Captain, mine's as big as a bucket." And goes off.'

Laughter exploded in the room.

'I don't get it.' Mira looked around appealing for help. 'Why did he want a cat?'

14

'He didn't like women!' Val cried, and Kyla attacked: 'Oh, the sophisticate!' and Clarissa grinned and said, 'That's juicy!' and Isolde shook her head: 'I can hardly believe it.' All at once they burst out after Mira had finished telling us about this party.

'I mean, how could you all have been so . . . naive?'

'I'm telling you, Iso, that was the point. That's the way we were. That's why I say things are so different now. To Sam, we looked like sophisticates. That was the fifties.'

'And you, you woman of the world, you!' Kyla taunted lovingly.

'Isn't it awful? I remember feeling so superior and cool, and then I wondered how it had happened, how I had suddenly become this knowing woman of the world when only that morning I was still feeling like a child. And so serious, so earnest, so moral! God! It was all just fun, good for the spirit. I really believed that. It would never have occurred to *me* to have an affair, so I assumed it would never have occurred to them. They couldn't! They were – *good*. God, how I'd internalized sexual morality.'

'But that Roger fellow,' Clarissa put in. 'You had a raised consciousness even then.'

'I had a raised *un*conscious,' Mira corrected her. 'I couldn't have articulated it; I had no words to describe what I felt.'

They went over it all, seizing on one person or

another, asking about motivation, the feel of their relationships, about consequences. They milked it dry. But Val was unsatisfied.

'You say this guy – Paul? – liked women. I say he didn't. He used them. They were just sexual objects to him.'

Mira shook her head back and forth slowly, as if she were debating. 'I don't know, Val.'

'Was he really expecting something to come of all his lines?' Clarissa suggested. 'I mean, you said it was just his social posture.'

'Yeah,' Mira sighed. 'I don't know, you see. Maybe he just sent out lines and didn't care who caught them. But Samantha stayed friends with Adele and Paul for a long time. And once, when she was having terrible trouble, and they were very kind to her, especially Adele, Paul started pressuring her sexually. She told me about it and I was furious because I thought he was trying to break up her friendship with Adele by introducing jealousy, you know. But she said no. She said he acted sexual because that was the only way he knew how to treat a woman with kindness. He was trying to tell her he was her friend, but couldn't do it without offering to become her lover. It made sense to me.'

Valerie snorted.

'At least he tried to talk to women,' Mira finished sadly.

'And like a good woman, you were grateful for that,' Kyla said nastily.

'Listen,' Iso started up. 'Look who's talking! Whenever Harley puts down his book and looks at you, you practically jump up and down with joy!'

'I don't, I don't,' Kyla protested, but they were all on her then. 'Well,' she surrendered finally, 'at least I'm a good woman.'

15

Natalie was on the phone to Mira before nine on the Monday morning after the party, but Mira could not get away before the afternoon. Natalie was humming in the kitchen when Mira walked through her back door. She looked different: her eyes were bright and her whole face seemed firmer.

'How about a drink? No? I'll make you some instant, okay?' She fished a stained plastic cup out of the dishwasher that Mira envied every time she looked at it. 'Boy, I really laid a load on Saturday night. I ruined my dress, tore it all down the side when I fell, ruined the shoes I had dyed to match it, everything's shot! And I paid ninety dollars for that dress, and seventeen for the shoes.'

Mira gasped. She bought one or two dresses a year and paid ten or fifteen dollars for them. 'Oh, Natalie! Can't you salvage them?'

Nat shrugged. 'No. I threw them out.'

'Poor Nat,' Mira said with real feeling.

'Oh, it was worth it,' she answered jauntily.

'Why? I thought you weren't having a very good time.'

'I was having a lousy time at the party!' Natalie laughed and smirked at her suggestively.

Mira just looked at her. She had no idea what Nat was talking about.

Nat rubbed Mira's face affectionately. 'You are such an innocent. You're so cute.' She sat down across the table from Mira. 'You didn't notice that Paul left the party?'

'Yes. That was kind of him. I was a little concerned myself, and I was glad he'd done that. It surprised me, I never thought him that sensitive....'

'Oh, he's very sensitive!' Natalie was laughing.

Mira stopped. 'Are you saying . . . ?'

'Of course! What did you think?'

'I like to think men and women can be friends without it always being sexual,' Mira said disapprovingly. 'I thought he was being a friend.'

'Friend, schmend, screw that. I don't need a friend, I've got lots of those! Oh, God, it was so romantic! I was stark naked, my dress was on the floor and my

152

underwear on top of it. I'd left the front door open for him. And suddenly he was standing there, right in the doorway: I hadn't heard him come up. All I had was a sheet over me and I sat up and gasped. I really *was* surprised. To see him there so suddenly, you know. I hadn't been sure he'd come. And he just comes toward me, walking slowly with his eyes on me the whole time, like Marlon Brando or something, and he sits down on the bed beside me and pushes me hard back against the headboard and kisses me, oh, God! It was fantastic! Pressing his body against my breasts and then he slid his arm around my waist and held me so hard I could hardly breathe and kept on kissing me. Oh, it was great!' Her voice had risen and her face was ecstatic.

Mira sat stony.

Suddenly Natalie's face changed. Nasty lines came into it, her voice grew sharp and hard. 'And that son of a bitch Hamp can just go straight to hell, he can kiss my ass, he can go fuck himself. He doesn't want to fuck me, I'll find someone who does, and he can go fuck himself.'

'He doesn't sleep with you?' Mira inquired timidly, some life coming back into her face. If there was a reason, of course, that was different. She had read it often and often: spouses don't roam unless there is something wrong with the marriage. And if it was Hamp's fault, why then it was all explainable and with time and patience and discussion, solvable.

'The son of a bitch hasn't slept with me in two years. I've been going out of my mind. But he can go fuck himself.'

'Why doesn't he sleep with you?'

Natalie shrugged and looked away. 'How should I know? Maybe he can't. He can't do anything else, God knows. I asked him to help me paint Deena's room Sunday and all he did was manage to spill a whole can of paint on the rug. Not only that but he leaves me to clean it up: he retreats back to his chair and the TV set. He's a child!' she said scornfully.

Mira pondered.

Nat kept going. 'He doesn't even take the garbage out. Probably afraid he'll fall in the pail and the garbagemen won't be able to tell him from the rest of the swill. He sits in that chair every night, night after night. He doesn't talk to the kids, he doesn't even talk to me. He sits there, drinking himself into oblivion and watching TV. He falls asleep there. One night he almost burned the house down – his cigarette burned a big hole in the cushion, that's why I have it slip-covered, but I smelled something burning and came down. Look at the rug, look at it! There are cigarette burns all around his chair.'

She made Mira get up and look.

She was into it now, and she kept it up. She had all Hamp's sins written in blood on her memory. Mira was speechless. Not at Natalie's revelations: they were familiar enough complaints. Natalie had joked about such behavior before, and all of the women had similar complaints about their husbands. It was that Nat was serious. Mira felt that she was entering a new realm. The women always lamented or complained with humor and lightness. Their personal relations with their husbands had remained private. They were all simply parts of the ongoing American saga of uncontrollable children, inadequate husbands, and brave women wryly admitting failure even as they piled one more sandbag on the dike. But Natalie was making it real, she was moving it from the realm of myth (about which one can do nothing) to the realm of actuality (about which, if one were American, one must do something). The women could joke about marriage and children the way Italians joke about the Church, because it is there, solid, unmovable, unopposable, undefeatable.

'Maybe I will have a drink.'

As Natalie poured it, she said, 'Why don't you leave him? If you're that unhappy with him.'

'Goddamn bastard, I should leave him. That would really serve him right.'

'Why don't you then?'

Natalie gulped down her drink and rose to pour

another. Her voice was getting thick. 'Goddamn bastard, I should.'

'Your father would give you money. You don't have to stay with him for that.'

'Damn straight I don't! That stupid ass, all he does is dictate form letters all day. If I had to live on what he earned . . . We'd all starve. Bastard! That would really serve him right, because if I divorced him, my father would fire him on the spot. All he does is dictate form letters all day. My father told me. That's all he does. Stupid ass.'

Mira was inexorable now. 'From what you say, the kids aren't much attached to him.'

'Of course not! Damned brats. He has nothing to do with them. Once a month he yells "Shut up!" and that's it. They just walk around him, stepping over that fat slob slumped in that chair. That's all he is, a fat body. Fat lot of good that fat body does me.'

'So they probably wouldn't miss him. They don't need him, you don't need him. So why stay?'

Natalie suddenly burst into tears. 'You know I hate those kids? I hate them! I can't stand them!'

Mira stiffened with disapproval, not at Natalie's feelings but her words. She had long noticed Natalie's behavior with her children. It was not that she abused them physically, but she always disparaged them in speech: they were 'the brats.' And she was always trying to get rid of them, to send them outdoors or upstairs, away, away. Anything to be rid of them. Natalie took care of the children's physical needs: she cooked for them as well as she could, she cleaned their rooms and did their laundry and bought them new underwear when they needed it. She just never wanted to be with them. But to some degree all the women were like that. Still Mira felt it was one thing to feel that way and another to say it. Saying it somehow made it hard and fast. In some dim place in her mind, Mira really believed that if you didn't say you hated your kids, they would not know it.

'Why did you have them?' she asked tightly.

'Good Christ, the way everybody has them! Accidents, my three little accidents. Christ. What a life.' She stood up and poured another drink. 'Actually, I liked them when they were babies. I love babies. You can carry them around and coo at them and they're warm and helpless and they love you so much. But when they grow up! My mother is the same way. I can't stand it when they start to talk back, be fresh, all that shit. My mother is the same way.'

'I certainly don't feel that way. I like my children better as they get older. They're more interesting,' Mira said primly.

Natalie shrugged. 'Good. Good for you. I don't happen to feel that way.'

Mira's mouth began to purse nervously. 'Well, what do they have to do with not leaving Hamp?'

The tears spilled over onto Natalie's large cheeks. 'Oh, God, Mira, what would he do if I left him? He's helpless; do you know I have to tell him to change his underwear, I have to draw his bathwater? He's so smart, God, he's smart – you ought to know, Mira, you've talked to him a lot at the parties – he really has a good mind, and does he do anything with it? He sits in that damned chair and watches TV. If I left him, he wouldn't have a job, he wouldn't have anything.'

Mira was silent.

'He wouldn't know when to blow his nose!' Nat burst out again.

'You love him,' Mira said.

'Love, love,' Natalie mocked. 'What is it? Years ago, before the kids were born, we were happy.' Her voice changed: it went higher and thinner, it sounded like a child's voice. 'We used to play. He'd come home and find some dust on something, and he'd spank me. Not hard, you know. He'd pull down my pants and put me over his knee and spank me, real hard, it would hurt. And I'd yell and cry.' She was smiling. Mira's face was horrified. 'He was my daddy and I had to do what he wanted. I was so happy then, so excited all the time. I'd run around all day doing things to please him. I loved

156

doing them. I'd buy all the things he liked to eat and records he liked to hear and I'd buy these real sexy nightgowns, and I'd always have a pitcher of orange blossoms waiting – unless I wanted a spanking.' She giggled. Her voice and face were entirely given over to the child. She had the dreamy sweet look of a child telling you the story of a book she has just read. 'And, oh! would he spank me. I'd cry and cling to him.' She stopped and sipped her drink. 'I don't know when it changed. When Lena was born, I guess. I had to grow up then,' she said bitterly. 'I had the shitty diapers to clean up. I couldn't run around buying things, I couldn't plays games so much. And now look. For God's sake I'm not just the mommy but the daddy too around here. He does nothing.'

'You grew up.'

Her voice rose. 'I had to grow up! I had no choice!'

'He either had to be a tin god or nothing. Sometimes,' and Mira heard bitterness in her own voice now, and wondered where it came from, 'sometimes I think that's all men are. Tin gods. They have to be all or they are nothing.'

'Nothing, nothing! Right. That's what that bastard is!' Natalie had recovered. She wiped her face and stood up and poured herself another drink.

16

Late that night, Mira told Norm the whole story. She was very upset; many things were working in her, but she was unaware of most of them. What dominated her account was shock at Natalie's adultery. Norm listened impatiently, with a look of disgust on his face. He said Natalie was stupid and a drunken slut. She didn't matter; she was not to be taken into consideration. Mira should just forget the whole thing; it was unimportant. Natalie was a whore and Paul was a bastard: that was that.

He went to bed. Mira said she would be up soon, but she felt restless; she paced around the downstairs rooms, gazing out at the night, at the moon over the rooftops, at the ominously rustling shrubs. She saw motion, furtive and frightening, everyhere. To calm herself, she poured a little of Norm's brandy in a juice glass, and took it into the living room. She sat there sipping, smoking, meditating. It was the first time she ever did that, and the beginning of a new pattern.

She wanted very much to talk to someone about the whole thing, especially to discover why it was bothering her so much. She considered: Was she jealous? Did she wish it had been she Paul came charging in on? But if Paul had come to her like Marlon Brando, she would have laughed. Was the resentment she had heard in her own voice reflective of her feelings about her own marriage? Was she urging Nat to leave Hamp because she wanted to leave Norm? She didn't know and couldn't seem to work it through.

She decided, however, not to tell anyone what Nat had told her. Nat had not enjoined her to silence, but it seemed a point of honor not to talk about it. That meant, though, that she could not discuss with anyone the things about the situation that bothered her. She decided to do some reading in psychology.

Time passed, winter melted into a rainy spring. Theresa bent over her swollen belly to plant a vegetable garden; Don got a job mending roofs. The Foxes finished the extension on their house and threw a party. Adele's pregnancy was beginning to show. Nat finished redecorating her bathroom and was thinking of finishing the attic. Mira had finished the Jones biography of Freud, and several Freud monographs and was reading various other psychologists. She wanted to read Wilhelm Reich, but the library did not have his books, and when she asked Norm to get one for her at the medical library of the university, he sternly forbade her to read Reich.

It was a slow drippy spring, and everyone was restless. The outside world, with Berlin and Cuba and a faded Joseph McCarthy, seemed far away. Bill got a raise and Bliss was elated: it meant she could hire a

158

baby-sitter once in a while, so she could go out at night when he was out of town. She enrolled in a bridge course.

Late in May, the sun came out. Nat came down one afternoon for coffee. In the months that had passed, Mira had never referred again to the business with Paul, and neither had Nat. But their relationship had changed: Natalie now told Mira in detail about her daily irritations with Hamp. She would rave against him for three-quarters of an hour, and then go cheerfully on to something else. Mira was bored and irritated; she began to avoid Natalie. And Natalie felt that and was hurt and angry. She stopped just dropping in, but would call once in a while. Mira was usually busy. Natalie failed to understand how reading some books when you weren't even in school could take precedence over her company. So she stopped calling. But one afternoon in late May, she strolled into Mira's back door.

'Hi! Guess what! I bought a house!'

'Nat! Great! Where?'

'West End.'

'West End! Wow! Really moving up!'

Mira poured wine and soda for them. The house, Nat told her, had ten rooms, two and a half baths, two fireplaces, dishwasher, and wall-to-wall carpeting. It backed on the country club golf course, had an acre plot, and they would become automatic members of the club, which Nat was already referring to as simply 'the club,' as if she'd been a member all her life.

The thing was beyond even Mira's envy. 'When did you decide to do this? Why?'

The Meyersville house was too small, they needed more room, and that meant finishing the attic or putting on an extension and that was expensive and you might not get a return on it when you went to sell. The girls were getting older and they argued all the time and should have their own rooms. 'Besides, I'm sick of this place. What is there to keep me here?'

159

Mira felt reproached. Without thinking, she asked. 'Do you ever see Paul?'

'Paul? No. Why? Oh! That bastard! No.' Then she smiled. 'But I am interested in someone else.'

'Who?'

'Lou Mikelson. I've known him for years, of course, and I always loved him, but . . .' She gave a childlike delighted smile.

'I thought Evelyn was your best friend.'

'She is! I love Evvy! Adore her! But she has those two creepy kids, she has no time for Lou.'

'The oldest one is in an institution, isn't she?'

'Yes, but Nancy's still home. And you know, she's big, she's eleven and an awful handful. Still has to have diapers changed, and although she's been walking for a couple of years now, she's always bumping into things – she doesn't see very well. She still has to be fed.'

'Nightmare. Babyhood protracted into forever.'

'And Tommy's no angel either. I mean, at least he's normal, but he's always in some kind of trouble. I don't think Evelyn would mind. She'd probably give me her blessing.'

'Well, are you actually involved?'

'No.' Natalie's voice lingered over the syllable. 'It's in the early stages,' she smiled. She was very nervous. She kept picking at her hands, which were covered with a rash and peeling skin.

'Well, that's great about the house, Nat. I'm glad for you.'

'Yeah. Of course it needs redecoration. I want to take you over there someday – as soon as the people move out. It has this really nice family room, you know, that I think would look gorgeous if I put in all sliding glass windows. . . .'

She was off. Mira listened to the thousand plans she had for the house, thinking that it was nice, that it was enough to keep her occupied for several years, enough to keep her mind from dwelling too much on the other. Mira did not take seriously the business about Lou. She'd seen Lou and Natalie at parties too often: they always flirted in a friendly, almost familial way. She mentioned Lou to save her pride, which seemed to require that a man find her attractive. But we are all like that, she thought. We all want it, anyway. It doesn't seem so important to men. Women, victims again. Why should men be so important to us and we not to them? Is that nature too? She sighed and went on reading her male psychologists.

<h1 style="text-align:center">17</h1>

Bliss searched the room. Hugh Simpson – 'Simp' – came sidling over to her with his glass in his hand.

'Looking pretty snazzy tonight, eh, Bliss?' He never made a statement without sounding as if he were intimate with one, and as if the grounds of the intimacy were some shared dirty secret.

'The old hair going pretty fast there, eh, Bill?' He had said the same thing at the three preceding parties, and Bliss was annoyed, but she smiled gracefully and said, 'I'm hoping he gets to look like Yul Brynner.' She looked at Bill with a loving smile as she said it, and he giggled and patted his bald spot. Bill was regaling Simp with his latest dirty story, which Bliss had heard four times in the past week. She made a face at him, an angry-Momma-scolding-little-boy face and said, 'Not again, Billy.' Then she smiled and he grinned a little-boy-is-being-naughty-but-he-knows-Momma-will-forgive grin back at her and said, 'Just one more time, Blissy.' She laughed and bent her body lightly, excusing herself and went into the kitchen.

Paul was standing with Sean near the sink; they were speaking in soft voices and laughing. Bliss approached them with her head cocked to one side, a knowing smile on her face.

'I can just guess what you two are talking about,' she said. Paul put his arm out and she walked into it, and he closed it around her gently.

'We were discussing the ups and downs of the market,' Sean smiled.

'It's unpredictable, you know. You throw a little into many investments, and suddenly one of them pays off.'

'I see,' Bliss smiled at Paul. Their faces were close together. 'You don't, I take it, have any favorite stock.'

'Of course.' Paul nibbled at her ear. 'But you can never be sure that one will bring a return.'

'And you'll accept any return that occurs.'

'I just love speculating.'

'Why don't you speculate me up a drink?'

'I'd have to take my arm away.'

'That isn't irreparable.'

Sean drifted off. Paul moved and poured two drinks.

'I remember one night you took your whole self away from me,' Bliss taunted. 'At least tonight you won't have to go anywhere.' The party was at Natalie's house.

Paul made a face at her. 'It wasn't you I left, it was Adele.'

'I was there.'

'And offering nothing. A man has to do something with it. If the woman who arouses him won't come through, he's got to find someone else.'

She grimaced. 'That's the poorest excuse I've ever heard for just not having any standards.' She took the drink from his hand. 'Of course,' she added airily, 'there's no accounting for tastes.'

'Some women are sexy and some only act sexy.'

'Oh? How can you tell?'

'I can tell.'

'It's possible to put it another way : some women have standards.'

He looked at her intensely. During their interchange, smiles had never left their faces. 'And do I meet yours?'

'Do you care?' She arched her body and let it ripple, and walked away.

Norm was in the study alone. He switched the television set off guiltily when Bliss entered. He gave her a naughty-boy look.

'Just checking the late scores. Mira has a fit if I turn on TV at a party.'

162

She gave him her mock-scolding look. 'And I'll bet you're afraid to take a walk unless Mira says you can. Aren't you?' She touched his nose lightly with her finger. 'And I'm going to tell on you.'

He cringed comically. 'Oh, please don't tell. I'll do anything!'

'Okay. I won't tell if you dance with me.'

He put his hands to the sides of his head. 'Oh, not that! Not that! Anything but that!'

She kicked him lightly with her instep, and he crumpled, bent, held his leg. 'Ooh! Ow! She's lamed me for life. Okay, okay, I give in!' And followed her, limping, into the big living room.

Natalie had rolled up the carpet in this room so people could dance. This was her farewell to Meyersville, and she had invited sixty people. Her house had more rooms than the others, and could hold such a crowd.

Mira was sitting with Hamp when Norm and Bliss came into the room. She watched them dance; it was a clowning dance, as it was whenever Norm danced with anyone but her.

'I think Norm would like to have an affair with Bliss,' she said.

'Do you care?' Hamp and Mira had become friends at these parties. If Hamp didn't read, at least he knew about books, and he provided her with what felt like a safe island. But they had not talked much personally.

'No,' she said, shrugging. 'It might do him some good.'

Hamp looked at her glitteringly. She was not looking at him. She was watching Roger put his possessive arm around Samantha and lead her to the dance floor. She wanted to leap up and protect Samantha, to push him away from her. But Samantha was walking with her little mechanical doll wiggle, and her doll's face held a wide smile.

'I feel so out of things,' she said to Hamp. 'So out of all the people I know. I guess I've always felt out.'

'You're too good for them,' Hamp said, and she turned to him with surprise.

'What does that mean?'

163

'Just what I said.'

'I don't see how one person can be better than another. I don't know what that means.'

Hamp smiled and shrugged. 'They're all bums.'

'Oh, Hamp!' She felt uncomfortable and tried to think of a way to get away from him politely. 'I think I'll get another drink,' she came up with finally.

She passed Nat in the kitchen talking loudly about the beauties of her new house. She had spoken of nothing else for the past months. Bliss was near the wall with Sean, talking in low voices, smiles on their faces. Bliss was taunting, teasing; Sean, superior, enjoying it, deciding whether or not to pounce. Roger was standing at the sink talking to Simp. He had his back to her, and she heard him say, 'Cunt is cunt. The only difference in it is some is wet and some is dry.' She walked to the sink and stood beside him to pour her drink. She did not look at him or greet him. She walked into the small living room. Oriane was sitting with Adele, talking about children. Oriane was looking almost as harassed as Adele: she had just had a long ordeal in which her two younger children came down in alternate weeks with measles, mumps, and chicken pox and her oldest child, a boy, had nearly ripped his hand off in a bicycling accident. Adele looked purely terrible. Mira sat down with them.

'You've had quite an ordeal,' she began.

Oriane laughed and rolled her eyes. 'Oh, it was charming!' The banter began again: whatever she had been discussing with Adele had been serious, and was now put away in favor of the public mode. Mira remained, restlessly, and got up as soon as she could. She wandered.

'No, Theresa and Don don't come to parties anymore. I don't even know if Nat invited them. Terry says she can't afford to give one, so she doesn't want to come. But I think it's silly to isolate yourself like that, don't you?' Paula said.

'Pride. You have it where you can have it,' said a firm voice.

Mira turned. She liked the person who said that. It was Martha, a newcomer to the group. Mira walked toward them. 'Theresa reads a lot,' Mira said.

18

Bliss flirted mildly with the bridge teacher. He would take her to a bar on nights when Bill was out on a flight, and talk to her about himself, his loneliness, and his marriage. Bliss smiled a lot and teased him. He would drive her back to the shopping center where she parked her car, and they would sit for a few minutes kissing. Finally he asked her to go to a motel with him. She said she had to think it over.

Bliss did not delude herself that her problem was moral. She had been brought up in a hard country, where people acted wild and even savage. Cars full of drunk teenaged boys had contained more than one of her high-school girlfriends. Her aunt, deserted by her husband early in her marriage, had had an unending series of lovers; some even said she made her living that way. Bliss had been too poor to afford the luxury of middle-class morality. She figured that if her aunt had gotten something out of those men, good for her. She had a deep snarling contempt for people who confused an essentially economic situation with a moral one. And the relation between men and women was economic.

Economic and political. Bliss had no fancy words for any of this: she would have had difficulty in expressing it abstractly. What she said to herself was, you have to play it, and you have to play it their way. She recognized the master class, she recognized its expectations from a woman. She played the game by the rules that had been laid down long before she was born, laid down, as far as she could tell, in ancient times. There was only one thing Bliss wanted: to win. Nothing mattered more, except in some fierce inner place with few occupants – her mother and her children, and her mother was dead now. But she would have fought for her children's survival just as her mother had fought for

165

hers. Somehow, her children knew that. Although it was their father who teased and joked with them, and their mother who usually was the one to scold, they sensed her fierceness and her love, and returned it. Their gay independence was settled on a foundation they knew to be unshakable.

Bliss had never been one of the girls in the cars. Sex and romance had been part of the great market basket of niceties she could not afford. But she had been eating a bit better of late, and her body was reaching out. She had sold herself to Bill knowing perfectly well what she was doing, and with honorable intentions. She would uphold her part of the bargain. She would be consort, maid, and brood mare, and he would pay for her services. She would be faithful, since that was one of the conditions. And Bill had upheld his part. They were not what is called 'comfortable,' but they ate. And he was faithful to her, of that she was sure, regardless – or perhaps because of – all his tales of stratospheric shacking up. He would, in time, earn decent money. He was Security.

To risk that was terrifying. She sat and pondered this deeply. She went over and over in her mind the possibilities. At the worst, he would divorce her: he was not a killer. If he divorced her, she might be able to get a job in New Jersey, but with her Texas diploma, so looked down on in the North, she might not be able to teach. Even if she could teach, all she could earn was six or seven thousand a year, a salary Bill had passed years ago. It would be hard for her and the children to live on that without someone to do what she did – the unpaid labor: she would have to pay after-school baby-sitters, pay for laundry done, pay someone to stay with the kids if they were sick. And if she could not get a teaching job, she would earn even less. Sometimes when Bill was away, she read all the Help Wanted Ads for women. Only crack secretaries earned more, and she could not even take dictation. She could be a clerk in an office, in a department store, or in a dry cleaning shop. She could work in a factory. She could go to New York with her diploma and be a fancier clerk, earning more but having to spend more on clothes and commutation.

There was no way out. A woman had to be married. But who would have her with two young children? As a mistress, yes, but Bliss did not delude herself that anyone was going to fall wildly in love with her and want to take her on with two kids. Of course, Bill might not divorce her. She might be able to play penitent, and he needed her so much that he might be willing to take her back, granting her forgiveness from his magnanimous male soul. But then he would become watchful, prying. That would be intolerable. The rest of her life she would be a virtual prisoner.

Of course, he might not find out. If she were careful and clever enough, there was no reason for him to find out. But even the best laid plans . . . an accidental encounter, a chance word dropped. No matter how careful she was, there was always that chance. It came down to that: she would have to be clever and careful, and even then he might find out. Then she would have to use all her skills to play it so that he would not believe it, and at the same time play it so that if he came to believe it, he would forgive her. It was overwhelming, and too costly for a bridge teacher.

She told her bridge teacher that she felt him to be terribly attractive, that she had, all this while, been lonely too, lonely for a kindred soul to talk to. But she loved her husband and felt she could not do this to him. She was sorry, but she thought they should not meet anymore.

He did not understand. The problem with games is that all players do not have an equal insight into the rules. He did not understand that she was salving his male pride, playing up to his male ego: he believed her words. He began to call her up at home. She was terrified. Luckily, he called at moments when Bill was not there. But the third time, she told him that if he called again, she would call his wife and tell her everything. That worked. Bliss never got beyond Blackwood in bridge.

167

But her body did not go away, and without the bridge teacher's pressure, she felt its pressure more and more. She played seductress at parties, knowing what she was doing, knowing the men knew too, unable to help herself. She played seductress, telling herself she was in control. Bliss the snake.

Bliss the ache. For when the parties were over, she went home with Bill and undressed in the bathroom while he, already in bed, was calling to her.

'Hey, come here, Mommy, Baby wanna suck your boobs. Little Billy cold, Mommy, need little Blissy come play with him.'

She would shower, remove her makeup carefully, brush her long hair a hundred strokes. But he would not stop. 'Mooooooommmy! Biwwy wonwy!'

She would stand there silent, or call out, 'Coming!' and gaze at herself. And slide her hands down her sides and wonder what it would be like to be held hard and firm and passionately by someone who wanted to *own* her, to take possession of her, to control her, someone who would embrace and encompass and hold her against him hard no matter what she did, and make her know that she was his.

19

Mira was washing windows when she heard the slam. It was hot, and sweat was running down her face and arms. She heard Natalie's voice call out, and silently said, 'Darn!' Natalie would want to talk and she wanted to get these windows done before midday, before the heat became intolerable. She got down from the stepladder. Natalie was standing in the bedroom doorway.

'I have to talk to you!' she said, sounding almost angry. She had something in her hand that she was waving around.

'Nat, can I come over later? I wanted to finish these windows.'

'No! I'm going out of my mind. I have to talk to you.' Mira looked at her and Natalie burst out, 'I'm afraid for my life!'

168

They went downstairs. 'Got any booze?' Nat asked, and Mira fished around in a cabinet and found some bourbon. She poured a drink for Nat, and made iced coffee for herself.

Natalie's face looked strange. She was holding a thick packet of papers in her hand, held together with a rubber band. It looked as if the packet contained some small memo books as well. Her manner was ominous.

'I was packing the stuff from the bedroom. I'd reached Hamp's chest. I never look at his things,' she said stiffly and then puffed nervously on her cigarette. 'I mean, I fold his underwear and socks and iron his handkerchiefs and put them all in his drawers, but I never look in his drawers. I never look at his papers,' she kept insisting.

'I believe you,' Mira said, realizing she never looked at Norm's papers either.

'But I had to pack them. The movers are coming tomorrow. So I emptied out his drawers. And there, in the back of his sock drawer, way in back, behind the ski socks he's had for years and never worn, were these!' She held the papers almost under Mira's nose.

'Of course, I wouldn't have looked at them, but I dropped them and they fell open to a page. And after one page, I had to read the rest.'

Mira stared at her. Natalie began to fan herself with papers.

'Mira, you wouldn't believe! I can't believe! Mild Hamp, sitting in his chair! When did he write them? They're in his handwriting. That I know. He must've done it on the train, or in the office, then come home and buried them back there. Why did he keep them? Mira, I think he's going to kill me!'

Mira said, 'Why? What's in them?' and held out her hand, but Natalie clutched the papers.

'Terrible! Terrible! Stories. They're all stories. None of them are finished, they're just beginnings, and they are all about him. He uses his own name. "Hamp did this. Hamp did that." And terrible!'

Mira bent toward her perplexed.

Natalie tried to describe them. After a while, she opened one of the little memo books and began to read, holding it close to her so that Mira could not see. But there was no doubt she was reading from the book. She opened another, then another, choosing at random. They were all the same.

In each of the beginnings, for that is what they were, a man named Hamp was involved with a woman. Sometimes the woman was named too: Natalie, Penelope ('his *mother*, Mira!'), Iris ('his sister!'), but there were other names too, Ruby and Elisia and Lee ('He loves Lee Remick, I'll bet that's who that's supposed to be') and Irene. The involvement was less sexual than violent. In each of the pieces, the man had the woman in a condition of submission: tied up, chained to a bed, chained to a hook in the wall. And each one contained a torture. In the one dealing with Penelope, he pushed a hot poker up her vagina. He singed Iris's breasts with curling irons, whipped Ruby with a cat-o'-nine-tails, racked Lee and screwed her at the same time. They were all variations on the same theme. They were not developed: no background scene had been sketched in, little description was offered. There was a man and a woman and the act: only the act was described lovingly, with detail. The number of strokes, the number of turns of the screw, the woman's cries, screams, beggings: all were recounted carefully. The man's emotions were not described. Whether he felt hate or love, whether he derived pleasure from his acts, or how the scenes ended, was not included. Only the act mattered. Mira was aghast. Mild, nice, pleasant Hamp! And all the time, underneath, such hatred of women.

'Do you think it was because of the war, Mira?' Natalie pleaded. 'You know, when he was captured and put in that prison camp? Heaven knows what they did to him there.'

Mira pondered. 'I don't think so. It seems to go back to his childhood.'

'God, Mira, do you think he'll kill me?'

'Not as long as he keeps writing.' Mira laughed

170

shakily. She got up and poured a drink for herself, and a refill for Nat. 'He probably thought he was writing pornographic stories. Probably had an idea he could make money selling them, money that had nothing to do with your father. Except all he was really doing was writing out his fantasies. And he hates. God, he hates. All of us. All women.'

'Not quite all,' an acid voice behind her put in.

She turned. Natalie was glaring at her, slowly waving the rest of the packet. 'There's one woman he likes. Just one.'

Mira frowned. She didn't understand Nat's tone. 'What do you mean?'

'Don't tell me you don't know!' Natalie accused. At Mira's look of incomprehension, she burst out. 'They're to you! Are you going to say you didn't know?'

Mira sank into a chair. 'What?'

'Love letters. Oodles of them. "My darling Mira," "My sweet baby," "My adorable child Mira." Oh, yes! But I don't need to show them to you, I guess.'

'Natalie, I never got a letter from Hamp.'

'Really?' she asked sweetly. She opened one folded paper. ' "My darling little Gigi, once you were a child but now you're a woman. You have grown up right under my eyes. To me you will always be Gigi." I could go on,' she ended, folding the paper back up.

'Natalie,' Mira said reasonably, 'if you found the letters, obviously they were never sent.'

'These could be copies.'

'They could be. But they're not. Natalie, someplace inside of you, you know Hamp never sent those letters to me.'

'All these years I thought you were my friend.'

'I was.'

'Sure. At every party you and Hamp would sit talking....'

'Just because both of us felt out of it most of the time.'

But Natalie would not be convinced. She had another drink. She went deeper and deeper into the affair as she imagined it, accusing Mira of treacheries and betrayals

171

at every step. 'I'll bet you told him about Paul too! That's why he overturned the paint can on the rug! And I thought you were my friend, I thought I could trust you!'

Mira stopped arguing. It was obviously useless. Natalie raved on and on; Mira sat drinking, smoking, waiting. Natalie poured herself another drink. Mira poured herself another drink. Finally, Natalie cried, and Mira knew it was ending. Nat put her hands up to her face and sobbed about how much she loved Hamp, and how she could not bear it that he cared about someone else. She sobbed for minutes, then slowly calmed.

'But he doesn't love me,' Mira said coldly.

'What do you mean!' Natalie was indignant. 'You heard those letters.'

Mira shrugged. 'They're the same as the notebooks. Why do you suppose he keeps them in the same packet? In the letters, I'm an adorable child he's going to master; in the notebooks he masters women who aren't adorable children. One step out of the role of adorable child and you get tortured.'

Natalie didn't understand. 'He loves you.'

'Oh, come on, Nat, you've loved other people.'

'I haven't! Never! I've screwed other people, but I never loved them.'

Mira sat back in the chair. It was hopeless.

'I believe you never got the letters,' Natalie said finally.

Mira smiled. 'Good.'

'I have to get back to packing. We'll have to get together sometime.'

'Yes.'

Natalie went off like a chastened child. But Mira knew. She knew that no matter what had actually occurred, the facts stood as facts. Hamp had thought of her that way, and that was what was hurting Natalie. It didn't matter that Mira hadn't known, or that, had she known, she would not have become involved with Hamp. In fact, that even made it worse: that she would dare to refuse Hamp, the man Nat loved, the man who rejected Nat. But instead of dealing with Hamp, Nat had attacked Mira, who had been, if not a faithful friend, an honorable one. Natalie would never forgive her.

'What do you care?' Norm said when she told him about it.

20

Natalie moved in July; in August, Adele's baby was born. Otherwise, it was an uneventful summer. The children were around all the time. The women had long ago learned to sit through the humid days with iced tea, listening to child noises. Mira had grown closer to Bliss; she even told her about the business with Natalie. It upset her, not because she was hurt — she wasn't — but because of what she saw. She tried to explain to Bliss: 'It's that they go round and round. They never get anyplace. Everybody, all the unhappy marriages. They go on and on doing and saying the same things, miserable and wretched, but they never try to understand what they're doing or why, they never try to do things differently so they can be a bit happier. I see it everywhere. It feels like hell to me. It may only be Dante's first circle, but that's hell enough. To go round and round like that forever.'

Bliss shrugged. 'Natalie *was* a bit of a bitch.'

'I know,' Mira said reluctantly, 'but she was more than a bit unhappy.'

'If she hadn't been so bitchy, Hamp might have been better.'

'Oh, Bliss! He was sick! We always blame the woman. That wasn't Nat's fault, it was his mother's.' Then she shook her head as she realized what she had said. But all the wisdom culled from all the books she had been reading sent her to no other source: it was Mother's fault. And it was easier to blame Penelope than her husband: she was large and domineering and able and he was a shriveled little man, kind and ineffectual.

Bliss did not want to talk about Natalie. These days,

she was acting oddly. She was always humming or singing, and would stop abruptly when you spoke to her, answer, then start humming again. It was as if she had closed herself away in a private place she hated to come out of: the singing was the wall she had erected around it.

'I wish somebody would give a party,' Bliss said suddenly.

'Yeah, I can't. The measly two days Norm and I had at Lake George broke us for two months,' Mira laughed.

Bliss smiled and began to sing 'Sand in My Shoes' under her breath.

In September, Samantha decided nervously to try her hand. She was very excited and frightened – she'd never given a party before. But it went well. Part of what made the parties so good was that at their center was a nucleus of people who knew each other well and felt secure, so that they did not simply cling together but were open to those who were less familiar. Mira thought about the arrangement of these parties as a kind of model for a community. They seemed to her to hold the secret of togetherness and separateness, closeness and strangeness. The problem with most communities is they are xenophobic; the problem in most modern places is too much separateness. She pondered that, having by now read the *Republic*.

Mira bought a new dress for this party, a white taffeta with a bouffant skirt and large purple flowers printed on it. It had cost $35 and was the most expensive dress she'd ever owned. She wore it as if she had borrowed it from her mother-in-law, and walked around as if she was afraid to brush against a wall.

'So I got out the ice,' Samantha said. 'I put the trays on top of the refrigerator, and I went to get the lemons. And all of a sudden, bam!' She put her hand on her head. 'The lump's as big as a marble!'

Mira thought about her increasing habit of going off into private thoughts when she was with people. She felt cut off from the events around her these days, even

174

from her friends and the parties. Things that happened no longer made her feel: they made her think. And she missed feeling, missed being nervous and excited. Things had changed. Natalie was gone, Bliss was in a private world, Adele was not as friendly as she had been – well, of course she was horrendously busy with the new baby – and, even more, Mira had grown tired of the game they had played. She did not think the things that happened to the women were funny, she was tired of making them out that way. She was tired of joking about the ineffectuality or absence of the men, who were absent even when they were physically present. That was not funny either. She was sick to death of Bill's obscene jokes, of Roger's behavior, Norm's naughty-child act. She liked Samantha, but her mechanical doll behavior jarred Mira, and Samantha seemed determined to remain a wide-eyed child. Also Samantha was still playing the old game, the aren't-we-funny-but-brave line. Mira had met two new women she liked, but they weren't part of the party crowd. In fact, the old group seemed not to like Lily and Martha. Mira moved from group to group at the party, feeling sullen and unsocial.

Then Bill asked her to dance. This was an occasion, for he rarely danced, and when he did it was awful. But one could not say no to such a rare request; one could not wound a male's vanity. So she smiled gratefully and let him put her through the one dance he did, a manic lindy. He jumped around on the floor like a monkey and tossed his partner with abandon. It was graceless, exhausting, and chaotic: there was no sense of the formed movement that was so satisfying in dancing. Bill had short hair and a cowlick, a freckled, open face: he looked like the all-American boy, and, she imagined, probably looked just as he had at twelve. He had no conversation except for a running stream of dirty jokes, each followed by a hoop of shrill laughter, almost a whinny. One of the grounds of Mira's respect for Bliss was that, intelligent as she clearly was, she always looked at Bill with respect and affection. She never showed in the slightest glance that she found him ridiculous, although it seemed to Mira that she could not do otherwise.

Bill was tossing Mira in circles and jumping from one foot to another, telling her a joke at the same time.

'So the captain says he's just gonna run back and get some sack time, and everybody laughs, you know.' He bent and gave his hysterical giggle as he approached the punch line. As he gave it, he stomped, and flung out his arms and hit a glass that was standing on the TV set and it flew off and straight at Mira and hit her in the breast and spilled its contents down the front of her dress. Bill bent double laughing, pointing at her. She must have looked funny, stuff dripping all down her front and that look on her face. Her new dress! She couldn't believe it, she couldn't accept it. After all these years she had finally gotten a good dress and the first night she wears it, that clown, that jerk, that stupid, giggling fool . . .!

She went to the bathroom to wash it off and saw that the liquid was Coke. It would never come off the taffeta. She washed it down as well as she could, but she was nearly in tears. Someone knocked on the bathroom door, so she vacated it, but she could not go back downstairs. If anyone spoke to her she was sure she would burst out crying. She did not want to act like such a fool, crybaby, caring so much about a trifling thing. She decided to sit for a while in Samantha's bedroom, and she swung open the door to go in. And stopped.

Bliss and Paul were standing there talking. Had they been kissing, she would have been less surprised: people did get sexy at parties. But they were standing talking, standing so close together and talking so seriously that it was clear that theirs was an intimacy of some length and some seriousness. Had they been kissing, they would have stopped and turned and made a joke and she could have laughed too. As it was, they just turned and looked at her and she had to find some excuse.

'Bill got too enthusiastic doing the lindy,' she said

176

pointing to the stain on her dress. 'I thought I'd see if Sam had anything that would fit me.'

It passed; they picked it up, they gave some explanation for their being there – something about plans for Adele's birthday – and they left. She sank down on the bed, her tearfulness forgotten.

She thought about it. She didn't blame Bliss. Being married to Bill must be constant torment for a woman of Bliss's mind and manner. And everyone knew what a horror divorce was for a woman: it meant poverty, stigma, and loneliness. So what else could Bliss do? She was awed by Bliss's courage: Mira would have been terrified to do what Bliss was doing. She didn't think much about Paul: the rumors were he was always having affairs. She had put the rumors down as untrue. She thought they arose out of his behavior at parties, the way he acted with women. She had assumed it was all innocent flirtation.

And that was what pained her. She felt as if she had been shot, as if there were a hole right through her forehead, and moreover, that she deserved it. She had believed they were all happy children playing ring-around-the-rosy. All except Natalie, and Natalie was different, she'd always been rich, she had her own rules because she could afford them. But now here was Bliss. All the flirting she'd seen Bliss do, all the going round and round that sometimes bothered her, had had real consequences. She sat there feeling stupid. For all her reputed intelligence, she was the stupidest person she knew, so stupid she could not function in the world. That was the reason she had retreated into marriage. She was too stupid to survive in the real world. Living in dreams, illusions about the way things were, she was so egotistical that she insisted they were as she wanted them to be. All her intellect and pride had ever done was to blind her. A category she never thought in, a word she never used, came flaming up at her : she felt like a sinner.

21

Bliss had none of Mira's stupidity. She had known the instant she saw Mira's face in the doorway that Mira had recognized the truth. She was terrified. It was not that, after all these years of friendship, she thought Mira would try to hurt her. She knew Mira was honorable. But she mistrusted her for that very reason. Mira had too many principles; she might decide that it would be in the best interests of all involved that the thing be made public, open. She might come up with some crazy idea about putting marriage on a new basis in which all concerned parties agreed to mutual infidelities. She might do anything. Unquestionably, she would tell Norm. She might even tell Samantha: they were pretty thick these days. And they would tell others. Of course, there was no evidence, but Bliss knew things like this did not require evidence. Even if she and Paul were not having an affair and the story got started that they were, she would end up paying.

But she did not know what to do. Luckily, Bill was going out on a flight on Monday, and she would be alone for five days and could do some real thinking. The first thing she had to do was sound out Mira's attitude toward the thing. If she were judgmental and reproving, strong action would be necessary. If not, they could be more subtle.

She did not have to wait long. She went to Mira's for coffee on Monday, and as soon as they were seated, Mira looked her in the eye and said, 'So.'

Bliss laughed and waved her hand in air. 'Yes, so.'

'How do you manage it?' Mira asked, really curious.

'Well, Bill's away.'

'I know, but the kids!'

'I give them tranquilizers when he's coming.'

Mira looked shocked.

'Oh, Bliss!'

'It doesn't hurt them. I just give them a little, so they sleep more soundly.'

'Don't you feel funny talking to Adele?'

'Not at all.'

As they talked further, Bliss saw that Mira on the whole approved, but she also saw the grounds of Mira's reservations: the children and Adele. Bliss did not exhort Mira to silence: she was too proud, and it would not have done any good anyway. Mira would talk or not as she judged right. And Bliss sensed she would not. But if Mira saw Adele upset, or saw the children's eyes looking glazed – there was no telling then. Action had to be taken.

Paul was supposed to be with her on Tuesday night. By then she had formulated a plan. He arrived a little early: 'I couldn't wait,' he said. Her heart leaped almost out of her chest when she saw him. As they embraced, she thought it would quite literally be death to be torn away from him. They could not let go of each other. Every time they tried, one or the other pulled them together again. Bliss had put some music on the record player, and their embraces and kisses felt like a dance. They floated in each other. For a moment as she lay against his chest, Bliss wondered what it would be like to be married to him, to have him all the time. But she brushed the thought away: it was impossible, and feeling brave and dry-eyed, she looked up at him.

'Come sit down. We have to talk.'

She feltched a pitcher of the martinis he had taught her to make and poured them into the two iced glasses. She was wearing a floaty new robe, emerald green, and had her hair down. He gazed at her as if she were some incredible treasure he had stumbled on and could not yet believe was his. He kept reaching out to touch her, gently, touch a strand of her hair, her cheek, run his hand lightly over her lips. Sometimes she would grab his hand and kiss it, and then they would be in each other's arms again. But she pulled away at last and moved to the couch beside him.

'Paul.' She put her hand over his. 'Mira knows.'

'How?' He put his glass down. 'You didn't *tell* her?'

'Of course not. Saturday night. She saw us.'

'We weren't doing anything.'

She made a face. 'You may be dense, but she's not.'

'Did she say she knew?'

'Yes.' There was no point in going into details, she thought, laughing to herself. Men were just dense, that was all there was to it.

'Do you think she'll say anything?'

'No. Not now. But I can't be sure. You know how het up she gets about ideas and principles.' Bliss stood and paced, her slender body held in the careful languor she aimed for, looking tense and sensual at once. She spoke rapidly and bluntly, then lowered herself back into the couch, her grace barely masking the terrific coiled-up energy caged in her slim ribs, the narrowly spaced pelvic bones. She sat looking at him, prepared for almost anything – protest, recoil, perhaps even contempt. Courage, she thought wryly, I don't lack. But he was laughing. He thought it a splendid idea.

'To her, of all people! That tight-assed virgin!'

Bliss laughed in satisfaction. She and Paul *were* of a kind.

It was a simple plan. It would take time and careful playing of roles, but both Paul and Bliss were adepts at that. And as it happened, Adele played right into their hands. Over coffee with Bliss a few days later, she repeated some remarks Doris had made about Mira. Roger and Doris didn't like her, Adele said. They thought she was neurotic. 'I know you're a good friend of hers, Bliss, and I don't mean to offend you, but I don't think I like her so much either.'

Bliss looked down, stiring her coffee. 'Why?' she asked in a tone that sounded concerned-trying-to-sound-offhand.

'Well, I don't know, I'm not comfortable with her,' Adele said uneasily.

Paul had been supposed to stand staring out toward Mira's house at a time when he knew Adele would see him, and to act startled when she said something to him. Bliss gathered he had done this, but Adele didn't mention it.

Bliss said nothing, kept stirring her coffee, looking down.

Adele gazed at her. 'Didn't you tell me something about her and Natalie? About letters Hamp supposedly wrote?'

'Yeah,' Bliss said carefully.

'What was that?'

Bliss sighed and raised her head. 'Oh, nothing. You know how Natalie was. She thought Mira was having an affair with Hamp.'

'Well, was she?'

Bliss shrugged self-consciously. 'How should I know?'

'She's close to you.'

Bliss gave a small shrug. 'Not that close.'

It worked. They kept it up. Paul looked out at Mira's house long and longingly; he would look guilty when Adele caught him. Bliss acted very kind to Adele – kinder than usual. She acted almost as if she were – sorry for Adele. Every once in a while, as if she were testing, Adele would make a small uncomplimentary remark about Mira to Bliss. She watched, but Bliss never responded. She did not defend Mira. One day, Adele asked how Mira was, and Bliss shrugged and said, 'Oh, I don't know. I don't see her much anymore.'

'Why?'

'Oh,' Bliss waved her hand, 'I don't know. It's just well, you know, friendship can go just so far.'

'What do you mean?'

'I can't talk about it,' Bliss said sadly. She took Adele's face in her hands. 'I'm sorry, Dell. But I can't.'

Before Christmas, there was a party. Adele watched Paul carefully. He danced almost all night with Mira. He kept going over to her, talking to her. That week, over coffee, she turned her gaze straight at Bliss.

'Mira's having an affair with Paul, isn't she?'

Bliss looked up startled, embarrassed. 'Adele!'

'Isn't she?'

'She's been my friend for over four years now, Adele. Don't ask me to stab her in the back.'

'Isn't she?'

181

Bliss put her elbows on the table and laid her head in her hands. 'I don't know,' she said in a muffled voice. 'I've heard stories. But I don't know. Honestly.' She looked up, straight at Adele. 'I honestly don't believe them. Honestly.'

CHAPTER THREE

1

One thing that makes art different from life is that in art things have a shape; they have beginnings, middles, and endings. Whereas in life, things just drift along. In life, somebody has a cold, and you treat it as insignificant, and suddenly they die. Or they have a heart attack, and you are sodden with grief until they recover to live for thirty petulant years, demanding you wait on them. You think a love affair is ending, and you are gripped with Anna Karenina-ish drama, but two weeks later the guy is standing in your doorway, arms stretched up on the molding, jacket hanging open, a sheepish look on his face, saying, 'Hey, take me back, will ya?' Or you think a love affair is high and thriving, and you don't notice that over the past months it has dwindled, dwindled, dwindled. In other words, in life one almost never has an emotion appropriate to an event. Either you don't know the event is occurring, or you don't know its significance. We celebrate births and weddings; we mourn deaths and divorces; yet what are we celebrating, what mourning? Rituals mark feelings, but feelings and events do not coincide. Feelings are large and spread over a lifetime. I will dance the polka with you and stamp my feet with vigor, celebrating every energy I have ever felt. But those energies were moments, not codifiable, not certifiable, not able to be fixed: you may be seduced into thinking my celebration is for you. Anyway, that is a thing art does for us: it allows us to fix our emotions on events at the moment they occur, it permits a union of heart and mind and tongue and tear. Whereas in life, from moment to moment, one can't tell an onion from a piece of dry toast.

Mira lived contentedly through the last months of 1959 without realizing that her life had already drastically changed. Natalie was gone; Theresa was a destroyed person, no longer accessible. Mira had not been close to Adele for some time, but because of her other friendships, had not noticed that until now. She had grown intensely close to Bliss, whom she loved second only to her family. Their intimacy was not especially verbal; it arose out of their feeling the same way in a situation, from their being able to look, simply glance at each other in a situation, and know they knew, knew the same things, felt together.

For some weeks in the fall, Bliss stopped in only once or twice a week; she had been distracted all summer, humming and off buying paint. For a while, she didn't stop in at all. Then, suddenly it seemed, she was busy when Mira stopped in to see her. She was spending much time on her house, painting the living room, making new drapes for it, painting her bedroom, making a new bedspread, new lampshades, new pale pink opaque curtains. Finally, Mira challenged her, asked her what was wrong, what had happened. Bliss hummed and raised her eyebrows. Nothing was wrong, nothing had changed, she was just busy. Mira went home with a numb spot in the middle of her forehead. What she had thought of as love and support had simply stopped, stopped with no reason, or at least, no reason given. She knew there was no point in pushing Bliss; she understood how tough Bliss was. Bliss was through with her and she did not know why and she would never know why. Maybe it was because she knew about Bliss and Paul. But even suspecting that, she still did not know why.

Late in the fall, before Bliss cut her off completely, Paula and Brett had a party. Mira had a vague feeling of being an outsider in her own group, and she got drunker than usual, faster than usual. She recalled, the next day, that Paul had come over to her frequently, more often than usual, to ask her to dance. She had thought it odd, and she had refused him many times. Yet he returned, over and over again. She had a strange feeling, but drunk as she was, disoriented as she felt, did not draw any conclusions from it except that she was disorganized. The feeling she had, not solidified into perception until later, was that she was being used as a decoy. But there was no way she could talk it out, no way to check her perceptions against reality. She no longer got more than mere social politeness from Bliss. Then, one blustery January day as she was removing the frozen bedsheets from the laundry line, Adele came out her back door to shake a dust mop. Mira hailed her. Adele looked up, looked straight at her, and turned and went back in the house.

Then she knew. She thought about it on many evenings, sitting up late in the dark with a snifter of brandy, and smoking. She worked it out that Paul's reputation was deserved; he had had affairs, and Adele knew it. But what could she do about it? With all those kids, alimony payments being what they were, she and the children would have to live like paupers. That is, if she even considered divorce. Someone who would not use birth control was not likely to use divorce. That in itself gave Paul enormous freedom. He might think twice if he felt he was risking loss of his family, his home, his wife. They are easy enough to ignore or abuse when one has them, but losing them is unpleasant. Adele's only alternative was to beat him up. Probably they had an unspoken agreement: he did not insist on using birth control, but the kids then were her responsibility and he retained his freedom. Nevertheless, Paul and Bliss would want to keep Adele from knowing about them so the couples could continue to have an easy social mingling; they figured the best way was to find a substitute target for Adele's suspicions. Bliss was not too worried about Bill, who was oblivious, but even if he did suspect, the story about Paul and Mira would serve to deflect him too. After all, how many women can a man handle at once? It was an ingenious plan. Mira thought bitterly about the two of them sitting together, plotting it, giggling.

But part of her understood. They were in love and they were protecting their love. It was understandable, and she did not much blame their motives. What hurt was Bliss's betrayal of her. Of course, Mira had to be the victim. Because she knew, she might talk. Well, let her

185

talk, no one would believe her now; Adele would not hear the story from someone she would not speak to. Oh, Mira supposed she could go charging over to Adele's, insist on being let in, shout out the truth. She could keep a watch on Bliss's house, and on a night when Paul was there, drag Adele bodily to find them together. But what good would it do? Adele might believe Mira was being vicious because Paul had left her for Bliss. Or she might believe Mira, but she would never again be her friend. Adele would hate Bliss; she might never trust another woman. She would go on living with Paul, humiliated and contemptuous. And Paul and Bliss would lose what they had, and Adele might tell Bill and Bliss would lose what she had, and only Paul would end up rather untouched, finding consolation in some new face and body. No, it was not worth it. Because the only thing Mira wanted was for things to go back to being the way they had been: and that was impossible. She wanted Bliss's love, something, she told herself, she had had, remembering their long, close talks. But one could not expect Bliss's love for Mira to be stronger than her desire to protect herself. She had had Bliss's love, but would never have it again, no matter what happened. Bliss could never like Mira again after what she had done to her.

Mira went over and over it until she understood it so well that the thing did not even hurt her anymore. All her love for Bliss had been translated into understanding, which was nonfeeling, and which she had chosen over hate. What was left at the end (when she knew it was the end – it came to her with a kind of surprise one day after she'd cleaned the house and had a free hour and wanted to go talk to someone) was loneliness. She had no friends left.

One night when he was home and in a good mood, she told Norm the whole thing, including her theory. He pooh-poohed it. She had too active an imagination. It was ridiculous: no one would believe that Mira would do a thing like that. He was uninterested in the rest of it, except he had some sympathy for Bill. 'Poor slob,' he said. 'When the O'Neills went to visit Adele's folks last summer, Bill even went over and mowed their lawn.'

Over the years Mira had come to feel it was useless to speak to Norm. Their ways of looking at the world seemed too different. Norm could not understand why Natalie or Bliss or Adele should matter so much to her. She argued that he got upset with certain patients, or with some of the big names in the local medical association, if they seemed to dislike him. That was different, he said, that was business, his livelihood was at stake. For their personal affection he did not give one straw. And he could not understand why she did, why she let stupid sluts and housewives bother her. She paled when he said that. 'And I? What am I?'

He put an arm around her affectionately. 'Honey, you have a mind.'

'So do they.'

He insisted she was different, but she pulled away from him. She knew there was something terribly wrong with what was being said, but she didn't know what it was. She defended the women from his attacks and he was puzzled about why she should defend the very people who had betrayed her. She gave it up.

She moved out in search of new friends, but without the enthusiasm she'd had years ago. She liked Lily, who lived a few blocks to the north, and Samantha, who lived a good ten blocks away, and Martha. But Martha lived in a different town, and without a car. Mira could not visit her. Mira visited Lily and Samantha on occasion, but it was a far different thing to walk some distance to someone's house and sit, almost formally, with coffee or a drink, than to run next door or two houses down where you can see the kids when they come home, or leave them a note telling them where you are, so if they need you, they can run over. Mira deeply missed that kind of community, the daily intimacy and companionship of people who lived close by. She thought she would probably never have it again.

As it happened, she would have lost it anyway. In the spring of 1960, Norm announced that he had finished paying back his family, and a month or two later, he

187

completed arrangements to leave the local practice he was involved in and join a group in the modern new medical clinic they were building. He would pay off his share of the costs over the next five years, out of his share of the profits, which were expected to be staggering. It was time, he said, for them to move to a 'real' house. Early in the summer he found a place that suited him, and took Mira to see it. It was beautiful, but it overwhelmed her. It was too big and too isolated. 'Four bathrooms to clean!' she exclaimed. He found her provincial and petty in her concerns. 'Three miles to the nearest store, and I have no car.' He wanted the house. He promised her a car and help in the house if she insisted, although he added, 'What else do you have to do?'

Mira debated. She would like to have the house, of course: she too had wanted material success. But it frightened her. She felt she was sinking, sinking – into what she wasn't sure. Norm's parents were proud of their son: to be able to own a house like that at only thirty-seven! But they were also a bit anxious: he wasn't getting himself too far in debt now, was he? Paying off the new partnership, buying the house and another car too. They glanced significantly at Mira. She was an ambitious driving woman, she supposed, in their eyes. She no longer cared what they thought, but the injustice nevertheless scratched her. Her own parents were more enthusiastic: Mira had really done well for herself, marrying a man who could afford a house like that.

Mira sank. She was thirty when they moved to Beau Reve.

2

Yes, I know, you think you see it all. Having shown you the nasty underside of life in the young, struggling white middle class, I will now show you the nasty underside of life in the older, affluent, white middle class. You are a bit chagrined. I start you off at Harvard, in the middle of an exciting period full of young exciting people with new ideas, only to drag you through an afternoon of soap opera. I'm sorry. Really. If I knew any exciting adventure tales, I'd write them, I assure you. If I think of any as we go, I'll be glad to insert them. There were important things happening during the years just described: there was the Berlin Wall, John Foster Dulles, Castro, who was the darling of the liberals until he shot all those people (having read his Machiavelli) and became suddenly the devil. And a senator of less than national fame took the Democratic nomination and forced Lyndon Johnson to go along with him.

Sometimes I get as sick of writing this as you may be at reading it. Of course, you have an alternative. I don't. I get sick because, you see, it's all true, it happened, and it was boring and painful and full of despair. I think I would not feel so bad about it if it had ended differently. Of course, I can't talk about ends, since I am still alive. But I would have a different slant on things, perhaps, if I were not living in this inconsolable loneliness. And that is an insoluble problem. I mean, you could go up to a stranger on the street and say, 'I am inconsolably lonely,' and he might take you home with him and introduce you to his family and ask you to stay for dinner. But that wouldn't help. Because loneliness is not a longing for company, it is a longing for kind. And kind means people who can see you who you are, and that means they have enough intelligence and sensitivity and patience to do that. It also means they can accept you, because we don't see what we can't accept, we blot it out, we jam it hastily in one stereotypic box or another. We don't want to look at something that might shake up the mental order we've so carefully erected. I have respect for this desire to keep one's psyche unviolated. Habit is a good thing for the human race. For instance, have you ever traveled from place to place, spending no more than a day or two in each? You wake up in the morning a bit unnerved, and every day you have to search for where you put your toothbrush last night, and figure out whether you unpacked your comb and brush. Every morning you have to decide where to have your *café* and croissant, or your *cappuccino* or *kawa*. You even have to find the right word. I said *si* for two weeks after I entered France from Italy, and *oui* for two weeks after I entered Spain from France. And that's an easy enough word to get right. You have to spend so much energy just getting through the day when you have no habits that you don't have any left for productive labor. You get that glazed look of tourists staring up at one more church and checking the guidebook to see what city they're in. Each day you arrive in a new place you have to spend two or more hours finding a decent cheap hotel: subsisting becomes the whole of life.

Well, you see what I mean. Every new person you meet and really take in violates your psyche to some degree. You have to juggle your categories to fit the person in. Here where I am, people see me some way – I don't know exactly how. Middle-aged matron, rabid feminist, nice lady, madwoman: I don't know. But they can't see me who I am. So I'm lonely. I guess maybe I wouldn't be able to say who I am myself. One needs some reflection from the outside to get an image of oneself. Sometimes, when I am really low, the words of Pyotr Stephanovich come into my mind: You must love God because He is the only one you can love for Eternity. That sounds very profound to me, and tears come into my eyes whenever I say it. I never heard anyone else say it. But I don't believe in God and if I did I couldn't love Him / Her / It. I couldn't love anyone I thought had created this world.

Oh God. (Metaphorically speaking.) So people handle loneliness by putting themselves into something larger than they are, some framework or purpose. But those big exterior things – I don't know, they just don't seem as important to me as what Norm said to Mira or Bliss to Adele. I mean, do you really care about 1066? Val would scream that it was significant, but my students don't care about 1066. They don't even care about World War II or the Holocaust. They don't even remember Jean Arthur. For them, Elvis Presley is part of the quaint, irrelevant past. No, it's the little things that matter. But when you're dealing with a lot of insignificant lives, how do you put things together? When you look back on your life, are there places where you can put your finger, like crossroads on a map or a scholar's crux in Shakespeare, where you can say, 'There! That is the place where everything changed, the word upon which everything hinged!'

I find that difficult. I feel like a madwoman. I walk around my apartment, which is a shithouse, full of landlord's odds and ends of leftover furniture and a few dying plants on the windowsills. I talk to myself, myself, myself. Now I am smart enough to provide a fairly good running dialogue, but the problem is there's no response, no voice but mine. I want to hear another's truth, but I insist it be a truth. I talk to the plants but they shrivel and die.

I wanted my life to be a work of art, but when I try to look at it, it swells and shrinks like the walls you glean in a delirious daze. My life sprawls and sags, like an old pair of baggy slacks that still, somehow, fits you.

Like Mira, Val, and lots of others, I went back to the university late in life. I went with despair and expectations. It was a new life, it was supposed to revitalize you, to send you radiant to new planes of experience where you would get tight with Beatrice Portinari and be led to an earthy paradise. In literature, new lives, second chances, lead to visions of the City of God. But I have been suspecting for a while now that everything I ever read was lies. You can believe the first four acts, but not the fifth. Lear really turned into a babbling old fool drooling over his oatmeal and happy for a place by the fire in Regan's house in Scarsdale. Hamlet took over the corporation by bribing the board and ousting Claudius, and then took to wearing a black leather jacket and German Army boots and sending out proclamations that everyone would refrain from fornication upon pain of death. He wrote letters to his cousin Angelo and together they decided to purify the whole East Coast, so they have joined with the Mafia, the Marines, and the CIA to outlaw sex. Romeo and Juliet marry and have some kids, then separate when she wants to go back to graduate school and he wants to go live on a commune in New Mexico. She is on welfare now and he has long hair and an Indian headband and says *Oooom* a lot.

Camille lives: she runs a small popular hotel in Bordeaux. I've met her. She has bleached blond hair, thick orange makeup, and a hard mouth, and she knows everything about the price of vermouth, clean sheets, bottled orange drink, and certain available female bodies. She's thicker all around than she used to be, but she still has a shape. She meanders around in a shiny pale blue pantsuit, and sits in her bar laughing with friends and keeping an eye out for Bernard, the married man who is her latest lover. Except for her passion for Bernard, she is tough and fun. Don't ask what it is about Bernard that makes her so adore him. It is not Bernard, but love itself. She believes in love, goes on believing in it against all odds. Therefore, Bernard is a little bored. It is boring to be adored. At thirty-eight, she should be tough and fun, not adoring. When he leaves her, a month or two from now, she will contemplate suicide. Whereas, if she had been able to bring herself to stop believing in love, she would have been tough and fun and he would have adored her forever. Which would have bored her. She then would have had to be the one to tell him to clear out. It is a choice to give one pause.

Tristan and Isolde got married after Issy got a divorce from Mark, who was anyhow turned on to a groupie at that point. And they discovered the joys of comfortable marriage can't hold a candle to the thrill of taboo, so they have placed an ad in the Boston *Phoenix* asking for a third, fourth, or even fifth party of any gender to join them in tasting taboo joys. They will smoke, they will even snort a little coke, just to assure a degree of fear about being intruded upon by the local police. Don't judge: they, at least, are trying to hold their marriage together. And you?

The problem with the great literature of the past is that it doesn't tell you how to live with real endings. In the great literature of the past you either get married and live happily ever after, or you die. But the fact is, neither is what actually happens. Oh, you do die, but never at the right time, never with great language floating all around you, and a whole theater full of witnesses to your agony. What actually happens is that you do get married or you don't, and you don't live happily ever after, but you do live. And that's the problem. I mean, think about it. Suppose Antigone had lived. An Antigone who goes on being Antigone year after year would be not only ludicrous but a bore. The cave and the rope are essential.

It isn't just the endings. In a real life, how can you tell when you're in Book I or Book III, or Act II or Act V? No stagehands come charging in to haul down the curtain at an appropriate moment. So how do I know whether I'm living in the middle of Act III and heading toward a great climax, or at the end of Act V and finished? I don't even know who I am. I might be Hester Prynne, or Dorothea Brooke, or I might be the heroine of a TV drama of some seasons back – what was her name? – Mrs. Muir! Yes, she walked on the beach and was in love with a ghost and originally she looked like Gene Tierney. I always wanted to look like Gene Tierney. I sit in a chair and I have no one to knit woolen stockings for so it's irrelevant that I don't know how to knit. (Val could, oddly. Nothing works the way it does in books. Can you imagine Penthesilea knitting?) I'm just sitting here living out even to the edge of doom – what? Valerie's vision? Except she forgot to tell me what comes next.

3

Mira had a new life. It was supposed to be glorious, it was supposed to be what all those hard years in the two- or three-room apartments were for. This was what it was all about. Norm had worked hard for long hours, so had she: for this. Not everyone who worked hard for long hours achieved this; they were lucky. She had her own car – Norm's old one; he bought a new little MG for himself – and a house with four bathrooms. She also had (after some wrestling with her conscience and some tense discussion with Norm, who did not want to say straight out that he did not want to pay for help in the house, so said instead that they could only get a colored woman and she would no doubt rob them blind – as if they had anything to steal) a washer-dryer, a dishwasher, a man to wax the kitchen floor every two weeks, and a laundry to do the sheets and Norm's shirts. Never again, frozen sheets in January.

She told herself this as she paced the large, mostly empty rooms. She stood in the wide foyer, with its impressive chandelier and the winding staircase, and told herself she must be happy, she had to be. She had no other choice: there was a moral imperative on her to be happy. She was not actively unhappy. She was just – nothing.

The rhythms of life were different in Beau Reve. She would get up at seven with Norm, and make coffee while he showered and shaved. He no longer ate breakfast at home. She would sit with him over the coffee for a few minutes while he gave her her chores for the day – suits to be cleaned, shoes to be mended, some business at the bank, a telephone call to the insurance agent about the dent in his car. Then he left her and she woke the children, who dressed as she prepared their eggs. She dressed as they ate them, then she drove them the mile to the school bus stop. Everyone but Norm was grouchy in the morning and they spoke little. Then she returned to the house.

That was the worst time. She would come in through the door from the garage to the kitchen and the house would smell of bacon and toast. The greasy frying pan sat on the stove, the spattered coffeepot behind it. Dirty dishes lay on the kitchen table. The four beds were unmade and there was soiled underwear lying about. There was dust in the living and dining rooms, the family room held used soda glasses and potato chip crumbs from the night before.

What bothered her was not that the tasks that had to be done were exerting. It was not even that they were tedious. It was that she felt that the three others lived their lives and she went around after them cleaning up their mess. She was an unpaid servant, expected to do a superlative job. In return, she was permitted to call this house hers. But so did they. Most of the time she did not think about it: only every morning, when she returned from dropping the kids at the bus. She made up little rewards for herself: I will do this and that, then I will sit and read the paper. She charged into it, sticking a batch of wash in the machine, cleaning the kitchen, making up beds and straightening rooms, and then attacked the rest of the house, in which something had to be done every day, it was so big. Down on her hands and knees in one of the endless bathrooms, she would tell herself that in a way she was fortunate. Washing the toilet used by three males, and the floor and walls around it, is, Mira thought, coming face to face with necessity. And that was why women were saner than men, did not come up with the mad, absurd schemes men developed: they were in touch with necessity, they had to wash the toilet bowl and floor. She kept telling herself that.

About eleven thirty, she made a fresh pot of coffee and sat down with *The New York Times*, which (another new luxury) she had delivered. She sat for an hour at least, savoring it. In the afternoon, she did her errands, or on days when there were no errands, she might visit Lily or Samantha or Martha. But she had to be home by three, when the boys got in. They were not yet old enough to be left alone. She didn't mind that too much, although it would have been nice, just once in a while, to feel free to stay out as long as she wanted. She didn't know what she would have done with such freedom – Lily's, Martha's, and Samantha's children came in around then too, and the women were involved with the children. It was just the feeling of freedom she craved. But she enjoyed talking to the boys when they got in. They were smart and funny, and she hugged them a lot. They would talk over a snack, then change their clothes and go out. She had another hour to herself. She would take the laundry out of the dryer and fold it carefully, patiently. She would take something out of the freezer to defrost. Then she would take a book and sit down. The boys ran in and out and she was frequently interrupted, so she read only light things in the afternoons. Then it was time to prepare dinner. Norm usually got in about six thirty, and nowadays they all ate together. But Norm continually picked on the boys at the dinner table: they were using the wrong fork, they had their elbows on the table, they were chewing with their mouths open. So dinnertime was always tense. Afterward, the boys would go off to do homework, Norm would settle in the family room with the paper, and Mira would clean up the kitchen. The boys took their own baths now, and all she had to do was remind them about it, keep track that they did it, and wash the tubs afterward. They would come in to watch TV for a while before bed, but they had to watch what Norm wanted to see. Once she insisted they be allowed to see a children's special, and Norm had sulked the rest of the night. She would sit with them, reading or mending. Then they would go to bed. Norm would sit for a while longer, and by ten he would be asleep in the chair. She would go over and shake him: 'Norm, don't fall asleep in the chair.' He would awake and stand and stumble groggily to the bedroom.

Then Mira would switch off the TV set. She was too tired now to read seriously, but she did not want to go to bed. She would pour a snifter of brandy and turn out all the lights and sit in the corner of the family room, by the window – sit and drink and smoke until eleven or twelve, then go to bed.

She was living the American Dream, she knew that, and she tried to get her mask on straight. She had her hair done at the right shop and when they saw gray and advised dye, she let them dye it. She bought expensive three-piece knit suits: she had her nails manicured. She had a holder full of charge cards.

There were moments of beauty. Sometimes, before she made the boy's beds, she would think about them, and love would gush into her heart, and she would lie down on their beds and smell the sheets, bury her face in them. Their beds smelled just like the boys. Sometimes, when she was having her coffee and reading her paper, the sun would slant in through the big kitchen window and pour across the wooden table and her heart would be still. And sometimes, dressed to go out, she would walk slowly through the large house and feel its cleanliness and order and would think that the comfort of order might after all be the best one could hope for, might even be enough.

She was not unhappy. She lived much through her friends, all of whom were having troubles. After listening to Lily or Sam or Martha all afternoon, it felt good to come home to her peaceful and orderly house. Given what she knew about others' lives, how could she complain about her own?

First there was Lily.

4

All the women were attractive when they were young, but Lily was gorgeous. She had a large-boned, classic face – wide-browed, strong-jawed – and large, well-spaced brown eyes, and a slender neck. Her body was perfect. That is, it was the kind of body you were supposed to have, but didn't: shoulders broad but not too broad, nice bust, slender waist, no belly, slim hips, and long slender legs, all perfectly proportioned. She had dyed red hair and eyebrows, and she was inclined to buy rather showy clothes: lots of sequins and chiffon and silver threads. When Lily walked into a restaurant or bar, all the male heads turned. That probably would have pleased her had she been aware of it. She wasn't. She wasn't even aware of her beauty. She worried about her looks all the time. She studied magazines to learn about makeup, and experimented for hours with different brands and kinds. She used darkish foundation for parts of her face, a light foundation for others, a special kind for the oily skin around her nose. She plucked her eyebrows, and dyed them with great care. She used three different makeups on her eyes. Over the foundations she placed special rouge and powder. She could discuss these

197

cosmetics with great intelligence and knowledge. Mira wondered why she bothered: 'You're so beautiful, you don't need them,' she said and Lily just looked at her. 'Oh, you've never seen me without makeup,' Lily said seriously. 'I'm a fright.' She described all the flaws in her appearance. There were, it appeared, nothing but flaws.

Her life was the same way. On the surface, it appeared fine. Carl, her husband, was a calm and affable man, who seemed never to get excited about anything. During any minor crisis with the children, he would always say, 'It's all right, Lily, it'll be all right.' Andrea, the older child, seemed to have her father's serene nature. Little Carl, whom they called Carlos, was more difficult. But Lily lived with a tearing wretchedness so severe that she had to have four-fifths of her stomach removed when she was only twenty-seven. In conversation she was always miserable, but it was never clear why. Her voice soared up and down; she was always tugging at her hair or wrenching her mouth out of shape. People said simply, 'Lily is emotional,' or 'Lily is nervous.' In another time, that might have ended discussion, but the culture Lily and Mira lived in believed that happiness was an inalienable right and tried to discover what was wrong if they didn't have it. So people added: 'Lily is neurotic.' That was not a description, it was a judgement. Lily did not question why she was unhappy: she seemed to know. But in conversation she tossed from problem to problem, making statements so elliptical and vague that it was difficult to deduce what was bothering her. She was never very concrete about anything.

Mira's earliest conversations with her, when both still lived in Meyersville, were about Lily's childhood, which had been cruel. One is always forced to pay for that. Economic theories are all based on the wrong principle. In life, you pay for pain and get rewarded for pleasure. Lily's father was a maniac, a sweet, slight man with an Italian accent, who on the outside was a Good Man, that is, one who supports his family and doesn't drink or do worse. His marriage to Lily's mother was arranged by her family when she was sixteen. She didn't want the

198

marriage or the man, and she ran away, but true to old dicta about women, she did it halfheartedly. Frightened and unable to take care of herself in the world, she returned to the family, telegraphing ahead to tell them what train she would be coming in on. They met her in Grand Central Station, with her fiancé in tow. And right there in the middle of the station, with her family standing there, he beat her up, blacked one eye and bloodied her nose. A month later, she married him. *Was das Weib will?* It was an old Sicilian family.

His mode of operation did not change. When children came, they simply provided more objects for his continuing and seemingly causeless rage. He supported them decently on his bricklayer's wages and they were never hungry, if often bruised. Over the years, he saved enough to buy a three-story house in the Bronx, renting out the top floor. The stories of his brutality in her childhood, and Lily's anguish over it, I will omit. Enough is enough.

When Lily was graduated from high school, she wanted to get a job in an artist's studio. She had always wanted to be an artist, although she had only a vague notion of what artists do. But her family regarded such an aim as proof of her rebellious and selfish nature. Her mother, who when the husband came in angry and searching for prey, cried out, 'Hit the kids! Don't hit me!' saw to it that Lily got a perfectly good job in a garment factory, earning $25 a week, $20 of which went to the family. But even after she was working, her father beat her.

One morning after a bad night, Lily looked at her puffed face and the bruises on her shoulders in a mirror, and went boldly to her mother. 'Ma, I'm eighteen years old. I bring money into this house. I'm not a child anymore. When is he going to stop beating me?'

The remark must have seemed ludicrous to the mother, who had bruises of her own. She roared, though, at Lily's arrogance, which did not seem tameable. 'As long as you live in this house, you get beaten!'

Lily decided silently then that she would get out.

She saved every penny she could, skimping on lunches,

sacrificing the Saturday-night movie with her girlfriends that was her only pleasure without really feeling it as a sacrifice: she had a goal that swallowed up anything else. She got a small raise at the factory which she did not mention at home. After some months, she had a little sum of money.

You will say that Lily was self-defeating, that she didn't really want to get out. You will say, if she had, she would have taken that money and bought a train ticket to Peoria or Chicago. But Lily had never in her life been out of the Bronx, had never been permitted to act without supervision. She was frightened and her horizons were limited. She took a room at the YWCA three miles from her home. Probably she did not want to sever her connections with her family, only to assert her independence, her individuality. She was clever. Every day, when she went to work, she stuffed a piece of clothing in her bag, which she would then leave in her locker at the factory. On Friday nights, pretending she was going out with a girlfriend, she would take the week's gleanings and carry them in a paper bag to her unslept-in room at the Y. Little by little, she garnered all she wanted: she didn't dare to take all her clothes – that would have been noticed. Then she began to take pieces of her sewing machine, her only and prized possession. She took the small ones day by day, but the motor was a problem. So she waited until the last day, and one Sunday, when her parents were down the block visiting cousins, she packed the motor and the last of her personal belongings in a paper bag and left. She wrote a note telling her parents not to worry about her, that she could no longer tolerate the conditions at home, that she was living elsewhere.

She thought her room at the Y a palace: she was free!

Foolish Lily. She kept her job at the factory. It did not take long. On Tuesday her father was there waiting for her as she left work, and with him the parish priest. Her father grabbed her out of the line of women threading out, pulled her out roughly by the arm. He shouted at her: she was a slut, a whore, a *mala femmina* who had dared to leave her father's house. He slapped her over

200

and over. The priest watched. She whimpered, she tried to explain, she defended herself, she affirmed her virtue, she was living in a Y, she wasn't cheap – it did no good. Her father looked to the priest for approval of his condemnation of the girl, and the priest gave it. Together they pushed and prodded her back to the Y, picked up her things, and dragged her back to the family home, where, after a glass of wine and some homemade cake and a general sense of virtue restored, the priest left and Lily was punished for her whorish ways. She never again went to church.

She understood then that there was only one way she was going to get out of her father's house, and she began to look around. Although she had a strong sexual nature, she had never put any energy into that forbidden field: there had been more pressing matters. She gained permission from her parents to 'date'; that, somehow, was all right. She was accepting her place. In time she met Carl; he was mild and gentle, totally unlike her father. He was also steady – in personality and in life. Her parents approved. Lily and Carl became engaged. At that moment, things changed. She was permitted more liberty, her father stopped beating her, although he might slap her around a little. She understood that she was now seen as the property of another man.

Because Carl was mild, this constriction seemed a liberation to her. She began to act more and more independently, and came home one night when she was twenty and announced that she had rented a store, that she was quitting her job, that she was going to open a dress shop. They didn't even ask her where she got the money – perhaps they thought Carl was giving it to her. But it was her own savings of a year and a half. They shrugged: she was no longer their responsibility.

Foolish Lily. What did she know about the clothing business? She went around to factories and bought what she liked, guessed at the markup, and worked in the store all day and into the night seven days a week. She was driven with energy; she was happy. On Saturday nights she would choose something from her own shop and paste inch-thick makeup on her face and she and Carl would go to a nightclub. Carl enjoyed taking her to nightclubs, he liked getting dressed up and showing her off and spending money with his friends. He was in no rush to get married.

But Lily's business did not do well. She was not hard enough, she had no experience. Women would buy a dress on Friday and return it on Monday obviously worn, and ask for their money back. She did not know how to refuse them. Her selection of clothes was not objective enough, it was based on her taste alone. For a while she kept the thing going, working alone in the shop, her energy unflagging. She kept it going until all her savings were gone, and the month arrived when she could not pay the rent. Her dream had lasted just a year. Tearful, she sold out her scanty remaining stock for less than cost, declared bankruptcy, and married Carl.

5

Carl's tranquil surface was the result of careful self-control as well as inherited temperament. Carl's father had abandoned the family when Carl was five. His mother, a passive and tranquil woman, got a job cleaning houses, but the five children were left mostly to themselves. She earned very little; arriving home late at night, she was tired, and her own house went uncleaned, her children unfed. The oldest daughter, Marie, took over as best she could, but she was, as Carl would put it later, 'selfish.' She wanted her own life. Half-heartedly, she cooked, but that was all. She did it for four years, and when she was eighteen, she took off to live on her own. Nobody cleaned, and marketing was as haphazard as the money. It was a dismal life for a child, and frustrating to someone as fastidious as Carl already was. Still, even when he was older, he did not attempt to help out in household chores; he deeply believed they were women's work. Carl had contempt for his mother's weakness, her inability to take over and run things, to give a decent background to his life.

All the children had to work. They did anything they could – sold newspapers, shined shoes, ran errands, swept up grocery shop floors. The middle son died of tuberculosis when he was twelve. After Marie abandoned them, Lillian took over. Carl, who was the youngest, followed his brother Edwin to the streets. The streets provided them with an outlet for some of what seethed inside them. Sports, mischief, and fighting filled non-working afternoons. Once, they got caught stealing fruit from a stand, and once they kidnapped a local 'sissy' and hanged him from a clothesline post. Someone saw the child, and cut him down before he strangled. In both cases, there was not too much fuss. But over the years, the boys on the street began to disappear into reformatories and, later on, prisons. Carl began to think about the future.

Carl always said World War II was the best thing that ever happened to him. He had some flaws in his body – nothing serious, mostly the result of his inadequate diet as a child – but enough, when added up, to mark him 4-F. So when all the other men had been drafted, Carl was able to get a job in a defense plant, where he learned, eventually, to be a skilled machinist. He was very good at it: his German father, perhaps, had left him a legacy of precision and order. He did well and was liked: he had learned on the streets how to act cool. He seemed easygoing, affable, bland, unjudging. What went on under the exterior, one can only guess. Even Lily was never sure. He never cracked.

Carl and Edwin and Lillian were all working so they moved their mother into a decent apartment, made her give up her job, and settled back to enjoy the fruits of her labors in their own behalf. But the woman was weak and worn out. She had long since given up; she cooked and marketed, but she never learned how to operate the washing machine they had bought her. She cleaned randomly, ineffectually. Carl's early contempt was heightened: it was her Italian nature, he thought, that made her slovenly. Although she died, simply worn out, within two years after her assumption into a life of luxury, he did not change his opinion.

Although Carl did not object to getting married, he did not want his life to change. Week nights, he hung out with his friends from the old neighborhood, playing cards; on Saturday nights he took Lily out, and he slept most of Sunday. He enjoyed his life. When his mother died, the home broke up: Edwin got married and Lillian got a job in Manhattan and moved. So when Lily said she was losing the shop, it seemed the right time. To Carl, marriage represented the perfect way for him to continue in his life as it was. He urged Lily to get a job. She was pleased at this; it seemed to her that he did not intend to constrict her as her mother had been constricted. She got a job as a receptionist in a fancy office. That was good, Carl said: she didn't earn much, but it was easy work. She discovered only gradually, for Carl never articulated it, just what he expected of her. He wanted her to work so that they would continue to have the money to go to clubs on Saturday nights; he also expected her to keep the apartment immaculate, and to handle the marketing, cooking, and laundry chores with silent efficiency. He did not say this; but if something were neglected, he pointed it out in a cold, contemptuous remark. 'You didn't get the laundry done,' or 'The kitchen floor is filthy, Lily.' He never helped. He sat in a chair reading his newspaper and watching TV, occasionally getting up to criticize her work. She argued with him, but somehow she always lost. Carl never raised his voice: he merely stared coldly at her. And if she were guilty of some sloppiness or neglect, he treated her with disdain, turning away from her in bed, not allowing her even to touch him, as if her body were defiled.

Lily's independence and courage crumbled under this oblique approach. If he had abused her as her father had, she would have found the strength to fight him. As it was, she fell into line. His contempt was so cruel to her that she would do anything to avoid it. She scrubbed and vacuumed; she labored over cookbooks. Still, he always found a flaw: a spot left undusted, a meal he didn't like.

Many nights he turned his back on her in bed. He had discovered on their honeymoon that Lily was sexual. It is odd, it seems to defy all textbook knowledge, but Lily enjoyed sex. She would have orgasm after orgasm while Carl watched her with incredible disgust. It was a worse punishment to her than any strap when she touched Carl with light fingers and he shivered and pulled away. She felt that he thought she was filthy. She tried to prove to him that she was worthy.

Despite the frequently turned back, Lily got pregnant. This really shook Carl up. A child would mean the end of his life. Lily would have to quit her job – there would no longer be money enough to play poker with the guys three nights a week, or to hang out with the bunch at Carmine's on Saturday nights. There would be a squalling kid to contend with. He insisted she have an abortion.

Slavelike, Lily obeyed. She went through it like a robot, barely seeing the dirty back room, the sleaziness around her. But that act changed her, and changed her relation to Carl. She never forgave him for the abortion. She did not talk about it, to him or to anyone else, until years later. It hardened her toward him. She wasn't sure she wanted a child: the thought terrified her. But the abortion had violated some inner part of her she had not even known to exist. Having a child became tremendously important. It was the sign of victory in the power struggle that her marriage to Carl had become. She got pregnant again a few months later and this time she was adamant. None of Carl's arguments touched her. Not even his refusal to have sex with her could touch her. She did not even have to quit her job: she was fired. Receptionists are not permitted to be visibly pregnant. Carl wanted her to find another, for a few months, at least, but she refused. She was fighting for her right to stay at home and do nothing but care for the apartment. She did still try to keep it to Carl's satisfaction. Carl muttered, and gave up two nights of poker and Saturday nights at Carmine's. Lily clamored to be taken out: Carl took her to a Chinese restaurant once every few weeks. 'You can't have everything,' he said resentfully to her. The baby was a girl, a calm, happy child. Carl ignored it, calling Lily if the baby fussed. Lily was confused. She felt she had won the battle but lost the war.

They moved, under Lily's prodding, to a small house in Jackson Heights. A couple of years later, Lily got pregnant again, and after the baby, an intense, clamorous, wild creature was born, they moved again. Carl had gotten a good job with a New Jersey-based firm; he had money enough to purchase a small house in a suburban neighborhood. He missed his old poker buddies. He sank into domesticity: reading the paper, watching TV, mowing the lawn. He fell into the habit of answering the increasingly clamorous Lily, no matter what she said, with, 'Yeah, Lily, it's okay, it'll be all right.'

6

Carlos was an enormous baby. He had a large head and at two was as big as some four-year-olds. He also had a tempestuous disposition: he was easily frustrated and threw tantrums continually. He reminded Lily of her father. She was terrified of him. He tried continually to climb up on her; he was always reaching for her, touching her, holding on to her legs. And she continually pushed him away. She did not want him on her. She would pick one hand off her ear, only to have him grab her around the neck, would pull that one off only to have him grab her arm. She would peel both his hands away and try to set him down on the floor and he would scream and turn blue.

Lily's denial of the infant (Carl had nothing to do with either child) had seemingly contradictory consequences. On the one hand, he was inordinately shy. He would put his hands over his face if a stranger came into the room; sometimes, although he could walk, he would crawl into a corner and hide from guests, even familiar ones like his grandmother. But he was screamingly aggressive with Lily. As he grew older, he carried both his shyness and his aggression into the outer world. He was violent and abusive with the children he knew, and would run and hide from any strange child.

At five, he no longer tried to touch Lily, and pulled away from her if she touched him. He had picked up his father's unspoken judgments with an acuity that was astonishing. 'You, what are you good for, you ain't good for nothin', you can't even wash the floor right. Why don't you go wash the floor, stupid?' Lily would flutter and scold. When Carl came home, she complained to him. Carl would say, 'He's just a kid, Lily, it's all right, he'll outgrow it.' He'd sit down at the dinner table, and add, 'Beside, he's right; look, you didn't even put forks on the table.'

It was true. Lily was guilty of being a poor housewife. She kept the place clean, but she was disorganized. Her mind was perpetually confused, because she knew she had wanted it, had wanted to be a housewife and stay home with the children, but there was something nagging at her from underneath, somehow she didn't like her life. She decided it was Carl's fault: he never talked to her, never played with the children. She began a campaign of complaint and nagging. Carl would sigh on the nights when she launched into this tirade: he would put down his paper and turn off the TV and sit with crossed arms in his chair and face her.

'Okay, Lily, okay. What do you want to talk about?'

She paused. 'Well – what happened at work today?'

Carl was silent for a long time, pondering. Finally, he said, 'Well, yes, something did happen today. These guys came into the shop with tools and wires and they made holes and they drilled and clasped and strung and worked for about an hour. Then they put a new telephone at the other end of the shop.'

Lily laughed nervously. 'Carl . . .' she began to protest.

He picked his paper up. 'That's it, Lily. That's what happened at work today.'

She would complain that he had nothing to do with the children. For instance, Carlos wouldn't eat anything except cookies and peanut butter sandwiches. He had to learn to eat. Carl would let it slide. 'Okay, Lily, it's all

207

right, he wants to eat peanut butter, let him eat peanut butter.' But every once in a while, when Carlos refused his dinner, Carl would rise up and grab Carlos and haul him up to his room and beat him with his belt. Then Lily would scream and cry and wring her hands. He would look at her blandly. 'Well, what do you want? You were saying he needs to learn. I don't know what you want, Lily.'

Lily was as stubborn as he; her complaints did not cease. The voice swooped up higher and down lower with every passing year. Carl could not stand it anymore. He called his brother and for three months the two of them and assorted friends built a room over the garage. It was a large bright room, with its own bathroom, and a staircase on the outside of the house. It could not be reached from inside. He moved in. He would come home from work and eat with the family. Immediately afterward, he would depart for his room, to which he had the only key. There he would watch TV and read his paper in silent tranquillity, and sleep undisturbed by tentative fingers. Lily clamored when she saw him, but he answered mildly, 'Look, you got the house, you got the kids, I pay the bills. We go out together, don't we? Nobody knows. What have you got to complain about?' It was at about this time that Mira met Lily and wondered at her flashy social appearance. Lily did not seem to be trying to attract men; it never occurred to Mira that Lily was trying to seduce her own husband.

7

Mira's experience was so different. She had completely settled into her new, easier life. The mornings were bad. She hated to get up. Norm had to call her, then shake her, and she would stagger downstairs and hang like an exhausted alcoholic over a clutched mug of coffee.

The children were unhappy in the morning, like her. They would argue and complain about the breakfast. They refused to eat an egg that was cooked too long or not long enough. They no longer liked this cereal. They

208

wanted English muffins, or they wanted toast. She left the kitchen to dress while they lamented their miserable existences, and more often than not, she came back from driving them to the bus stop to throw their breakfasts in the garbage.

After her return, after that heart-sinking moment of coming back to the greasy frying pan and the littered table, there was cleaning. The afternoons, though, were better. Money was plentiful despite all the loans, and one thing Norm was willing to spend it on was the house. So Mira's afternoons were spent in an orgy of planning decor and buying furniture, rugs, draperies, lamps, pictures. Slowly, the house filled up. It got to be hard to handle, so she bought herself a small file box and some packages of 2 x 3 cards. On each card she wrote one task that had to be performed, and filed them in sections. The section headed WINDOW WASHING would contain cards for each room in the house. Whenever she washed the windows in one room, she would mark the date down on the card, and place it at the end of the section. The same was true for FURNITURE POLISHING, RUG SHAMPOOING, and CHINA. Regularly she removed all the dishes from the dining room china closet, washed them by hand – they were good china, not to be entrusted to the dishwasher – and returned them to their freshly washed shelves. She did the same in the kitchen; she did the same thing with the books, removing them, dusting them carefully, and returning them to clean, wiped, and waxed shelves. She did not make cards for ordinary, daily cleaning, only for the large, special tasks. So each day, after the small chores of cleaning kitchen, making beds and cleaning the two main bathrooms, she would also perform a thorough cleaning of one room, washing mirrors and windows, waxing any visible wooden floors, cleaning the small ornaments, dusting ceilings and walls and furniture surfaces, and vacuuming. She would then mark on the appropriate card the large task accomplished. That way, she reasoned, she would always keep up. It took her two weeks to go through the whole house – ten working days. She did not clean on weekends. And extraordinary tasks, like cleaning every dish in the kitchen and pantry, she did only twice a year. The same was true of the curtains. It was good housewifery, performed in the old way. Mira's mother cleaned this way, although without the cards. And had scrubbed sheets and shirts on a scrub board, and walked two miles each way to the market. The Wards' house was always shining and smelled fresh, of lemon oil and soap.

Mira would feel tremendously satisfied when she finished her morning's work. She would bathe then, using expensive bath oil, and smooth an expensive lotion all over her body when she was through. She felt luxurious. She would stand in the door of her enormous closet in a thick velour robe and choose her outfit for the afternoon. She chose her perfume and makeup to complement the outfit. She would walk through the house, dressed to go out, relishing the silence, the order, the shine of polished wood in the sun. Her mother-in-law had given her a clock similar to one she owned, an old-fashioned clock with a great glass dome over it, that struck the hour with chimes, the quarter hours with little bells. It ticked loudly: you could hear it in most of the downstairs rooms. She walked listening to its ticking, feeling the order and the peace, the cleanliness, the comfort. She would walk to the kitchen; the morning light had slid away, and the paler light shone on the old hutch, making the clean china pieces, old pitchers and cups, charming unmatched plates standing on end on the shelves, gleam and reflect. The beauty was her doing. The clock ticked.

She would go out then on a shopping expedition, or to do errands, or on an infrequent visit to one of her friends. The boys were older now; she could tarry a bit, and not get home until four. But she was usually annoyed when she did get home. There was always something, it seemed: muddy footprints, finger marks on a clean wall, a blackened towel. She would rage at the boys; they largely ignored her. They did not understand, she knew that. The cleanliness and order were her life, they had cost her everything.

210

When she came home, it was usually to go out again: the boys had appointments with the dentist, the orthodontist, games with Little League, Scout meetings, Clark had violin lessons, Normie, trumpet lessons. On Saturday mornings she took them for riding lessons, waited and took them back, while Norm went out to play golf. Her nights were calmer than they had been. Norm was very busy these days, and often did not come home for dinner. She fell into the habit of feeding the boys early, and continued it even on nights when he did come home. It was better: they could eat and go off and do homework and then watch TV, or on summer evenings, go out and play ball for a while before baths and bed. Norm was more pleasant at the dinner table when the boys were not there. After about nine o'clock, she was free. Norm would sit watching TV, she would glance up at it and back at her book, but he tired early and went to bed. She liked sitting there alone, listening to the silence of the sleeping house, the night noises outdoors – a barking dog, a car starting up – all measured by the ticking clock.

In nice weather, she worked in the garden. She would drive to the nursery in the spring and pick up boxes of spring flowers, pansies, violets, crocuses, iris, lilies of the valley, daffodils, and jonquil, and set them lovingly in the damp sweet-sour earth. The air was soft and a little wet, and she enjoyed feeling the cool, damp, dungy earth in her hands. She stood, looking around, planning the garden. She would buy white wrought-iron pieces with delicate tracery, and set them there, by the rock garden. She bought lounges for the patio, and glass-topped tables. She hung a bird feeder.

When Norm did not come home for dinner, or when he ate and went out again to a meeting, Mira would spend the evening reading. Then, at about eleven, she would pour herself a drink and turn out the lights and sit and think. He never came in very late, always by twelve, and he always tripped on the doorstep from garage to kitchen hall, and he always yelled out complaining, 'Why the hell don't you keep a light on?' Still, she never left it on.

She would offer food, but he was never hungry. He would pour himself a rye – Canadian Club – or a brandy, and sit across from her with the light turned on.

'How was your day?'

'Okay,' he'd sigh. His collar button was undone, his tie pulled loose, and he looked tired. That burn case was coming along better; that case of hives was more serious than they'd thought – it was internal now. Poor Mrs. Waterhouse, whom he'd sent over to Bob, had CA, it had spread, there was no hope. They could give radiation treatments, but that would only prolong the agony. Her children wanted to do it, however. He'd explained, and so had Bob, that it was a great expense and could do little but prolong. But they insisted: they wanted to feel that they had done everything possible.

'They feel guilty because they want her to die.'

He burst out in exasperation. 'Why do you say a thing like that? That's ridiculous! You don't even know these people and you say a thing like that! They just want to feel they've done all they can for her, left no stone unturned. She's their mother, for God sakes!'

Mira had formed a habit of making little nonsense rhymes in her head. She never wrote them down; she was hardly even conscious she did it. She did it now.

Some birds fly and some birds sink and some birds don't know how to think. She said, 'Because they know it can't help. So the only reason they would want it is to alleviate guilt. And the obvious guilt is their wish for her to die.'

'Mira, that's ridiculous,' he said in disgust. 'You know, some people aren't like you, they have simple motives, they just want to do everything they can for someone they love.'

Love, love, heavens above, we all destroy in the name of love.

Norm changed the subject when she was silent. 'Maurie Sprat was in, remember him? I guess he was two years ahead of you. I knew him because his brother was in my class, great basketball player, Lennie. Maurie says he's vice-president of an aluminum company now, sells house siding or something.' He laughed. 'God, I can't picture that! Skinny Lennie Sprat a successful businessman, that really gets me. Maurie came into the clinic for what he calls a scalp condition – a scalp condition! He's completely bald, can you picture it? Bald as a billiard ball. Funny! He works for a soft-drink company, gave me a good tip: Sunshine is going to merge with Transcontinental Can company, put out soft drinks in cans. I may plunge a little.'

'Plunge?'

'Buy some stock.'

'Oh.'

Silence.

'And what about you? What did you do all day?'

'I cleaned – in here. Doesn't it look shiny?'

He looked around. 'I didn't really notice.'

'And I planted some flowers.'

'Oh, good,' he smiled at her benevolently. She had such a simple, sweet life: she could do things like plant flowers and get pleasure from it. Because he provided her the means.

> *What do you do with yourself all day,*
> *Said little man to little maid,*
> *You have nothing to do but play*
> *Move about dust and tea on a tray*
> *And sing aloud to your heart's content,*
> *While I'm out struggling to pay the rent.*

She cleared her throat and launched into what in her mind she called her column of Family Notes:

'Normie broke a window playing baseball this afternoon.'

'I hope you told him he'd have to pay for it out of his allowance!'

'He didn't mean to do it.'

'I don't care. He's got to learn responsibility!'

'All right, Norm. I'll tell him you said . . .'

'Why do you always have to make me the heavy? I'd think you'd be just as interested in his getting a little

213

sense of responsibility! That kid thinks money grows on trees.'

In my yard is a little money tree;
It flowers and it flowers, but none of it's for me.
I rake and hoe and water to keep the tree in health,
And all the neighbor women envy me my wealth.
But all the little dollars growing on that tree
Belong to Norm the Doctor, none of them to me.

'Yes, Norm. And Clark got an A on a math test.'

'Good, good.' He rose. He sighed. He was tired. He put his glass down on the wooden tabletop. 'I'm going to bed,' he said. 'Big day tomorrow.'

Big day tomorrow. She heard him finish in the bathroom, was aware of the bedroom light being turned off. She rose and picked up his glass. She rubbed the table with the sleeve of her robe, drying it and erasing the watermark. She carried his glass into the kitchen, returned, poured herself another brandy, and turned off the light. She never went to bed when he did if she could help it.

8

Big day tomorrow: she wondered what that felt like. All her tomorrows were big days – tomorrow, for instance, she would tackle the living room. Yet they were not big days. What would that be like, a big day? The only way she could envision such a thing was to imagine going out early, just getting in the car and driving – oh, driving anywhere, to Manhattan, say, and going to – oh, a museum, or on a boatride around the island. Just not doing her work, letting it go. Not coming home on time, leaving the kids, letting them fend for themselves. Coming home late, as late as Norm, a little drunk, maybe.

No, of course she would not do such a thing. She did not even want to. The kids would be worried, frightened. Norm did his part, she would do hers. She did.

214

Some nights, the conversation ran differently. Norm would come home perhaps a little earlier; he would be in a gay mood. She always recognized, with a little heartfall, the occasion. Then, after she'd asked him about his day, he would turn to her with a special sweet smile on his face and say, 'And what did the little mother do today?'

Mira knew that Norm thought she was a wonderful mother. Not that he said so to her, but she'd heard him say it to other people, and he frequently mentioned it when he was scolding the boys: 'Why did you do something like that to worry your mother, when you know what a wonderful mother she is?' He himself had no patience with them. They always seemed to spill the milk when he was sitting at the lunch table with them; they always came home crying about some childhood tragedy on days when he was there to lay contempt on them for it. But somehow, whenever Norm asked her this question, her insides curled up. And he always had that same smile on his face, coy and fatherly at the same time, a smile you would use on a little girl who had just climbed up into your lap. It always made Mira blush, or at least feel hot in the face. And she'd stammer out something about the price of loin lamb chops or meeting Mrs. Stillman at the dry cleaner or the vote to buy Christmas trees for each classroom taken by today's meeting of the PTA. Whatever she said she would stammer out with the high color and tongue-tripping of the novice adulteress. But he never seemed to notice. Perhaps he expected her to be nervous when he interrogated her, like the string of young receptionists continually being hired and fired at the office, or like the young women who consulted him whispering about vaginal rash and who were breathless, blushing, and soft-spoken in response to his shot-out questions.

He would listen, patiently, tolerantly to her trivialities, wanting to show his affection, waiting for her to finish. Then he would gaze at her kindly, stretch a little, and say, 'Coming to bed?' as if it were a question. Sometimes she would say, 'I think I'll look at the paper

215

first,' or 'I'm not really tired yet,' but he would simply put his hand out to her and she knew, she knew she had to stand up, to take his hand, to go to bed with him. She had no other choice. She knew it: so did he. It was an unwritten law. Maybe it was even a written law: he had rights over her body even when she did not want him to. Dutifully she would rise, but something inside her squirmed and squealed. She felt like a peasant girl commandeered by a noble in the *droit de seigneur.* She felt bought and paid for, and it was all of a piece; the house, the furniture, she, all were his, it said so on some piece of paper. He'd check lights and locks as she stood there, then come back and put his arm around her and gently propel her up the stairs and into the bedroom. Her reluctance seemed to please him.

And she would feel her body moving differently from usual. Sometimes she would see a woman in the beauty shop, sometimes in the street, who moved the way she felt she was moving, as if their hips and arms and necks were borrowed pieces of porcelain that had to be taken special care of, as if they were jewels that belonged to someone else, as if movement did not arise in muscle and bone but was dictated by some outer music. Such bodies were not connections of bone and muscle, fat and nerve. Like slave girls brought in to dance for the sheik, they were soft tender skin oiled in warm baths and perfumed: for him. Their bodies existed only in the eye and hand of the owner even when he was not present. She remembered seeing Bliss move this way in the days when she had started to sing all the time. Mira had thought Bliss was moving to the music she sang. She did not know how her own movements looked, but they felt like that.

Norm always insisted she come into his bed, and he always insisted on using rubbers. Her diaphragm lay drying in a box in her bed table. She would lie there waiting for him to get it on – he always had trouble with them – already feeling helpless and violated. Then he would lie down and lean toward her and take her nipple in his mouth and suck it until it hurt and she would push

216

his head away. He assumed that meant she was ready, and he entered her, came in a few seconds, head thrown back, eyes shut, hands on her body but mind a thousand miles away, and she would lie there watching him with grim sarcasm, wondering what he was thinking about, what movie star or patient's body, or perhaps just a color or scent, he was imagining. It was over fast and he never looked at her. He got right up and went into the bathroom and cleaned himself thoroughly. By the time he returned she had gone to her own bed and closed her eyes and was soothing her genitals into relaxation. He would say, 'Good night, sweetie,' get in bed and fall instantly to sleep. She would lie there soothing herself for a half hour or longer until she became aroused, than masturbate for fifteen or twenty minutes until she came and when she came she would cry, hard, bitter tears that she did not understand, for at the moment of orgasm the thing she felt besides relief was emptiness, an agonizing, cruel, and hopeless vacuum.

Over the years, Mira had picked up a little sexual knowledge. She had, for some months, tried to get Norm to make love in a somewhat more tender way, but he was totally resistant to change. He believed that anything other than what he did impeded his pleasure, and that seemed to him wrong, unnatural. The only other act he was willing to perform was fellatio, and that Mira firmly vetoed. On the whole, Norm probably felt that what was pleasant for him was pleasant for her, or if it were not, it was because like so many women, she was frigid. Mira gave up her attempts to change him, but she sought other ways to make the whole thing less wretched for her. She would try to think of other things, to let him do what he wanted and keep her mind elsewhere. But she was never successful at this because the moment his head came down on her breast, she was so full of rage that she could not concentrate on anything else. And no matter how short it was, she felt violated and used and willess, and every month, every year, this feeling grew. She dreaded the least sign of desire in him. Fortunately, these signs appeared less and less often.

9

Things were changing for Mira's friends. Paula and Brett were divorced and Paula remarried a man remarkably like Brett, only a shade more alive and considerably better off. Roger and Doris were divorced and Doris was grim and bitter, working in a state office typing out forms all day. Samantha had announced gaily that she was bored and was getting a job. Mira was appalled: the baby, Hughie, was only three, and even Fleur was still really a baby at six. She put it down to greed. Samantha no longer had dyed hair, and her cheek color was her own, but she still walked like a mechanical doll. And things kept happening: Fleur was taken sick at school while Sam was at work, and a neighbor had to care for the child, who was running a high fever. Hughie, whom Sam left all day with the same neighbor, fell out of a tree house and broke his wrist and was languishing for hours in the hospital emergency room before Sam could get there and sign the permission to treat him. Mira pressed her lips together at such news. It was all because Sam wasn't home that these things happened. If she had been home with her children as she should have been, things wouldn't have been so bad, and they might not have happened at all. She, Mira, would certainly never have allowed a three-year-old son of hers to play in a tree house. Mira was cool and disapproving whenever Sam called with the latest catastrophe.

Sean and Oriane had moved to the Bahamas and bought a boat and were living, according to her letters, the paradisal life of the rich on Sean's inheritance from his father. And Martha had gone back to school. She started part-time, and when she did well, matriculated as a full-time student. She wanted, she said, to be a lawyer. Mira pressed her lips at that too. It was absurd. Norm agreed. By the time Martha finished all her training, she would be thirty-seven or -eight. Who was going to hire a middle-aged, novice female lawyer? She wouldn't even get into law school, Norm assured Mira. Mira believed it. All she had to do was look around her to know it was true. 'Well, if it amuses her,' Mira would say finally, brushing past the real reason for her unhappiness. For few of her friends were available anymore: everybody was at work, at school, at study, or just gone. She saw them mostly at an occasional evening get-together. Then something happened to end that.

It was Lily's idea. She had not been out in ages, she said, and neither had her friends Sandra and Geraldine, so why didn't they all get together, the old crowd, and all go bowling together? Martha and George, Samantha and Simp, Mira and Norm, Lily and Carl, and the two new couples, old friends of Carl's and Lily's. It sounded like fun; they agreed.

They sat in the bowling bay, talking when it wasn't their turn, ordering great trays of drinks from the bar. Mira was glad to see them. She wondered at Sam, who looked tight and tired, but who bubbled over as much as ever about the latest catastrophe in her household. Simp was suave in his usual slimy, intimate way; he was drinking double martinis at a great rate, but alcohol never showed on him. Martha looked happy. She was tiny and delicate, with skin like porcelain and large deep blue eyes. She looked sweet, which was possibly the reason she so shocked people.

'Oh, what a fucking idiot!' she was saying, laughing at George. 'That asshole! I told him it was wrong but he wouldn't look, he wouldn't come down and step back and *look!* He just kept on going like a blind fucking idiot! He stopped when the panel he was about to put up slanted so much it was almost parallel with the staircase molding. God!' she laughed. 'Each one had slanted just a little more. I screamed at him, but, oh, that man is useless.'

George sat looking at her without expression, but Sam was uncomfortable with the form of Martha's criticism. Had it been couched in the usual laughter and in milder language, it would have been a funny story, but there was too much real anger in Martha's voice amid

219

the laughter, and her diction was too strong.

'Oh, well,' Sam's voice swooped comfortingly down, 'George is a poet, not a carpenter. Simp had an awful time hanging a lamp and my father finally had to come over to help us. Remember, Simp?' she turned to him brightly.

'Sam, I could of gotten it up myself. It was Hughie – he kept picking up the screws and losing them.'

'Oh, Simp!'

'It's true!' he almost whined. 'That kid gets into everything.'

'Well, at least George tries,' Mira said stiffly. 'Norm doesn't even bother. Last week I had to restring a venetian blind all by myself. Norm sat there watching a football game.'

'Well, he works all week, Mira,' Carl said lazily.

'What do you think I do?' she retorted sharply.

'And this way,' Carl continued as if he hadn't heard her, 'he got to watch the football game and your ass all at once.'

George kept out of the conversation triggered by his inadequacies. He usually kept out of conversations, and when he talked, it was to the women. George worked in an anonymous job for a large corporation. He wrote poetry in his spare time, but never showed it to anyone. He had fixed up primitively some space in the attic where he kept his collection of mystical books and where he spent most of his time when he was home. They had two children and a nine-year-old jalopy that Martha never set foot in without first kicking and cursing. George was considered strange by the men and some of the women. This was because he never stood in the kitchen talking about football and cars. He always sat with the women, sometimes talking, more often silent. He had confided to Mira that he preferred women – they were, he said, more alive, more interesting, more sensitive. They were involved with other people – the men were not. When George did talk, he always hooked the conversation to some mystic doctrine or other: he could talk for hours about the Kabala or the

Vedas. No one was interested; no one listened. And if that were not enough to disqualify him from manliness, he wore his body like a slippery garment hung on a wire hanger. His arms dangled, his knees dipped; he often looked as if he were about to fall over. Mira thought he was ashamed of having a body at all, and that when he was in his 'study,' he lost it. Yet George liked to dance, and did it well, and he was, Martha said often, a great lover.

'You ought to try George,' Martha said whenever Mira complained about her sex life with Norm. 'I'm serious. He's good.' Mira would gaze at her a little incredulously. She had never heard a woman say that about her husband. 'Any problems we have in sex are my doing,' Martha would insist. 'The lovemaking is great; I just can't get it off.'

'What about when you masturbate?'

'I can't. Can't masturbate. I can't have an orgasm no matter what, and George is willing – God, he's even happy – to spend hours helping me. Nothing works. I think I may go to a shrink.'

After their turns, Mira and Martha sat down together apart from the others.

'Lily's friends are a strange lot,' Mira said disapprovingly.

'Yeah, unusual.' They examined the four surruptitiously. Harry was short and fat and gray-faced. They had heard that he did something illegal, was a bookie or something, but he didn't fit any movie-criminal image they knew. He seemed sad and tired, and lifted his eyelids with effort. Tom was huge; tall and muscular, he looked as if he used his body for heavy work. He was dark-haired, and sat or stood apart from those who were strange to him, glaring out under heavy dark eyebrows. His wife also remained aloof, not near him, but not far from him. She was wearing a pale blue dress with silver threads through it, made of a sleazy fabric, formfitting. She had a good body. She had exchanged pale blue satin heels for bowling shoes, but they stood on the floor under the bench where she'd lain her silver bag.

She had dyed blond hair piled high on her head, and false eyelashes. It was a strange outfit to go bowling in.

Lily managed to knock down three pins, and sighing, turned and joined Martha and Mira. She sank on the bench. She too was dressed for a party, wearing a satin blouse with her slacks and a rhinestone comb in her hair.

'That Geraldine is really something,' Martha said.

Geraldine was short, like her husband, and a little plump, but shapely. She was tremendously energetic: she spoke, handled her ball and rolled it down the alley all in gusts of strength that didn't seem to end.

'Yes, she's sexy. She always was,' Lily said.

Mira looked at the woman intently. What was that – sexy? What was it about her that made people call her that? She was no more attractive than any of them, certainly not more than Lily. Her body was, in Mira's thin view, overweight. She did not wiggle it, or arch it, or any of the things Mira had seen other women do. Yet the men seemed fascinated by her.

'That – what's his name, Lily? – the big man? . . .'

'Tom.'

'Yes. He looks as if he hates her.'

The man was watching Geraldine bowl, his face smoldering.

'Yes,' Lily sighed. 'He's strange. Geraldine is a good kid, she's fun, alive, you know? Tom is just – oh, I don't know. They're all from the old neighborhood, Carl and Tom and Harry and Dina, they all grew up together, except Dina's much younger. They're all strange, those men, they all believe in the old ways. Carl is bad, but Tom is the worst. They don't know how to live, those men. They only know how to kill. Harry's okay, he's pretty good to Geraldine, except these Mafia types in big black cars keep coming around to terrify her every once in a while. I guess Harry gets in trouble with them. Poor Sandra, she never gets out of the house. Tom keeps her under lock and key. That's why I planned this evening – I though it would help her, give her a little break.'

'You don't mean he literally locks her up!' Mira exclaimed.

'Well . . . She lives in a little house in Farmington, miles from stores, and she doesn't have a car.'

'She must have friends with cars.'

Lily looked away evasively. 'Ye-es, I suppose.'

Geraldine got a strike. She jumped up and down and clapped her hands and turned to Carl with glowing eyes and cried, 'I'm great, ain't I, Carlie?' and hugged him and George, who was standing next to him, and ran over to Sandra and hugged her. She pranced over to the three women and flopped on the bench beside them.

'Did'ja see that?'

Her warm brown eyes smiled directly at you. She babbled on happily about her poor bowling, her improvement, and watched the others in their turn, crying with joy at a good score, oohing in pity at a poor one. When it was her turn again, she marched to position singing *ta-da!*

She was, in fact, the center of more emotions than she knew. Everyone watched her, and everyone responded. Samantha envied Geraldine's spontaneity and gaiety, but she did not like the way Simp acted with her: 'She's desperate, that's what I think, frantic, you know?' Sam appealed to Mira and Martha. Mira agreed, but thought she was also innocent. 'That's a dangerous combination. I'm a little worried for her.'

Martha cackled. 'Christ, what a fool you are! She's a calculating bitch in heat!'

'Oh, she just likes attention,' Lily demurred mildly. 'She's always been like that. She doesn't mean any harm.'

'She's great!' Martha said. 'I love her! But she's still a calculating bitch in heat.'

The men's response was not verbal. Simp, seeming not to notice that she acted the same way to everyone, slid beside her and insinuated an arm around her, smiling his intimate smile close to her face. Norm held stiffly aloof from her, but his eyes followed her; Carl, too, was distant, but whenever she came up to him, he smiled and put an arm around her. But Tom watched her gloweringly, and when she hopped up to him, teasing him about something, he spat some words at her and turned away. Harry sat on the bench smiling mildly and sleepily at everything. Whenever she came up to him, she put an arm around him, or hugged him, or touched him in some way. He remained impassive, but smiled at her blankly.

They finished bowling and went into the restaurant for more drinks and some food. The restaurant was a large blank room with long tables and a jukebox. A bar extended the length of one wall. The place looked poor and not especially clean; only a few teenagers stood at the bar. Norm curled his lip and glared at Mira.

This is the sort of place *your* friends frequent, he was saying, silently.

'No husbands next to wives!' Samantha ordered. It was an old tradition with the friends, adopted in an effort to improve conversation. The group dutifully changed places, although they had been friends for so many years now that the split provided no real novelty. But Tom glowered at Sam. He sat his wife at the end of the table, and himself beside her next to Lily. He spoke to no one. Mira found herself at the end of the table next to Harry, with George on her other side. Geraldine was already on the floor, feeding coins into the jukebox. She danced back to the table.

'Who wants to dance?'

Simp jumped up. Other couples followed. Norm led Samantha to the dance floor. Tom and Sandra were left at one end of the table, Harry and Mira at the other.

'You're different, huh?'

'Different?'

'I'm different too.'

'Oh?'

'I live in a sewer. Don't I look it?'

She gazed at him disapprovingly.

'I'll bet your husband is a lousy lover.'

'I beg your pardon!'

'I can tell, I can always tell,' he said easily, his sleepy

224

eyes sliding around the room searching for the waitress. He signaled for another drink. He turned back to Mira. 'You don't have to get on your high horse with me. It ain't worth it.'

She sipped her drink. Her words had sounded priggish even in her own ears. She stared down at the table.

'I'm a lousy lover too,' he continued easily, speaking in a soft foggy voice, barely moving his lips, his face impassive. He was not even looking at her; he seemed to be gazing tiredly into space. 'Yeah, poor Geraldine, she didn't know, she married me when she was sixteen, she begged me to marry her so I did, poor kid, she had a father that was always beating up on her, she had to get out of the house. I was twenty-five, I'd known her all her life, on the block, you know? She has three kids now, look at her, you'd never know it, would you? Just a kid herself. But I can't do nothin' for her, not anymore. For years now it's like this. If I'm away from her, I call her up, I come all over the place just talkin' to her, you know? Just hearin' her voice. I don't do anything, it just happens by itself. It pours out all over my pants and down my leg. But when I'm with a woman, I can't do nothin'. It isn't just Geraldine. I've tried. I can't do nothin'.'

The dancers returned when the music changed to rock. Simp asked Mira to dance; she stood up instantly. Geraldine was leading Carl in some combination of lindy and the twist. When the dance ended, Mira pulled a chair over from another table and sat between Martha and Samantha. Harry sat alone at the end of the table, gazing at the wall. Geraldine was riding high. She flew around the room with any partner she could drum up.

The pizzas arrived, and everyone but Geraldine began to eat.

'Food, food, how can you think of food!' She danced by herself, hovering near the table. 'Hey, Harry, come on, sweetie!'

Harry did not turn to her, but nodded his head no.

'Carlie?' The music changed to a slow tune. 'Oh! This is my favorite song!' Geraldine exclaimed, near tears.

225

Sandra gazed at her with love. 'I'll dance with you, Dina,' she said pityingly.

Tom's large hand came down swiftly on her midarm, pounced and pulled her back hard into the chair.

'Ow!' she wailed.

'You SIT!' he commanded.

George stood up. 'I'll dance with you, baby,' he said kindly, leaving his half-eaten slice of pizza.

Geraldine pressed her body into his, and they swayed together. More drinks arrived. When the pizza was gone couples stood to dance. A group of young men in black leather jackets, carrying motorcycle helmets, invaded the room. They gathered at the bar. Norm looked meaningfully at Mira. She ignored his lowering, but prepared herself to leave soon, gathering her cigarettes and lighter from the table, stuffing them in her purse. Geraldine replayed her favorite song. The other couples sat down. She and George remained on the floor boredly moving, swaying, pressed closely together. Martha leaned forward and tried to talk to Sandra, but Sandra could barely raise her eyes. She mumbled brief answers. Every once in a while, Tom would remove his eyes from Geraldine to check on Sandra, the way one might check a prisoner taken earlier in the battle to make sure he did not start something while the fighting was still going on. The prisoner's hands were tied behind his back and his feet fastened together, and you had thrown him in a corner of the trench, but meanwhile they were shooting at you out there and you had to shoot back and your face was smudged with mud and soot and was furious and watchful, but you had to turn around every once in a while to make sure the prisoner hadn't loosened his bonds, wasn't just then struggling to his feet ready to pick up a fallen rifle with bayonet attached and stab you through the back. Although she was looking at the table in front of her. Sandra's eyes flickered every time he looked at her; she perceived it from a corner of her eye.

The music changed to a rhumba. Geraldine and George were still dancing close together, but now, instead of simply swaying, they were moving their hips together, bumping each other gently as if they were screwing. Sandra had just mumbled an answer to Martha's question about her children when suddenly Tom leaped up so fast and hard that his chair fell over, strode across the floor and began to punch George. George put his hands up over his face. Everyone else leaped up. Carl and Simp tried to grab Tom's arms. Samantha cried out, 'Simp! Your teeth! Watch your teeth!' She grabbed Tom's jacket; Tom flailed out at Simp, who ducked, then Tom pulled at Simp's arm and tore the sleeve right out of his jacket. The women crowded in, pummeling Tom and trying to push him away from George, who was now sitting on a barstool with his arms crossed over his crouched head. The bouncer came from behind the bar. He was smaller than Tom, but he was able to grab his arms and propel him toward the door. At the doorway, Tom turned, said something to the bouncer, who did not let go of him. Tom looked back at the table, at Sandra, who was standing paralyzed and white.

'Get your ass out here!' he shouted. Sandra grabbed her bag and coat and scurried out.

'He didn't even pay for their fucking drinks,' George said afterward in disgust.

10

Norm tightened his mouth, took Mira by the elbow so firmly it hurt, and said good night. She was grateful that the next day, when the phone rang for hours, he was out playing golf. That was it, he had said. He would no longer be involved with such a crude bunch. She argued that it was Tom who was crude and he was not one of their friends. He refused to argue. He would no longer go to parties, invite, or in any way associate with any of them. That was that.

'They're my friends, Norm!' Mira protested.

He looked at her coldly. 'That's your problem. They're not mine.'

'I go to all your boring doctor dinners,' she said almost in tears.

'My friends are polite and proper. I don't impose rowdiness and riot on you.'

'If you won't go to their parties, I'll go alone,' she insisted stubbornly.

'You will not,' he said in a low, grim voice.

She thought about Sandra's face when Tom pulled her down, and thought she knew how the woman had felt. There was no way out from them. Just no way out. She would not, of course she would not. He would not permit her to. She was a full-grown woman of thirty-two, but needed permission to do something just as if she were a child. She sat smoldering, feeling helpless.

But the next day, when the phone rang, full of explanations, interpretations, and compared notes, she felt herself retreat from all of it. It was too gross.

Samantha bubbled on about it with glee and excitement. She had had only one thought, she admitted giggling: Simp's new bridgework. He had had all his teeth capped in the past year, and it had cost them fifteen hundred dollars. She was shocked at George's cowardice, she felt sorry for Martha. And wasn't that Tom crazy!

Lily was full of sorrow for Sandra: imagine what her life was like, she said.

'One night, me and her went to a Tupperware party. Oh, it was nothing, stupid, for the stupid housewives, you know, but it was a chance to get out, so I asked her if she wanted to go, and she worked on Tom and finally, she came. I picked her up and drove her to my friend Betty's, and they had the party, and when it was over and everybody else had gone home, Betty brought out a bottle and we had some drinks. Oh, we had so much fun! We talked and laughed. It felt so good. Anyway, we stayed sort of late; I guess it was around midnight when I took Sandra home. We walked in the house – we were having so much fun, we didn't want to stop, so Sandra said I had to come in for coffee because I was too drunk to drive – and Tom is sitting there on the couch in front of the TV, and he takes one look at her and leaps up and smacks her across the face so hard he knocked her down. Then he started for me. I ran.'

'He would have hit you?' Mira was appalled.

'Sure. He'd think he was doing Carl a favor.'

'Lily!'

'Oh, that's how they are. You don't know. The old ways, the old neighborhood.'

Mira told Lily what Harry had said to her. Lily was not surprised.

'Yeah, poor Harry. He's not a bad guy. We all come out of nothing, you know? Brutality was the way of life. Without it, the men felt like they were nothing, you know?'

She felt sorry for George, but had a little contempt for him.

'When you're dealing with people like that, you have to deal in their terms,' she said with grim strength.

Sandra and Tom were never heard from again. Harry and Geraldine popped off rather cheerfully once George's face had been cleaned off, and Lily and Carl continued to see them.

But Mira was deeply preoccupied by the response of her friends to the event. She mulled it over for weeks. Whatever their opinions, they felt the evening to have been high drama. Something had happened: something true. It was almost as if – she hated to give expression even to the thought – they envied Tom his directness. Their own lives were filled with subtleties: subtle power games, subtle punishments, subtle rewards. This Tom might be a barbarian, but there was something clean and clear about his way of proceeding.

Only Martha disagreed. Alone of the friends, Martha did not blame George. Geraldine had been coming on strong, George had taken her up on it. He wasn't pressing her, wasn't abusing her. That was all natural. So Tom has the hots for Geraldine and punches George in a puritanical projection of his own lust. What is George to do? Tom has seventy pounds and many thicknesses of body over him. He defended himself by protecting himself: the intelligent, the nonviolent thing to do.

Mira hesitantly confessed her confusions to Martha, her sense that most of the women had enjoyed the scene, had found it revitalizing. Why, do you suppose?'

Martha smiled grimly. 'Well, you ought to know, Mira,' she said with sweet acid.

Mira stared at her.

'They see in the relation of Tom and Sandra the truth about their own, the concrete form of their relations with their husbands. Isn't that what you see?'

Mira shook her head. That was ridiculous. Norm would never strike her, nor was she terrified of him. She went home from Martha's feeling irritable. Norm was right. Her friends had no manners, no grace. Why couldn't they be more . . . acceptable! She really felt Norm had a point. She would have to accept his decree. She decided she would see her friends only during the days. But she didn't want to see Martha for a while. Martha was entirely too bitchy. She would see only Lily and Sam.

But even that became difficult.

By the age of six, Lily's son Carlos was pure monster. He was alternately abusive and almost catatonically timid. When he went to school his timid side showed. He spoke rarely, did not do his work, and would not even answer the teacher when she spoke to him. But once out of school and back on his own block, he taunted the other children, he beat them up, he called names, threw rocks, rang doorbells, and ran away.

His behavior did not improve with age. By the time he was eight, he was known and labeled in the neighborhood. The children his own age, all of whom were smaller than he, ran away from him at sight. Over the years they had communicated their problem to their older brothers, if they had them. The older children began to retaliate. They would get him on the way to school, for he was always most timid then; they would gang up on him, hit him, throw him down, tear his clothes. He would run home crying; he refused to go to school. Lily, hysterical, ran to the school and asked them

230

to do something about it. She cried to Carl to find a way to stop it. She took to driving Carlos to school and picking him up afterward.

But sometimes he had to be alone. One afternoon he walked by himself around the corner to a candy store to get an ice-cream cone. A gang of kids saw him and followed him, and when he came out, they surrounded him. Taunting and jeering, they forced him to walk some distance from his house to an empty lot behind a deserted gas station. They smeared the ice cream on his face. They sent one of their number for rope. They waited, still taunting, jeering, threatening. Carlos was hysterical, but they were too many even for his fierce strength. When the rope arrived, they tied a noose around his neck and tried to hang him from the branch of a tree. They had trouble because he was so large and was fighting so hard. The tree branch proved too slender to hold his weight, and they were unable to climb to a higher one and drag him at the same time. They argued and talked in high angry voices that pierced the dusky light of the autumn afternoon.

They finally decided to use the edge of the sloping roof of the gas station building. They dragged him over to it, he screaming, punching, kicking. They put the noose around his neck and one of the children climbed up on the roof and fastened the rope around its chimney. He clambered down and they looked. They couldn't figure out how to make him hang. All the movies they had seen on TV had horses. One decided to run off for a bicycle.

A woman who lived nearby heard the arguing and crying; she was used to it, glanced out from her front windows and saw only a bunch of kids, arguing as usual. But it kept up, which was not usual. She looked again and saw a child with a noose around his neck standing in front of the abandoned gas station. She called the police. They arrived like the cavalry; the children fled, except for Carlos, who stood there crying hysterically, the loose rope dangling on his body.

The policemen crouched down, they pulled the rope

off him, they tried to calm him and to ask him who he was and where he lived and who had done this to him. But Carlos only cried. They tried to get him into the police car and he kicked them and called them bastards and broke loose and ran. The policemen leaped into their car and followed him. They went up to the house nearest to the yard he had darted into and rang the doorbell. Lily answered it, Andrea standing behind her. Yes, she had a son with blond hair and blue eyes, yes, he was home, yes, he'd just come in – She tried to follow what they were saying. They insisted on coming in to see if he was all right. She led them to Carlos' room; he looked up when they entered, staring, defiant, outraged. One of the policemen crouched beside the bed on which the child was lying and spoke gently to him. The policeman examined his neck, asked him calmly who the other children were, asked if they had hurt him, if he was all right. Carlos would not open his blue lips.

Lily was confused. Carlos had come flying in the back door, she had turned to him with a smile, saying, 'Hello,' and he screamed, 'Bitch! Useless bitch!' at her and flew to his room and slammed the door. She had been about to go to his room when the doorbell rang, and now here were these policemen, and they were talking to him and he was not answering. What had he done? Her large eyes deepened in her skull. The dark circles around them absorbed them until her eyeholes looked like the sockets in a fleshless skull. The police left. She turned to Andrea. 'What? What was it?'

Eleven-year-old Andrea explained what had happened. She explained it over and over again, as Lily asked, 'Yes, what was it? What did he do?' Finally Lily understood. Some boys had tried to hang her child. Hang him. Literally. Kill him. Lily began to mutter.

By the time Carl came home from work, Lily was pacing the house, talking wildly, crying, thrusting her fists at the air, screaming at some invisible enemy who seemed to live in the ceiling. She would stop walking suddenly, raise her face and fist and scream at him. Whoever he was, he was a bastard, he was a fucker, he was a shit. Carl tried to find out what was the matter, but he couldn't understand what she was saying. Andrea watched, said nothing until he turned to her.

'What the hell is going on?'

She did not understand either, but she told him what she knew. Carl tried to steer Lily to a chair.

'It's okay, Lily, it'll be all right. Come on, sit down. Come on.'

She sat, but she raved. Carl went to check on Carlos, who was still lying on his bed. He would not speak to his father, but he did not vilify him. He never vilified his father. Carl assured himself that Carlos was all right, and returned to Lily.

'Listen, Lily, it's nothing. I did the same thing when I was a kid. Me and the kids in the neighborhood tried to hang some pansy on the block. It was all right. No harm done. Just kids. That's the way kids are.'

His voice was soothing, smoothing, shrugging. It was nothing. Lily got wilder.

He shrugged. 'Kids are rotten, Lily, people are rotten, nothing you can do about that. He's okay.'

Lily quieted a bit. She would not look at him, she was still staring out at some malevolent being, but she quieted. As her noise diminished, Carlos, perked up his ears. He got off the bed and opened his door.

'Come on now, Lily, I'll get you a drink,' Carl was saying.

Carlos slipped down the hall and the steps, and sat on a step just out of sight of the living room. His father brought his mother a drink. She sipped it. He sipped his. She was no longer gasping or crying; she was quiet.

'But listen, Lily,' Carl began again, 'why did you let him go to the store alone? You know you should have gone with him. And when he didn't come back right away, how come you didn't go out looking for him?'

Lily began to breathe deeply again. Carlos moved down two steps. His large feeling eyes, eyes like his mother's, watched. Carl's voice, as smooth as ever, shifted from comfort to complaint.

'You know the kid has troubles. So how come you let him go out alone?'

She started to answer. She sat up straight and said, 'My God, Carl, he's eight years old, he can walk to the corner store and get an ice cream, he has to, what will he do if he's never allowed to be free . . .' and then her voice rose again and she was off, crying, screaming, tearing at her hair. Carl rose, disgusted.

'For God's sake, Lily,' he protested, but it was useless. Her clamor filled the house. Carlos came down to the bottom of the stairs and watched. He felt satisfied. He had known it was all his mother's fault.

11

At seven thirty, Carl called Mira. Could she come over? At the time she thought he had called her because he simply didn't know what to do. Later, she thought he had called her because he wanted someone else to do it, he wanted to be justified.

Lily was pacing and raving when Mira entered. When she saw her friend, she ran over to her, crying, gesticulating, and Mira embraced her stiffly, then Lily broke away. Her eyes were tragic and earnest; she was trying to tell Mira something. Mira concentrated on Lily's face. She listened, nodding. Lily calmed a little. Mira said, 'Let's sit down, and then you tell me.'

They sat together on the couch; Carl sat across the room. Lily talked and jumbled everything together. Mira would stop her, patiently, and ask questions. Sometimes Lily would start to rave again. Then Mira would put her hand out and touch Lily's arm lightly, gently. Lily would start and look with terror at Mira, who would then smile kindly and ask Lily to explain again. Finally, Mira got the story, but she still did not have the explanation for Lily's state.

'Well, of course you're upset, some kids tried to kill your child.'

But that was not it. Lily raved and cried. 'Roots, roots, roots!' she screamed. 'You need roots! But how

234

can you have them when everywhere they try to kill you? I tried to make a home for them, in a neighborhood, and what happens? Where do we go now? A strange place, no roots! I need roots!'

After a long time, Mira began to make some connections. Home, security, terror, and violence were all connected in Lily's mind. The contradictions among them, or perhaps their consanguinity, was driving her mad. Without someplace where one can feel safe, where one can sleep, one goes mad. Mira tried to say this to Lily.

'So you feel you and your children are unsafe, that you have no place to go, that . . .'

But Lily wasn't hearing. Her voice reached another register. It swirled around them like a noose. She went round and round and round, repeating herself, unhearing, clamorous, in agony. She was dizzy with her own feelings, her own voice. She was flying around on a carnival machine that would not stop, she could not make it stop and she screamed and screamed.

'Oh, my God, let me die, I want to die, please, somebody, kill me. Carl, kill me! Mira! Somebody! Kill me! I can't stand it anymore!' She leaped up and ran to the kitchen, Carl and Mira behind her. She had pulled open a drawer, there was a large knife in it, Carl grabbed her, he held her, she was wire and taut against him, she was screaming, 'Kill me, kill me, kill me! I can't stand it!'

After Carl had her wrists tightly in his hands, she stood there slender and vulnerable, her whole body shaking, weeping, 'Please, please, please. Please kill me.'

'I think,' Mira said softly, slowly, amazed at the ease with which she had found the solution. 'you had better take her to the hospital.'

Carl was suddenly in control. It was not until later, much later, that Mira realized this. Yet he probably did not know what he was about. In fairness, that was probably true. The question is, are you responsible for what you do not let yourself know you are doing? Suddenly, everything was different. Carl had Lily's coat in his hands, he had it on her. A moment ago she had been violent, but now she was paste.

'Do you want me to go with you?' Mira asked, anxious. How would he drive and control her at the same time? 'We can put the kids in the back seat and I can hold Lily in the front seat.'

'No, no, Mira it's okay, it's fine, I can manage. If you'd just stay with the kids until I get back . . .'

'I can't. My kids are alone. I'll take them back to my place. You can pick them up there.'

'Sure. Okay.' He put his hand on Lily's back and pushed her gently. 'Okay, Lily, it's okay, come on now,' he kept saying as he pushed her gently toward the door and down the front steps and into the car. He treated her as if she were a bomb that might explode indoors. She had subsided. She must have known the moment Carl took control. She must have been waiting for it; she accepted it totally. Meekly, only whimpering a bit, she left and walked down the steps and got in the car. She was sitting hunched over in the front seat when they drove off.

12

Lily was given a sedative and placed in the violent ward of the hospital for the night. They kept her there for a few days, then told Carl they would either transfer her to a state mental hospital or he could put her in a private one. He put her in an expensive and luxurious private hospital.

Mira thought about it. She concluded it was all Lily's fault. Mira remembered Lily pushing Carlos away, peeling him off her body; remembered Lily giving him cookies when he would not eat lunch; remembered Lily's wild complaints and impossible demands. She pressed Carl for money for clothes, went to the Bargain Shop and bought something, bringing it home saying it wasn't much, in fact it was crap, but with her sewing machine she could turn it into something fine. She would cut and sew and piece, and end up ripping it to

236

shreds. No, in Mira's judgment, and judgment then meant apportionment of praise and blame, or rather blame and blamelessness, Carl had done everything he could. He was kind and tolerant, and Lily was mad. It was all understandable of course: Lily was insane because of her childhood. But she was clearly insane.

After some months, Lily got out of the hospital. Mira didn't even know it until Lily called one day. Mira could not see her that day, or that week, in fact. She was spring cleaning. She visited Lily the next week: they had coffee and discussed clothes. Lily kept trying to break in, to tell Mira of the horror of shock treatments, about her terrified letters, 'HELP!' written in lipstick on toilet paper, plastered on her windows until the nurse came in and found it. Or notes dropped from the window on the heads of visitors on Sundays. Or her frenzied pleas to Carl to get her out, whenever he visited. Mira smiled, nodded. Of course. She did not visit Lily soon again.

She saw almost no one. She was busy with her housework, chauffeuring the boys, with the PTA and a bridge club of doctors' wives and with their social life, which had become very formal. Other people entertained twenty for a sit-down dinner and had a maid and a butler. Mira had to do the same without help. She learned how. She was busy. Occasionally there would come a phone call. Sean had abandoned Oriane in the Bahamas, simply disappeared with all funds and left her there with the three kids, a rented house, and two unpaid-for boats. She had had to appeal to the governor of the island, to the American Embassy or whatever it was. They had paid air fare for her and the kids to the States; she was staying with Martha. Paula had divorced her rich man and was working as a medical receptionist somewhere, trying to support herself and her children. Theresa had gone mad with her eighth child, had drowned it in the bath, and was now in the state mental hospital.

The phone calls came from another world. They had nothing to do with her. Out there, all was chaos. Her world was orderly, clean and shining. It was also – and to do her credit, it must be admitted, she knew it – mean and small and angry. The boys snarled at each other, she snarled at them for every violated towel; Norm was mostly absent, and when he was there it was clear that he felt that everything there must contribute to his pleasure or be damned. He was supporting the whole thing, wasn't he? It was his sweat, his unfreedom that kept it all going, wasn't it? So it all had to contribute to his pleasure or he roared, he damned, he consigned to the prison of their rooms the underminers of his plan.

Mira was fall cleaning when John Kennedy was killed. She heard it on the radio, and did not believe it. She had voted for him over Norm's extreme opposition: the difference in their votes had caused the worst fight they'd had in years. It was not possible that he was dead. She hung on the radio: reports varied. He was dead; he wasn't. He was. Mira remembered when Marilyn Monroe killed herself. Somehow the two events fit together in her mind. She didn't understand how. Images, she thought. She mourned. She neglected her housecleaning to watch television depictions of the funeral, of Jackie Kennedy's stoic strength, of Charles de Gaulle walking behind the horse-drawn funeral carriage. She even managed a smile at the thought of Charles de Gaulle walking in horseshit.

Life went on. A phone call came: Sean had divorced Oriane, or gotten her to agree to a divorce. He was willing to pay $10,000 a year to support her and the three children: an opulent settlement, compared to what most divorced women get, but not enough, in those opulent times, to support four people. Sean bought himself a small estate on the water in East Hampton, and moved his mistress in.

One afternoon, in a spurt of loneliness and lifelessness, Mira went to visit Lily. The mechanical face Lily had worn at Mira's last visit was gone, but Mira was not prepared for the new one. Lily was old. She was the same age as Mira, thirty-four, but she looked – well, anything, actually. You could not name an age for her, you could only say she was old. She was terribly thin, even haggard. Her hair had grown out and was a number of colors – dark at the roots for a couple of inches, dark interspersed with gray, getting red, then paler toward the ends. Lily was wearing a thin cotton housedress with no belt. She looked like a maidservant in some primitive village, underfed, overworked, used to blows and despair. Mira stood appalled: the visual image of Lily had more potency than any words. All her rationalizations, her explanations, her condemnations vanished: if this was how Lily looked, this was how Liily was. Suddenly she believed in the misery of Lily's existence, felt it, perhaps. It was stark fact and beyond judgment, apportionment of blame; appearances of rectitude. It required no justification, no explanation. It simply was.

Lily poured coffee with a shaking hand and forgot the milk. When their coffee was almost drunk, she leaped up and unboxed a cake she had bought especially for Mira. 'I forgot,' she said anxiously. One more failure.

'Look at me, look what they've done to me,' Lily said, but her speech sounded like song, like wailing controlled and brought into form. She held out her hands: they were almost orange, and Mira noticed then that Lily's face too was jaundiced. 'They have me jaundiced with their pills,' Lily sang, 'they have me oozing. Feel my hands.' They were slippery moist. 'My whole body oozes sweat. I shake all the time. I hate them, those doctors. They don't care what they do to you as long as they can get you out of the office. I'm just a crazy woman, what do they care about me? Mira, I cut down the dosage but I don't dare stop taking them. I can't go back there, Mira, it will kill me, it will drive me crazy.'

Mira stood and walked over to the cabinet and pulled open a drawer searching for cake forks. Lily didn't notice. Mira was shocked by the jumble of things thrown in the drawer. She rummaged through it, though, and found some forks.

'Carl says I can't do anything right. I don't know, Mira, I try. I clean and clean and clean. If I don't, they'll

239

send me back. And I couldn't stand it, Mira, it's torture, it's medieval, you wouldn't believe what they do to you! Now my memory is gone. Every time Carl came I begged him to get me out of there, and he kept saying, "It's all right, kid, it'll be all right." He did NOTHING! Nothing! He didn't care what they were doing to me. Every day they come and get you and take you to that room and they strip you naked, stark naked, Mira, as if you were nothing, and they throw you down on the table and tie you down, Mira, they strap you to it! Then they give you this shock, oh, it's terrible, it's such a violation! They don't care what they do to you, you don't matter, you're just a crazy woman, you have no dignity.'

Lily had picked at her cake with her fork, but hadn't eaten it. It was a mess of crumbs on her plate. Her face was wrenched; there was a terrible line between her eyes, and the eyes themselves stared out as if they still looked at horror. Her whole face was strained; the lines around her mouth looked as though they had been drawn with black pencil by a makeup man, and the skin was stretched tautly across her cheekbones.

'So I come home and I try. I know they'll send me back if I don't. But Carl, what does he do? All he does is sit in that chair in front of the TV set. I ask him, I beg him to take us out on the weekend, on a picnic or a camping trip, something. The kids are growing up and we never do anything together. You need a family, it should be a home. All he says is that if I keep it up he'll move back into that room over the garage. What difference would it make? One less body cluttering up the family room. He comes home at night like a Nazi, he comes in here and stands in the doorway and says, oh, he's so cold, like a drill sergeant, "Lily, why aren't the dishes dried?" What's the point of drying dishes? They dry by themselves. But then I have to run and dry them, or else I have to argue with him, I have to say I didn't have time, or that I don't want to dry them, it's silly to dry them, and then we're in an argument, and I'm always wrong, it doesn't matter what I do or what I say,

I'm in the wrong before I begin, I don't know how it happens.'

She was mashing the crumbs in the plate into a paste. Mira watched her. Mira's mind was suspended. She felt as if she were in the deep seas on a raft.

'I forgot to wash his socks. They're dark and I didn't want to put them in with the whites, you know, and there were only a few, and I forgot to do a separate load. Is that crazy? Is that so terrible? He acted like I was ready to be carted away. He was livid, he could hardly move his lips, his mouth was so tight. So I said I'd wash them by hand, and he had to leave, he only had half an hour, so I said wear your white socks, they're clean, and he acted as if I had hit him or something. Or he could have worn dirty socks, couldn't he, Mira? Am I crazy? So I washed them by hand, and he's parading around the house acting as though there was a knife sticking out of his back, and I got so flustered I put the socks in the oven to dry, then Carlos threw a tantrum, oh, I don't know, he didn't want a soft-boiled egg, something like that, and I forgot the socks and they burned in the oven. What a smell!' She began to giggle. 'Burned socks! Have you ever . . .?' Now she was really laughing, laughing with delight, tears streamed down her face. 'You should have seen Carl's face!'

Lily's movements were jerky and sudden, but not always directed. She jumped up to get more coffee, but then when she was up, she hovered, seemingly unsure of why she had risen. She kept talking. 'I think men are dead. You know, they have no life. I read all the magazines, I watch all the TV shows, the women's panels, you know. Those women are so wonderful, they have so much strength, such vitality. Do you know Mary Gibson? She's great! She was saying how she flunks all the tests. I do too. The tests in the magazines, you know, score yourself on how good a wife you are, how good a mother, how feminine. I always flunk them. Mary said she thinks it's the fault of the tests!' Lily announced this as some outrageous, delightful piece of arrogance, laughing as she said it. 'I love her. You ought to watch her, she's on at ten o'clock, and then there's Katharine Carson, she's divorced and she really knows the score.' Lily chattered on about her television friends, for that is, Mira thought, what they were, and probably the only friends she had.

'Oh, they save me, really, they save my sanity. I know he wants to drive me back there, but I'm not going to let him do it. I won't. I won't,' she ended, stubborn, recalcitrant as ever. Her chin jutted out, and those terrible eyes stared at some fire in the distance, and beneath the shapeless housedress, her thin body tightened and looked hard and angular as steel.

13

'She hasn't learned the lesson,' Martha said in that direct way that managed to combine grimness with humor. 'Fucking bastards are only telling her one thing: YOU HAVE NOT LEARNED TO ACCEPT YOUR LIFE. And she had damn well better do it, or they'll have her back in there so fast she won't know what hit her.'

'She's fighting so hard.'

'Fuck it! Adjustment is the thing. When the world is crazy you had better be crazy along with it or they'll stick you in the madhouse. Fucking psychiatrists. I'm surprised they didn't try to fuck up more than her mind. Every attractive woman I know who's gone to a shrink, including myself, ended up bare-assed on that couch.'

Mira had a problem with Martha's language and her directness, but somehow Martha brought something refreshing into her life. After a conversation with Martha, Mira felt she had a little more room to breathe. But sometimes she felt like a voyeur on Martha's life.

'Really! What happened?'

Martha recounted it easily, laughing at the psychiatrist's line, laughing at the ease with which she had swallowed it, laughing at her own expectations.

'I knew he was a turd. But I *adored* him! Transference, you know. So I figured this was my chance. If I screwed him, it might happen, I might finally make it to orgasm.' She laughed heartily. 'He was such a klutz! My God, I don't think he understood the first thing about a woman's body. But I imagine he thinks he did me a great favor: physical therapy, you know? They're all convinced that the sacred prick can solve all ills, and I'm quite willing to believe that, being a worshiper of the sacred prick myself. The only problem is I still have to find one that's sacred!'

Mira felt her lips purse.

'Well, Martha, I don't know about what you're saying, but when Lily got out of the hospital, I thought that because of her bad feelings about men it might be a good idea for her to go to a woman psychiatrist, and I talked to Newton Donaldson about it – Norm's psychiatrist friend, you know? And he said that would be the worst thing in the world. He acted really shocked. He said that would lead to homosexuality.'

'Oh, he did? And did you ask him what happens when male patients go to male psychiatrists?'

'No,' Mira said uneasily.

'No,' Martha cackled back at her. 'Of course not! You just took his word as the word of God, the way you take Norm's. You should hear yourself: Norm said this, Norm said that. The Great God Norm!' She sat back laughing, waving her drink around.

Sometimes Mira felt a strong dislike for Martha. 'How's school?' she asked tightly.

Martha giggled. 'Getting too hot for you, huh? Okay.' She launched into a discussion of how school was, and although she was talking only about herself and the people she met and the structure she had entered into, Mira felt just as uncomfortable as she had when Martha talked about her, Mira's, life. She wondered if she was masochistic, if that was why she held on to Martha. Martha did slash and jab. But Mira knew that was not it. Martha was a touchstone. She had an unfailing shit detector. She did not pick up every truth, but she picked up every lie. It was, she said, because she had been such a liar all her life. 'I lied my way from kindergarten to

243

twelfth grade. Successfully. So now I know the creature when I meet it.' And with anything except lies, she was generous. She listened and she tried to see – only that, to see. She did not have immediate slots for all behavior – Lily's crazy, Carl ought to put his foot down, Natalie's a whore, Paul's a bastard – the kind of thing Norm came up with as the final significance of every event. If someone said to Martha, 'I feel so useless,' she would not, like most people, immediately answer, 'Why should you feel like that, that's silly, of course you're not useless.' Or stupid, or inadequate, or wrong, or whatever it was. She would just say, 'Why?' and listen to the why and try to see how that felt. One could trust Martha to challenge one's lies and yet not to deny one's reality. That made Martha very rare.

Still, she made Mira uneasy. She broke all the rules and she got away with it. Years ago, Mira had envied Martha the easy way she could curse out George and tell him what a klutz he was, and the easy way he could laugh at her attacks, crying out laughing, 'I know, I know!' Yet when everyone else condemned George for a coward and a lecher, Martha shrugged off the world's judgment and supported him: he had done the best thing possible under the circumstances. She could talk about going to law school and either not notice or not care that the people around her regarded her as deranged and deluded. And going back to college had given Martha confidence and authority in spheres other than the personal. This was especially difficult for Mira, who had always seen herself as *the* intellectual in every group. Martha had entered into not just a new sphere, but one larger than the one women usually occupied. At the university, relations were professional: feelings were the same, but rules were different. The politics of the kaffeeklatsch, if similar in nature, were more personal in reference than the politics of the classroom, the dean's office, the teacher-student conference. When Martha talked about this, her descriptions had the verve and awed humor of the one kid in the neighborhood who has been permitted to venture off the block, or the one villager who has returned to tell the others about the big city. School was great and terrible, wonderful and awful, but it was exciting. And there was the double challenge of crossing lines. Martha's French professor had, after a conference on her term paper, invited her out for drinks. He was tall and tanned, a skier. His name was David. They had laughed a lot and he had let his large brown eyes wash over her. One evening after class she went up to ask him a question; they talked for a while, and again he invited her out for drinks. This came to be a habit, every Tuesday evening. One Tuesday, he suggested a dinner, and since George was out of town and she had only a cup of soup before class, Martha accepted. In time, the suggestions moved further. Martha was perturbed. Today was Monday, and she had promised to give him an answer the next night.

'He's really cute, a real doll, you know? And I like him a lot, even if he isn't as smart as he imagines he is. And of course, it flatters me that he should pick me out of a class full of girls a hell of a lot younger and thinner than I am. But the politics of it bothers me. If I screw him and I get an A for the course, I'll always feel – not that I didn't earn the A, I know I did – but that I am subject to the accusation that I earned it on my back. I don't like that.'

'Why not tell him that?'

'Yeah, yeah. That's it. I'll ask him to wait until the term is over, and if he's still interested, then we'll see. Yes, that's it.'

She left, cheerful, busy, confident. Mira sat. Her mind felt like a red sea, swirling and hot as fire, liquid fire. She understood for the first time what it meant to be consumed with jealousy. Martha was perturbed, Martha had problems. But what problems! It was not just that Martha had such an attractive-sounding man interested in her; it was not even that she was accomplishing something, getting a degree and making plans for law school. It was that Martha, who up till a couple of years ago had been confined to the same narrow circle Mira inhabited, now felt ease and confidence in that larger world, that she could move through it without terror, could go so far as to let herself in for difficulties by going out for drinks with David, by risking that the acquaintance might turn sexual, and felt able to deal with it even after it had.

It staggered Mira. She felt deeply that it took some special qualities to move out of the little circle, and whatever they were – courage, confidence, energy, resiliency – she did not possess them. She sat that night and many nights after, considering. She felt ashamed, a coward. She remembered her teachers' high estimate of her intellect and abilities the way an aged athlete might remember the touchdown that had won the trophy for his high-school team. Her childhood ambitions rose again in her memory. She brushed them away, but they stuck like threads of cobweb that get trapped in a shred of broken plaster even as you try to dust them off.

Above all, she had to get rid of the jealousy: it was too painful. So she sat with two, then three, and even sometimes four brandies, watching the moon weave through the clouds, and applied her mind to the subject of human effort. Ashes to ashes, dust to dust: what did it all mean in the end? She reminded herself that what gets called accomplishment in the world is often meretricious, and even when it is not, it is futile. All the works of men's hands and minds come to dust in the end. Consider, for instance, how much time and concentration it must have taken to come up with the idea of the lever, or what a stroke of imaginative brilliance had been required to come up with the notion of putting those little green leaves around the meat as you roasted it. Everything was so hard, and took so long. Mira remembered writing papers in school, spending months reading, thinking hard, coming up with a conclusion that seemed astoundingly original and perceptive, only to run across it a year later in an essay published before she was born. What did it cost to build a kingdom? An empire? Only to have it, in time, disappear like Mari beneath a nameless desert. People violated their insides by murdering others by sword or gun, poison or starvation, to set up a dynasty that would fall in a year or ten or a hundred. What difference did the extra zeroes make when the thing was doomed to fall sometime?

It was men who did these things. Pompous and self-aggrandizing, they tried to erect permanently in the outside world symbols of the penile erection they could not maintain in their flesh. Delusion, hideous delusion, to which they had sacrificed millions of less insane humans. The Great God Norm: was it true she quoted him like a god? She could remember when she thought him less intelligent than herself. What had happened? He had moved from frightened boy to authoritative man, but she knew he was still as hollow as ever. Still, she'd allowed his position to dictate hers. Suppose now she moved, slid out from under him saying, 'I'm not comfortable here.' What was the point, what was to be gained? She would cause suffering to others and herself, and for what? Did she dare disturb the universe?

And if she succeeded in extricating herself, then what? She might have the excitement and joy Martha seemed to be living with, but everything in Mira told her there was only one direction for that excitement and joy – increasing loneliness. You could break society's rules, and you might even get away with it, but after such success, what return? Forever and forever you would be alone. Perhaps then you could make great art, or good art. But for what: in a world where poems are used to start fires and paintings are bombed off walls, where libraries are destroyed and monuments crumble, and even the art that survives is just so much dead stone sitting in a room in a museum where no one goes because they don't understand what they are looking at. Would it matter to the people of 1964 if *Beowulf* had simply vanished forever? Would the world be different?

Life passed: the trees changed color, the flowers bloomed and died, the air was soft or chafing. The best one could do was sit and watch them and take pleasure in the inevitable one could not change. This was what women did. It was women who kept the world going, who observed the changing seasons and kept the beauty high, women who cleaned the world's house, who kept the cobwebs off the windows so that people could keep on seeing out. Enduring continuation, the hard lot. No one pinned medals on you or gave you honorary degrees; you didn't get to wear fancy costumes and walk in processions; your bust would never be set up in any hall of greats. But it was her task. The rest was the sound of puny voices raised against the wind.

That winter and spring, Mira developed a serenity, a calm transcendence that shone from her face. People praised her for looking well, and she felt somehow blessed. She had, for all her confusion and unhappiness over the years, attained harmony and grace with herself and her life. Adjustment, Martha would have called it, but it felt tinged with divinity. She felt more feminine. She could sit silent at parties, listening to the men talk, smiling at them with tolerance and benevolence, instead of arguing and having to assert herself. Men moved toward her like a magnet: she felt beloved. Somehow, she thought, she had managed to make the right choices. She had escaped the old continuing pain. She felt like one of the elect, and unconsciously she believed that having now attained this grace, she would never lose it. She had achieved not just grace, but invulnerability.

14

She maintained her equilibrium even after Martha fell in love. It was David, the French teacher, who had understood perfectly Martha's reluctances, who had been 'just right,' had waited until the term was over, had been passionately assertive afterward, but without being overbearing. He wanted her, but he did not think he had a right to her. He was wonderful. It was hard for Mira to listen, but listen she did, through hours and days and weeks of Martha's joy, the joy that glistened in her eyes and glowed in her face and made her look ten years younger – his age, in fact. Mira listened to every shared

248

coffee hour and lunch, every cocktail hour, every bedroom scene. He was Martha's brother, her twin, her other self: Mira thought about the dangers of narcissism. He was a great lover, had a great prick and thrust and gave Martha the thrill of his, if not her own, orgasm: Mira thought about projection and forms of homosexuality. He was everything she, Martha, wanted to be but wasn't – assertive and confident in the world, yet graceful at the same time: Mira thought about the theory that love is envy. They could tolerate each other because they were both obsessive, fanatical about details and about personal cleanliness. The worst argument they had had concerned whether the shampoo and conditioner bottles should be permitted to stand permanently on the tub ledge, or whether the ledge should at all times be kept immaculate and free from clutter. The argument had nearly led to blows, yet afterward they were both able to laugh at it.

Martha was on an endless high, with her mouth always full of David. (One way or another, Mira thought nastily.) David was also married and the father of one child, a two-year-old girl. But it sounded to Mira as though Martha, undaunted by such details, was thinking about David not as a lover but as a permanent condition of her life. 'I almost get it off with him. Sex is glorious, and just talking is glorious, and being with him makes me feel full all the way down. I don't have to be anything, I can just be. I can't tell you how great it is.'

But Mira knew. Don't we all? Isn't that what they feed us, what our imaginations are full of from the time we can think about love? Mira was happy for her friend, although her sense of personal lack was heightened by this perpetual bliss going on in the very next room and unable to be blotted out. She had to work to keep her detached perspective. She had to remind herself of how transitory love was, how fragile; she had to put the thing in its social context and remember claims of spouses, children, the entire social fabric. But nothing could keep the buoyancy of Martha's feelings from spilling over all of it, like well-tended farmland simply wiped out by a

249

flood. The flood, while it lasted, was all there was, and was such an intense reality that transcendence was difficult to maintain in the face of it. Mira felt perched on the roof of a shaky chicken house being totteringly borne downstream. But she kept her balance, and worked much in her garden.

She was working in her garden with a little transistor radio perched near her, listening to a broadcast about the three young civil rights workers who had disappeared in Mississippi, when the phone rang and Amy Fox, an old friend from Meyersville, came screaming on about Samantha. Mira did not understand but it sounded as if she were saying that Sam was going to be put in jail. Amy kept saying, 'I know you're a good friend of hers, and maybe you could help.'

Mira tried to phone Samantha, but was told the telephone had been disconnected. That was odd. She had not heard from Sam in weeks. Mira showered and dressed and drove to Samantha's house. It was a seven-room house in a pleasant suburb, hundred-foot plots with some old trees left behind by the builder. Children were bicycling in the street, but the place had the deserted look of most suburbs. As she approached Samantha's front door, she noticed something – a notice of some sort – tacked onto it. Were they sick? She moved closer: it was a notice of repossession signed by the sheriff's office. Repossession? She rang the bell, wondering if Samantha were at work, but she answered the door. Mira just stood looking at her. Was this Samantha, the mechanical doll? She was wearing old slacks and a shabby shirt. Her hair was short, uncurled, and unkempt and its color was a mousy brown. She wore no make-up and her face was pale and haggard.

'Sam,' she began, putting out her hands.

'Hi, Mira.' Samantha did not take the hands. 'Come in.'

'Amy called.'

Samantha shrugged and led Mira into the kitchen. The house was full of boxes.

'You're moving?'

'I have no choice,' Sam's voice said acidly. This was sweet, bubbly Samantha, who wiggled through the days getting delight from everything?

She poured coffee for them.

'What happened?'

She told her story tonelessly, as if she had told it many times before, but she lingered over every detail. It was her epic, etched in her memory by sheer pain. It had started years ago, soon after Sam and Simp moved from Meyersville. 'But we didn't tell anyone. Pride, I guess. It all seemed too shameful.' Simp had lost his job and had taken months to find another. They had gone deeply into debt. She took a job, trying to help out. Eventually, he found something but they were still impoverished trying to pay back the debts. Then his teeth had needed repair and it had taken them two years to pay for that. Meantime he lost his job again. That time he got another before too long, but Samantha was beginning to feel worn down, even doomed. Everyone else was doing well, or so it seemed to her: moving up and out into larger worlds. She skimped on everything, but they never were able to break even. Then Simp lost his job again. There were arguments: Sam wanted him to get out of sales and go into another field. He would make a good junior-high teacher, she thought, and he had a college degree. He could substitute and take some ed courses and eventually get a teaching job. But he was adamant. Sales was where the money was and one day he'd get his break. It wasn't his fault. He got orders. But there was always something: the manufacturer didn't deliver on time, the manufacturer went out of business, the territory he'd been given was a poor one. This time, though, he did not make such an effort to get another job. He'd sit at home poring through the newspaper and wouldn't go into town unless he saw an interesting ad. He was underfoot all the time and they were living on a tiny unemployment check.

Mira remembered that she had condemned Sam in her mind for leaving her children, and she recalled Sam's pert appearance and manner, recalled not liking it, finding it artificial, brittle even. She had thought Sam greedy.

'But where was Simp? I mean, I remember some accidents that happened then when no one was home. . . .'

Samantha shrugged. 'Who knows?' She turned away. The toneless monotony of her voice gave way, and she put her face in her hands. The rest came from deep in her throat, a voice like a clot of tears. She couldn't earn much, she had no training, she got a job typing for $75 a week, Simp got unemployment, she stretched but it was impossible to pay the mortgage and eat. The situation was aggravated by her coming home every night to find him sitting there with his third martini, not having made any effort at all. 'He couldn't lower his pride, wouldn't even think of taking a job pumping gas, anything, anything at all, to feed his kids!' Then her checks started to bounce and she made inquiries and found that during the days he went out, God knows where, and wrote checks, God knows for what, at all the local bars. Their mortgage payments went further and further into default.

'It got to be too bad. Every night I'd come home and scream at him. The kids never came home if they could help it. It was terrible. I had to cancel our joint checking account and warn the bank not to cash his checks. I couldn't stand it anymore. It was like living with a monstrous child. So I made him leave.'

She blew her nose and poured more coffee. 'So.' She sat back, her eyes in dry hollows, her mouth a rubber band pulled out of shape. 'The other day the sheriff came. I got hysterical and I tried to keep him from nailing that thing to my door. My poor kids! The neighbors. Well, everyone knows now. There's nothing left to lose. I don't know where we'll go. Simp is living with his mother in her big house in Beau Reve. I called him and he said we should go on welfare. While I was packing, I cleaned out his closet – there were some boxes on the shelf, and behind them was that.' She pointed to a giant stack of papers, which would have been several feet high if it had been put in one pile. 'Bills. All bills. Some of them are two years old. Most he never even opened. Just stuck them up there as if they'd go away by themselves.'

She took the cigarette Mira offered her, lighted it, and inhaled deeply. 'Ummm. Luxury. I've given it up for the duration,' she said smiling. It was her first smile. 'Thing is, altogether we owe out about sixty thousand dollars. Can you imagine that? I can't. Whenever Simp borrowed money, I always cosigned the notes. So now, they can't get anything from him because he doesn't work, but I do, and so they're putting liens on my pay. I mean, I have two kids to feed! On my pay!' Tears rose to her eyes again. 'I'm thirty-one years old and the rest of my life is already signed over to that debt. The only thing that's saved me is my friends. They are so wonderful.'

The women in the neighborhood had gathered together when they learned about Samantha's difficulty, and with great delicacy had done what they could. 'Made a great pot of spaghetti tonight, Sam, but I made too much and you know my family and leftovers. I was wondering if you'd do me a favor – your kids like spaghetti, don't they? – and give it to your kids for lunch or something.' 'Sam, Jack went fishing yesterday and I'm drowning in bluefish. Could you use a couple? Please?' 'Sam, Nick and I are going to the club tonight and that place is so damned boring, why don't you come along with us and liven it up?' Delicacy, care, not to appear to be giving charity; tact about the hand-me-down clothes, the little recreations, about being sure always to pick her up so she wouldn't have to put gas in her car. 'The thing that hurts me most is the thought of leaving them.'

'What will happen now?'

She shrugged again. 'Unless I can come up with three hundred dollars for one month's mortgage payment, we're out on the street as of Friday. If I could have a month, Nick – May's husband, he's a lawyer and he's been just great – might be able to get something out of

253

Simp and make some arrangement to tide us over until I can find a place.'

'What about your parents?'

'My father died last winter. His retirement annuity ended with his death. My mother is living on Social Security and his insurance – he didn't have much. She barely gets by. I haven't told her any of this. She's in Florida living with my aunt. It would just upset her and there's nothing she can do.'

'My God.'

'Yeah. You know what really gets me – I like working. I mean if I had been the man – I wouldn't have minded. And Simp could have stayed home. You know? But everything hangs on them. You're no one without them. If they flub up, you're finished. It's like – you're *dependent*, you know what I mean?'

Mira did not want to think about that.

'Totally dependent,' Samantha went on, 'I mean on everything. If they work or not, if they drink or not, if they go on loving you or not. Like poor Oriane.'

'Oriane?'

'You know, they were really living great, and she'd moved all the way to the Bahamas with him, and then one day he decides he doesn't want to live with her anymore and he just takes off and leaves her with a rented house, two boats unpaid for, three kids, and no money in the checking account. You heard about that.'

'Yes. It's because they don't care about their kids. They just don't care about them. So they're free. Women are victims. All the way through,' Mira heard herself say.

'And now she has cancer.'

'What?'

Sam shook her head. 'She's going in for surgery next week. Breast cancer.'

'Oh, my God.'

'It just goes on and on. Last year the woman who lives two doors down from me tried to commit suicide. Nick said women are unstable, but I know she did it because that was the only way she could control her husband. He's an awful runaround, and he's not nice to Joan. Everything seems to be falling apart. I don't unstand it. When I was a kid, things didn't seem to be like this. It's as though there's more freedom, but all it means is more freedom for men.'

Samantha reminded Mira a little of Lily. She went on and on talking almost oblivious of her audience, and the expression on her face under all the strain was bewilderment, the total bewilderment of a person who wakes up to find herself a dung beetle.

'You know, I really liked being a housewife. Isn't that crazy? I did. I love doing things with the kids, and when we were broke and had no money for Christmas gifts, I enjoyed getting together with the children and Alice and her kids and we'd all make things to give as gifts. And I didn't mind cleaning and cooking; I loved to have company and set the table and arrange flowers and cook something really snazzy. Isn't life ironic?'

Mira murmured something.

'I never really wanted very much. I mean, I wanted a home and a family and a decent life, but I was never very ambitious. I'm not smart enough to be ambitious, I guess. And now . . .' She let it hang, opening her hands like someone who has suddenly realized the small palmful of water she has carried so carefully from the well has already seeped through her fingers.

Mira, though, was barely listening. Three hundred dollars. It was little enough. Norm spent that in a month and a half at the golf club. She had her checkbook in her purse. All she had to do was take it out and write a check to Samantha. It was nothing. But she could not do it. She tried. She worked her mind down to her bag, she imagined her hand pulling out the checkbook. If she could get that far, she couldn't turn back. But she couldn't get that far.

But she left Samantha promising to see if she couldn't do something. Samantha smiled tiredly. 'Listen, thanks for stopping over and listening to my sad tale. I'm sure you didn't need it. The world is full enough of them.'

Not my world, Mira thought.

15

'Absolutely not,' Norm said.

'Norm, poor Samantha!'

'I feel very very sorry for Samantha,' he said solemnly, 'but I'll be goddamned if I'm going to lay out my hard-earned money to help that creep Simp.'

'You wouldn't be helping Simp. He doesn't even live there now.'

'He owns the house, doesn't he? It would be different if I thought he'd ever repay it, but from what you say, he's a loser and a stupid bastard, and I'd never see that money again.'

'Oh, Norm, what difference does it make? We have plenty.'

'That's easy for you to say. That money comes out of my hide.'

'What do you think I do all day? What have I done all these years? I work as hard as you do.'

'Oh, come off it, Mira.'

'What do you mean, come off it?' Her voice rose wildly. 'Am I not an equal participant in this marriage? Don't I contribute to it?'

'Of course you do,' he said placatingly, but there was an edge of disgust in his voice. 'But you contribute different things. You don't contribute money.'

'My work enables you to make that money!'

'Oh, Mira, don't be ridiculous. Do you think I need you to do my work? I could live anywhere, I could have a housekeeper, or live in a hotel. I support your way of life by my work, not the reverse.'

'And I have nothing to say about how it's spent?'

'Of course you do. Don't I give you everything you want?'

'I don't know. I never seem to want anything.'

'Do I complain about your bills for clothes, or the kids' music lessons or camp?'

'I want this, then. I want three hundred dollars for Samantha.'

'No, Mira. And that's the end of it.' He stood up and left the room, and in a few minutes, she heard the shower running. He was going out to a meeting that evening.

She stood up too, and only then did she realize her whole body was shaking. She held on to the back of the kitchen chair. She wanted to pick it up, she wanted to race upstairs with it and smash open the bathroom door and crash it down on his head. She glanced at a carving knife lying on the counter, and imagined picking it up and stabbing it into his heart, stabbing it over and over. She was breathing in little gasps.

She felt that he had eradicated her. He was annoyed that she did not understand her powerlessness. How had it happened, that he had all the power? She remembered the evening she had sat in a rocking chair deciding to die. She had power then. The power to die, anyway. She felt that she could not fight him. She could not give that money to Samantha without his permission. Yet somehow if she didn't, that would be the end of something. She had allowed him to close out her friends from their life, and that had shrunk her, but if she allowed him to do this, she would be eradicated. But she could not move.

When he came back downstairs dressed freshly to go out, he glanced at her standing in the kitchen.

'I may be late, so don't wait up,' he said in a normal voice, as though nothing had happened. He pecked her cheek as he passed her and went out the kitchen door to the garage. She thought of running out and locking the garage door, forcing him to sit in the car breathing in carbon monoxide. She was astounded at the images that were popping into her head.

One of the boys came tearing into the kitchen. 'Hey, Mom, the Good Humor man's here, can I have a quarter?'

She turned on him like a vindictive fury: 'No!' she shrieked.

257

16

She moved through the evening like a sleepwalker. She sat in the family room while the boys watched television and didn't even turn it off when they went to bed, just sat there, and the news came on and people were still talking about Schwerner, Goodman, and Chaney, and everyone thought they were dead, and that roused her. Dead for a cause. In her youth she had spouted integration lines but had long since given up even thinking about it. What was the use? She thought though that it must be nice to die for a cause. Since you had to die anyway. Better for a cause. Because otherwise. Her mind was a numb jumble. She rose and switched off the set, and poured a brandy, but that was the wrong thing to do because as the brandy settled and heated her insides, the heat came washing over her, and she began to cry, but it wasn't crying, it was wild, tempestuous, gusty sobbing, she could not control it, it felt as if all her insides were coming up with the sobs.

As she settled down – it took a long time – she wondered about them, those three young men who believed they could change things. They had probably not expected to die, had not sought it out, had not plotted martyrdom. They had simply believed the cause was worth the risk. But when the cause was yourself, all the guilts rose up. How dare you fight for yourself? It was so selfish. Maybe Chaney was fighting for himself, though, and one didn't think that selfish. She had another brandy, and another. She got drunk. She began to imagine scenes. Norm would come in from his meeting and she would stand up and say . . . She made up noble speeches in her head. She argued him point by point and he was astonished at her logic and capitulated, apologized, asked forgiveness. Or he would come in and she would smash him over the head with the cleaver and watch him die, hopefully slowly. Or he would not come in, he would get drunk and crack up his car and be killed. He would be assaulted in the street and stabbed by a street thief. Then all her problems would be over.

The sky was starting to get light when she realized that Norm was not coming home at all. At the same time she realized that Norm was not the enemy, only the embodiment of the enemy. Because what could he do to her if she wrote that check? Would he beat her up, divorce her, deny her money for food, make her pay it back? There was nothing he could do. She began to see that his authority over her was based on mutual agreement, that it was founded on nothing but air, and that that was why he had to assert it so often in such odd ways. It could be broken by her simply turning her face away from him. Why was she so terrified of doing that? There was something more, out there, out in the world, something that gave him the power, wasn't there? Or was it just that she feared losing his love? What love? What was it, their marriage? She sat rocking drunkenly on the solid chair and watched the sun come up over the trees. She had fallen asleep when the boys came bounding in crying out at her, 'Mom, you didn't wake us up! Mom, we're gonna be late!'

She shook herself awake and gazed at them.

They were running around grabbing books, yelling at her and each other.

'We didn't even have breakfast,' Normie said reproachfully.

She sat and looked at him. 'You never eat it anyway.'

He stopped and blinked at her. He recognized some change. But there was no time to pursue it, and they took off to run the mile to the bus stop since obviously she was not going to drive them. She sat there with a nasty smile on her face, then got up and fixed herself some coffee. Afterward, she took a shower and dressed and took her checkbook and went out to the car and drove to Samantha's house, and handed her a check for $350. 'A little extra to tide you over,' she explained. 'Actually, I can't explain, but it's for me, not you.'

She entered the amount and recipient in large letters in their joint checkbook. But Norm did not mention it, not ever.

17

All this while you are asking, 'What about Norm? Who is he, this shadow man, this figurehead husband?'

You may not believe this, but there isn't much I can tell you. I did know him, I even knew him fairly well, but there still isn't much I can tell you. I can tell you what he looked like. He was tallish, about six feet; blond, blue-eyed. In the early years he had a crew cut. As he aged, he got red in the face and put on some weight, but not too much. He kept trim playing golf and squash. He looked very handsome in turtleneck sweaters and white buck shoes. When the styles changed in the seventies, he kept up. He let his hair – what was left of it by then – get a little longer – and he grew sideburns and started to wear colored shirts and wide ties. He had a pleasant face, still does. He has a pleasant personality, knows a few jokes, nothing too salacious. He watches football games and sometimes goes up to West Point to see one. He reads what he has to to keep up in his profession, and nothing else except a few front pages of the newspaper. When he's home, he watches TV and likes cowboy and detective shows. He has no vice to an extreme. He was in many ways the ideal man of the fifties.

You think I am making him up. You think, Aha! A symbolic figure in what turns out to be after all an invented story. Alack, alas, I wish he were. Then he would be my failure, not life's. I'd much prefer to think that Norm is a stick figure because I am not much of a writer than because Norm is a stick figure.

I have, over the years, read a lot of novels by male novelists, and there is no question in my mind that their female characters – except for those of Henry James – are stick figures with padding in certain places. So maybe the problem is just that we don't know each other very well, men and women. Maybe we need each other too much to be able to know each other. But the truth is, I don't think men knew Norm any better than I did.

And it's not just Norm. I don't think anyone knew Carl either, or Paul, or Bill, or even poor Simp, although I have more of a sense of him than of the others. When you slip out of respectability, when you fall below the line, somehow you become clearer. Do you know what I mean? It's as though being a white middle-class male is a full-time occupation, like being a colonel in the army who was trained at West Point. Even when you aren't wearing your fancy costume you have to stand like a ramrod and talk without opening your mouth too wide and make jokes about booze and broads and walk like a machine. And the only way out is if you get kicked out for some terrible breach and end up on skid row talking to some kid in a Salvation Army soup kitchen; then you can afford to let yourself show. Simp slid down: that's an unforgivable sin to the other white middle-class males – almost as bad as going gay. And so I can imagine him sitting there in the bars he still frequents with his mother's money, sitting elegantly with his second double martini, talking easily about the big killing he expects to make this afternoon, expecting a call at three (in the bar? you wonder) that should do it, and he's no more hollow than the others who sound the same way except in his case you know it isn't true and you peer in at him and figure that somehow he doesn't know it isn't true, he isn't clever enough to be a good liar; he bought an image and it was all he bought and now it's all he has, and he is going round and round in it, living in it the way children live in daydreams.

Anyway, the others kept their uniforms, and so that was all anyone ever knew of them. Soldiers, like niggers and chinks, all look alike.

Still, I'll try to tell you what I do know about Norm.

He was a happy baby. His father was a pharmacist, his mother a housewife, and gregarious. He had a younger brother who became a dentist. Both Norm and his brother were fairly bright in school, fairly athletic, fairly social. They were not extreme in any way that I know of, and it is that very moderateness that makes it so hard to talk about them.

He was not much devoted to sex. His mother had seen to it, from his earliest years, that he slept with his hands on top of the blankets, even going so far as to pull them out if they slid under during his sleep. She never never permitted her boys to lie abed in the mornings and warned Mira often and direly of the dangers of such indulgence. When Norm was five, he engaged in a contest with some other boys in the neighborhood to see which of them could pee farthest. His mother caught him and threatened him with the loss of his organ if he ever did such a thing again: the threat probably made less of an impression on him than her dead white face and her gasps for breath as she dragged him home. He fell in love when he was nineteen, with the first girl he'd ever dated. They became engaged, but while he was away at college, she eloped with the mechanic at the Esso station in their town. Norm carried his tragic betrayal for many years after that. A group of his friends set him up with Antoinette, the town pump, and he lost his virginity on the back seat of a '39 Ford. The experience was accompanied with enough guilt and a variety of unknown unpleasant sensations or emotions that he did not actively seek it again. There was in Norm, in those days at least, a certain delicacy: he laughed along with his friends about the experience, and about Antoinette, but he had a vague sense that somehow that wasn't the way it should have been, wasn't the way he would have chosen it to be.

When he was a child, he loved to draw, but his family did not encourage such activity. They did not actively forbid it either. It was just that the entire family was geared in a different direction. The only pictures they hung were Currier and Ives prints; they neither read nor listened to music. And they felt no lack. Such things simply did not exist in their world. Norm was given riding lessons – his father had been in the cavalry in the first war. He was encouraged in his desire to go to West Point. His temper tantrums were always of the same variety: he kicked in the radio every time West Point lost a game. It was hard on their radios, but somehow

262

this was accepted by the family, which permitted no other expression of anger. Any other rage was treated as an aberration, and Norm was sent coldly to his room and given no dinner.

Norm learned to be what his father would have called a gentleman. He did everything, but nothing extraordinarily well. He did nothing with passion. He studied, and made C's. He played ball, but rarely first string. His social life was pleasant, but not wild. He dated, but was not sexually aggressive.

He met Mira through their families. She seemed to him very pretty, fragile, and innocent, yet at the same time somehow sophisticated. It was probably her mind that seemed sophisticated to him, because she had thought about things and he had not; but as he became more involved with her, he began to hear things about her from his friends at the university, and got the impression that Mira was not the innocent he thought. He never tried to resolve the conflict of two impressions: when he wanted to keep her to himself, he mentioned the outside world as the mass of teeming agressive maleness he felt it to be and that he knew frightened her. When he was angry with her, he hurled at her accusations of whoredom. For him she had the mythic quality of virgin/whore in one, although that is not the way he thought about it. He did not think about it at all. He did not think about anything dangerous. His feelings toward his parents, about his profession, about the world he moved in, were always proper, tinged with humor, shrugged off. This avoidance of penetration into the difficult, the dangerous, was as characteristic of him as his moderation. He walked always on the wide, the beaten path and found those who chose narrower ones either crazy or unmannerly. Those words, in fact, were almost synonymous in his vocabulary, craziness being only a heightened degree of lack of manners. In a sense, he was the ideal gentleman of an age older than the fifties.

Mira seemed the perfect partner for him. He was the scientist, the one who dealt with facts, understanding the wordly areas of sports, money, and status; she was artistic, literary. She could play the piano a little, knew something about art and theater. She had a refined quality that seemed to be inborn. She would reflect well on him. It never occurred to him, despite her two years at the university, that she woud act differently from his mother: she would care for him and their children, and she could provide the cultural note, the finish, so absent in his own family. And in all surface ways, their marriage was acceptable. Both came from middle-class, Republican families. If she had had some training in Catholicism, neither she nor her family was now religious, and would not evoke his own family's contempt for non-protestants. She had some education, she was healthy, she had not been brought up with wealth and would not object to the labor required of her in the early years. And besides, Mira had a helplessness, a vulnerability that touched his deepest core. It seemed perfect.

And indeed it was. They had been married for fourteen years, and Norm would avow that they had no serious problems. She was a wonderful mother, an excellent housekeeper, a good hostess. She was not very sexual, but Norm respected that in her. He felt that his choice of her had been wise, and looked down complacently at those of his colleagues who had domestic problems. He felt good about himself and his life, good about Mira. His face had set, over the years, in good, kindly lines. They had lived out the life that had been expected of them, and for Norm, it was fairly fulfilling. Only sometimes, when they went to a movie or a musical comedy playing on Broadway, and an attractive woman moved her body in a certain way – not just any attractive woman, but one who had a certain helplessness and vulnerability about her even as she wiggled her flesh – then something would rise in him like a cry, a longing to reach out and grab hard, to hold and pull even over objections, to – but he never even thought the word – to rape, to overcome and possess and keep in possession. It had been his earliest feeling about Mira, but he had never acted upon it. Nor would he now. He would laugh at himself and his cosmic desires, laugh them away into absurdity, and go home and insist quietly and factually on having sex with the reluctant Mira, and never equate the act with the feeling.

18

What is a man, anyway? Everything I see around me in popular culture tells me a man is he who screws and kills. But everything I see around me in life tells me a man is he who makes money. Maybe these two are related, because making money in our world often requires careful avoidance of screwing and killing, so maybe the culture provides the unlived part. I don't claim to know, and I don't even care much. I figure that's their problem. Women are trying hard these days to get out from under the images that have been imposed on them. The difficulty is there is just enough truth in the images that to repudiate them often involves repudiating also part of what you really are. Maybe men are in the same boat, but I don't think so. I think they rather like their images, find them serviceable. If they don't, it's up to them to change them. I do know that if that is what men are, I'm willing to dispense with them forever and have children only through parthenogenesis, which would mean I'd have only female children, which would suit me fine. But the other side of the image, the reality, is just as bad. Because if the men I've known haven't much indulged in killing and are no great shakes at screwing and have made money (for the most part) in only moderate amounts, they haven't been anything else either. They're just dull. Maybe that's the price of being on the winning side. Because the women I know have gotten fucked, literally and figuratively, and they're great.

One advantage to being a despised species is that you have freedom, freedom to be any crazy thing you want. If you listen to a group of housewives talk, you'll hear a lot of nonsense, some of it really crazy. This comes, I think, from being alone so much, and pursuing your own odd train of thought without impediment, which some call discipline. The result is craziness, but also brilliance. Ordinary women come out with the damedest truth. You ignore them at your own risk. And they're permitted to go on making wild statements without being put in one kind of jail or another (some of them, anyway) because everyone knows they're crazy and powerless too. If a woman is religious or earthy, passive or wildly assertive, loving or hating, she doesn't get much more flak than if she isn't: her choices lie between being castigated as a ball and chain or as a whore. What I don't understand is where women suddenly get power. Because they do. The kids, who almost always turn out to be a pile of shit, are, we all know, Mommy's fault. Well, how did she manage that, this powerless creature? Where was all her power during the years she was doing five loads of laundry a week and worrying about mixing the whites with the colors? How was she able to offset Daddy's positive influence? How come she never knows she has this power until afterward, when it gets called responsibility?

What I'm trying to understand is winning and losing. Now the rule of the game is that men win as long as they keep their noses comparatively clean, and women lose, always, even extraordinary women. The Edith Piafs and Judy Garlands of the world become great by capitalizing on their losing. That part is clear. What is not clear is what game we're playing. What do you win when you win? I know what you lose, having some experience with that side. What I don't know is what rewards are involved with winning besides money. Maybe that's it; maybe that's all there is. I guess so, because when I look at all the winners, all the Norms of the world, I can't see much else: money and a certain ease in the world, a sense of legitimacy.

You think I hate men. I guess I do, although some of my best friends . . . I don't like this position. I mistrust generalized hatred. I feel like one of those twelfth-century monks raving on about how evil women are

266

and how they must cover themselves up completely when they go out lest they lead men into evil thoughts. The assumption that the men are the ones who matter, and that the women exist only in relation to them, is so silent and underrunning that even we never picked it up until recently. But after all, look at what we read. I read Schopenhauer and Nietzsche and Wittgenstein and Freud and Erikson; I read de Montherlant and Joyce and Lawrence and sillier people like Miller and Mailer and Roth and Philip Wylie. I read the Bible and Greek myths and didn't question why all later redactions relegated Gaea-Tellus and Lilith to a footnote and made Saturn the creator of the world. I read or read about, without much question, the Hindus and the Jews, Pythagoras and Aristotle, Seneca, Cato, St. Paul, Luther, Sam Johnson, Rousseau, Swift . . . well, you understand. For years I didn't take it personally.

So now it is difficult for me to call others bigots when I am one myself. I tell people at once, to warn them, that I suffer from deformation of character. But the truth is I am sick unto death of four thousand years of males telling me how rotten my sex is. Especially it makes me sick when I look around and see such rotten men and such magnificent women, all of whom have a sneaking suspicion that the four thousand years of remarks are correct. These days I feel like an outlaw, a criminal. Maybe that's what the people perceive who look at me so strangely as I walk the beach. I feel like an outlaw not only because I think that men are rotten and women are great, but because I have come to believe that oppressed people have the right to use criminal means to survive. Criminal means being, of course, defying the laws passed by the oppressors to keep the oppressed in line. Such a position takes you scarily close to advocating oppression itself, though. We are bound in by the terms of the sentence. Subject-verb-object. The best we can do is turn it around. And that's no answer, is it?

Well, answers I leave to others, to a newer generation perhaps, lacking the deformities mine suffered. My feelings about men are the result of my experience. I have little sympathy for them. Like a Jew just released from Dachau, I watch the handsome young Nazi soldier fall writhing to the ground with a bullet in his stomach and I look briefly and walk on. I don't even need to shrug. I simply don't care. What he was, as a person, I mean, what his shames and yearnings were, simply don't matter. It is too late for me to care. Once upon a time I could have cared.

But fairyland is back beyond the door. Forever and forever I will hate Nazis, even if you can prove to me that they too were victims, that they were subject to illusion, brainwashed with images. The stone in my stomach is like an oyster's pearl – it is the accumulation of defense against an irritation. My pearl is my hatred: my hatred is learned from experience: that is not prejudice. I wish it were prejudice. Then, perhaps, I could unlearn it.

19

I guess I should get back to the story, but I turn in that direction with such weariness. Oh, those lives, those lives! Those years. You know how you feel when someone whispers to you that so-and-so is ill and you say, 'Too bad,' and ask what the matter is and they whisper 'Women's troubles'? You never pursue it. You have this vague sense of oozings and drippings, blood that insists on pouring out of assorted holes, organs that drip down with all the other goo and try to depart, breasts that get saggy or lumpy and sometimes have to be cut off. Above all there is the sense of a rank cave that never gets fresh air, dark and smelly, its floor a foot thick with sticky, disgusting mulch.

Yes. And for every story I'm telling you, I'm leaving out three. For instance, I didn't tell you all of what happened to Doris and Roger, or Paula and Brett, or Sandra and Tom, or poor Geraldine. I know, but I'm not telling. There's no point in telling, it is all just more of the same. I'm not going in detail into what happened to

Oriane, although I will tell you that after they cut off her breast, Sean went to see her in the hospital and turned his beautiful face away with disgust.

'Don't let Timmy see that thing when you get home,' he said with a twisting mouth. 'It's disgusting.'

He shouldn't have worried. When she got home, she committed suicide. Not his fault, though: she just shouldn't have loved him as much as she did, shouldn't have let his opinion matter so much to her. Should. Shouldn't. For every great woman I know now, there's an Oriane, an Adele, a Lily, or an Ava. Someplace.

Wrecked, wrecked. All survivors, all of us. We survived the battlefield of our own lives, and the only help we got came from each other. It was Alice who sat night after night with Samantha until she got over the hysteria, the sense of betrayal, the awful hurting hate. It was Martha who came and found Mira lying on the floor with her wrists slit. It was Mira who put Martha to bed and got rid of the rest of the sleeping pills and sat with her as she realized that she would live. No one could save Lily, though. She was beyond us.

Do you believe any of this? It is not the stuff of fiction. It has no shape, it hasn't the balances so important in art. You know, if one line goes this way, another must go that way. All these lines are the same. These lives are like threads that get woven into a carpet and when it's done the weaver is surprised that the colors all blend: shades of blood, shades of tears, smell of sweat. Even the lives that don't fit, fit. Ethel, for instance. You don't know Ethel, but she was a college friend of mine who wanted to be a sculptor. She got married, of course. She's gone quite queer in the head and collects shells. Her house is full of them and she doesn't talk about anything else. No one visits her anymore.

Sometimes as I try to write this all down, I feel as if all I'm doing is a thing I used to do as a child, draw paper dolls. They all looked pretty much the same except one had blond hair, one red, one black. And I'd draw sets and sets of clothes, all of them interchangeable: evening gowns, tailored suits, slacks, shorts, negligees. When I'd much rather be able to draw a Medea or an Antigone. But they, you see, had sharp edges and endings, and the people I know don't. And their lives don't. I see, I saw, the slow wearing down of the years. Not lives lived in quiet desperation: no, there was nothing quiet in these lives. There was passion, and extremity, screeching, and lacerations of the flesh – one's own, of course. And all of us ended up wrecked. So it seems more a general than an individual problem. Oh, if you are looking for flaws, they are there, but this is not tragedy, after all. Or is it? I mean, Mira's prissiness and smugness and superiority and coldness, or Samantha's dependency, her childlike leaving of everything to Simp until it was too late, or Martha's arrogant assumption that she could live the way she wanted to and have what she wanted, or Oriane's intense and undeviating love for Sean, or Paula's driving ambition . . . Yes, those were all there.

But think about this: none of the men is wrecked. Well, Simp, of course. But he's quite happy there in his mother's house, with his martini allowance for the day, his delusions, his barroom audience. But the others all have pretty good jobs, some are remarried, all of them live, to varying degrees, what is called the good life. It's true, they're dull, but after all that bothers other people, not them. They probably don't find themselves dull. Sean lives on a little estate on Long Island and has two boats again. These days Roger has a swinging pad on the East Side and takes his vacations at Club Med, while Doris is on welfare. Can you figure that out? Is there any cause in nature for these things? Maybe the men are worse off than I think. Maybe they're going through all kinds of inner torment and just don't show it. It could be. I'll leave their pain to those who know and understand it, to Philip Roth and Saul Bellow and John Updike and poor wombless Norman Mailer. I only know the women are all middle-aged and poor as shit and struggling with things like trying to get the oldest kid off heroin, get the girls through college, pay for the shrink who's trying to treat daughter's anorexia or son's depression, or the orthodontist who's trying to help Billy to close his mouth. It depresses me. I remember Valerie saying once, 'Ah, don't you see that's why we're so great. We know what matters. We don't get caught up in their games!' but it seems an awfully high price to me. I look back to my own life and all I see is bombed-out terrain, full of craters and overturned rocks and mudholes. I feel like a survivor who has lost everything but her life, who wanders around inside a skinny shriveled body, collecting dandelion greens and muttering to herself.

20

Samantha survived. She went through a year and a half of legal and economic hell, but she ended up in a small apartment on the wrong side of the right town. She knew that staying near her friends was all that would save her, and she was saved, whatever that means. She started back to school at night, aiming to get a better job. How she paid for it, I don't know: talk about squeezing money from stones, Samantha knew how. Or rather, learned. They ate, and the kids were healthy and sometimes even happy. They helped Sam a lot, young as they were. They understood. In 1964, Fleur was eight and Hughie was five. Now, ten years later, Fleur is in college. Somehow, they managed it. Of course Samantha changed. She grew very thin and there was a severity about her appearance that remains to this day. She was on welfare for only a few months: it shamed her horribly. But later she would say thank heavens it was there for those few months. Men like Sam, and sometimes she says she would like to get married again. But there is something. She draws away from them just a little, she's hardly aware of it. She is not prepared yet to put her life in the hands of one of them, and that, after all, is still what marriage asks. So she goes on being single, has a pretty good job now as an office manager in a small local firm, and the three of them live as if they were rich on her $200 a week before taxes. But I am jumping ahead. Then, in the summer of 1964, there were only anguish and change and loss and hardship and the hideous question of whether they would survive, and if so, how? What would happen to deprived children in an affluent suburb? Who has not heard horror stories? Well, her children are the finest I know, but perhaps that is because of Samantha. That couldn't be predicted, and had to be suffered through just as if the ending were different.

Mira did not feel as if she had a part in that. Samantha's friends lived near her; Mira was in Beau Reve, polishing furniture. The money she had given to Samantha (who, incredibly, tried to pay it back a year and a half later) was the closest Mira ever came to a declaration of independence. Norm understood that. He never mentioned it, but for several weeks after he looked at the checkbook, he regarded Mira as from a great distance. His eyes on her were cold; she felt he was looking at a stranger. She often wanted to bring the whole thing up, to have it out, but she didn't dare. She remembered her feelings the last time they spoke about it, and was terrified of what more might be said, terrified of finding out what Norm really felt, and of feeling herself the emotions of that horrible night. So they went on. In August the bodies of the young civil rights workers were found, and the futile and laughable search began for someone to blame. So much for that, Mira thought bitterly. Her mouth, she noticed, was coming to have a thin and bitter aspect. She went on polishing furniture.

Martha's life, however, was turbulent, and in those months she came often to Mira, who was the only person she could talk to. David still filled her eyes, her laugh, her voice. You could not call it adoration, though. She saw David whole. She knew he was arrogant and selfish and magnetic and commanding and intelligent and occasionally dense and incredibly mean and petty. She accepted all of it. 'Who am I to ask for more?' she laughed. They had a terrible fight one evening in the Xerox room of the library when he wanted to copy a paper he had written for publication and she wanted to copy a paper she had written for a course she was taking and he wouldn't let her go first even though her paper had to be in by five o'clock and he ended by tearing it to shreds. Mira was appalled. 'You took that!'

'I hit him,' Martha said. 'I punched him in the face and kicked him.'

'What did he do?'

'Hit me back.' She removed her sunglasses to show the black eye.

'My God!'

'Well,' she went on complacently, 'then he retyped my paper for me. And he explained to Professor Epstein, who is a friend of his, that it was his fault my paper was late. I can't imagine what Epstein thinks – probably that we're both crazy – but he didn't dock me for lateness.' She laughed again. 'It was a power struggle, the kind of thing we're in all the time. But I understand that, I can live there. The problem with George is he doesn't fight back and leaves me always wrestling with my own guilt. George just gets sullen. I much prefer a good sock in the eye myself.'

'Oh, Martha!' Mira shuddered. It was things like this that made her retreat.

'Well, George is pulling his usual routine right now,' Martha went on breezily. 'You know, I told him about David as soon as I was sure it was more than a passing thing.'

'You said he took it fine,' Mira said, wondering where she found the coolness to talk so. She could not imagine such a thing in her own life.

'Yes. Then. I mean, what could he do? He's been sleeping with his secretary off and on for a year now. Whenever he stays in town overnight, he stays with her. We've always been honest with each other.'

'I know.'

'But the problem was David. He's so goddamn jealous.' Martha said this with a certain relish. 'He can't bear the thought of my sleeping with George. He holds my body, he talks about it . . . well, as if it were the center of the universe for him. I really think it is. It

273

isn't my body anymore. But it isn't possessiveness either that makes him act that way. It's that the two of us really are one. He stopped using a soap because I didn't like it, he's even given up a deodorant I don't like. He had a rash on his chest a couple of weeks ago, and he didn't want to make love because he didn't want me to see it. He wants to be perfect for me. And it's true, we feel the same way about everything, we feel the same feelings. That's why things are so turbulent with us. We're so close, we really want to be one person, and that means neither can allow the other to disagree about anything. The slightest difference in opinion feels like a chasm. And both of us are fighters, neither of us will give in. I feel as if for the first time in my life I've met my equal in a male.'

Martha was still glowing. She was dressing these days with thoughts of David, who had lovely taste, and she looked exquisite, her skin shades of paleness moving into pink, her hair simple, straight and long, her clothes simple and tailored. Mira gazed at her beyond envy, as if she were watching a miracle.

'So he's been after me to separate from George. I can't do that. George has been good to me, we have a good marriage, we like each other. And there isn't enough money – there's barely enough for us to live together and pay my tuition. If George had to live by himself, it would be difficult.'

'David lives with his wife.'

'Yes, but he says that's different. He doesn't like his wife. He uses her for a servant. He comes in late, never tells her where he is. She cleans the apartment, cooks his meals, and doesn't complain if he doesn't turn up for dinner after all, and she takes care of the kid. The brat, I should say. She was with David one day when I met him "accidentally" in the park. Yugh! Well, I hate kids anyway, they're all monsters, but she's worse than most. He says he doesn't sleep with his wife.' Martha laughed the braying laugh she used whenever her shit detector was working. 'Anyway, he's been giving me a hard time about it, but I was holding my own. And now, suddenly,

I get it from the other side. George has decided I'm really in love with David. I mean, at first I guess he thought it was just an affair, and after all I was with him more than with David, and he and I were other things besides lovers – you know. But when he decided that I loved David, he suddenly became impotent. George! That great lover! I was flabbergasted. I mean, he can't handle it after all! So now, in addition to everything else – I have a major paper on German socialism in the twenties and thirties due Wednesday, a real bitch! – in addition to David's grumblings and attacks, I have to put up with goddamned George's sullenness – because of course it's all my fault – and my own fucking guilt. Christ! Why is it all my fault? Did I get impotent when he started sleeping with Sally?'

They both giggled.

'Of course, I've been impotent all my fucking life. It doesn't matter!' she brayed, laughing. 'You know, it's convenient being a woman!'

'If you're impotent, what am I? I don't even get any pleasure from sex.'

'But you can masturbate.'

They pondered.

'It sucks, being a woman,' Martha finally announced.

After she'd left, Mira thought about it all. It was like another form of fairy tale. She pictured Martha making love to George – 'I may not get it off, but I'm a damned good whore,' she would say – moving around him, over him, on him, caressing him with hands and tongue, and George, usually so responsive, lying there limp. Like me, she thought, then forgave herself. Norm, after all, was hardly a good whore. And she pictured Martha making the best of George's impotence, carrying it to David like a gift, food set in plantain leaves to please the strange white man who had landed on the island. He would smile, his eyes would light up at the exotic stuff, he would eat and lie back content, and all their problems would be over.

But that is not what happened. David, darling David, difficult David became a walking explosive. First he accused her of lying to him. They argued that out for several weeks. Finally, in a weepy violent session, he admitted that he believed her. But then he grew even stranger and more wary. He began to make cutting remarks about George. Martha, of course, defended George staunchly. After a month and a half of passionate conversation followed by violent sex (which Martha loved), she probed and poked at him until he spat it out that if her husband could live with her without wanting to screw her then he had to be a faggot and if her husband was a faggot what was she and besides he'd always felt in himself a strong urge toward faggotry. This violent current carried them into Thanksgiving. Mira, listening, drifted away. They were so passionate, so involved. She'd met David several times, had lunch with him and Martha, and had found him almost irresistibly attractive. Well, what did that mean? Was she really in love with Martha and wanting to screw David because she couldn't screw Martha? Her mind rebelled. She was disgusted. It all seemed so ludicrous, so absurd. It was hard to believe that people lived and died about things like this, that they were really hurt or upset or crushed, that they could delude themselves that the things they felt mattered.

Just before Christmas, Mira had lunch with Martha.

'It's all decided,' Martha said, and she was grim and glowing at the same time. 'There's no other solution, there's nothing else to be done. We're both going to get divorced and later, when things simmer down – we don't want to hurt David's career – we'll get married.'

Martha's face was serene; it gave forth light. Then it grew grim again.

'I feel terrible about George. But he'll just have to learn to live without me. It will be hard for him, he depends on me for everything. But he'll make it. I hope. I can handle only so much guilt.'

'You're sure that's the right thing ...'

'Absolutely!' Martha announced transcendently. 'Absolutely right! We belong together.'

She waited until after the holidays to tell George, however. Early in January of 1965, George moved out.

Mira felt sorry for George, and invited him for dinner over Norm's objections. But Martha had been right. George could not live without her. He came to dinner, drank too much, and whined. He had taken to going to a shrink. He lived in a shabby rented room near his office. He had no life, no money. He was miserable. Mira invited him twice, then stopped. George stopped sending Martha as much money, saying he deserved to live too. Martha could not pay the bills on the house, could not buy shoes for the kids. It went round and round. Still, Martha was happy. David could come to the house now, they could spend full evenings together and go to bed, luxuriously, in her room. She introduced him to her children and watched with fascination and love as they, as she put it, 'learned to relate.'

'He's ten times more there for the kids than George ever was. He *talks* to them, Mira, he listens to their answers!'

There were problems. David had not left his wife, and now this was important to Martha. David had made the thing into a test – a test of love, almost. And she had passed it, she had separated from George, whom she loved, at some cost. David explained he had money problems. And his wife presented no difficulty, did she? She was a helpless little thing, and would go to pieces when he left. He had to wait until . . .

The end of that sentence varied, but Martha still trusted him. Mira sat wondering bitterly about women's credulity, but the few hints she dropped were not picked up by Martha. It was true that David almost lived with her as it was: he was at her house nearly every day. And it was true, Mira admitted as she saw them together, that he was in love with Martha. Then why? But it was the same old story. Mira was tired of it. Women and men. They played by different rules because the rules applied to them were different. It was very simple. It was the women who got pregnant and the women who ended up with the kids. All the rest stemmed from that. So women had to learn to protect themselves, had to be wary and careful. The way the rules had been set up, everything was against them. Martha was courageous and honest and loving, but she was also a damned fool.

Mira told herself this, sitting in the dark with her brandy. She felt mean and small, foreseeing tragedy for Martha. And tragedy it would be if David failed her. Her emotion for him was too intense and engulfing for it to be anything else. Maybe it won't happen, her other voice suggested. Maybe he's telling her the truth – after all, she believes him and she has a built-in shit detector. Maybe it will all work out and they'll live happily ever after. David had applied for a job in a college in Boston. It was better paying than the one he had, and if he got it, he and Martha would get married and move up there and he could still provide for his wife. That's what he said. Perhaps it was true. But the other part of Mira's mind nagged and picked. Why did he force Martha into something he wasn't ready for?

But both voices came together when she thought about herself. She knew what was right for her, and she had done it. She had hedged her bet. She had not understood the rules when she started playing, but she had managed to play right. It must have been feel. All her intelligence, that brilliance she presently applied to file cards listing windows to be washed, had not in fact gone to waste. In a world where women are victims, she was surviving on the winning side. She had a magnificent house, two fine boys, beautiful clothes. She and her husband had dinner at the club at least one night a week; if she had chosen, she could have played golf there every afternoon. She cleaned the house herself out of choice, not need. Wasn't that winning? Look at Samantha, and Lily, and Martha too now, forced to ask *David* for money.

She sat, her lips nervously pursing in and out, when she heard the garage door slide up, and Norm come in, stumble over the doorsill, mutter 'Shit!' and come into the room where she was sitting. 'Hi,' she said, and he said, 'Hi,' and he entered and poured himself a drink, but he didn't turn on the light.

She said nothing, but the entire surface of her skin came to attention. Something was going to happen. God knows she had imagined it often enough. He would come in one night and see her outlined against the window and he would remember the days when he respected her, and he would sit down on the hassock at her feet, and sip his drink and look at her dark profile and she would not be able to see his face, but she would remember the eager light and youth he had had back in the days when he was asking her to marry him and it would be there on his face and he would say, 'I understand why you sit in the dark, I want to do it myself, perhaps we can do it together, perhaps we can do it and touch each other's hands, not hold them, just touch, lightly. I would like to ask you what you dreamed last night. And why, when the moon goes beyond the clouds you watch it almost with terror, waiting for it to come out again. And why it is, whenever I put my hand out to touch Clark's head, such a beautiful little head, bent over his game, I always end up giving him a cuff instead, a friendly cuff, you know, but a cuff just the same, and I always say something like "How's tricks, big fella?" and he looks around at me as if I were an annoying fact of life, like bathtime, that had to be placated and is to be dealt with as shortly and easily as possible. And Normie. God, I hate that kid. Why is that, Mira, when I love him so much? But when he stumbles down halls with exactly the awkwardness I had as a kid, I want to kill him. Part of me wants to run and catch him so he won't hurt himself, and to carry him, carry him everywhere so he'll never hurt himself, and part of me wants to storm down the hall and smash him against the wall because he's such an idiot that he will hurt himself, and I end up doing nothing except making some nasty crack and he turns to me with contempt and hate on his face and my insides curdle because that wasn't it, I don't want to do

279

that to him, what is that all about, Mira, do you know? Does it happen to you? And I wanted to tell you that last night I had a dream, a nightmare. Can I tell you about it?'

Who knows, maybe Norm thought things like that. It could have been.

So when he sat down and was silent she could hear her heart beating because she knew it was about to happen, that her expectations were coming true, and she tried to help, she tried not to help too much, it was difficult to find the right balance, she didn't want to push him and repel him by her pushiness, she only wanted to welcome him, to tell him he was welcome in her dark world where you could look out at the night and be part of it at the same time, and so she said in a low voice, 'The moon is so beautiful tonight.'

And when he didn't answer she could hear her words in her head, hear them over and over, words of an asshole, a gushing idiot, gurgling, 'The moon is so beautiful tonight,' like something out of an Italian opera, except thankfully in Italian so that when the lovers went into their duet you could believe it because you couldn't understand what they were saying. Feeling stupid, feeling denied, she opened her mouth obediently to say the usual words, 'How was your day?' but they wouldn't come out.

'I love to watch it from this angle in winter,' was what she said. 'When the tree branches are outlined against it. It is all so fine, so complex. Just one tree. Look, see what I mean? Just one tree, but look at the interconnections. Like the most delicate lace. Imagine what the roots must be like.'

He sipped his drink. She could hear the ice cubes tinkle in his glass. He cleared his throat. Her heart felt tender, overflowing. It was so hard for him. She wanted to put her hand out and touch him, but she restrained herself.

'Mira,' he said finally, 'this is very hard for me and I don't expect you to understand it at all, I don't understand it myself, and I don't want you to think it reflects on you at all, it's just me, just me. . . .'

She turned her head toward him, puzzled. A deep line invaded her forehead.

'Well, I guess you've noticed that I haven't been home much recently and that's because . . . oh, hell, what's the use of dragging it out! Mira, I want a divorce.'

CHAPTER FOUR

1

As I understand it, the medieval view of sin was very personal. Dante placed his murderers in a higher circle of hell than those who committed fraud. A sin is a violation not of a law but of a part of the self; punishment is meted out according to what part of the self has been abused. In the neat hierarchy of Dante's hell, sins of concupiscence are less severe than sins of irascibility, but the worst are those that violate the highest faculty, reason.

This seems strange to us, who think about crime (not sin – the only sin left is sex) according to the degree of harm done to the victim. Only that strange category, the victimless crime, remains to remind us of earlier ways of thinking. But I find the old notions somehow appealing. Not that I want to go back to them – it is outrageous to have some outer authority tell you what is proper use and abuse of your own faculties, and it is ludicrous to hold reason higher than body or feeling. Still there is something true and profoundly sane about the belief that acts like murder or theft or assault violate the doer as well as the done to. We might even, if we thought this way, have less crime. The popular view of crime, as far as I can deduce it from movies and television, is that it is a breaking of a rule by someone who thinks they can get away with that, implicitly, everyone would like to break the rule, but not everyone is arrogant enough to imagine they can get away with it. It therefore becomes very important for the rule upholders to bring such arrogance down. So television crime is a contest between two powers, and in a way this conception subtly encourages the spirited to defy the rules. Some of the most popular rule upholders are liked because they too break the rules, are unorthodox in approach, although they are on the side of the angels.

Whereas in fact, I imagine it costs someone something to break and enter, to steal, to murder, costs something quite apart from the fear of discovery or punishment. I don't know what exactly – my experience with ordinary criminals is nonexistent – but I think that one's way of perceiving himself and his relation to the world must be jarred, must contain some hurt, some rift, a germ of hopelessness. Of course, lots of people besides those who commit crimes feel that way too, I suppose. And of course the worst crimes are perfectly legal. So maybe none of this makes any sense, maybe it is impossible to talk about crime. But then the old categories come flaming up, looking better than ever, although in need of revision: a good life is one in which no part of the self is stifled, denied, or permitted to oppress another part of the self, in which the whole being has room to grow. But room costs something, everything costs something, and no matter what we choose, we are never happy about paying for it.

Mira was thrust into freedom just as she had been chuted into slavery, or at least that is how she thought of it. She could have refused Norm a divorce or she could have acceded easily, demanding nothing, but she agreed to the divorce and submitted a bitter bill, totting up the cost of her services for fifteen years. Norm was horrified that she could view their marriage in that way, but at the same time he argued that she had not deducted her food, lodging, and clothes.

Their separation and divorce did not feel like good freedom to her, it felt more like being thrown out of the igloo in the middle of a snowstorm. There is lots of space to wander in, but it's all cold.

She alternated between cold bitter moods in which she sat at a desk listing pages and pages of labors she had performed, and checking out with employment agencies the going rate for such workers, and simply falling apart. Some days she raged like an out-of-control train, charging through the house, cleaning it with compulsive ferocity, purging basement and attic and every closet of fifteen years of shit. Still pieces of Norm remained: there were the boys, to begin with, and at times she turned that fury on them. Other times she wept, inconsolably, ceaselessly, and would have to wear sunglasses to the market next day. Some days she would spend in the bathroom, bathing and oiling her body, shaving her legs and underarms, touching up her hair dye, applying makeup, studying herself in a variety of costumes, then undressing and putting on a shabby old robe.

She began to drink during the days. Several times she was staggering when the boys come in from school. Norm found her drunk once when he came in to get something he had left behind, and he warned her severely that if she did not 'shape up,' as he put it, he would take the boys away from her. She was disheveled, her hair sticking out at all angles, and she slouched, in old baggy pants she used for gardening, in her usual chair. She leaned back and laughed.

'Go ahead!' she crowed at him. 'You want them so much, take them! They're yours too. They're built like you. They both have the great manly appurtenance!'

Shocked and apprehensive, Norm backed out of the room and did not return to the house again. Mira giggled every time she thought of it. She told the story to Martha, told it over and over. 'Hah! "I warn you, Mira, I'll take the boys away from you!" Hah! He wants them like he wants me. They'd put a cramp on his style with his little chippy.'

At night, though, the drinking led her into depression. One night Martha called. They had taken to calling each other at any hour: there were no husbands to complain. She called at one, one thirty, and two, and still there was no answer. She got worried, and dressed, and drove over to Mira's. The car was in the garage. Martha rang the doorbell and kept ringing it until Normie, eyes full of sleep, finally answered. Martha acted as though it were not unusual for her to come visiting at three in the morning, and sent Normie back to bed. Both boys had adopted, in the face of the inexplicable chaos that had suddenly entered their lives, a kind of ignorance. They saw, heard, and said nothing. They gazed blankly and went their own ways. So Normie went back to bed and even to sleep, while Martha wandered through the house looking for Mira. She found her finally, on the floor of her bathroom. Her wrists were cut. There was blood on the floor, but not a great deal. Martha washed off Mira's arms and made tourniquets for them. The cuts in the wrists were not really deep. Mira had managed to cut the smaller blood vessels but miss the large vein in the wrist. Still, she was unconscious. Martha cleaned up the bathroom and washed Mira's face with cold water. Mira began to come to.

'What did you do, pass out?'

Mira stared at her. 'I guess so.' She glanced at her arms. 'Oh, yeah. Gee, I did it. I really did it. I've been wanting to do it for a long time.'

'Well, you didn't do it very well,' Martha said.

Mira stood up. 'I need a drink.'

They went downstairs.

'Are your kids alone?'

Martha nodded.

Mira looked at her watch. 'Is it okay?'

'Lisa's fourteen, for God's sake, it ought to be.'

'Yeah.'

They sat drinking, smoking.

'I kept thinking I ought to care about the boys, but I didn't.'

'No. I know. Nothing else matters when you feel that much pain.'

'No. Not even getting even with Norm. Because, you know, he might feel guilty for a little while, but mostly he'd be annoyed at the crimp I put in his plans, saddling him with the boys. But he could even handle that: he has enough money. There's just nothing I can do to him except kill him. If I could beat him up, I'd feel better, but I can't, I'd have to shoot him or something. And that's not very satisfying. What I want is to make him cry, to see him living in pain the way I am.'

'I imagine that's the way George feels about me.'

285

'Oh, George is so full of self-pity he can't even think about anger. It would be refreshing if he could.'

'Yeah. Listen, Mira, you have to do something.'

'I know,' she sighed.

'What about going back to school?'

'Yes.'

'Okay.' Martha stood up. 'I'll be at school tomorrow. I have a nine o'clock class. I'll meet you at the student center at noon for lunch, and then we'll wander around and see what we can find out.'

'Okay.'

So it was settled. No further discussion of anything was necessary: by this time they knew the insides of the other's mind so well that they never had to explain an action or a motivation.

2

There was a march that spring from Selma to Montgomery; and a new music was being heard, made by strange-looking creatures who called themselves the Beatles. The march seemed admirable to many of Mira's generation, an admirable symbol of an impossible aspiration. The Beatles just seemed loud. Neither seemed to have greater import: the generation that reached adulthood in the fifties had no comprehension of the possibility of change.

Mira enrolled for the fall term at the university, which agreed to grant her full credit for her two years of earlier work. The episode with her wrists had calmed her down. She had done her best not to survive and had discovered she could not do well enough. So she settled down to trying to survive. She worked a lot in the garden. She had little to do with the boys. They came and went, and asked of her only meals and clean clothes, being not terribly fussy about either. She would gaze at them sometimes, wondering when and how it happened that she had lost her feeling for them. She had memories that did not seem very old, of holding them on her lap and talking to them and listening to what they said. But the further she tried to push her memory, the further it receded. They were twelve and thirteen now: the last physical affection she could remember showing them was in the old house, which meant at least five years ago. Clark had been pounced on by a gang of boys and had come in sobbing and bruised, and she had set him on her lap and sat there holding him while he cried, and in time he calmed and just sat leaning against her shoulder, his eyes sunken into reddened sockets from crying, still catching his breath, and then he'd put his thumb in his mouth, which he still did at night, and suddenly Norm walked in and exploded.

'Are you trying to make a faggot out of that kid, holding him on your lap, Mira? Letting him suck your thumb, for God's sakes! What in the hell is the matter with you?'

Scurried getting down, Mira's protests, storming from Norm, more tears by Clark followed, and Clark was sent to his room in disgrace, while Norm shook his head, pouring himself a drink, muttering about the stupidity of women and the unconscious possessiveness of mothers. 'I'm not blaming you, Mira, I know you didn't think. But I'm telling you you have to think! You can't treat a son that way.'

Had she, after that, had impulses, wanted to reach out and touch them, wanted to hold them when they touched her, and restrained herself? She could not remember. That had been another world, a world dictated by Norm. Everything seemed different now. She did as she pleased. She cleaned only when it was necessary, she wore old clothes around the house. Meals were simple and relaxed and suited to the boys' taste. In time, as calmness was restored around them, they spent more time at home, and sometimes they even sat down near Mira and started a conversation. But Normie was the image of Norm, and Clark had his coloring and his eyes, and when she looked at them, something in her felt hard. They were part of Them. She remembered Lily tearing Carlos' hands away from her body, fighting him off as if he were full-grown and trying to attack her. She found herself, as they spoke, continually correcting their grammar, reminding

287

them of homework or chores, telling them they were filthy and needed showers, reproaching them for not cleaning their rooms. It was effective. They did not stay long and soon stopped sitting down with her. She did not care.

The only person she had deep feeling for was Martha, who was having a terrible summer. Money problems were mounting: she feared losing the house. 'It wouldn't matter, except apartments are even more expensive than the house is. Where are we going to live? I can't blame George, although I suspect he is being a bastard about it. I suppose that's his way of showing anger. He has his apartment and he sees his shrink twice a week: that's expensive. I have to get a job. But with the house, the kids, and school, I don't know where I'll find the time. And David. I'm starting to get really upset with him. It's been almost nine months now, and he's still living with Elaine. He does give me money every once in a while, that's the only way I've survived this long, but now that's his excuse for staying with her. The Boston job fell through. It seems to me he's used whatever excuse was handy. He has the ideal world: two women, two families, both centered around him. He has a fucking harem, for God's sakes!'

But she was afraid to bring the argument to a head.

Mira started back to school, extremely nervous, taking only two courses, unsure of how she would be able to manage after all these years. But there was a whole group of them at the local university, middle-aged women back at school. She was astonished to find them and they to find each other. All had the same trepidations, all had domestic concerns. Mira was not alone. Her courses seemed amazingly easy, and she did three times the work necessary, not out of anxiety but from interest. She had the time. She had plenty of time.

She began, for the first time in years, to think wistfully about sex. She replayed Martha's stories in her mind, imagining Martha and David together, wondering if she could feel the way Martha felt. But Martha and David were strange, she thought. Not everyone was like them.

Each of them loathed their own body. They took showers three times a day. Martha shuddered at her own genitals and tried to fight David off the first time he tried to kiss them. He adored her cunt, he insisted on cunnilingus, and after she relaxed, she liked it. But there was always a period of distaste first. And she adored the penis, worshiped it almost, while he felt it to be absurd and repulsive. She enjoyed fellatio more than intercourse, and David learned to lie back and enjoy it too. When they had intercourse, it was his thrust and the feel of his organ that sent her swooning; and it was the sight of her swoon, the sense of her liquidity, that sent him over. Each of them experienced ecstasy through the other, almost *for* the other. And out of bed too, it was as if each of them lived in the other, wanted to be the other, experienced life much of the time as the other would experience it. It was, Mira thought, enlarging, as if you could live outside yourself. But too intense. The 'too' never left her mind. How could you keep that up?

Late in October, late, very late at night, Mira's telephone rang. A thin, distant voice called her name. It was Martha. She was not recognizably talking, or crying. She called faintly, 'Mira,' then seemed to fall away from the phone. Then, 'Mira?' again, then a silence that seemed to hold distant sighs or sobs or wire noises.

'Martha? Are you okay?'

The voice grew a little stronger. 'Mira!'

'Do you need help?'

'Oh, God, Mira!'

'I'll be right there.'

She threw some clothes on and went out into the chilly October night. The moon had been orange earlier, but it was fading now. The stars glittered overhead just as they would for young lovers with the world before them. Or so they think, Mira thought bitterly. She knew Martha's trouble had to be David.

Martha's front door was unlocked, and she went in. Martha was sitting on the edge of the bathtub leaning over the toilet, seat up. She had a bottle in her hand. She looked up when Mira came in. Her face was swollen and her cheek was black and blue. One nostril was red and swollen, and a thin line of blood trickled down from it. Her shoulder, exposed in the nightgown, was also black and blue.

Mira sighed. 'My God.'

'Don't call Him, He's on their side,' Martha said, then suddenly crumpled, let her face fall in her hand, and began to sob wildly.

Mira let her cry, and gently removed the bottle from her hand and looked at it. It was Ipecac. Mothers know it; it makes babies vomit, and you use it on those terrible nights when you suspect a child has swallowed half a bottle of Grandma's sleeping pills.

'What did you do?'

Martha couldn't talk. She was sobbing. She just shook her head back and forth, and then suddenly, vomited gigantically, a rush of liquid with feathery bits in it. Mira waited until she was through, then washed her face with a cool cloth. Martha would not let Mira wipe up the toilet. 'Look, I know what it's like. I've done it for the kids enough times.'

'So have I. I'm used to it.'

'You never get used to it!' Martha insisted, and got down on her knees and cleaned the bowl. When she was through, she stood up. 'I think that was it. I feel okay.'

'What did you do?'

'Took a bottle of sleeping pills.'

'How long ago?'

'About ten minutes before I took the Ipecac,' Martha said, and laughed.

'I need a shower, then I'll air this place out,' she said.

'You're an agreeable suicide, I must say,' Mira smiled. 'Mind if I have a drink?'

'No. Pour me one too.'

Martha got into the shower. Mira sat in Martha's bedroom, drinking, smoking. Everybody should clean up their own vomit. Everybody should clean up the toilet they use. Why not? Problem was kids. Can't ask them. I wonder why not? Martha's bedroom was austere and delicate at the same time. Plain and stark, but with delicate prints, gracefully framed, straight-hanging draperies in delicate fabric. It was very restful, very nice. Why not? Balances, balances. Things didn't have to be the way they were.

Martha emerged looking horrible. Her delicate face had deep lines in it, unpleasant lines. There were bitter lines along her mouth, a deep frown on her forehead; her eyes were puffy. She sat down on the end of the bed and took the drink Mira handed her. Mira waited, looking at her. She sipped. She looked up.

'Well, that's that,' she said.

Mira looked listening.

'David came for dinner tonight,' she said, breathing deeply, launching into the just quieted wound. 'It was a little celebration. His paper was accepted by the *Journal of Comparative Literature*, and he was so happy. I was so happy for him. You know, I haven't been doing much cooking lately – no time since I've been working – but this afternoon I ran around getting filet specially sliced for tournedos, fresh asparagus. I boiled a chicken yesterday – my kids hate boiled chicken! – just so I'd have broth to make risotto. I bought a little jar of caviar – really splurging – and hard-boiled some eggs. And I bought fresh strawberries – the last of the season and I paid an arm and a leg for them – and red wine. And it was great. If I do say so myself. It was beautiful, and I felt so happy, and everything felt so right. I felt so happy doing it for him, I felt I could do it forever and ever. And he looked so beautiful sitting there. He was very funny, talking about his colleagues' reactions to the news about his article. It's such a jealous, backbiting department. He was funny, but he really understands them. He's not like most men, you know? He thinks about what people are feeling as well as what they're saying. So he's interesting.'

She sipped her drink again and bent over to wipe her nose. She was sniffling. Blood was trickling out along with mucus. She blew it and wiped it and sat up, but the sniffling continued.

'And we were sitting with snifters of the cognac he'd brought, and Lisa was in her room doing homework and

291

Jeff was asleep, and we were sitting in the living room, on the couch, not too close because I wanted to be able to look at him, and we had coffee on the table in front of the couch, half-drunk...'

She began to cry then. Mira waited.

She pulled herself up again. 'And then Lisa went to bed, and I leaned back against the arm of the couch, looking at him, basking in it, in him, feeling warm and sexy and comfortable and just loving looking at him, and all of a sudden he turns to me with a serious, solemn face, and says, "Martha, I have something to tell you."'

She was crying as she spoke now, interspersing words and gasps.

'But I was still drifting, floating, in that miraculous place, and I didn't pay attention, I put out my hand and said, "Yes, darling," or something stupid like that, and he took my hand, and he said, "Martha, Elaine's pregnant."

'Then he put his head in his hands, and I sat up, and I screamed "What!" and he shook his head, still in his hands, kept shaking it, and then I realized he was crying, and I moved over to him and I held him, held his head and back, and rocked him, and he talked, he said it was some kind of accident and he didn't know how it happened, she was trying to trap him because she knew he wanted out of the marriage, and I was crying too, and rocking him and saying, "Yes, I understand, baby, it's okay, it'll be okay," and in a while he started to calm down, but all the while my mind was whirring and it got hotter and hotter and hotter, and when he stopped crying I threw him away from me, I sat back and shrieked at him. Accident? When they weren't sleeping together? How did that come about? Okay, lie number one, but I always knew that was a lie. But she knew about me, she knew he wanted out, how come he trusted her with birth control, I mean didn't he have any idea? And then I remembered him saying how much he would like to have a son. He loved his daughter but...' Martha laughed bitterly. 'And I looked at his face and I knew. I knew it was what he really wanted. He never intended to divorce her. He made me wreck my life for him, but he never had any intention of damaging his. I looked at him and I could have killed him. I just roared and went for him. I pounded him, I kicked him, I scratched him. He defended himself. I guess I look like a mess, but believe me, he's a picture too. Then I threw him out. That motherfucker, that cocksucker, that fucking bastard!' She was gone again, screaming in rage and pain, sobbing. The children's bedroom doors remained adamantly closed. Martha cried for half an hour. 'Oh, God, I don't want to live anymore,' she gasped out finally. 'It hurts too much.'

3

By this time, all of us had a word. It was THEM, and we all meant the same thing by it: men. Each of us felt done in by one of them, but that wasn't it. Because each of us had friends, and our friends were also being done in by them. And each of our friends had friends . . . But it wasn't only husbands. We had heard about Lily's friend Ellie, whose husband was a brute, who finally got a separation from him, but then he would break into the house and beat her up in the middle of the night, and she couldn't stop him. Literally. The cops wouldn't do anything because he still owned the house. Her lawyer said there was nothing he could do. Maybe there was, but Bruno had threatened him too and maybe he was frightened. She couldn't get anyone to help her. She didn't want to go down to the police station and sign a complaint about Bruno. She felt he would lose his job, and she didn't especially want to see him go to jail. But finally, that's what she had to do. And he did lose his job. He didn't go to jail. But he stopped paying her anything. So big deal. She won. Won what? Status as a welfare mother.

Or Doris. Roger wanted the divorce, and she was angry, so she really soaked him. She asked for fifteen thousand a year for her and the three kids. But after all, he was making thirty-five. And she had quit school when they got married and supported him for three years

293

while he finished. She'd agreed to put her eggs in his basket, which is what he wanted, and then he breaks the basket. You can't blame her. She was thirty-five and hadn't worked in years. When she had worked, she'd been a typist. She had no pension plan, no seniority built up. But Roger got furious at the judge's decision, and got himself transferred out of the state. She can't touch him. He sends her a hundred a month for the kids. Three kids. She can't do a thing.

Or Tina, who dared to have a lover after she was divorced. Phil had one too, but of course, that's different. He didn't have the kids. He said he wasn't going to give her money as long as that man was hanging around, and if she wanted to give him legal trouble about it, he'd take the kids away. 'Any judge,' he said threateningly, a judge himself emerging from the heavens, 'any judge in this country would take those kids away from a woman who lets a man stay in her house overnight. A whore is a whore, and don't you forget it.' Maybe he wasn't right about that, but Tina was too terrified to find out. 'Phil,' she said, 'he's a nice guy. The kids like him. He pays more attention to them than you ever did.' That was not exactly calculated to work. It might have mattered if what they were having was a human encounter as she thought, but he was just nose-thumbing in a power struggle. Tina didn't sue him, he didn't pay. She's on welfare too. If you want to find out who all the welfare mothers are, ask your divorced male friends. It sounds easy, you know, going on welfare. But apart from the humiliation and resentment, you don't really live very well. In case you didn't know. Which is unpleasant for a woman, but sends her into fits when she looks at her kids.

The point is that we all heard these stories, we kept hearing them. It seemed everybody was getting divorced. After a while you stopped asking whose fault it was; after a while you even stopped asking why. We had all, without reason, got married, and now we were all, without reason, getting divorced. After a while it didn't seem abnormal. We didn't feel the world was falling apart.

Anyone who's been married any length of time knows how rotten marriage is, and we'd listen to the news commentators deploring the high divorce rate as just so much more pious hypocrisy. It wasn't that we were or were not married that bothered us. It was that we were all so poor that we could be invaded (even Norm would come into the house and read Mira's mail – he had the right, he said, he owned the house), we could be beat up, we could be done anything to and no one, no one, from the cops to the courts to the state legislatures, no one was on our side. Sometimes even our friends and families weren't on our side. We gathered together uneasily in little groups of twos or threes, muttering, bitter. Even our shrinks weren't on our side. We excoriated THEM to the point of nausea, but that was all it was, vomiting the immediate cause of indigestion. The sickness, though, was chronic. We understood that the laws were all for THEM, that the setup of society was all for THEM, that everything existed for THEM. But we didn't know what to do about it. We half believed there was something terribly wrong with US. We crept into our holes and learned to survive.

4

George and Martha got back together, at a cost. They did it mainly because of money problems, but George had never really been able to function alone, and was grateful for Martha's difficulty. And George is a good guy. He did not ever use what happened against Martha, not even when he was very angry.

But the truth is, he didn't need to. The affair with David finished her. She was never the same afterward. But I'm getting ahead of myself again. Will this story never end? My God, on and on and on. Only an atomic blast would end it. Sometimes I understand hawks: they too, like me, have moments of such intolerable pain that they would be willing to see it all go up, and would even cheer the mushroom cloud.

Christmas came, then Easter, then summer. Norm insisted on a divorce, Mira held him up. She counted the years, counted what he would have had to pay a housekeeper, nurse, laundress, chauffeur, prostitute – for that is what she felt, now, to have been her most painful role – and presented Norm with the bill.

'The money is all yours. You told me some time ago you could live just as well in a hotel. Consider that you have lived with paid services for fifteen years. That is what it would have cost you.'

Norm was outraged, his lawyer was outraged, her lawyer thought she was insane. They went over and over her account. In the end, they settled: Mira as well as her lawyer knew the judge would never grant her what she asked, despite Norm's high income. What she got was the house as long as she lived in it (there was a mortgage, and joint ownership – if she moved, she would receive half of their parity), the car (paid for: a '64 Chevrolet), six thousand a year in alimony and another nine in child support (until the children reached twenty-one). She figured it out. With the house and furniture and her clothes, she figured she had been paid two thousand dollars a year for the fifteen years they had been married, and would receive six thousand a year every year they were not. It was a strange arrangement, but by now Mira was as thin and brittle as a saltine. 'Not quite slave labor, I guess. I got something besides room and board.'

Mira did well in school, and liked being back doing scholarly work. Martha was surviving. Samantha was surviving. Lily was barely surviving. The boys went on. The years went on. Mira's work was good, even brilliant. Her teachers advised her to go on for a Ph.D. Mira listened to 'Eleanor Rigby' and thought that something had happened to popular music. Lily had another breakdown. Martha finished her B.A. and was accepted at the university law school. She had not been deranged after all. Mira made out applications, asked for recommendations. Martin Luther King was killed. Bobby Kennedy was killed. My Lai happened, although we didn't know it yet. The mail arrived. Mira had been accepted at Yale and Harvard. She sat there looking at the letters, unable to believe them. Norm was remarried, to the woman Mira had once called his little chippy. Mira was about to put the house up on the market when Norm called and told her he would buy out her half. He was willing to pay her $5000 less than she thought her half was worth considering what the house would bring on the open market. They quarreled. She accepted his offer when he came up $2500. After all, she would have been the one who would have had to clean it up every morning, expecting buyers. Sigh, sigh. Shit, man. Enough, I can't understand anymore. What happened was bad enough without reviewing it. I'm sorry I started this. But I guess I had to do it. And now I feel I have to finish it. It's only July 26. School doesn't open until September 15. Besides, as they used to say, what else do I have to do?

Mira sold all the furniture to Norm. She got the boys enrolled in a good private high school. And one morning in August of 1968, Mira packed her suitcases in her car to drive to Boston. She stood for a while in front of the empty house. The boys were with Norm. They were all coming back tomorrow, when Norm and his new wife would move in. She wondered what that woman would feel like, moving into her house, full of furniture she had chosen and cared for and devoted her life to. Yes. She saluted it.

'Good-bye, furniture,' she said. And the furniture, being furniture, sat.

5

Before she left, Mira made two visits. The first was to Martha. Martha knew she was coming, but when she arrived, Martha was wearing an old, stained wrapper that made her look pregnant, and had a kerchief wrapped around her head. She was down on her hands and knees, holding a small tool, scraping the wax off the kitchen floor.

'You don't mind if I do this while we talk. I have so little time these days,' Martha said.

Mira sat on a kitchen bench. She sipped the gin and

tonic Martha had given her. Martha talked. She was through her first year of law school. She didn't know what she wanted to specialize in. She was interested in international law, but that was an impossible field for a woman. She talked much of the intricate politics of the school. Martha had gained much weight. Her delicate frame looked odd under all that flesh. Martha rarely looked Mira in the eyes these days. She talked to walls, floors, knives and forks. She never mentioned David. George was unhappy. During their separation he had learned some independence. Now he felt constrained by Martha's competence. He thought he wanted a divorce.

'Funny, isn't it? He's having an affair with a woman in his office, but that's not why he wants the divorce. He wants a swinging pad in Manhattan. He wants to try what he never had. You can understand it, except it's all so goddamned adolescent.' She laughed. She worked at the wax, square inch by square inch. She worked very slowly.

'If you have another of those putty knives, I'll help you,' Mira said. 'At the rate you're going, you'll be done in two weeks.'

'It's okay. I'm such a perfectionist that I'd redo what you did anyway.'

'Is George serious?'

'About the divorce? I don't know. He's serious about having an apartment in New York. He misses his bachelor bliss,' she laughed, 'although he didn't think it was such bliss when he had it.'

Scrape, scrape.

'But it would be messy for me. I have two years of school to go. My job is only part-time, I barely pay for food out of it. And what George wants now is a fancy place, not the dump he had before. I can't imagine how we'll pay for everything. He got a good raise a couple months ago, but he's a dreamer if he thinks that will cover it. We still have two thousand dollars in debts from the separation, one thousand of it being what he owes the shrink.'

'Does he still go?'

'No. He's got me now,' Martha laughed humorlessly. Martha had not yet looked directly at Mira.

They talked about their children, about the future. Martha's voice was monotonous; it had neither highs nor lows.

'Do you ever see him?' Mira asked finally. Martha stopped scrapping and pushed the kerchief back on her forehead.

'Not often. The law school is across campus from liberal arts. Sometimes I see him in the student center. He doesn't seem to see me. He looks just the same. I hear rumors about him: he's involved with a married woman student. French major. So they say.'

She resumed her scraping. She'd completed about two square feet.

'And you? How do you feel now?'

Martha stood up. 'Ready for a refill?' She walked to the counter, stood with her back to Mira and poured two drinks. 'How I feel.' She said it as a statement. 'I don't know. I don't feel anything, really. I feel as if I'll never feel anything again. He's a bastard but I love him. I feel like all the slobs in the song, "My Man Bill," you know? I'd go back to him tomorrow if he asked. I know I would. I'm not saying I wouldn't give him hell, but I'd go back. But he won't ask.'

'Why don't you look for someone else?'

Martha shrugged. 'I do. At least I think I do. But my heart isn't in it. Right now all I care about is getting that degree and getting out. I've been in school too long. My God, I'm thirty-six years old.'

'So am I and I'm just starting.'

Martha laughed. 'No one can say we don't try.'

'But I feel the way you do – as if nothing can ever matter again the way things used to matter. As if nothing again could touch the heart that closely, hurt that much.'

'Maybe that's getting old.'

'Maybe.'

She left Martha still crouched on the floor, five square feet of the kitchen floor dewaxed. 'Good luck,' Martha said tonelessly. 'And keep in touch.'

In touch. What did that mean, send Christmas cards? How can you keep in touch with someone who is beyond touch, who has cut the nerves before they reached the skin, so as not to feel a touch, any touch at all. She understood what Martha was doing, and why, but it made her feel terribly alone. But what was Martha's alternative? To go on feeling? As Lily did?

Mira walked across the grounds of Greenwood Mental Hospital. It was made up of many open squares of grass surrounded by trees that obscured the chain-link fence that rose twelve feet high around it. There were trees in the squares too, and benches. There were a few beds of flowers. People wandered or sat, nicely dressed people. You could not tell if they were patients or visitors. At Lily's dormitory, Mira inquired for her, and a nurse smilingly led her out to a corner of the grass where several young women sat on benches talking. Lily jumped up when she saw Mira and as they met, they embraced awkwardly, Mira's stiffness and Lily's hard tension meeting at the same time as their affection did.

Lily was terribly thin, but she was dressed nicely, much better than she dressed at home, in neat brown pants and a beige sweater. She was wearing makeup, a lot of makeup, and her hair was freshly dyed. The other young women were introduced. They too, were well-dressed and heavily made up, with brilliant eye shadows, false eyelashes, orangey pancake makeup, heavy rouge, deep red lipstick. Mira did not know if they were patients or guests. They talked for a while about the weather, and then the three young women left. Lily had cigarettes but no matches, and was delighted with Mira's lighter. 'You always have to ask the nurse for a light. One of the rules here. They're afraid the crazies will burn the place down.'

'Those women,' Mira nodded to the departing figures. 'Are they guests?'

'Oh, no. They're like me.' Lily laughed. 'What this place really is is a country club for women whose husbands don't want them anymore.'

Mira looked around. That sounded like Lily's insanity,

300

but almost everyone around them was female, between thirty and fifty.

'Aren't there any men?'

'Oh, yes, but they're mostly old alcoholics.'

'Are there old alcoholic women too?'

'Yes, lots of them. We're all people nobody wants.' Lily smoked hastily, as if she were anxious to finish her cigarette so she could have another and light it herself. 'All my friends are like me, though.' She talked about them, about herself.

'Before I got sick I went to see my aunt. She said I was a spoiled brat, she said her husband was worse than Carl. She said Carl was a good husband compared to most. My aunt said I should be grateful for Carl, he doesn't push me around. Sometimes I think she's right, but I can't stand it, I can't stand living with him. I wanted a divorce, that's why I'm here. I wanted a divorce, but then when he walked out of the house I ran after him, I ran all the way down the street screaming for him, trying to hold on to his jacket. I couldn't be alone, I didn't know how to do things. How could I do it? Pay bills. I've never paid a bill in my life. And the bulb in the kitchen light went out and I just sat there and cried. I thought I'd be living in the dark. I cried and I begged him to come back, but then when he came back I couldn't stand him, the Nazi, the martinet, and I kept trying to get him to act human. So he had me locked up again. My aunt, she belongs to a suicide group. A suicide group! She wanted me to join.' Lily laughed richly.

'Suicide group?'

'Yes, they call each other up, you know, late at night, they say things like, "This is a gray day and tomorrow the sky will be bluer," or "I'm here pulling for you, I know you'll have the courage to come through this."' She laughed again, the old rich laugh, and there was no hysteria in it. Nor did she seem to be shaking. 'I saw an ad for a group like that once. It had big letters CALL US IF YOU NEED ANYTHING, something like that, and then it said if you had a drug problem or if you felt suicidal or if you had any problem at all you wanted to talk to someone about, to call them, and they had this telephone number. Then in small print it said, "Mondays through Thursdays, noon until 10 P.M." I took the number down but I never used it. I never felt bad at those hours.' Laughter.

'The trouble is,' she continued, breaking often into laughter, 'I'm not suicidal! It's like having a cold instead of pneumonia: there's nothing anybody can do. The psychiatrist – what a joke! He has us all wearing make-up, dolled-up like Mrs. Astor's horse. We walk around with all this makeup, going to tea, my dear.'

A small plump woman meandered across the lawn and dropped alone on a bench. She had frizzy hair and a bewildered look. 'There's Inez,' Lily said. 'Her husband doesn't come to see her much, not like Carl. He shows up with the kids almost every Sunday. They don't stay long, but nobody is going to be able to say he didn't do everything right. Inez's husband only comes once in a while. I listen to them talking. She cries, the tears run down her cheeks, she cries softly, you know, not huge sobs or shrieks, just like a continual soft rain. And she whimpers, she says, "Please, Joe, let me out. I promise I'll be good this time, I'll try to be a good wife, honest, I'll really try, I'll learn how." But she's too smart, you know? She could never retard herself enough to be a good wife.'

Inez suddenly got up from the bench and knelt on the ground behind it. It looked as if she were worshiping the tree.

'She loves bugs,' Lily said. 'She watches them all the time. She used to read books about bugs when she lived at home, but her husband thinks that's crazy, she doesn't vacuum the rug or wash the dishes, all she does is read about bugs. The psychiatrist agreed with him. They think she shouldn't be encouraged in crazy ways, so they won't let her have any books. But she still watches the bugs!' Lily crowed triumphantly.

'And there's Sylvia.' She pointed to a very thin woman, tiny, neat, and plain. Her hair was done in an elaborate beehive, and her mouth was a brilliant red gash. 'Her

302

husband never comes. She's been here for eight months. She got married fifteen years ago and she wanted kids, but her husband couldn't have any, so she went to work, she was an art teacher in a grade school. She just lived for her husband. Then about a year ago her husband walked out on her and went to live with a fat Puerto Rican woman who had five kids. They lived just a few blocks away from her, she kept seeing them. She tried to go it alone, but she was miserable. She was so bitter, because she'd wanted kids and hadn't had them because of him. She begged him to come back. She was so lonely. He wouldn't do it, he just kept telling her how ugly she was. So she looked at the Puerto Rican woman and she looked at herself and she figured it out and she took all her savings and went to the hospital and had an operation, silicone, you knew? To give her breasts. Two thousand dollars it cost her. But when she was recovering, the nurse looked at her and said, "You poor thing, did you have a mastectomy?" It was a terrible failure. She cried, but the doctor took his money just the same. Then she put on suntan lotion and went to her husband, and finally he came back, but every time they had sex he put a pillow over her face because he said he couldn't stand to look at her. She started to feel sick. She thought he was poisoning her. She said he was still seeing the other woman. He said she was crazy. She got worse and worse, she was crazy suspicious, she would call him up at work. She couldn't sleep. She kept thinking he was trying to kill her, she was scared when he had the pillow over her face that he would smother her. He took her to a psychiatrist and the doctor asked him if there was any truth to her suspicions and he swore there wasn't and the doctor said she was paranoid and she ended up here. She is sort of peaceful, but she cries a lot. They give her medication for that. No matter what life does to you, if you cry, you're crazy. Even animals cry, don't they, Mira? Anyway, for a while now she hasn't been crying, so they thought they'd let her out and they notified her husband. And he came tearing over, he didn't want her let out. What a damn fool! He came in the open convertible with the Puerto Rican woman and her five kids, and the nurse saw them and told the doctor and the doctor confronted him and he admitted it, admitted he'd been seeing her all along and the doctor was furious and said that it was his lie that kept her locked up for eight months. He blames the husband. But I say, how come he believed the husband and not Sylvia? I mean, it's just as possible she might be telling the truth. But they'd never think that. They always believe the man. All women are a little crazy, they think. So she's getting out next week, and she's going back to live with him. Her husband!' Lily laughed. 'I told her I thought this place had made her *go* crazy!'

'The problem,' Mira began firmly, trying to hold at bay the wave of insanity she felt washing over her, 'is that these women think too much about men. I mean, their men are everything to them. If the men think they are attractive, they are; if they don't, they're not. They give men the power to determine their identities, their value, to accept or reject them. They have no selves.' She finished, pursing her thin, severe mouth.

'Yes,' Lily said, her tragic eyes scanning the lawn for another example to tell Mira about.

'Why don't they just forget about the men and be themselves?' Mira insisted.

Lily turned her terrible eyes toward her as if she were foolish. 'Yes,' she said again. 'We all know that. How do you do it?'

'You just cut them out of your heart, the way I did Norm,' Mira said self-righteously.

'Oh, Carl is so cold, so cold. He makes me feel so worthless.' She talked on about Carl for a long time, telling tale after tale.

'Stop talking about Carl! Stop thinking about him!' Mira cried finally.

Lily shrugged. 'He was most of the life I knew. I lived life through Carl. I was in the house and he was in the world. When I was young, I had energy, but they put it all out. The kitchen light went out and I didn't know how to fix it. It was a funny bulb, you know? That long thin

304

kind, what do you call them? Fluorescent? I didn't know you could buy them in stores. I thought they lasted forever. Carl went to the store and got one, and he stood on a stepladder and took out the plastic square in the ceiling and took out one bulb and put in another. I couldn't get over how he did that. How did he know to do that? All I could do was sit in the dark and cry.

'Carl, the mechanical man, killed himself so he could kill me. Why did he need to do that? He walks around like an automaton: I kept screaming, I shrieked. So he locks me in here. In Harlem the government pushes heroin to keep the niggers down and doctors by the thousands give barbiturates and tranquilizers to all the housewives: keep the natives quiet. When the drugs don't work anymore, they put the blacks in jail and us in here. Don't make noise. I read a poem once, it had a line, something like "You keep stiller when everytime you move something jangles." This time he won't get me out. He never had enough money to take us out to dinner, but he has the twelve thousand dollars a year it cost him to keep me in here.

'Why should he miss me? All I ever was was trouble. He takes the kids to McDonald's; he pays a woman to clean the house. He doesn't miss sex, we never had sex. I went to see a lawyer about it once and he said if you have sex once a year you can't divorce your husband for that. Is that true the other way round too? Once a year. It was the one thing I liked, so he turned off. Sometimes after I had my shower and was lying in bed, he'd go in to take a shower too, and I'd get really excited because he never took his shower at night, and I'd hop out of bed and put my best nightgown on and I'd lie there waiting and he'd shave, and he'd be humming, and I'd be getting all aroused and then he'd come into the bedroom and get in bed and turn over and switch off the light and settle himself down and say, "*Good* night, Lily!" real happy, you know? A sadist, he is, a Nazi. So of course I'd scream and shout. What would you do? Why did he have to do that? I wouldn't have cared if he put a pillow over my face, I was that desperate. I tried, but I couldn't have an

305

affair. I just felt too guilty. I tried to masturbate. My doctor told me my insides were all drying up, they were like the insides of an eighty-year-old woman. He tried to tell me how to masturbate, but I could never do it. Carl, who knows what he is? It's as though he put me in a box and inside it was all the color and the passion and sex, and then he spent the rest of his life holding a hose over the box, putting me out. What did I know about him? I married a suit.'

She is still there, Lily. Mira hasn't seen her in years. I haven't either. It's not because I don't care about her, it's that I sometimes get confused about who is who, I think I'm Lily, or that she's me, and when I'm there I'm never sure which of us is supposed to get up and bend and kiss the other and walk down the stone paths to the gate and go out into the parking lot with all the other people who look just the same as the ones inside who get into cars and drive away. And even when I'm in the car I'm not sure I'm supposed to be, I don't feel as if I'm in my body. My body is driving the car, is sitting on the seat, but I'm still in the hospital, my voice is going on endlessly, wildly, I can't stop it, it keeps running on and on. She had boundless energy, Lily, but it all went into her eyes and her voice. She never tires, she never even flags, she never runs out of material. She talks about Moslem women, Chinese women, women in the macho countries, Spanish Italian, Mexican women: 'All women are our burden,' she says, and I know she didn't read that in a book because she doesn't read. 'I don't feel separate when I hear about them, I feel as if it's happening to me. I think we are reincarnated and I can remember being other women in other times, in other places. I carry the weight of that with me, I bend under the load of faggots slowly climbing a hill in Greece; I slink down the streets furtively in purdah, feeling wrong that I'm seen at all; my feet are crippled from being bound; I have the clitoridectomy and become my husband's possession, feeling nothing in sex and giving birth in agony. I live in countries where the law gives my husband the right to beat me, to lock me up, *disciplina.*'

306

Actually, Lily and I aren't so different: she's inside those gates, I'm inside these. We're both insane, both running on and over the same track, around and around hopelessly. Only I have a job and an apartment and I have to clean my own place and cook my own meals and I don't get to have electric shocks twice a week. It's strange how they think that giving you electric shocks will make you forget the truths you know. Maybe what they really think is that if they punish you enough, you'll pretend to forget the truths you know, you'll be good and do your housework. I've known for a long time that hypocrisy is the secret of sanity. You mustn't let them know you know. Lily knows that too, and the last two times she used it, she pretended to be docile and sorry for her sins and they let her out. But now she's too angry, she won't pretend. I sent her a letter, I told her what happened to George Jackson. But she hasn't answered.

Mira sent Lily a book on bugs to give to Inez, but a nurse found it and took it away from her and Inez got wild and violent and tried to attack the nurse and she was sent to a different ward where they use straitjackets and give them electric shock every day, and they don't get dressed up and made up every morning. So much for good intentions. In Russia they put you in insane asylums if you disagree with the state: it's not so different here. Keep the natives quiet.

6

'It's not that way for us,' Kyla insisted. 'We were lucky, we were born later.'

'Yeah,' Clarissa agreed. 'I mean, I never thought about myself as being constricted. I played football all through high school.'

'And I always knew I'd have a career.'

'I will admit,' Clarissa added, 'that they managed to shunt me from science to the humanities. But it's not terribly important to me where I use my mind, as long as I use it. And in fact, I'm sort of glad they pushed me in this direction.'

307

'The humanities,' Iso put in, 'being more humane.'

'The field is, if not all the players,' Kyla said.

Val was sitting silent, which was unusual enough that we all turned and looked at her.

'No, I'm not disagreeing. Certainly things are better for your generation. But I am wondering how much better. You all come from top schools, you're all privileged, given the general state of women, and none of you has any kids yet. I don't want to be a doom-monger, but I think you may be underestimating what you're up against.'

'In a way it doesn't matter. We have to believe that we can do anything we want to; otherwise we're fucked before we begin,' Clarissa argued.

'Yes. If you don't fall head over heels into the trap because you didn't see it beforehand,' Val warned grimly.

'You really are being a doom-monger,' Iso protested.

'Maybe. But you are being naive if you really believe that a situation that has existed as long as written history has changed so much in fifteen or twenty years that you are not going to have to deal with it. You feel lucky. You've escaped. The hell you have. You're still in the convent. Along with all the little boys. Who was saying before that all the male grad students at Harvard seem to be missing the basic organ? Everybody wants to stay locked in here, because nobody wants to become what they know they're going to have to become when they get out there. And the chances are they'll become it: you don't have much chance against IT.'

'The IT theory of history!' Kyla proclaimed.

'We need Milton here to explain how we're free.'

'Sufficient to have stood but free to fall,' Kyla laughed.

'Are you? Are you?' Val stormed hugely.

'Maybe not, but . . .' Kyla began again to tell us of her wonderful marriage, their agreements, their arrangements . . .

'Their filthy refrigerators,' Mira put in.

'Oh, Mira!' Kyla said with testy affection. 'Why do you always have to bring us down to the level of the

mundane, the ordinary, the stinking, fucking refrigerator? I was talking about ideals, nobility, principles . . .'
And leaped up and charged across the room and threw herself on Mira and hugged her, kept hugging her, saying, 'Thank you, oh, thank you, Mira, for being so wonderful, so awful, for always remembering the stinking, filthy refrigerator!' She caroled on, the others in laughter, that serious conversation ended.

Mira grimaced. 'How can I forget it?' she wailed.

'Oh, poor Mira!' Kyla cried. 'Stuck forever through history with the stinking refrigerator!'

'Write a paper about it,' Clarissa suggested. ' "The Image of the Refrigerator in the Twentieth-Century Novel." '

' "The Frost-Free Syndrome in 'Fire and Ice,' " ' Iso called.

'No, NO!' Mira shouted. 'It has to be a filthy refrigerator, one that needs to be cleaned, not just defrosted. Not that defrosting isn't bad enough!'

'That could be a song,' Iso decided. ' "It was bad enough when I had to defrost you, baby, but now I have to clean you out." '

'Or, "You ain't nothin' but a filthy frig, but I love you just the same," ' Kyla sang.

They all clamored, shouting titles at her. She laughed, and then, as titles flew around the room, echoing many that had recently adorned the first pages of papers written by this very group, she hung her head, her eyes streaming, gasping with laughter. She pulled her head up, finally.

'You can all go fuck yourselves!' she shouted, and they shrieked, they hooted, they whistled between their teeth. Kyla began to applaud, then the others; Clarissa stood up, they all stood up, she was surrounded by a circle of applauding madwomen all shrieking with laughter: 'You did it! You said it!' they cried.

'Have I passed a test?' she yelled. 'An initiation rite?'

'See how many you know,' Kyla challenged, bending down and baring her teeth at Mira.

'Oh, for God's sake, how many are there? There

aren't many, that's the problem. Now in Shakespeare's time . . .'

'He made his up!' Clarissa declared. 'You have to use those available to you from IT!'

'The IT theory of language!' Iso agreed.

'Shit,' Mira said, and they all applauded and hooted again. 'Listen, there just aren't many. Poverty of language. There's damn and hell and bitch and bastard and shit and fuck and motherfucker. Now there's an interesting word . . .'

But she didn't have a chance then, in that room. Amid the applause, the animated talk, Iso had put the record player on and soon Janis Joplin was ripping across the room and they had broken into groups of two having tête-à-têtes that would, in time, become the subject of other tête-à-têtes, and in time, everybody would know everything about everybody else, and everybody would talk about everything they knew about everybody else, and everybody accepted everything about everybody else. That was the way that was.

7

It wasn't always that way. Mira and Val and I were part of what one eminent professor of English in this exalted institution had referred to sneeringly as the 'Geritol crowd.' There were a few older men, too, mostly Jesuit priests. I don't know why Harvard accepted us at all; it was not its usual practice. Perhaps because of the war – we were eminently undraftable. But we were few enough in number to feel terribly alone in that mass of undirected faces, all of which looked under twenty. They weren't of course: Kyla was twenty-four, Isolde, twenty-six, Clarissa, twenty-three. But Mira and I were thirty-eight and Val was thirty-nine. That was quite a difference. Many of our professors were younger than we were; the chairman of graduate studies was thirty-five. It is strange. All of us had lived much alone and had great confidence in our own perceptions, and were not used to being treated like fools, or patronized. When the graduate chairman treated us like recalcitrant children, it made us very uncomfortable. But we didn't know what to do about it. You couldn't seem to assert human equality within the limitations of institutional relations. If you know what I mean. So you dropped out. At least I did. I mean, you just didn't talk much to them, you did your work and got your grades and had nothing at all to do with them if you could help it. When you were finished and asked for recommendations, you got nice letters about your excellence as a mother figure, or your elderly stability.

Anyway, it took us some time to find each other, and in the beginning, Mira walked the streets of Cambridge feeling like a foreign and condemned species. With her tinted, curled hair, her three-piece knit suits, her stockings and girdle, her high heels and matching purse, she felt like a dinosaur in the Bronx. She passed them, one after another, mostly young faces, bearded if male, with long hair if female, wearing shabby jeans or Civil War uniforms or capes or long granny dresses or saris or anything else their imaginations had come up with. No one looked at her; no one looked at anyone else. If they did happen to look at her, their eyes clicked her into her category and clicked off. She went berserk.

She was forced to look at things about herself she had never seen before. Her years at the university in New Jersey had not prepared her for this. The university was sprawled right in the middle of suburbs; the people there were used to suburban matrons, they were used to suburban life, they were suburbanites themselves. There, she was considered a member of the human race. Men's eyes sometimes flickered as they passed her, reassuring her that she was still attractive. Sometimes she could sense a head turn to look at her as she passed, or even after she had passed.

It was only after she moved to Cambridge, which is so insistently young, which was, in 1968, so insistently opposed to everything Mira seemed to represent, that she began to realize how much she depended on those flickers of eye, those head turnings for her sense of im-

311

portance. The first few days she was there, she would run out for shelving paper or thumbtacks to fix up her apartment a little, and run back and stare wildly in the mirror, work with her hair, try different makeups, put clothes on and off in front of the mirror. She ran out and bought pleated skirts and white socks; she took her pearls out of their dusty box. But nothing worked. For the first time since her divorce from Norm, she felt utterly and utterly without a face. In New Jersey, she had had her friends; some of the couples they'd been friendly with continued to invite her for an occasional dinner, always, of course, inviting some single man of their acquaintance at the same time. She'd been a known quantity: a divorced woman who lived in a fine large house and had two sons and was going back to school.

But Cambridge was full of young people who moved like arrows toward a target; they were angry, they couldn't understand how the old world could be so rotten and still insist on continuing. They couldn't understand why it didn't die of its own disease, or preferably, seeing its own disease, commit suicide. They moved toward targets not seeing each other, bumping into each other by accident on Mass Ave, and not even remembering to say, 'Excuse me.' They were young people who had had everything, had had much, anyway. They knew about everything except limitation.

But Mira did not see that. She saw everything in terms of herself. She felt it was she, her person, that they were rejecting. She sat late at night with her brandies, realizing how all her life she had maintained her ego by things like the butcher smiling when he saw her, complimenting her on her appearance; or the floor waxer looking at her with a glint in his eye; or a male head turning as she walked across the campus at the university. It appalled her; she remembered Lily. How do you stop doing that? How can one maintain oneself by such absurdities? How can one rid oneself of them?

She sat in the dark, smoking. In the dark, she could not see the shabby furnished apartment she lived in, the peeling wallpaper, the tottery Formica tables. She remembered sitting in the dark in her fancy house in Beau Reve, the year after Norm left, trying to get to the root of her bitterness, the uncontrollable rage that kept spurting out at the boys, at the butcher, the floor waxer. She felt so wrong in Cambridge. But then she'd always felt wrong. She had worked hard, had used all her intelligence, and she had discovered the secret of how to seem right, and had found out that the seeming was all. She had spent her life maintaining the appearance, like Martha poring over *The Ladies' Home Journal* and *Good Housekeeping*.

All those years, those years, she had done it too. If she had not gone so far as to buy the magazines and rate herself on the tests, she always pored over them at the dentist's office. Rate yourself: are you a good wife, are you still attractive? Are you understanding, compassionate, nutritive? Do you keep your eye shadow fresh? Have you, in the boredom of the long lonely hours of dusting and ironing his shirts, allowed yourself to consume a whole coffee cake? Are you OVERWEIGHT?

Mira had pitted herself against the standard. She had dyed and dieted, spent hours trying on wigs to be sure her hairstyle suited her face, had learned the proper tone of voice in which to ask nasty questions: 'Did Clark do something terrible, Norm, that you spanked him?' 'Oh. Well, do what you want, of course, dear. But we did promise the Markley's we'd come – yes, we did talk about it, dear, last night after you came in, remember? I don't care about it at all, but I would feel bad calling her to say we won't come because you forgot and made a golf date.' She had been properly ginger with his male ego, his fragile pride. She needled rather than raise her voice, she never threw tantrums. She was a perfect mother: she never struck her children, they were clean and well-fed. Her house shone. Her meals were edible. She kept her figure. She had done it all, everything the magazines, the television, the newspapers, the novels, everything they told her she was expected to do. She never carped when Norm was out late night after night; she never expected that she and the boys should come

313

before his work; she never asked him to do anything around the house.

She had done everything right, she had been perfect, and he had still come home saying, 'I want a divorce.' Thinking it, she was filled with outrage, she threw her glass across the room, spilling brandy on the carpet, splashing it on the walls, and the glass flew into shreds and spattered her mind. She remembered the last time thoughts like these had invaded her perfectly made-up mind, and she had stumbled crying upstairs and seized a razor blade and hacked at her wrists, even then attacking herself, still Mrs. Perfect Norm. When IT gets to you, you take yourself out of the scene, making way for a new Mrs. Perfect Norm, in the modern form of suttee. Bury yourself in darkness, you are no longer necessary. By day, watch your step, obey the rules or they may call you castrater, bitch, slob, pig, cow, slut whore prostitute chippy tramp. You are not a prostitute, even if once every ten days or so you go through the motions of sex with someone you have no desire for. You are not a prostitute because you aren't getting paid. All you get is room, board, and apparel. And Norm got what he paid for.

Down on her hands and knees wiping up brandy, sweeping up glass splinters with a paper towel, thinking that women always have to clean up their own messes, wondering what it would feel like to have someone clean up after you, unable to remember that far back in her childhood, feeling the bitter sagging of the sides of her mouth, she suddenly sat back on her heels. She thought: It is useless to demand justice. She sat down with a fresh brandy, her mind feeling as if a door had opened and fresh air was blowing through. She had been presented with a set of terms: your function is to marry, raise children, and if you can, keep your husband. If you follow these rules (smile, diet, smile, don't nag, smile, cook, smile, clean) you will keep him. The terms were clear and she had accepted them and they had failed her. Ever since the divorce, she had grown more and more bitter at that injustice, at the injustice of the way the world treats women, at Norm's injustice to her. And all she was doing was getting more bitter, destroying her own life, what was left of it.

There is no justice. There was no way to make up for the past. There was nothing that *could* make up for the past. She sat stunned for a while, freed of a burden, feeling her mouth soften, her brow unline.

And what slid into her mind now, seeing it all as she did from a distance and so, whole, spanning time and space, but complete, discrete, finished, was that what was wrong was deeper than the set of terms of their falseness. What was wrong was the assumption beneath them that she could have a life only through another person. She felt her wrists, her arms, rubbed her hand over her breasts, her belly, her thighs. She was warm and smooth and her heart beat calmly, fine pulsing energy was being driven through her, she could walk, she could talk, she could feel, she could think. And suddenly it was all right, the past, even if it was all wrong, because it had freed her, it had placed her here, still alive, more alive than she had been since the days long ago when she had taken off all her clothes and gone for a stroll to the candy store.

There was no justice, there was only life. And life she had.

8

Unfortunately the world around us does not necessarily change in tempo with changes in us. Mira went back to school the second week and looked around her, seeing, wondering, judging, instead of creeping through it encapsulated in an image and being aware only of how she was seen, judged. She knew she would not again hide in a toilet unless Walter Matthau really was after her. But she had yet to speak to anyone.

Then one day after Hooten's Renaissance lecture, a short red-haired girl with wide blue eyes, long straight hair, and a creamy oval face approached her: 'You're a grad student in English, aren't you? My name's Kyla Forrester. Would you like to have some coffee?'

315

Mira was so grateful for the overture that she kept her mouth from pursing at the girl's appearance. Kyla's hair was cut with bangs across the forehead, and she was wearing a flared miniskirt and a white turtlenecked sweater. She looked just like a cheerleader.

Kyla took her to Lehman Hall, a cafeteria for students who did not live in Harvard Houses. She talked constantly as they crossed the yard, talked about loneliness and the horrible Harvard system, about the horribleness of Harvard graduate students, about all the zombies and creeps walking around in the world. She talked with flair and zest and energy, punctuating her remarks with wide flings of her free arm – the other being full of books – and expletive 'Ughs!' and 'Yicks!' Mira was completely charmed.

Lehman Hall was a large dining room with carpet, twenty-foot windows, crystal chandeliers. The carpet was cheap tweed, the tables were plastic cafeteria type, the smell was of canned tomato soup. One long table near the east wall was the usual resort of graduate students in arts and sciences between the hours of twelve and three. Kyla introduced Mira to the group at the table.

There was Brad, an intense young man with a wide mobile mouth, who interrupted his imitation of some professor long enough to say Hi; Missy, a short-haired girl scout from Iowa who was charming and interested, and who explained to Mira her urgent desire to computerize all of Milton; Isolde, a tall, very thin woman with mousy brown hair pulled back in a tight bun, a pale frozen face and manner, who sat with a book often before her; Val, a large woman around Mira's age, who talked loudly and wore a flowing cape and who, it turned out, was in social science; and Clarissa, a silent young woman with long chestnut braids and watchful eyes. Kyla and Mira sat at the far end of the table and Kyla launched into a set of questions to which she already knew the answers.

'How do you feel about being in this crummy place, well it's obvious, it doesn't touch you, you're serene. I wish I had your kind of dignity, I get crawly about all the slimy creeps, how did you get that way? I mean I keep flipping out, I feel as if I'm climbing the walls, it's a freak-out, man, just walking around in this place with all the zombies. What happened to life, did it disappear with the development of the brain? Well, obviously that didn't happen to you, which means there's hope, I mean, I don't want to think I am going to end up like them, like all the rest of them . . .'

After that, Mira went every day to Lehman Hall; although its environment was not welcoming, there was at least always someone to talk to, or listen to.

'I have these dreams,' mild, handsome Lewis said anxiously. In his hands was the antiwar petition he was circulating. All the men were in danger of the draft. 'I hate violence, so why should I have these dreams?' He recounted them without any change of expression, his voice mild, his speech a steady modulated stream. He had sent hot pokers up the vaginas of the closest female members of his family, had arranged and gloated in disembowelings, electric shocks applied to delicate portions of anatomies, had tied people to stakes and poured honey over them and waited until the ants arrived, had castrated, mutilated, maimed, and killed. 'Kill, kill, kill,' he said with mild wonder, 'there's blood all over my dreams. Last night I lined up all the Harvard faculty and machine-gunned them. Do you suppose,' he peered into Mira's face, 'there's something wrong with me?'

Mira glanced over at Iso, and was surprised to see that frozen face dancing with laughter. Isolde had strange eyes – pale green and dead looking, the eyes of an ancient person, someone who sees all human effort as futile. Mira, whose own face had been carefully set in concerned-sympathetic, burst out laughing too. Val blurted out, 'Half your problem is that you're male,' and strode off for coffee. Lewis turned worriedly back to Mira and Iso: 'Even my mother! And I love my mother!' Iso cracked up.

Beside them, Clarissa gazed silently at Morton Awe as he explained in detail the respective merits of various

317

available and unavailable records of *The Abduction from the Seraglio*, and Missy listened, with detailed questions, to Mark's recipe for home-baked bread. Kyla, who was trying to kick smoking, sat alone at the end, sucking on a plastic spoon and reading Greek. To the questions of each newcomer, she rapped out like a drill sergeant: 'Oral fixation, innocuous substitute.'

'I'll never get in. No first-year people will. Jones limits his seminars to two and three G.S.'s.'

'Sonia Toffler got in.'

'She did!!!?'

'Don't go, hang around. I want to go to the Coop and buy some records.'

'I have to go. I have to study Latin. I study ten hours a day.'

'You're crazy.'

'No, I'm an overachiever. No brains, pure grind.'

'What do you think of Purdy?'

'Man, he's an asshole.'

Mira finally had something to say and leaned forward to join the conversation. 'He wrote an excellent book on Milton.'

'Yeah, if you like verb clusters.'

'You mean there are *verbs* in *Paradise Lost*? Shit, man, all these years and I never knew that.'

'Listen, man, how else can Adam and Eve make out? *Fuck* is a verb.'

'Maybe for you. For me it's an adjective. I never made it to the verb stage. Pass the fucking salt, will you?'

'I really gotta go.' Hollow eyes, hollow voice. 'I'm a wreck. I'll never make it here.'

'Shit, man, you went to Swarthmore. I come before you a *manga* from P.C.'

'P.C.?'

'See? Providence College, man. You think you got troubles?'

'So I took the room in the graduate dorm. You know how the undergraduates live in the Houses, suites of rooms, those libraries with grand pianos and Oriental rugs and chandeliers and shit? Well, my room's so small it holds a bed and a bureau. Period. There's a window, but it's so high I have to stand on a chair to look out. And the plumbing leaks, so all my books are piled on the radiator to dry out. I'll keep them there, I guess. There's no room for a bookcase.'

'Did you hear that Lawrence Kelly got into Bailey's seminar on Renaissance Humanism?'
 'How'd he manage that?'
 Awed silence.
 'He must be sharp.'
 'He's from Berkeley. Worked with Malinowski.'
 'Oh. Malinowski's an old friend of Bailey's.'
 'Oh.'
 'I have always thought there were disadvantages to having attended Our Lady of the Swamp.'

'When's the language exam?'
 'Which one?'
 'This place sucks with elitism. Three languages. Christ! They've gotta prove their superiority.'
 'Oh, it sucks, man.'
 'Why did you come here then?' Mira heard herself ask sharply. But they ignored her.
 'Yeah, but remember it used to be five. Old Norse, for Chrissakes. And Gothic and Icelandic. Real living culture.'
 'I wonder if they'd accept an obscure Bantu dialect? I've got that down letter perfect. Interesting language – only two hundred words.'
 'Inflected, I take it?'
 'Yeah. All roots. To make a verb you add *fuck*, to make a noun, you add *it*.'
 'You're gross, Brad.'
 'Damn fuckers. Three languages, a general exam in the entire literature of the English language, and we're

319

supposed to study all the time living on the measly two thou they give us. I mean, they got to be kidding.'

'Listen, at least you have the two thou. I have a job tending bar at night and I still had to borrow money.'

'Yeah, it shits, man.'

'Everything shits.'

'Yeah.'

It was after three. Mira rose and left for the library. No one said good-bye.

9

One day, about a month after school started, Iso took Mira aside shyly, and invited her to come to dinner. 'I have a roommate – she doesn't go to Harvard – and she's really lonely – this place is so lonely. So I thought – well, I've invited a few of the better people, you know?' Iso's mouth barely moved when she spoke. For some reason, she touched Mira deeply.

It was the first invitation Mira had received since her arrival, and she was excited by it. A possible future was opening up. She stopped at Kupersmith's that afternoon and bought some cheap plants for her windowsill; when she arrived home, she unwrapped the contact paper she had bought the week before and cut it out and plastered it over the stained top of the cocktail table. She ripped down the brittle plastic curtain from the kitchen windows, and measured the frame: she would buy a heavy red cotton curtain, a red tablecloth, new towels. She would be entertaining soon.

The night of the dinner party, she set her hair and bathed in oil, and dressed in a girdle and heels and a Kimberley suit. She spent twenty minutes applying makeup. She eased her way down the stairs, thinking she had forgotten how miserable high heels felt, and tottered down the uneven brick sidewalks for four blocks to reach Iso's.

Iso lived on the third floor of an old three-decker on a tree-lined side street. The scarred front door was open and one could simply walk into the house. She climbed the creaking steps to the third floor and knocked timidly. She tried not to feel as if she were slumming. The house had cracked walls and peeling paint; the banister between the second and third stories was loose. She tried to relax her arms and back, but a thin noise made her shudder. She expected a rat to leap out at her.

Iso came to the door in the same bulky sweater and baggy pants she had worn earlier in the day.

'Well, don't you look nice,' she said with surprise.

Mira could hear talking from within, and her heart began to beat hard. What did she expect? A new life, a group of fascinating brilliant charming sophisticated people? Iso led her into the living room. It was like Mira's: the wallpaper was varying shades of brown, a huge radiator dominated one wall, the windows were gray and looked down on some cars parked in a neighboring yard. But one whole wall of Iso's place held books stacked in homemade bookcases, and the floor opposite it held five feet of records. Over the record player hung a huge oil painting of five women standing in an embrace, a rough imitation, Mira thought, of Matisse's 'La Danse.'

And there in the room were Brad attacking Harvard elitism, Lewis describing a gory war novel he had just read, Missy asking Davey Potter about the best way to drive to New York from Boston, and Val, looking glazed as Morton Awe discussed the respective merits of various available and unavailable recordings of Mahler's Ninth. A bearded young man sat crossed-legged on the floor holding on to a bottle of wine. Mira let herself down into an overstuffed chair of maroon velour, and crossed her legs at the ankle. She lighted a cigarette and leaned slightly to throw her match into an ashtray that lay on the floor in front of the bearded man, and the arm of the chair fell off. She gasped.

Iso darted over and replaced it. 'Sorry,' she said between closed lips. 'My furniture all comes from Goodwill.' She left the room and returned to the kitchen.

The bearded man cocked an eyebrow at Mira. 'Just like home,' he said sarcastically.

She fluttered. 'Yes, my place too. Do you live in Cambridge?'

'Doesn't everybody?' he responded wearily, and turned away from her.

'Grant,' Iso called from the kitchen, 'pour Mira some wine, will you? And see if anyone needs a refill.'

Mira decided Grant was Iso's boyfriend.

The wine passed around, but people drank slowly. Grant was putting records on the turntable and people were talking about somebody, some woman singer. Mira thought she was horrible. Her voice went all over the place, she did not seem to be rooted anywhere. She had a strange name too: Aretha. Then they began to talk about somebody with a stranger name, and they put her record on. She was even worse, and Mira wondered about these people: how could they like such sounds? This person – it was a woman, but you couldn't tell whether she was male or female from her voice – was called Odetta. Mira did not dare to ask what they thought of Peggy Lee.

She turned to Grant, breathing in, trying to try again, and asked him what he was majoring in. He made some crack, mentioned Galbraith, waved his arm in air. She was confused. 'Economics,' he said curtly, turning away again.

The music played, the wine passed, the conversation floated by her. Val got up and went out into the kitchen for a while. When she returned, she sat down on the floor beside Mira, tapping Grant's knee, telling him to pull in his tentacles. Mira decided Grant was Val's boyfriend.

'You look out of it,' Val said.

Mira had not realized how close to tears she was, but words now came pouring out. 'It was a mistake, I guess, coming back at my age. I don't know what they're talking about, I don't know who they are, I don't know how to talk to them, and I thought – just the other night I thought I saw, thought I understood, knew what had been wrong with my life, but you don't change by just

322

deciding something, and everything is just the same, who is that, Grant, anyway? And does anyone like Brad, he's so obnoxious, doesn't he realize how obnoxious he is? I don't know what they're talking about,' she concluded, liquid-eyed, looking at Val.

Val was broad and handsome with bright eyes that were almost black and she looked straight at you. 'I know, I know. They're talking about music, they talk about music a lot. That's because they don't have anything else to talk about, they don't know how to make conversation, music is their one common bond. You may not realize it, but they're in worse shape than you, more disjointed, more frightened, more bewildered.'

Mira stared at her. 'You understand them.'

Val shrugged. 'Well, I've lived in Cambridge for ten years now.'

'You've been at Harvard for ten years?'

'No. Just started. I've been living in a commune in Somerville. I've had an assortment of jobs, was involved with the peace movement, sometimes lived on welfare. When they decided to use my politics against me to cut off my income, I decided to use my wit against them. I applied for fellowship at Harvard and got it. So here I am.'

Mira gazed at her wistfully. 'I guess it isn't age. It's – I feel as if I come from a different world. The suburbs – not that I liked them, I never felt part of them really – but they have different rules. I don't feel part of it here, either.'

'Maybe you will, in time,' Val smiled. 'I think of Cambridge as a home for the homeless.'

A new woman entered, tallish, very slender, with a body that really was willowy – long and graceful, and seemingly full of bends and curves. Iso came from the kitchen, a little flushed, and introduced her. It was Ava, the roommate. Ava lowered herself to the floor, where she sat cross-legged, her upper body rising from the lotus of her legs like a stem, her head like a daffodil. She glanced shyly at the strangers. Grant leaped up and handed her a glass of wine, which she accepted with a

323

flutter of eye, a demure, self-deprecating smile. Her head was bent forward, and her long shiny black hair hung straight and silky, almost hiding her face. She looked once at Val and Mira, raising her eyes as if looking were a significant act, then lowered them again. She gazed at her wine. She did not speak. The room at large was talking about the war.

Iso had set up a bridge table in the entrance hall, which was just large enough for that, had covered it with a bright cloth and a vinegar jar full of daisies. She announced dinner, which was spaghetti and cheese and salad and Italian bread heated with garlic. Everyone filled a plate and returned to their places. Mira was careful with the arm of the chair. They ate and spoke desultorily; the wine passed. Someone questioned Ava: no, she was not a student, she was just a secretary, she answered in a soft voice. Her replies to other questions were saved from curtness only by her soft shy manner. After she had helped Iso clear the plates, Ava left the room, went into a bedroom and closed the door. A few minutes later, music poured from the room, a Brahms Intermezzo, flawlessly played. Everyone looked up. It was Ava, Iso explained, almost apologetically. She was shy with strangers.

'Can we open the door?'

'She'll stop. She won't play for people, only for herself,' Iso said, and there was something hedged in her voice, a warning, perhaps, the tone one might hear in the voice of the mother of a problem child talking to critical neighbors.

Conversation returned to the war. Iso was talking about Vietnam, which, it appeared, she had visited several years before, getting into the country illegally, and escaping by hitching a ride on an Air Force plane. She spoke in her stiff, expressionless manner, and it was difficult to believe that this reticent stiff woman had done such adventurous things. The group questioned her. She had, it seemed, been everywhere, to Africa, Asia, and Mexico, had spent months in an ashram in India, had lived with Indians in Yucatán.

324

'I used to get restless. I'd waitress for a while to make some money, then put my pack on my back and take off.'

Mira was overwhelmed. 'Did you go alone?'

'Oh, sometimes. But you always meet people when you travel. I'd carry a camera and take pictures, and sometimes I was able to sell them to travel magazines. That helped.'

People began to leave. Studying, they said. Grant left suddenly, curtly. Mira decided he was nobody's boyfriend. Mira and Val remained and offered to help with dishes, but Iso refused. Ava stopped playing and came shyly into the room, accepting praise with a sweet smile, as she lowered her body to the floor.

'Have you been playing long?' Mira asked.

'Since second grade. My second-grade teacher let me stay after school and play the piano in the classroom.'

She spoke with shy glances at her auditors, then dropped her eyes again. She did not seem to want to talk anymore.

'She didn't have lessons until she was twelve,' Iso said with pride. 'Her daddy bought her a piano then.'

'Yes, but he sold it when I was fifteen,' Ava giggled.

'They were having hard times,' Iso explained as if she were Ava's interpreter. But Ava shot her a warning look, a hard fiery glance that lasted only half a second, and Iso fell silent. In the awkwardness, Mira stood up, knocking the chair arm off again.

'Oh, dear!' she wailed, and the evening ended with smiles.

10

'Valerie isn't a person, she's an experience,' Tadziewski said after knowing her only a few weeks.

She was tall – over five foot ten – and big-boned and well padded. She also had a big voice, so that even when she was talking naturally, you could hear her halfway across Harvard Yard. She probably couldn't help that, Mira thought, pursing her lips in distaste. Although she was Mira's age, she did not seem to feel the slightest

325

awkwardness at Harvard. She strode unselfconsciously across the Yard with her inevitable cape flying out behind her. She had capes from everywhere – Spain, Greece, Russia, Arizona. She wore boots, and her feet turned in as she walked, and she laughed a lot and loudly, and she would start a conversation with anyone, anyone at all. And she was obscene.

Mira was drawn to Val because of the similarity in their ages, and because Val seemed to her to have experience and knowledge she lacked. But she was appalled by Val's language, and somewhat put off by something direct, something – blatant – she did not know exactly what. She felt a little threatened, as if Val were simply not accountable to the rules in the way other people were, as if she held nothing sacred. This threat was not apparent, but very sensible; Mira could not have said how Valerie could harm her, but she felt vulnerable. She called it in her mind Valerie's potential for saying or doing 'anything, anything at all.' Sometimes Iso and Val and Mira, bored with Lehman Hall, would go across the street to the Toga for lunch. Mira would order coffee, Iso milk, but Valerie had beer: she drank it by the quart. Valerie would never drop a subject when it grew too personal, and every subject seemed to grow personal when she was talking. She related everything to sex and used sexual words as casually as any others. Mira could bear to hear the word *shit* because Norm had been fond of it. But anything stronger caused her a small tremor and an anxious peering around to see if people were staring at them with shock.

She was very drawn to Iso in spite of – or because of – Iso's expressionless face, her dead eyes, her deadpan recital of interesting tales. Iso touched her, and Mira, herself reticent, inclined to be nonphysical, felt a deep urge to reach out and touch something in her friend, to touch her physically as well as psychically. But Iso's impersonality made this impossible. Iso would talk about any subject except herself. She did ask other people personal questions, but they were so seemingly innocuous that they offended no one. 'Who was your favorite

326

cowboy star when you were little?' or 'What kind of books did you like when you were in your teens?' or 'If you had lots of money, what kind of car would you buy?' These questions invariably stimulated a lively discussion, and the talk often had a free, childlike quality, the feeling of play, because they dealt with what seemed to be childlike subjects. But Mira could see Iso's eyes watching faces as they grinned and giggled about Roy Rogers, The Lone Ranger, and James Arness, watching, listening, hearing far more than the speakers imagined. Later she might say, 'I think Elliott is one of those sensitive guys who got scared into acting authoritative because he was never man enough for the other kids. Underneath his superciliousness beats the heart of Tonto,' thus granting more charity and understanding to a particularly unpleasant young man than anyone else could offer.

The three of them, Mira, Val, and Iso, came to be a group. They knew and liked Kyla and Clarissa, but both of them were married, and lived somewhat differently as a result. Other students threaded in and out of parties and coffees, but the three women felt a special kinship. Ava rarely attended any Harvard party, but she would often visit Val or Mira with Iso, and in time, spoke more freely, glanced less surreptitiously, remained longer in the room.

In time, too, Mira ceased to feel her appearance. She dressed casually, not in jeans, but in pants and soft shirts or sweaters and low-heeled boots; she let her hair grow out to its true darkish blond color; she walked around the streets seeing what was on them instead of searching for images of herself. She felt alone, apart, but it was not a bad feeling. She would have been completely happy if she had only had someone to love.

She confided this to Val, who did not seem very sympathetic.

'Ummm. You've had someone to love?'

'Well, I was married.'

'Yes, but did you actively love him, whatshisface?

327

Norm? I mean did you feel love when you saw him, talked to him? Or was it just habit?'

'It was a sense of security.'

'And you want that again?'

They were in Val's kitchen. Mira and Iso – Ava had a dancing lesson – had come for dinner. Val's apartment was also in a three-decker, but it had high ceilings and long shuttered windows. It was clean and white, and the windows held a jungle of plants, hanging, standing, set on low wicker tables. There were no curtains, only bamboo blinds, but the plants sent a cool green light through the room. There were two low couches covered in brilliant throws and heaped with cushions, some white wicker chairs with cool green and blue cushions, a wall of bookshelves, and many posters, prints, African masks, carved wood figures.

'It's beautiful, Val,' Mira said when she arrived. 'How did you get it to be so beautiful?'

'It was a pigsty when we moved in. But Chrissie and I,' she put her arm around her daughter's shoulders, 'sanded and plastered and sanded and painted. We had fun, huh, Chris?'

The girl was slight and slender, very pretty but sullen. She pulled gently out of her mother's embrace.

'Chrissie's going through a phase: she hates me,' Val laughed, and the girl blushed.

'Oh, Mom!' she said, and left the room.

'*You* sanded and plastered and painted?'

'Sure. It isn't hard.'

Mira followed Val into the kitchen. 'I just have to cut some things up,' Val apologized.

Chris was sitting at the kitchen table talking to Iso in low, serious tones. They rose when Val and Mira entered, and walked slowly out of the room. 'We need privacy for this conversation,' Iso said, rolling her eyes at Val. She turned back to Chris. 'Yes, well, for instance, if you compare fifteen-century Flemish art with sixteenth- and seventeenth-century Flemish paintings, you can see it. There comes to be an obsession with things, possessions. And his point is that wealth was the

328

mark of the worldly elect, so in a sense Calvinism became secularized, was transformed into capitalism . . .' They were gone.

Val cast a strong amused look toward Mira. 'My precocious daughter.'

'How old is she?'

'Sixteen. She'll be seventeen in February. She's a senior in high school. She is precocious.'

'She's very pretty.'

'Yeah.' Val was chopping onions.

Mira wandered around the kitchen. It too was large and bright; plants stood on the windowsill and hung at the window. The round table was covered with a gaudy striped tablecloth, and there was a large bright rug in front of the sink. One whole four-foot wall was given over to racks of spices, dozens of them, including some Mira had never heard of. Shiny bright canisters lined the counters, plastic-looking things in reds and purples and oranges.

Another wall had been 'papered' with prints. Mira walked over to look at them. They had been cut out of a book or magazine. They were Persian, Indian, or Chinese, and they were all pornographic. Mira pulled her eyes away and walked back to the window and breathed out. 'How long were you married?' she asked tightly.

'Too fucking long.' Val poured wine over simmering meat. 'Four years. He was a bastard, like all men. I've given over hating him, any of them. They can't help it: they're trained to be bastards. We're trained to be angels so they can be bastards. Can't beat the system. They can't, anyway,' she ended, laughing.

'Are you saying,' Mira began carefully, 'that you'd never get married again?'

'I can't imagine why I would,' Val answered a little absently, involved in measuring some spice in a tiny spoon. She stirred it into the meat, and turned toward Mira. 'Why, would you?'

'I've thought so. I mean, I sort of just assumed I'd get

married again. Most divorced people do, don't they?' her voice asked a little anxiously.

'I think so. That's what the statistics say, anyway. But most of the women I know don't want to be married.'

Mira sat down.

'I'd think they'd be lonely. Aren't you? Well, you have Chris, of course.'

'Loneliness is all in the way you look at it. It's like virginity, a state of mind,' Val laughed.

'How can you say that?' Mira's voice was tinged with sharpness. 'Loneliness is loneliness.'

'I gather you're lonely,' Val smiled at her. 'But weren't you often lonely when you were married? And isn't it nice to be alone sometimes? And sometimes when you are alone, aren't you feeling sad mostly because society tells you you're not supposed to be alone? And you imagine someone being there and understanding every motion of your heart and mind. When if someone were there he – or even she – wouldn't necessarily be doing that at all? And that's even worse. When somebody is there and not there at the same time. I think if you have a few good friends and good work to do, you don't feel lonely. I think loneliness is the creation of the image makers. Part of the romantic myth. The other part being, of course, that if you find your dream person, you'll never feel separate again. Which is a crock.'

'You're hitting me with that a little too quickly,' Mira said. 'I'm not sure I follow it.'

Isolde came charging into the kitchen, smiling broadly. 'Jesus, that Chris! She was poking holes in Tawney. I had to tell her to go read him, to fight with the book, not with me. She's too much!' She poured more wine in her glass and in Mira's. 'How about you, Val?' Val nodded. She was measuring cream in a glass measuring cup. 'What do you do to her, anyway?'

'Leave her alone,' Val said shortly, but with a smile. 'My theory about children.' She turned to Mira. 'I have a theory about almost everything, I'm afraid.' She gave Mira such a graceful, almost apologetic smile, that Mira almost liked her. 'Actually, Chris's problem is shyness.

We've moved around so much. She has no friends her own age. I've urged her to get out a bit – but you know what it's like to be shy and sixteen.'

Dinner was served in the kitchen – there was no dining room.

'I hope you like cream of watercress soup,' Val said.

Cream of watercress? But it smelled good.

'I can never serve this without remembering a guy I knew once. I was really interested, you know, and things were at the beginning stage and needed a little push from me, you know? They're always so dense. Anyway things were at *that* point – I was nervous, and anxious to please, and I thought he was golden boy himself . . .'

Chris slipped into her place. 'Talking about men again?'

'Why not, they're half the human race, aren't they?' her mother snapped.

'Men, men, men,' Chris said in a hollow mocking voice. 'I get so sick of women talking about men all the time. Why don't you talk about capitalism? I might learn something.'

Iso was giggling, hiding her mouth in a napkin.

'I've already taught you everything I know about capitalism, Chrissie,' Val said easily. 'It's simple, it's a game, you know? First round, the people who are good at grasping get most of the chips. Second round, they make the rules of the game, and make them so they're sure to keep most of the chips. After that, it's really simple. The rich keep the poor in line and the rich get richer and the poor get poorer. I've even played that game, someplace or other.'

Chris gave her mother a disgusted look. 'Some people, Mommy, might accuse you of oversimplification.'

'You got something better to suggest?' Val gave her a superior look and waved her spoon at Chris. Mira realized they were playing.

'You can read my paper when it's finished,' Chris said. 'It's for social studies and the teacher's a real pig. I mean, he thinks the black kids are animals – he even calls them

331

that – and he thinks Joseph McCarthy is a maligned saint.'

'Well, you think *he's* an animal too : you called him a pig.'

Chris made a face at her mother. 'Touché. Anyway, you might find my paper interesting. He'll surely give it an F.'

Val gazed at her daughter and her face looked soft and loving and almost hurt.

'The Cambridge schools are a horror scene,' she said to Mira. 'Class squabbles. Lower-class whites trying to keep the niggers down. The black kids are angry, the whites are scared, the place is a bombshell. One of these days . . . I just hope Chrissie's out before it explodes.'

'Oooooh?' Chris quizzed her. 'I thought you were a good radical.'

'Shit, piss, and corruption,' Iso said. 'Your mother might want to throw a bomb herself, but she sure doesn't want to see you in range of one.'

'I'm a lousy radical,' Val said. 'All I am is talk. You ought to know that by now.'

Chris was pleased. 'You said it, I didn't.'

Val stood to remove the soup bowls. Chris leaped up to help her. Val put more bowls on the table – a salad made of spinach and mushrooms, with cheese dressing in a little bowl, some noodles, and a beautiful fragrant red-brown Bourguigon. Chris helped her mother; they did not speak. They worked together as if each knew what the other would do without speaking. There was French bread, more wine. Chris rinsed the soup bowls under running water and sat down. The meal smelled delicious.

'That soup was terrific,' Mira said. 'What were you saying before about preparing it for someone? You said you were really in love with someone . . .'

Iso began to giggle. 'Tell her about love, Val.'

Chris groaned. 'Wait until after dessert.'

Iso's laugh was quiet, almost under her breath, but it kept coming, like a giggle. 'Go on,' she urged, still laughing.

'May I please enjoy my dinner, Mother?' Chris stormed, sounding serious.

'Go to hell, Chris,' Val said. 'What are you so up-tight about?' She turned to Mira. 'Oh, it was nothing. He threw up. After he ate it, I mean. Not because of the soup; he'd gotten drunk before he arrived. It was one of those nights when you pace the floor because HE, magical HE is coming. You know.'

'I don't. Really.'

'Love. Being in love. Yuck!' Val poured more wine in their glasses.

'Val hates love,' Iso explained, a wicked smile on her face.

Mira blinked at Val. 'Why?'

'Oh, shit.' Val sipped her wine. 'I mean, it's one of those things they've erected, like the madonna, you know, or the infallibility of the Pope or the divine right of kings. A bunch of nonsense *erected* – and that's the crucial word – into Truth by a bunch of intelligent *men* – another crucial word. What the particular nonsense is, isn't important. What's important is why they did it.'

'Come on, Val, skip the theory this time.'

'Well, love is insanity. The ancient Greeks knew that. It is the taking over of a rational and lucid mind by delusion and self-destruction. You lose yourself, you have no power over yourself, you can't even think straight. That's the reason I hate it. Not, understand, that I am a rationalist. I think everything is rational; the word irrational simply applies to rationales we don't totally understand. Nor do I believe that reason is separate from appetite, or any of those neat little fences in the desert that mankind likes to erect. Everything comes from all parts of the self, but we understand or think we understand some parts better than others. But love is an insanity created outside us – by the structure. There are lots of others . . .'

'Val . . .' Iso shook her fork at Val.

'Okay. Love is one of those things you think is supposed to happen, is a fact of life, and if it doesn't happen to you, you feel cheated. You're walking around feeling rotten, you know, because it's never happened to you. So one day you meet this guy, right? And, ZING! He is gorgeous! It doesn't matter what he's doing. He may be making a point in a debate, he may be chopping up concrete on a city street, with his shirt off and his back tanned. It doesn't matter. Even if you've met him before and not thought much about him, at some moment you look at him and everything you've thought about him before goes straight out of your head. You never really saw him before! You realize that in a split second! You never saw how totally gorgeous he was!

'But you suddenly see it. That back, those arms! The strength in his jaw when he leaned forward to put his opponent down. That brilliance in his eye! What an eye! So careless he is, as he runs his fingers through his hair. What hair!'

Iso was bent over the table, laughing. Val's face as she spoke was a complex network of acting: she was full of adoration and mockery.

'His skin, my God, that skin is like satin. You sit there hardly able to contain yourself, you want to get your hand on that skin. And his hands! My God, what hands! Strong, delicate, thick, and powerful, it doesn't matter what they are, they are gorgeous hands. Every time you look at them you start to sweat, your armpits get soggy ...'

Iso choked on her wine and had to leave the table. She went only as far as the kitchen door, however. Val paid no attention.

'You can't look at his hands without imagining them on your body. Looking at his hands becomes a forbidden act, an act of lasciviousness. His hands are full of touch and your body is tingling just as if they were on it. And on it in such places! Heavens! You move your eyes away from his hands. But those arms! God, such arms! So strong, so gentle, made to hold, to enclose, to protect and comfort, but they could also break you in half, that's part of the fun, those arms are unpredictable, they might twist your body, they might be able to turn you into a piece of clay ...'

'Tsk, tsk,' Mira heard her mouth go.

'And his mouth! Oh, that mouth. Sensual and cruel-looking, or full and passionate, he looks as if he could devour you with his mouth. You want that mouth, no matter what it will do to you. You long for even its cruelty. And when he opens it! My God, what pearls! Everything he says has a halo, it radiates brilliance. He is pithy or symbolic; everything he says means a hell of a lot more than the surface. He turns to you and says, "It's raining out," and you see a glitter in his eyes, you see him figuring if the two of you are going to be able to get together somehow that night, and you see him devising means, you see passion and desire, you see unconquerable will, and all that will is directed towards *you*! Or he is talking about politics and everything he says is brilliant, you can't understand why the other people in the room don't leap up the way you want to and kiss his feet, the savior. When he turns to you and smiles, you want to curl into a little ball and fall down and snuggle under his feet like a footrest. When he turns away from you, you feel as if the world had just stopped, you want to die, you want to pick up a knife and stab it through your heart, standing up in the room and shouting, "If he doesn't love me, I don't want to live!" Any turn of head in another direction devastates you: you are jealous not just of other women, but of men, of walls, of music, of the fucking print hanging over the couch.

'Well, in time, you sort of get together. Your passion is so extreme that no other possibility exists. And someplace you know that. You know that somehow you made this happen. So you don't trust it. You keep feeling that somehow you got him to ask you out for coffee, or lunch, or dinner, or a chamber music concert, or whatever it is, but that if you lose control for more than a minute, the enchantment will be broken and you'll lose him forever. So whenever you're with him, you're high, you're brilliant, your eyes look a little mad but very beautiful, you act just right, but the way you're acting has nothing to do with you, you're acting, just like someone on a stage, acting the part you think will get him,

335

and you're terrified because you're also exhausted and you don't know how much longer you can keep it up, but every time he appears, you manage.

'Mostly, if you're female, you smile a lot and listen a lot and cook a lot. You adore him during the whole twelve minutes it takes him to stuff your whole afternoon's work down his throat. And in time, you get him where you want him, which is in your bed. If you don't – well that's a different trip, and I haven't been on it. I can only tell you what I know. You get him in your bed and for a while, everything's glorious. You never had sex like that before: he's the greatest lover you've ever had. And in a way, it's true. The two of you lie in a warm bath of love, you make love and you eat and you talk and you walk together and there's not much of a dividing line among those things, they all flow together, and it's all warm and hot and brilliant colors, and it's all right, you're floating in it, nothing has ever been so right in your life before. The two of you are one togetherness, one attenuated lovingness, your skins flow into each other, you can feel him get chilly even when he's in another room. And every time he touches your skin or you touch his, the heat strikes as if you carried lightning around inside you, you were both Zeus.'

Mira was gaping now. Isolde had returned and was pouring more wine, but she was silent, if grinning. Chris was sitting with her head bent over her half-full plate, playing with the food with her fork. She looked glum. Val was in full sail. Her face with a little pink from the wine and the cooking, she held her wine glass aloft and gesticulated with it, she was staring at a point on the wall just above Iso's head.

'You can't think about stupid practical details like making money or going to school. It is as if the sensual surface of your skin and the innards of your body had a direct connection, and that was all the life there was. Nothing else matters. You go along like this for a long time, months, maybe, flunking courses, losing jobs, getting kicked out of your house, whatever. Nothing matters, because nothing else exists. You get a little paranoid, you think about the world versus lovers. You think it's all horribly unfair, you think everybody else is stupid and crass and lumpy and doesn't understand the flame that life is.

'Then one day, the unthinkable happens. You are sitting together at the breakfast table and you're a little hung over, and you look across at beloved, beautiful golden beloved, and beloved opens his lovely rosebud mouth showing his glistening white teeth, and beloved says something stupid. Your whole body stops in midstream : your temperature drops. Beloved has never said anything stupid before. You turn and look at him; you're sure you misheard. You ask him to repeat. And he does. He says, "It's raining out," and you look outside and it is perfectly clear. And you say, "No, it isn't raining out. Perhaps you'd better get your eyes checked. Or your ears." You begin to doubt all his senses. It could only be a flaw in his sensory equipment that would make him say a thing like that. But even that flaw isn't important. Love can't be stopped by locksmiths, contact lenses, or hearing aids. It was just that you were hung over.

'But that's only the start. Because he keeps on, after that, saying stupid things. And you keep turning around and looking at him strangely, and my God, do you know what, you suddenly see that he's skinny! Or flabby! Or fat! His teeth are crooked, and his toenails are dirty. You suddenly realize he farts in bed. He doesn't, he really doesn't understand Henry James! All this while, he's been saying he doesn't understand Henry James, and you've thought his odd, cast-off remarks about James showed brilliant perception, but suddenly you realize he's missed the point entirely.

'But that's not the worst part. Because all these months you've been adoring him like a descended god, he's been being convinced he is. And now he's parading around with a smug superior expression on his face, cocksure and blind and insensitive, just like all the other males you rejected, but this time it's your fault! You did it. You! All by yourself! My God, you created this monster! Then you think, well, he helped. I couldn't

337

have done it without cooperation. And you hate yourself for having deluded yourself about him (you tell yourself it was HIM you were deluded about – not love), and you hate him for having believed your delusions, and you feel guilty and responsible and you try, slowly, to disengage. But now, just try to get rid of him! He clutches, he clings, he doesn't understand. How could you want to separate from a deity? He saved you, you told him that. He was – when was that, anyway? – the best lover you ever had. He keeps on believing all the things you told him, and he doesn't believe when you try to untell. And after all, what can you say? He wasn't the best lover you ever had? But he was, once. "So it's just now," he says, nodding his head judiciously. "I've become mechanical. It needs more thought. I've come to take you for granted, and women don't like that." What can you say without destroying his fragile male ego forever, or making yourself out a deluded fool or a liar?'

Val paused to drink. Mira was hanging on her. 'What *do* you do?' she asked, barely breathing.

Val swallowed and put down her glass, and spoke in the most matter-of-fact possible voice. 'Why you bring in another man, of course. That's the only thing they understand. Territoriality, you know. If you turn them down by yourself, that's inconceivable and horribly ego-deflating. If you move to another man, that's bad, but understandable. They always knew they weren't up to par, that somebody else could beat them. And then you're not rejecting them period, facing aloneness alone, you're just one more promiscuous bitch of a female. It all fits that way. That's the way the game are played. You must know that.'

'I don't know if I've ever been in love,' Mira said doubtfully, 'or if I was, I was so young . . .'

Chris looked at Mira sympathetically. She turned to her mother. 'Not everybody's like you, Mom.'

'Sure they are,' Val said cheerfully. 'They just don't know it.'

That's the way Val was. Absolute. There was no point in arguing with her. And in fact she was so right so often

338

that one simply shrugged off her gigantic arrogances. They were part of her, like the sprawly way she sat, her large movements of arm as she spoke, the way she held her cigarettes high in the air. And in time one came to feel that Val's extravagances of statement were harmless. She did not impose her categories on other people any more than anyone else does: she was simply louder in announcing them.

11

October is the month in which Cambridge is most beautiful. The brilliant gold and crimson leaves tint the sunlight dusky and soft on the redbrick sidewalks and the sky is very blue. The soft, ashy, burning sad autumn air, the sad sound of brittle leaves crushed underfoot that makes autumn a dying time in most places is offset here by the thousands of new young faces, bodies hurrying to a thousand events planned for one more new year.

Mira found her classes uninspiring, but the reading lists a challenge. She spent hours in Widener or Child library, poring through bookstores, and felt her mind expanding with this opportunity to read in depth, as well as width. The emphasis was on primary texts; anthologies were regarded as no more than study guides. It was a pleasant change from what she was used to.

She hung her curtains and bought some throw pillows and a few more plants, and planned her first dinner party. She invited Iso and Ava, Val and Chris, and struggled in the tiny kitchen over the blackened stove to do something as graceful as what they had done. She was not able to think of anything more exotic than baked chicken, but they all acted as if she had created a feast, and when it was over, she was flushed with pleasure. She had bought red carnations for the kitchen table, and Ava oohed and hung over them, saying how much she loved them, saying it as if the flowers had taken root in her soul and her body was enveloped by them.

'Please, take them home with you.'

Ava's eyes widened. 'Me? Ooh, Mira, I couldn't. It's just that I love them so.'

'It would make me happy if you took them.'

'Really? Oh, Mira, thank you!' Ava acted as if Mira had given her something large and valuable. She embraced Mira, buried her face in the flowers, thanked Mira over and over. Ava's mannerisms were so extreme that it was hard to believe them, but it was clear, even in the short time Mira had known her, that she believed them, that somehow they really expressed her.

After dinner they sat in the living room drinking wine.

'Well, look at your life, for instance,' Val was saying to Iso. 'You grew up on an orange plantation, or whatever they call them, you surfed, swam, skied, you've been all over the world with a pack on your back, you've done white water canoeing, you bicycled across Kenya. Or me: my life hasn't been that glamorous, but I've been everywhere. Chris and I traveled through Europe in a VW bus; we helped register voters in the South; we've lived on Indian reservations doing teaching and rudimentary nursing; we worked in Appalachia trying to mobilize opposition to the strip mining companies; we've been working with the peace movement, with Cambridge school and city problems, for years now . . .'

'You have, not me, Mom.'

'Or Ava . . .'

She raised her eyes from the flowers. 'Oh, I haven't done anything.'

'You have. You've been living on your own for years now, working, supporting yourself at a boring nine-to-five job and living in ratholes so you'd have money to study ballet four nights a week and all day Saturday. That takes courage, energy . . .'

'It's just all I care about,' Ava demurred in a tiny voice.

'But what do you find in the movies, in TV? The same old figures, the sex bomb and the housewife – that is, when they even bother to have female characters . . .'

'They come in three types: the heroine, the villainess, and the crossbreed. The heroine has blond hair, is utterly

340

moral, and has as much personality as a soft roll; the villainess has dark hair and gets killed in the end. Her crime is sex. The crossbreed is a good woman who goes bad or a bad woman who goes good. She always gets killed too, one way or another,' Iso laughed.

'I always wanted to be the villainess,' Ava said. 'But sometimes the heroine has dark hair.'

'Actually, there's another type,' Iso said thoughtfully. 'The asexual. You know, asexual Doris Day acting like a little boy clowning around with asexual Rock Hudson acting like a little bigger boy. Presley is like that too, and the Beatles.'

'That's true,' Mira agreed. 'Asexuality or maybe androgyny. Like Katherine Hepburn.'

'Or Garbo. Or Dietrich.'

'Or Judy Garland with that child's face, wearing tails.'

'Or Fred Astaire. You could never imagine him screwing.'

'Why is that, do you suppose?' Mira asked them.

'Maybe because real women have to be either angels or devils. And real men have to be macho, can't be sweet. Maybe the inbetween figures, the asexuals and androgynes are freed from the moral imperative,' Iso suggested.

'I always knew I was a devil,' Ava murmured.

'You act more like an angel,' Mira smiled.

'When I was five, I had a new party dress and I went out to the yard to show it to my daddy and I was so happy, I felt so pretty, and I swung all around to show him and my skirt flew out and my panties showed and my daddy picked me up and carried me into the house and beat me with his belt.'

They gazed at her. Val's forehead was furrowed, as if she were in pain. 'How do you feel about him now?' she asked.

'Oh, I love my daddy. But we fight a lot. I don't go home much because we always fight and that upsets Momma. Last time I was home was Christmas two years ago and Daddy hit me because I said I didn't like Lyndon Johnson, he just reached across and smacked me in the face real hard, it stung, you know, it brought tears to my eyes, so I picked up a fork that was lying on the counter, one of those long ones that you turn meat with, and I stabbed him in the stomach.' She said this in her soft-edged Alabama voice, confiding the events the way a child would, her long-lashed eyes trusting, questioning.

'Did you hurt him?' Mira asked horrified.

'Did you kill him?' Val laughed.

'No.' Ava's eyes danced. 'But I sure made him bleed a lot!' She burst into giggling, and kept laughing. She doubled over with laughter. 'He was sure shocked!' she added, pulling herself erect again. 'And I told him if he ever hit me again, I'd kill him. But now I'm afraid to go home, because if he hit me – and he might, he's such a bull – I'd have to do it. I'd have to kill him.'

'Does he hit your mother too?'

'No. Or my brother either. Anyway, not since my brother got bigger than him. But he always hit me the most.'

'Love pats,' Val said dryly.

'That's true,' Ava looked up at Val. 'That's it. He always loved me the most, and I knew it.'

'Training,' Val added.

Ava was sitting cross-legged on the floor, holding the jar of carnations. She buried her face in the flowers. 'Well, I don't know what it trained me for, because I'm not good for anything.'

'Ava, that's not true!' Iso protested.

'I'm not! I'm really not! I want to play the piano but I get too scared to play for people, and I want to dance, but I'm too old. All I can do is pound on that old type-writer all day, and I do that pretty good, but it gets boring.'

Iso spoke to Val and Mira. 'Ava only had a few years of lessons, when she was around twelve, and then again in college for two years. But she was so good, they put her on the stage and let her play with the Cleveland Symphony.'

342

'Oh, Iso, I won a contest,' Ava corrected irritably. 'You make it sound so great. It was just a contest.'

'But that's great!' Mira exclaimed.

'No, it wasn't,' Ava curled her head down, examining the flowers. 'Because I got so scared I knew I could never do it again. I couldn't go through that again. It was too terrible. So that was the end of the piano.'

'And why can't you dance?' Mira continued. 'You aren't old.'

Ava looked up at her. 'Oh, yes I am, Mira, I'm twenty-eight. I only started dancing a couple years ago. . . .'

'She's great,' Iso interrupted.

'Well,' she glanced at Iso briefly, then back at Mira, 'I think I do pretty well for a beginner, but it's too late.'

'She should have had lessons when she was a child. She sat down in second grade and played the piano. Just played something. The teacher thought she'd had lessons.'

'Well, I'd heard it on the radio.'

'You should have had lessons.'

'Well, Momma and Daddy, they weren't always doing too well. And I don't think they ever thought about it. You know? It just never occurred to them.'

'I wish my mother was like that. When I was seven, I used to draw a lot so my mother goes tearing out and gets me an art teacher, some creepy guy who lived down the block and did it in exchange for a meal. What a creep!' Chris held her forehead.

'That was one of my few mistakes,' Val admitted.

'It was your mistake, but I had to suffer for it,' Chris threw back banteringly. 'The sins of the fathers . . .'

'I'm not your father.'

Chris shrugged. 'You have to admit, Mommy, you're the only father I have permanently. The rest are just father figures – Dave, Angie, Fudge, Tim, Grant . . .' She was counting on her fingers, grinning wickedly at Val.

'Maybe you're better off,' Ava said wistfully. 'Do you ever wish you had a father?'

Chris looked at her seriously. 'Sometimes. Sometimes

343

I sort of imagine, you know, somebody coming home at night with the paper under his arm.' She giggled. 'You know, like hugging you and shit.' She giggled again.

'That's called a lover, Chris,' Iso laughed.

'Well, to take me places, you know, not like my mother, taking me on marches against the war, but real places, like the zoo.'

'I never knew you wanted to go to the zoo.'

'I don't. It's just a place.'

'Good, because I hate zoos.'

'Well, what about the circus?'

'I hate circuses.'

'You hate everything that doesn't have words in it.'

'That's true.'

'I love circuses,' Iso said. 'I'll take you, Chris.'

'Really?'

'Promise. Next time it's in Boston.'

'Great!'

'Oh, can I go too? I love circuses,' Ava sighed.

'Sure. We'll all go.'

'I was a real devil when I was little. I used to sneak into the circus without paying,' Ava giggled.

'You really do feel like a devil,' Val murmured.

'Her real name is Delilah. How would you feel if you were named after Delilah?' Iso grinned.

'Iso!' Ava pulled herself up and glared briefly at Iso. Then she turned to the others. 'It's true. I changed it to Ava after Ava Gardner. My momma called me Delilah Lee.'

'It's who you are,' Iso said lovingly. 'A cross between Delilah the temptress and Annabel Lee.'

'I'd rather be Margot Fonteyn,' she said swiftly, in anger, her back like flexible steel, her eyes flaming at Iso. 'It's you who want me to be those things, it's you who think I'm a temptress. Do you think I'm dying too?'

'You are a temptress, Ava! You flirt all the time, you bat your eyelashes, you really do, and you smile and act coy. You even get your car greased for nothing. The whole gas station stops work when you come in.'

344

'Good!' came the flaming reply. 'What else are they good for? Men are only vehicles for getting things. If I know how to use them, good for me!' Her body was taut, her fists clenched, and her face looked suddenly ravaged, the pretty pouty shy look gone. She looked noble and powerful and beaten all at once.

'Well, you sure know how to use them,' Iso said grudgingly.

Ava bent her head back down into her carnations. 'You make it sound as if I was always trying to get something from men. I'm not. That's not very nice of you. You know it's men always at me, even when I don't look at them. You know what it's like on the subway. Or that guy yesterday when we were walking to the grocery store. Or the guy in the downstairs apartment. I don't ask them for anything. I don't need them. I don't need men, mostly. All I need is music.'

They were all silent, gazing at her.

'And I'm uncomfortable because everybody's looking at me,' she added without looking up.

'If you could do anything in the world, what would you do?' Iso said in a new, cheery tone.

'Dance. In a real ballet. On a real stage.'

Iso turned to Val. 'What would you do?'

Val laughed. 'I don't want much. I just want to change the world.'

Iso turned to Mira. 'I don't know.' She was a little surprised. 'When I was young, I wanted to . . . *live*. Whatever I meant by that. Whatever it was, I still haven't done it.'

'Chris?'

'I don't know either.' Her young face looked sober and almost sad. 'I'd like to make everybody happy. If there was a way to do that. I guess I'd like to help people who are starving. All over the world.'

'That's a noble thought.' Iso smiled at her.

'What about you?'

Iso laughed. 'I'd go skiing. Really. Whenever I think of intense satisfaction, I think about skiing. I'm not serious, like the rest of you.'

'But that's serious,' Ava said sweetly. 'It's as serious as dancing.'

'No, one's art and one's just pleasure.' She sipped her wine. 'But it makes me wonder what the hell I'm doing here.'

Val groaned. 'Do we have to go through this again?' She turned to Ava. 'All day long, every day, everybody sits around in Lehman Hall drinking coffee and smoking cigarettes and beating our breasts and probing our souls trying to decide what the fuck we're doing here.'

'Well, I wonder what you-all are doing here too. It's such a terrible place,' Ava shuddered. 'Nobody talks to anybody else and when they do, it's always about such strange things.'

'Why don't you all leave, then?' Chris looked at them. 'Why don't you,' she turned to her mother, 'buy a big farmhouse in the country? I'd love to live in the country with all the cows and pigs and shit.'

'Literal,' Iso shot in.

'And we could all live together. I really liked living in the commune except some of the people were so spacey. But it would be cool with all of you. We could take turns chopping wood and shit.'

'Chris, did you know that *shit* was not synonymous with *et cetera?*' her mother said.

'And Ava could dance all day, and Iso could ski all day, and Mom could go out every morning and change the world and Mira could sit around and figure out what she wanted to do and I could ride the horses.'

They all agreed that would be wonderful indeed, and set about planning it: the size of the house, the location, what animals they would have and who would be responsible for which. They got into an argument about pigs, Iso insisting they were clean and Ava insisting she would not have them. They had another argument about household chores, all of which Ava refused to do. In fact the only thing she was willing to do was feed the chickens.

'I love chickens,' she sighed, 'when they go cluck, cluck!'

346

The arguments ended in screaming laughter and a few wry comments on the bleak possibilities for human social harmony.

When they had gone and she had finished the dishes, Mira took the bottle of brandy into the living room, turned out the lights, and sat beside the window, breathing in the chill damp October air. Footsteps passed on the sidewalk below, a man's footsteps. She listened until they vanished.

She felt swirled up in something rich and alive but also strange. She wondered about the relationship between Iso and Ava. It was almost as if Iso were Ava's mother. And about the list Chris had ticked off: were they the names of Val's lovers? Did Val bring men right into the house in front of her daughter? Did Val not mind the language Chris used? Of course, she used it herself. But Chris was only sixteen. She thought about Chris's suggestion they all live together. It was only a pipe dream, of course, but why had they all felt so free, so excited, when they talked about it? It was a thought: she was not particularly happy living alone, yet it had never occurred to her there was any alternative but marriage. It could be fun living with a group of friends like these, so full of ideas, so full of life, not like men, always trying to insist on themselves and their dignities. Norm would have been horrified by the evening she had just spent, at the subjects discussed, the language used, at some of their notions – especially Val's – and at its frivolity, its playful pleasure. He would have stood up looking disapproving, looked at his watch, spoken gravely of tomorrow's important schedule, and left at eight thirty.

Yet it had been so much fun. She felt rich, full of energy, she wanted to plunge into her work. She felt as if things were continually being freed in her, as if her imprisoning those things had made her tired all these years. But what things they were she did not know. It was just that somehow with these friends you could be *honest:* that was the only word she could come up with.

She thought about Val and Chris. Under their banter

or squabbling you could sense the closeness, the trust. It seemed enviable. Her own sons, those babies who had come out of her own body, whom she had loved so much once, she hardly knew now. She remembered how her heart had felt as she gazed at them when they were toddling, when they came home from school able to read the first pages in a book, when they looked at her with a child's clean gaze and told her a story about school. She remembered burying her nose in their sheets, smelling their bodies.

And now. She wrote them every week, short polite letters telling them about the weather and what she was reading and where she had gone. She had had one short note from each of them at the beginning of school, nothing since. They were probably not sorry to be away from her. She'd been so terrible those first months after Norm left, and just distant since. It was all so mixed up: her rage at them for being Norm's children, for resembling him; her guilt toward them for failure – for surely if she had been better, the marriage would not have dissolved: and resentment too. Once Norm had gone, her position was clearer than ever: servant to a house and two children. And did they appreciate? Yes, she had felt all that, and more too, probably. So she had abandoned them, not physically but psychically. And now physically too.

Suddenly she was overwhelmed with grief. There was no way to apologize, no way to go back, no way to wipe it all out of their memories. There was no justice, she remembered. But maybe there could still be love.

She decided she would insist on their spending Thanksgiving with her.

12

In the fall of 1968, Normie was sixteen and Clark fifteen. They were quiet, shy boys. They had been more outgoing before their parents' separation, but something had happened to them after it. They were typical suburban monsters, however, expecting every luxury, expecting to be driven everywhere, terrified of independence and full of blame of their parents for this terror. And both were slow developers; neither had hair on his chin yet, and Normie's voice still squeaked out of control at times. Private school had shaken them somewhat. Normie's response to the change had been to become extremely gregarious, and his grades were suffering. Clark's had been to become withdrawn, and to sit watching television for long periods, and his grades were suffering. When Mira called saying she had cleared it with their father and they were to spend Thanksgiving with her, both had only one question.

'Do you have a TV set?'

'NO!' Mira stormed, insulted.

They arrived at Logan with two canvas bags and a boxed-up portable TV.

Valerie was having a big Thanksgiving feast and had invited fourteen people, but Mira was apprehensive about Val's effect on her sons, and explained that she had not seen them in a long time and preferred to be alone with them. She had, indeed, a plan in her mind. They would talk, really talk. She remembered the times they had tried to talk to her and she had cut them off, and the memory wrenched her heart.

They arrived late on Wednesday, and were tired, so she was not upset when they sat sleepy-eyed in front of the TV set, and went to bed early. Thursday, she was busy cooking and they wanted to watch a football game. But when they wanted to keep the set on during dinner, she protested. The game was not over, they shrilled at her, outraged.

'Dad lets us keep the TV on when we're there!' they yelled. That was a tactical error.

'Does he! Wonderful! Well, I don't!'

They sat glumly through the meal, responding to her continual questions with the briefest possible answer, and as soon as the meal was over, they looked at her.

'May we leave the table, ma'am?'

She sighed. It was hopeless. 'Go ahead. But I expect you to dry the dishes.'

They leaped up and went into the bedroom, which

349

Mira had given over to them for their visit, and lay on the bed and watched TV. The dishes, she noticed after they had gone to bed, still stood in the rack.

Friday she took them along the Freedom Trail. They dragged, they looked reluctantly as she explained the importance of one building or another; they looked at each other with faces that said she was crazy when she grew excited about the people buried in the old cemetery. They did like *Old Ironsides*, though, and the Italian ices they bought in the North End. Once home, they headed for the TV set.

Saturday she walked with them through the Yard and in the Square. They liked the Coop and spent considerable money on records. She took them to a French restaurant for lunch and they wanted double cheeseburgers.

'Quiche, you're having,' she hissed at them. 'That's why I brought you here. Quiche and salad and wine!'

But they left most of it, tasted the wine and left it, asking for Coke, and complained about the salad dressing, which was made of vinegar, oil, and tarragon.

They looked strange to her too. They were handsome boys, and still tan from playing tennis. Their hair was clipped very short, and both had come up in navy blue blazers and flannel trousers. She had seen nothing like them in several months: at first she looked at them as if they were Arabs at a B'nai B'rith convention. And they said 'sir' and 'ma'am'. Norm had wanted them to speak that way, but she had never insisted upon it. Apparently the school agreed with Norm's position. They were clean-cut and polite and blank. She tried to think of what they reminded her; it was Ken, the doll who went with Barbie.

By Saturday night she was simmering. She picked up a bagful of cheap cheeseburgers and French fries, and a couple of bottles of cola. They ate with relish: it was, they said, the best meal they'd had. She eyed them coldly.

'May we be excused, ma'am?'

'Damn it! Will you stop calling me ma'am?' she screamed. They were shocked. 'Anything else will do,'

350

she added with sweet acidity. But they did not laugh. They looked at each other with bewilderment.

'Look,' she pleaded, 'I don't see you very often, and I'd like to talk to you. To find out how you are, and how you like school and . . . everything. Do you understand?' Her voice was a little shaky.

'Sure, ma – Mom,' Normie said quickly. 'Only we already told you. We're fine.'

She insisted on going through the litany again. Their answers were the same: 'Okay.'

'Well, let's talk about other things, then. How do you feel about Daddy and me getting divorced?'

They looked at each other, then at her. 'Okay,' Normie said.

'Do you feel funny? Do you feel different from the other kids?'

'Naw. Everybody's parents are divorced,' Clark said.

'How do you like Daddy's new wife?'

'She's okay.'

'Nice. She's nice.'

'How did you like Cambridge? What do you think about my apartment?'

'Cambridge is okay. Your apartment – I guess it's okay for an apartment.'

'You oughta have a TV though.'

'I suppose you have more fun when you're with Daddy.'

Clark shrugged. 'Yeah, you can play ball.'

'And he lets us watch TV with dinner,' Normie reminded her casually.

'And do you talk to him?'

They looked again at each other and back at her, silent. Finally, after thinking about it, Clark said, 'Well, he's never there.'

'And what do you think about my going to graduate school? Does it seem strange to you?'

'No,' they both murmured unenthusiastically.

'You certainly are articulate,' she said and stood up and went into the bathroom and cried. She told herself she was suffering from self-pity and that Rome was not

351

built in a day. She tried to fight down the rising gulps in her throat. She washed her face with cold water and reapplied makeup. She returned to the kitchen. In her absence, they had brought the TV set into the kitchen. Unwilling to defy her – they had not been excused from the table and they were polite children – they had brought the monster right into the kitchen. At her look they turned down the sound, and she started again.

'Look, what happened between Daddy and me had to have some impact on you. I would really like to know how you feel. I'm not trying to run an inquisition. I'd really like to know.'

They gazed at her blankly, and suddenly Normie hit Clark on the shoulder. 'Did you see that pass?' he cried with real animation.

Mira stormed over and turned the set off. She whirled on them. 'I'm TALKING to you! I'm trying to talk to you!' They both looked down. She saw they were embarrassed at her lack of control, and resentful, possibly fearing a wild scene like some three years earlier. The tears came again. She sat down across from them and put her head in her hands. They sat silent, watching her intensely. 'Okay, okay. If you won't talk to me, I'll talk to you. I'll tell you how I am. How I am is Miserable!' She saw their eyes meet, but they did not move their heads. 'I hate this place, I hate the kids, they're such spoiled brats, and everybody is disconnected and if it weren't for a couple of people, I'd have gone stark raving mad! And this goddamned school is antifemale, they look down on women, especially women my age. It's a goddamned monastery that's been invaded by pople in skirts and the men who run it only hope that the people in skirts are pseudomen, so they won't disturb things, won't insist that feeling is as important as thinking and body as important as mind. . . .'

She could see the glaze in their eyes, but they were staring at her as if they understood that something important was happening, even if they did not understand her words. She persisted.

'They make me feel just as rotten as your father did.

352

As if I'm nothing, invisible, or if not, that I ought to want to be. And sometimes I do. And even worse, I'm lonely, I'm so damned lonely. . . .' She was crying again. 'Do you know that in three months not one man has so much as asked me to have a cup of coffee with him? Not one!' She was sobbing now, half surprised at herself, having been unaware that her feelings were so strong, that she was as miserable as that, that these were the feelings buried in the darkness and the brandy. She was no longer looking at the boys. She had buried her face in her hands and had turned away from them. She remembered sharply now how she had felt toward them during the year she had been in despair, feeling that they were just there, flesh of her flesh, perhaps, but unconnected to her. They did not know who she was and did not care as long as she serviced them. They were only accidentally of her production. She remembered hating them for that and berating herself for her irrationality, expecting consolation and concern from boys so young who did not understand what was happening. But she had felt that they turned their faces away from her purposely. She felt so now: she was utterly alone.

Then she sensed something warm and solid near her. She looked up. Clark was standing beside her. He put his arm awkwardly on her shoulder. She leaned her head against his body, and he patted her back lightly, unrhythmically, unsure in the role of consoler. 'Don't cry, Mommy,' he said, and there were tears in his voice.

13

The snow began to fall the day before Thanksgiving and it never went away until spring. Cambridge was covered all winter; there were permanent walls of snow along its sidewalks. I walked in it thinking about snow symbolism in literature, something I had never found persuasive. But that year I did feel that nature was trying to purify what men had done, to cover over the blood-gorged earth and let it rest.

Maybe no single year is worse than any other; maybe

353

just as much flesh is slashed and scarred, just as much blood driven violently into the soil in every twelve-month span. It would be hard to get statistics on violent death – what do you count as murder? When people starve to death because of the policies of governments and corporations, is that murder? Nature does a fair amount of murdering itself, which is why this whole notion of dominating nature arose: it was one of those things that seemed a good idea at the time. No one ever believes a cure will prove worse than the disease. And maybe it isn't. An invasion of microbes that destroys a body could also be called murder. All deaths are violent deaths, I suppose. You can see that when you think the way I do, you never reach any conclusions.

Still, 1968 felt more terrible than other years. I felt as if I was a cell in a huge convulsed body sprawled across a continent, jerking in spasms from the shots that killed King, Kennedy, and some nameless folk in a ditch in My Lai. One suffered from being the murderer – for hadn't they come from among us, hadn't they learned what we learned? – and the murdered. Of course one is always both: the killed – body shrieking the trail of hot metal through brain or chest or stomach, the heat, the burn, the pain expanding through every sensible member, the slow-motion turn and fall, one thin line of hot lead in a body sufficient to undo all of it, standing and understanding; and the killer – the nervous itchy boy's finger on the trigger, the soft sweating armpits of the conspirator, the mindless eyes of the paid murderer, the taut back of the saver of the world from Jews or Communists or Albigensians – the one, for it must always finally be one who kills, one who is killed. That year, 1968, was a slow-motion murder, spanning the year, spanning the continent, a photograph capturing an eternal falling.

But we all die, and all death is violent, the overthrowing of the state of life, so why did that year seem so terrible? Are King or Kennedy or some peasant folk in a village more important than the starved-out of Biafra, the names on the Detroit homicide list? Maybe I'm playing an intellectual game, marking out one year or two on a calendar as special in horror so I can add that they were also special in significance, and thus compensate for the horror, or even redeem it. Humans are fond of finding ways to be grateful for their suffering, calling falls fortunate and deaths resurrection. It's not a bad idea, I guess: since you're going to have the suffering anyway, you might as well be grateful for it. Sometimes, though, I think if we didn't expect the suffering, we wouldn't have so much of it.

Whatever my head is doing, I can't help it: I do see the violence of that year and the years following as symbolic, but not in the usual sense. What I see – and it frightens me – is that all action may be simply symbolic, and only the death part is real. It's as though the prop dagger they stab Caesar with onstage keeps getting transformed into a real one the minute it encounters real flesh, in some grotesque variation of Midas' terrible gift – which is after all the true legend of our time.

Some people use bullfights, some the Mass, some art in order to ritualize or transform death into life or at least meaning. But my terror is that life itself is a ritual transforming everything into death. People criticize what they call the media for shaping – they say distorting – events. Lots of events are held just for the media – marches and sit-ins and people chaining themselves to fences. I think it's a good idea. A long unforced march is better than even a short siege, a symbolic protest better than a real bomb. And, when you thing about it, there were always media events. All the pomp and ceremony, the trumpets blaring, the ermines and velvets and jewels men of government and clergy encompassed themselves with, the medal declaring position, the ring requiring a kiss, the scepter requiring genuflection – all of them were part of what nowadays we call PR events, except that those celebrated the people with power and the events complained about in our times draw attention to people without power. I suspect there lies the problem. Who ever had a better eye for PR than that Holy Roman Emperor who walked barefoot for miles through the snow to make obeisance to Pope Gregory at Canossa?

But when does the symbolic leave off and the real begin? The symbolism changes according to whether you believe that King was killed by the FBI, by black militants who wanted a martyr, or by some simpleton who believed in the devil; but the death doesn't change. Bobby Kennedy sympathized with Israel; some of the people in My Lai may have given succor to the soldiers of the north. Those facts or possibilities have little relation to what happened. What was murdered in those cases was an image, but what died was real. And the whole movement of those years was the same way: all the long-haired, bearded freaks and dope addicts we maced and sprayed from Berkeley to Chicago, all the lazy lying niggers we stoned and shot from California to Chicago to Alabama to Attica, all those slanty-eyed commie charlies we machined-gunned and napalmed, all of them were saying they weren't what we insisted they were and would be if we had to kill them to make them be it, if you follow what I mean. Nixon went to Madison Avenue and bought a new image. Maybe if they'd treated the whole thing as a media event, they'd still be alive too.

What is real beyond the muscle, bone, and blood, beyond body? The image can become intrinsic, can shape the mouth, the vision, the posture. If you're a waiter all your life, maybe you always stand a little bent forward. But it's disconnectable too; Galileo didn't see himself burning. And even body is not fixed. There's age, weight, accident, nose bob, hair dye, colored contact lenses.

I see us as all sitting around naked, shivering, in a huge circle, looking up as the sky turns black and the stars flare out and somebody starts to tell a story, claims to see a pattern in the stars. And then someone else tells a story about the eye of the hurricane, the eye of the tiger. And the stories, the images, become the truth and we will kill each other rather than change one word of the story. But every once in a while, someone sees a new star, or claims to see it, a star in the north that changes the pattern, and that is devastating. People are outraged, they start up grunting in fury, they turn on the one who noticed it and club her to death. They sit back down, muttering. They take up smoking. They turn away from the north, not wanting it to be thought that they might be trying to catch sight of her hallucination. Some of them, however, are true believers, they can look straight north and never see even a glimpse of what she pointed to. The foresighted gather together and whisper. They already know that if that star is accepted, all the stories will have to be changed. They turn suspiciously to sniff out any of the others who might surreptitiously turn their heads to peer at the spot where this star is supposed to be. They catch a few they think are doing this; despite their protests, they are killed. The thing must be stopped at the root. But the elders have to keep watching, and their watching convinces the others that there's really something there, so more and more people start to turn, and in time everyone sees it, or imagines they see it, and those that don't claim they do.

So earth feels the wound, and Nature from her seat, sighing through all her Works, gives signs of woe, that all is lost. The stories all have to be changed: the whole world shudders. People sigh and weep and say how peaceful it was before in the happy golden age when everyone believed the old stories. But actually nothing whatever has changed except the stories.

I guess the stories are all we have, all that makes us different from lion, ox, or those snails on the rock. I'm not sure I want to be different from those snails. The essential human act is the lie, the creation or invention of a fiction. For instance, here in my corner of the world, a major story is that it is possible to live without pain. They are removing hooks from noses and psyches, gray from hair, gaps from teeth, organs from bodies. They are trying to remove hunger and ignorance, or so they say. They are working on a pitless peach, a thornless rose.

Is there a thornless rose? I'm confused. I'm confused because part of me thinks a thornless rose would be really nice, while another part of me grips puritanically the thorn, even as blood drips down my palm. And all of me thinks it would be nice if there were no hunger or ignorance – the latter a bit of a joke, I fear: One man's ignorance is another man's wisdom. And I don't want to insist on suffering, that self-realizing prophecy. It must be that the snows wash it away, or rain, or wind. Otherwise, how could the world get about with all those scars, those mutilations on its body? We have forgotten the Siege of Paris, the Albigensians, and hundreds of other old stories. The pennons, the decked-out, high-stepping horses, the ermines and velvets are all part of fairy tale now.

The point is that if only what endures is real – something Shakespeare, say, believed – then only death is real. All the rest is image, transient, mutable. Even our stories, although they last longer than we do. So what makes them – what makes anything – worth dying for? When everything but death is a lie, a fiction.

People on both sides claimed ideas were worth dying for back then in 1968, although the ones who made the loudest claims were rarely the ones who died. One day in Lehman Hall, which was festering with talk of revolution, Mira dared to suggest that revolutions weren't especially fun. Brad Barnes, who had lately joined SDS, sat beneath chandeliers, a cheeseburger and French fries before him, his Coke halfway to his mouth, stopped, stared at her, and said: 'Well, Mira, when the revolution comes, I'll try to prevent them from lining you up against the wall. I know you're well-intentioned, after all.'

14

Grief and revolt notwithstanding, ordinary life went on, classes and parties which Mira dutifully attended. Graduate student parties were noisy, centerless, and disconnected. They were held in shabby apartments decorated with posters. One room was usually emptied of furniture except for the stereo which blasted the usual Stones or Joplin songs. The grad students might go without food, but they had music. Sometimes there was a strobe light in the room, and always people danced. In the kitchen there would be beer and wine, pretzels, potato chips, sometimes cheese and crackers. One bedroom door was always closed. Mira thought people went into that room to, as she put it, 'neck.' This seemed strange, since a number of them were in there at once, and all of them could simply have gone someplace else and had privacy. It was several months before she was invited into the room and discovered what was really going on. They were smoking, passing the joint or pipe in a casual, indifferent way that was betrayed every time they heard a police siren, or whenever the music grew too loud. Someone would open the door then and yell: 'Hey, keep it down, you want the pigs to come?'

Grass seemed to send each of them into their own private circle of senses. They inhaled deeply, sitting on the floor or lolling on the bed; they gazed outward, but did not seem to be looking outward. They were calm, talked desultorily in low voices. It seemed to her that they were together only because they were in the same room and were participating together in something that was called a crime: it was 'Us' against 'Them.' It was just like their dancing, she thought. They danced together to the same music, but no one touched anyone else, no one led, no one followed, you could not call any pair a unit. Cambridge seemed a world of complete disconnection and isolation.

She would leave the smoking room and wander through the other rooms. Some apartments were large, shared by three or four students. There were people everywhere, but everywhere they were saying the same things they said at every other party. She passed Steve Hoffer giving one of his monologues:

'It's a bird, it's a plane, it's Superbreath! Here he comes, with a sound like thunder, his aim to relieve the oppressed and defeat evil and to establish Daddy Warbucks as King of the Universe! He flies into the room where Dr. Caligari bends over the inert form of who else but . . . Barbarella! He opens his supermouth and blows. Pow! Everyone in the room passes out, unfortunately including Barbarella. Careful to close his mouth, he leaps to her side and snatches the beautiful woman from the torture table. In a flash he is gone, wafting her high above skyscrapers. The gorgeous woman recovers and opens her eyes, twittering delicately her six-inch eyelashes (aided in their length by her indispensable Belliball eyeliner and mascara), and perceiving her rescuer's handsome face, presses her mouth warmly and wetly against his: only to pass out again! Poor Superbreath! A tear mists his eye: the terrible curse laid upon his powers cannot be evaded! Never can he know the love of woman! Forever and ever he will fly the skies seeking out evil and establishing the Kingdom of Daddy Warbucks so that the world may be covered with busily humming factories and sprinkled with happy workers and dotted with even happier millionaires! But until the day the world is secure, when he will resign his cape, he cannot enjoy the pleasures of mere mortals. But when that day comes, boys and girls, when he has firmly and forever established the kingdom of money and machines, he will finally be allowed to brush his teeth with Crest and gargle with Listerine – something, you, boys and girls, can do right now! – and live a normal life in a ranch house in Levittown with Barbarella in a little white apron and nothing else. . . .'

'Natura naturans,' Dorothy said.

'No, *naturata*,' Tina argued.

'I'm going to scream,' said Chuck Spinelli mildly.

'First cause is the same as final cause, no? I mean metaphysically, or if you go beyond ordinary categories into mystic reality . . .'

'It wouldn't be efficient cause.'

'It's sufficient cause to leave,' Chuck said.

'Hi, Mira!' said Howard Perkins, as if he were really glad to see her. He was a skinny young man with an eye twitch. He curved and dangled his body. Thin and tall

360

as he was, his body seemed a particular burden to him, as if it were a long string of cooked spaghetti and he could not find a way to make it stand upright. He was always draping himself over or around something.

'I can't believe half a year is over. Only six months to go. This has been the worst year of my life.'

Mira gave a motherly murmur.

'You're so lucky.'

'Why?'

'You're older, you're sure of yourself. The rest of us . . . oh, it's been horrible.'

'Do you mean you were afraid you wouldn't get through?'

'Sure! All of us! I still am. You know, we were all superstars in undergrad school. Straight A's and all that. Never failed anything. But all the while, in the back of your mind, you know you're really stupid, because you know how much you don't know. The teachers – even the best ones – don't know because they haven't thought to ask you those questions, and so they keep on giving you A's. But you know the day of retribution is coming. Then you get it, the acceptance to Harvard! You got it because those teachers recommended you, the teachers who don't know. But you can feel in your bones that it's coming. When you get to Harvard, they'll find out. You'll fail miserably. Then everyone will know.' He groaned.

'So you study like hell to make up for your stupidity.'

'Of course.' He looked at her appealingly, trustingly. 'When do you think they'll find me out? At the general exam?'

She laughed. 'When I was little I thought my father knew everything. That was because he wasn't around very much. It was upsetting because I knew he would know who made those muddy footprints down the hall. Then, when I got a little older, I figured anybody would have known who made them since there was only one person in the house who wore a size five shoe. I also figured that my father didn't know much at all, because my mother told him everything, and she was the one to be feared. But then I discovered that neither of them could multiply twenty-seven by fifty-six as quickly as I could, and I cast both of them off in contempt. I thought that it was the teacher who knew everything. Well, that didn't last too long, but by then I was in college, and I really figured the professors were the ones who knew everything. That doesn't last too long either. When you get your first A, you're overjoyed, then you get another, another, and another. You are convinced by now that none of those professors knows anything at all. You keep going, you move through the minefield on tiptoe, waiting for the explosion. But it never comes. Years and years go by and nothing happens, nobody finds out. You keep being successful, you keep getting promoted. One day you wake up and you're President, and then you're really scared. Because by then you know that nobody knows anything and they think you do. It's at that point that you begin to worry about the future of mankind.'

He laughed, a full rich unselfconscious laugh, and everybody turned around to look at them. Then his face fell again.

'Sometimes I wonder what I'm doing here,' he moaned.

God. Again. 'What else could you be doing?'

'I could be out killing gooks.'

'Yes.'

'That might be better.'

'If you enjoy that sort of thing.'

'Maybe I'll join the Peace Corps.'

'How would you like a diet of fishheads and rice?'

'All I eat is brown rice and beans and yoghurt. I have to get out of here. This place is full of walking-around zombies. Everybody tries to compete with each other and tries to impress Hooten hoping he'll be impressed enough to recommend them for the Harvard appointment, or maybe to Yale or Princeton. Nobody's real.'

'Maybe that's what real is.'

'No. You're real. You say what you really feel.'

362

No, I don't, she thought. Or I'd tell you how bored I am.

'I think I'll get some more wine,' she said. That's how you get to be an alcoholic, she thought, always heading for the booze when the party gets dull.

A young woman with long straight red hair was standing at the table pouring wine into her glass. She kept pouring until the glass overflowed.

'Oh, Christ!' She looked up at Mira and laughed nervously. 'I don't know why I'm drinking this stuff, I'm zonked already.'

'Well, if you enjoy pouring for its own sake, here's another glass.'

Kyla laughed. 'I never see you anymore, Mira.' She filled Mira's glass, managing to spill only a little. Mira saw that her hands were shaking.

'No. I guess I don't go to Lehman Hall as often as I used to.'

'I don't go at all. God, I hate this place!' She turned her head and looked around nervously. Her eyes were anxious.

'Yeah.' Mira offered her a cigarette.

She tapped it for some seconds on the kitchen table. 'You're so wonderful, though, so calm. As if it just meant nothing to you, you just sail through it.'

Mira was surprised. 'Someone else just said something like that. It's strange. The impressions other people get of us, I mean.'

'Don't you feel calm?'

'Well, I suppose so, yes, I don't feel nervous. But I'm not very happy here.'

'Not very happy here. Well, of course, who could be? But you have the whole thing in perspective, you know what's important.'

'Me?' She looked closely at Kyla.

'Yes!' Kyla insisted. 'The rest of us run around like idiots worrying, terrified. It's our whole future, our lives.'

'Is what you're saying that your entire sense of self-worth depends on your doing well here?'

'Beautiful,' Kyla said, smiling benignly at her. 'Right.' She held up the cigarette, and Mira lighted it. She puffed nervously. 'Not just getting through, but doing brilliantly. We all want it, we all expect it. It's sick. We're sick.'

'Then my health is a consequence of my lowered horizons,' Mira said. 'I'd like the appointment at Harvard or Yale too, but I don't see any chance of them giving it to the forty-odd-year-old woman I'll be when I get out of here. So I just don't think about it. I don't think about the future much at all. I can't imagine what it will be.'

'It's a rat race, a rat race,' Kyla insisted, puffing on the cigarette and staring intently at the wine bottle. 'And if somebody cared. I am married to this absolutely magnificent man, but he really doesn't give a damn whether I do well or not, oh, yes he does, but he's not willing to help me, do you think it's wrong of me to ask him to help me?' She turned to Mira with moist eyes. 'I help him. I really do. When he's depressed, I listen, and when he needs it, I boost his ego, and I love him, I really love him.'

'I don't think I've met your husband,' Mira said, looking around.

'Oh, he's not here. He's a physicist, and he's finishing up his dissertation. He's down at the lab almost every night. Do you think I have the right to ask anything of him? I know he's busy.'

'Of course,' Mira heard herself say. 'Of course you do.'

Kyla looked at her.

'You might as well,' Mira laughed grimly. 'If you ask nothing you'll get nothing. You may get nothing anyway, but at least you will have tried.'

'Oh, thank you!' Kyla cried out, and hugged Mira, spilling some of her wine on Mira's blouse. Mira was touched and embarrassed.

'What did I do?' she laughed.

'You told me what I had to do!' Kyla exclaimed, as if it should have been obvious.

'You told yourself,' Mira corrected her.

'Maybe. But you helped me to figure what I had to do. Can I come over and see you someday?'

'Of course,' Mira said, bewildered.

Someone came to the table and tapped Kyla on the shoulder. It was Martin Bell, a silent, intense, dark young man.

'Want to dance?'

Kyla put her glass down. 'Sure, fine.' As she was leaving, she turned to Mira. 'Remember, I'm coming over someday,' she said, and Mira smiled and nodded.

Mira wandered again. She stood near a few groups that went on talking without looking at her; she stood near a few that looked around and admitted her to conversations about how terrible it was at Harvard. She went for her coat. In the hall, she brushed past Howard Perkins, who was talking to a beautiful young woman dressed in a long, multicolored skirt and gypsy beads. As soon as Howard touched Mira's sleeve, the young woman turned and walked away.

'Mira, you're going? Listen, would you mind if I came over and talked to you someday? Some night, maybe? Would it be okay?'

'Of course.'

She left shaking her head. She felt as if she had suddenly become the Old Wise Woman of Cambridge, when all the while she knew nothing, nothing.

15

Howard Perkins knocked on her door the next afternoon. He slumped, slouched in, and hung his body over a chair.

'I'm really depressed. I need somebody to talk to. I hope you don't mind.'

She murmured something and offered him coffee.

'I never drink it. It's poison. I'll have tea, though, if you have good tea, not that American mold in teabags.'

'Sorry, that's all I have.'

'Nothing then.' He rearranged a limb. Mira lighted a

cigarette and sat down across from him. 'I really can't stand it anymore, this pace, this paper world. I really sort of hope I get drafted. I wouldn't kill anyone, I'd refuse to do that, but at least I'd be out of this cocoon.'

'You'd rather endure ordeal by combat than ordeal by paper.'

'Nothing could be worse than this.'

'What about working on an assembly line? Collecting quarters at a toll booth? Cutting wheat with a scythe?'

'At least you'd be out in the real world.'

She wondered what he would do with his body in the 'real world.' Many of the male grad students were like him, bodiless, as if they did not live inside their flesh, but hovered somewhere above it, as if it were a garment necessary to put on when going out in public, but which they removed at night when they returned to their dark little apartments. Body was a social necessity, like the white gloves she used to wear to formal occasions. How did they look when they were alone? Ectoplasm ranging awkwardly around an apartment, reaching for the supper can of soup, sprawled on a daybed reading, draped around a chair; no joints to impede its suppleness, no matter to impede its progress through walls, chairs, windows.

Howard was talking about the Romantics seminar. He was particularly bitter about Kyla, whom he called 'a little, tight-assed bitch.'

'Did she give a paper recently?' Mira asked shrewdly.

'Oh, sure. Christ! Typical! She wrote about the plays written by the Romantic poets. Can you imagine? I never even knew they'd written plays. And who cares? Morrison, of course, loved her paper: it was full of disgusting forgotten details that deserve their oblivion. But some termite had to drag them out into the light of day.'

'Kyla's very bright.'

'She's good at that crap. Is that what we're here for? The world is falling apart and we're haggling about Hugh of St. Victor's comments on Chalcidius' commentary on Plato!' His voice was outraged, his arms flailed about.

Mira laughed.

366

'I can see it now! The bomb goes off, the sky lights up, and Kyla Forrester and Richard Bernstein swing into argument about whether that precise formation was predicted by St. Stanislaus of the Steamy Sump, or in the adaptation made by Pynne of Pynne Head. L. Morrison listens with sober attention, undiverted by the flames which are consuming Boston, and finally interrupts gravely: "Very interesting," he says, "but both of you are overlooking a little known but interesting tract by a great scholar, famous in his own time, Dr. Asininum Scholasticum Claus of Sancta Claus, which modifies the final apocalypse described by Pynne by adding a spreading flower in the shape of *Agaricus campestris*, the common mushroom, a shape very like that we see before us. I refer you to Part III, article 72, A1 – I believe. It may be A2." Forrester and Bernstein quickly scribble the reference down, and as the flames reach Cambridge, Morrison is quietly continuing his monologue about Claus, including publication dates of every copy of every manuscript of his ever published.'

'At that point, why not? It's as good an occupation as any for last moments.'

'Maybe. But only for last moments.'

Mira stood up. 'I think I'll have a drink. Do you want one? Or some wine?'

He took the wine.

Mira was bored and irritated. 'It seems to me that you're frightened of failure and are just being nasty about people you think might be better than you are.' She said this a little nervously. She had never intentionally attacked someone this way.

'Of course I'm frightened. And you're probably right about my nastiness. But still I think what Forrester and Morrison do sucks. It's useless, parasitical work.'

She was surprised by the calmness of his response, and decided to go further.

'Then why are you here trying to do it?'

'That's what I'm asking you. Why am I here?'

'Oh, Christ!' She did not try to keep the disgust out of her voice. 'All of you! It's really outrageous! You are

367

all impressed as hell with Harvard; you all would like nothing better than a life like Morrison's. All this soul-searching is just protection for yourselves in case you don't make it.'

He crumbled. 'It's true,' he mumbled. He looked up at her. 'Don't you think it's disgusting – to have goals like that?'

'No,' she said quietly. 'What's so wrong? You enjoy using your mind, you want the approbation of society, you want a pleasant life. Why does everyone seem to think the only proper goal is to mortify the spirit?'

'Well, I think it's disgusting. I hate myself for it. I just hate myself period. Do you know I'm twenty-three years old and still a virgin?'

'No,' she answered gravely, switching on the lamp on the table beside her. Dusk was falling outside; the street-lights switched on.

'Well, it's true. I guess you think I'm some sort of freak.'

'Not at all. I'm sure there are many others like you.'

'What do you mean, like me?' he shot at her swiftly, suspiciously.

She shrugged. 'Virgins at twenty-three. Or -four, or -five. Or thirty.'

'You think so?' He watched her carefully, untrusting.

'I know so,' she said firmly, wondering what data she possessed to support her statement. But she did know it, somehow.

He sat back, his ectoplasm curling into the seat cushion. He talked on about his deficiency, and Mira began to realize he was placing a demand on her. She felt a mounting resentment. How dare he ask this of her without giving anything of himself? Even if he had come to her with passion, she would feel reluctant. But he gave nothing. He expected her to do all of it. She was to make a miracle, to create not only the experience but also the desire for it. I could dance naked, she thought, and suddenly understood a whole set of things that had previously bewildered her, bunnies and strip houses and skin flicks and other strange arrangements between men

368

and women. I could wear a black halter and garter belt and come through the door with a rose between my teeth like some woman in a novel by Saul Bellow. Arouse the erection so that you may have the pleasure of satisfying it. My God.

He talked on, seemingly rambling, but there was, she sensed, a center he was circling around, not hitting on. She listened hard to what was not being said. Suddenly she had it.

'So you think you might be gay.'

He stopped dead. His eyes were sharp and focused on her. 'Do *you* think I'm gay?'

'I have no idea.'

He relaxed a little. 'How can you tell?' his voice trembled out.

She stared at him. 'About yourself, you mean?' she faltered.

'Yes. Or about anybody. How do you know if you are or aren't?'

Mira was shocked. She did not know how to answer him. She realized, at that instant, that her closest ties had always been with women, that it was women she loved, not men. 'I don't know, Howard,' she said slowly. 'I don't even know about myself.'

'Oh, you gay?' he laughed. 'That's crazy!'

'How do you know?'

'Are you?' He looked horrified.

She laughed. 'I told you, I don't know.'

'How can you laugh about a thing like that!' He was outraged.

'Oh, Howard! At my time of life, you don't worry about what you are, you only worry about being able to go on being it.'

'I think that's pretty cynical, Mira. I think that's gross. I think that's disgusting.'

'And that,' she leaned forward nastily, 'is why you are in trouble.'

Again, he crumbled. He had, she thought, nothing whatever to hold him up. 'You think so?' he asked anxiously.

'You're afraid of what you might be, so you can't be anything at all.'

He sat stunned, rambling on with half his mind, staring around the room as if he were looking for something. She watched him anxiously; she had gone too far, she had said things she should not. She had only spoken the truth, though, part of her protested. And who are you to know the truth? the other argued. She searched her mind for something consoling, something that could mollify what she had said. But he was rambling out some excuse, was rising. He wanted to run; she couldn't blame him. She felt very guilty. She rose too. At the door, he turned, and looked directly at her.

'Listen, thanks. It's been great. Really. I've never said things like this to anyone before. Thank you. You've been great.'

And his ectoplasm wound around the door.

Mira immediately telephoned Valerie.

'I'll come over there,' Val shouted. 'Chris has half of Cambridge here and the place is a madhouse.' Rock music was pounding in the background.

'God, I'm glad you called,' she announced whirling in ten minutes later. 'From now on I'm spending Sunday in a nice quiet church somewhere. Damned libraries are closed. Did you ever try to read *Poly-Olbion* over *Revolution?* I wanted Chris to make friends but this is ridiculous. And when those kids leave, I have to sweep the floors and I pick up – no exaggeration – three-quarters of a dustpan full of dirt. You'd think they were farm kids. It's because they walk so much, I guess. Of course, they're all getting stoned.'

'You let them smoke in your house? You could get in trouble.'

'They're going to smoke someplace. They might as well be warm and comfortable.'

She settled herself in the same chair Howard had occupied. The contrast was startling. There was so much body to Val: she filled the chair, she overflowed it. And she was inside her body, her body was her. She was wearing one of her flowing dashiki-type things. Mira wondered where she found them. Beneath it, in the summer, she wore nothing at all. The thought made Mira uncomfortable, made her feel wet and floppy. Val kicked her sandals off.

'Val,' Mira burst out, 'how can you tell if you're gay?'

Val laughed. 'Have you had a proposition?'

'Yes. Not that kind.' She told Val about her conversation with Howard. When she was finished, she leaned forward earnestly. 'You see, it made me wonder about myself. Maybe I am gay, maybe that's why I never enjoyed sex with Norm.'

'From what you say, that was Norm's fault, not yours. But it could be, of course. I don't know. A friend of mine says you can tell by the way your heart beats when someone walks into the room. If it beats harder for women, you're gay.'

'But what do you think?'

Val shrugged. 'I don't know. I think we're all bisexual, in the ideal. But only in the ideal. People do seem to develop strong preferences one way or another. It's something we don't know anything about: there's been too much *ought* for us to find *is*.'

'Have you ever . . . ?'

'Screwed a woman? Yes.'

'What was it like?' Mira was fascinated.

Val shrugged. 'Nothing much. Neither of us got much out of it. We loved each other, but we had no passion for each other. We still laugh about it – or did, last time I saw her. She lives in Mississippi. I met her when I was doing civil rights stuff down there.'

Mira sat back, perplexed.

'If you're so fascinated, why don't you try it?'

'Yes,' Mira said in a small voice. 'But you can't just do that, can you? Just go out and experiment.'

'I have.'

'I don't think it's right.' She looked directly at Valerie. 'Sex is too important, it touches us too closely. You

371

haven't the right to do that to someone else, just use them that way.'

Val smiled at her.

'I couldn't, anyway,' Mira finished. 'You could because you don't think of it that way. Sex isn't important to you.'

'Oh, it's important. It just isn't sacred.'

'It isn't sacred to me either!' Mira protested.

'Sure it is,' Val smiled.

16

To this day I feel uncomfortable about Valerie. I don't know if she was simply the greatest egotist I ever knew, or whether her operations came out of a high energy level and as she said, a messianic drive. She had everything organized in her head, as if she and she alone possessed secret knowledge about how and what things are. She could tick life off on her fingers like a laundry list. And I not only can't do that, I don't even believe life is open to such an organization. Still, I find the things she said coming back to me all the time. A situation will occur and Val's comment on something that happened in the past returns to comment upon what is happening now. Her way of seeing did make sense.

But Mira somewhat resented her because she always thought she was right, she never seemed to feel unsure, and she expressed things so loudly that she was like a tidal wave coming at you. Every one of her experiences had been transformed into a theory: she was full of ideas. You had the choice of running or getting drowned in ideas. Yet it isn't true that she never felt unsure. After she broke up with Tad, she went into a depression for a while, and sometimes when she drank too much, she would start to cry. She said the thing she was most afraid of was ending up like Judy Garland or Stella Dallas.

'Oh, God! I'll never forget that last scene, when her daughter is being married inside the big house with the high iron fence around it and she's standing out there –
I can't even remember who it was, I saw it all when I

372

was still a little girl, and I may not even be remembering it right. But I am remembering it – it made a tremendous impression on me – anyway, maybe it was Barbara Stanwyck. She's standing there and it's cold and raining and she's wearing a thin little coat and shivering, and the rain is coming down on her poor head and streaming down her face with the tears, and she stands there watching the lights and hearing the music and then she just drifts away. How they got us to consent to our own eradication! I didn't just feel pity for her; I felt that shock of recognition – you know, when you see what you sense is your own destiny up there on the screen or on the stage. You might say I've spent my whole life trying to arrange a different destiny!'

But she often made Mira feel as if she were some female Pope, and Mira just a child being given the Word. For instance, a few days after their conversation about Howard, Mira brought up the subject of sex again. They were having lunch at the Toga, just the two of them, and Mira was loosened, having had two Dubonnets.

'You know what we were saying the other day. I don't mean to argue with you, you have much more experience than I do, but I think you put too much emphasis on sex.'

'Not true. We spend half our lives thinking about sex. Say that the two mainsprings are sexuality and aggression. I don't think that's what they are, but say it's true.'

'What do you think they are?' Mira interrupted.

'Fear and desire for pleasure. Aggressiveness comes out of fear, predominantly, and sexuality predominantly out of the other. But they mix in the middle. Anyway, both of these impulses can destroy order, which comes out of both drives, and which is another human need I haven't yet fit into my scheme. So both have to be controlled. But in fact, despite religious commands to the contrary, aggressiveness has never really been condemned. It's been exalted, from the Bible through Homer and Virgil right down to Humbert Hemingway. Have you ever heard of a John Wayne movie being censored? Did you ever see them take war books off the

373

bookstands? They leave the genitals off Barbie and Ken, but they manufacture every kind of war toy. Because sex is more threatening to us than aggression. There have been strict rules about sex since the beginning of written rules, and even before, if we can believe myth. I think that's because it's in sex that men feel most vulnerable. In war they can hype themselves up, or they have a weapon. Sex means being literally naked and exposing your feelings. And that's more terrifying to most men than the risk of dying while fighting a bear or a soldier. Look at the rules! You can have sex if you're married, and you have to marry a person of the opposite gender, the same color and religion, an age close to your own, of the right social and economic background, even the right height, for God's sake, or else everybody gets up in arms, they disinherit you or threaten not to come to the wedding or they make nasty cracks behind your back. Or worse, if you cross color or gender lines. And once you're married, you're supposed to do only certain things when you make love: the others all have nasty names. When after all, sex itself, in itself, is harmless, and aggression is harmful. Sex never hurt anyone.'

'That's not true, Val! What about rape, or seduction? Lucrece was destroyed by sex.'

'Lucrece was destroyed by aggression. The line does cross. Tarquin's aggression against her, and her own aggression against herself. If she could stick a knife in herself, I don't know why she couldn't stick one in him. Rape is aggression that happens to involve the genitals. There are methods of torture that do that too. But those are not primarily sexual acts.'

'What about sexual depravity? ...'

Val leaped at her. 'What is sexual depravity?'

Mira sat in shock.

'What is it? Is it homosexuality? Cunnilingus? Fellatio? Masturbation?'

Sophisticated Mira, who had experienced only one of these, shook her head.

'Then what is it? What sexual act can you name that is depraved? that is harmful?'

'Well . . . in pornography . . . well, pornography itself . . . and parties where men wear lipstick . . . well, heavens, Val, you know!'

Val sat back. 'I don't know. Are you talking about S and M?'

Mira, pink-faced, nodded.

'S and M is only the expression in the bedroom of an oppressive-submissive relation which can happen also in the kitchen or at the factory, can happen between people of any gender. There is obviously something titillating about these relationships, but it isn't the sexual component that makes them ugly, they're uglier elsewhere. Nothing sexual is depraved. Only cruelty is depraved, and that's another matter.'

Val lighted a cigarette and continued. She talked about polymorphous perversity, and how the whole world was just like a litter of puppies who want to curl up together and lick each other and smell each other, and about exogamy and endogamy and the absurdity and destructiveness of notions like racial purity, and about the ways property, the whole idea of property, had infected and corrupted sexual relationships.

Mira had another drink and listened uneasily. She was overwhelmed. It wasn't just Val's readiness with words and arguments, but the enormous energy she put into them, the energy radiated by her mere physical presence, her voice, her face. She closed her mind to Val. Val was extreme, she was a fanatic, she was like Lily, talking on and on about the same thing as if it were as inexhaustibly interesting to others as it was to her. She felt small, silenced: Valerie's power nullified her own.

'You'd like to nullify the world,' she muttered. 'You'd like to be Dictator of the World.'

Nothing fazed the woman. 'Who wouldn't?' she laughed.

'I wouldn't.'

'Actually, I'm really an old-fashioned preacher at heart. I'd like to get up in a pulpit every week and teach the world how to save itself.'

'And you really believe you know how.'

'Of course!' Valerie crowed, laughing.

Mira went home smoldering.

Nevertheless, she thought about what Val said, and sometimes it helped her. Val really did know a lot about sex, partly because she had had so much experience and partly because she was intelligent and thought about it. For her, sex was almost a philosophy. She saw the whole world in terms of it. She used to say that only Blake had known what the world was really about. She used to read Blake at night: the book lay always on her bedside table. She said that even if he was an mcp, he knew what wholeness comprised. Val slept with people the way other people go out for dinner with a friend. She liked them, she liked sex. She rarely expected anything from it beyond the pleasure of the moment. At the same time, she said it was overrated: it had been so tabooed, she claimed, that we had come to expect paradise from it. It was only fun, great fun, but not paradise.

And she was a happy person; she was one of the happiest people I ever knew. Not happy in the sense of smiling and gay: she was a crank. She loved to crank about politics and morals and intellectual idiocy. She enjoyed cranking. There was a wholeness in her, I guess. She went breezing through, and even though she was sensitive and aware of what was going on around her most of the time, it rarely flapped her. She laughed at absurdities, went home and cooked a great meal, had a good talk with somebody, then made love until two in the morning and next day got down to the books again. She was unflappable. Until the end.

17

Ava had gone home to Alabama for the holidays; Iso went with her 'to make sure nobody kills anybody,' she laughed. They did not return in two weeks, as Ava had been supposed to. At the end of January, their phone still went unanswered. Mira was worried about Iso, who was supposed to assist Wharton in the medieval course. It was strange: close as they were, none of them would have known how to find another, to contact parents or family. If Iso and Ava had never returned, Mira would simply have lost them. In mid-February, when the new semester had already begun, Brad Barnes said he saw Iso coming out of Wharton's office. But the phone still rang empty.

The following week Iso called sounding tight, almost curt, and Mira agreed to have lunch with her and Val the next day. She stood on the street near the back gate of Widener, where they'd agreed to meet. Gazing down Mass Ave, she saw Iso walking, a couple of blocks away. She had a long stride, but she paused in her step as if with each one she were debating turning back. This gave her a loping, sideways walk, ungainly. Her head was down, her hands plunged in the deep pockets of the shapeless pea jacket she wore, a remnant from her adolescence. As she came nearer, Mira studied the tight face. Her mouth was pursed, her cheekbones looked more prominent than ever, and the skin stretched tight across them as if the tight, pulled-back hair were drawing the skin too. She looked like a middle-aged nun worrying about coal for the school as she walked swiftly to her next duty.

Val came up behind Mira, greeting her. When Iso saw them, she stopped still. She did not smile. They approached her without haste, cautiously, both understanding without any communication that it was important not to rush over to her. She looked as if she were swaying, standing there. When they reached her, Val put a large arm lightly around her and said to Mira, 'Let's go to Jack's,' a bar that served food and was always deserted during the day. They sat at a back booth. A few people stood at the bar in the front of the place, and music was playing, but the back was empty.

Iso sipped the whiskey sour Val had ordered for her, and looked at them. Her mouth was twitching. There were dark circles under her eyes and her hair looked as if it would pull all the skin off her face. It was tight and smooth and tied in a tight, smooth little knot on top.

She looked like an aging schoolmarm who has just been fired. 'Ava's gone,' she said.

In the fall, Ava's dance school had held a recital. Just before Christmas, Iso told them, a woman who had attended the recital had called Ava and offered her a 'scholarship' to her ballet school in New York. This meant free lessons, and the possibility of dancing in the corps de ballet of an opera company with which the woman was connected. It also meant Ava would have to move to New York, find an apartment, a new job, a new life.

'But that's wonderful!' Mira exclaimed.

'When did she leave?'

'Yesterday.' Iso kept looking at her drink, rolling it in her hands.

'How long have you two been together?' Val continued.

'Four years off and on. Steadily for the last three years.' She tried to pull her mouth back into shape.

'You can still see each other', Mira suggested uneasily, unsure about what was going on.

Iso shook her head. 'No. No.'

'It's really a divorce,' Val said gently, and Iso nodded yes, vigorously, as tears began to splash down the tight cheeks. Controlling her weeping, she tried to tell them, gasping out phrases, blowing her nose, sipping her drink, pulling at her hair until its smooth front was a mass of webbing. Intense, passionate, all-consuming, their love had sprung up instantly. They had tried to fight it off, Iso going around the world, Ava moving to a new place, a new job. But always they returned to each other, and three years ago had given in, had decided to live together, to brazen it out, although pretending, always pretending that they were mere roommates. Ava curled up inside Iso's mothering like a kitten, but she clawed like a cat when she wanted to jump down, when the arms grew too warm, when the nest felt oppressive.

'I could never give her what she wanted. I could never be right. She pounded on me all the time, demanding,

378

pleading that somehow I do something, something to make things all right.'

'How could you when what she wanted was to dance?'

Iso nodded. 'I know, but I felt there was more she wanted, I wanted to give it, I wanted to be able to give it, and I resented her because I couldn't, because she needed it so much. For the last year, practically all we've done is fight.'

But that wasn't all. Except for a few casual 'flings,' they had been only with each other. 'We knew, nobody else, it was our secret, it kept us together and the world outside, it kept us glued together, like having a deformed child, as if each of us had a limb that had to be strapped on and off that nobody else knew about except each other. And if we split up, either we'd have to let other people know or we'd have to live alone, isolated, completely cut off . . .'

Val ordered sandwiches. Iso stopped when the waitress brought them. Val ordered another round of drinks. Nobody ate.

'We never went to Alabama. We didn't go anyplace. Ava didn't go to work. We went late at night to the market and didn't answer the phone. We've been sitting in that apartment for two months, arguing, talking, pacing, fighting, accusing . . .' She put her forehead in her hand. 'It was crazy, I thought I was going crazy, maybe I did, maybe we both did.' She looked up again, appealing to them with her eyes. 'Is everything in life like that?'

Ava wanted to go, wanted the chance; she did not want to go and leave Iso; she felt guilty about wanting to go, so accused Iso of wanting to be rid of her; she resented Iso's unwillingness to leave Harvard and go with her when she had left every place to be with Iso; she was frightened of going alone; she wanted to go alone, she was sick of their fights, their hopeless circle of accusations.

'And me too, it was the same for me. I wanted her to go for her own sake, but I didn't want to lose her. But I didn't want to leave Harvard, it's taken me so long to

379

settle down to something and besides, I love what I'm doing. And I felt angry that she wanted to go off without me, and frightened for her : how will she get along without me? She's so . . . vulnerable, so fragile. We went around and around and around. There was no solution. Except night before last we had a real bang-up, blast-out fight and she packed her bags and called the woman and said she was coming. Then we both cried and held hands. It was finished. Like a war. It ends when everybody's dead.'

She stood up suddenly, clumsily, and walked swiftly across the room to the toilet. Mira fiddled with her glass.

'Val . . . did you know?'

'I knew they loved each other.'

'I'm so dense. I have cutoff points in my head. I just won't think about things beyond a certain point.'

Iso returned. Her hair was restored to order, but her face was splotchy, and the red blotches emphasized her freckles, usually invisible in her pallor. Her eyes were pale and very dead. She lighted a cigarette.

'And now?' Val began.

Iso spread her hands and shrugged. 'Nothing. Just nothing.' She puffed nervously. 'Although I'm sure Ava will find someone to take care of her fast enough,' she added grudgingly.

'Was that part of the problem?'

Iso nodded, eyes lowered. 'It's embarrassing. It's humiliating to be jealous. And of course she claimed that I was just dying to be rid of her so I could get involved with a whole flock of women . . .' She pursed her lips tightly. 'I'm much too old to start being promiscuous. Besides . . .' She twisted her mouth again and sipped her drink.

'Besides, anything might happen,' Val laughed.

Iso looked up surprised.

'I remember when I divorced Neil. I was too young, even younger than you, to imagine living a celibate life for the rest of my years, but I had Chris and couldn't quite figure how to handle just the mechanical arrangements, you know? Because I loathe lying and sneaking.

380

And I set my lips the way you're doing now—'

Iso instantly untwisted her mouth.

'– and said I wasn't going to be promiscuous, and I'd worry about finding the One and Only when I found him. Actually, I was dying to screw around. Everybody looked attractive to me. And if a guy came on to me, I wanted to try him even if he wasn't all that attractive to me. I was really hungry for experience.

'And I had it. Once, I remember, for about six months, I had five lovers at once. The thing is, it's just too time-consuming. You can ignore a husband, but you have to spend time with a lover – talking, eating, touching, making love all afternoon or all night. You can't get anything else done. So after a while, I cut it out. Nowadays, apart from a casual encounter – they're always nice, sort of sweet – I only see Grant. And not that much of him, the grouch.'

Iso was staring hard at her drink. There were two tiny pink spots on the corners of her cheeks. Her mouth was tight, almost angry. When Val finished, she looked up; her eyes were hard, hurt.

'You act as if it were the same thing. As if I don't have special problems.'

'You have the problem whether you do anything or not. As you no doubt know. If people are going to snipe at you as a lesbian, they'll do it whether you're involved with anyone or not.'

Iso's flush deepened. 'I have the name so I might as well have the game?' Her voice was hard, cold.

'I don't know if you have the name. I've never heard anyone say anything. Besides, around here, who can tell what anyone is?'

They all giggled: it was a sad truth.

'I'm talking about the long run.'

Iso relaxed a little. She picked up her sandwich and took a bite.

'It's a matter of costs,' Val resumed. 'Aloneness, careful watchfulness, suspicion – it's a horrible way to live. Always squelching impulses for fear the truth may show.'

'But the risk,' Iso objected.

'Gossip? It can be damaging, I suppose.'

'Oh, if that were all!'

'Why? What do you think?'

'Survival.'

Iso trudged off, when they parted, toward her home. She was in hiding, she told them, and came out only to attend Wharton's class – she'd made peace with him – and to see them. Mira had tears in her eyes as she watched her go, head bent forward, hands plunged deep in the pockets of her old pea coat, loping along as if she were never precisely sure she wanted to go in the direction she was going in. She was going home alone, to think about all of this alone, to decide or avoid decision, alone. Like me sitting with my brandy, she thought, and felt gushy and sentimental, thinking that everyone must do that, face alone the worst truths, the worst terrors. Yet we do do something for each other, she protested, we can help. How? a grim voice insisted. She meditated on this on her swift walk home through the biting February cold. As she neared her house, she saw a small figure sitting on her front steps, reading. It was Kyla.

'Aren't you freezing?'

'Well, I had just two hours between my class and a meeting, and I wanted to see you so when you weren't home I thought I might as well wait, you might come in and if you didn't I didn't have anyplace else to go anyway, of course I could have sat in Widener or Boylston, but my meeting's up this way anyway and besides, you might come home,' she announced smiling.

She came in, lugging the heavy green bookbag she always carried, and got warmed up with two gin and tonics which she gulped down like water. She chattered about the differences between German and English Romanticism, and a paper she was writing. 'It's so *interesting*, Mira, almost as if you could talk about differences in the German and English souls, as if you could define national characteristics. I don't believe it, yet I do. Like Harley and me, you know? He's really German, despite the name, and I'm really English, well, with a little Scots, both Teutonic, I guess, but so different!'

'Are your differences like those between English and German Romanticism?' Mira laughed.

Kyla paused, taking this seriously. 'No, no, well, I don't know. I haven't tried to align us with them. But that's a thought, you know? It might be illuminating. It might help.'

And she burst into tears.

She tried, but she could not stop crying. She kept gasping, and raising her head, and blowing her nose, and drawing in sighs, and sipping her third drink, and talking, but through it all, she sobbed. Harley was brilliant, so brilliant, Mira should meet him, he was really wonderful, his work, his professors had said, no question about it, someday the Nobel Prize, nuclear physics such a difficult thing, a consuming thing, it was understandable, she was a dog to complain, she should be proud, she was proud, to be even the smallest part of it, if she just made his life the teensiest bit easier, happier, more comfortable, it was enough, she should be grateful just to have the chance, she was a rotten complaining bitch. And why should she complain? She was so busy herself, a member of four organizations, president of one, studying for generals, taking two seminars and Hooten's demanding conference course, she had so much to do in the house, of course Harley helped, she had to say that, he was really wonderful, he always made breakfast, but there was the shopping and the cleaning and the cooking and it seemed too much, but that wasn't the problem, she could do it, she could do everything, she wouldn't have minded, if only if only if only

'If only he'd talk to me!' she burst out in a sob, leaped up, and ran into the toilet and shut the door.

Mira waited. After some minutes, she stood up and walked to the bathroom door and stood there. After another minute or two, she knocked. She could hear Kyla sobbing. She opened the door. Kyla lunged at her, threw her arms around Mira's waist, buried her head in her bosom and cried. They stood like that for a long time. Mira had never heard anyone cry so long so hard.

383

She thought that Kyla's heart must really be broken, and then thought that the old worn-out phrase did mean something. Kyla's heart was not broken, but breaking. After the break, there is silence. She thought too that she had never loved anyone as much as Kyla loved Harley, and she felt humbled, awed in the face of such love.

After a time, a long time, Kyla's sobs subsided. She asked to be left alone, and Mira went back to the kitchen, where they had been sitting, feeling dizzy from so much emotion and so much drinking in one day, and put on a pot of coffee. Kyla came out, her face somewhat smoothed out, her bouncy manner returned.

'I'm sorry. I shouldn't drink.'

'I'm making coffee.'

'Good. I have to give a report at the meeting, and I'd like to be in control.' She looked at her watch. 'God, I have only forty minutes.' She gulped down the rest of her drink, and tossing her hair over her shoulder with a shake of her head, began to tell Mira about her first experiments with alcohol back in Canton, Ohio, in her teenybopper days. She had been a cheerleader, the most popular girl in the class, twice vice-president of it, 'never president, they always gave that to a guy,' and had been nicknamed Lightning. Her parents were wonderful, purely wonderful, her father a professor in a local college, her mother a champion baker of pies, their house in the middle of farm country looking out over hills and sunsets, wonderful, wonderful, peaceful. But then she had gone to college in Chicago, so different but wonderful too, but suddenly it had become harder to go home.

'I don't know why. They're so wonderful, they love me so much. Then when I married Harley! Oh, they adore Harley! Dad builds a fire and Mom sets a little table in front of it all done up with a lace-edged cloth and silver, you know, late Christmas night, then Dad plays the piano and we sing and Mom brings out all sorts of wonderful things, they have such a nice life, they're so happy, I don't know what's wrong with me, why I hate to go there ...'

384

She broke off, her head full of tears again, but this time she did not sob, but merely blew her nose for a while. 'And last Christmas it was really terrible – all my fault, I'm sure, I shouldn't drink, I had three eggnogs and I gulp so, just an alcoholic at heart, I have to watch it, but somebody – oh, I suppose it was me – brought up the Democratic convention, I was so upset by it, Daley and his white gestapo and Humphrey complaining about the whiffs of tear gas he was getting up there in his protected hotel suite, and my father blew his stack, he screamed and raved about the unwashed hippies, the ungrateful filthy wastrels . . . oh, all that sort of thing, you know. And Harley was wonderful, he kept coming in as interpreter, and he made me shut up and by then I couldn't hear what anybody was saying, I was screaming at my father. I wasn't even talking about Chicago anymore, I was talking about something he'd done when I was little – I can't even remember, and my mother was very angry with me, her face was so big, I could see it glaring, and my father was shouting, and Harley got it all under control, I don't know what he did, he made me go to bed when we left everything seemed to be okay, everybody was smiling and my father kept clapping Harley on the back and saying, "I'm glad she's got someone like you to look after her, she needs a level head," and I was still confused, because I'm the practical one, Harley's always off at his lab or in his study, I look after him, and besides I'm more articulate than Harley and he and I agree totally on politics, so I couldn't understand what was happening, it was as if everything I knew was shifting under my feet, as if nothing was what I thought it was, so I decided I just couldn't drink anymore, I just can't, but here I went and did it again, so now you know, and I'm terribly sorry.'

She overstayed her time, and left, almost literally flying out the door, her green bookbag in air behind her, ten minutes late for her meeting. Before she went she hugged Mira. 'Oh, thank you, Mira, thank you so much, you're so wonderful, I feel so much better, you are wonderful, thank you, thanks!'

Mira took a nap, woke, heated a TV dinner, and prepared to study late into the night to make up for what she called a wasted day. She read for several hours, but her concentration was poor, and around one in the morning she stopped, carried her brandy bottle into the living room, and sat by the window huddled in flannel pajamas, a wool robe, and a blanket pulled up around her chin – the landlord turned the heat down at ten. She sat as still inside as she could, trying to let whatever it was she was feeling rise up and show itself. What kept coming into her mind was a scene in Lehman Hall a week or two ago, when Val had embarrassed her horribly. A group of them were sitting around talking about the months, or year, or two years ago when women had not been permitted in Lamont Library, or in the main dining room of the Faculty Club.

'It was a problem,' Priss was saying, 'because there are classrooms upstairs in Lamont, and female teaching assistants still couldn't use the front door, they had to go in the side entrance and climb the back stairs to teach their classes. Like in Rome, you know, slaves teaching the children of the freeborn.'

'The same thing happens at Yale,' Emily said. 'Mory's is such an institution they hold committee meetings there, but no women are allowed to eat there, so they have to go in a back way and climb a back staircase to where the meetings are held.'

'Well, that won't last long,' Val said dryly. 'God, the whole world's going to pot. I mean, once they let women in, heaven knows what will come next! It's a terrible degrading of standards. I mean, you have to consider the real reason they keep women out. You know, they say to let women enter med school, or Harvard, or whatever, means lowering their standards, but you know as well as I that women do better than men in high-school grades. So *that's* not what they mean. And women don't mangle books or dirty the card catalog any more than men do, right? So they're just being polite, the men, when they talk about standards. It's an euphemism. They don't want to embarrass us. The real reason is sanitary. You let women through front doors and what will they do? Splat, splat, a big clot of menstrual blood right on the threshold. Every place women go they do it: splat splat. There are little piles of clotty blood all over Lamont Library now. There are special crews hired just to keep the place decently mopped down. That's an expense! And they have to put in separate toilets. That's an expense too, and it takes up space! But what can you do? Women *will* do it: splat splat. Just one more example of the decaying standards of the modern world, letting women in. Nobody,' she concluded bitterly, 'cares about decorum anymore.'

Despite her embarrassment, Mira had ended laughing. Val had caught precisely her feeling about herself at Harvard. She was defilement – how, she wasn't sure – but a defilement of pure thought, pure mind, pure marble busts of pure marble men. The aetheriality of Harvard made her conscious of flesh and feeling in a way she had not been before; her earlier life, back in the suburbs, so full of flesh and feeling, had made her hyperconscious of her intellect, her connection with ideas and abstractions. Never right, she thought without self-pity. Was anyone? For here, underneath all the intellect, the abstraction, the disconnection, were the same old salt tears and sperm, the same sweet blood and sweat she'd wiped up for years. More shit and string beans. The anguish of Howard, of Iso, of Kyla were only more obvious than her own. They thought her balanced and content because she'd lived longer and was more used to pain. She bore it better, or at least more silently. All the fancy words – adaptation, maturity, sublimation – all they really meant was learning that the empty gaping need in you was never going to be filled, that one was doomed to live forever with unfilled cunt, unemcompassed prick. The need was not just sexual: cunt and prick were in every mind, and receptive and twitching or dry and limp, the need was pain.

They called her wonderful. Thank you, thank you, Mira. You've helped me so much. I feel so much better. You're wonderful. When she did not know, really, what they were feeling, did not understand their particular pain, their particular need. How then could she help? She had not helped, she had done nothing but listen. Yet they were not lying. She had helped, listening. She had not denied their truths. She had not asked, by flicker or gesture, that they consor themselves. She had not insisted that they be happy people with happy problems, that their problem was that they had not learned how to fit into a rational and comprehensible world. All she had done was, unblinking and uninterrupting, let them be whatever horrible creature they thought they were.

That seemed little enough. Mira's friends had always done that for each other. But for Howard, Iso, and Kyla, that seemed a great gift. That meant no one did such things for them.

The idea seemed a great truth when it descended upon her around four in the morning: a space to be and a witness (flawed as any witness had to be). It was enough, or if not enough, it was all, all that we could do, in the end, for each other.

18

Val belonged to a great many political action groups, and Mira would sometimes attend meetings with her. She was no longer desperate in her aloneness, but she always went with the half-hope of meeting an interesting man. However, the men in these groups were idealistic, intense, egotistic, and asexual. At least, they didn't look twice at Mira. And although she was still unconsciously placing the entire onus of initiation on the male, in fact, she was not in the least interested in them. They struck her as adolescent egomaniacs, Tamburlaines and Edwards IIs in little.

The meetings were held in shabby Cambridge apartments, with coffee served in polyetheylene cups that everyone would end up cracking and squeezing. Mira was often asked to serve the coffee.

One Thursday, Anton Werther, a brilliant student at the school of government, was arguing with Val. Anton was remarkable for his beautiful dark complexion and his utter contempt for the entire world. Val was talking ruefully of the follies of idealism – the Left's refusal to vote for Humphrey after the 1968 convention, the belief of some left-wingers that a Nixon victory would be a catalyst to revolution – would result in a Nixon Supreme Court, which would, she lamented, put the country back forty years.

'That's no politics, that's religion,' Anton said, managing to look down on Val even though both of them were seated on the floor.

Val was silenced. 'My God, you're right!' she said.

A man sitting in a corner, a dark man in a white shirt with rolled up shirt-sleeves, spoke up. 'Yes, and of course one must be able to proceed politically. But ideally – and I think we're all idealists, or we'd be out doing something more fruitful than this – politics and religion are the same thing. Or politics and ethics, if you prefer. Politics is simply one sphere of application of morals.'

Anton had enough respect for the speaker that he turned his head slightly toward him. 'Let's leave morals for the women and children where they belong, Ben. How successful was moral thinking in Lianu?'

Ben laughed. He had a spontaneous, hearty laugh. He seemed to find himself as amusing as anything else. He pulled on the sodden end of a filterless cigarette. 'I'll have to admit, Anton, that Lianu is not at present concerned with finding a usable human morality. Its only interest is survival, which means power, and that's of course what you're talking about. But I think that unless in all our deeds we remember the ultimate intention, whatever we do will be as poisoned as anything else done in history.'

'Libraries are full of pious precepts; they've never had the least effect on political reality,' Anton snarled.

'Well,' Mira shouted, knowing she would not be heard if she did not, 'there was Christianity.'

Anton swung around and let his cigarette fall out of his mouth. Some people laughed. Mira flushed. 'And what did *that* accomplish besides inquisitions?'

'Whatever it did,' Mira said a little waveringly, 'it was

an ethical system that had an effect on political reality.'

'It was,' Anton sneered, 'a superstition used by the outs to get in.'

'It left a legacy,' Val said. 'At least now we feel guilty for the rotten things we do.'

'Tell that to the Nazis.'

'An ethical tradition kept the British from murdering Gandhi,' Ben put in. 'Imagine what the Nazis would have done to him.'

'Pre-cisely!' Anton crowed precisely. 'And in any fight between the British with their so-called ethics (simply overlooking the horrors of British imperialism), in any fight between these ethical British and the Nazis, who would have won?'

'That has nothing to do with ethics. That depends on resources, preparation, armament, population . . .'

'Exactly!' Anton summed up. 'Power. Now let's get serious, children.'

The problem on the agenda was praxis: should the group spend the little money they had on handouts? If so, should they be distributed in the Square and certain other key locations, or distributed door-to-door in Cambridge? If the latter, where would they get the man-power?

Mira sat stewing. For all our wealth and armament, we were not winning the Vietnam War, she wanted to shout at Anton. Nor did we win the Korean War. And for all his talk of practical politics, he was a lousy politician: how would he ever get people to vote his way when he simply overrode them, slapped them down without any regard for their dignity? Politics, she thought, remembering the Greek tragedies, begins at home.

In fact, when the time came to vote, Ben, Val, and Mira, as well as most of the others, voted for Anton's proposal.

After the formal part of the meeting was over, Mira went over to Ben and told him her thoughts, laughing at herself. He smiled at her with a broad smile that included his eyes; he looked at her, really looked, as if she were a person. 'I have this problem,' he laughed, 'I know it's true, but Anton is always right. Besides,' he added wryly, 'we *are* all idealists, and no matter how Anton knocks that, he counts on it.'

'Idealists always seem to be at a disadvantage. Do you suppose it's possible to be both idealistic and practical at once?'

'Sure it's possible. There's Mao.'

'One to a generation?'

'Not even that.'

Someone called Ben's name: 'We need you on this,' Brad yelled from across the room where the inner circle of the group – all men – were having an animated discussion. Ben excused himself and joined them, saying, 'I can't imagine why.'

Mira and Val left. Almost everyone was gone except for the inner circle and a few young women who were cleaning up.

'I really hate that Anton,' Mira said.

'Yeah. You wouldn't be too happy at his being Dictator of the World.'

'I wouldn't be happy at anybody's being Dictator of the World, but I'd rather have that guy Ben, or any bumbling idealist.'

'I don't agree – quite apart from Ben. Bumbling idealists invariably get overthrown by nonbumbling fascists. What I keep wondering is why we always have to choose between obnoxious alternatives. I mean, we live in moral schizophrenia: there are certain ways to behave at home, in town, in the nation, and entirely different ways of behaving politically. I mean, if the president of General Motors got treated at home the way he treats the world, he'd collapse. It's all because of the man-woman split, I'm convinced of it. They get women to act humane and decent so they can sleep at night even though all day they're out screwing the world. If Anton were a little humane – he really is bright, you know – if he were female, say ...'

'Impossible!'

'Right! It's his socialization that makes him so impossible.'

'Oh, Val, that's just fanatic. There are women who aren't humane, and I guess somewhere there are men who are. Hypothetically, at least.'

'Sure. The point is that the roles are split on the male-female model. I'll bet you if you ever meet a humane guy, ten to one he'll be gay.'

'Oh, Val!'

'I mean, suppose Lenin had been female.'

At that, Mira broke into giggling, and they both laughed all the way home, imagining improbable combinations – a female John Wayne, Henry Kissinger in skirts, Gary Cooper, Jack Palance as women. At the door, Mira was reluctant to have the evening end. 'You know this guy, Ben? Come in and have a drink and tell me about him.'

'Why not? I don't have a class tomorrow. How about Nixon as a woman? Joe Namath?'

They climbed the stairs giggling, and Val put her arm through Mira's. 'Ah, it's wonderful being a woman. You can have so much more fun.'

'If you've only one life to live,' Mira intoned, 'live it as a woman!'

Mira fixed drinks, insisting avidly. 'Tell me, tell me!'

Ben Voler had been at a few meetings a year ago, but then he'd won some sort of grant to go back to Africa, to Lianu, where he'd spent years doing research. He was a combination political scientist, sociologist, and anthropologist. He was older than most of the grad students, probably in his early thirties. He'd been married, but his wife couldn't take Africa, and they'd split up. He'd recently returned, just this semester, in fact. He was teaching a seminar on Africa and writing his dissertation, but was considered even by the faculty to be the expert on Lianu in this country. He said the days of whites were over in Lianu and much of black Africa, and he said it was about time.

Mira poked and prodded. What about his wife, what was she like? What had she done after the split? Were there children? What was he aiming to do, teach? Was he really intelligent or just an expert?

'My God, gal, are you planning to marry him?'

'Val, he's the first interesting man I've met since I've been here!'

Val sighed and sat back, gazing at Mira affectionately. 'I just don't know anything more to tell you.'

'Tell me about Grant. I hardly know anything about Grant.'

'Oh, he's a pain. Grant is a pain. I've had it with him.'

'Why?'

'Well, you've seen him. He's socially a klutz, he's too egotistical, he's a grouch, he's . . . he's a man, for God's sake, he thinks only about himself, self, self, and his fragile, precious ego.'

'Why did you like him? How did you meet him?'

'Oh, a couple of years ago I was working with a group that was involved with Cambridge politics. We were trying to do something about the way they treat blacks in the school. Although we didn't say that. For instance, they have a class for foreign-speaking students. That sounds okay, but in fact, it's all black. The kids mostly speak French – they're from the islands. They put them in this room with whatever teacher happens to be in disgrace this year – usually a new teacher who tried to side with a black student about something the year before – and leave them there. The teacher doesn't speak anything but English, the kid's don't speak English. Some people tried to get some of the kids in the French class at least, but the Cambridge school system – a real peach, I tell you – vetoed that. But their day will come. They're going to have a problem on their hands one of these days. The point is the kids will suffer for that too. Anyway, we were just looking in, trying to see what could be done, trying to get black parents involved. And for some reason, Grant came to one of the meetings. Afterwards he came up to me, his eyes really glowing, and he said, "I just want to tell you I think you're great." Something like that. We talked for a while. I didn't find him very appealing – why don't I stick with my first impressions? – but I thought he was intelligent and had decent values. He said he didn't like where he was living and was looking for a commune. At the time I was living in a commune in Somerville, and we were down to six people. It took eight to keep the place going. So I told him about it, and he came over one night and looked it over and he liked it and he moved in.

'And one night – oh, a long time later – I went into his room and got in bed with him. We've been lovers since, although since I moved out we've been less close. He still lives there.'

'Why did you go to his bed?'

Val thought. 'It was because of the ants.'

'Ants!'

'It was one night at the dinner table. The whole group of us was sitting around. I don't know how the subject came up. But Grant had apparently spent some time studying ants. He was fascinated by them. He talked about them for a long time, their kinds, their characteristics, their social organization, their mutual rules – morality, if you will. He was fascinating. And while he was talking, he forgot himself. He was completely unselfconscious, something Grant isn't very often. And he looked so beautiful. It was before he grew the beard. He was radiant, his eyes glowed, he was expansive, excited, passionate. He wanted us to know, to understand, to love the ants! And I loved him for that, that night anyway, and for some time after. Unfortunately,' she concluded, 'it only happens about ants.'

Then Mira asked Val about Neil, the man she'd been married to; then Val asked Mira about Norm. Then Mira told Val about Lanny, and Val told Mira about some of her other lovers. The conversation grew more and more intimate, more and more honest. They were laughing so hard their pants got damp. They drank, they laughed, they talked. They felt lusciously wicked, wonderfully free, saying to each other things neither of them would say to anyone else.

At about three, Mira said, 'Will you listen to us? We could be a couple of teenagers talking about all the boys we've had crushes on.'

'Yeah. And for all the raking over they're getting,

394

they're still at the center of our conversation.'

'Well, Val, that's natural. I mean, your work is central to you, but if you talked to me about it, I'd probably fall asleep. And vice versa.'

At four, Val rose wearily. 'It has been really great, Mirabelle.'

They kissed good night and held each other for a moment as if each were the only solid object in the world. Then Val left and the light began to pour into the apartment and Mira said, 'Damn!' and went around pulling shades down and cursing out the fucking birds.

19

Contrary to her custom, Mira went to every meeting of the peace group after that. 'I can't imagine why,' Val drawled sarcastically.

'I have found a real dedication to the cause,' Mira smiled with mock hauteur.

But Ben did not appear, and Mira was in despair. After a month, when she was ready to quit, he showed up. The moment she saw him in the room, her heart began to beat wildly. In irritation, she scolded herself. Anyone who's the least bit likely you build into a knight on a horse. Still, she could not keep her heart still or her vision straight. She heard nothing at all of what happened at the meeting that night. She kept saying to herself, he probably has smelly feet, and I'll bet he sits in the john for an hour with a magazine and stinks the place up. He probably voted for Nixon, or else he's a vegetarian and lives on soy curd and brown rice. Or he thinks Ernest Hemingway is the greatest American novelist. Her self-exhortations did not, however, have any effect on her pulse rate. And since she had heard nothing during the meeting, she also had nothing to go over and talk to him about afterward. She sat feeling like a lump, trying to look poised, wondering if he would come over to her, and now her heart was really thumping. But he was surrounded by a group of people, and did not move. Out of the corner of her eyes, she saw Val go over to

Ben and join the group. She could not hear them: her ears were thumping too hard. But she could notice Val gesticulating, hear Val's voice, Val's laugh. Val was being brilliant, she thought, and hated her. Why? she almost cried. She has Grant, she doesn't need Ben. She sat in the middle of her pulsing blood and felt tears in her eyes.

Suddenly Val was beside her, touching her on the arm. 'Ready to go, kid?'

Mira rose stiffly and followed Val out. She did not know what to say or how to say it; she was not sure she would be able to speak at all without bursting into tears.

'Well,' Val said cheerfully, 'I hope you're free Saturday night.'

'Why?' she asked numbly.

'Oh, I'm having a few people for dinner. Chris and Bart and Grant and me and you and Ben. It just came to me, like a stroke of light! Actually,' she turned to Mira, 'I looked at you during the meeting and saw you were gone. I figured it would take you months to get off your ass. And God knows you can't expect *them* to figure anything out. They just go home and daydream and masturbate. Or don't masturbate. So I took things into my dishpan hands. Hope you don't mind.'

Mira was not sure what Val was saying. She tried to absorb the words, she stuttered out questions, and finally understood. 'Val!' she cried, and turned and hugged her friend. They were on the sidewalk, and people passing turned and looked at them. But Mira didn't care.

'Listen, Mira, don't get so hyper yet, okay?' Val pleaded. 'You don't really even know him.'

'Okay, I won't,' Mira said obediently, and Val laughed.

'Right,' she said, and they both laughed.

The evening of the dinner she arrived early. Only Val and Chris, and Bart, Chris's friend, were there. They were all in the kitchen. Val was stirring something, Chris was cutting something, and Bart was setting the table. They were also arguing.

'I can do anything I want,' Bart was protesting. 'Even though I flunked chemistry twice, I could get into Harvard. Man, we got them so buffaloed!'

'Wonderful,' Val commented sarcastically. 'When they kept you out it was because you were black; when they let you in, it is because you are black. That's progress?'

Bart looked at her with affectionate eyes. 'You might as well use the current while it's going for you.'

'Sure. But I don't see you doing that.'

'I'm involved in more important things,' Bart announced haughtily, then doubled over in laughter.

'Yeah, dealing dope,' Chris drawled.

'That's an act of social concern!'

They were all laughing when Grant walked in. Suddenly Bart leaped to his feet, flew across the kitchen waving his fist, and yelled, 'As I was saying!'

Mira's heart stopped. Chris's involvement with Bart challenged all her nicely erected mental structures. Always opposed to any sort of prejudice, always insisting on complete intercourse between groups, Mira had been a liberal since her childhood. Her liberalism had been made easy by the fact that she knew no black people except the maids of some of her friends, no Orientals except for a physician who was a colleague's of Norm's (and whom she disliked), and no American Indians or Chicanos at all. She had been shocked the first time she met Bart; she remained nervous at the easy argumentativeness – always present in Val's house – between Bart and Chris and Val. Someplace in the back of her mind, she realized, she expected the banter or discussion to erupt into violence, expected Bart to pull a knife and kill them all. She had not, despite some mind-searching, been able to get over this sense of things. So when Bart – as she saw it – went for Grant, she paled. But the others were all laughing. Grant was shaking his fist at Bart. 'You're just a stupid ass, man!' he yelled back, and Bart was yelling back.

They sat down opposite each other at the table, Mira standing at the counter pouring wine, eased herself toward the wall. Val looked at her. 'They have a continuing argument,' she said softly. Mira watched them.

They did not talk, they yelled. Each of them picked up a piece of the silverware Bart had recently laid down, and shook it at the other. They – no, Bart – was half-laughing. Grant was serious. They were arguing about – it took awhile to decode – the proper form for minority protest. Bart was in favor of tanks and guns; Grant was in favor of law school.

'Get into the power structure, that's the only way to defeat it!'

'Shit, man, you get into it, it'll eat you alive! By the time it's through with you, you're as lily white as it is! They buy your soul, and wash it, bleach it, until it's whiter than whitey's.'

Suddenly Val yelled 'OUT!' they both looked up. Calmly, preparing to peel a carrot, she said, 'Would you care to continue in the other room? I can't stand the noise.'

Still talking, arguing, Bart standing around while Grant poured himself some wine, they walked together into the other room. Mira looked at Val. 'I'd have thought you'd want to get into that.'

Val groaned. 'They have been over that and over that and over that. At least ten times. They just like to argue. And I don't like to waste my energy on futile arguments. They're both just talking. What's the point of their sitting around deciding on the proper way to change society? Some people are going to use guns, some are going to use different forms of power. And it's also ridiculous. Bart is a really gentle guy: he'd fight if he had to, but he'd rather not. And Grant – underneath that monastic, ascetic exterior, is a killer. He has the temper of a savage, old style, when they swung from trees.'

'Yeah,' Chris mused. 'That's true, you know? Remember the night, Mommy, when he got mad at you and threw over the whole cocktail table? The heavy one? With everything on it. He smashed a lot of things,' she turned to Mira, 'and completely ruined the tabletop. Then he stalked out and left the mess for us to clean up.'

'One of his more heroic moments,' Val said dryly.

'But, Mom,' Chris turned her soft young face to Val seriously, 'how can you say that? How can you say there's no point in talking about the proper way when you're always talking about the proper way to build a society?'

Val sighed deeply. 'Look, honey, I know this is going to sound like rationalization. But there's a difference between asking what people need and trying to come up with some inadequate blueprint or other – which is what I do – and saying, "Everybody should do thus and so." Which is what they're doing.'

'I don't see that they're so different.'

'Maybe they're not.' Val rested her hand in her chin. 'But I'm not doing it in order to have battle with somebody. And they are. I'm trying to find . . . find a piece of truth. They're trying to one-upman each other. Or outshout each other.'

'Ummm.' Chris considered.

'Will you look at us?' Mira laughed. 'The men in the living room and the women in the kitchen. Just like always.'

'I'd rather be here,' Chris said.

'Cooking!' Val exclaimed, and leaped up and began to stir something.

Someone knocked at the door. Mira, who had totally forgotten Ben, felt her heart knock. One of the men opened the door, there was conversation in the hall, steps approached the kitchen. She was gazing out the window. Her face felt hot.

'Hi, Ben,' Val said, and Mira turned smiling but Ben was kissing Val on the cheek and then he handed her a bottle of wine in a paper bag, and she thanked him and they were talking and the smile felt stiff on Mira's face and finally he turned and Val turned and Val said, 'You know Mira, don't you?' and he smiled and moved toward her with his hand outstretched and said, 'Yes, but I didn't know your name,' and Val introduced Chris and they talked and the smile was petrified on Mira's face and she could not say a word.

They took their wine and went into the living room. 'What do you say we play a different game?' Val said as they entered.

'Which one are we playing now?' Grant asked ominously.

'Empty rhetoric,' she said cheerfully, and passed around a tray of canapés. Bart giggled.

Grant grimaced. 'You really are too much, Val. You get up in the preaching box at the slightest whim, but anybody else's arguments is just empty rhetoric to you.'

'I talk about real things.'

'My ass!'

'Yeah, I guess your ass is real. Sometimes,' she glanced at him threateningly. 'Ben's an expert on Africa, I'm told,' she said in a social voice.

'The only thing I can claim to be an expert on is my own digestive system,' Ben grinned. 'I'd be glad to tell you all about that.'

Grant turned away. Bart leaned forward with interest.

'Were you in Africa? Where? How long? What was it like? How did they feel about you?' Bart had a bagful of questions, and Ben answered them easily, leisurely, anecdotally, yet underneath his narrative ran a passionate interest, a loving commitment. Everyone listened intently. It felt as if they were hearing truth, not absolute truth, but one person's considered, honest truth. Mira, remembering the conversation between Chris and Val in the kitchen, thought she understood what Val had meant. So many conversations consist of a position prejudicially adopted, and defended to the death. This was different: Ben was saying things that hurt him to say, things he wished were not true, and things he gloried in. Her stomach stirred for him. But he did not once look at her. He was talking to Bart, and whenever possible, to Grant.

Mira had another drink, and another. She went out to the kitchen ostensibly to help Val. 'What do you think?' she attacked.

Val grinned. 'I like him. He may be a little mcp. But

400

maybe not. Social modes and all that. I think he's decent.'

'Decent' was Val's highest term of praise short of greatness. Mira was satisfied. But when they went back, Ben still did not look at her. Mira was getting drunk. She leaned her head back, her head floaty, far from the conversation.

Ben was attractive – very. She would like – she blushed as she felt it, although she did not let the words enter her mind – she would like to screw him. Her vagina felt wet and open just looking at him. And she *was* lonely. But it dawned on her as she sat there that her loneliness had, over the past months, become a formula more than not. She was not actively feeling lack these days. Her loneliness – my God, had this always been so? – had been largely caused by her sense that she was supposed to have a man, supposed to have someone, or else be the pathetic woman in the rain, staring into a lighted house. Yes, Ben was attractive, and intelligent, and he seemed decent. Mira did not know why Val had said he was an mcp. She tried to make a note to ask Val about that. But suppose Ben did not find her attractive? Suppose he was involved with someone else? Suppose nothing came of tonight?

She would be fine. She was fine. A weight seemed to drift from her heart. It's because I'm drunk, she thought. Things don't matter so much when you're drunk.

They went into the kitchen for dinner. Val sat Mira between Ben and Bart. They had a shrimp bisque, praised it, and talked about food. Ben described Lianese food. Grant, still sulky and eating greedily, finished and wiped his beard, and described the rotten dried-out food his mother had cooked. Bart laughed.

'Man, you don't know dried-up food until you've eaten my aunt's. She isn't really my aunt,' he told Mira, 'she's just the only person who's willing to take me. Anyway, she's a nice old lady, and she gets the check from the welfare, and she cooks spaghetti. On Monday, she cooks spaghetti, and she leaves it in the pot. She cooks two pounds, and it sits there. She never puts it away. By

Friday, man! the spaghetti is ready to sprout. It is so dry, it crackles!'

They laughed. 'You exaggerate!' Mira exclaimed.

'No, he doesn't,' Chris said in a low, dry voice, sounding like her mother.

'She's a good lady, though,' Bart added. 'She doesn't have to have me. It's 'cause she's so old, I guess. She hardly eats anything herself. She gives me practically all the money she gets for keeping me. For clothes, she says.'

'You do have beautiful clothes, Bart,' Mira said.

'He's got great taste,' Val assented.

'Clothes. Who the fuck cares about clothes,' Grant intoned.

The conversation turned to the meaning of style. Style was an expression of the ethos, of the person, of culture, subculture, rebellion — they arued and ranted and laughed. Bart, though, was the expert.

'Now you,' he told Val, 'really have a style. You understand your body, yourself, and you dress great. You,' he turned to Mira, 'dress a little uptight. But you're getting better. I really like those pants you have on. What fabric are they?' He reached out and took an inch or so of fabric from the thigh portion of her pants and rubbed it between his fingers.

'Cotton and polyester.'

'Nice. Now you two,' he said to Grant and Ben, 'between you have the taste of a Zulu. Not to knock my own kind!'

'Fuck clothes,' Grant repeated.

'You can fuck clothes because you got a closetful from your daddy.'

'All I ever got from my father was a rap on the head.'

'And a few on the tail too, if I recall,' Val put in.

Grant looked at her dangerously. 'And I seem to keep getting those.'

'Then you should be calloused by now.'

'I'm the only one I know who had a great father,' Ben said. 'He worked on the railroad, and he was away a lot. But when he was home, he was really there. He talked to me and my brothers, and my little sister too. And to my mother. I remember the two of them sitting out-side on the back step on summer nights, holding hands.'

'Maybe absence was the secret,' Val laughed.

'Maybe! But you know what sociologists say about the absent father.'

'Man, I'm glad my father's absent,' Bart said. 'I only met him once, but he scared the shit out of me. My aunt says he used to beat my mother blind and he does the same thing to his wife and kids now.'

Through all this, Mira sat paralyzed. Her thigh still tingled where Bart had touched it, barely touched it, as he picked up the fabric of her pants to feel it. Her heart had stopped when he did that. How could he dare? How did he dare? The blood pulsed in her head, it was a con-stant beating rhythm. Slowly, it slowed. She calmed. He was unpolished, he did not know that men did not do such things to women they were not intimate with. But, she argued, suppose Grant had done that? She would not have liked it, she would have felt it a violation, but she would have shrugged it off, attributing it to Grant's lack of social finish. Her thigh would not have continued to tingle, as it was doing. No, there was more to this. She sat watching Bart talk and laugh, so young, only a year older than Chris, yet so much older, willing to take on Grant and Ben, and even Val, although he generally de-ferred to her. Yet, look closer, forget the dark skin which automatically made him old and wise, one of the witches and demons of the earth who know everything the moment they are born and spend the rest of their lives undermining us, the innocent, the privileged, the genteel. ... He had soft round cheeks, like Chris's, and his eyes were still dewy with faith, or hope, or was it charity? It was his color. Her teeth set as she faced that. Her real protest was: how could he dare touch her with his dark hands? His hand was lying on the table beside his plate; she lowered her eyes and looked at it. What would it be like to have a dark hand like that on your body? And suddenly she put her head back, silent, but

403

in her throat, a cry, a cry of agony and awareness and lament: of course, her brain pounded, of course!

But it was not bigotry. It was the strangeness. She had never jumped rope with a black child, never held hands walking home from first grade. And over the years, she had, despite her nice neat liberal ideas, absorbed the sense of horror of the big black buck. Prejudice lay in the body.

Bart's hand lay on the table beside his plate. It was a short thick hand, chocolate colored, its palm paler, almost pink. It had short nails, and its fingers looked somehow like a child's fingers, curved naturally, with an unselfconsciousness it is impossible to affect, looking vulnerable and sweet and strong and capable. Mira put her own pale thin hand over it, settling down very lightly on Bart's. Bart turned quickly. Grant was raving about his rotten father. Mira whispered: 'Will you pass me the bread, Bart, please?' She removed her hand, he smiled and passed the basket. It was over. She settled back into herself.

She wondered if he knew, if he had guessed her agitation at his touching her, and the way she had chosen to confront her problem. She wondered if he would forgive her if he did know. He would forgive her if he had felt the same way about white flesh, but suppose he had not? White was the master race, after all. If he had not? Her eyes misted. Perhaps he would not forgive her. If he knew. But of course he knew, if not about her, about her race. Was there forgiveness for that?

'You look misty,' a voice said in her other ear. She turned to Ben's sweet kind face.

'Do you believe in forgiveness?'

He shook his head. 'In forgetting, maybe.'

'Yes. Forgetting.'

'Do you have something specific in mind?'

'Oh, well, what you were saying about Africa. Or any-place that's been oppressed, any people who have been oppressed, black people, any people, women, for instance,' her voice faded out.

'There's only one way,' he said softly. Grant and Bart

404

were currently arguing about the Proper Family Structure. Both agreed that a male should be dominant in the house, and that every house should contain a father, a mother, and some children. Beyond that, they agreed on nothing. 'And that is – well, independence. I don't know how else to put it. People – the Lianese – will forgive us only when they don't need us anymore, when they're equal to us.'

'But that won't be – in terms of power, I mean – for a long time. Probably never. Lianu is a small country.'

'Yes, but there will be a federation of black African countries. I don't mean absolute equality. When they or their league is equal in bargaining power.'

Mira laid her head in her hands. Tears were streaming down her face. I drank too much, she kept thinking, I drank too much.

'What is it?' Ben's voice didn't sound annoyed or impatient. It sounded kind, concerned. Still, she could not stop crying, and she didn't know why she was crying. After he laid his hand on her back, she lifted her head.

'What is it?' he asked again.

'Oh, God! Life is impossible!' she cried, and jumped up and ran to the bathroom.

20

'Oh, I just got drunk. I was nervous and I drank too much. So I blew it,' Mira shrugged, as if she didn't care.

'I've never seen you like that before,' Val insisted.

She tried to tell Val all of what had been going on in her head about Bart, ashamed of it as she was.

Val listened soberly, nodding her head. 'It seems strange to me,' she said finally, 'that although you thought of Bart as the stranger, the foreign element, you were feeling like a stranger yourself. As if you were saying – I want to love you, man, but can I forgive you for what you've done to me? – as if you were perceiving similarities between Bart's relation with whites and your relation with men.'

'Oh, Val, that's ridiculous! God, you insist on interpreting everything according to your fanatic, your mono-maniacal beliefs! I just got drunk and soupy and feeling sorry for myself! That's all there was to it!'

Val gazed at her for a moment, then moved her head slightly. 'Okay. Sorry,' she said, her voice sounding a little tight. 'I have to go to the library.' She picked up her books and left.

Mira sat there in Lehman Hall feeling slightly guilty, slightly relieved, trying to feel justified. Val had been kind to her. She'd had the dinner party, invited Ben. But why did she have to insist that everybody see the world in the fanatical way she did? Mira picked up her books and walked out of the building, head down, ru-minating. She decided she would never speak to Val again; she decided she would call her that night and apologize. Tears came to her eyes again. I'm having a nervous breakdown, she thought. Why was it so hard to know anything, anything at all?

'Mira!' a voice floated to her, and she looked up. A vision drifted toward her, a beautiful woman who looked like a young Katherine Hepburn, her hair, honey brown and glistening, floating out behind her in the sunlight, tall and slim, in pants and a sweater and a jacket that was open and flying behind her in the wind. It was Iso.

'Iso!'

'You look very sober.'

'My God. You look gorgeous. What did you do?'

'This is my natural self,' Iso crowed, turning in a com-plete circle. 'What do you mean, what did I do?'

They laughed. 'It's wonderful!' Mira exclaimed. 'What *did* you do?'

'I let down my hair and I bought some new clothes,' Iso grinned.

'Oh, God, if it could be that easy for me!'

'You don't need it,' Iso flattered her.

'Iso, have dinner with me tonight,' she pleaded, find-ing a way out of her problem. If she could talk to some-one, it would all become clear.

'Oh, Mira, I'm sorry. I'm going to lunch now with Dawn Ogilvie – you know her? And I'm having dinner with Elspeth. And lunch tomorrow with Jeanie Braith. I'm sorry if I sound snooty. I'm just so delighted.'

She looked it. She beamed and glowed, she couldn't stop shining.

'You're trying to be promiscuous,' Mira ventured, a little smile around her mouth.

'I'm trying to reach a place where I can be promiscuous,' Iso corrected her. 'I feel so good! I'm going to have a party, Saturday night, you'll come, won't you?'

'I'll come,' Mira said, admiring.

'Anybody you want me to invite?'

'You look beautiful.'

Iso turned a vulnerable child's face to her. 'Do you really think so?' she asked, looking frightened.

'I really think so,' Mira said firmly. Iso glowed.

'Well, I'm going to try.' Her voice wavered. 'I don't have anything to lose, right?'

'Right,' Mira said, her voice as wavering, full of tenderness, full of Val's kind of perception of the human race as a bunch of terrified children. 'Oh, yes,' she added, including herself in her teary pity for the race, 'your party. Invite Ben Voler. You know him?'

'The African guy. Yeah. Okay! Wish me luck!' Iso drifted away.

The party was mobbed. Iso, obviously, knew everybody. Mira stood in the doorway of the dark living room which had been emptied of furniture, watching the dancers. Val was out on the floor making a fool of herself dancing with Lydia Greenspan; Iso was dancing, and Martin Bell, and Kyla, and even Howard Perkins, and the beautiful girl who looked like a gypsy, and Brad, and Stanley, who was dancing with Clarissa, who never looked at him and seemed to be dancing by and for herself. She was a marvelous dancer, and eventually, everyone else stopped and just watched her. She danced with her head bent, her eyes nearly closed. Her long dark hair fell across her face; her tautly muscled body wound and curved. Her dance was extremely sexual, but not sexy. Her body moved for its own pleasure, not for display, it joyed in sexuality as its own expression. Mira watched, suddenly perceiving the difference, although she could not have done what Clarissa was doing. How, she wondered, could Clarissa have so blanked out the room as to feel free to be herself? On the other hand, if one could not blank out rooms, would one feel free to be one-self when one was alone, a record blasting, dancing in one's own empty apartment? Everything these days seemed too hard.

Iso was dressed in a long white Moroccan robe trim-med with red and gold braid. Her hair floated behind her. Her face had been transformed just the way they do it in the movies: the girl with the hat, the glasses, the pinched mouth, removes hat to reveal flowing blond locks, takes off glasses and military jacket and is revealed as sex bombshell. Iso's change was less dramatic, but the long hair – down to her shoulders – made her face look fuller, and her heightened color, her glamorous clothes gave what had been the face of a schoolmarm a cast of great sophistication, wisdom, experience. Mira was entranced.

'Come on,' Iso said. 'It's time you tried this.' She reached out her hands.

'I'd feel like a fool. I don't know how to do it,' Mira protested.

'Just move your body the way the music feels,' Iso said, and took her hands, and led her gently onto the floor.

She was dancing. Her awkwardness and self-con-sciousness vanished as soon as she realized that no one was looking at her. As the music blasted, she fell into it: she forgot herself and felt into its rhythms and moods. Iso drifted away from her, and Kyla drifted to her: they did a *pas de deux*, grinning at each other. She danced opposite Brad, Howard, Clarissa. She began to understand. It was a wonderful kind of dancing. It was totally free. She was not dependent upon a partner, she did not have to bite her lip in irritation at his ineptness, or rage because she would like to spin and fly around the floor and he lifted and set his feet in the same single spot. She could do whatever she wanted, yet wherever her motion carried her there was someone there, she was in a group, she was one of them, they were together, all full of delight at their own bodies, their own rhythms. Suddenly, her eyes squeezed shut, then opened, she found herself opposite Val. Val was large and smiling, but her face flickered a little when she saw Mira, and Mira felt hurt, hurt for Val's hurt, and she moved toward her and put her arms around Val and whispered in her ear, 'I'm sorry, I'm sorry,' and moved back, and Val shrugged, grinning, glowing, and they danced, and moved apart to face someone else.

It was a tiring dance, and in time, Mira left the floor to find a beer. The kitchen was nearly empty. Only Duke, Clarissa's husband, stood leaning against the refrigerator, and two people she did not know talked quietly in a corner. Mira had to ask Duke to move in order to get her beer.

'You look a little lost,' she said, understanding the feeling.

Duke was a large heavyset man. He would be fat in a few years. He was pinkish and puffy; he looked like an aging football player. In fact, he was a West Pointer. He had recently returned from Vietnam and was stationed now in New England.

'Well, a Harvard party isn't exactly my idea of the best way to spend a weekend pass,' he said.

'How do you feel when you come here? I guess Cambridge is the center of the peace movement.'

'That doesn't bother me,' he said seriously. 'I wish the war would end.'

'How did you feel when you were over there?'

His face betrayed nothing. 'I was doing my job. I wasn't near the front. But I don't like this war.'

Although Mira had not liked him simply because of the way he looked, she felt now a sympathy for him. He too was trapped. She wondered how he felt.

'It must have been hard for you,' she said sympathetically.

He shrugged. 'No. You just have to keep things in separate categories. I believe in this country. I believe in a well-trained army. Sometimes the politicians make

409

a mistake. You just have to do your job and hope the politicians will find a way to correct it.'

'But suppose your job had involved killing? Suppose you felt it to be morally wrong?'

He looked puzzled. 'I didn't sign on as guardian of the morals of the world. Who knows when something is morally wrong?'

'Suppose you lived in Germany and they assigned you to putting Jews on trains?'

He looked annoyed. 'This isn't the same thing at all. These things are always so simple for you people. It's a bad war because a lot of Americans are getting killed, and there's nothing to be gained by it. It's costing us millions and we're getting nothing for our money.'

'I see. Do you plan to stay in the army?'

'Maybe. It's a good life. I enjoy it. I even enjoyed Vietnam. I bought some great stuff there, you have to come over some time and we'll show it to you. Sculptures, some rugs, and wonderful prints. I have one print . . .' He launched into a precise description of one print after another, enumerating subject matter, color, linear rhythms. 'They're really great.'

'Yes. They get beyond facts, which are always so false.' She sipped her beer.

'Oh, I wouldn't say that.' Then he launched into a long argument supporting factualness. He talked about things like sightings in bombsights and rifles, mapmaking, charts, graphs, and inventories of men and arms. He spoke long, and perhaps even well. Mira could not judge. But he spoke from a height. It was clear in his tone and his language that he was speaking from authority and knowledge to a simpleton who knew nothing of such things. Since this was indeed the case, his tone was all the more offensive. She wondered if he would listen for ten minutes while she explained the subtleties of English prosody.

'Yes, but my point is that what you like about the prints is that they get beyond the facts.'

'Hell, those prints are worth a fortune,' he exclaimed. Then he launched into a precise explanation of how much he had paid for each one, and how much they had been evaluated for after he returned to the States. 'The rugs, too,' he continued. 'I took each of them to three different dealers . . .'

Mira felt a little numb. Duke was incapable of conversation. He was a monologuist. He was probably incapable of dialogue with any equal. He could talk down, and since he was in the army, no doubt he could talk up: 'Yes, sir. The enemy are deployed at . . .'

She looked around. The kitchen was completely empty now. She reached for another beer. She did not know how to get away. Duke was now talking about the uses of computers. He talked long and intricately, and she tried to listen. After a long time, she asked, 'But what's the point? I mean, what is it you're trying to do?'

He did not seem to understand the question. He continued talking, but what he said made no sense to her.

'I mean, you must have a project. An aim. What is the goal of all these manipulations?'

'Why to see how well the computer can project, can predict. And to see how well we understand its uses.'

'The opposite of the ends justify the means,' she interrupted as he tried to talk further.

'Pardon?'

'The means is all. You have no end. You're just playing with a big toy.'

'Mira, this is serious stuff.' His irritation was controlled.

Mira was grateful when Val came barging in, red-faced and pounding her chest. 'At my age, at my weight, with three packs a day down my lungs, I should put away childish things!' she announced, reaching into the refrigerator.

Avery, a sweet, soft-faced young man, slipped into the room and stood enthralled by a stack of cans of soup on a kitchen counter.

'Admiring homemade pop art?' Val intruded.

'The configuration is . . . interesting.' There were five cans on the bottom row, three on the next, and one on top.

'Do you think Warhol could learn something?'

'No, but maybe I can penetrate into the deep, mystic heart of things.'

'You're teaching Conrad,' Mira concluded.

'No. Mailer. *Why Are We in Vietnam?*'

'Do you seem to hear a thunderous cry from inside those cans?'

'Absolutely. "Fulfill my will! Go eat this swill!"'

People drifted into the kitchen. Harley and a strange bearded man came for beers. They stood there for a time talking. Mira listened to them, but she already knew better than to try to talk to Harley. He was probably as brilliant as Kyla said, and he was handsome in what Val called a 'Swiss Alps Nazi' way, tall, blond, severe, and usually wearing a ski sweater. But Harley could only talk about physics. He simply had no other conversation. He was interesting as long as he was explaining things that had some meaning to his audience, but like Duke he was essentially a monologuist, he would carry any talk far past his audience's limits. He could not talk about the weather, or food, or movies, or people. He fell silent when others did. She listened, then, to see what kind of conversation he was carrying on with the stranger. He looked over at her.

'Oh, hello, Mira. This is Don Evans. He's from Princeton, here on a visit. We met last time I was out at Aspen.'

'A physicist too, I take it,' she smiled at him.

He smiled abstractly back, then turned again to Harley. He was talking. Suddenly Harley interrupted him and corrected something. He backtracked, explained, continued. Harley interrupted and spoke. This went on. It was not dialogue, it was one-upmanship. They were not talking to reach some common ground of experience or to find some limited truth, but to show off. It was two monologues carried on simultaneously. Disgusted, Mira turned away. Duke, still standing by the refrigerator, put something into the conversation. The two stopped, looked at him, then Harley said, 'Let's go into the bedroom, it's quieter,' and the three left.

The kitchen had become crowded. Clarissa and Kyla

were talking to the gypsy. Mira approached them. They introduced her as Grete.

'Yes, I saw you dancing with Howard Perkins,' Mira smiled.

Grete made a face. 'He follows me everywhere.'

'Poor Howard,' Kyla said. 'Somebody ought to be kind to him. *I'm* going to be kind to him!' she announced, and left the room.

Grete rolled her eyes. 'I don't think she knows what she's in for.'

They talked about studying for generals, a subject of consuming interest to those presently studying for them. Mira noticed that none of the young women in the room wore bras. It seemed to be the new style, but she found it a little raw. You could actually see the outline of some of their breasts.

Clarissa was talking very soberly. 'I mean it's interesting, I enjoy literature, but sometimes it seems frivolous to be doing something like this when all around us things are in chaos, when you think you could do something that would help, something to advance change in the right direction, instead of leaving it to those who care only about power.'

'I don't think you can,' Grete said. She had quick, penetrating eyes. 'Nothing changes except styles.'

'But styles are significant,' Mira said. 'They mean something. I have a stack of white gloves in my bottom drawer that are slowly turning yellow.'

'And what does that mean?' Grete asked.

'Well – things are easier, more casual. We aren't so much out to impress each other.'

'I think we are just as eager to impress, but we have different ways of doing it,' Grete argued.

Val came up behind them. 'My God, things never change. The men are in one room planning the future of the world, and the women are in the other talking about styles.'

Clarissa laughed. 'What men?'

'Your husband for one. And Harley, and that guy from Princeton. They're talking about computerized

413

techniques for predicting the fate of the country. All of them want to be part of a think tank to plan the future of America. God save us from that!'

They all laughed, even Clarissa. Mira wondered what she thought of her husband. He seemed so different from her. 'It would be a world of facts,' Clarissa said smiling. 'That's all Duke knows.'

'How did he get that name?'

Clarissa tilted her head confidentially. 'He was christened Marmaduke, but that's a deep, dark secret.'

They returned to the subject of style and whether it has meaning.

'I insist there's a difference in significance of various styles,' Mira argued. 'If a woman has to encase her body in a constricting corset, wear tottery high heels, spend hours dressing and powdering her hair and making up, just in order to go out, well, that says something about both the position of women and the class structure of a society.'

'That's true,' Grete admitted frowning. She frowned whenever she thought hard, and had a deep line between her dark eyebrows. 'But that styles become more casual doesn't necessarily mean that no class structure exists, or that the position of women is very much changed.'

They all got into it and were talking with great animation, sending whoops of laughter out into the room, when, suddenly Ben appeared.

'I gather this is where the party is,' he smiled.

Mira smiled radiantly at him because she was happy and enjoying herself, then finished her statement. 'It's broadening, you can experience everything. You can put on blue jeans and let your hair hang loose and see what it's like to be treated like a "hippie" or you can put on your fur coat and heels and go into Bonwit's and see what it feels like to play society matron . . . it's just freer, that's all. Expansion.'

'Expansion! That's it!' Val agreed. 'The only possible progress. Everything we've called progress is just change, bringing its own horrors. But there is progress, it's possible, it's an increase in sensibility. I mean,

414

imagine how the world seemed to cave people: it must have been full of terrors. We've domesticated a lot of those. Then along came Christianity . . .'

'That's quite a leap,' Clarissa smiled.

Ben touched Mira's arm lightly. 'Would you like something to drink?' he asked softly.

She turned to him and looked in his eyes. They were a warm golden brown. 'I'd love something,' she said feelingly.

'Beer? Wine?'

'Now, Christianity was a great step in progress: it made us feel guilty. The trouble was the guilt made us act worse than ever . . .'

Mira stood radiant. Her arm still tingled where Ben had touched it. He returned with her glass of wine and one for himself and stood beside her listening to Val.

'What we have to do is get beyond the guilt to the real motivations of the things we do. Because the motivations aren't evil: wishing harm on another is always a secondary, a substitute emotion for being unable to get what we want ourselves. If we could learn to figure out what it really is we want, and to forgive ourselves for wanting it, we would not have to do terrible things.'

'It sounds good,' Clarissa grinned, 'except for a few little leaps here and there. I imagine primitive people acted on their feelings—'

'And primitive people don't like to fight,' Val interrupted.

'What about war masks, war dances?' Grete intruded.

'Yes. Okay. They may not have liked fighting and had to psych themselves up for it – armies still do that,' Clarissa thought out loud. 'They fought because aggression is necessary for survival. It has an economic base.'

'It has to have a psychological base as well or the race would have gone the way of the dinosaurs. And obviously it occurs in inappropriate contexts. I like aggression, I think it's fun to be aggressive. That's what I'm talking about. If we could figure out what cause aggression – or sexuality – serves, accept those emotions, stop trying to hide them, then we could find a way to use them that wouldn't be so destructive.'

'Just how do we manage to find out these basic motivations?' Grete asked, unpersuaded by Val.

'Experiment. Science. But I already know what they are.'

Everyone laughed.

'I don't know,' Clarissa said reflectively. 'The conflict I see as basic is between spontaneous and free feelings and feelings requiring order, imposed order, structures, habits . . .'

'Order is ugly in the face of feeling,' Mira said fervently, too fervently, but not even embarrassed, so intensely conscious was she of Ben's body beside her, of his dark arms covered with dark hair, emerging from the rolled-up sleeves of his shirt. She could almost feel his body warmth, could almost smell him. 'But on the other hand, everything is order. What else is there? There are simply different kinds. I can't conceive of such a thing as anarchy.'

'Anarchy,' Ben said to her, 'is a cubist painting.'

Everyone cried out in delight. 'Explain, exegesis, *explication de texte!*'

'It's true that anarchy is simply a variation of order. You know, gangs of black-jacketed motorcyclists tearing up little towns might be a horror, but that isn't anarchy; each of those gangs has a leader, each of those towns does, too. It's a conflict of two different orders. Most threats about anarchy are fears of an order different from the one presently constituted. I'll admit that it's easier to live with one order than with two or three different ones, but not necessarily if the one order is a totalitarian state, say. Anyway, anarchy – I looked it up—' he grinned, 'means *without ruler*. That's hard to envision politically. But if we move to another discipline, we can imagine it.'

Everyone was listening with interest, but Mira was losing much of what Ben said. She was looking, under her eyes, at his arms, and at his hand on his glass. His shoulders, under the thin white shirt, looked broad and

416

tanned. His hands were large, with a little dark hair on their backs. The fingers were broad and stubby-ended yet delicate at the same time. His hair was full and dark. She did not dare as yet to look at his face.

'Think about a traditional painting – of a table, say. Most of what you see is the top, the things piled on it, the cloth, or a bowl of fruit, a vase of flowers, the bread and cheese – you know. Say it's a painting of the entire table, not just a still life. If there's a long cloth, you may not even see the legs. Or take another example – a building. You see the facade: you don't see the back unless you walk around it, and if it's a working building, chances are the back isn't attractive, it has sliding garage doors and ramps, it's the receiving and warehouse part of the building. But even if you see the back, you never see the foundation, the basement, the part that holds everything else up. Well, that's our usual view of society.'

Mira raised her eyes. His face was brilliant, his eyes were light. He was enjoying himself and his audience's attention. He had a large round face with prominent cheekbones and dark eyebrows. He looked intense.

'We are aware of the people at the top – in our present society and in those of the past. We know about the wealthy, the powerful, the famous. They make the rules, their standards and manners and styles set the tone. It's as though they are the flower the whole plant was designed to produce. But in fact, the flower is only one phase of the process that is a plant, and the purpose of the plant is to endure and to reproduce. Production of a flower is only one step in the process. The stem, the supports of the table, the foundation pillars of a building are also essential to the whole. So are the roots, the feet of the table, the basement walls. These are like the lower classes of a society: they are necessary, but they don't get much attention, they are not often seen as beautiful, they are taken for granted.

'But in cubist painting, everything is important, everything is paid attention to. Even the underside of the table, the insides of desk drawers, the space around the table – each thing is seen and seen in the round, each is shown

417

in its essentiality, each is given room to exist. What dominates the painting is not the top, the flower, but the whole, the design of the whole. Well, society could be like that. With laws designed for people rather than for property, we could have a government without a single dominating ruler. There is no single thing in a cubist painting that dominates the whole, yet the whole coheres. It might be possible that each group, each person, could be granted its own inherent autonomy, its space. The foundations would be admitted to be as important as the top.'

'If there were a top,' Grete said.

'Well, there will always be a top if it is a table, a facade in a building, people who are better known than others. But each would have only its own space and would stay in it.'

'But in cubist painting,' Mira argued, 'things don't stay in their own space. That's one of its main points. Each little section infringes on every other around it, everything overlaps.'

'Is that right?' Ben gave a delighted gasp. 'That's even better! Because we do violate, intrude upon, each other's space all the time – life would be awfully sterile and boring if we didn't. We do it in speech and in action – we do it when we touch each other. So we learn to violate each other's space a little, but we know when to return to our own. There is contact without conflict.'

Clarissa shook her head. 'I'd like to believe such a thing is possible, Ben, but I can't imagine eliminating conflict.'

'We don't want to eliminate it. It's a wonderful thing. We grow by it. We just learn to contain it. We learn to jiggle!' he laughed, carried away by his own high spirits.

Clarissa was thinking. 'Yes, okay. But isn't that exactly what the human race has been trying to do for centuries? Games, sports, debates – that sort of thing. Provide sublimation for aggressiveness?'

'Yes,' Val shot in, 'but all the while it has been piously mouthing that aggression is wrong, it has been exalting the hero, the warrior, the man who kills.'

418

'That's true.' Thoughtfully said, but Clarissa was not persuaded.

'You think it's time we got our shit together and stopped being moral schizophrenics,' Val said to Ben. 'A man after my own heart!'

Everyone began to talk at once then. Mira touched Ben lightly on his arm to get his attention, then pulled her hand away instantly, as if she had been burned. He looked at her smiling. He had seen.

'That was wonderful, Ben,' she said.

21

Mira got a little high that night, and so did Ben, and somehow – later she could not remember whose suggestion it was, or if there had been no suggestion at all, but simple single purpose – he ended up in her car, driving her to her apartment and when they arrived, he got out and saw her to the door and of course she asked him in for a nightcap and of course he came.

They were laughing as they climbed the steps, and they had their arms around each other. They were designing the perfect world, trying to outdo each other in silliness, and giggling to the point of tears at their own jokes. Mira fumbled with her key, Ben took it from her, dropped it, both of them giggling, picked it up and opened the door.

She poured them brandies. Ben following her to the kitchen, leaning over the counter and gazing at her as she prepared the drinks, talking, talking. He followed her out of the kitchen and right into the bathroom, until she turned with a little surprise and he caught himself, cried *'Oh!'* and laughed, and stepped out, but stood right beside the closed door talking to her through it while she peed. Then sat close beside her on the couch, talking, talking, laughing, smiling at her with shining eyes. And when he got up to get refills, she followed him into the kitchen and leaned across the counter gazing at him as he prepared the drinks, and he kept looking at her as he did it, and poured too much water in her glass. And they sat even closer this time, and there needed no fore-thought or calculation for the moment when they reached across and took each other's hands and it was only a few moments later that Ben was on her, leaning against her, his face searching in her face for something madly wanted that did not reside in faces, but searched, kept searching, and she too, in his. His body was lying on her now, his chest against her breasts, and the close-ness of their bodies felt like completion. Her breasts were pressed flat under him: they felt soft and hard at once. Their faces stayed together, mouths searching, probing, opening as if to devour, or rubbing softly together. Their cheeks too rubbed softly like the cheeks of tiny children just trying to feel another flesh, and hard, his beard, shaved though he was, harsh and hurtful on her cheek. He had her head in his hands, and he held it firmly, possessively, and gently, all at once, and he dipped his face into hers, searching for nourishment, hungry, hungry. They rose together, like one body, and like one body walked into the bedroom, not separating even in the narrow hallway, just squeezing through together.

For Mira, Ben's lovemaking was the discovery of a new dimension. He loved her body. Her pleasure in this alone was so extreme that it felt like the discovery of a new ocean, mountain, continent. He loved it. He crowed over it as he helped her to undress, he kissed it and caressed it and exclaimed, and she was quieter, but adored his with her eyes as she helped him to undress, ran her hands over the smooth skin of his back, grabbed him from behind around the waist and kissed his back, the back of his neck, his shoulders. She was shy of his penis at first, but when he held her close and nestled against her, he pressed his penis against her body, and her hand went out to it, held it, caressed it. Then he wrapped his legs around her, covered her, holding on to her tightly, and kissed her eyes, her cheeks, her hair. She pulled away from him gently and took his hands and kissed them, and he took hers and kissed the tips of her fingers.

She lay back again as he pressed against her, and he caressed her breasts. She felt that her body was floating out to sea on a warm gentle wave that had orders not to drown her, but she didn't even care if she drowned. Then, rather suddenly, he put his mouth to her breasts and nursed at them, and quickly entered her and quickly came, silently, with only an expelled breath, and a pang of self-pity hit her, her eyes filled with tears. No, no, not again, it couldn't be the same, it wasn't fair, was there really something wrong with her? He lay on top of her, holding her closely for a long time afterward, and she had time to swallow the tears and paste a smile back on her face. She patted his back gently and reminded herself that she had at least had pleasure from it this time, and maybe that was a good sign. He had given her, if nothing else, more pleasure than she had ever had from her body before.

After a time, he leaned back and lay on his side close to her. They lighted cigarettes and sipped their drinks. He asked her about her girlhood: what kind of child had she been? She was surprised. Women ask such things, sometimes, but not men. She was delighted. She lay back and threw herself into it, talking as if it were happening there and then. Her voice changed and curled around its subject: she was five, she was twelve, she was fourteen. She hardly noticed at first that he had begun to caress her body again. It seemed simply natural that they would touch each other. He was gently rubbing her belly and sides, her shoulders. She put her cigarette out and caressed his shoulders. Then he was leaning over her, kissing her belly, rubbing his hands on her thighs, on the insides of her thighs. Desire rose up in her more fiercely than before. She caressed his hair, then his head moved down, and she tightened up, her eyes widened, he was kissing her genitals, licking them, she was horrified, but he kept stroking her belly, her leg, he kept doing it and when she tried to tighten her legs, he held them gently apart, and she lay back again and felt the warm wet pressure and her innards felt fluid and giving, all the way to her stomach. She tried to pull him up, but he would

421

not permit it, he turned her over, he kissed her back, her buttocks, he put his finger on her anus and rubbed it gently, and she was moaning and trying to turn over, and finally, she succeeded, and then he had her breast in his mouth and the hot shoots were climbing all the way to her throat. She wrapped her body around him, clutching him, no longer kissing or caressing, but only clinging now, trying to get him to come inside her, but he wouldn't. She surrendered her body to him, let him take control of it, and in an ecstasy of passivity let her body float out to the deepest part of the ocean. There was only body, only sensation: even the room had ceased to exist. He was rubbing her clitoris, gently, slowly, ritually, and she was making little gasps that she could hear from a distance. Then he took her breast in his mouth again and wrapped his body around her and entered her. She came almost immediately and gave a sharp cry, but he kept going, and she came over and over again in a series of sharp pleasures that were the same as pain. Her face and body were wet, so were his, she felt, and still the pangs came, less now, and she clutched him to her, holding him as if she really might drown. The orgasms subsided, but still he thrust himself into her. Her legs were aching, and the thrust no longer felt like pleasure. Her muscles were weary, and she was unable to keep the motion going. He pulled out and turned her over and propped her on a pillow so that her ass was propped up, and entered her vagina from behind. His hand stroked her breast gently, he was humped over her like a dog. It was a totally different feeling, and as he thrust more and more sharply, she gave out little cries. Her clitoris was being triggered again, and it felt sharp and fierce and hot and as full of pain as pleasure and suddenly he came and thrust fiercely and gave off a series of loud cries that were nearly sobs, and stayed drooped over her like a flower, heaving, his wet face against her back.

When he pulled out, she turned over and reached up to him and pulled him down and held him. He put his arms around her and they lay together for a long time. His wet penis was against her leg, and she could feel semen trickling out of her onto the sheets. It began to feel cold, but neither of them moved. Then they moved a few inches and looked into each other's faces. They stroked each other's faces, then began to laugh. They hugged each other hard, like friends rather than lovers, and sat up. Ben went into the bathroom and got some tissues and they dried themselves and the sheets. He went back and started water running in the tub. Mira was lying back against the pillow, smoking.

'Come on, woman, get up!' he ordered, and she looked at him startled, and he reached across and put his arms around her and lifted her from the bed, kissing her at the same time, and helped her to her feet, and they went together to the bathroom and both peed. The water was at bath level by then. Ben had put Mira's bath lotion in the water, and it was bubbly and smelled fresh, and they got in together and sat with bent knees intertwined, and gently threw water at each other and lay back enjoying the warmth and caressed each other beneath and above the water.

They dried each other off. Mira put on a heavy terry robe, and Ben wrapped a towel around himself.

'I'm hungry,' she said.

'I'm famished,' he said.

Together, they pulled everything out of the refrigerator, and produced a feast of Jewish salami and feta cheese and hard-boiled eggs and tomatoes and black bread and sweet butter and half-sour pickles and big black Greek olives and raw Spanish onions and beer, and trotted all of it back to bed with them and sat there gorging themselves and talking and drinking and laughing and touching each other with tender fingertips. And finally they set the platters and plates and beer cans on the floor and Ben nuzzled his face in her breast, but this time she pushed him down and got on top of him and, refusing to let him move, she kissed and caressed his body and slid her hands down his sides and along the insides of his thighs, held his balls gently, then slid down and took his penis in her mouth and he gasped with pleasure and she moved her hands and head slowly up

423

and down with it, feeling the vein throb, feeling it harden and melt little drops of semen, and wouldn't let him move until suddenly she raised her head and he looked startled and she got on top of him and set her own rhythms, rubbing her clitoris against him as she moved and she came, she felt like a goddess, triumphant, riding the winds, and she kept coming and he came too then, and she bent down her chest and clutched him, both of them moaning together, and ended, finally, exhausted.

They fell back on the rumpled sheets for a while, then Mira lighted a cigarette. Ben got up and smoothed the bedclothes out, and fluffed up the pillows, and got in beside her and pulled up the sheets and blankets and took a drag of her cigarette and put his arms behind his head and just lay there smiling.

It was five o'clock, and the sky above the houses was light, lightening, a pale streak of light blue. They were not tired, they said. They turned their heads toward each other, and just smiled, kept smiling. Ben took another drag of her cigarette, then she put it out. She reached out and switched off the lamp, and together they snuggled down in the sheets. They were still turned to each other, and they twisted their bodies together. They fell immediately asleep. When they awakened in the morning, they were still intertwined.

CHAPTER FIVE

1

Strange. I can see now, writing this all out, what I never saw before. Everything that characterized Mira's and Ben's relation was there from the very beginning. It was formed in a mold. But even seeing that, I don't know what to say about it. Is there any relation that is not formed in a mold? I remember Clarissa saying – after she and Duke had been divorced for over a year, and Duke badly wanted a reconciliation and was pleading with her to believe that he had changed, had become more sensitive, more able to see other people – 'He says he's changed, and maybe he has. But in my head and feelings, he has the same shape he always had. I think I'll always see him that way. So even if I could bear to go back to him – which I can't – and even if he has changed – which is unlikely – I'd turn him right back into what he was, because that would be what I expected from him. It's hopeless.'

I find it a desperate thought that people can't change, can't grow together. If that's true, people should be required to reenact marriage every five years or so, like signing a lease. Oh, shit! No rules: we have enough as it is. But if it is true that relationships are formed in molds, then how do people live together? when time brings change, and change inside a mold either breaks the vessel or agonizes the bound foot.

But people do live together: men and women, women and women, ancient ladies with lace curtains at the windows who dress up in rayon print dresses and high heels to go to the market for a half-dozen of eggs and a quart of milk and two rib lamb chops. Do those women, like some elderly married couples I know, sit in silence at dusk, chewing the insides of their lips with irritation at Mabel or Minnie?

'Scratch a woman, find a rage.' Val said that so often that her voice still says it in my ear. Does Mabel's habit of using so much talcum powder after her bath that she leaves the bathroom floor dusty, which bothers Minnie's nostrils, does that lead inevitably to explosions, during which all of Mabel's other annoying habits – peering at the name of the sender of all Minnie's letters, never vacuuming behind the sofa, and missing the eyes when she peels the potatoes – are thrown at her like a set of knives, sending her into tears and counteraccusations? Because of course (Mabel announces the terrible truth tearfully), Minnie herself is not perfect. She always asks who is calling when the telephone rings (ah, so rarely!) for Mabel, and that is pure nosiness. Minnie pulls out her smelling salts at the slightest provocation, as if she were frail, when the truth is she's healthly as a horse. She even did it that day the neighbor's dog, in heat, met a stray on their front lawn. Yet surely, Minnie, at seventy-four, has seen such things before! And Minnie, never, never, puts the newspaper back together again the way it was after she reads it: it is enough to drive one mad.

It is true they both cluck and tut at any news story about children being mistreated; that they both tighten their lips and look away when there is a sex scene on television; that they both live uncomplainingly on canned soup and eggs and a lamb chop or hamburger every third night, which is all they can afford on Social Security and their tiny pensions; that they both disapprove of smoking, drinking, gambling, and any woman who engages in them; that they both love the scent of lavender and lemon oil and freshly laundered sheets. Neither of them would think of going out with curlers in her hair, the way some of the young women do, and each spends a chunk of her little allowance to have her hair set and blued every week. And neither of them would ever go outdoors, or even walk about the house, for that matter, in disarray. Their ancient knobbed arthritic fingers struggle every morning with the iron-tight girdle, the delicate hose. And both of them

426

remember, as if it were yesterday, the Baum family that used to live next door.

But I ask you: is that enough?

Across the street are Grace and Charlie, also in their seventies, married over fifty years, who are the same way. Except Grace gets angry at Charlie for every day consuming three cans of beer and constantly belching, and Charlie gets angry with Grace because she doesn't let him watch all the TV programs he likes, insisting on watching those stupid game shows. Both are proud and smug about the neatness of their front lawn – not like some people's, they tellingly remark to Mabel and Minnie, who of course feel the same way, and all four of them look downstreet at the Mulligan house. Yes, but is it enough?

What holds people together? And why do we have to hate each other so much? I ask this not to have you shake your head piously and pronounce that we must certainly not hate, not hate our fellow-man. We do. What I want to know is, why? It seems necessary, you see, like breathing out after you've breathed in. Okay. I can accept that. The true mysteries of the true church, if there ever were one, would be those: Why do we love and hate? How in hell do we manage to live together? I don't know. I already told you: I live alone.

It's easy enough to blame men for the rotten things they do to women, but it makes me a little uncomfortable. It's too close to the stuff I read in the fifties and sixties when everything that went wrong in a person's life was Mother's fault. All of it. Mothers were the new devil. Poor mothers, if only they realized how much power they had! Castraters and smotherers, they were unpaid servants of The Evil One. It is true that men are responsible for much of the pain in women's lives – one way or another, whether personally or as part of a structure that refuses to let women in at all, or keeps them in subordinate positions. But is that all of it?

If anyone ever had a chance for a good mutual life, it was Mira and Ben. They had enough intelligence, experience, goodwill, and enough room in the world –

whether you call that opportunity or privilege – to figure out what they wanted and to achieve it. So what happened in their relationship ought to be paradigmatic somehow. It seemed so at the time. It seemed to glow with the divinity of the ideal. They had the secret, keeping both intimacy and spontaneity, security and freedom. And they were able, somehow, to keep it up.

It was April when Mira and Ben became lovers. Mira's first Cambridge April, and her mood was perfectly attuned to the little green balls that appeared on the trees, the thin feathering of forsythia, and the lilacs in the Yard, hanging over the brick wall around the president's house. As the sun grew warmer, the tiny green balls expanded, then opened, and cast green light on the warm uneven red brick. The days smelled warm; light perfume of dogwood and lilac drifted down from Brattle Street, from Garden and Concord, and penetrated even the crowded, fumy Square. People thronged on the streets, jackets open, smiling, unselfconscious, carrying a bunch of daffodils from the Brattle Street Florist, a rolled-up poster from the Coop, a polished apple from Nini's.

Mira was studying for generals and finishing up papers; Ben was trying to organize the ten crates of notes he'd brought back from Lianu. They met almost every day, for lunch or coffee at the Patisserie or Piroschka or Grendel's, where they could get a table outdoors. When everybody was broke, a group of them would meet for a drink at the Faculty Club, where Ben or another teaching assistant could charge things. They always spent the most money when they were broke.

Mira was working very well: the sense of home she had in her relation with Ben freed her mind. She could focus intensely for hours without feeling restless or getting up to pace her apartment or the top floor of Widener. She could be as organized and efficient as she had always been without having to feel she was substituting order for life.

The lovers spent Saturday night and Sunday together, in an extended honeymoon. They ate dinner out on

Saturday night, trying every interesting restaurant in Cambridge. They had guacamole, the Szechuan shrimp, and vegetable curries, and Greek lamb with artichokes and egg lemon sauce; they tried a variety of pastas, baba ganoush, hot and sour soup, sauerbraten, quiche, rabbit stew, and one special night, suprêmes de volaille avec champignons. They tried buffalo stew at the Faculty Club. They tried for variety and goodness of food and surroundings. They found everything good, and some wonderful things.

On Sundays, when most restaurants in Cambridge are closed, they cooked in. Sometimes this became quite a production, as when Ben insisted on cooking a beef Wellington that took him all day and left the kitchen a shambles. More often it was simple: soufflés and gratins, stuffed crèpes, or pasta, and salad. They had friends in or ate alone with chamber music on the stereo Mira had bought.

And off and on all weekend, they made love. They did it for hours, and sought for constant variation. They tried it standing up, hanging over the edge of the bed, sitting down, or with Ben holding Mira onto his standing body. Many of their experiments ended in giggling failure. They played games, pretending to be characters out of old movies, varying the power roles. She would be Catherine the Great and he, a serf; he would be a sheik and she, a slave girl. They acted the parts with verve. She played the woman of her masochistic fantasies, he played the man of his masochistic fantasies. It was like being a child again and playing house or cowboys and Indians. It liberated their imaginations and freed them to live out all the mythic lives they had rejected, like playing dress-up in all the costumes they had stored in the attics of their brains.

They went for long walks, down along the Charles, up to Fresh Pond, all the way along the Freedom Trail, ending in the North End with an Italian coffee or ice. And they talked, and they argued about everything conceivable, about poetry and politics and psychological theory, about the best way to make an omelet and the

429

best way to rear a child. They shared enough of the same values and assumptions to make their arguments rich and exhilarating, and both were old enough to know that small differences of opinion kept things interesting.

In May, there was a student protest against the war led by a group more militant than the peace group Val and Ben belonged to. The Yard thronged with students; the protesters surrounded University Hall and spoke to the crowds through loudspeakers that distorted their voices. Sounds wavered across the Yard: it was moral to use forcible means to try to stop the war because the war was immoral. That was the crux of the argument. They urged the students to strike. Mira, listening, watched the crowd. People stood, considered, wandered. Some argued with the speakers, who tried to argue fairly in response. But the arguments were over logic and legality: it was against the law for them to take over University Hall; it was immoral to act against the law; but it was more immoral not to act against the law when the law supports an immoral war.

Mira could not take the thing seriously. It was intellectual game-playing, juggling concepts that were valid only as long as the speakers chose to grant them validity. The real contest was between the powers of government and armies and the vulnerability of young flesh. This was not, she thought, how revolutions happened. Revolutions happened in the guts, in fury and outrage so deep, so long endured, so killing to the self, that they could issue only in complete rebellion. The cadres in Algeria, in China, in Cuba, had perhaps sat around finding ways to justify morally, intellectually, the overthrow of the government, but their impulse had been rooted in their daily existences, in years of watching the oppression of their people, in the muttered knowledge of an oppression so severe that life became secondary to a cause. The young people shouting on the steps of the Hall were right; they were committed; they grew hoarse yet still shouted through the loudspeakers, trying to reach the rest. But their audience was not hungry enough, not frightened enough; their families were alive and well and living in Scarsdale, not dead of a bullet, maimed by torture, enslaved, or locked up nights inside a compound. Ben said American imperialists were smart : they enslaved the population by giving them two cars, two television sets, and a case of sexual repression. Val and he argued Marcusan theory. Mira sat and watched. The thing was not taking off; there was simply not enough passion in enough people. Then one night, the president of the university called the police, who pulled the students out of University Hall. There was violence. Some people were hurt, many were jailed. The next day the campus was in a state of shock. Overnight, it had been radicalized.

It is easy to forget the feeling of those days just because the passions that were aroused came from principles, not existence, and so were evanescent. I remember sitting in Lehman Hall feeling the fragile air; voices floated by sounding like broken glass; one touch, I felt, could shatter the whole building. Some people – mostly older male graduate students – were tough and grim and full of words, repeating over and over the rhetoric of revolution, trying to build up the threats of the previous fall, muttering in corners over dirty coffee cups about guns and tanks. The younger students were tremulous, near hysteria. Their eyes were permanently startled, and as they handed out leaflets, circulated petitions, their hands shook. Rumors – later verified – about materials found in administration files burned like a desert wind through the buildings, tinkling, shattering the delicate balance necessary to hierarchical organization. A lot of people old enough to know, but sheltered long enough and well enough inside privileged walls that they never learned, discovered in those years that power is not something you possess, but is something granted to you by those you have power over. The genteel pale men who quietly, blandly, courteously ran the university were revealed to be unapologetic, sexists and racists, who considered prejudice their right, and their right to be identical with the good of the nation. It was impossible to accuse them of conspiracy, for their collusion

431

occurred on a subconscious level. It was, Mira thought, like her old confusion about Norm: can you blame someone for something he doesn't let himself know he's doing and even when you point it out, sees nothing wrong with it, although it demeans or oppresses you, calling it 'natural'?

But if for Mira this was an old story, it was not for the young students. They had been taught, from their earliest years, that America was the land of equality, of democracy, of equal opportunity; although they knew there were flaws in the system, people of goodwill were attempting to repair them. Their superiors, their teachers and deans and parents, all sounded well-intentioned. But in the privacy of their offices, they wrote these sorts of letters. They hadn't known, hadn't seen, and in the shock one feels when it is partly one's own blindness and easy acceptance that one blames, they went around screaming, crying, shaking. They realized suddenly that this had been obvious all the while if they had cared to look, that this was the ugly underside of the very ideals they had been taught, the aspirations they had inherited. This elitist thinking, so close to the thinking of Hitler, was precisely what their luxury was founded on, required, assumed. The cost of ease is another's slavery. It was intolerable.

They tried to work it out. They clung to the ideals, the aspirations; they tried to renounce the luxury. But this they could not bring themselves to do completely. A few of them left school, went on the road, went to live in communes, repudiating their backgrounds. There were arguments, full of rhetoric which was a kind of short-hand, on both sides. If you want to change things, you need power: poverty was not a power base. Some joined militant groups doomed to ineffectuality, continual splintering, and infiltration by the FBI so extreme that some groups had only a few nongovernment members. All the sensitive among them found insupportable the loss of innocence, the guilty and responsibility which are the price of knowing that you eat because another starves. For such a problem there is little solution, and no consolation. A saint may choose to starve so another may eat, but that doesn't change the situation.

But Val said that was all bullshit. She said to reduce the world's power alignments to that sort of simplicity was to turn a political problem into a metaphysical one, as if, she protested, it was a given that there should be more people than food. This was not necessary. There were alternatives. Suppose people gave up eating too much; suppose they gave up – she'd met a man once whose family of four owned four cars and four snow-mobiles, and that had remained her image – three of their snowmobiles and two cars. But how can you force him to do that, Clarissa argued, except by dictatorial fiat? Socialism is wonderful in principle, horrible in practice. Not so! We think so only because we look at socialism in countries which were undeveloped, in which, without socialism, the mass of the people would have been starving. But it does seem to repress initiative, creativity, individuality. Not in Sweden, Val said. The arguments raged. The thing ended, as it began, in words.

2

The strike petered out as examinations began, and things returned to normal. This does not justify the claims of those cynics who believe that the uproar and protest of the sixties and early seventies had no more meaning than the rage for the lindy. The things that were revealed, discovered, and discussed in those years were driven deep into people's minds; what happened in those years affected the way we think. Nevertheless, I do not expect that one day as I return from the beach, I will hear on my car radio that Eden has been proclaimed, except, of course, when an incumbent is running for re-election to the Presidency.

The night of the dinner party at her house, Val had broken up with Grant. She was a little upset about it. 'Here I am, for God's sake, almost forty years old and I still do these things!' What upset her was that she and Grant had not much liked each other for some time,

433

but had done nothing about it. 'He's really resented me – for a lot of reasons. He wanted someone steady, someone always there, someone to minister to his hurt soul, and I wasn't willing. But instead of walking out on me, he hangs around, sniping and griping at me, being useless in bed, always starting stupid arguments. And I, who wanted from him only a companion to have fun with, in bed and out, have not had fun with him since – well, for God's sake, since before I left the commune. Yet I didn't break it, I didn't call it quits. I don't know why I let myself fall into these depressing habits. I feel ten years younger and much more cheerful since Grant is no longer among my responsibilities. And that's just how I'd come to think about him – as a responsibility, like a dog that has to be taken for a walk every night. Jesus! What's wrong with me!'

'It's not just you,' Iso said consolingly. 'Ava and I hadn't been happy together for a long time too. Even so, I was devastated when we split. At least you're not that.'

'My relationship with Grant never had the profundity of yours with Ava. You two really loved each other. We just like each other.'

'What about me?' Mira droned. 'I have the worst track record around. Fifteen years with a man I probably stopped loving after six months.'

'You had kids,' Iso offered, always nourishing, salving.

'I've thought a lot about it. You know, since Ben and I have been together. At first, I really wanted it kept private – I just wanted to be with him.'

'We noticed,' Iso grinned.

'But after a while – when I was sure I loved him and he, me – I wanted – what do they say in the popular songs – to shout it from the rooftops. I wanted to go out with him in the world, to announce us as a unity, to say, we love each other, we are together. Not for the sake of showing off, but out of, well, joy. And of togetherness. I mean, it's as though you have a new identity; you're Mira, and you're Mira and Ben. You want the world to recognize both. It's a corporation of the heart, a new emotional identity. Then, I guess, you want that identity

434

legitimated, you want it to be legal identity as well. So you get married, you have these ceremonies and official seals so that people have to treat you as a unity. But then, of course, you – well, women, anyway – lose the other one, the private one. Men don't seem to, quite as much. I don't know why. But once you have this unified identity, once it is an entity in the world, it's hard to give up.'

Val shrugged. 'I never had that with Grant.'

Iso laughed. 'Could anybody? He came in sullen and left sullen, wherever he went. And he came and went alone.'

'That's because he was angry with me all the time for not living with him, for not always meeting first and going together.'

'So why couldn't you break up with him sooner?'

Val was exasperated. 'I don't know! That's exactly what I don't know!'

It was only about a month later that Val appeared with someone new in tow. People talked about this. Her friends accepted it as they accepted everything any of them did unquestioningly, but even they wondered about it. It was not his age, although he was only twenty-three. It was his personality. In the year that he had been at Harvard, he had developed a small reputation for insanity.

Tadziewski was tall, fair, blond, blue-eyed, and beautiful. He was also extremely erratic. He was still gangly, and his eyes wandered, as you talked to him, in various directions. He, like Anton, was in the school of government, but people wondered why. He was a member of the peace group but his attendance was erratic, and when he went, he sat in the back and spoke little. When he did speak, he expressed himself so incoherently that everyone discounted what he said. Only a few women seemed to understand him, and they regarded him with affection and respect. On the rare occasions when his name came up, they defended his humanity, his sensitivity. Those were qualities incomprehensible to Anton and his colleagues, and they wrote his appeal off as sexual. It was not. His beauty was angelic, his body disconnected. One could not imagine him being sexual. The reason he sounded incoherent, Val said, was that he was so sensitive, so acute about people's vulnerabilities, that whenever he spoke, he went round and round, trying to find ways to say what he wanted to say without offending anyone, not because he was afraid of their disliking him but because he shrank from wounding them. 'He's not for this world,' she concluded. 'It's funny to hear myself say that. What he is is humane. But there are damned few people with any humanity at all in that crew dedicated to saving lives in Southeast Asia. Men,' she added with disgust.

One evening after a long meeting, Val walked down the two flights of rickety wooden stairs in the house Julius lived in, and found Tad standing in the entry. For a moment she thought he was waiting for her, then decided she was mistaken, and started out.

'Can I talk to you?' His voice jutted out so rapidly she did not understand what he'd said, but she stopped and turned. His eyes were shining at her. 'I never believed it, but the metaphor is true,' Val told Iso and Mira. 'His eyes looked like stars.'

He stumbled, stuttered something about how he enjoyed her remarks at meetings, and that he would like to know her better. She gazed at him gravely.

'I just didn't know where he was coming from. He could have felt that I was one of the few people in the group who listened to him – which is true – and wanted in some way to express gratitude for that. He might have wanted sympathy, support. He might have been drowning and grabbed out at me as a life jacket. He might have been coming on sexually – although that seemed unlikely. But I couldn't tell – he is so awkward, so unworldly, that he has no notion of trying to create an image – which I like, but which makes it difficult to read someone – anyway, I didn't know how to respond.'

'Thank you. I find your remarks interesting too.'
'No one understands them. I'm on a different plane.'

436

'That could be.'

'They don't know how to get beyond ego.'

'Oh? What does that mean?'

'They're so involved with their own egos, they have no room for larger concerns.'

'Yes,' Val said doubtfully. Although she damned the men in the group for their egotism, she had a strong suspicion that she and Tad did not mean the same thing by the word.

'You get beyond ego,' he said eagerly. 'That's what I like about you.'

'Umm.' Val was puzzled. It seemed to her that she was as self-involved as the others; the difference was only that her self-involvement included others, and theirs did not. When they talked about the good of humanity, they meant what they thought humanity ought to consider good. When she did it, she spoke gropingly, as one trying to discover what felt good to people, using herself as an example.

'I get beyond ego,' Tad insisted. 'I am killing the ego.'

'Are you sure that's a good idea?'

He paled and pulled back. 'Well of course! Don't you?'

'No.' She was weary, and not up to a mystical discussion. 'But keep up your effort,' she smiled, and walked swiftly out of the door.

After that, she paid even more attention to the things he said – when he spoke – at the meetings he attended. She heard more acutely his carefulness not to violate another's standing place, and although she thought it was wasted effort, liked him for it. 'Can you imagine worrying about Anton's feelings? That's like an Appalachian farmer worrying that his stream might interfere with TVA!'

During the Harvard strike the meetings were long and tumultuous. Brad and Anton, who were members of SDS, wanted to merge efforts with other groups; others agreed to a degree; others did not. The group had a series of frustrating and finally destructive meetings.

One night there was a meeting of representatives of all camps at Brad's house. Val left late, discouraged. It was clear to her that the effect of the strike would be to fragment the group. She descended the stairs heavily. Tad, who had attended for a while, but left early, was standing in the entry. This time it was unmistakable; he was waiting for her. She sighed. She was not up to metaphysical discussion. She smiled a little, tried to pass him, but he put his hand on her arm.

'You were brilliant tonight.'

She turned to him, smiling tiredly, but suddenly he had his arms around her. He pushed her against the wall, he kissed her. His passion was so strong that her body reacted, uncertain as her mind was. He kept kissing her, and she kissed him back. His eyes and face were moist. She put her hand on his arm.

'Tad . . .'

'No! No! I won't listen!' His eyes were large and starry and moist. 'I don't know how else . . . I tried to tell you . . . I tried to do it politely, but I don't know how . . . Don't push me away, you can't push me away, you pushed me away, you just slid by me last time. I don't know how to tell you.'

He stood there, looking intensely into her face, his right hand gently, gently caressing her hair. 'I love you,' he said. Now, Val was an old hand. She knew the range of interpretation possible to those words. But the boy touched her. She was intensely aware of their position. She did not know why, but she would have been unhappy had Julius or Anton descended the staircase at that moment. Their mocking, brilliant eyes, their twisting mouths – she did not want to look at the two of them, Tad and her, through the eyes of Julius or Anton. But she could not, in humanity, simply push the boy away.

'We can't stay here,' she said. 'I have my car. Why don't you come back to my place and we can talk?'

He went with her as if it were the most natural thing in the world that he do so, as if it were to be expected. He walked down the outside steps and down the sidewalk to the car, with his arm around her, as if something were settled between them. Val felt this, and was able even to think it. She did not quite know how to handle it. What was she doing with this boy?

Chris was asleep when they arrived, and Val fixed drinks for her and Tad and sat down in the living room in a single chair, rather than taking her usual place on the couch. Tad sat on a couch at a right angle to her, pressing against the table that stood beside it, as close to her as he could get.

'I've loved you from the beginning,' he said. 'You're so beautiful!' His eyes and face were shining. 'I knew it had to end this way.'

'End? It hasn't ended,' Val said seriously, kindly. 'I don't know how it will end. How can you?'

'It had to,' he insisted, and then was on her again with his passion and his delicacy, and Val's body at least responded, and it ended as he had anticipated.

'And he's a great lover,' Val said thoughtfully. 'Isn't that strange? You wouldn't expect that from him. He seems so disconnected. But he cares above all about me, about pleasing me. Which makes him, in my book,' she laughed, 'a great lover!'

'This is one time,' Mira taunted her, 'when it wasn't the guy who was dense.'

'True,' she shook her head. 'I'm not sure, if I'd had a choice, I'd have chosen to get into this. But I didn't have a choice. Not given who I am. It was all so clear for him ... he had fantasized it, I guess, so often ... the ending, as he called it, was so inevitable. How can you ruin the endings of someone's fantasy?'

'His fantasy is enough for you?' Iso challenged.

'It seems so,' Val said, puzzled.

3

Tad and Val became a togetherness in a way she and Grant had not. People snickered and whispered, but Val really didn't care. She was aware, because under her assertiveness Val was perceptive, of the tone of people's remarks about her and Tad. They saw her involvement

439

with him as a descent, whether they blamed her for being a cradle-snatcher or for lowering her intellectual standards. Tad was viewed as a nut by the small circle who knew him.

But Val came to love Tad, not just because he adored her, but because he was so discriminating, had such high standards for behavior, and although she did not agree with him about much, she admired his attempt to get beyond the narrow needs of what he called ego to a place of larger understanding.

Everyone was happy that summer. Most people were taking summer courses, trying to get language or seminar requirements out of the way. Iso and Kyla were reading Dante, Mira was reading Spenser, and Val was taking something to do with statistics – hideous but necessary for her degree. Ben was on crate three of his notes.

The women met for lunch every day. Often they were joined by Clarissa, who was reading Faulkner with a celebrated visiting professor. Others drifted in and out. But it was during this summer that the women really meshed into a group.

Political action had moved elsewhere : most students and faculty had gone, and the movement went on in basements and attics in New York, Boston, and Chicago. The summer people drifted in and the scent of the reefer was smelled in Holyoke Center. Those were the days of runaways and road people. Some looked very young, some past middle age, but their faces all had a timeless quality, as if things had stopped for them, or rather, if they lived in an eternally extended now, and had neither past nor future. One or another would be seen sitting against the brick Yard wall along Mass Ave, in front of the Coop, against the wall near the Holyoke Center. Their eyes were both blank and hostile : perhaps those are the same thing.

The women's days were exciting, hot, and easy. Their work was fun, their coming together was fun, and since it was summer, and they felt entitled to allow themselves some days off, they would occasionally drive together to the beach. The life of graduate students may sound easy.

440

In fact, most of them worked harder than most people. But because their work was self-generated and self-controlled, they did not have to find relaxation at the water cooler or the food truck, on fifteen minutes – stretched to twenty or thirty – of company time. They could save up their leisure, working for long hours at a stretch, and allowing themselves a day of complete freedom from work every eight or ten days : in the summer, at least.

Iso's apartment was nearest the Square, and in the late afternoons they would stop in there, carrying soda or wine. There was always somebody there. Iso shone. She was wearing white shorts and tight white jerseys, and as she grew tanner, her hair fairer, her freckles deeper, she looked more and more like the all-American girl. The women sat around talking about things they never talked about elsewhere, playing games that were not games.

'What games did you like to play when you were little, Clarissa?'

'Oh, hopscotch and jumprope and king of the mountain. I especially liked king of the mountain until I got into football. But football is my all-time favorite.'

'What about you, Mira?'

'After that, you ask me? Memory – it's a card game. School – I was always the teacher. And Monopoly.'

Around they would go, laughing at themselves and each other. Iso's game was softball; Kyla liked racing, tag and taking care of tropical fish; Val didn't like games, but remembered loving to build an Oriental tent in the backyard and lie on cushions eating her lunch, drinking homemade lemonade with fresh mint leaves in it, and reading and writing novels.

And on the special day, they would drive up the coast, sometimes with Tad or Ben – Harley and Duke never went with them – to Gloucester or Crane's beach. They swam, read, played cards; sometimes they packed chicken and salad and beer and eggs and ate on the beach. Such days seemed utter happiness to them : a car was a luxury, a day out of the city was royal magnificence.

Occasionally, Mira and Ben went off by themselves.

They went to Walden and walked around the pond holding hands and swam illegally, out of sight of the beach, in a little cove they pretended was private. They looked at the stone remains of Thoreau's chimney and tried to imagine what it had been like here a hundred-odd years ago. They visited Concord and Lexington, Salem, Plymouth, traveled with the full satisfaction of people who are excited by each other but who are not totally caught up only in the other. Things are more fun shared if they are shared so.

In August, most people disappeared. Iso made her annual trip back to California; Kyla and Harley, Clarissa and Duke made their parental visits. Chris returned from visiting her father and went with Val and Tad to a place Val had rented on the Cape. Mira and Ben went down to visit for a few days.

It was delightful. They went riding, they swam in the mild bay water or drove across to the surf and rolled and dove in that. They sat around late at night giggling and drinking and Indian wrestling and leg wrestling and playing cards. Tad and Ben cooked the meat on the outdoor grill that had come with the cottage and Val and Mira and Chris had a wonderful time making potato salad and coleslaw together. The cottage was on a pleasant street with many trees and they sat outdoors at night, their empty paper plates getting soggy, and listened to the insect noises and watched the sky slowly turn lavender and purple, and smelled the rustling clear summer evening air and spoke idly, in low voices. After Cambridge and its noise and soot, it seemed paradise, at least until the mosquitoes came out. Then they went in and started drinking and got rowdy.

Mira and Ben just stayed. They mentioned, after two days, that they ought to leave, but Val shouted 'Why?' and that was that. They chipped in for food and liquor, but after four days, they began to get apprehensive. 'We really have to go,' Mira insisted, not wanting to, one night as they sat in a circle on the floor playing cards.

'Listen, the landlord called me today. The people who were supposed to take this place for the last two weeks of August have pooped out. The landlord has their deposit, of course, and he asked me if I wanted the cottage at a cheaper rate for the rest of the month. I can't afford it, but why don't you two take it, and we'll come down and visit *you*?' She looked at them grinning. 'Just so you won't get lonely.'

Mira smiled broadly and reached over and grabbed Val's arm.

'It wouldn't have been the same without you all here.' She sat looking at her friend with love. The four days had been a brief but beautiful experiment in communal living. But the boys were coming up for the last two weeks in August. There was no way they could . . .

'Great!' Ben said. 'How much is it? We can surely scrape up two hundred bucks between us.'

'Mom,' Chris said in a low voice, but sharply, 'I thought we were going shopping for clothes for college next week.'

'We will, we will,' Val smiled, rumpling Chris's hair. 'How long can it take to buy a pair of jeans and three tops?'

'And boots.'

Mira shuffled the cards. They were all sitting on the floor in a circle, playing poker. Ben had looked to Mira when he made his suggestion, and he was still looking at her, but she had not looked back at him. He had made the suggestion that they take the place with joy in his voice, and had expected her radiant smile to meet his, but she was looking down, shuffling.

'You don't seem too enthused.'

'I wish you wouldn't use a nonexistent word, Ben,' she said sharply.

'What the fuck's the matter?' His voice rose.

'Nothing,' she said with a tight mouth. 'Nothing at all.' Then she stood up and went into the toilet. Ben looked at Val. Val shrugged her shoulders. They all looked at each other. The noisy fun they had been having evaporated into silence. They sipped drinks; the ice clinked in the glasses.

'You think she wants to keep playing?'

443

'It's her deal.'

'Well, we'll wait.'

'Anybody ready for a drink?' Val rose and went into the kitchen. 'Tad, is there any more tonic?'

'How should I know? I don't know.'

'Jesus, the gin is finished.'

'No, I bought more, Val,' Ben called. 'It's under the sink.'

'Mom! And a jacket. A blue denim jacket. And some sweaters. And underwear. And I guess I should get a dress.'

'What in hell for?' Yelled from the kitchen.

Chris began to protest. 'Listen, Mom, how do I know? There may be some college thing I have to go to where I should wear a dress.'

Val returned with the drinks, smiling broadly at her daughter. Chris looked at her and relaxed. She patted her mother's hand. 'A long dress. Real sexy.'

'And a mink stole. What you really need is some pajamas and a robe.'

'What for?'

'Chris, in some places it is conventional to wear something to bed.'

'Do you?'

'I don't live in a dorm . . .'

Ben stood up and walked toward the bathroom. The conversation stopped, then Val continued. Ben went into the bathroom and closed the door. Val looked at Tad and Chris.

'How about a slam-bang game of three-handed solitaire?'

They played hearts. Finally Mira and Ben came out of the bathroom. Mira's face was swollen and pink. Ben was tense and taciturn. They rejoined the group. Val tried to talk to them, and they answered her, but they did not look at or speak to each other. Finally, Val folded up her cards.

'Mira, did I do something? I know I have a big mouth. What's wrong? Please tell us.'

Mira shook her head, biting her lower lip. 'No,' she

444

answered tremulously. 'It's no one's fault. It's me. You just can't transcend the past, I guess.' She stood up, her voice a liquid lump in her throat. 'My taste was bitter, my taste was me,' she added desolately with the soupy despair that alcohol can bring to the surface. 'I'm going for a walk. I'll be back.' And left.

They were silent until her footsteps stopped echoing on the flagstone path that led from the front door to the street. Then all of them turned and looked at Ben. He shook his head, looked down at his drink, looked up at them with liquid eyes.

'She says I'm insensitive.'

'To what?'

'To her feelings about her sons. She says she could never, not in a million years, stay with me and her sons in the same house. I asked if she had been planning to banish me from her life when they came. She said she expected me to come over for dinner one night: that was it. I said it was nice of her to tell me. I guess I got nasty. I mean, what am I, a sex maniac or something? They're sixteen and seventeen years old, not exactly ignorant of the facts of life.' He gulped his drink. He shook his head like a dog that has come in out of the rain. 'She acts as if she's ashamed of me.'

'More likely of herself,' Val murmured.

'She made it sound like a disgusting thing – to have your children and your lover under the same roof.' He looked up at Val, then at Chris, then blushed. 'Not in principle, just for her,' he amended.

'Well, it is a problem,' Val said, letting him off the hook he thought he was caught on. 'For all of us, the women who end up with kids. It takes a lot of thought.'

Chris leaned forward with her chin in her hand, lying across the cards. 'Did you give it a lot of thought, Mom?'

'Yes.'

'How old was I?'

'About two. I'd been divorced from your father for about a year when I met this guy . . . there were choices. I mean, I could have gone out to a motel with him. I didn't have to bring him home.'

445

'But you did?'

Val nodded, and Chris laughed, 'And you've been bringing them home ever since.'

Ben looked at Chris. 'And how do you feel about that? If it's not too impolitic a question,' he added, looking at Val.

Val spread her hands. 'That's up to Chris to say.'

Chris shrugged. 'It's okay. I guess if I had to choose between having Mom home and having her go out, I'd choose the first. I guess maybe I would have liked it if she had decided to become what do you call it?' She appealed to her mother.

'A nun? A gray-haired grandmotherly type sitting home waiting for you to come home and knitting you long woolen stockings.'

'Yeah,' Chris grinned. '*Celibate!* You know, devoting her whole life to little old me.'

'Do you have any idea,' Val said making a fake mean mouth, 'what I would have *charged* you for that?'

'Some,' Chris agreed. 'Lisa's mother is divorced and she does that. It's a heavy trip. Anyway, sometimes it annoys me when there's somebody around I hardly know, and I have to be sure to close the bathroom door, or to have clothes on when I walk around the apartment, or when I want to talk to Mom and she's occupied with somebody else. That's when I walk around slamming doors and other objects. But sometimes it's nice to have a guy around, even if he is feebleminded,' she pushed her face, making slit eyes, toward Tad, who pushed in her nose. 'It sort of feels like having a family. But the times I really can't stand it are when I don't like the guy . . .'

'Yeah!' Val leaped in. 'Some people have trouble with their parents, I have it with my kid! If I invite somebody she doesn't like, she is so mean and vicious that he doesn't stay long.'

'I'm always right, aren't I?' Chris asked seriously.

'You're always right in your estimate of them. But you don't understand me. I mean, sometimes there's just nobody around who is up to one's standards, but I, I get lonely, I want to make love, I want to talk to a man –

much as I love women, I like some balance – so I bring home a limited creature. After all, everybody can't be God's gift to the human race . . .'

'That's all academic now,' Tad said authoritatively. 'You have me now.'

Val swung around to him with astonishment. He looked in her face with devotion, and reached out and took her hand. She let him take it, but she turned away looking thoughtful.

Ben frowned. 'I don't know. Mira just kept saying – crying – that it was disgusting. She said it over and over. I asked her if she thought it was disgusting that you lived with Tad – out here, at least – and she said that was different, Chris was just a baby when you got divorced, and that she was a girl and that was different – but then she burst out that she was shocked when she first realized Grant was your lover and stayed with you sometimes.'

'Well,' Val said wearily, 'one thing is sure. She loves you.'

'How do you make that out? Love is a blackboard eraser? When I'm inconvenient, she can wipe me out of her life?'

'That's another thing. But I don't think she'd be so upset if her feelings for you were not so intense. You know, she hasn't much of a relation with her sons. It's probably all the emotions around that are pulling her apart. She's thinking about how they would feel, knowing the three of them aren't that close, seeing her with you . . . You can understand that, can't you?'

'I guess.'

Val sat up and crossed her legs, lotus position. She leaned her head toward Ben. She was a little drunk, and her voice took on the childish tone that was common when she was in that state. 'Well, now, Ben, I'm serious, and you'd better listen to me.'

He leaned forward and kissed her lightly on the lips. 'I'm listening.'

Tad's arm jerked, and his head became very erect.

'Oooookay!' she pronounced, sitting back. 'Who's for

447

a slam-bang game of . . .' She peered around, counting them slowly. 'One, two, three . . . oh, well . . . oh! I'm four! How about a slam-bang game of bridge?'

<h1 style="text-align:center">4</h1>

Ben's suggestion that they rent the cottage had so appalled Mira that for a time she could not think. It outraged her in some place she never before knew to exist, and was suddenly forced not only to recognize, but also to explore. She walked down toward the beach; the night was warm and the crickets were singing love songs. The sky was dark here, far from the neon-lighted city, and the stars stood out brilliantly against it. She asked herself question after question. Was it because her life had been so sheltered, so *normal*, so much what popular morality said it was supposed to be, that she had never been forced to make a moral choice, and so was helpless in this terrain? She could remember mentally castigating people who regarded adultery as mortal sin. But she also remembered her shock when she realized that Bliss was actually having an affair with Paul. At the time, she had told herself that what upset her was the betrayal of Adele, who considered Bliss her best friend. She reminded herself that she had not been horrified when Martha got involved with David. But of course, Martha and George were honest with each other, there was no deceit involved.

But what deceit was involved here? Her sons knew she was divorced, they lived in the same house with their father and his second wife whenever they visited. They would understand that she too . . . They would have to understand! Who were they to judge her? Was she not entitled to her own life, to *a* life, to friendship and love?

She reached the beach. The bay was still, only rippling under the moon. The sand was deserted, although there were some cars parked at its rim, cars with people in them. She averted her head stiffly, and walked down toward the water.

She could not come up with a single logical reason

why she should be so upset by the idea of the boys staying with – no, it was not even that – just knowing about
her and Ben. She prodded and poked this area of her
mind, this newly discovered territory, and risked pain
with each motion, but she could not find answers. She
walked and walked. In time, weary and wanting to
sleep, she decided to return to the cottage, but by this
time, she felt like a walking toothache, and she blamed
Ben for her pain. After all, she had lived all these years
without ever having to feel precisely this way, without
ever having to ask such questions, all these years she had
gone her happy calm way without having this dentist's
pick probe at her sore spots. Why couldn't he understand
her delicacy? He was insisting, pushing her, being un-
conscionable and insensitive.

Poisoning my existence, she thought.

She walked back slowly. The image of Ben in her
mind was horrible. She never wanted to see him again.
It gave her agony to think she was going to have to walk
back into the cottage and face him and even sleep in the
same bed with him – perforce. There were only three
bedrooms. Perhaps she could sleep with Chris. Or on the
living room couch. It would be horrible to have to put
one's body in the same bed with that creature.

In two days her sons were coming to visit. They would
stay only two weeks. She saw them rarely. They were
her children. They took up little enough of her time.
Why did he have to intrude on that, why did he have to
barge in as if he belonged there?

She stopped. Tears were streaming down her face. She
tried to remember how she had felt yesterday, when she
was so full of love for Ben. She tried to recall the first
night they made love. It was useless. The memory was
like a news story about a foreign place: full of facts
with no texture. He did this, he did that; she felt this, she
felt that. She had an orgasm. Yes. It had probably been
good. But that was in another country and besides, the
wench is dead. It would be tinged with bitterness forever in her memory because it had led up only to this,
inevitably to this. She had not seen what he was. He was

an intolerable pressure. He was a hulking darkness, trying to take over her life.

Her heart felt like a bruised prune. Miserably, she returned to the cottage. The lights were on, but everyone had gone to bed. When she opened the front door, Val came stumbling out of the bedroom, pulling a robe loosely about her.

'You okay?' she asked sleepily.

Mira nodded.

'I'm sorry I can't talk to you. I'm just so tired,' Val apologized.

'It's okay.'

'Well – it's an old saw, but it's true. Things do look different in the morning.'

Mira nodded stiffly. She was too timid to ask Val if she thought Chris would mind if she slept with her, and too timid to barge into Chris's room, so she undressed in the bathroom and put on a nightgown and crept into the bed where Ben lay sleeping. She was quiet and stiff, trying not to make the bed move. He was lying on his side, facing away from her. She lay stiffly on her side, facing away from him. She was aware, after a few moments, that he was not asleep. His breathing was awake breathing. But he did not, thankfully, speak. She lay stiffly, trying to keep her body from relaxing and filling up more space and possibly touching his. After a long time, his breathing became heavier and his body relaxed a bit and curled up. He can sleep, she thought bitterly. Because she could not. She dozed on and off in the course of the night, but in the morning felt as if her insides had taken poison and her outside showed it.

Nothing was better in the morning. Silently, Mira and Ben packed their things and loaded her car, said muted good-byes to Val and Chris and Tad, and silently they drove back the long quiet road along the Cape and back to Boston. Ben drove to his place and got out, and took his suitcase and casting rod out of the back seat. He stood beside the car for a moment, while she slid over to the driver's seat, but she would not look at him. She was afraid her face would betray her true feelings, would reflect its hate for this huge intruder who was nothing to her, who was trying to jam himself into her life, to take it over, yes, that was it, a typical male, trying to run her life, to mold it into his image, to press into it the imprint of his huge thumb.

She drove off. He did not call. The boys arrived, and she tried to act happy. She took them to Walden and Salem and Gloucester and Rockport. Numb, she walked with them the paths and streets she had walked only in the last two months with Ben, feeling such joy. She took them to a Szechuan restaurant and they enjoyed it: their taste had broadened a bit. She took them to an Italian restaurant and they ordered something besides spaghetti. Numbly, she spoke to them; they answered from a distance. They had not brought the TV set up with them, but after two nights of watching them fiddle restlessly, she rented one for them. But they did not watch it as much as they had the last time. She even saw each of them with a book at one time or another.

One night, after they had been with her for a little over a week, Mira was sitting in the dark living room with her brandy and cigarette. The boys were in the bedroom watching TV, or so she thought. Because Clark idled in and sat down across from her. He did not speak, he only sat there, and Mira's feelings reached across to him, thankful to him for sharing her isolation, her silence, the dark.

'Thanks, Mom,' he said suddenly.

'Thanks? For what?'

'For taking us around to all those places. You have a lot of other things to do. And you've been to them before. You must've been bored.'

He had picked up her mood, and interpreted it as boredom. 'I wasn't bored,' she said.

'Well, anyway, thanks,' he said.

It was no good. He had picked up her mood and if she didn't explain, would assume she had been bored, and now was merely being polite. She did not know what to do. 'It was the least I could do,' she heard a prissy voice

451

saying. 'I haven't much to offer you boys. Your father ...'

'He never spends any time with us,' Clark cut her off in a new, sharp voice. 'We were there all summer. He took us out on the boat three times, with his wife and a whole bunch of friends. He doesn't ever talk to us. He sends us out of the room when the conversation starts to get ... well, you know.'

'No, I don't know.'

'Well ...'

'You mean when they start to talk about sex?'

'Oh, no! No, Mom,' he exclaimed, and his voice was full of disgust. 'Those people never talk about sex. I mean – well, when somebody talks about someone who got divorced, or a guy who cheated on his income tax ... you know. Whenever they talk about anything *real*,' he concluded, 'anything beside politenesses.'

'Oh.'

They were silent together.

Clark tried again. 'Anyway, it was nice of you, especially when we don't act very – well, interested, you know.'

'You were better this time than last. At least,' she added sarcastically, 'you gave signs of life this time.'

She thought: he handed me a weapon and I used it. She wondered why. She wondered what she was really saying. It came to her that she was profoundly reproaching him, her son, reproaching him for existing, for being her son, for being, over the years, so much trouble and so little reward, for having needed to have his diapers changed, for waking her in the middle of the night, for chaining her to a kitchen and bathroom and house, for being her life as well as his own and not being worth it. What would be worth it? If he were a Picasso, a Roosevelt, would that repay her? But he was sixteen, and untalented. Above all she was blaming him and Normie for her misery. She had to face it: she felt it was them or Ben. She'd chosen them but she'd never forgive them for that.

Clark stood up finally. He would, she knew, sidle out

of the room. She had to say something, but her mind whirred. She did not know what she should say.

'Clark.'

He took a step toward her. She stretched out her arm, and he moved forward and took her hand.

'Thank you for thanking me.'

'That's okay,' he said generously.

'Would you like to have dinner with some of my friends?' she said nervously.

He shrugged slightly. 'Sure. I guess.'

'I'll invite them for dinner. I don't know who's in town, but I'll call them. I have the most wonderful friends here, Clark – well, you've met Iso – they're all really interesting people.' She heard herself babbling.

They were still holding hands, and he raised and lowered his arm, so they were shaking hands, arms, gently, slowly.

'The reason,' she began in the same almost hysterical babble, 'the reason you thought I was bored was because I have been very unhappy.'

He let go her hand. Her heart stopped. He must, of course, be sick of hearing about her unhappiness. He sat down at her feet and looked at her. In the darkness, the streetlight shone in right on his young, clear face. He was looking at her, his eyes like blotters.

'Why?' he asked gently.

Norm's rangy form appeared in the doorway, silhouetted by the lights in the hall. He moved into the room and switched on (just like his father, she thought) the overhead lamp.

'In or out!' she announced, and heard Val's voice. 'In either case, no light!'

He switched it off.

'You're welcome to come in, Norm. If you want. We've just been talking.'

He edged in and sat on the arm of the couch, near the door.

'The reason,' she recapitulated for Norm's sake, 'I may have seemed bored to you this past week is that I have been unhappy. I've been unhappy because,' she

453

paused, trying to figure out what the reason was, 'I think I made a mistake.'

They said nothing, but Norm slid off the arm and onto the seat of the couch.

'I have a boyfriend,' she began, then paused.

'Yeah?' Norm's new deep voice – for it had deepened further this year – came from the corner.

'I have a lover,' she amended. 'At least I did. And he wanted the four of us to take a cottage at Cape Cod for these two weeks. And I got very upset with him for that. I was too embarrassed. I was afraid of what you might think or feel.'

There was a heavy silence. All I have done, she thought, is to shift the burden to them.

'Why were you embarrassed?' Clark asked finally.

'Yeah,' Norm said. 'It's nice you have someone to love you. I wish I did,' his voice trailed off.

I love you, she was about to say, then closed her mouth. Her heart hit hard against itself. That was it. That lay beneath all the lies. Mother loves you, son, but she can't screw you, you can't screw her. It's against the rules. But she knows that to prove her love, she must not screw anyone else; you must therefore not screw anyone else either. And we will all live happily ever after in a paradise where no one even has genitals.

'It's true, he does seem to love me.' Her voice sounded high and childlike and incredulous.

'Why shouldn't he?' Clark's voice out of the darkness sounded tough compared to hers. 'You're beautiful!'

'I'm not beautiful, Clark . . .'

'To me you are!' he answered fiercely.

She listened; she heard love and loyalty and she felt almost as if she had been wearing a mudpack and had sat in the sun, and the thing had hardened and cracked and all of a sudden, fallen off.

'Maybe I'll call him.'

They were silent. It was after eleven, and no doubt they were not eager for visitors. But suddenly she did not care what they wanted. They had asked her to be. They would accept that. And what she was, wanted Ben. She

454

stood up, excited, the excitement coming through in her voice. 'I'll call him. He may be asleep, or he may be out, but I think I'll just give him a ring.'

5

He answered the phone in a tired voice, and when she said, a little timidly, 'Ben?' his voice went tight and hard.

'Yeah.'

'Ben, I see it all now. Oh, well, maybe I don't see it all. But I see something. I would very much like to have you come over and meet my boys.'

'You're sure I won't pollute them,' he said bitterly, and it was only then that she realized how hurt he had been.

'Oh, Ben.' Her voice was full of tears. 'I'm sorry.'

'I'll be right there,' he said.

And came in twenty minutes later, charging like a brisk wind, and talked to them about football and baseball and school and lousy teachers. They were stiff at first, then grew easier and talked in a lively way, then started to yawn – it was after twelve – and grew, finally, simply bored. Enough adult talk. They drifted off to bed, and Mira looked at Ben and he at her, and they moved toward each other the way they had the first night they made love, gracefully, naturally, both moving toward the couch, and sitting, a little apart, just looking at each other for a while, then reaching out for the other's hands. They did not speak at all. They heard one boy, then another, in the bathroom, heard the light click off, the bedroom door close, and after a few minutes, total silence. Then they embraced, and Mira found her cheeks wet and herself blubbering, 'Oh, God, how I've missed you!' and Ben rubbed his cheeks against hers so one could not tell if he was wet from her or from himself and blubbering too, said, 'I felt exiled to Siberia.'

Then they could not contain themselves, they could not contain their hands, and soon they were making love, right there on the living room couch and in a living room without a door, with the boys sleeping just down the

455

hall. She could not understand herself, but she did not stop to try: at the time, making love was the only thing that mattered to her. But afterward, after many hours and a few cigarettes, and a drink, Ben got up and dressed to go home.

'You don't have to go,' she said desperately, clutching his arm. 'I don't feel that way anymore . . . I . . . I don't want you to go.'

'Sweetheart, this couch isn't even very comfortable to sit on, much less to sleep on. But if two of us try to sleep on it, we'll both need a chiropractor tomorrow. And since I don't approve of chiropractors, I think I'd better go home.'

'Go home then, you shit,' she murmured lovingly, sleepily. 'Knowing,' she turned over on her back and spread her arms and legs, 'knowing you have abandoned the woman who loves you to the cold, the isolation, the loneliness of an empty bed.'

He bent and kissed her gently. 'Good,' he hissed viciously. 'It serves her right.'

She kissed him back. 'Just be sure to be here at six tomorrow night for dinner, or else! . . .'

Next day, she asked the boys for their reactions to Ben. They agreed he was 'okay.' He was even nice, they finally admitted. They had met some boys in a neighboring house: would she mind if they did not go sightseeing that day, but went to the neighborhood park and played ball?

Wonderful!

She got on the phone and called all her friends, but only Val and Iso were in town. She invited them for dinner. Then she went to Savenor's and loaded up her shopping cart. She had not bought so much food since she was married and planning a party. She was in an ecstasy of bliss. The sun shone, she hummed, she drove back like a blessed madwoman, narrowly missing accidents by swerving the car with the tempos of her body. She carried the heavy bags up the two flights to her apartment without gasping for breath. She turned on the radio: violins poured out a waltz. She danced into the

456

kitchen, unloaded her purchases, put beef bones in a great pot to simmer, and began to wash and chop vegetables. Sun was pouring through the kitchen windows. Outside she heard small children playing, arguing down in the yard over the water hose.

Peace cupped her heart and held it gently.

Smiling, she stood at the kitchen sink, holding a bunch of string beans in her hand, letting herself be part of it: part of the gold streaming over the kitchen, part of the mellow surge of the waltz, part of the green of the trees bowing outside the window. It was beauty and peace, the child noises outside, the delicious simmering aroma of the soup, the fresh liquid green smell of the string beans. Her home was humming happy and bright, and Ben – sexy, exciting Ben – was coming at six. It was happiness.

She brought herself upright. My God! She dropped the string beans, dried her hands, sank into a chair, and lighted a cigarette. It was the American Dream, female version. Was she still buying it? She didn't even like to cook, she resented marketing, she didn't really like the music that was sweeping through the apartment. But she still believed in it: the dream stood of the happy humming house. Why should she be so happy doing work that had no purpose, no end, while the boys were off playing and Ben was off doing work that would bring him success, work that mattered?

She got up and skimmed the broth, pondering the question, but she could not keep the joy out, it invaded her again like sun pouring over her head and arms. The boys came home for something to drink.

'How about keeping me company?'

'Sure! Can we cook?' Norm asked eagerly.

She handed him the string beans and a vegetable knife and told him how to cut them. She set Clark to chiffonade the cabbage. She was careful not to watch them work, remembering her own mother's untrusting surveillance of her at chores, and her resulting hatred of helping in the kitchen.

'Yick!' Clark shouted in disgust. She looked up dismayed from the onions she was peeling.

457

'What is it?'

'That soupy music! Wet-dream music: isn't that what Iso calls it?'

She laughed. 'Get what you want. Just not too loud.' He went into the living room, fiddled with the radio, and found Joni Mitchell. He came back into the kitchen singing with her, softly, under his breath. Norm joined in. They finished the song with her, singing in faint sweet voices. Mira's eyes were wet as she sliced. One of them noticed it.

'Just the onions,' she smiled radiantly, then dropped her knife and embraced them both with her oniony hands, and they embraced her, the three of them standing there for some minutes. Then Mira went back to business.

'Shit! There's not enough oil.'

'Want me to go around to Zolli's?'

A small grocery store stood only two blocks from where Mira lived. However, on their first visit, her spoiled suburban children had refused to walk so far for more milk; they went only when they ran out of soda. But this time, Clark went with no complaint. Then she discovered she was out of salt: Norm went. An hour later, Clark went for more soda, then Norm went when she discovered she was low on coffee. The fifth time – Clark had used up the last fragment of toilet paper – both of them balked. She looked at them ready to sermonize, to remind them of their past spoiledness and laziness. But she had to laugh first: 'I guess I have a rotten memory.'

Clark said, 'I don't mind going, Mom, but that's a little store and the old guy that runs it is a grouch and when you come in again,' Clark began to giggle, 'he looks at you like you're crazy!'

Norm croaked, his voice still breaking, 'Yeah! Three times in one day!'

She laughed and forgot her sermon. They weren't lazy, they were embarrassed. She lifted her chin and pretended to grande-dame-ism. 'Tell them your mother is eccentric.'

The boys laughed and went off together.

Ben came at five-thirty with a bottle of wine, and she kissed him in front of her sons. Iso came in smiling and cornered the boys with talk of baseball, and a bet. Val came alone: Chris was having dinner with Bart's 'aunt', and Tad was visiting his parents for a few days. She challenged Ben immediately on some political issue, and Mira grinned over the stove as they argued. It was not the American Dream: it was much freer, much wilder.

She was proud of her dinner. They had a fine Brie, and good black olives with their drinks; then minestrone; then veau poêlé and brown rice and asparagus and a salad of spinach, avocado, and mushrooms with blue cheese dressing; then chilled grapes and melon. The meal went splendidly, and after dinner, the boys accepted the chore of dishes without balking. She went into the living room with Val and Iso and Ben and the remains of the wine, feeling warm and filled and content, and tried, in the back of her mind, to figure out what it was, content. And what it had to do with the American Dream. But her mind was too limpid with pleasure to work sharply. They talked; in time the boys joined them. They did not speak, but they did not yawn. They did not excuse themselves to go watch television. Of course, Iso kept getting them involved, asking them questions about their favorite television programs, their favorite sports, what kinds of clothes they liked. But the conversation kept moving away from the inarticulate boys. Still they sat there unblinking, unblinking through *subsume* and *recidivism* and *revisionist* and *cunt* and *ass* and *motherfucker*. Mira felt the evening had been some sort of triumph.

Val and Iso left before two: the boys were still sitting with them. After they left, Ben looked at her liquid-eyed. He was making no demands, but she felt herself demanding. She turned to her sons: 'Boys, I'm going to kick you out of the bedroom tonight. One of you can sleep on the couch, one in a sleeping bag. You can toss a coin. You're camping out tonight, okay?'

They agreed easily. She helped them make their beds,

Ben carried the TV set into the living room. They made drinks and went together into the bedroom and closed the door. They sprawled out across the bed, their drinks and an ashtray between them, and talked. The boys knocked a couple of times. Norm had forgotten his pajama bottom. Clark wanted his book. They wanted to know if it was okay to eat the leftover minestrone. Each time, they opened the door shyly, but with curiosity. Each time, Ben and Mira talked to them easily, desultorily. Once they were holding hands when Clark came in: and they went on holding hands while they talked to him. And the boys stood there looking down at their mother with her lover lying on the bed, looked, and did not blink. Mira wondered at the inexpressiveness of young faces. What were they feeling, if they were feeling anything?

Eventually lights went out in the apartment, silence fell. Then Mira tried to tell Ben about her experience that day, about her confusion about the American Dream. But he did not understand. No matter how she phrased it, he simply did not know what she was talking about. Besides, he was not very interested. He felt ardent, he kept tugging at her blouse; she wanted to go on talking. In time, she gave in, but she did not give in. Whether because he did not understand the profundity of her experience that day, or because of the presence of the boys, she felt a little isolated, apart from him. Their lovemaking that night was brief and quiet. She was grateful when Ben lay back and fell asleep.

6

When the boys were gone, and they were alone, Mira told Val about that day. Val understood immediately. 'It's that you can, for a moment, believe in enduring happiness.'

'Yes. And you think if you clutch it – whatever it is – you can, well, stop time, freeze the moment, preserve the joy.'

'But that's true of every happiness, not just this one.'

460

'Yes. But part of what brought me up short was that I was afraid of falling into the impulse toward permanence. But I was also shocked at how I was still buying the package, the *happy humming domesticity*, you know?' she cooed the phrase.

'But it was, wasn't it?'

'Val, we had so much fun that afternoon, the boys and I. We laughed, we sang . . .' She gazed wide-eyed at her friend. 'The vegetables smelled so fine and fresh, the sun was so bright! But I don't like to cook!' she insisted.

Valerie laughed. 'It's like me never really learning to type. I type all the time, of course, but even after all these years, I'm lousy at it. I didn't want to be excellent at something I was *supposed* to be able to do.'

'Oh,' Mira mock-moaned, 'nothing is ever simple. What do you do when you discover you *like* parts of the role you're trying to escape?'

They both laughed hopelessly.

'You're closer to the boys, aren't you?'

'Much. But still – I don't know. I worry. I still have such trepidations, Val. Guilt, I guess, but I can't seem to eradicate it. I do still feel it's shocking to have Ben here with them. And they – well, I don't know – they never mention him, they're noncommittal when I ask them what they think of him. And when we're all together, they tease him – but, well, there's a little – well – an edge to it. . . .'

'Hostility.'

Mira nodded.

'That's inevitable, you know? Strangeness, jealousy: he's an intruder in their house, in their lives. It's good they can let it out with a casing of good humor.'

Mira sighed. 'Of course. Why do I always panic if people aren't getting along perfectly? The least discord throws me for a loop, I start to think I'm doing something wrong, that I have to do something to eliminate it.'

'Now *that's* really the American Dream, female version.'

'Complete harmony, all the time. Oh, God, why don't

I remember that a little chaos is good for the soul? You know,' a smile crept around the edges of Mira's mouth, 'late last night, the phone rang. It was Clark. He wanted to ask me what courses he should sign up for next semester. He'd been with me for two weeks and said practically nothing, but last night he talked for two hours. Collect, of course.'

'Ooooooh!' Val laid her head in her hand. 'Ooooooh!'

Chris was leaving for college in a week, and Val, independent, antifamily Val, was in a moderate panic. She and Chris had been alone together for fifteen years; now that was ending.

Iso, sensing Val's anxiety, and imagining that Chris might feel anxious about leaving her mother and going off alone to Chicago, got the women together and planned a celebration. They piled into two cars and drove Chris to Logan – Val and Chris and Tad and Mira and Ben and Clarissa and Duke and Kyla (Harley couldn't come) and Bart. Following Iso's directions, they all dressed in costumes and carried signs and blowers and horns. Chris was pink with embarrassment and pleasure as they walked into the terminal.

They followed Chris on the round of ticket and baggage check, seat reservation. They were a group of oddments behaving oddly, who were nevertheless together. They stood outside the low railing surrounding the seats for customers (there were no barriers in those days, no bomb or gun checks) until the word came to queue up for boarding. Chris kissed them all, kissed and held her mother, then hurried to a place in line. Then they all hooted and hollered, whistled, cheered, blew blowers, waved signs.

Kyla was wearing her old cheerleader outfit; she kept jumping in the air and shouting, 'Yay, yay, who's okay? Chris, Chris, Chri-i-i-s!' Clarissa, in tight woolen pants and Indian blanket and headband, smiled enigmatically and waved a sign: 'Oh, Chicago, here Chris comes!' and occasionally blew the party blower she had locked between her teeth. Bart was done up from head to foot in shiny white leather; he too blew and while he was blowing, held his arms, clasped together in a victory sign above his head. Duke wore a sheet and a helmet like a Norse god's, and carried a trident and a sign: 'To Valhalla with you.' Tad seemed to be losing his costume, a sheet that was a cross between a toga and a loincloth. He looked bewildered, but occasionally tooted on his tin horn. Iso, in a sequinned jump suit and an aviator's cap pushed back on her head, waved a sign, blew a blower, whistled, yelled; and every once in a while adjusted Val's feather boa, which kept slipping down off her shoulders. Iso was the director, and waved her hand in command, urging crescendi as the line of passengers grew shorter. At the end they all shouted and blew and tooted and waved at once, they cried, 'Yay, Chris!' and Chris stood, looking at them, for once in clean blue jeans and a neat top and her hair combed, looking fifteen, and she tried to smile but her mouth trembled and she turned her head swiftly away and disappeared.

'Oh, my God, she's gone!' Val cried, and the group formed around her and embraced her and led her away and loaded themselves back into cars and drove back to her house and had a party that lasted until two in the morning.

My sister has a life like this. She lives in a small community; it has the usual discords, but when one of her friends is in trouble, the others gather round and lift up the hurt one, bandage her in love. They do little homely things that can't save, but salve. Probably everywhere there are little groups like that, groups whose order isn't legislated, can't be codified; they're flexible and shifting, people leave, people arrive, people die, but the group goes on, ruled by spirit, not codes, adapting to what happens.

My friends in Cambridge were like this, and more than anyone, it was Iso who taught us this kind of love. Her grandmother, whom she loved more than her own parents, had lived with her family all through Iso's childhood. She was a vivid, intelligent woman who always had time enough to play, imagination enough to pretend, and mind enough to speak the truth, even to a child. But through all those years, Lamia Keith had been ill with several diseases; that she was dying was certain. Yet she was always celebrating something, baking a cake, festooning the living room with crepe paper ribbons because she'd seen some frost on the grass, or the first fruit on the lemon tree in the front of the house. She bought horns and blowers and little gifts for every holiday from St. Patrick's to Columbus Day. Clarissa Dalloway said, 'Here's death – in the middle of my party.' Lamia Keith said, 'Here's a party! in the middle of my dying.' And Iso remembered.

The celebration at the airport gave them all ideas. Everyone planned parties. The problem was saving up enough money, and finding good dates to give them. They had plenty of ideas: come as your favorite fantasy figure; come as your favorite fictional character; come dressed as your favorite author and act out his/her personality all night.

The surroundings were sometimes shabby and the refreshments sparse, but the parties were brilliant. They played games: three or four members of a team would be assigned a plot and told to act it out in the styles of various authors. Val, Grete, and Brad were told to act out a husband's discovery of his wife's infidelity in the style of Henry James, Tennessee Williams, and Dostoyevsky. Val was assigned the husband's role because she was tallest. Iso, Kyla, and Duke had to act out the same subject in the style of Fielding, Scott Fitzgerald, and Norman Mailer, but Duke reneged, and Clarissa took his place. They would gather at Iso's, who had a great collection of old records, and all get down on the floor on one knee and sing 'Swanee' with Al Jolson, or moan 'The Man That Got Away' with Judy Garland. Couples would dance like Fred Astaire and Ginger Rogers to the music of the thirties and forties, and Iso perfected a dance in which she leaped up on the sofa cushions, stepped on its top, pushing it over, and leaped off and pirouette-tapped away. They came with canes and top hats and other strange equipment gathered from junk piles and attics. Ben and Tad perfected a sketch that was a takeoff on Beckett's *Waiting for Godot*; Grete and Avery acted out a love scene in the styles of French, Italian, British, and American movies. They lined up and danced the soft-shoe, or pretended to be the Rockettes. They made up poems, line by line, going around the room; they thought up plots for pornographic novels they never wrote, or for detective stories they planned to write.

The crowd attending the parties fluctuated, but at its center always were Iso, Clarissa, and Kyla, Mira and Ben, Val and Tad. Duke came when he was home, but he did not participate happily; Harley never came, although sometimes he would stop by late in the evening to pick Kyla up. Grete and Avery, who had become lovers, often came and acted out roles and played games with real gusto: Grete, especially, was a marvelous performer. But central to all the parties was Iso. It was from her the creative impulse came, and in a subliminal way, she dominated the gatherings. She'd grown very tan over the summer, and her hair had lightened in the sun. Tall and tan and slender, just like a song, her pale green eyes brilliant in the tan taut face, her hair floating around her shoulders, she moved through rooms like a visitation. Everyone stopped to turn to her, she was a magnet.

Iso's seeing always the positive side of people was not an affectation: it came out of her sense of herself and her own life. She had been tight and frightened, she had decided to risk, and here she was, doing work she loved, surrounded by friends who accepted her. She glowed with satisfaction, she believed in possibilities. And everyone in the circle was in some way in love with her. All faces lighted up – even Harley's – when she walked in. It was not just her beauty or her charming manner; she was fascinating because she was undefinable. People felt that they could never really know her, never fully pin her down.

Even Mira, who knew her well, felt that. She and Iso

465

spent many evenings together talking; Iso tried to give Mira some sense of her life.

'I don't know when I first knew I was different – maybe always. Yet at the same time, I didn't know I was different. How can I explain that? Like, some kids have brown eyes, and some blue. You may realize you're the only kid in the neighborhood with green eyes, but that fact has no significance. You don't think of it as a difference. Like one kid can run faster, another throws better, somebody is terrific on a skate board – you know – and those things make them special, but not different. It is not the difference but the significance placed on that difference that is important. I knew how I felt about girls, knew it early, but I assumed everybody else felt the same way. I assumed I'd get married and have children, just like my mother, like my aunts.

'But someplace along the line I became aware that my feeling about girls wasn't shared by other females. And I discovered that my feeling, my difference, had a name, that it was a nasty name, that the way I was was considered wicked, depraved, sick. That shook me up. That was when I started to withdraw, to watch myself carefully, to dress and act so as not to draw attention to myself, hoping my depraved deviation wouldn't show. It did, though, you know. It showed to other women who were like me. I can't tell you how many of them tried to make friends with me in college. I was terrified by it, I pulled away from them in a cruel way. I didn't want to be what I was.

'I thought maybe I could make it go away. I began to accept dates, I necked in cars, I allowed myself – rather coldly and calculatingly as I recall – to be seduced. Finally, I got engaged. My parents were ecstatic: they must have sensed something was wrong with me. I was engaged to a very handsome guy, a law student at the University of California. He was a gentle fellow, a little bland and uninteresting, but a great sailor, and he had a boat. We went out on it every weekend. That made up for everything else. I thought I could hack marriage to him. I don't know what I was thinking – that marriage

466

was a lot of sailing weekends, I guess. I hated screwing, but I didn't let myself think about that. He was not pushy, and I kept him off me most of the time. When I did give in, I was very drunk.

'One night he came over to my place late at night, un-expectedly. I was studying. I had an exam in economics the next day, not my strong suit as you might guess,' she grinned. Iso's improvidence was famous. 'He was out of his mind drunk – he'd been out with a bunch of guys, macho guys, I imagine, who'd been talking about "broads" and screwing all night. He'd gotten worked up about my dislike for sex, and he'd come over to, as he put it, have his rights. Another night I might have given in just to shut him up and get rid of him. But this night I wouldn't. I was outraged. I had this eco exam. I had to study, it wasn't a question of working for an A, it was a question of not failing. But that didn't mean anything to him. He was ugly and he stunk of liquor and vomit. He pushed me around the room, he smacked me. I hit him back, tried to push him, but he had eighty pounds on me. In the end he raped me. That's what it was, al-though it would never stand up in court. Rape is the right of husbands and lovers.

'When he was finished, he passed out, and I went back and studied, but I couldn't concentrate. I was so out-raged my pulse was pounding, my head was full of booming blood, I couldn't think. Next morning I went to take my exam. When I got back, he was sitting at my kitchen table drinking coffee. I just looked at him, but he didn't seem to notice that anything was wrong. He laughed and groaned and held his head; he talked about getting "smashed" as if he'd done something cute and funny. I asked him if he remembered what he'd done. He put on a small boy apologetic face and said he knew he'd pushed me. Pushed me. But then he laughed, he looked delighted with himself: "You don't have the hottest pants in town, you know," he said. That justified everything.

'I stood there very slowly taking off my engagement ring – it was a little diamond, can you imagine me with something like that? – and I walked into the bathroom. He got up, he was puzzled. I stood there over the john, waiting for him to come into the doorway. Then I dropped the ring in and flushed the john. He tried to stop me, but I was too fast. He stood there yelling, he couldn't believe what had happened. By the time he came to himself and came after me, I had the phone off the hook. "You lay one hand on me and I'll press charges," I said. "For assault and rape. That will look nice on your record when you come up to the bar." He stood there furious. He called me every name in the book. He was figuring his chances. He really wanted to beat me up. But then I felt the same way: I'd have liked to kill him. He saw that. Eventually he left.

'That was that. I've never gotten involved with a man again. But I still felt strange about myself. That's why I took off, traveled so much, trying to find other ways, trying to escape myself. Then I met Ava.'

'How did you do in the exam?'

'I flunked it. I've always felt that was a small price to pay for discovering the true nature of the beast before marriage. He could complain, I guess, that I wasn't honest, that I didn't come out. But until that night, neither did he.'

'I've often wondered what Norm would have done if I'd simply said *no*. Just *no*. God knows he deserved a *no*.'

'What do you think he'd have done?'

'I don't know. I don't think he'd have been violent, not right away. Maybe if I kept it up. . . . But he always felt screwing me was rape, because I disliked it so much and he knew that, felt that. I think that turned him on.'

'Oh, God, men.' Iso shook her head. She stretched out her body and let her hair fall back against the chair. 'Oh, it feels so good just to be what you are, just to feel good. It feels good to feel good,' she giggled at Mira.

Iso's eyes were brilliant, her lips were shiny, her hair was a halo of honey. Mira wished Iso would hold out her arms to her. She wanted to go to her friend and embrace her, to be embraced. But she couldn't move.

She doesn't care about me, she thought, not that way. I'm old, I'm unattractive.

They gazed at each other for a long moment. Then it passed. Iso turned and yawned. 'It's late,' she said. 'I'd better go.'

7

Mira went to her parents' home in New Jersey for Christmas. She went without joy. The Wards were elderly and very proper. In the forty years they had been married, neither of them had ever appeared at the breakfast table in a robe, nor had either of their children until last Christmas when Mira visited them. She had not only come down in a robe but sat around in that robe for an hour or two. They were so shocked they could not speak.

Mr. Ward had never appeared at the dinner table without shirt, tie, and jacket, even on weekends when he spent the day working on the lawn, and Mrs Ward never appeared without a 'good' dress and jewelry. When Mira wore her slacks and sweater, they drew their breaths in sharply. It was particularly difficult for them, since it seemed somehow indecorous to reprimand a thirty-nine-year-old daughter with grown children of her own, who came to visit only once a year. They were silent, but tense and jarred.

The Wards had fixed habits. They changed for dinner at four, had drinks at five: two manhattans. That was the only thing they drank and they could not understand anyone drinking anything else or anything more. Dinner always consisted of things like a single lamb chop and two teaspoons of peas with canned potatoes, and perhaps a salad of sliced lettuce with a peach half, heavily dosed with mayonnaise. Or there might be a broiled chicken breast and two teaspoons of canned string beans. Or a slice of roast beef and a baked potato: but that was only on special occasions. There was always cake afterwards, one of two kinds, black and white, one of which Mrs. Ward baked every week, and had done for nearly forty years.

Their house was much like their food. Everything was of good quality, but drab, chosen with an eye to durability and what the Wards called 'good taste' which meant nothing they would call 'flashy.' The faded Wilton carpet was a deeper brown than the beige wallpaper; the tweed chair coverings had lasted eighteen years. One reason their furniture stayed in good condition, they rather pointedly reminded Mira, was because they did not smoke. They opened windows vividly when Mira was visiting.

Not that they did not love her. But their house was so clean, so quiet, so orderly when she was not there, that it caused them both physical pain to endure the disorder she created. Oh, she was careful, they'd agree to that: she emptied her ashtrays at night, brought her own brandy and gin, and washed her glasses. But the cigarette odor hung in the lemon-waxed living room for several days after she left. There was a trace of the smell of alcohol in the kitchen every morning. Her toothbrush cluttered up the bathroom sink, to say nothing of her comb and brush, and sometimes, even stray hairs. They didn't complain. But she sensed their difficulty in accepting what felt to them like defilement; she violated the narrow patterns of their life.

She wanted to violate more. She wanted to talk to them. But that was impossible. The rules guiding conversation were strictly abided by. There were various levels of propriety. Mrs. Ward's friends might stop in for coffee of an afternoon and whisper a shocking story. Mr. Ward might meet someone at the hardware store and hear a ghastly tale. They might, alone in their bedroom, communicate these horrors to each other, and sometimes Mrs. Ward would whisper the tale to the wife of a visiting couple, when she went into the kitchen with Mrs. Ward to help her put out the coffee and cake which was served after the men had had three highballs. But such tales were never, never discussed publicly, and never in front of the children. Mira, hardly a child, might now be granted her mother's confidence as they sat in the living room in the afternoon, hearing Mr.

Ward hammer at something in the cellar. But that confidence would be conveyed in a low voice, with an eye cocked toward the cellar door, and it was understood that the information would not be brought up later, when the three of them were together. As a child, Mira had understood these distinctions implicitly. She had not given them much thought, but it seemed clear to her that the line was between men and women. There were certain facts of life that men either were not strong enough to bear or were not to be bothered with, that women whispered among themselves. Yet she felt sure that her mother occasionally, privately, related these incidents to her husband. It seemed to her a ritual game with no point at all, and she wanted to break it, to open it up to the air.

When Mira was young public conversation could include only certain stipulated topics. One might discuss one's children, but unless they were very small, there could be no mention of problems. Toilet training, yes; failing out of high school, no. Carousing at night, never. One could discuss one's house endlessly, and might mention money but not money problems. The cost of the new water boiler was okay; the hike in taxes was okay; but difficulty in meeting payments was not. One could discuss one's husband or wife, but again, only in certain ways. It was acceptable to mention that he had just joined the golf club, bought a new lawn mower, received a promotion. You were on shaky ground if you mentioned he'd been called in for an income tax audit. And if you related that on Saturday night he'd gotten drunk at the club and gotten into a fight, the shock would be less at the deed than at the fact that you told it. Certain things could be suggested, but must not be specified. So when the Adams girl three houses down had been raped one night last summer, everyone knew that she'd been walking from the bus stop at ten o'clock when a man came at her and well . . . you know . . . the poor thing screamed, but no one came . . . she's in the hospital now, but she seems to be all right. Sigh. Tsk, tsk. The result of these lacunae was that everyone

471

imagined the incident in the most violent, the most degraded way their imaginations could find. 'She was attacked' no doubt meant many things to each of Mrs. and Mr. Ward's friends and the unspoken pictures each formed rose like a vivid sublife hovering beyond the pale.

The Wards disapproved of Jews, the colored, Catholics who had many children, divorce, and any unusual behavior. Mrs. Ward, on her own, had low opinions of the Irish (shantytown habits), Italians (dirty, garlicky), the English, who were cold (she never said whether she included her husband in that category), Germans (drinkers and bullies), the French (sexy: although she did not know any), and Communists, who hovered as a vague but powerful devil. Other ethnic categories were too strange even to be considered members of the human race. However, in the past twenty years their neighborhood had changed, and people of all sorts moved in. Mrs. Ward, who was curious and gregarious, would stoop to coo over a baby in a carriage, and find herself in conversation with its mother. She could explain this to anyone. She would say constantly: 'Well, they're —— [fill in the blank], but they're really very nice.' She even had a Jewish friend.

Mira's divorce was a terrible blow to them. They could not forgive Mira for being the first member of the family so to disgrace it. Although they knew that it was Norm who wanted the divorce, and that Mira had been an exemplary wife, they still believed deep down that a woman's first job is to hold on to her husband, and that Mira had failed. It hurt them that Norm was now living in that magnificent house with a second wife; they would mention it only briefly to Mira, but always with a pained line between their eyes.

'We passed your old house the other day on our way to the Baxters' and Norm's putting in new shrubs,' they would say.

When Mira arrived, there was always a flurry of hugs and kisses, an offer of lunch, and then they would sit around the dining room table drinking coffee. How

472

was her trip down? Much traffic? Was the car holding up? How was school? This was another difficult spot, since Mrs. Ward could not for the life of her understand why a middle-aged woman would want to go back to school, and always had to forbear when the subject came up. What was she doing now? Orals. Yes. And what was that? Oh, and after that? When, the questions insisted, are you going to be finished and rejoin the adult world? Dissertation. Oh, yes, of course. And what did that involve? They had asked the same questions last year, and would ask them the next.

Friends were acceptable subjects of conversation, and so Mira told them whatever news she had about her friends. But they could never remember anyone but Val, despite the number of times Mira mentioned Iso, and recently in her letters, Clarissa and Kyla. It seemed that Val was her own age, and thus could be classified as a friend, while the others got lumped in with 'the young students.' Mira decided to tell them about their parties. They listened in puzzlement. Mrs. Ward did not understand why these young students, none of whom had very much money, would want to waste what little they had on such foolish enterprises.

'For fun,' Mira said, but that was a word neither of the Wards comprehended.

As she talked on, she slid in 'Ben' several times, but neither of them asked who he was.

Then it was Mrs. Ward's turn. The Wards had many friends, couples they had known for thirty years or longer. They knew these peoples' children and grandchildren. They knew their friends' cousins, aunts, and uncles (mostly dead now). There were stories galore. This one's daughter had moved, her husband having received a promotion and a transfer to Minneapolis; that one had died. A baby had been born. Someone had gone off to college. And someone – her voice lowered – had gotten a divorce. And someone's son was – even lower – on drugs.

Mira was astonished. Things were changing even in Bellview. She remembered from her childhood how pure and unsullied the immediate world of her parents had seemed. She always felt tainted in it, knowing herself not up to its standards. She was, of course, always sent from the room when her mother's friends stopped in for a visit. After she was married and visited her mother on an occasional afternoon, she remembered being aware of an aura of sin hovering just above the heads of some of her parents' oldest friends. There was a rumor of divorce in the Martinson family – a brother, she thought. There was a period when silence fell at the mention of Harry Cronkite's name, but eventually they began to speak of 'it' being over now. But here they were speaking of divorce right at the dining room table, and of drugs too. Both Wards shook their heads. The world was in imminent trouble. It was true, Mira thought. Their world was, when things like drugs and a rumored abortion could break through the carefully wrought surface of their social life. Life breaks out everywhere, Mira thought.

But still she had to listen to the boring recital of actions performed by strangers, or people she could barely remember. They were actions without motive and without consequence, and about as interesting as a parts list for an atomic submarine. But the Wards derived pleasure from the telling. Occasionally Mr. Ward would interrupt his wife with, 'No, it wasn't Arthur, it was the other brother, Donald, the one who lived in Cleveland,' and sometimes there would even be a little argument about just which brother it was. But on and on they went. They could fill three days with it. It began to remind Mira of a pornographic book she had borrowed from Iso. It had a male narrator, and on just about every page, he had intercourse. There were some details: he was having intercourse with A, B, or C, on a fur rug in front of a fire, on a swing, in the bathtub. But most of the story was given over to the dull, repetitious recital of the physical details of the act.

'That's how they arouse themselves. They masturbate to it. They want it ritualistic,' Iso explained.

'It's a mind-fuck,' Kyla added.

474

'I thought you liked them,' Mira said, still unable to use the word.

'Oh, I do when they're with other people. You know, when you come together and two minds just set each other off and you can feel the sparks. It's great! But this is a different kind.'

Mira wondered what her parents would do if she told them she thought they were having a mind-fuck.

'How about a gin and tonic?' is what she did say. They were shocked anyway.

After the good news had all been told, the bad had its turn. Since misbehavior and money problems were forbidden, the only bad news allowed was of sickness and death. And the Wards were a walking encyclopedia. They knew every detail of every symptom of every sickness of every friend. They knew each one's doctor bills. Since the Wards and their friends were in their seventies, these were considerable. The hospital expenses were indeed staggering. The Wards were horrified by sickness itself, and by the extravagant costs, but beneath this, they were puzzled, although they could not articulate their problem. 'I don't know what's happening to the world,' they said worriedly.

Most of the Wards' friends had been like them, poor during the Depression. They had lived frugally and worked hard and by the late forties, with the help of the war, they were fairly well off. They had not considered the implications of needing a war to improve an economy; they felt no moral question implicit in their new prosperity. They all believed in technology and were certain that progress, as they would call it, had been a good thing. They shuddered at the word *socialism*, and even socialized medicine seemed to them something tinged with evil. It was a strange society, Mira thought, that destroys the very people who support its principles. For these people were being wiped out by medical bills, and even the Wards, who as yet had no serious ailments, were having trouble living on Mr. Ward's pension with all the inflation. Mira's feeble interest in politics had been somewhat increased by Ben, who talked about it constantly, but for the first time she saw it in practical application. Apart from any moral consideration, a system that does not support the people who support it is doomed. She tried, in simple language to suggest something of this to her parents, but they could not hear her. The things were in two different categories in their minds: capitalism was good, high medical bills were bad, but they had no connection with each other. She gave up.

By nine thirty, Mira's head ached. She longed for ten o'clock, when the Wards would turn on the news, after which they would go to bed. She was no longer really listening. Tomorrow was Christmas Eve; she had a few little things to buy, gifts to wrap, and in the afternoon the boys would arrive. They would stay overnight and into the afternoon of Christmas Day, when they would go to their father's house. Then there would be a second Christmas dinner, then there would be cleaning up to do, talk about the gifts. She would have to stay only one day after that. The Wards would not be too unhappy to see her go. They could air out the house, polish the brandy snifter and return it to the back shelf of the china closet. She was trying to figure if she could leave even earlier, unlistening to the calamity that had befallen Mr. Whitcomb's second cousin's liver, when suddenly her mother stopped talking.

The silence brought Mira's head up. Mrs. Ward was sitting in a straight-backed chair near a low, dim lamp. Her mother's knotted hands lay very still, lightly clasped in her lap.

'We'll all be dead soon,' she said.

Mira looked at her with shock. Mrs. Ward did not look old. Her hair was gray, but it had been gray since she was in her late twenties. She was a brisk, energetic woman; she ran around the house cleaning it in high heels and earrings. Her movements were quicker than Mira's. Her father had always been slower, and since his retirement he slumped more. He broke rules to the point of wearing carpet slippers around the house at least until dinnertime. He spent his time now putter-

476

ing: he insisted there was plenty to do around here.

She looked at them. They were not old, no older than they had ever been. They had always been old. She could not remember them any other way. She recalled a photograph of her mother, taken before she was married. She had been dark-haired and very beautiful: she looked like Gloria Swanson. In the picture, she was wearing a floppy, wide-brimmed hat, and holding it on her head with one hand. Her hair was blowing. It must have been windy. And she was smiling, and her eyes were brilliant and alive, her smile was vibrant, she looked full of energy and joy. And there was one of her father too, taken in his World War I uniform, before he had gone overseas. He was slender and fair; she imagined him pink-cheeked, much like Clark now. He had longing eyes, was shy and delicate looking, like a Romantic poet.

What had happened to those people? Surely they were not now in this room, encased in this utterly different flesh, the vibrant triumphant girl, the yearning sensitive boy. All of life had constricted for them into a mortgage payment. Was that it? Had simple physical survival been so difficult for them that any other kind was a luxury? Was she, who felt herself to be miraculously still living, simply luckier? There was no question that survival of the spirit depended upon survival of the flesh: but hardship did not kill all its victims. Or did it? Was their hardship *so* hard? Was it perhaps the way they had conceived of life, of their duty, of their expectations? Yet, going over in her mind what their acts had been, and the space they had to move in, she could fault them on nothing. They had not had enough room. And now, it was not just what they had become that was oppressive, but that they would not allow that anyone could become anything else. That's the price, she could hear Val saying, that's the price they exact for having paid too much themselves. What had they wanted? To serve tea from a silver pot on an embroidered cloth just as nice as Mrs. Carrington's of the Bellview Carringtons? The silver tea set was covered with plastic, standing unused inside the china closet. To rise in society. Yes. Which required certain objects, certain manners. They had risen. They had reached the heights. They were now the old society of Bellview, the Carringtons and their friends having long since left it for Paris, Palm Beach, Sutton Place. The old Carrington mansion was now a private school, the Miller place a home for the aged.

Her parents rose the moment the news reporter said, 'Good night,' and turned off the set and turned to her and said, 'Good night, Mira.' And she stood too and embraced them, really embraced them, not giving the usual polite peck of a kiss. They were surprised, and both of them stiffened a little. They smiled at her, her father shyly, sweetly, her mother with a certain vividness. But her mother could only say, 'Don't stay up too late now, will you, dear?' and her father, 'You'll remember to turn the thermostat down, won't you, Mira?' Then they went up to their dreams.

8

The Wards had always 'had Christmas' early Christmas morning: a quick unwrapping which was followed by Mrs. Ward's wild flurries in the kitchen aimed at producing a dinner by midafternoon. Later everyone would sit, stuffed and lethargic, in the living room. Some man or other – it could only be a man – might snooze for a while. The others would chat until eight, when turkey sandwiches and coffee would be brought out, food taking up the slack in the conversation. Mira's divorce and the necessity of splitting the boys with their father on the holidays had caused a break in this tradition, a break her parents had not yet accepted and which never went unremarked.

Now they had a little party on Christmas Eve, inviting part of the family 'so the boys will at least *know* their family,' Mrs. Ward would say, swallowing her pain. The boys would leave before midafternoon the next day and so miss Mrs. Ward's Christmas dinner. She invited the

478

rest of the family to come then to help her get through the unnatural event.

Mira met the boys at the bus station. They understood the decorum, and were combed, jacketed, and tied, although their hair was getting a little long. They were lively enough in the car, but as soon as they walked into the Ward house, they became more subdued, even stiff. Pecked kisses all around, exchange of traffic information, weather reports, polite inquiries about school. They settled down with Cokes in the living room, and Mira said, 'Wait till you see what I bought!'

She ran upstairs and dressed quickly. With Val's help, she had bought a brilliant green and blue dashiki. She slipped it over her pants, neglecting to wear a bra. She laid brilliant blue eye shadow on her upper lids, making her eyes even bluer, and she hung enormous gold dangling earrings from her ears. They hurt, but she gritted her teeth. I want to tell them something, she said fiercely to herself. I want to tell them who I am. For the family, she knew, would be dressed as usual: the men in dark suits, white shirts, and red and blue, or red and gold, or blue and gold striped silk ties; the women in three-piece knit suits and teased, sprayed hair, and high heels matching their purses. A daring one might appear in a knit pant-suit.

She came down the steps as if she were making an appearance, and stood, grinning, before her sons. They grinned back. 'You look nice,' Clark said. 'Where'd you get that thing, anyway?' Norm asked, sounding irritated, and when she did not answer, he pursued it. 'Did you get it at that little store on Mass Ave near the place that sells bowls? On Brattle Street?' He really wanted to know. 'Why?' she asked him finally. He looked shamefaced. 'Well, they have them for guys too, don't they?'

'You mean you want one?'

He shrugged. 'Well, maybe.'

Mrs. Ward's eyebrows went up as she surveyed her daughter, but then she smiled a little. 'Well, it's different,' she admitted. Mr. Ward said something about Mira looking as if she had come from Africa, but after shaking his head a little, he subsided.

The Wards' small house had a narrow porch in the front, separated from the living room by folding glass doors. To keep the mess down, they stood the artificial Christmas tree out there, placing it on a wooden settee that stood beneath the front windows. The presents were strewn on the settee around the tree. The room held only the settee and a slant-doored secretary. The living room sparkled with wax and clean ashtrays, so when Mira wanted to talk to the boys, she led them out to the porch, carrying an ashtray, and they all sat on the floor. Mira called out to her mother that she would do all the vegetables in an hour, after she'd visited with her sons. But Mrs. Ward, tight-lipped, stood in the kitchen peeling and chopping. Mr. Ward had gone down to the basement to ready the whoopee room (as they called it) for visitors. Mira knew that this, this sitting on the floor filling the rooms with cigarette smoke before company was expected, was an act of defiance, and angered them. But she refused to give in.

Norm and Clark seemed much older than they had in the summer. They talked easily now, telling her about someone's funny error in a soccer game, a martinet math teacher, some guys who sneaked beer into the dorm. Norm said he wanted to have a long talk with her about college: his father insisted he go to a good premed school, and become a doctor. But he didn't want to be a doctor. The problem was he wasn't sure whether he didn't want to be a doctor because he didn't want to be a doctor or because his father wanted him to be a doctor. Mira laughed and said he probably wouldn't find out the answer to that in time. Clark wanted to tell Mira about an argument with his father that had confused him. As she listened, it became clear that Clark was perturbed because he'd shouted at his father. 'He was yelling at me,' he concluded sulkily. 'I guess you're allowed to have a temper too,' Mira said, patting him. 'Everybody else does.' Norm had had an encounter with a Girl at a prep school mixer. He wanted to know if Girls were always

480

like that. Mira got up and poured herself a gin and tonic.

'Really, Mother, the boys and I will do the rest,' she said, but Mrs. Ward went on grimly peeling and chopping. Mrs. Ward hated to cook and blamed the world for the necessity of her doing it.

She returned to the porch and the three of them talked and laughed. She told them about the parties; she told them about the change in Iso. They were fascinated, they asked question after question. They wanted to know, clamorously, what women did with women, men with men. They told her rumors at school about fags; they told her jokes and stories they had heard but did not understand. They asked, a little warily, how one could tell if one was gay. Mira had never seen them as interested in anything before, and she pondered the subject's fascination.

'Val thinks everybody's gay and straight, but that we get conditioned, most of us, to be one or the other early in life. Iso thinks that's not true, that she was always only gay. I don't know, I don't think anybody knows. When you think about it, it doesn't seem terribly important – I mean, what does it matter who you love? Except that I guess it causes identity problems. But that happens anyway, doesn't it?'

They were mystified.

'Well, you are both so fascinated by this. You're wondering what you're like, aren't you?'

'Well, there's this guy, Bob Murphy, Murph, and he's really a great guy, he's a terrific soccer player and just a great kid, you know, and everybody likes him a lot, and I do too, sometimes my heart fills up looking at him, and everybody's always touching him, you know, in the locker room and all? Always patting him on the back or poking him in the arm. He just laughs, but one day some guy – a real jerk, Dick his name is, said we were a bunch of queers. Do you think that's true?'

'I think you all love him. Do you think it's peculiar that I love Val and Iso?'

'No, but you're a lady.'

'Do you think ladies and men have different feelings?'

They shrugged. 'Do they?' Norm asked suspiciously.

'I doubt it,' she smiled and got to her feet. 'Come on.' Mrs. Ward had given up trying to make them feel guilty and had gone upstairs to dress. Mira and the boys went into the kitchen. She made herself another drink, offered them one – which led to hysterical giggling – and they talked on. She peeled and chopped while they set the table, fished down platters from high shelves, stirred the cream sauce, fetched vinegar from the pantry, laughed, talked.

'The older guys in my class – some of them are older, and some of them just seem older, you know? They're always talking about booze and broads, booze and broads,' Norm imitated a deep male voice. 'You think they really do those things?'

'What things?'

'Oh, you know, with girls and all.'

'I don't know, Norm, what do they say they do?'

'Well, screwing and all,' he said with a red face. The tension in the kitchen was high. She could hear them waiting for her answer.

'Maybe some of them do,' she said slowly. 'And some of them probably make it up.'

'That's what I think!' Norm exploded. 'It's just all lies.'

'That could be. But say some of them are really screwing.' Mira heard her father's step descending the staircase. 'You have to figure they don't know much about what they're doing, and are just as scared and uptight as you are. They're no doubt clumsy. To hear Val talk, a lot of them stay clumsy.'

Mr. Ward was in the hall leading to the kitchen.

'They say girls like it,' Norm frowned. 'They say girls want to.'

'Maybe some of them do. But most of them are probably pretending. Sex doesn't come naturally to many of us. Not in this world. Maybe back when people lived on farms, I don't know.'

Mr. Ward's step veered quickly in the other direction and disappeared into the living room rug.

The boys glanced toward the hall, then at their mother. They blushed, they giggled silently, holding their hands over their mouths. Mira stood smiling at them, yet grave.

'Which is not to say that people aren't sexual early,' she continued imperturbably, turning back to peel a carrot. 'I remember masturbating when I was fourteen.'

They were silent at that, and she was standing at the sink with her back to them and could not see their faces. Norm came over to her and laid his hand lightly on her back. 'Do you want me to pour the water out of the onions, Mom?'

The family arrived at six on the dot, all of them at once. There were Mrs. Ward's sister and brother and their spouses and their three grown children and two spouses and five grandchildren, and Mr. Ward's brother and his wife and one of their grown children with her husband and their three kids. After the briefest of greetings, the small children were shunted downstairs to the whoopee room, which Mr. Ward had built for these occasions alone, to watch TV or play Ping-Pong or darts. The adults crowded into the living room and Mr. Ward served them manhattans. Only Mira drank anything else. Clark and Norm went downstairs for a while, but came back up within half an hour and sat on the fringes of the room. No one seemed to notice, but it did not matter. The conversation was entirely proper: sex was not mentioned once.

Other things were, however. Mira was not sure whether she had never really listened to them before, whether they had changed, or whether her being at Harvard gave a focus to their attacks. People seemed very upset these days. These people, familiar aunts, uncles, cousins, seemed united in a most virulent hatred. They talked with outraged contempt about drug addicts and hippies, about ungrateful spoiled kids who grew beards and long hair and did not appreciate their parents' sacrifices. Jews seemed to have become more evil than ever in the past year or two, but they did not occupy center stage anymore. It was the niggers. When

Mira complained, that was changed to the coloreds. They, the coloreds and the hippies and the war protesters, were ruining the country. 'They' were getting in everywhere; 'they' got scholarships to colleges while poor Harry, who earned only $35,000 a year, had to pay to send his children to college. And then, when the coloreds and the hippies got in, not on merit, you can be sure of that, they tried to overturn the school. Harvard kids were the worst. They were the most privileged group of kids ever known, and still they complained. 'We' had to work for what we got; 'we' didn't get anything and didn't dare to protest; but 'they' were still unsatisfied.

Mira listened. She tried to muster arguments against them, although she saw bits of truth in what they said.

'You can't judge them by the standards of a past world,' she said, but they leapt on her in fury. Those standards were eternal. Hard work, frugality, suppression of desire: that was the recipe for success and success was goodness and virtue. And one stayed faithful to one's wife, and one made one's mortgage payments, and one created a semblance of order because if one did not, the world would fall apart.

'Do you know,' asked a cousin, a woman almost Mira's age, married and with three children, 'the students in my school, the Negro students – there are all of ten of them in a school of two hundred and thirty – had the gall to ask the principal for a course in Black Studies? Can you imagine? I was flabbergasted! As soon as I heard it – and that idiot of a principal, he was thinking about giving it to them! – I marched right down to his office and said that if they could have a course in Black Studies, I wanted to give a course in English-Irish Studies! If they could have theirs, I want mine!'

'That's pretty much what they've gotten up until now,' Mira said, but her cousin did not hear.

'And the teacher in the room down the hall from me is French. I told him she could give a course in French Studies! Hah! How would he like that? Sixth graders learning *that* sort of thing!'

'What sort of thing?'

'Well, for heaven's sakes, Mira, she's *French*!' She glanced around the room and saw the boys. 'You can imagine!' she said, with a sarcastic smile.

It went on like that. Through dinner and afterwards, it went on like that. Mira probed her memory: had it always been like this? At some point in the evening, she poured herself a rye on the rocks. Norm was pouring Coke for himself, and noticed.

'Switching drinks?'

'I can't seem to get drunk enough on gin and tonic.'

'Why don't you have a brandy?'

'That's for later. For sitting up late with.'

'Can I have some tonight? If we stay up late?'

'Sure,' she smiled, and slipped her arm around his waist. He put his around her shoulders, and they stood there for a time.

They did stay up late, long after everyone had left. They each had a brandy snifter, although the boys had only a drop each and did not like it and were soon gulping Coke again. Mira asked them, was it me, or were they worse this year?

They didn't know. Apparently all three of them had been not listening all these years. Mira blasted her family. She took their politics apart and damned them, she blasted their bigotry. The boys listened. When she asked for their opinions, they did not have any, not even on bigotry. They knew, they explained, that prejudice was supposed to be bad, but they heard it everywhere they went. And they knew scarcely any Jews, and no blacks at all, so how could they judge?

'I mean, it sounds crazy,' Clark explained. 'But I don't know. Maybe black people really are what they say. I know you say all that's not true, and I believe you, but I don't know. For myself I don't know.'

Mira shut her mouth. 'Yes,' she said finally. 'You're right. Of course. You have to wait until you know for yourselves.'

But the boys had other complaints. There had been so

much hate. They had never before seen so much hate, so much anger.

'She was so bitter.'

'He seemed so mad.'

'Is he that mad all the time?'

'Does Uncle Harry always sound that way?'

They gave her a new perspective. She thought of all those faces, faces she had known since childhood, faces she never thought of in terms of beauty or lack of it, and which she never looked at anymore, never tried to see the character under the familiar. But as the boys spoke, she saw them again: hard, lined, angry faces, with deep bitter lines, eyes furiously popping out of heads, mouths tight and hateful. And she remembered her first days at Harvard, looking in the mirror and noticing the bitter thin scar of her mouth.

'Do I look like them?' she asked her sons with a trembling voice.

They hesitated. Her heart constricted. She knew they would find a way to tell her the truth.

'You used to,' Norm said. 'But you got fatter.'

She wailed. It was true.

'You got softer,' Clark said. 'I mean your face is like – rounder.'

Her vanity would not let it pass. 'I look fat?'

'No!' they both insisted. 'Really, no. Just . . . rounder,' Clark repeated, searching for words.

'Your mouth isn't so hurt,' Norm said, and she raised her eyes to him.

'My mouth looked hurt?'

He shrugged. He felt incompetent. 'Yeah, sort of. You looked as if you had to be mad or otherwise you'd cry.'

'Yes.' Then she glinted her eyes at them. 'You want me to tell you how you've changed?'

'NO!' they shouted, laughing.

She reverted to the evening. She wanted to emphasize certain things. She did not want them to grow up unthinking, echoing the words they had heard that night. She wanted to underline a moral. But they would have none of it. They could not, they insisted, judge the opinions, the positions taken that evening.

She was a little liquorish, down to basic impulse. She wanted to pound the table with her fist, to insist vehemently on the evil of bigotry, stereotyping, prejudice. She wanted to insist on her rightness. She began angrily, 'Yes, that's all fine, you won't prejudge, that sounds wonderful. Except as you yourselves have admitted, everything and everyone around you is infected with bigotry and stereotyping, and by the time you actually meet and know some of its victims, you won't be able to see them except through the lenses you've been handed.'

They continued to demur, to argue. 'Why should we let *you* brainwash us?' Norm demanded.

She wanted to rise up like a Victorian father and proclaim THE TRUTH, to boom and pound them into submission. How dare they refuse to submit to her greater knowledge, her larger moral experience!

Suddenly she crumpled; she sat staring at her drink, her throat full of tears. They didn't trust her moral judgment because she had forfeited her right to be their guide by letting them know she was a sexual being. She sniffled, engulfed in self-pity. Never again would they look up to her; never again could she guide them gently with a mother's firm but loving hand. She blew her nose. They, however, paid no attention to her. They were talking to each other, repeating remarks made that evening, giggling together.

'Yeah, and the look on Uncle Charles's face when he leaned forward and sneered at Mommy and said how would she like it if her grandchildren all had slanty eyes!' They both roared.

She listened.

'And Mommy said slanty eyes might be better than some she saw around her, and his popeyes nearly popped right out of his head!'

They continued, laughing through most of their survey. They were talking about ugliness. That was what bothered them: the people were ugly. They would not like to be like them. The boys perceived there was something wrong with their lives, with their thoughts, with

487

the world, if it made people as ugly as that. She let out her breath. The boys were all right.

9

Mira and Ben spent New Year's Eve alone. There were parties going on, but they had not seen each other since before Christmas, and wanted only to be together. Ben brought over his TV set and plugged it in in the bedroom. They sprawled on the bed half dressed, drinking bourbon – Ben's drink – talking over the family visits. The subject was profoundly interesting to both of them. Both had noticed a difference in atmosphere in their families, an increase in anger, hate, and fear. And each felt that they had been somehow different, and that had been noticed.

'After thirty-four years, my mother just stopped calling me Benny.'

Mira recounted at length her discussions with the boys, and Ben, far from being bored at hearing about mere children who were not even his own, listened intently and asked serious questions. He recalled his own youth, and drew comparisons; he offered suggestions. He wondered if they were feeling this or that which he had felt at their age. It was beautiful talk and made them both feel rich and full and close.

Ben opened the champagne as the countdown began, and when the balloons broke in Times Square, they wrapped their arms together and drank it from wide-mouthed, stemmed glasses. But the position didn't work: they spilled champagne on each other and themselves, and giggled, and ended by laughing and kissing, with champagne spilled all over the bed. A change of linen was necessary if they were not going to sleep on a damp mattress, and they went about it gazing more at each other than at what they were doing, loving each other's every bend, every motion. Then they had to bathe themselves, their skin sticky with the sweet drink, so they filled the tub and poured in half the box of bubble bath Mira's aunt had given her for Christmas. It stunk: it was acid sweet and lavendery, but that seemed funny too. They took the champagne bottle into the bathroom with them, and set their glasses beside the tub and immersed themselves. They bathed each other, loving every limb, every curve and angle, the jut of neck muscle and the knob of collarbone, the sheen of flesh, the fine lines under the eyes, the sad ones around the mouths. They poured water on each other, and every handful was a handful of love.

'It's like bathing in warm sperm,' Mira laughed.

'No, it's like bathing in what comes out of you. Something does. What do you call it?'

Mira did not know. 'Lubricant,' she decided finally, and that struck them both as hilarious.

'Mira,' Ben said suddenly, 'I have to tell you something?'

He was serious, and she felt her heart slow: thinking how terror always lurked just under the surface of joy.

'What?'

'I hate champagne.'

She giggled. 'So do I.'

He picked up the bottle. 'I christen thee Mira Voler,' he said, pouring it over her head. She wailed and mock-cried and grabbed her glass and poured its contents over his head, and they wrestled rather weakly in the slippery tub, their bodies already intertwined, but ended in an embrace. Then they dried each other vigorously, with some rump-slapping and bear-hugging, and padded naked into the kitchen and got out the feast they had prepared earlier, and carried overloaded plates of food back to the bed to stain the fresh bed linen. And talked and talked, exchanging, interrupting, arguing, laughing, and suddenly Ben said, 'I meant it, you know. Let's get married.'

Mira stopped. She realized that for some time now, they had rarely spoken of the future in terms of the singular personal pronoun: it was almost always 'We.' It might be 'when I get my degree,' but it would be followed with 'we can take a trip.' Their vague plans included taking a cottage in Maine with the boys, going to

England and driving through the countryside, applying for travel grants for the same year.

'We don't have to get married. We're wonderful as we are. Maybe marriage would spoil what we have.'

'We could be together all the time.'

'We could do that now if we wanted. We seem to prefer being together only some of the time.'

He bent toward her. 'We don't have to do it right away. But someday – I'd like to have a kid of my own.' He touched her fingertips lightly. 'And you're the only person in the world I've ever felt I'd want to have it with.'

She did not answer then, could not have answered then, nor the rest of that night. And next day the subject seemed to be forgotten, as Ben returned to his card files, his blank paper, and his typewriter, and she to the joyful abandon of seventeenth-century sermons.

After the holidays, the friends decided to have a second New Year, together. Kyla offered her house, the finest of the graduate student residences. Kyla had hunted, in her swift, unerring way, and had found the bottom floor of an old mansion, all parquet floors, carved moldings, high painted ceilings, and a fireplace in every room. There were stained-glass windows over window seats, and old-fashioned, heavy sliding doors between the rooms. The kitchen had a separate breakfast nook which looked out on an overgrown garden full of wild flowers.

Kyla had hung plants at the sunny windows, had sewn brilliantly colored hangings for the others, and covered the window-seat cushions with the same fabric. The bedroom, a corner of which was Kyla's study, held a huge fur rug before the fireplace. They had turned the dining room, which was large, into the living and dining room, and the living room proper was given over to Harley for a study. The couple had collected prints and paintings done by friends who were artists, and the walls were covered with witty and elegant designs.

The group decided to dress formally: they all got into it, and the men went so far as to rent dinner jackets. The women shopped the 'reduced' racks and found swishy, low-cut things. Kyla wore a white Grecian dress and a rhinestone-studded band around her hair; Clarissa wore sea-green chiffon; Iso came in flame red satin, long and narrow, with a slit up the side. Val wore low-cut black velvet with a feather boa, and Mira found a pale blue bare-backed gown which was the sexiest thing she'd ever owned.

They were delighted with themselves and with each other. The evening began quietly, with drinks and talk and Segovia playing Bach on the record player. Harley looked beautiful in a black velvet dinner jacket and a white ruffled shirt that softened his severe pale face and heightened his white-blond hair. Duke looked elegant; formal clothes suited him. His weight disappeared inside the dark jacket. Tad looked as if his arms were a little too long for his jacket, and Ben looked uneasy, like a mechanic at a wedding, but a sense of elegance touched them all, and their gestures showed it. Everything felt graceful.

The women had much to talk about, because most of them had made Christmas visits to their parents or a relative, and they talked intimately, almost as they would if the men had not been there. Mira talked about her conversation with the boys, omitting the discussion of Iso and their fascination with sex; she described the hatefulness and vindictiveness of her relatives. Kyla and Harley had had a similar experience; the rage of their elders against the young, against war protesters, seemed excessive, seemed, Kyla thought, to have a different source. The men listened, speaking rarely, but they did not withdraw. Their interest could be felt: they were *there*, and the activeness of their participation made the conversation rich with a vibrating intensity. Harley suggested that what the elders were feeling was rage at the freedom of option open to young people: 'It's a luxury to refuse to go to war. They wouldn't have dared. They imagine everybody young is gaily shacking up with everybody else. They're jealous.' The whole room got into it: everyone had some personal experience with a parent or relative that illuminated the situation. Everyone agreed that the feeling in the air 'out there' in the 'real' world was dire, full of hate and anger. 'I wonder what will happen when they explode,' Duke said ominously.

But they were too happy to feel threatened. Clarissa, whose family was also angry, had done some investigating of family history on her visit. 'I was asking so many questions my mother brought out an old family album I'd never seen. It shows five generations of my forebears, farm people mostly, from North and South Dakota. Their faces are fascinating; they're so strong, worn and lined, and you can tell they're tanned from working outdoors, and their mouths are a little grim. But so strong! You just don't see faces like that now. My parents don't look like that – well, of course they don't farm – but neither do my aunts and uncles, who do keep up the farm. They are America, those faces. They're what people mean when they talk about moral virtue and the backbone of America. They were tough. My great-grandmother had twelve children and lived to be eighty-seven, working on the farm right up until the end. My grandmother is ninety and still does the cooking for the aunts and uncle who live on the farm, and all their kids. But my forebears weren't like the image we have. One relative was run out of town on a rail for embezzling money from the bank to spend on his fancy woman, who lived right there, over the dressmaker's shop. One uncle was an atheist and the town scandal. He'd stand outside the church on Sundays, on a big flat rock, and when the congregation came out, he'd start ranting and sermonizing on the evils of religion. He died at eighty-three by falling into a pigpen and the town said it was the judgment of God. My great-great-grandfather had three wives at once, one of them an Indian, a Kiowa. I like to think I'm descended from her. There's a little confusion about the children, who belonged to whom. There are no pictures of her, but there's one of him looking very prosperous and respectable in a black suit and a gold watch chain. Hardly your image of a trigamist.

'They were utterly bourgeois; they kept their butteries clean and their pantries in order, and their barns full of hay, and I imagine the women walking around with clean white aprons and a ring of keys hanging at their belts, feeling very contented because of the bacons and hams hanging in the larder, the fresh eggs in the white bowl, the vegetables stored in the root cellar, enough to get them through the winter, and them all sitting at the round parlor table doing needlework while the men carved wood or read aloud to them, and the fire blazed, and the lamp hanging over the table swayed slightly when the wind blew fiercely. They were bourgeois, but they weren't like our picture of them. Morality meant something different to them. They accepted the peculiarities of the people they lived with.'

'The men,' Val interrupted.

Clarissa nodded thoughtfully. 'That may be. I don't know any legends of atheistic or polygamous grandaunts. But Grandaunt Clara – I was named for her – was a crack shot with a rifle and ran her farm alone for thirty years after Uncle Tobias got his foot caught in a cart wheel and died of gangrene. I think because they were tougher, because they had fewer choices, because they worked so damned hard, they could afford to be freer in some ways . . .' Her voice drifted off. 'I don't know. I can't quite articulate what it is I feel about them. They were, most of them, very religious. But their eyes – the eyes in those photographs – the eyes in those grim, worn, stern faces – are like the eyes of visionaries. And the vision wasn't of hams and bacon sides hanging in the larder, and a full root cellar.' She breathed in deeply and threw back her head. 'OH! They took me to this crazy place, unbelievable! It's in West Bend, Iowa, and it's called the Grotto of the Redemption. It's supposed to be a Christian monument, some priest started it in 1912. It's quite mad, it is made up of tiny stones piled on each other, and it's a cross between a monastery, a Buddhist temple, and Disneyland. It has twisting towers and carvings and grotesqueries like Victorian houses. It is crazy, wild, but *it* came out of them too, along with the plowed fields, the silage nicely stored for winter, the fat cows out in the meadow. They made it.'

'And you wonder what they were seeing.'

Clarissa nodded.

'You should know,' Iso said softly. 'What do you see?'

Clarissa just stared at her.

'You have the same eyes. I often wonder what it is you're looking at. As if your eyes were so filled up with vision you didn't have room to look around. Your dreams are prophetic. You're always finding coincidences in things. Remember the day we were walking on Quincy Street and you found a feather and said that meant you should be an Indian at the costume party. And then the costume shop had exactly the same Indian headdress you'd dreamed about?'

'You think that's mystic?'

'Well, it sure isn't old-fashioned pragmatism. You're always having strange dreams.'

Clarissa considered. But Kyla leaped up then and dragged in a giant alarm clock set for midnight, and Harley and Ben fetched the champagne, and they pretended it was the week before and all counted out the countdown and poured out glasses and at the ring everyone toasted the new year.

'Happy 1970! Happy 1970!'

And everyone kissed everyone else, and everyone glowed because they were all happy and the future did seem good. They loved and were loved; they liked their work; they loved their friends, and they celebrated life, just being alive, in what they all believed, despite their intellects, to be the best of all worlds past and a new decade that was the beginning of a better one.

More dancing, drinking, food, louder music. They were sitting in a circle made of the couch and some chairs, with the center space cleared for dancing. Kyla put a Joplin record on, then stood up and began to dance mildly, gracefully, swaying and turning. She was dancing to them, at them; her dance was an invitation to all of them at once. Her face glowed, her red hair flew, the white gown swung out widely when she turned. In a few moments, Clarissa got up and stood behind her, putting her hands on Kyla's waist, adding to the picture her own

494

shining dark hair, her own blue eyes full of vision, her sea-green dress. They danced together, Clarissa following Kyla's movements almost as if the thing had been choreographed; they were two people dancing to the same spirit. Then Iso rose and joined them, and they were three steps; Iso the tallest, with her honey-brown hair, her red dress, put her hands on Clarissa's waist, and followed their rhythms and movements easily, then Mira too, not knowing what moved her, got up and attached herself to the chain and the four of them glowed and moved and snaked around, all radiant, smiling, speaking to the room. And a sound came out of a throat – it was Tad's, and sounded choked: 'My God, how beautiful! How beautiful you are!' The others sat watching without moving, and the women smiled at Val, who sat there gazing enraptured, and finally she got up and joined them too, and called Tad, and the men joined on and they snaked around the room and into the kitchen and back, then formed a circle and made up a dance that had pieces of the hora, of old square dance motions, and much sheer invention. They weaved and wound, and everybody glowed with love toward everybody else, and clasped hands and felt clasped, and faces sometimes brushed together, and the room whirled, the green plants, the red hangings, the blue cushions, the blue and green chair, red, green, blue, green, blue, red, the whole world was color and motion and love. When they were exhausted, they stopped and hung on each other, all at once, arms around backs, together, accepted, joyful to be part of such beauty.

The group was silent in the car going home. Only Mira, midway there, suddenly said, 'I think that was the most beautiful night of my life.'

10

Val said: 'It was a vision.'

The women were gathered at Val's one afternoon, chatting after the long hours of silent study up in Child, drinking coffee, Coke, beer, gin. They were all still

495

bathed in the feeling of the party, still glowing: they could feel it still around them. They fell silent when Val said that, waiting for her to continue.

'It was a vision of community. Of the possible. Of the person merged with the group, yet still separate. Of harmony. Not order, unshakable order at least; everybody was moving in a slightly different way. Everybody was dressed differently, looked different. Even the men had a little individuality – Harley's ruffle-front shirt, Tad's tie, Ben's red lapels. And we made the group because we wanted to, not because we had to, not because we were afraid . . .'

'Why didn't you join sooner?'

'Because I wanted to *see*. I wanted to join, very much, but I had to *see* first.'

'And what did you see?' Clarissa sounded intently curious.

'The way things could be,' Val said abruptly, sadly, and stood and went for another beer. On the table near where she sat was a report on conditions in prisons for political prisoners in South Vietnam. She was helping a group that was trying to put it together. More and more, Val was neglecting her schoolwork.

'I don't understand,' Iso said when she returned. 'What did that have to do with people apart from us?'

Val shrugged apologetically. 'Well, you know, I have a lot of visions. I grew up in the late forties, the fifties, when the best minds believed you couldn't make it as a person if you got too involved with the world. Oh, there were the socialists too, and they had a dogma, at least, but they'd been fairly well silenced by the early fifties. My generation grew up reading Joyce and Woolf and Lawrence and those crummy poets of the fifties. And granted maybe Lawrence wanted a community of three, and Woolf tried to get beyond the isolated self, still all of them felt the world was grimy and power was disease, death itself. And in everyday culture too. All the lovelorn columns gave the same advice: if you're having trouble, get away from your mother-in-law, move out of town where all those acid aunts and pompous uncles can't get at you.'

'It's true. We all learned to live emotionally alone,' Mira put in.

'Yes. Salvation was a personal affair. But look at us! We have a community, a real community. We share almost everything but still have our privacies. We can love and nourish one another without oppressing each other. It's fantastic to realize that it can be done. It makes me think my vision can come true.'

'Which vision is this?' Clarissa smiled.

'Okay.' She lighted a cigarette and sat back looking like the chairman of the board about to deliver the annual report. We all settled down for what we knew would be a lecture.

'Wait!' Kyla giggled. 'I want to get my pad and take notes!'

'The old neighborhoods didn't work. The Italians hated the Irish and the Irish hated the Jews, and neighborhoods warred with each other. But the breakdown of the neighborhoods also meant the end of what was essentially an extended family: only blacks still have it. With the breakdown of the extended family, too much pressure was put on the single family. Mom had no one to stay with Granny, who couldn't be depended on not to set the house on fire while Mom was off grocery shopping. The people in the neighborhood weren't there to keep an idle eye out for the fourteen-year-old kid who was the local idiot, and treated with affection as well as tormented – I'm not saying the old neighborhoods were all good. So we came up with the idea of putting everybody in separate places. We lock them up in prisons, mental hospitals, geriatric housing projects, old-age homes, nursery schools, cheap suburbs that keep women and the kids off the streets, expensive suburbs where everybody has their own yard and a front lawn that is tended by a gardener so all the front lawns look alike and nobody uses them anyway. Did you ever see a family using their front lawn? Anyway, the faster we lock them up, the higher up goes the crime rate, the suicide rate, the rate of mental breakdown. The way it's going, there'll be more of them than us pretty soon. Then you'll have to start asking questions about the percentage of the population that's not locked up, those that claim that the other fifty-five per cent is crazy, criminal, or senile.

'We have to find some other way. The kids who go off to communes have a good idea, but the idea isn't usable in that form because most communes reject technology. And we can't do that. We need it and we have to learn, somehow, someday, to love technology, to live with it, to humanize it. Because not only couldn't we live decently without it, we're not going to live without it. That's not a possibility. It's second nature – I mean that – it's our environment now, and no more artificial than the first cultivated ground, the first domesticated animals, the first tools. But communes are a good idea. People criticize communes because they don't last, but why in hell, will you tell me, should they last? Why does an order have to become a permanent order? Maybe we should live one way for some years, then try another.

'Anyway, for a long time now. I've been thinking about this, and talking to people, and I don't claim originality for my ideas because I'm sure I've stolen them from everywhere, and I don't even claim to offer a good idea, but just, maybe, another track. So I was thinking – I was in Spain, I guess – and you know, some of the poorest, the sorriest Spanish towns are beautiful. The houses are all connected, at least it looks that way from the road. They are little white stucco houses, built at crazy angles to each other, but connected by one wall, and they're built in a circle. They have those red tile roofs, and they look like a bunch of people with outspread arms holding to each other to stay warm and safe. Well, we can stay warm, and comparatively safe without doing that, but I'm not sure we can stay sane without that. They sit up there, the houses, baking under the sun, and they're cool and dim inside, and the dust settles down at the threshold. I'm sure they smell, and lack bathrooms, and all the things we'd want – and most of those, by the way, I think we're right to want, unfashionable as it is to say so. But they cluster on the sides of those hills looking as beautiful and as natural as the olive grove just beyond.

'So I started imagining, suppose we did that. Suppose we built houses in a circle, or a square, or whatever, connected houses of varying sizes, but beautiful, simple. And in the middle would be a garden with benches and trees and people could grow flowers, it would be a common. And outside, behind the houses, all the space usually given over to front and back lawns, would be common too. And there could be vegetable gardens, and fields and woods for the kids to play in. There'd be problems about somebody picking the tomatoes somebody else planted, or the roses, or the kids tramping through the pea patch, but the fifty groups or individuals who lived in the houses would have complete charge and complete responsibility for what went on in their little enclave. At the other side of the houses, facing them, would be a little community center. It would have a community laundry – why does everybody have to own a washing machine? – and some playrooms and a little café and a communal kitchen. The café would be an outdoor one, with sliding glass panels to close it in in winter, like the ones in Paris. This wouldn't be a full commune: everybody would have their own way of earning a living, everybody would retain their own income, and the dwellings would be priced according to size. Each would have a little kitchen, in case people wanted to eat alone, a good-sized living space, but not enormous, because the community center would be there. Maybe the community center would be beautiful, lush even. With playrooms for the kids and the adults, and sitting rooms with books. But everyone in the community, from the smallest walking child, would have a job in it.'

Mira looked incredulous.

'Kids can do things!' Val insisted. 'It makes them feel good. True, you have to risk an occasional accident. But those happen anyway. They can rock the carriage, they can fetch and carry, they can clean up the toys, set the table, help pod the peas.'

'In Europe lots of little kids work. They help out in their parents' shops and cafés,' Iso said.

'Sure. They would be allowed to do whatever they wanted to do. Since everybody would be doing something, they'd want to too. There wouldn't be a rigid hierarchy of tasks, only of hours. Little kids might only be expected to give, say four hours a week to the community, twelve-year-olds and over, maybe eight, and adults, oh, I don't know, say twelve or sixteen. But if there was somebody who wanted to spend more – somebody retired, say, or a poet who didn't want to hold a regular job – they could put in extra time and it would give them a reduction in rent. Older people might want to spend time watching over the children, or growing vegetables. But the community would have its own government, everyone having one vote, and would be responsible for its own garbage, its own rules, running its own kitchen and its – I insist on this,' Val grinned, 'outdoor café.

'One important thing that might cause trouble: it should have a quota system. There has to be a mixture of ages, so young people grow up knowing older people. I think there will also have to be a mixture of kinds, otherwise we'll run into the same problem the old neighborhoods did. Like, I don't go for these swinging singles apartment complexes. A certain proportion of various religions, colors, families, singles, pairs, you know.'

'I see trouble,' Iso said. 'What about that swinging single?'

'Yeah.' Val stopped and wrinkled her forehead. She seemed to be thinking about this just as if it were a possible reality. 'Well, have to decide that later,' she said finally, and we all laughed.

'Okay. There are a certain number of clusters of these communities, the number to depend on the natural topography, and where people chose to put them. Each group of communities would center in a larger town. There are buses running back and forth all the time, all hours. In the larger center are some schools, but the schools wouldn't be like ours. They wouldn't divide people strictly by age. They would be voluntary, and people of all ages would attend them. The divisions among rooms would be based on activity. Some rooms would hold little animals, some plants, some paints and paper. And some would be devoted strictly to reading and writing, but reading and writing for fun, not for filling in workbooks. You know. Well, that's another thing. The town center would also have shops, churches, local government buildings, offices for services. And you'd have to walk through it. There would be mini-buses in the larger ones, but most of them would be smallish, and would be built with narrow lanes, trees, outdoor cafés, maybe even a square with a fountain, or a covered galleria like the one in Milan. And one of the schools will have an auditorium good enough to hold concerts in, for town meetings, for traveling theater groups, or ballets. And for amateur groups, too. And someplace in it – in the galleria, I guess, there will be an art gallery. Maybe just with local art.' She stopped, and frowned. 'No, with a combination. Some local, some from the city. But I suppose you'd have to have some glass, until the little kids learned not to touch them with ice-cream fingers. But open, not shut in. So everybody could see the pictures.'

'Val, have you read *Walden Two*?'

'Umm. You detect thefts?'

'Just a bit.'

'Well, I don't put babies behind glass. And there really weren't any kids in *Walden Two*. There were babies under glass and nubile boys and girls. No kids. That's because it was written by a man. I once heard Mortimer Adler say that in the ideal world nobody would have to do the shitwork. Babies would be diapered by machine. My God! I hope he doesn't have anything to say about the next world. Not that I so much love diapering. But the things babies need are to be held, fondled, crooned over, touched. And left alone. We do everything bass-ackwards. We don't want to hold them

501

much when they're little, but when they're a little older, we won't leave them alone, we're so busy protecting them. When Chris and I were living in the South, we stayed for a while in a well-to-do suburb, and those kids had their afternoons scheduled! Really! Doctor, dentist, orthodontist, dancing lessons, confraternity, temple, Scouts, Little League, music lessons – they never had a free wicked minute. I don't know what will become of them.

'Anyway,' she resumed, businesslike, 'these centers are still communities of a sort. They're not very large. They also have their own governments, their own medical centers and so forth, but people work in them, they don't give their labor, they get paid. People around, oh, ten or twelve work one day a week, people between, say, fifteen and nineteen work two days a week, people over that work three or four days a week, depending on their other interests and how much money they want to earn. Older people can drop down if they want to, can work less. Really old people, or infirm people who don't want to work in the center, can work in the community only. But there's always some sharing of shitwork. Like a person who's a doctor four days a week may be put on the garbage detail of the community for a couple weeks, and the person who works in the factory may be put in charge of decorating the community center for a holiday. You know? Everybody would cook sometime except the ones who really hated it. And everybody would clean sometime, ditto. Anyway, every so often, depending on population spread, there would also be a city. Oh, by the way, industrial centers would be just like the towns and cities: they would be built for pleasure as well as work, and they would be surrounded by country-side, so the ecological balance would stay in kilter. The way the Swiss built Geneva, you know? Anyway, the cities would hold the universities, the museums of note, major offices for businesses, concert halls. There are people living in the cities just as there are in the towns, but they live in little clusters, just like the ones in the country. They will also have a certain amount of open

502

space, small open spaces for each cluster. And if you want to hear Gunther Schiller's music, or see avant-garde theater, you may have to go to the city. Although you never know. The community theater group may decide to put on something unusual. 'Well,' she sighed, and sipped her drink.

They all stared at her. How many hours had she spent thinking up this daydream? Mira wondered.

'It sounds nice,' Kyla said, preparing to tear holes in it.

'I know,' Val answered sadly. 'I don't mean to suggest we should engineer perfection. Or even think about trying to do that. Only that we think about finding a more humane way to live, a way that feels better to us. I remember when Chris was little. I had a hard time for a few years after I left my husband. I had no money and he was holding out, thinking he could get me back that way. The damned fool never realized he'd have had a better chance if he'd been fair. Men always seem to think power is more attractive than lovingness. I suppose they have some reason to think so. Anyway, my life was pretty bad and hard and the only thing good about it was that he wasn't in it with that unpredictable temper and that loud voice of his. I'd pick Chris up at the sitter's and go home and cook dinner and clean up and I'd be exhausted from working in that crummy office all day, from stopping at the supermarket and carrying home a heavy bag of groceries in one arm and holding on to Chris with the other. And she'd be tired and cranky then too. And at last I'd draw a bath for her, happy it was her bedtime, and sit her in it with some toys and go back to the kitchen and wash the fucking dishes. And then I'd go back to her and I was tired and harried and I hated my life, and I'd just look at her sitting in the tub, crooning to herself and a rubber boat, maybe, hardly noticing me, I was just an appliance, and her skin was all shiny from the water, and her hair had curled up, and she was talking to her toys, babbling away, and then she'd deign to notice me, and she'd grin and pound her toy in the water, smashing it all over me and getting soapsuds in my eye and I'd just have to reach out and hug her, she was so beautiful, so free, so much herself. . . . I don't know. Taking care of Chris, problem that it was, somehow kept me human. And if we all did that, all took care of each other, if that became, oh, not a requirement, but a custom, something people just did unless they really didn't want to . . . I have this scene in my head. I see a rose garden tended by an elderly man who tends to be grouchy. And some children coming to see him, visiting him once in a while, as he tends the roses. And he always shoos them at first, growls at them, but he's been there so long they're not afraid of him, they stand around and talk to him and one day, one spring day after a couple of years, he starts to teach them how to tend roses, and even puts the clipper in one child's hands and helps them to clip off the dead or dying sprouts. Well.' She spread her hands out, and laughed a little. 'You have to let me be a fool. Somebody has to do the dreaming.'

Kyla ran across the room and held Val's head; Iso got up and got her another drink; and Clarissa grinned across at her.

'I think we've just elected you our community fool,' she said.

11

The image of the party remained in Mira's head. She thought about it in terms that belied her atheism, as a moment of grace vouchsafed them by something divine. They were all touched by it, and they would never be quite the same as they had been. There had been many wonderful parties, many comings-together, but this one transcended, it was an image of complete human harmony and love. Would it endure? Would they all, when they came together in the future, mesh in precisely that way, feel the grace of connection? Such grace could not be arranged or forced or even hoped for; there was no structure capable of creating it. Val would try: she would spend her precious time trying to come up with a

504

structure that did not kill spirit. Bless her for trying, but it was hopeless, Mira felt. Best to swirl in the dance when it occurs, let yourself become the music, the motion, and then just remember. But they had all been touched by it: they could not ever be quite the same as they had been. She was sure of that much.

The winter was long and cold and lonely. No one was taking classes any longer. Lehman Hall was empty of familiar faces. Everyone was holed up in Child or a carrel in Widener or at home, plowing through lists of books, taking piles of notes, scratching out book after book, only to add another thirty to the bottom of the list. Mira had tens of folders with lists of things like the various arrangements of *The Canterbury Tales*, the order of items in the Martin Marprelate controversy, or the dates of all editions of *The Laws of Ecclesiastical Polity* and *The Anatomy of Melancholy*.

Only Val was not studying for orals; she operated under different rules, and was working on an elaborate project which required her interviewing several hundred carefully selected people. But she seemed these days to be always running from meeting to protest to meeting. She was agitated and more and more single-minded: the situation in Southeast Asia became more intolerable to her as the bombings were increased, American forces increased. But all of us were distraught: Kyla was pale, and her face looked crumpled; Clarissa's eyes were sunk in her head; Mira was worried and withdrawn; only Iso bloomed.

The major luxury the women permitted themselves was a visit at Iso's two or three times a week. But Kyla stopped in almost every day. She went whenever the impulse struck her – sometimes at eleven in the morning, sometimes at two, or four, or even six o'clock. If Iso was not there, she would sit on the steps waiting, a forlorn little figure, her face knotted and twisting from one expression to another. She would sit reading, her mouth twisting even while she read. When she spotted Iso striding home, she'd look up and smile, and her face would smooth out.

Iso had no money, but she tried to keep her refrigerator full of soda and wine and beer for her friends. She too was studying for orals, but she never seemed to resent her friends' intrusions on her time. She would grin at Kyla and sweep her up, as if Kyla's visit was the most important moment of her day. She saw the twisting mouth, the knotted fingers. She gave a drink appropriate to the hour, and sat easily, listening, listening. She asked Kyla questions, not about the present but about the past, about her childhood, her two successful brothers, mom and dad, grade school, high school. The subjects were innocent, and Kyla talked easily. She poured out stories, memories, hurts, triumphs; she talked as she had never talked to another human being, wondering at herself as she did it. But Iso seemed interested, really interested. 'I'm not boring you, am I?' Kyla would break off often, biting her lip. Words blasted out of her as if the past had been bottled up so long and so tightly that given a pinhole of escape, it had blown out cork and all.

'Even when I was very little, I remember reading things and saying, "This is how I want to be." Or "I don't want to be like that." When I was nine or ten I started to keep a journal – a ledger, really – listing qualities I wanted to possess and those I wanted to avoid, and grading myself day by day. Like Ben Franklin's, you know? Except I wasn't so successful. Unlike him, I did not achieve every virtue including humility in thirty days.' They laughed. Kyla twisted her mouth. 'Or whatever it was,' she amended nervously. 'In fact, I never achieved any of them. I kept backsliding. It was so disheartening, I can't tell you, it was so important to me to achieve these things.'

'Like what?'

'Oh, honesty. Honesty was first, always. And justice – fairness, whatever you want to call it. And cheerful obedience. I really flubbed that one.' Suddenly she changed her tone and leapt into a seemingly irrelevant story about her days as a high-school cheerleader, tearing up the road on a friend's borrowed motorcycle, and crashing into a ditch for no reason. 'I had the thing in control. I never understood that.' She sipped gin. 'And excellence. No, perfection. In whatever I was doing . . .'

'What were the baddies?'

'Cowardice, deceit, shoddiness, lack of control,' she rapped out. 'Ugh, how I hate those things. That's why I love Harley so much. He has none of those things.'

Talk about Harley always began on this kind of high note, and always deteriorated, after a couple of glasses of wine or gin, into inarticulate, hysterical weeping. Kyla's conclusion was always the same when the fit was over: Harley was wonderful, everything was fine, she should not drink.

Then she'd leap up, invariably late for something, grab her things and run out, down the stairs, down the block, except for those sessions at Iso's always running, even in class, always in motion, crossing and uncrossing her legs, lighting cigarettes, puffing, then tamping them out, tapping cigarettes in ashtrays, gesticulating widely with arms, sometimes so passionately that she threw whatever she held in her hand – a pen, a filled glass, a cigarette – clear across the room. She scratched her head, she grimaced, she raised her eyebrows, she lowered them, she moved in her seat, she fiddled with papers. Her movements were as perky and abrupt as the course of a hunted animal scurrying from one familiar hole to another and finding each one blocked, yet repeating and repeating the round in panic. As often as not, when she arrived at Iso's she would sit there for ten minutes telling Iso she should not have come because she had thus and such to do, listing impossible schedules which she was going to fulfill, she insisted, as soon as she finished this cup of coffee, this Coke, this glass of wine, this gin. The latter two invariably led to more, and thence, invariably to tears. She did not seem conscious that she visited Iso every day, or that she stayed for hours. Often when she arrived in the afternoon, she would remain late into the evening. Harley came to know where she was, and sometimes there would be a phone call at seven or eight or nine, and Kyla would emerge from the bedroom with drawn white face, and nervous mouth twitching and puckering. 'I did it again,' she would announce hollowly, having missed another dinner party. Twice she missed dinner parties she had been supposed to prepare. Her mind was full of blank spaces.

One day, Iso confronted her with them. It was a bad time, a month before Kyla's orals, a week before Iso's. Kyla had chewed her lips bloody, and her hands were covered with eczema. These days she got drunk on one gin and tonic or even a small glass of wine. She was sipping wine and relating in a trembling voice her unspeakable behavior the night before at a party at MIT for graduate students in physics.

'I mean Kontarsky! The great Kontarsky! He's Harley's superviser on the dissertation, he holds Harley's future in his hands! To anyone else it would be bad enough, but to say it to him! Harley was livid – he wouldn't speak to me all the way home, and when we got there he packed a bag and stormed out. Wouldn't speak. I was crying. I was apologizing. I guess he's sleeping at the lab. I don't blame him. I don't know how I manage to do these things.'

'What exactly did you do that was so terrible?'

She tried to tell her story, but kept breaking into tears. Her right fist was knotted so hard the knuckles were blue. She kept smashing it into her knee. 'How could I? How could I?' she kept crying in a thin high voice, barely audible. Eventually she calmed down. 'I'd had a couple of drinks. Kontarsky was talking to me, standing over me, he's big, you know, and beaming at me with his fatherly benevolent look, but I know what that posture, that look means – he was leering at me, wondering how far I'd go to aid my husband's career. There were a bunch of other people standing around, mostly professors, and on the fringes, behind them, all these greedy little graduate students, dying to make a point, dying for God's sakes to breathe in the carbon dioxide the great man breathed out. And he was talking about Academia and what a wonderful life it was and how nice it was that Harley and I were in it together, and I just looked up at him and flicked my ash and said

508

I didn't think it was so great, that as far as I could tell all the men in Academia were prickless wonders.'

Iso started to gurgle in her throat; the gurgle exploded into laughter; the laughter continued until there were tears streaming down Iso's cheeks. Kyla stared at her horrified. 'Don't you see, I couldn't be sure he was putting the make on me! I mean he hadn't said anything! If he had, it wouldn't be so bad! I can't be sure!' She kept protesting, Iso kept laughing, and Kyla began to titter, and then broke out fully in a deep joyful laugh. 'Oh, the bastard!' she gasped. 'He's such a bastard, really. I'm glad I said it!' Then instantly sobered. 'Oh, but poor Harley. It was terrible of me to do that to Harley. I'm not fit to be taken out in public.'

'I think it's great,' Iso sighed, wiping away tears. 'That pompous mass of inflated ego, that horses's ass of a human being, Kontarsky! They think they're doing something so great – how can you do anything great for the human race if all you have is a detached mind? Mira would say they ought to clean the toilet once a week. They need that, they require it.'

'Oh, Iso, do you think so?' Kyla chewed her lip. 'But how could I do that to Harley?'

'Listen, Kyla, for a person who worships honesty and courage, you are amazingly immersed in deceit and cowardice.'

'I?' Kyla struck her chest with her flat hand. 'I?' She put her glass down hard on the table, spilling wine on her skirt. She leaped up and fished in her bag for some tissues. 'I'm a drunk and I'm a rotten bitch, but I'm not dishonest! That's not fair!' She wiped up her skirt.

Iso gazed at her kindly. 'You're the worst liar I ever met.'

Kyla perched herself on the edge of the chair. There were tears in her eyes again.

'You lie to the world, you lie to yourself. You keep saying over and over again, as if you could make it come true, that Harley's wonderful, that you're happy, that your marriage is great. But you're falling apart, you're utterly miserable – it's obvious to anyone who

509

looks. I don't understand why Harley doesn't see it. God knows you even cry at parties when he's around. You're always crying.'

Kyla burst into tears. This time they continued for a long time. Kyla's small body heaved, it looked as if it would be destroyed by the spasms passing through it. Iso moved closer to her and took her hand. Kyla buried her head in Iso's bosom, and kept crying. She clutched onto Iso, gripping her arm so hard she left bruises. Still gasping, she began to talk. She poured out a story hedged at every turning with self-deprecation. Harley was wonderful but he did not seem to love her but that was because she asked too much because Harley himself was grand. Of course he would be upset when he came home from the lab full of excitement at some breakthrough and wanted to talk to her and she was not there. And of course when she was there and wanted to talk but he was busy in his study he would not want to be interrupted. His work was so difficult, so important. It was all understandable. It was just that she was a rotten bitch. She kept chewing her lip, and blood was trickling down her chin. 'But I get excited too and want to talk to him about it, but he's always busy, he doesn't want to hear. And then orals. When he was studying for orals, I took over everything, I did everything, I freed him to study. I had classes and committees too, but I shopped, cooked, cleaned. I didn't vacuum unless he was out; I answered the phone in a whisper. I acted as if his studying for orals were a sacred act and I was the votaress in charge of sweeping up the chapel.

'But now, I'm studying for orals and what does he do? Nothing. He expects me to go on doing all the work and he brings home friends for me to entertain. He's not so busy now, his work is nearly finished, he has time for friends, oh, I understand, I don't blame him, I love Harley, he's worked so hard, he's entitled to a little pleasure. He doesn't mean any harm – he just doesn't realize how scared I am. He thinks English is a snap subject, and that I'm smart enough to pass without really working.' She was still perched on the edge of the chair, but her legs were still. 'I think that's what frustrates me the most. It's as though he doesn't take me seriously.'

'Does he feel that way about everybody in English?'

'Yes. He has less respect for English than anything. He likes art and music and he says history has some reason to exist, and philosophy, and even philology – he respects linguists. But not people in literature. He says anybody can read. He thinks he knows as much about literature as any of us. And it's true, he does know a lot. It's hard to fault Harley. He's usually right. Still it makes me feel lousy.'

Around eleven, Iso went into the kitchen and opened a can of soup, and put some crackers and cheese on a plate. She had been arguing with Kyla, telling her how bright she was, how interesting her work. 'I've heard Harley talk about books, and he's just eccentric. He thinks James Branch Cabell is a great writer: that's okay, it's good to hear eccentric opinions, but that doesn't have much to do with what we do, after all. We work with a critical and literary tradition with changes in ideas manifested in changes in style . . .'

Kyla kept giggling: 'Tell that to Harley! Oh, you make it sound so legitimate!' Iso was standing at the stove, stirring the soup, and Kyla slid her arm around Iso's waist, and Iso put her arm on Kyla's shoulders, and bent and kissed the top of her head lightly.

They ate, they drank more wine, they talked. Kyla was exultant. 'I haven't felt so good in years! You make me feel as if I'm worthwhile, as though what I'm doing is worthwhile.' Iso was sitting on the couch, sprawled out over its length, and Kyla went and sat in the curve of her arm, which closed around her. At two they went to bed, and Kyla slept wrapped in her friend.

Kyla went home the next day to water her plants. She stayed in the empty apartment for two full days and nights, trying to study, but then she went back to

Iso's. After that they alternated, sitting in one or the other apartment to read, asking each other lists of dates, looking up at each other occasionally to smile in the other's eyes, making coffee, pouring soda, and around four, pouring wine for each other.

When they went out, they floated down streets together. Their exaltation was obvious; a stranger could have seen it, Mira thought. Iso floated through her orals as well, and a group of them went out and celebrated. Kyla was amazingly different – still lively and vigorous, still given to knocking over wineglasses and throwing spoons, but her mouth was calm, and mostly smiling or talking.

A few days later Kyla and Iso were reading at Kyla's, Iso checking her out on medieval sources for Renaissance writers, and Harley walked in. He did not, of course, understand the relation. He was pleasant to Iso, coldly polite to Kyla, who immediately sat up stiffly and began crossing and uncrossing her legs.

'If Iso doesn't mind, I'd like to talk to you.'

'I'm busy, Harley. I'm studying.'

'It is rather important,' he said mildly, sarcastically.

Kyla bit her lip and looked pleadingly at Iso.

'I have to go anyway. I'm meeting Mira at Child at four thirty,' Iso lied.

Kyla leaped up and threw her arms around Iso. 'Thanks so much. Thanks for helping me. Thanks for everything. I'll call you.'

'I'd like to return to my home,' Harley began, combing his hair with his fingers, a gesture that betrayed more nervousness than he had ever shown. Harley's father had been trained at West Point and had trained his sons in what he called 'composure,' which meant the avoidance of any expressive gestures.

'I haven't kept you away.'

'Yes, you have, Kyla,' his voice rose firmly. He recited his wrongs without emotion, like a judge reading off the counts of an indictment. There were plenty of them: times the defendant had been absent when she was supposed to be home; engagements, even dinners missed; the unforgivable missing of dinners she had been supposed to cook; weepy drunkenness at parties, continually; and the final, the terrible remark to Kontarsky. 'Luckily, his first wife had several nervous breakdowns—'

'I'll bet she did!' Kyla shot in.

'– so he understands,' Harley continued calmly, only frowning at her. 'I had a long talk with him—'

'About me? You talked to him about me?' she shrieked.

'Kyla! What are you trying to do to me? I think you're trying to destroy me! I think you're insane – certifiable!'

'So!' she exploded, throwing out both her arms and knocking over a glass vase that stood on a side table. 'It's all my doing, is it?'

His face carefully expressionless, his movements conspicuously patient, Harley rose, retrieved the fallen vase, and placed it on the mantelpiece, out of a child's reach. Kyla leaped up, charged into the kitchen, and poured herself a glass of straight gin.

'If you're going to get yourself smashed, I'll leave. There's no talking to you when you're like that.'

She charged back and threw herself on the couch and began the recital of her litany. He was never home, and when he was—

'That is illogical.'

'You know what I mean!' When he was he was uninterested in her, in her work, in her excitements, her discoveries, he wanted her only as an audience. She had done everything for him when he was studying for orals, but he had done nothing for her. And, and (biting her lip, turning away her head) sexually he was – inconsiderate.

Harley sat looking like a Greek sculpture, his fine noble profile serene, but at the last charge he blinked and turned.

'Inconsiderate how?'

'You know how. You know. You're always in such a hurry, you don't get me excited enough and you thrust

513

yourself into me before I'm ready and it hurts and you know all that. How can you ask me how when you know?'

Harley looked straight at her, and there was fear in his eyes. Then he dropped his gaze, but his face had changed, it had shadows of pain in it. That tinge of suffering on his face stabbed through her. She tried to ease it for him: 'Well, we've talked about it before. I've asked you. But you always seem to forget.'

He was staring at the floor, his hands lightly clasped between his legs. 'So it's really that. All this while you've been storing up hate for me because of that. All this crazy behavior . . .'

'No,' Kyla heard herself sounding calmly assured, in control. 'No. It's that you don't take me seriously. In any area.'

'That's ridiculous.'

She launched another litany, but this time her voice was quiet, dignified. He regarded her work as frivolous, her nature as emotional and therefore invalid, her concerns as insignificant. She offered him example after example. Harley stood up and ran his hand through his hair again. He came closer to her, but did not look straight at her. Gazing half out the window, half his face visible to her, he said, 'I didn't mean to hurt you, Kyla.'

She closed her eyes and a tear splashed on her lashes. Harley stood before her, looking down. 'I'll try, Kyla.' It was the most unsure she had ever heard him, and she knew what that cost him. He looked like an angel standing there, his hair white in the last glow of sun. He was an angel fallen because of her, dragged down by her into the world of flesh and pain and limitation and inadequacy where he was not at home. He belonged in the world of pure thought. His face had never looked sad like that before, his voice had never trembled before. She grabbed his hands and kissed them and laid her cheek against them, and he bent and kissed the top of her head, and she rubbed her cheek on his hands and as she did so, she smelled her underarms, and when he crouched down to embrace her she became conscious of

514

her sweatiness, it seemed she could smell her crotch, her period must have arrived, she felt rank and stained, and she pulled away from him, she ordered him back to his chair, she scratched her head and felt its grease. 'I'm having an affair with Iso,' she said.

Harley stared at her. She explained how it had happened, how upset she had been, how sympathetic Iso had been, how she had clung to Iso desperate for love.

'Ummm.' Harley said nothing, although he watched her acutely during her explanation. 'Are you telling me I've been replaced by a woman in your affections?' he asked finally, his mouth twisting a little.

'No. It's different. It doesn't replace you, it complements you.'

'Then let's forget it.' He stood up. 'Is it all right with you if I come back?'

She was overpouring with love, it flowed from her eyes as she looked up at him. 'Oh, yes, Harley, yes, darling.'

'Then I'll get my stuff from the car.'

'Okay. I'm going to take a quick shower.'

She hummed as the water washed away her sweat, her effluvia, her grease; she washed, thoroughly, all her orifices. He was more wonderful even than she had thought; he was large, he could accept criticism, he could forgive and understand. They would have a fresh start. Maybe what they should do was have a baby. She could have a baby and write her dissertation at the same time. It might be fun.

That afternoon, as they made love, Harley was careful and painstaking, caressing her body, nuzzling her breasts, rubbing her clitoris. He did not push himself at her, only twice he asked her if she was ready. The third time he asked, she was too embarrassed to say no again, and she said yes, and he thrust into her painfully and she was so grateful for his care and remorseful at her slowness and embarrassed by her failure that she pretended orgasm, and Harley lay back afterward glowing with pleasure and a sense of achievement.

Kyla's mouth twitched.

Kyla, smoking nervously, explained to Mira the arrangements she and Harley had worked out. He would take over the house completely for the next two weeks, until her orals were over, and after that they would divide the chores in half. She was to get home at whatever hour she had said she would; he would help her in her studying as she had helped him; and she would no longer be sexually involved with Iso, although they were still friends.

Lehman Hall was nearly deserted, but the tables around them held a clutter of filled ashtrays, empty coffee cups, balled-up cellophane potato chip bags, cigarette packages. Mira listened to Kyla, trying to reflect in her eyes and smile the elated confidence, the loving joy Kyla was expressing, but she felt dragged down. This was a depressing place with all its leftovers, she thought, all the dregs of the past, the lunches and afternoon coffees that left such a mess but hadn't been worth it, hadn't satisfied anything except the barest hunger. Val, sitting next to Mira, kept things going, and in time Kyla jumped up, looking at her watch, and went off to some duty.

'I just can't believe in it,' Mira said sadly.

'I know.'

'I should be able to. Ben and I are still good. But Harley's different.'

'It's significant that he was able to accept the business with Iso so easily.'

'That was remarkable.'

'Hah!' Val snorted. 'It simply means he doesn't take it seriously. A woman as a lover doesn't count.'

'Do you think so?' Mira was surprised. 'Oh, Val, have a little charity.'

Val grimaced. 'It gets harder and harder.' Val looked haggard. She was working, almost all the time these days, on the antiwar committee. She insisted to anyone who would listen that without our knowledge, the war was being extended into Laos and Cambodia, that we were on our way to destroying all of Indochina. She was grim and angry much of the time. She sighed, and turned to Mira. 'So how are you and Ben?'

'We're fine. At least I think we're fine. It must be this place,' she looked around, 'so full of crap, all the leftovers, as though you could never get rid of things . . .'

Val's brow clouded. 'What things?'

'I don't know. I don't know why I'm feeling so low. It was listening to Kyla, to her enthusiasm. She really foresees a rosy future, and I can't foresee that for her with Harley. And then that talk about maybe having a baby. . . . You know, you go around feeling good about things and maybe to somebody else you look as deluded as Kyla looks to me,' she finished questioningly.

Val laughed. 'I take it you're asking. You don't look deluded to me. I think Ben's great.'

'But,' Mira said warily, 'he wants a baby too.' She watched Val's face.

It did not change. 'How do you feel about that?'

It was Mira's turn to smoke nervously. 'Well,' she laughed half-heartedly, 'it may seem strange coming from me, but I'm not sure I even like the idea of marriage.' She developed it; Val watched her intently. She had forgotten that most of the things she was saying now she had heard first from Val, a long year ago. Marriage accustomed one to the good things, so one came to take them for granted, but magnified the bad things, so they came to feel as painful as a grain in one's eye. An opened window, a forgotten quart of milk, a TV set left blaring, socks on the bathroom floor could become occasions for incredible rage. And something happened sexually in marriage – the swearing to forsake all others, despite its slight observance, had a profound effect. Some people felt trapped by it, impelled to assert what they called freedom. Some accepted it like a rein, and in the effort to avoid pain in the form of hopeless desire, cut off occasions of desire, avoided having long talks at parties with attractive members of the opposite sex. In time, all feeling for the opposite sex was cut off,

517

and intercourse limited to the barest politenesses. The men then gathered talking business and politics; the women talking people. But something happened to you when you did that, a kind of death seeped up from the genitals to the rest of the body, till it showed in the eyes, the gestures, in a certain lifelessness. On the other hand, it would kill her if Ben got sexually interested in somebody else, and she hoped, yes, she hoped, he felt the same way. But if they were to marry, then what? Would Ben feel he was cut off from the feast of life? She would not. She had no desire for anyone else, of course there was no one else much around, perhaps in a different place . . . but would she lose her friends? The great nights she and Val, she and Iso had spent, talking wonderfully far into the morning, would they still be possible? She and Ben would start to be just a couple. Then their time together would lose its intensity, would become mere dailiness.

And – she hesitated, and her voice deepened – a baby. A baby. She shook her head vigorously. 'I couldn't go back to that, I couldn't stand it. I love my kids, I'm glad I have them, but no, no, no! But after all, he's entitled, isn't he, to want a child? Except he wouldn't be the one to take care of it. If all I had to do was have it – well, I wouldn't be thrilled, but I'd do it. But I'd have it forever, you know how it is. And if he left me, when I was sixty and he was fifty-four and the kid was still in college, I'd still have it. Still, he wants a child, and if he insisted . . .'

'Yes. If he – well, he doesn't have to insist. Just press.'

'Yes. What would I do?' She puffed nervously. 'I don't know, you see. I know I shouldn't have a baby. I know that for myself. But I love Ben so much, I might give in. Just the thought of being without him gives me the sensation of being on an elevator that suddenly drops ten floors. He's my center: everything is good because he's in my life. But if I did it – oh, God, I don't know.'

Val looked at her, and Mira saw in Val's face what it was that made her so extraordinary. There were whole networks of shapings and turnings, age lines, not deep,

518

just complex. And Val's expression at this moment had everything in it: understanding, compassion, the knowledge of pain, an awareness of the impossibility of what, when we are young, we consider happiness, and at the same time, an amused, ironic gaiety, the joy of the survivor who knows the value of small pleasures.

Mira spread out her hands. 'There's nothing to be done,' she shrugged.

'The trouble is that something must be done.'

Mira raised her eyebrows questioningly.

'You must do something. You will go on together or you won't. You'll marry or you won't. You'll have a child or you won't.'

Mira sank. 'That's what I can't deal with.' She appealed to Val. 'Do you think he'll forgive me in years to come if we stay together but don't have a kid?'

'Do you think you'll forgive him in years to come if you stay together and do have a kid?'

Mira laughed then, they laughed together heartily. 'Fuck the future!' Val crowed, and Mira grabbed her hand, and they sat looking at each other's not-young faces, lined with time, bright with life, survivors grinning at a joke that in this young place was not widely shared. And Mira was reminded of Val's entrance at a costume party they'd had months before, wearing a sexy black pantsuit trimmed with feathers, and with silver sprayed in her hair, and sparkling blue eye shadow over her eyes, carrying a long black cigarette holder. Everyone stopped when she walked in and took an extravagant pose: she laughed too. She stood there unperturbed by her bulk, her age, posing like a vamp of the thirties, laughing, triumphant, at herself and her illusions and desires, at the foolishness of glamour and its joy, and the colorlessness of a world without it. Some of us understood. All of us were contained in that laughter, all of us who knew that our necks had grown thin, our chins soft, our legs too heavy, our hairlines diminishing. Even the young were part of it, who didn't yet accept that they would grow old or that the beautiful life they had imagined would not occur, but who did know that there was something not quite ideal about the length of their bodies or the knobbiness of their knees; even the youngest and most beautiful of us had an eyebrow or a nostril we were not happy with, all of us beautiful and aging, walking forth preening in the middle of our dying, preening with life, shrugging off death. She made us see that. She came in glowing and laughing and gay. Ah, indomitable Val!

13

The first time she had the nightmare was a week before her orals, and she had it every night after that. She would wake up damp and shaking and get up and smoke and pace around the apartment. But she did not tell Harley. She did not tell anyone.

She dreamt she was in the room where orals were held, a wood-paneled room with small paned windows and a broad shining table. The three men who were to examine her were sitting at one end of the table quareling as she walked in. She had just stepped inside the door when she spied the pile in the corner. Instantly she knew what it was, but she was incredulous, she was so ashamed, she moved nearer to check it out. It was what she thought. She was horrified. Those stained sanitary napkins, those bloody underpants were hers, she knew they were hers, and she knew the men would know it too. She tried to stand in front of them, but there was no way she could conceal them. The men stopped quarreling, they had turned to face her, they were peering at her....

Her apprehension became severe anxiety. She made more lists, swiftly, grimly; she ran to the library first thing in the morning and read until Child closed, but at the end of the day she knew she had absorbed nothing, that she had read words, words, words. She did tell Harley about her panic, but he could not take it seriously.

'Kyla, for God's sake! That's ridiculous! You have nothing to worry about!'

He was impatient with her repeated fears; he insisted

her examiners were all assholes and she would run circles around them. Beneath his impatience, she sensed his disdain for grown men who would involve themselves with something as trivial as English literature, but she was too panicked, too caught up in terror, to talk about it. She barely spoke to Harley: she read, day and night, made lists, crossed things out, and every night, dreamed the same dream.

The day of her exam, she entered the wood-paneled room and saw the shining broad table and the three eminences sitting at it. They were quarreling about which window, if any, should be open and how wide. Their quarrel lasted some minutes and contained surprising snarliness: over a window? she thought. They were like an aged trio who have lived together squabbling for fifty years. She glanced at the corner, but it was empty. She sat down. Her whole body was shaking.

A little over two hours later, the judgment having been whispered in her ear by the director, she trembled down the wooden stairs of Warren House. She could not see, but she held her chin firm. She would not cry here, not in front of them, not in Warren House. She walked down carefully, holding on to the banister. She would not fall here, not here. Objects glimmered and swam in her vision; but there was a group of people, they did look familiar, it was, yes, it was Iso and Clarissa and Mira and Ben, and someone asked, 'How did you do?' and she said, the words gurgled out of her wet throat, 'I passed,' and they cheered, but they must have seen, must have been able to know, because they gathered her in their arms and helped her out and things were gray, but then there was fresh air and she was being held up and they were walking, they were all walking together and the air was fresh and sweet and it was April, and things were in bud.

They took her to the Toga and ordered drinks, and asked her about it, and she repeated some of the questions and watched their horrified faces, and then she was able to laugh too. 'Wasn't that impossible? They only asked it to shake me up, but it did shake me up!'

They drank and drank. Someone got up to phone Val, who showed up a half hour later, and someone, she had a vague feeling – it was Mira, she thought, after Iso whispered to her – telephoned Harley. But Harley never came. Kyla did not ask why, she did not ask about it. They ordered food, and after a while they left and stopped to buy a gallon of cheap wine and went back to Iso's and sat talking and drinking until late. Kyla did not leave.

It was after one when Iso shut the door on Val. She came back to see Kyla perched like a tiny child on the edge of a wooden chair, her arms around herself, hugging herself, shivering.

'I really failed. That's the truth,' she said.

Iso paled. She sat down. 'You mean you lied?'

'Oh. No. No, they said I passed. Hooten came up and whispered to me that I passed.' Iso sighed. 'But I really failed.'

Iso poured them more wine. 'Iso, it's no use. I can't do it. I can't make it in their world. I can't stand it.' She told Iso about her dream.

'Did you talk to anybody about it? That might have helped. Did you tell Harley?'

She shook her head. 'He would only have had more contempt for me than he has.' She described Harley's response to her panic. 'It's all of a piece – Harley, Harvard, the whole fucking world, for God's sake! I'm just going to go home and have a couple of babies and spend the rest of my life baking bread and growing flowers and sewing gorgeous clothes. I can't stand this, I can't.'

'Shit!' Iso breathed.

'You think that's wrong?'

'Oh, Christ!' Iso stood up and started pacing. 'I can't stand what you're feeling.'

'They demoralized me, they had that kind of power, I gave them that kind of power. And you can tell from the dream what the grounds were. I can't feel legitimate in the face of them. I'm sick of trying. I'm sick of trying to prove to Harley that I'm as rational and intelligent a human being as he, I'm sick of trying to prove to Harvard that I too can write disembodied intellectual tours de force.'

Iso paced, holding *her* arms around herself, hugging herself. Kyla saw, and knew, that Iso was feeling her pain as keenly as she was. 'The thing is,' Iso said, her voice obviously fighting for calmness, 'you'd be bored baking bread and growing flowers.'

'No, I wouldn't. They're great things to do.'

'Yes, they are. And most everything in me wants to say they are the best things to do, that they are the things that really matter.'

'Not according to Harvard. Or the Pentagon.'

'No. And the thing is – it isn't that I think Harvard or the Pentagon is right – or the male establishment, in any form – or that if you stay in it, you'll do more important things than baking bread or growing flowers, because most of what they do is even more transient, less nourishing, less creative – and having babies has to be the greatest thing there is – but,' she turned to face Kyla, 'the seeds were planted in you so long ago. There's no escape for you. Don't you see that?'

She sat down, trembling, and sipped her wine.

Kyla started at her.

'I know because they're in me too,' Iso shivered.

'Seeds.'

'I'm bright. You're bright. Maybe we're even brilliant. We have had opportunities lots of women never get. Our aspirations are equal to our intelligence and our backgrounds. We want to make it in their fucking world. But suppose we quit, suppose we say the hell with it, let them destroy themselves, I'm going to go off and cultivate my garden. Well, suppose *you* do that. It would be different for me. Suppose you go off with Harley or somebody and quit the shit and just have babies and grow flowers and bake bread. You still won't feel legitimate. You'll still feel resentful, even more so, of the world out there. You'll hate it twofold because you'll feel you failed in it. And you'll hate him – the man – the one who is legitimate out there, who can make it without its seeming to devour his soul.'

'Only seeming to,' Kyla said hardly, sarcastically. 'Mira did call Harley tonight, didn't she?'

'Oh, I don't know,' Iso said evasively.

'And he wouldn't come. Well, I suppose because you were there. But why wasn't Harley at the foot of those steps?'

Iso looked into her drink.

'So I'm in a bind?' Kyla grinned and stretched out her legs. 'The paradoxical seeds of destruction have me in their grip?'

Iso laughed.

'Come over here and give me a kiss, you doom-monger, you!'

Iso strode over. 'Listen,' she said, smiling, 'I don't want to be a substitute. You know – if Harley doesn't come through, there's always Iso.'

Kyla's face wrenched out of shape. 'Oh, God. I tried to make it the respectable way! Iso, I love you. I can't promise anything. But then, can you?'

Iso laughed and sat on the floor and Kyla slid from her chair and sat with her, and they held each other, and kissed, for a long time.

14

'It's hard to keep up,' Mira said, gazing around Val's cluttered living room. Everywhere there were papers, piles of mimeographed leaflets, pamphlets. 'As far as I know, she's staying at Iso's, and Harley's blowing his top. He's saying some really vicious things. I guess you were right. He didn't, originally, take it seriously.'

'Men,' Val said with disgust.

Mira gazed at her. 'I haven't seen Tad for a long time. Is something wrong?'

Val's mouth twisted. 'Oh, that's over.'

'Are you okay?'

Val puffed on a cigarette. 'We all seem to be going through the doldrums these days. Hey, what's the etymology of that, English major? Doldrums.'

'I don't know. What happened?'

524

'It isn't Tad. I mean, I don't think so. There's always the possibility I cared about him more than I knew. That's *my* problem. Some people's problem is that they think they care a lot about somebody and they really don't. Mine is that I always figure I don't care that much, that I can do fine without them, and discover I love them or need them more than I knew. But I don't think that's what it is this time. It's guilt, it's letting in the guilt fairy. Once you start to question your actions, once you begin to let yourself think you might have been wrong about something – then everything topples, because one wrong action last week was founded on a choice made fifteen years ago, and you have to question everything, everything.'

Val laid her head in her hands.

Mira stared at her in terror. It had never occurred to her that Val might be vulnerable like the rest of the race; she had obviously, unconsciously, been attributing to Val some superhuman impermeability. But here Val was, shaken.

'What happened?'

'It was during Easter break,' she began.

Chris had come home for the vacation. It was the first time she and Val had seen each other since Christmas, and they were completely wrapped up in each other. They talked late into the night that Chris arrived. They did not want Tad there, they wanted to talk alone, but Tad insisted on staying. It was awkward, they were annoyed, but Val did not want to hurt him. Finally, about two thirty, he went to bed, and they could talk alone, which they did until morning, kissing and holding each other before they drifted off into different rooms.

But next day, Tad was angry. The women slept late since they had not gone to bed until seven, and he was awake and adrift until the middle of the afternoon, when they arose. He was angry because of their exclusion of him the night before. And tactlessly, he hit Val with his anger as soon as she got up, before she'd

525

even had her coffee. He glared at her and made a sarcastic remark about her sleeping late. She ignored him, and sat down with her coffee. He was silent then, except for noisily ruffling the sections of *The Times* he pretended to be reading.

'And you make me feel like a goddamned outsider,' he said suddenly. 'Last night, you and Chris didn't want to talk to me at all. You didn't talk to me at all. You acted as if I wasn't even there. You *ignored* me!' he said, leaping up and walking to the stove and cursing the empty coffeepot and noisily putting the kettle on the heat. He turned back to Val, glaring, and announced, 'I'm either a part of this family, or I'm not.'

Perhaps if Val had been fully awake, she would have handled things differently. As it was, she lifted her eyes up and looked at him sarcastically. 'Obviously,' she said in a cool dry voice, 'you're not.'

He acted as if she had slapped him. His whole face flinched, and for a moment she thought he was going to cry. She felt sorry as soon as she saw him. She wanted to run up to him and hold him, and say she was sorry, but it was too late. He stood there unsteadily.

She tried to modify. 'At least,' she said more gently, 'when it comes to my relation with Chris. After all, she is my child. We are very close, and we haven't seen each other in a long time. There are times we want to be alone.' It might perhaps have been all right; she couldn't tell. She had hurt him, and was going to have to pay a price for that. He might in his head understand, but would not be consoled easily. It might have been all right, yet perversely, as it seemed to her even at the time, she added, 'In fact, you are a very small part of my life, Tad. You must realize that. I'm almost forty-one, I've had a complicated life. You come barging in and decide we should be lovers, and I agree, and you seem to feel that gives you carte blanche to move into my life permanently. Where the hell do you come off? Did you ever ask me if I wanted you as a permanent fixture in my life? You just move in. You are completely insensitive to other people. You either retreat totally or you assert yourself totally, and it never occurs to you how other people are feeling. You act as if we were married or something. You talk as if you expect I would never again have sex with anybody but you. Fat chance!'

By the time she was finished, Tad's face was a petrified blank. He looked at her with no expression, and walked out of the kitchen into the living room and just sat holding his head.

She finished her coffee. She was hot and angry, and surprised. She had not realized she was that angry. 'Love,' she muttered to herself. It makes you, she felt, hide your own anger from yourself, out of fear, so that by the time it does come out, it is poisonous. But she was not sorry. She felt just as she had when she was reaming him. Chris stumbled into the kitchen, sleepy-eyed and grouchy.

'What's the matter with Tad?'

Val told her. 'Ummm,' Chris mumbled. Last night she had been annoyed with her mother for not sending Tad away. This morning she felt her mother had been unduly unkind. 'That was pretty raw, don't you think?'

'Yes, it was pretty raw!' Val exclaimed in exasperation. 'You think I can manage to do everything perfectly?'

'You act as if you could,' Chris said, and Val wanted to slap her.

She fixed some breakfast for Chris and herself, and sent Chris into the living room to ask Tad if he wanted any. He did not. The women ate and read *The Times* in silence. By this time, both were awake and talking in brief snatches. Val was still angry with Chris, and gave her short answers.

'I'm sorry,' Chris said. 'It's just that he looked so miserable. When I came through the living room, I even thought he was crying. I guess I always think that you should be able to kiss every sore and make it well and if you don't, it's pure malice on your part.'

'Yes,' Val said bitterly. 'And of course, I could have. All I had to do was deny my feelings. That's what people expect *Mother* to do!'

527

'I know, I know! I said I was sorry.'

'Kids. Mothers,' Val muttered. 'You're not supposed to feel your own feelings so that you can be a perpetual bandage to everybody else's.'

Chris looked at her. 'If I didn't know you better, I'd swear you felt guilty.'

Val put her head in her hands. 'I do. Anyway, I feel bad I hurt him.' She lifted her head up. 'And what's more, I wanted to hurt him. I guess I've been feeling more hemmed in than I knew. I've wanted to slap out at him for a long time.'

Late in the afternoon, Val began to get over her anger at Tad. She smelled marijuana from the living room, and knew that he was smoking to dull his feelings. Her heart melted with pity for him: he seemed, in her eyes, so helpless. There was something unforgivable about hitting a helpless person. She went into the living room. She sat down near Tad, but in a different chair.

'Tad, I'm sorry I was cruel,' she said. 'I was angry, and I guess I've been angry for a while without really knowing it. It built up and came out that way. I do feel that you are part of my life – if you care now.'

His head jerked up. 'Have you had sex with anyone else?'

'What?'

'You heard me, Val! Have you been sleeping around?'

'You bitch!' She was astonished. 'What the hell business is that of yours?'

'You said it! You said if I thought you wouldn't, I was crazy. I want to know if you have. I have to know,' his voice cracked, and her blood pressure went down a little.

'What difference would it make?'

'All the difference. Do you think I'd stay with a whore?'

She gazed at him coolly now. 'If that's the way you see things, you might as well leave now. What do you think I've been doing the past twenty years?'

'I don't care about that. That was before you met me.'

'I see. You've broadened yourself enough that you can accept someone who has not always been yours alone, but not enough to accept that once you enter the picture, she does not become your sole property.'

He did not seem to understand. 'Have you?'

'Yes,' she answered.

'Who?' He was sitting back against the sofa cushions, his head dejected, his air despairing.

'That is not for you to ask. I would tell you if I wanted to tell you.'

His face was suddenly intense. 'Who? Who? I have to know, Val, I have to know!'

'Oh, for God's sakes!' She was disgusted. 'Tim Ryan.'

Tim Ryan was a member of the peace group, an undergraduate at Tufts.

'Val, he's eighteen! Eighteen! Younger than Chris!'

'So what? You're only a few years older than Chris. Since when did that become important?'

'I'll kill him,' Tad said between his teeth.

'Oh, for Christ's sake.' Val stood up. 'Go ahead, play every stupid game in the book. But I am sure as hell not going to waste my time playing them with you.' She left the room, and went into her bedroom, and sat down to work on the prison report. Hours passed. She heard Tad come into the kitchen a few times and pour drinks, but he said nothing to her, and returned to the living room. Around nine, Chris got hungry and prepared dinner. Chris asked Tad if he wanted to eat, but he refused her. But while she and Val were eating, he came into the kitchen twice to pour drinks. He was walking crooked, and almost slipped once. Each time, he said nothing, and returned to the living room.

Chris raised her eyebrow. 'Mom, I wanted to go out tonight. Some friends are getting together. They said Bart might be there. I haven't heard from him in months, and I'd really like to see him.'

'Don't worry about it, honey, I can handle Tad. What can happen? He's falling down drunk already. He'll

529

probably pass out. If worse comes to worst, I can run and he can't,' Val laughed.

They were finishing dinner when Tad staggered into the kitchen again, but this time after he had poured his drink, he staggered past them into Val's bedroom and fell on the bed. Then he started to speak. He called out, ritually, endlessly, a stream of imprecations. 'Bitch, whore, slut, cunt, filthy cunt, I believed in you, I thought I loved you, but I tell you, Val, I don't love you that much, not that much, I'll never forgive you, you filthy slut, you whore, you bitch. . . .'

He kept it up. Val stood up and went to the bedroom doorway. 'Take your filthy perverted values and get out of here,' she said. But he only yelled louder. She slammed the bedroom door. He rose unsteadily – they could hear him almost fall – and threw it open again, then lay back down in the bed and continued his litany.

Val shook her head. 'Funny, the thing he seized on. I can understand his being hurt at my saying he wasn't part of my life – I would have been hurt if he'd said that to me. But this!'

They sat looking at each other over coffee. He did not stop. 'We could throw him out. The two of us,' Val said. 'In his condition, we could do it.'

They looked at each other. It was inconceivable. Throw out on the street a drunk who could not walk straight, who was hurt in the way he was hurt? No. It must be endured. They did not discuss it, they simply dismissed the possibility.

'I could call the police,' Val said, her eyes on her coffee. Chris did not answer.

They sat there for a while. Tad never stopped. 'Whore, filthy whore, cunt, bitch,' he went on, as if his language could destroy her.

Suddenly he started to cry. He sobbed for a while, then cried out weakly: 'Chris! Chrissie!'

Her head came up and she glanced at her mother.

'Chris, Chrissie, come talk to me, please, please, come to me, will you?'

Val frowned, puzzled, suspicious, but Chris stood up.
'Chris, come here, please come here.'

Chris went, ignoring her mother's vigorous negative shake of head.

She stood beside the bed, looking down at him. Val could look directly into the bedroom from where she sat.

'Sit down, Chris.' He patted the bed, and she sat. 'Come to bed with me Chris, will you? You and me, Chris, don't pay any attention to the slut in there, just close the door, come and screw me, Chris, I've wanted to screw you always, ever since I first saw you. We don't have to worry about her, she can go find ten other people to screw, come on, Chris, lie down, kiss me.'

Val did not move. She could see Chris sitting there. Chris did not look angry or frightened. She was smoothing his forehead with her hand. He did not seem to notice that his words were not having effect. He kept repeating them, and he clutched her wrist a few times. She sat there calmly, gazing down at him with pity. After a long time, Chris rose. She bent over him and kissed his forehead. 'I have to go out,' she said softly.

She came into the kitchen. 'Where are the car keys?' she asked her mother, her face expressionless.

Val nodded at her purse. Tad struggled to his feet.

'Okay, bitch, you want me to leave, I'll leave, I'll go with Chris, Chrissie and me'll go out and have a drink.'

He caromed across the room and staggered out the door. Val stood and followed him. The thing she would get violent about was if he tried to drive the car with Chris in it. She was unsure about Chris, about how much pity she had, about where she would draw the line. She stood in the doorway, out of their sight, watching. Chris had already started the car; when she saw Tad, she rolled down her window. He wanted to drive. He was insisting. He was arguing with her, telling her to slide over. Val did not want to interfere: this was Chris's scene. But she held her body in readiness, like a runner. If she saw Chris's arm move to open the door, she would fly out and stop the thing. If she hesitated even a

531

moment then, it might be too long. But she could not hear Chris, only Tad's voice in tirade, not even what he was saying. It seemed to her that Chris moved, and Val put her hand on the knob and started to open the door. But Chris had rolled up the window. Tad would not let go of the door of the car. Then suddenly, he let go, but before she felt it safe to back up, he had staggered around to the other side and entered the car. Chris turned the motor off. They sat there in the dark car. They were still talking, Val guessed. They sat and sat. Val could not see well: the streetlight illuminated only the outside of the car. Chris's face was a white blur inside it. Val had to pee, but she stood there watching. It seemed endless, and Val was muttering against Chris under her breath.

'Damned kid. Why does she have to be so delicate?'

But then the car door opened, and Chris got out and walked up the steps and into the house. Val had by this time retreated inside, not wanting Chris to know how concerned she had been. Chris dropped the car keys on a table.

'I'm going out the back way,' she said, coldly. 'I'll walk.'

And disappeared before Val could stop her. She worried about Chris walking alone at night in Cambridge, but Chris never understood why she should not. Her friends all did, she said. Val talked about the dangers. Chris shrugged. She believed that if you did not want anything untoward to happen to you, it would not happen. She felt safe, inviolate. In any case, she was gone. Val picked up the keys and hid them, hoping she would remember tomorrow where she hid them tonight. Then she cleaned up the table and began to wash the dinner dishes. In a while, Tad staggered back in, headed for the counter and poured himself a drink, spilling Scotch on counter and floor.

'You've had enough Tad,' Val said curtly. 'You'll be sick.'

'Just shut up, you fucking whore,' Tad managed, but was too exhausted to continue. He aimed his body toward the living room, but it would not turn, and so he followed it, staggering toward the bedroom. He fell on Val's bed, and lay there with the light on. She finished in the kitchen, locked the doors, leaving the front light on for Chris, and went into the living room. She planned to sit up until Chris was safely in. But she drifted off to sleep in the chair. She was wakened by a bang, and leaped up and ran down the hall. Tad was in the bathroom, vomiting, and there was vomit on the hall floor. She went back to the living room and lighted a cigarette. Tad came out of the bathroom and slipped on his own vomit, cursed, then staggered back to bed. She thought: he's going to lie down in my bed with vomit all over his clothes; she cursed him, cursed herself, cursed all men. About five, Chris came in softly. Val opened her eyes as Chris came through the living room to her own room, but Chris did not even glance at her.

'Next day, he felt rotten, of course. At first he apologized just for the mess, as if that were all he'd done. I told him the rest. He was very upset. He cried. But truthfully, Mira, I felt nothing at all. Or rather, I felt I had to get him in shape before I threw him out. Chris slept most of the day. It was Easter Sunday. The three of us were supposed to go to Brad's for dinner. He was having a crowd to celebrate, as he put it, the birth of the New Year, reminding us that it used to open on Lady Day, March 25, which was in the vicinity of Easter. Anyway, I had to settle with Tad some way. He cried, he mourned, he grieved, he apologized. He wrote notes to Chris, then tore them up.

'The thing he did not do was listen to what I was saying. Because he kept apologizing for trying to seduce Chris. I couldn't make him understand that that wasn't what I was outraged about. He never had the slightest chance of seducing Chris.'

'But, Val, that was terrible! Terrible! To treat her that way!'

'Yes. It was terrible,' she said in a low voice, her face full of softness and tragedy, a terrible face on its own.

533

'But not for the reasons he thought. I mean, he thought it was terrible because he broke rules, because he offended Chris's honour, or her morality, or some stupid thing like that. I mean he's all fucked up.'

Mira looked confused.

'Look, he's angry with me, right? He has a right to be, I hurt him, I'm not knocking him for that, I'm not expecting he should sit there like a fucking saint and turn the other cheek. I expect he will get angry. But, how he does that is important. And the way he chooses is to figure – what can I do that will hurt Val most? I can screw her kid. Or else he figures the thing that will hurt me most is to hurt my kid's feelings. It doesn't matter which it was: he thinks he can get to me most painfully through Chris. Which on its own is rotten and cowardly. But if you add to that that Tad and Chris had a relationship, they loved each other, it takes on another dimension. I mean, they really loved each other. Chris didn't love him in the same way she did me – it was more sexual than that, and less personal. She didn't always want to talk to him, she didn't always want him around when she was talking to me. But they cared about each other. And he never thought twice about that. It never occurred to him while he was busy getting even with me that he was sacrificing his relation to Chris, that he was treating her feelings for him as if they were just so much expendable matter.

'And she understood everything. She felt sorry for him, for the way I'd treated him. She felt – I suppose she always feels – that a guy involved with me is at a disadvantage. I won't say she's fair in that, but because she is my child and feels that way herself, she has sympathy for anybody – well, any young guy I get involved with. At least those she doesn't hate on sight. In such cases, she is quite capable herself of being cruel in exactly the way she felt I had been cruel to Tad. But when she came in with the car keys – I could see it on her face – there was something numb and furious in her. She didn't know how to direct it. She felt, I guess, just general disgust – with both Tad and me. And a desire to get away. Understandable.'

'I don't understand why you didn't stop him, Val. Why did you let him talk to her that way? I would have gone in there and . . . I don't know. I think I would have hit him!'

Val shook her head. 'Yes,' she nodded, as Mira held up the wine bottle questioningly. 'Mira, Chris is eighteen. He was talking to her. If I'd gone in, it would've been like saying she wasn't capable of handling it herself. As it turned out, she was very capable. If she'd asked me for help, I would have helped her. She didn't.'

Mira shook her head slowly, not understanding, but did not argue.

'Look,' Val said wearily, 'I long ago gave up the protection of the rules. If I'm not going to live by them, I can hardly invoke them in time of need. "How dare you, sir! Unhand my child!" Nonsense. Chris and I have lived through things almost as bad, worse, maybe. Humanly. You don't need to call in the law.'

'How did Chris feel afterward?'

'General disgust. Tad got himself together and I told him to leave. He argued about that. He wanted to stay. He wanted to talk to Chris, but she was still asleep. I insisted, because he was okay, I could see that. He wasn't going to fall in front of a car on the way home. Chris got up after he left. I guess she had been waiting for him to go. And we just looked at each other. She had some coffee and we talked. She still felt sorry for him, but she didn't want to see him or talk to him. I didn't tell her what I just said to you. I told her I thought he was trying to hurt me in the worst possible way, and had decided that was through her. Once she looked up at me and said, "He really did want to screw me, though. I mean, before last night. And I wanted to too. But I decided not to. Tad didn't try, but I could have. I would have liked to. . . ."

' "Why didn't you, then?"

'She shrugged. "I didn't want to be compared with

535

you. No matter how it came out. I would have felt rotten being compared with you. But he *did* want to." She insisted on that. I agreed. That was the end of it. She stayed until the end of the vacation. Tad called a couple times and wanted to talk to her but she wouldn't speak with him. She was fine when she left.

'But, oh, Mira, when I sit here thinking about it, I get the shakes. All kinds of guilts come towering over me. I think, if I hadn't done that and that and that, this would never have happened. I think, this happened because I broke the rules. But how could I live without breaking the rules? Still, I can't avoid the feeling that my kid has had to pay because I broke the rules.'

'And mine had to pay when I didn't. Their lives were more shattered by Norm's and my divorce than Chris's was by this. And I broke no rules, none at all.'

'Your kids never got dragged into such an ugly scene.'

'No. But if it hadn't been for Martha – or maybe I really hadn't cut deeply enough, I don't know – they'd have been dragged into an uglier one: finding their mother dead with her wrists cut, on the bathroom floor.'

'I never knew you did that.' Val raised her eyes, re-appraising Mira.

'Does it change your evaluation of me?'

Val put a hand on Mira's shoulder. 'A little. When I first met you, I thought you were a little – shallow, maybe. I don't think so now, haven't for a long time. But I guess I had assumed you'd deepened in the past couple years. That you tried to knock yourself off tells me you always had strong feelings.'

'But you're right. I had them but they were buried. I buried them myself, and planted flowers over the grave. It was the divorce that upset the funerary arrangements.' She paused, thinking. 'And heaven knows what effect that had on the boys – an absent father and a mother with only half her feelings operating. Chris is a lot wiser, a lot tougher – in the good sense – than my kids.'

'Maybe. You're right, of course, it's incalculable.

Still, they hurt, attacks of guilt. Do you suppose they do any good at all?'

'Oh, little ones. Like when you were rude to some-body at a party last night and feel guilty this morning. Keeps you human.'

Val shook her head. 'I hope so. They're so fucking painful I hope they have some use.'

The doorbell rang and Iso came in. 'God, everything's falling apart!' she said looking worried 'I just met Tad in the Square and he said you two are on the outs.'

'Not on the outs. Finished.' Briefly, Val told Iso the story.

'Wow. Heavy, as they say.'

'What else is falling apart?'

'Oh, that Kyla! She's been with me a week, during which Harley is going around telling everybody I'm a bull dyke out to seduce everybody's else's wife and to watch out for me, and nice stuff like that, you know? And she goes back to him! I just can't get over it. We were so happy together, she's so happy with me. I'm not being arrogant, am I? Couldn't you see the difference?'

'It shone out—'

'Like shook foil.'

'What did she tell you?' Val asked, uncorking the wine.

'Oh, a whole lot of shit. At least it sounded like shit to me. She said she came to me in a fit of pique because Harley hadn't shown up after her orals. I mean he's really rotten – he had to know how terrified she was. If he didn't, he really doesn't care about her. And that that was no way to make a decision, it should be thought out, one should be sure it was the right thing to do.'

'But that's how Kyla is. She never trusts her feelings.'

'I know.' Iso put a hand on her head and wiped her forehead, as if it were wet. She kept doing it. 'And he handed her some line about she has to learn to be in-dependent and that's why he didn't come, and he wouldn't come later because I was there, and now that the pressure was off her, they should try again, and be-sides she has to rent the apartment for the summer because they're committed to go to Aspen to some physics conference. And she went!'

'To Aspen?'

'No Back to sublet the apartment. And to try again. Shit!' She shook her head as if she were trying to free it from something. 'I know she doesn't trust her feelings, but I wish she cared a little more about mine. On-off, on-off. You know, I love her!' Iso added this with surprise. 'I had to tell her, I had to say I thought she was being cruel. And she hugged me and she stroked me and she treated me like a two-year-old with a cut knee. She sat me down calmly and explained very rationally how she owed her first obligation to Harley because she'd known him first and committed herself to him first, and besides he was her husband that was a contractual bond! Can you imagine?'

'I can see her doing that. She has a moral account book in her head, with priorities clearly outlined: I, A, 1, a.'

'It won't last,' Val said. 'Two or three weeks with Harley and all her rationality will be thrown to the winds again. With him she's all emotion.'

'Anybody would seem to be all emotion with Harley!'

'Do you think she'll come back?' Wistfully.

'Well, I'd bet she won't last out the summer with him. Unless she has even more determination and self-hatred than I think.'

Iso sighed. 'I thought we'd have such fun this summer. . . .'

Val patted her hand. 'Well, Iso, you and I can go to the beach, take long walks. . . .'

Iso laughed. 'I know what kinds of long walks you mean, man! Marching on Washington! No thanks!'

The mention of politics brought a frown to Val's face. 'God, I forgot! I have to prepare a report for tonight . . . this was so good. I never see you two anymore. For an hour I forgot all the shit.' She gathered some papers together. 'I'm sorry,' she said, dismissing them.

They left cheerfully, but on the street they looked at each other. They were a little hurt, and more than a little concerned about Val. 'Do you think it's healthy to worry so much about something so distant? I mean, don't you think it's a sublimation or something?'

Mira shrugged. 'I don't know. Val doesn't seem neurotic to me.' They walked home slowly. 'I guess it's good somebody is doing something.'

'Even if it does no good,' Iso concluded sadly.

15

In February of 1970, Duke was transferred to a base in New England within commuting distance of Cambridge. He was elated: since their marriage, he and Clarissa had never really lived together. Their time had been limited to snatched weekends or furloughs, and so were always tinged with the bittersweet, the special joy and special sorrow of separated lovers. For months at a time he might not see her; although his tasks kept him occupied, he always longed for her as soon as they were over. Clarissa seemed to Duke a hot center, a vivid living fire that warmed his numbed fingers. This feeling was not just sexual; her mental ardor warmed him too.

But in the year and a half she had been at Harvard, he felt – he could not pin it down – as though she were slipping out of his hands, as though he could no longer fully grasp her. He laid the blame on his nine-month tour in Vietnam and on the influence of her friends. He saw Harvard as penetrated by intellectual elitism and radicalism. So he looked forward to their new arrangement not only with pleasure but with a sense of purpose: he would reforge the links between them. He bought a Porsche and settled into Clarissa's apartment.

Clarissa's reticence and thoughtfulness, her intent watchfulness, gave her an air of great maturity and experience, and intellectually she was developed. But the softness of her face, her inclination toward shyness, and her unselfconscious carriage showed her younger than her twenty-five years.

Clarissa was the flower of her time, the kind of product the magazines, the psychologists, the educators, the

539

parents, are all aiming to produce. She was a source of continual amazement to the women because she did not seem to have any problems with herself or her world, and she admitted without pride or shame that she had never in her life suffered pain beyond that of a pulled tendon. Born to educated parents, she and her sister were loved, nourished, gently disciplined, liberally educated, treated as persons and never shunted toward the doll corner of the kindergarten. They lived in a fine old house in Scarsdale, but Clarissa not only evaded the contagion of snobbery in the place, she did not even know it existed. Both sisters did brilliantly in school, were fine athletes, were popular. Her sister had gone on to become a pediatrician, get married, have five children, and practice with her husband out of an enormous house in southern California. The relation between the two sisters seemed perfect: there had been no sense of competition or any envy because there had been no reason for such things to exist.

When the women first knew her, they would listen to her rare recitals of her past in silence. It was incredible: they repeated that frequently. It was awesome. They stared at it as at a miracle, and returned to their own shit and string beans. Clarissa, on the other hand, was fascinated by their stories. She would often ask: what did that *feel* like? Her ideas of emotional pain were derived from books and her imagination; in her later adolescence, she would sit for hours trying to feel what Anna Karenina or Ivan Karamazov or Emma Bovary was feeling. Although her family was religious, and she had spent many of her summers on the family farms in the Dakotas, where the most religious members of her family lived, she did not even suffer a religious crisis. She moved from total acceptance of Catholic doctrine, to simple faith in God, to nonbelief, to an awareness of absurdity as easily and smoothly as she moved from geometry to algebra to trigonometry to calculus. Both were just series of steps of ascending difficulty concurrent with her increasing ability in comprehension.

She had attended Radcliffe, had met Duke at a party

given by some friends of her parents', and so had managed even to fall in love in the most proper way possible. Duke's family was old and famous, with a tradition of West Point or Ivy League training, political service to the country, and old manners, with a former governor of New York and a former secretary of state among their forebears. Their marriage pleased both families. Their life together was destined, it seemed, to partake of the highest sort of happily-ever-after. And Clarissa's serene brow, her quiet contentment after four years of marriage, suggested that it did.

But there was an underside to Clarissa that she rarely spoke of and most people did not know about. All through college, she had worked with a neighborhood program in Roxbury intended to help ghetto children to learn to read. She carried herself so well in this usually hopeless situation – not acting, as some people do, as if she were there to confer the grace of her whiteness and culture on the poor benighted, but like someone who had come to them to learn, come there to know them and be known. She grew to be a part of the extensive 'family' network of the neighborhood. They trusted her, and she was able to bring other people in. The reading programs she was involved with had great success. After college – Duke was overseas – Clarissa and some of the Roxbury people got federal funding to extend the program, and for two years, she spent most of her life in Roxbury. She lived there, she worked there. Duke was very upset; he insisted she keep an apartment in Cambridge for times when he was on leave. He hoped its comfort would lure her to it most nights. Clarissa loved Roxbury, though; she felt alive there in a way she never had before. And she saw pain enough there to make up for her ignorance. Whenever she spoke about those years to us, her eyes glowed, her face became animated. She had even had lovers there, a thing she did not tell us until much later.

Despite the success of the program, the funding was cut off under Nixon – one of his first acts in office – and Clarissa had to leave. She had already begun graduate school at Harvard. More than any other of the English majors, she questioned her purpose there, albeit, silently. But sometimes, late at night, she'd bring it up.

'You know, you think if you help to educate young scholars, young teachers, that you can have an effect on things, can change the way people think. But I really question whether memorizing the kings of England or knowing the cruxes in Shakespeare or, for that matter, most of what we do here, is calculated to develop that side of you. It's more likely to kill it off as you get involved in competitive scholarly debates about the better reading of a text.'

'And you wish you were back in Roxbury,' Val smiled.

'No. There's no point. The money is dried up, the people I had collected are dispersed, the neighborhood has gotten more dangerous for whites – there's nothing to go back to, not for me, at least, maybe not for any white person. Besides it was parasitical: I'm glad I did it, but in a way I was getting my nourishment from them, living through them instead of generating life in myself. But I can't see that Harvard's going to help me to do that.'

Still, she did brilliantly in courses and exams, and seemed headed for a plum. There are three plums for English graduate students at Harvard: an assistantship at Harvard, Yale, or Princeton. Since in 1970 it was inconceivable that any woman would get the Harvard appointment, and unlikely that a woman would get one at Princeton, the Yale appointment was what most people anticipated for Clarissa. It simply fitted in with all the rest. What her brilliance and demeanor did not do, her family connections would.

After Duke's transfer, we saw less of Clarissa. Like the rest of us, she was studying for orals. She had to be home at dinnertime, and because she wanted to spend her evenings with Duke, she did not take any time off from reading during the day. But in early April, still before her orals, she began again to appear at Iso's in the late afternoon. She did not seem as serene; it would

542

be hard to put one's finger on the difference; Mira said she had shadows in her face. But Clarissa said nothing.

Her orals went splendidly, and the group of friends went out to celebrate. Duke joined them as soon as he got home; he glowed with her triumph – unlike Kyla and Mira, she felt exultant afterward – and with pride. He had managed to get a couple of days leave to spend with her, and everyone who stopped in to visit them during those days found them both rosy and round; Clarissa especially looked pink with sensuality. Iso said you always felt you'd just gotten them out of bed. Then Duke went back, and Clarissa poked around in the library seeking a dissertation topic, and began to gather with her friends again. But now she mentioned difficulties. Things were hard for Duke.

'Okay, he's forced to live a schizophrenic life. He comes home and takes off his uniform, he puts on jeans and a Moroccan shirt and an Indian headband that he has to wear because he can't let his hair grow long. Actually I like it, but he'd rather have long hair. He puts on his beads and we go down to the Square to eat or go to a movie, or just walk. But next day he's back in his uniform, saluting and standing at attention, listening to his peers talk about weirdos and hippies in Indian bands. I think he's having trouble with this constant switching.'

'How does he show it?' Iso asked with a wicked glint. 'Does he expect you to stand at attention when he walks in the door? Do you have to fill out a work sheet in triplicate every day?'

The women laughed, but Clarissa raised her eyebrows. 'That's closer than you think. Okay, at the same time he wants to be part of his generation, part of my world, he does regard Harvard as a hotbed of radicalism.'

'He should hear what we usually talk about,' Kyla said dryly.

'No, no, he's right!' Val protested.

The rest of them hooted. They were, they insisted, as

disgustingly apolitical as it was possible to be – except for her. Their political apathy was shameful.

'I agree, I agree,' Val laughed. 'But still you're political. You aren't very active, I confess. But one reason you're not more active is that the political concerns around here are too mild, too detached from your own radicalism to interest you.'

'We? We?' Four voices cried at her.

'Damn straight!' she insisted cheerfully. 'Why did we all get together? Why are we friends? We share hardly anything: we come from different parts of the country, we have very different interests, we are of different ages, our backgrounds have little in common. Why do we hate so much about Harvard? Why do most of the graduate students turn us off the way they do?

'We hate the political, the economic, and the moral structure of Harvard, of the country for that matter, just as much as SDS does. But even I am not a member of SDS: I went to two meetings and left. God, what a group! It isn't their militancy that bothers me. It's that they have the same fucking values as the people they want to destroy. They're as patriarchal as the Catholic Church, as Harvard, as General Motors and the United States Government! We're rebels against all establishments because we're rebels against male supremacy, male surface bonding, male power, male structures. We want a completely different world, one so different that it's hard to articulate, impossible to conceive of a structure for it—'

'A world where I could bake bread and grow flowers and be taken seriously as an intelligent person,' Kyla murmured, biting her lip.

'Yes.'

'Or where Duke would not feel he had the right to insist I cook dinner every night because somehow what he does all day is work and what I do isn't. Even though he loves to cook and I hate it,' Clarissa said with a little asperity.

The women all turned to her. She hadn't mentioned that before.

'Yes. We're all rebels against the pompous, self-aggrandizing, hollow white male world and its delusions of legitimacy; we all sympathize with illegitimates of every sort because we all feel illegitimate ourselves; we're all antiwar, antiestablishment, anticapitalism—'

'Yet we're not Communists,' Kyla argued, crossing and uncrossing her legs. She turned to Clarissa. 'We really are shamefully apolitical.'

'For Christ sakes, what's in communism for us? It's – in practice at least – just one more variety of the same animal.'

'Okay,' Clarissa said thoughtfully. 'But I think most of us accept socialism in principle.'

They looked at each other. All of them nodded.

'Do you know, this is amazing!' Kyla leaped up. 'We have never discussed this before, never gone around the room itemizing pieces of belief! I wouldn't have been able to say what anybody here believed, except I knew we all shared something profound. . . .'

'But everybody believes what we believe,' Mira said puzzled.

They howled. 'What was it you were telling us about Christmas with the Wards?'

She giggled. 'I've been here too long. The rest of the world has totally disappeared.'

'And Duke doesn't believe what we believe. I wonder if any man does,' Clarissa said, a pained frown on her face.

Val gazed at her sympathetically. 'I know. That's what makes things so hard. And of course, our sort of radicalism is the most threatening sort ever to come down the pike. Not because we have guns and money. They tried to laugh us out of existence, now they're trying to tokenize us out of existence – the way they've done with blacks, not very successfully, I think – but their refusal to take us seriously at all is a measure of their terror.'

Kyla sat straight up and stared at Val. She was puffing alternately on two cigarettes without knowing it.

'Because what we threaten is male legitimacy itself.

Take a man and a woman both born to WASP families of note, both well educated, monied – both, in other words, with all the badges of legitimacy our society has to offer. And the man will be seen as serious, and the woman as trivial, no matter what she does or tries to do. Look at the way they treated Eleanor Roosevelt. And when a man loses his sense of legitimacy, what he is really losing is a sense of superiority. He has come to find superiority over others necessary to his very existence. Illegitimate men, like blacks or Chicanos, follow the pattern, but they can assert superiority only over women. When a man loses superiority, he loses potency. That's what all this talk about castrating women is about. Castrating women are those who refuse to pretend men are better than they are and better than women are. The simple truth – that men are only equal – can undermine a culture more devastatingly than any bomb. Subversion is telling the truth.'

The women sat in silence.

'Oh, God,' Kyla moaned softly.

'Some men escape. Some men do,' Mira insisted.

'For a while, maybe. And by themselves, as individuals some men would. But the institutions get us all in the end. Nobody escapes,' Val said grimly.

'I won't believe that!' Mira said, her eyes misted.

Val turned to her. 'You will. Someday.'

Mira flung her face away from Val.

'Okay,' Clarissa began slowly. 'So Duke, for instance, has a sense of something inimical in his environment. In fact, it's awfully close to home, but he can't admit that, so he blames it on Cambridge or Harvard. And he's frustrated, because he's used to shooting at enemies, and he can't even find this one. He just feels it around him like a fine mist, and he's constantly swinging around to try to grab something that just went by, but there's nothing there.'

'But he always feels damp.'

'Yes. So when something appears in a newspaper, or a magazine, or on TV – he launches into a lecture, hectoring me about the evils of sloppy liberalism. And

546

sometimes his thinking is very sloppy too and I have to point that out. And invariably that leads to a fight.'

'Well, of course I'm not the person who tactfully should say this, but I am the person who can say it: is it possible to live with somebody whose values you don't share?' Iso was leaning forward, gazing very hard away from Kyla.

Val looked at Clarissa. 'What do you think? Duke will be in the army for the rest of his life.'

Clarissa's face froze up. She spoke through tight lips. 'I think love can change people,' she said, but her voice was tight. Everyone knew that things had gone too far. The subject was changed, the wine bottle was passed, but no one took any except Iso. All of the women except Iso disliked Val that night, and strangely, they did not feel good about each other either. They did not want to have to look at their own concessions, their own complicity in the thing Val had described, through the life of another. Their move apart from Val and each other was subtle, barely traceable, yet it was sensible, and all of them felt it. But the breach brought a lack, and all of them moved closer than ever to Iso, who somehow in this thing was innocent, unable to harm.

16

It was spring again in Cambridge and people bloomed like flowers along the sidewalks; coats were left off or thrown open, and wonderful absurd clothes flared up – embroidered shirts, appliquéd pants, long skirts, short skirts, boots, sandals of all sorts, and the man in the kilt was seen in the Coop. The Hare Krishna people sparkled white and orange again, their old raincoats and jackets removed; and the sound of the guitar was heard in Holyoke Center.

Val had been having trouble breathing: there was a pain in her chest that wouldn't go away. She was sure it was simply anxiety, or not-so-simply anxiety. She was neglecting her schoolwork and work on the antiwar committee, and she felt guilty, and frustrated, and terribly angry at the reports she was reading that no one else paid any attention to, or cared about. Somehow things had not gone well these past months. She didn't take the time to think about it. She was too busy, too involved with ten different groups, but somehow, things had not gone well. She was losing touch, she felt, with what she vaguely called 'life,' but she could not help it. *Somebody* had to care about slaughtered people in Southeast Asia.

It was a gorgeous day, and she decided to walk into the Square before going home from her meeting. She didn't need anything, but a walk would feel good. Maybe her breath would ease. Maybe it was just lack of exercise and too much smoking: that would be good. That was something you could do something about. She walked idly, stopping to look in shop windows – a luxury for her. She browsed at a bookstore, bought a record, stopped at the market for a pound of spaghetti. It was good to be so idle, to wander around. Her breathing was coming easier, she thought. She could feel a faint smile on her face.

The light had faded as she started home. People's faces were dusky and cheerful, passing her like tiny dots of life pulsing along the dim street. Their conversation or laughter drifted before them, after them. She thought about how important that was: the way people on the street feel. In Warsaw, people ran, ran, with tense faces; in Washington, people did not walk talking together in light, gay voices. She realized she was humming. She decided to do this more often.

Yes, she would do this more often, every day, in fact. But now, tonight, she was going home to write up the minutes of this afternoon's meetings. But first she would cook some spaghetti sauce, cut up carrots and onions and garlic and parsley into slivers, and simmer them with tomatoes and salt and pepper and basil and oregano, and pour in beef gravy and the chunks of beef she'd had a couple nights ago, and simmer it all together – her mouth began to water. And she would put on her new record and write to Chris – she hadn't written in two weeks, it was shameful – and then get into a warm robe and sit down and write the fucking report and try to stay calm while she did it. Calmly, in abstract language, she would protest the invasion of Cambodia, while in her head were stories and images of what she had heard this afternoon. People, people everywhere just wanted to live. What was it they wanted, the ones who started wars? It was something she felt she would never understand.

Still humming, she sautéed the vegetables, covering the pan, poured herself a glass of wine, and crossed the kitchen and switched on the TV set for the evening news. It was too early, some old Western was on; she ignored it, making her sauce, setting the table for one, drinking her wine. The sauce was simmering, it smelled delicious, she picked up the pot to smell it – she always did that – and then somebody was saying it, she heard him say it, it couldn't be but he was saying it was, she turned around to look at the screen, it couldn't be, but there it was, there were pictures, it was happening right before her eyes, she couldn't believe it, and then the picture stopped and someone was pointing at a dirty shirt collar and talking about something else as if there were anything else to talk about and she heard this screaming, it was ungodly, it was coming from the back of her head, she could hear it, it was a woman screaming in agony, and when she looked, there was blood all over her kitchen floor.

We didn't know then that it was only a beginning. It was the time when the nightmare broke out into public vision, when you could really see, put your finger on, those subtle and tenuous currents that a lot of people besides Duke had been feeling but couldn't see clear enough to shoot. Sometimes, when I walk the beach, and everything seems so quiet, so settled, I wonder what happened to that nightmare. I think nightmares are like the heat bubbling inside the earth: always there, but only occasionally erupting to show the gaps, the murderous breaches.

Val got her wits back eventually. She stopped screaming, although she was still sobbing, tears were streaming down her face as she got down on her hands and knees to wipe up the spaghetti sauce she'd spilled all over the floor, and to stay there, crouched down, crying in her hands, unable to believe it, unable to disbelieve it, crying out, 'We're killing our children! We're killing our children!'

There were telephone calls, meetings. Those days are all jumbled in my brain. But suddenly the tiny peace groups sprinkled around town were one group; suddenly their numbers expanded, tripled, quadrupled, passed count. A few days later – it *was* a few days, wasn't it? – they killed children at Jackson State, unwilling, damned, in fact, if they were going to kill off white kids without killing off some black ones too.

Everyone walked around in a daze. Some felt the hour of the wolf had arrived. Something worse than 1984 had happened. The government, a government elected into office just as Adolf Hitler had been, had suddenly shown itself to be a gang of murderers. The thing was a *fait accompli*, we had not even noticed. Some of the younger students were close to hysteria: who was next? If they could kill them, why not us? Older people walked with the step of survivors, wondering what next. Mothers walked with the knowledge that those killed kids could have been theirs. Just an accident, the telegram reads, so sorry. The three years you wiped up shit and poured in string beans, the fifteen years you developed more elaborate techniques for same are declared null and void, along with the product, one nineteen-year-old male or female with —— eyes and —— hair, weighing one hundred and —— pounds more than it did when it pounded its way out of your uterus. A breathing person has been transformed into an unbreathing person: that's all.

Letters were written, telegrams sent. The group set up tables in the Square and offered telegrams for a dollar: all you had to do was fill out a form. People who two years ago, a year ago, had been muttering knowingly about arms caches and revolution went silent now, peering over their shoulders. There was a march; we gathered on the Cambridge Common and listened to speeches shouted through loudspeakers, unable to hear what was being said. It didn't matter. The older people, expecting truth in the traditions they had been taught, stood erect, marched with firm heads. The younger ones, expecting betrayal at every corner, cowered and watched warily what was going on; it cost them more. They ducked when suddenly small boxes were thrown into the crowd from somewhere out on the perimeter. Small groups gathered as someone courageous opened what was a used cigarette box resealed with Scotch tape: each one contained three or four joints. The receivers lighted up, but still warily. Can marijuana be mixed with gunpowder? Would the FBI be that clever? The march began, down to Mount Auburn Street, up Mass Ave and across the bridge into Boston, down Commonwealth to the Common. All along the way, people stood watching, people in business suits with cameras, men in work clothes and hard faces. The whole world had been transformed into FBI agents and hardhats. They were equally dangerous. People marched, talked, joked, but the young shivered every time a helicopter hovered overhead. Some of us had been at People's Park at Berkeley when the crowd was teargassed; all of us knew about it.

We reached the Common and wandered, threaded through. It looked as if millions of people were there. We found a place to sit and rested on the grass. The sun was warm, the air was soft, the grass and trees smelled green. People on a podium we could not see were singing songs and giving speeches we could not hear. We sat there, barely looking at each other. There were only a few possibilities: they would destroy us here, now, with whatever means they chose; they would pay no attention to us at all; or we would manage, through our gathering together, to tell them to stop, stop, stop, stop, stop! None of us really believed the last. All of us wanted to believe the last. We sat watching the new arrivals, some bearing Vietcong flags, some pictures of Mao, some obscene condemnations of Washington, of

551

Nixon, of that old devil, the military-industrial complex. Yes. Devils have a way of surviving. We were mostly silent. Slaves do not have much respect for each other, and the young among us felt like slaves that day – people alive and wanting to live whose government would as soon murder them as not, and would much rather murder them than listen to them. Voiceless, impotent, frightened, the young people sat on; the older people sat on, developing arthritic cramps and rheumatic aches, and then it was over, nobody had even tried to sell anything, and thousands, thousands of us walked toward the MTA. No one rushed: there was no point. People were walking as if they had been to church, really been to church. In time, we got on the subway. I remember wondering how the subway system managed. The train was crowded, but nobody was pushing, no one shouted. We all got off in a group and walked to a sub shop and picked up sandwiches. Then everybody went back to Val's place – Mira, Ben, Iso, Clarissa, Kyla, and Bart too, whom they'd met along the way and Grant was there too, and some others – and they sat around Val's kitchen watching TV, watching the same news shots on channel after channel, drinking coffee and eating sandwiches and every once in a while someone would say, 'They'll have to listen, there were so many of us,' and then silence would fall again. I am afraid we felt a little virtuous. It was they who were killing the children, the yellow, the black, the red, the white children. It was they, not us. We had set ourselves against them. We had proven our purity. If we, poor as we were, lived well, it was not because we held with exploiting the folk of Africa or Asia; our fellowships had nothing directly to do with Mobil's holdings in Angola, or Ford's profits on arms. At least we hoped not. It is easy to scoff at our morals. I can do it myself. But what else could we do? Storm the Pentagon? Do you think that would have helped? We were willing to be poorer if that would help stop the killing. Poor as we were.

There are no answers for this bleak mess. None that I know, anyway. Some days later, the governor of Ohio, who had sent the National Guard out armed that day, was defeated in a primary, and Mira turned to Ben, who had his arms around her as they watched TV, and cried out, 'See! See! The whole country feels the way we do.'

Quietly, grimly, Ben said, 'He was slated to lose that primary by more percentage points than he did. He gained popularity by doing what he did.'

Mira turned back to the TV set with a staring white face.

But that was later. Then they were all sitting in Val's kitchen, talking about the size of the crowd, the spectacle of the aerial shots, trying to estimate numbers. They were really all sitting around waiting for the eleven o'clock news, and just killing time between. Most of all they wanted to feel – not good, that wasn't possible, or even powerful, no, that wasn't possible either – but just as if they had at least enough power to make a statement; they wanted to feel that they had been tiny parts of a communicative and therefore significant act. They had sent up their burnt offering and were waiting for a small rain of reply.

In the midst of this tension, the phone rang, and everyone froze. We were silent as Val stepped across bodies to the wall where the phone hung, silent as she picked it up. So we all heard it, the voice on the other end. Because it screamed, it shrieked, it was a high, little girl voice, and it cried out: 'MOMMY! MOMMY!'

'What is it, Chris?' Val said, her whole body taut. Her fingers, Mira noticed, were twisted together and white. But her voice was calm.

'MOMMY!' Chris's voice screamed. 'I've been raped!'

17

It seems incredible now, looking back, that all of that could have been jumbled together the way it was. I am amazed that any of us survived it. But I guess the human race has survived worse. I know it has. The question is, at what cost? Because wounds do leave scars, and scar tissue has no feeling. That's what people forget when they train their sons to be 'men' by injuring them. There is a price for survival.

Val spoke calmly to Chris. Quickly she got details, told her to lock her door, to hang up and call the police, and she, Val, would be waiting, would be standing by the phone, and Chris was to call her as soon as the police came, or before, as soon as she had stopped talking to them. Quickly, briskly, she spoke and Chris kept saying, 'Yes. Okay. Yes, Mommy. I will.' She sounded twelve.

Val hung up the phone. She was standing beside the wall, and she turned and laid her head against it. She just stood there. Everyone had heard; no one knew what to do. At last, Kyla went up and touched her arm.

'You want us to stay with you? Or do you want us to get out of here?'

'There's no reason for you to stay,' Val said, still facing the wall.

Swiftly, silently, people stood to leave. It was not that they did not care. It was a sense of delicacy, of intrusion on some part of Val's life that was more private even than her sexual adventures, or an account of her menstrual cycle. They went over to her, they touched her lightly, they said good night.

'If there is anything I can do . . .' everyone said.

But of course, there wasn't. What can you do with grief but respect it? Only Bart and Ben and Mira stayed. Val stood by the wall. Mira made drinks for all of them. Val smoked. Bart got her a chair and sat her in it, and when the phone rang again, he picked it up, and Val gasped, as if she thought he was going to take the call, but he handed it to her, and then he brought her an ashtray. The voice on the other end was softer now, and they could not hear it. Eventually, Val hung up. The police had come to Chris's apartment. The boy who had raped her was gone. He had raped her a few doors away from her house, and she had somehow gotten home and called the only person she could think to call, who happened, Val said grimly, to be a thousand miles away. The police were taking her to the hospital. Val had the name written on the wall. She dialed Chicago information and got the number of the hospital.

'It's crazy, but I have to do something,' she said, smoking nervously. 'Someone has to look after her, even if it's at a distance.'

They sat there until three. Val kept calling. She called the hospital, where they left her dangling so long that she hung up and called again. And again, and again. Finally they told her Chris was no longer there. The police had taken her down to the station. Val called the Chicago police. It took some time and many calls to find out what precinct Chris had been taken to, but she found it finally, and got through, and asked what was happening to her child. They were not sure. They kept her dangling, but she held on. Eventually Chris came to the phone. Her voice sounded, Val said later, hysterical but controlled.

'Don't press charges,' Val said.

Chris argued. The police wanted her to do it. She knew the name and address of the boy who had raped her. They had other charges against him and they wanted, as they put it, to nail him.

'Don't do it,' Val kept saying. 'You don't know what it will cost you.'

But Chris was oblivious. 'They want me to, and I'm going to,' she said and hung up.

Val sat stunned. 'She doesn't know what she's doing,' she said, still holding the receiver in her hand. The dial tone buzzed through the room. She stood up and dialed again, got the station again. The man who answered was annoyed now: Val was becoming an irritation. He told her to hang on. He did not return. She waited ten minutes, then hung up and dialed again. In time, someone answered. He did not seem to know what she was talking about.

'I'll see,' he said. 'Hold on.'

She held on for a long time, and eventually he returned.

'Sorry, ma'am, but she's gone. They took her home.'

Val thanked him, hung up, and sank back into her

chair. Then she started up, fished in a cabinet for the phone book, and riffled through the Yellow Pages. She dialed an airline and made a reservation for the following morning. She turned to Mira.

'Do you think you could drive me to the airport?'

Of course, Mira and Ben too would drive her.

Val waited, smoking. After twenty minutes, she dialed Chris's apartment. There was no answer. She waited ten more minutes and dialed again. No answer. The group sat there with her for another hour. There was no answer, although she dialed six times. Bart's knuckles were pale pink.

Val sighed and slumped. 'She's gone someplace else. Sensible. Probably staying with a friend.' She stood and reached to a shelf for a small notebook, riffled through it, and dialed another number. It was four in the morning. Someone answered, because Val was talking. Her voice was subdued, but tremulous. She was telling someone about the rape. 'Yes, I'm flying out in the morning.' There was a silence, then she said 'Yes,' again, and hung up. She turned to her friends.

'That was Chris's father. I thought he ought to know. I thought he'd want to know. She has spent holidays with him for the last fourteen years. She's not a stranger to him.' Her tone was odd.

'What did he say?' Mira asked.

'He said it was good I was going to her.'

She went to the counter and poured a drink. She sipped it, and tried to smile at them. The smile looked as if it were cracking her face, so strained were its lines.

'Go on home and get some sleep. And thanks for staying. Thanks for feeling that you would stay whether I wanted you or not. Because I didn't want you to stay and I'm grateful that you did, and I realize the only people I wanted to stay were those who didn't give a shit whether I wanted them to or not.'

They laughed: such complexities after such strains!

She was packed and dressed by nine-thirty and Mira and Ben drove her to Logan. Her plane left at eleven. She admitted that she had not slept, but Val did not look too bad after a sleepless night. It was the day after that she showed wear. So when she left, she still had some glow, some sheen.

When she returned, that was gone. Actually, her friends did not see her when she returned. She and Chris had taken a cab from the airport, and it was several days before Val called any of her friends. She had been gone only a few days – four, or five perhaps. Everyone went over to see her and Chris, but both of them acted very strangely. Chris would barely speak, and glared at the people she had kissed good-bye last fall. She sat in a corner of a chair looking sullen. Val was strained and brittle. She tried to make conversation, but it was obviously an effort. She did not encourage them to stay, and not knowing what to do, they left. They were concerned and talked among themselves. They decided to leave her alone for a few days, until she unwound, and then visit one at a time.

I saw Val around that time and what struck me were her eyes. I have seen eyes like that since: they were staring at me out of the head of a Polish Jew who had spent her young adulthood in a concentration camp. The causes hardly seem parallel, but perhaps they were not so dissimilar. For I heard the story of that time, later.

Chris had been on her way home from a peace demonstration in Chicago, and was in high spirits, thinking she had done something good, and having had a good time. After the demonstration, she and some friends and a teaching assistant at the university had gone out for a pizza and a couple of beers. Chris's apartment was in a fairly safe neighborhood, and she walked home from the subway. Her legs were tired and she was wearing bad shoes – they had high wedges and thin straps around the ankles. She was a few doors from her apartment, walking along the sidewalk, when a boy leaped out at her from between two parked cars. He had leaped, not stepped, and he stood directly in her path. She was instantly terrified and thought about her rotten shoes. There was no way she could run fast in them, and no way she could slip them off her feet. He asked her for a

557

cigarette. She gave him one, and tried to pass coolly by him, but he grabbed her arm. 'What do you want?' she shouted. 'Match,' said, wiggling the cigarette at her. 'Let go,' she said, but he didn't, 'I can't get a match unless you let go.' He let go of her arm, but moved his body so that again he stood directly in front of her. Behind her, she knew, were the two empty blocks back to the subway. It was only about nine thirty, but there were no people on the street. She handed him the match-book, her mind whirring. The apartment buildings rose darkly around her. She did not want to scream. Perhaps he was just trying to frighten her – her scream might frighten him, turn him violent. People were killed every week on Chicago streets. She decided to play cool. She asked him to get out of her way, then tried to walk around him. He grabbed her and pulled her off the side-walk; he had one hand over her mouth. He pushed her down in the street between the two parked cars and held his hand over her mouth. He leaned down toward her ear and said softly that in the last months he had killed three people along these very blocks, that if she screamed, he would kill her. She did not see a weapon, she did not know whether to believe him, but she was too terrified to challenge him. She nodded, and he let her mouth go.

He pulled her pants off and put his penis, which was already stiff, into her. He thrust hard and fast and came quickly. She lay there wide-eyed, unable to breathe. When he was finished, he lay on top of her.

'Can I get up now?' she asked, hearing the trembling in her own voice. He laughed. She was thinking hard. It was not unknown for rapists to kill their victims. He was not going to let her go easily. Chris searched her mind. She never once thought of the possibility of using physical force to fight him; it never entered her mind that there was any way to get away from him except by outwitting him. She tried to imagine what would make a person a rapist. She thought of all the excuses for crime she had already heard, and all those she could imagine.

'I bet you've had a hard life,' she said after a while.

The boy got off her then, and asked her for a cigarette. They sat there smoking, as he talked. He told her wild, disorganized things; he told her about his mother, who was violent, and the things she had done to him as a child. Chris clucked and murmured.

Suddenly there was a noise, and the boy threw her down again with his hand on her throat. Some people had come out of an apartment building and were standing on the sidewalk talking. Chris hoped they would see the cigarette smoke rising from the street. She did not dare to scream. She felt if she had tried, her voice would have frozen in her throat. The men got in a car, one parked a few cars down, and drove off. The boy kept her head down, though, and stuffed his penis in her mouth. 'Do it,' he ordered, holding her head down and moving up and down over her. She was choking, she thought she would swallow her tongue, but he kept going, and he came right in her mouth, and the salty stinging semen burned her throat. She got her head up when he was through and choked and spit out the semen. He smiled. She tried to stand up, but he grabbed her arm.

'You're not going anyplace.'

She sat down again. She felt totally defeated. She tried to gather her wits and get him talking again. If she made him think she was his friend . . . She talked sympathetically, and he opened up. He talked about school, his block, his knowledge of the neighborhood, of much of Chicago. He knew, he boasted, all the alleys and dead ends for miles around. She listened with high sensitivity. She felt it would be fatal to make a move before he was in the right frame of mind. The moment had to be perfect. Once, she moved her body a little, and he threw her down instantly and was on top of her again, with his stiffened penis in her. It was clear to her that the thing that turned him on was his own violence, or a sense of her helplessness.

They sat up again, and smoked. 'Listen, I'm awfully tired. I'd like to go home,' Chris said finally.

'Why? It's early. This here's nice,' he said.

'Yes, but I'm tired. Look, let me go home now, and we can get together another night. Okay?'

He smiled at her incredulously. 'Really? You mean it?'

She smiled back. Oh, the wily female of the species!
'Sure.'

He grew excited. 'Hey, gimme your name and address and I'll give you mine, and I'll call you tomorrow, okay?'

'Okay,' Chris swallowed. They exchanged papers. Chris was afraid to put down a false name, because he could see her true one standing right there on her note-books. And she was afraid to put down a false address: he would no doubt watch her enter her apartment. But she put down a false telephone number, somehow imagining that that would save her. He let her get up then. She pulled her clothes together as well as she could, and stood there facing him for a moment. It was imperative, she thought, not to run.

'Well, so long.'

'Yeah. See ya, Chris.'

'Yeah.' She turned gently, and stepped up onto the sidewalk. 'Bye,' she said again. He stood watching her as she walked rigidly toward her building, fiddled with her key – her hands were shaking – all the while trying to hear over the beating of her heart if he was coming after her, if he was just then right beside her, if he would force his way in, throw the door open and her inside. But he did not. She got the door open, got inside it, pulled the bolt and ran toward the inner door. She un-locked that and got inside and slammed it and bolted it. She was too terrified to turn on the light; she was too terrified to look out, as if he had the power to destroy her even from the street. She could not think what to do. She ran to the phone and dialed her mother in Bos-ton. But then as soon as she opened her mouth, all that would come out was screams and sobs.

After she spoke to Val, she carefully, methodically followed her instructions. She was still screaming and crying: it would not stop. She dialed the operator and asked for the police. Somehow she told them what had happened and where she was. They were there in a short time; she could see the flashing light of the police car reflected in her room, even without going to the window. They knocked at the door, and despite the trembling of her hands, she was able to let them in. Her mouth kept crying; the sobs were coming from her depths.

They got her story and the slip of paper with the boy's name and address on it, and their eyebrows raised. They told her they would take her to the hospital. They treated her gently. She remembered she had to call her mother. When she hung up, she turned to them feeling as though she had severed all moorings and was now letting herself go into a frightful ocean. They took her to a hospital where she was put on a stretcher on wheels and left in a room alone. She was still crying. She hadn't stopped. But her mind had begun to work again. People came in and began to look at her body. They examined her vagina; she had to put her legs up in stirrups. And all the while she was crying and feeling demolished, people at her, all interested in the same place, that was all she was, vulva, vagina, cunt, cunt, cunt, that was all, there was nothing else, that's all there was in the world, that's all she had ever been in the world, cunt, cunt, cunt, that was all. They examined her and ignored her. They did not give her a sedative, or try to talk to her. She kept saying over and over in her mind, while her throat kept crying, I am, I am, I am, I am Christine Truax, I am a student, I study politics, I am, I am Christine Truax. I am a student, I study politics, incantationally, hypnotically, as they led her out, still ignoring her sobbing, and put her back in the police car.

Her hysteria had abated a little; she was still crying uncontrollably, but the sudden agonized screams came less often. Her head kept going. I am, I am Christine Truax, I go to school. They took her to the police station and sat her down. She could hear them; they were speaking gently to her. They wanted this kid, they said. They had him on three other charges, they wanted to nail him. She started suddenly, her eyes horrified. He had her name, her address, he knew where she lived, he'd seen the notebooks with University of Chicago printed on them, there was no way she could get away, he'd find her...

Her mother was on the telephone. 'They want me to sign a statement,' Chris said in a dead voice between sobs.

'Don't do it! Don't press charges! Chris, I'm telling you!'

He has my name, he has my address, he knows where I go to school.

'They want me to and I'm going to,' she said, and hung up. She went back. They started again, urging, begging. She nodded. She signed. They relaxed. They asked her where she wanted to go and she just looked at them. She began to cry again. They were growing impatient. She could not think. She could not go home. He has my name, he has my address.

Behind her, phones rang, policemen sat at desks, policemen walked through the room. Name, address. What is your name? I am Christine Truax, I am a student. I was out at a restaurant with some friends and my teacher, Evelyn, and was walking home at about nine thirty in the evening...

'Take me to Evelyn's,' she said.

18

When Val arrived, she took a bus from the airport and found a subway that would take her near Chris's apartment. She walked from the subway, looking around. Was this where it happened? Or here? It was a pleasant street in the lovely May afternoon. There were trees and women with baby carriages out walking. Chris was sitting in the dim living room; a friend was with her, Lisa. She ran to her mother and embraced her hard and they stood together for a long time.

'Well, you look okay,' Val said, gazing at her face.

'I am okay,' Chris said smiling. 'I went to Evelyn's last night and she was great. She's my teacher, she's a graduate student in English, I have her for my intro course. She was so great, Mommy! She said I was the fifth girl she knew to be raped this year. This year! She stayed up all night with me. I was pretty hysterical. She fed me Scotch,' Chris giggled, 'and I actually drank it!' Chris turned to Lisa. 'And Lisa too. I called her from Evelyn's and she came over. They were both great. Evelyn drew a bath for me and put in the nicest stuff, bubbly and perfumed, and then after, she sat me down and combed my hair for me, just kept combing and combing. And talking. And she made me a sandwich and tucked me into bed. It was like you were there,' she said, and her voice broke, and she clutched her mother again.

'We came over to pack up Chris's things,' Lisa said.

'Yes.' Val sat down and Chris hurried into the kitchen and came back with a cup of coffee for her mother.

As she told me this story, Val stopped here. 'It was as if she knew then. As if we both knew. What we were going to do with this thing, how we were going to arrange it. I kept doing things for Chris and she kept doing things for me. But they were different things.'

Val asked Chris for the story, and interrupted her often, insisting on knowing every detail, stopping her whenever the details became imprecise. She listened carefully. It took a long time. Lisa left; she had an appointment. It was starting to get dusky outside, and Chris began to look around nervously.

'Yes,' Val said, rising. 'Pack a little bag, honey, and we'll go to a hotel.'

Chris was delighted with such a simple solution. Everything was all right, now that Mommy was here. Mommy would take care of her. She locked the apartment and they walked out into the street, each carrying a small suitcase. Chris wound her arm through her mother's. They walked down the street that way, Chris leaning toward her mother, her body pressed closely against Val's. At the intersection of the main street, Val hailed a cab, and they went to a small hotel for women only. They had dinner in a restaurant only a couple of blocks away, and walked to it, Chris clutching her mother. Then they got into nightclothes, and Val took a bottle of Scotch from her suitcase and they sat down to talk. They had already, while dressing for dinner and eating, settled all the practical details. Because Chris was a student and was going home soon, she had been given an early date for court appearance. Val laid it out in quick, efficient strokes. They would go early tomorrow to pack up Chris's apartment. They would stop at shops along the way to get packing boxes: the supermarkets would probably help them out. It would take two days to pack; they would ship what they could not carry. Val called shipping companies and got rates. It was all set. In three days Chris was to appear at court. Since they could not tell how long that would take, they would plan to leave on the day following. Val called the airline and made their reservations. They would stop at Chris's bank on this day; take Evelyn out for dinner on that. Chris felt good. She kept hugging her mother. It was so good to have everything organized, to know where you were, to have it all neatly plotted, this day this and that day that and the next day court and the next day home. . . . Chris began to feel safe.

Val poured herself a Scotch, asking Chris if she wanted one, but Chris laughed. 'I didn't get raped today,' she said.

Val sat on the bed. 'There are some things I want to ask you. Did the hospital give you a sedative? Did they do anything for your hysteria?'

They had not.

'Did they give you a syphilis test, a gonorrhea test?'

No.

'Did the police offer you any protection if they were unable to pick this guy up?'

No.

Val leaned back. Chris was anxious. She leaned toward her mother. They were lying on the bed together, and Chris curled up in her mother's arms.

'Is that bad, Mommy?'

'It's okay,' Val said, but her voice was hard. 'I mean, we can have the tests done when we get back to Cambridge. It'll be all right.' She patted her child. 'Christ,' she began in a different tone, 'did you try to fight back?'

Chris's head jerked up, her eyes wide. 'No! Do you think I should have?'

'I don't know. What do you think might have happened if you had pushed him aside and stalked past him, and screamed?'

Chris pondered. 'I don't know.' She thought for a long time. 'I was too scared,' she said finally, and Val said, 'Of course,' and hugged her. But later, Chris said thoughtfully, 'You know, Mommy, there was something else I was feeling. Do you remember that time I was walking down Mass Ave and that man, that middle-aged man drove up and stopped and called me? And I just walked right to him, off the sidewalk. And he asked if I'd ever done any modeling, and I said no, but I was flattered, and he said if I'd get in the car he'd give me his card and I could come to his office, he had a modeling agency, and I did it, I got right in his car, even though you'd told me a thousand times when I was a kid never to do that, I did it just as if I was in a trance, like I had to do it because he said so, as if the minute he spoke to me, I had no will of my own. Remember, we talked about that? And that was okay, because I came to at some point, and got out of the car before he was able to go too far – you said thank heavens for the traffic jams on Mass Ave. Remember?'

Val nodded. 'You were about fourteen.'

'Yes. Well, there was something like that in this. Like us sitting there when Tad was so ugly. Like it would have been a crime for us to do anything about it, to throw him out or call the cops. I mean, nobody else says it's a crime, but we would have felt it was. We would have felt terrible, like we hadn't done what we felt was right to do.'

'In that case, I think we were right.'

565

'Yes. You felt you had to suffer it. But why did *I* feel I had to? You know?'

'Yes.'

'Well, there was that kind of feeling about it. Almost as if he had the right to do what he did. As if, once he'd attacked me, there wasn't anything I *could* do. You know, like in the movies, or on TV. The women never do anything, never. They cry and they shrink and they wait for a man to help them. Or if they do try something, it never works, and the guy catches them and then it's worse. I'm not saying I was thinking about that at the time. Just that that was how I felt. As if there was literally nothing I could do. I was helpless. And wiped out. He had the power to wipe me out. Oh, that wasn't all of it. He said he had a knife, and I was scared enough to believe him. But I didn't have any courage, Mommy.' She sat up when she said this, as if she had discovered something important. 'I've always felt courageous. You know, I'd always argue with my teachers. But I didn't have any courage that night.'

Val put her arm around her and talked for a long time, and Chris settled down into her mother's love, and her mother talked about conditioning and courage and common sense. She told Chris she had done the most sensible thing possible under the circumstances.

'I kept thinking he'd stab my face,' Chris said. 'I wasn't worried about the rest of me.'

They spent the next days working hard, packing up Chris's belongings and cleaning the apartment. Chris still clung to Val on the streets, and although there were two beds in their room, Chris slept with her mother each night. Val took over and supervised the work, and in fact, did most of it herself. But Chris felt there was something wrong with Val. She felt that Val was tensed, as if some terrible thing were going to happen. Val sounded and acted calm enough. Still Chris kept running to make her cups of tea or coffee, to bring her little cheese pieces and crackers on a plate. She was alert to every expression on her mother's face, and often went over and put her arm around her. 'As if she were protecting me from something,' she told me. 'As if she already knew she would have to.'

And when they were walking on the streets, Val's eyes were darting everywhere. Sometimes, cars stopped right in the middle of the street, and men would call out to Chris, 'Hey, baby!' Chris was beautiful. She clung to her mother, almost hiding inside her, hoping they would all go away. For of course, she was used to it, it had been happening to her since she was thirteen. She had never known what to do: she would walk on and ignore them. When she asked her mother, Val had said, 'Tell them to go fuck themselves.' Chris had been shocked. 'You wanna screw, baby?' some man would say, passing her, and she would look away. Now, clinging to her mother, she saw it. It was rape, rape, rape, and she saw that Val saw it that way too. She practiced fighting back. Go fuck yourself, she said over and over in her mind. Val actually said it out loud one night when they were walking back from the restaurant. They had their arms wound together, and they passed two youngish men on the sidewalk.

'Hey, girls,' one said.

'Wanna have a good time? We can show you a real good time.'

'Go fuck yourselves,' Chris's mother said, and swept by, holding Chris's arm.

Chris giggled all the way back to the hotel, but there was a little hysteria in her laugh.

The morning for court arrived. They had to take a bus. They passed through sections of Chicago Chris did not know. She looked out, but she also looked at Val's face. She was somehow worried about Val's face. Outside the bus, there were apartments built of yellow brick. Each one had a concrete courtyard, and around that, a high cyclone fence. They must have been built for black people because inside the yards there were black people, tens and tens of them, just standing there looking out. Chris saw Val's face and looked again. She felt it too. A wave of hatred came out from all those faces and washed over the bus, a laser beam of hatred that would

567

wipe out all it encountered, bus, street, cars, all.

'Daley knows how to keep the niggers down,' Val muttered bitterly. 'He really does. Build them a bunch of prisons and pretend they're free to leave them, and stick them all in there and give them welfare. Anyone who's ever read a fairy tale knows that when you have a dragon and you lock him in a dungeon, he gets out and ravishes the country. I guess Daley never read a fairy tale.'

Chris shuddered. 'Do you think they hate us, Mommy?'

'I can't imagine why not. I would if I were they. Wouldn't you?'

Chris shuddered again and was silent.

'What is it?'

'The boy . . . the one who raped me . . . Mick . . . he was black.'

'Was he? So is Bart.'

Chris relaxed. 'That's true.'

When Val and Chris entered the police station, every head turned. The men's eyes took in Val appraisingly, but lingered long over Chris. Val tightened, and Chris clung more tightly to her mother. Val was staring. Chris followed her eyes. She was looking at the men's hips. Their hips and asses were broad and ugly in the shapeless police trousers, and each of them had, hanging around his hips, a gunbelt with a holster and a gun hanging down. They walked swaggeringly, their pants sagging with the weight of the weapon. Like a pair of balls and a prick. They didn't care how ugly they looked, as long as the weight and size of their weapon was visible. Val's mouth was twisted.

They finally found the courtroom. But once inside, Chris kept making noises in her throat. 'He's there,' she would gasp, staring at the back of a head, then look around and, 'No, he's there!' She kept it up for some time, then Val said, 'I'm going to leave you for a moment. I'm just going to the front of the room.' She got up and talked to the man standing in front of the room, then called Chris and led her into another room. It was a locker room, long and narrow, with lockers along both walls, and benches in the middle. There were several large windows looking out on a pleasant, leafy street. They could hear dogs barking, a lot of dogs, too many for a neighborhood. They sat there smoking. After a half hour, Chris curled up on a bench and fell asleep. Policemen would occasionally walk through, glancing at them suspiciously. Val decided the men's room must be at one end of the locker room.

After three hours, two men in ordinary dress entered briskly and approached them. They glanced at them briefly, then one said to Val, pointing to Chris, 'Is she the one?'

'The one what?' Val flared, but they ignored her. Chris sat up. She looked very young, more like fifteen than eighteen, her face soft and pink from her nap, her eyes wide. The men sat down. Both carried clipboards with papers on them, both had pens. They tossed questions at her at random, and barely waited for her to answer. Val watched with horror. Chris was immobilized. She answered their questions mildly, in a small voice without explanation. She did not insist when they argued with her. They attacked and jabbed and tried to get her to retract her story. She did not seem to realize how they were treating her. She blinked and answered, and kept answering. She changed nothing, but she did not get angry, she did not fight back. They were bullying her now. 'You don't really expect us to believe that, do you? You sat out there with him for an hour!' 'He says you're his friend. He had your name. Come on, girl, tell the truth!'

Val understood that they were trying to see if Chris would hold up as a witness, but she also knew that their behaviour went beyond what was necessary in a case like this. The boy was only a boy, not a millionaire's son with lawyers staking reputations and high fees on their ability to get him off. They would ask Chris a question, interrupt her while she was in the middle of answering it, then before she could utter two or three words of answer for the new one, hurl a third question at her. Chris was calm, sickeningly calm. She did not seem to see them, although she was looking at them. She would start to answer a question; when they interrupted her she stopped politely, listened, thought for a moment, then answered the next; when they interrupted that, she simply stopped speaking and looked at them, her face impassive, her manner submissive and obedient. They had not once called her by name. There had not been any suggestion that she might possess one. When she stopped speaking, they started in again with the same questions asked before. She looked at them like a robot built into the body of a sweet child, and began again to answer, her voice calm, emotionless, her answers the same, her eyes unblinking.

After fifteen or so minutes of this, one of them turned swiftly to Val. 'You the mother?'

She glared at him. 'And just who are you?'

He paused for a moment, looking at her as if she were mad. He spat some words at her and turned back to Chris.

'Just a minute,' she commanded, pulling a small book out of her purse. 'Repeat your name and position.'

The man looked at her incredulously. He repeated his name – Fetor; his position – assistant state's attorney.

'And bully. I am writing it down,' Val said.

Both men stared at her. They whispered to each other. Then they rose and left. Chris sank back down on the bench and fell asleep. Val watched the men. The attorney was young, in his early thirties, she guessed, and would have been attractive if his manner were not so ugly. Near the door they stopped and conferred again. The attorney strode back toward Val and looked at her with a face full of loathing.

'Look, lady, you know what that kid is saying? He's saying she's his little friend, see? She wanted it just as much as he did. You may find it shocking,' he sneered at her, 'but lots of pretty little white princesses want to try a little black meat.' He closed the file he was carrying and left the room, followed by the other man.

Val walked to the window. The dogs were barking, barking. The noise seemed to be coming from the building they were in, from the basement perhaps. There must be a dog pound in the building. She stood there, smoking. She thought about that attorney. She wondered if he was the same way when he went home. Did he look at his children and wife as if they were criminals? Did he carry on interrogations over creamed chicken? Val knew she was losing her grip. She was slipping over and there was no way she could stop. She did not want to stop, because stopping would have meant telling herself a lot of lies, would have meant denying the truth she saw staring out at her, all around her, from every corner.

Several hours passed. Val and Chris were hungry, but did not know if they could leave to find a place to eat. The smoke of their cigarettes blew evilly in their stomachs. Finally, another man entered, also in ordinary clothes. He had the same brisk walk as the other, the walk of one who feels he has power in his little world. He was dark and slender and came up to Val, who was still standing beside the window. He was more polite than the other.

'Are you the mother of the rape case?'

'The rape case, as you call it, is my daughter, Christine Truax. Who are you?' She pulled out her little book again.

He gave his name and she wrote it down: Karman, assistant state's attorney.

He began to ask her questions, the same questions the first one had asked, but more politely. She said, 'The other one, beast-man, already asked all that.'

The lawyer explained he had to ask again.

'Well, why ask me? Ask Chris. She's the one it happened to.'

They walked over toward her. She looked tiny and fragile sitting alone on the bench, her thin body huddled up, her long hair hanging around a face that seemed permanently startled. The lawyer started again, but he was more polite than the other. He did not call Chris by name, but he seemed almost sympathetic.

After a time, Val realized what had happened: she offended Fetor and he had refused to handle the case.

571

Karman had been warned about her. She laughed out loud suddenly and Karman glanced at her uneasily: *she* had offended Fetor!

The questioning ended, the lawyer left saying he would be back. Then a group of men came in arguing with each other. They were police. A piece of procedure had been forgotten, Chris had not identified the boy. The boy was not there, he had to be picked up, identification had to be made from a lineup. There were comings and goings, but mostly waiting. The afternoon sun was growing weaker. The dogs kept barking. Some policemen came into the room and brusquely ordered Chris downstairs. Val followed.

'In there,' a cop pointed.

'Oh, no, you don't!' Val exclaimed. They all looked at her. They had already heard about her, she could see.

'You can't make her go into the same room with him without a screen,' she said. 'That's the law.'

They turned away from her and gave Chris a little push.

'Chris!' Val cried, but Chris turned to her with a blank hostile stare, and went inside. Val was standing behind her, and the police barred the doorway, as if she would have gone into the room with Chris. Val looked in. Chris stood with her back to Val. There were six black boys in the lineup. One cop rapped out orders to them.

'Right! Front! Left!'

The boys turned. They seemed listless, except in the muscles of their arms, the cut of some of their backs. They already knew, she thought. She would have rushed toward the cop and struck him if he had talked to her that way. But then she was privileged, white, and female. They would only have knocked her out, or pinned her arms and taken her to the insane asylum. They would have different methods for these boys. The boys turned. The police – all that she had seen that day – were white. The boys had blank faces. They did not dare even to look their hate.

Chris said something to one cop, then came out and

572

slid her arm through her mother's. Val understood and Chris knew that she understood. You must let me get on with this, Chris was saying. I must finish this business. Until I do, I will be afraid to walk out on the street. Let me do what I have to do. I don't care if it is legal or not.

They walked back up to the locker room.

After a time, Karman came to them and said he advised dropping the charges. Chris was stunned. They argued for over an hour. It seemed the boy claimed she had been willing. Karman said that as if somehow it was final, as if it had gone to the highest court and been decided. Unfortunately, he explained, Chris had not been stabbed. She had some bad bruises, he believed (he checked his notes) – at least so she claimed. The best they could do in any case, since she had not been stabbed, was to charge battery, for which the boy would get six months. But the boy was adamant in his story that she was his friend, and he doubted they could make the charge stick. It was best not to put her through it, he kept advising Val, not looking at Chris. Chris had the same glazed stare; she did not seem to understand what was really being said. The boy was coming up for trial on two other charges of battery, and one of rape – that time there had been some nice clean knife wounds – and he would no doubt be sent to jail anyway.

Chris gazed at him. 'No,' she said.

The lawyer argued and argued. Chris just said no. The lawyer said he didn't want to handle it.

'If you don't,' Val stormed, 'I'll get civil counsel and prosecute the government. Or maybe the best thing would be for me to buy a gun and shoot the kid so my daughter can feel safe on the streets.'

He laughed uneasily. He was sure – fairly sure – that she would never shoot anybody. He was graceful, conciliatory, but he kept arguing. And Chris kept saying no. He kept looking to Val, but Val would not budge. She would not say one word to try to influence Chris. And Chris said no.

'Okay,' he sighed finally. It was ironic, Val thought.

He was reluctant to try the case for Chris's sake: because he did not want to see her humiliated in the trial. So completely did he believe the boy. The boy had not challenged any of the details. He did not deny that he had jumped out at her from between two cars, that he had thrown her down. No one asked to see Chris's bruises, but she had a number of them, a large deep one on her shoulder, where several layers of skin had been scraped away, and one along her spine, not large but deep and bloody. No one questioned any of that. And Val thought that only a male could believe that a woman approached in that way could actually enjoy it, could find her will in the rapist's. She'd read such things too, in novels by men. Submission. Yes, that they might get. Kings, emperors, slavemasters got it too. And wiliness. Isn't that what women and slaves are known for?

Her mind was wandering. Chris led her into the courtroom. Chris sat her down and put her arm around her. She was muttering. In the courtroom she could not smoke, and smoking was all that had been holding her together. She kept muttering. All around them there were men: cops, lawyers, criminals, victims. They watched the proceedings and Val began to mutter more loudly. Heads began to turn. There was a striking difference between the judge's and lawyers' treatment of blacks and whites: it was so obvious that Val wondered it did not rise of its own strength in the middle of the room and stifle them all.

'Sexist pigs,' she said, then 'Racists!' Chris had her arm around her, she was patting her gently.

'It's okay, Mommy,' she whispered in Val's ear.

'Kill, kill, kill! That's the only thing you can do! There are too many of them,' she confided in Chris. 'There's no way you can take them on singly. You need weapons. Kill!'

Chris kissed her, and laid her cheek against her mother's.

'We'll have to bomb them. It's the only thing,' Val said. 'We have to get them all in a bunch. All at once.'

Their case was called. Word was sent to bring the boy

in. Their lawyer came over to them one last time. He had a kind face, he was concerned. But he was still a sexist pig. Val kept her hands over her lips as he spoke so she would not shout it at him. Chris had Val's elbow clutched tightly in her hand. She was begging her mother not to do it. Val then heard what the lawyer was saying: he was warning them both against the humiliation Chris was just now going to endure. He was trying to soften it, but at the same time saying that they had brought it on themselves. 'You're sure you want to go through with this?' he asked Val. 'We can still call it off.'

Val took her hand away from her mouth. Her mouth was twisted with hate. 'A little black meat, that's the way you say it in the back room, no?'

The lawyer looked shocked. He gazed at her with loathing.

'Well, if she'd wanted to screw a little black meat, she could have done it in a nice soft bed in her own apartment. She didn't have to get all bruised up in the street. If you think it's her virginity or her chastity we're concerned about, forget it. We're fighting for her safety, for her right to exist in the world. A world full of *you*. Men!' She stopped. His face was incredulous and horrified. His forehead was wrinkled. He thought she was insane perhaps, hideous certainly, and evil without a doubt. But he was a pro. He walked back to the bar and went through his papers. The public defender, a large, red-faced Irishman, asked: 'Who's the next one?' and Karman murmured an answer.

'Oh, Mick!' he laughed. It was all there in his laugh: the little wicked glint in the eye, the knowingness, the pleasure. We all know about cunt, much as the little prisses try to pretend. 'Come on, you're not going to try this one, are you?' he smiled at Karman. 'You got to be kidding. This chick had hot pants.'

The boy was brought out. He was young. He looked no more than nineteen, but was twenty-one. He had a sweet baby face. He was larger than Chris, and more muscular, but he was far from a giant. He glanced briefly at Chris, but she did not look at him. She looked tiny and frail standing there all hunched over, her long hair hanging about her thin face, her eyes sunken in.

The judge asked Chris what happened, and briefly, she told her story. The Irish lawyer stood behind his client, his profile to the courtroom. He was grinning broadly.

The judge turned to the boy. The public defender had his file in his hand, and was ready to open it, to contest the accusation. He was all ready.

'And how do you plead?' the judge asked the boy.

'Guilty,' the boy said.

It was over. Both lawyers were surprised, but they folded their files up calmly. Only Chris did not move. She waited until the judge had sentenced the boy to six months for battery, and then she said, in a faltering little voice, that she had expected more of American justice, that she had been studying it for years and had intended to make it her life's work and what she had encountered today had crushed every notion she had had. She was little and looked very young and her voice was high and unsure, and they let her finish and the judge slammed his gavel for the next case, and they paid no attention whatever to her. What was she, after all?

Chris came shaking back to her mother. It was over. Justice was done. A black boy who had believed everything his culture had taught him and had acted on it was to go to jail for six months. Of course, there were other charges pending against him. He might spend his life in jail. And he would go in bitter hurt and hate. She had said she was his friend and he had believed her. Like all other men, he had been betrayed by a woman. He would not remember the rest, the jumping out at her, the hand on her throat. He would remember only that she had played him for a fool and he had believed her. Someday, perhaps, because of Chris, he would kill a woman.

Val sat there remembering that downstairs she had felt sorry for the black boys in the lineup, knowing that such sympathy was gone in her, and that it would never return. It didn't matter if they were black or white, or

576

yellow, or anything else for that matter. It was males against females, and the war was to the death. Those white men would stand up there and make Chris a victim rather than disbelieve a male who was a member of a species they heartily despised. What, then, did they think about women? One of their own women? What did they see when they looked at their daughters?

She rose stiffly. Her bones felt as if all the juice in them had dried up. Chris led her out of the room as if she were a cripple; Chris somehow got them back to the hotel. Chris arranged to pay the bill and get a cab. But there was trouble with everything. The man at the desk argued about something; the cabdriver yelled about the amount of their baggage; the steward on the plane yelled at Val that if her daughter did not keep her shoes on he would throw them both off the plane. And everywhere they turned they saw the broad blue pants, the gunbelts, the heavy pricks that shot real bullets, or the others, the neat, short-haired men in gabardine suits and white shirts who looked just like the attorneys, who were ever so nice and never said shit in front of ladies and always pulled out your chair when you went to a restaurant. They even, Val kept thinking, shivering, they even had little daughters of their own, they maybe even played with them, talked to them when they were in good moods. And they had little boys. What did they teach them?

Chris took care of Val all the way home. When they were back, Chris collapsed. She curled into a ball and crept into the corner of the couch and did not speak. She could not stand to have anyone but her mother near her. She slept in her mother's bed, but had trouble sleeping nevertheless. She kept waking up, imagining she heard strange sounds. Since she slept so badly at night, she was tired all day and napped frequently. She tried to read, but could not concentrate. She would sit for hours every day in her room with a mirror propped up before her, cutting split ends from her hair with a nail scissors. If people came – people she had loved before, Iso or Kyla, Clarissa or Mira – she would sit there absently, speaking little to the guest, snapping at her mother, or else she would retreat to her room and close the door. If Val asked for help in preparing a meal or cleaning the apartment, Chris would respond passively, sometimes obeying, but more often simply drifting off to be found, twenty minutes later, asleep in her bed.

Val took her for vd tests and a general physical. There was nothing wrong with her health. Chris went everywhere with Val, because she would neither go out or stay alone. But Val went to few places: the market, the laundry. She dropped out of all her organizations curtly, with no explanation. People kept driving up to the house to pick up stacks of mimeos, notes, pamphlets. Grimly, Val handed them the paper as if it were so much shit. The two women could do nothing. They would, on occasion, turn on TV at night, but within a minute or two there would appear a commercial, a line, a scene, a snatch of dialogue that was intolerable and without looking at each other, one of them would get up and turn it off. When Val tried to read, she would get through a few lines, then throw, literally throw the book against the wall. They could not even play music. Chris growled about rock lyrics and Val growled about Beethoven. 'Daddy music' she kept muttering. The entire world seemed to them polluted. When Tad stopped in one day, neither of them would even look at him.

The only person Chris wanted to see was Bart, and when he stopped by, she and Val sat with him drinking tea and Chris told him the story. His eyes filled with tears, he stared gloomily at the table, but when she was through, he looked up and told them in dire tones how black men felt about white women, how the women were only the vehicle of their revenge against white men.

Chris and Val looked at him. He left shortly.

Val realized that it was up to her to do something, but she had no heart. She felt she had no friends left: they did not seem to understand the real meaning of what had happened. They tried to act cheerful, to talk about other things as if rape were not much more than having your house broken into and your stereo stolen. She was not angry at them; she simply didn't want to see them. She cast around in her mind and remembered a group who had lived in the Somerville commune and had gone off, a year and a half ago, to start a communal farm in the Berkshires. They grew vegetables and herbs, had chickens and goats, a grape arbor, some bees. They made their own cheese and yoghurt, wine and honey. They spread themselves out along the main roads and sold home-baked bread, their own pottery and knitted things. They were surviving.

She wrote to them about Chris, and their reply was positive. She was welcome to come, and the calmness and naturalness of the place were bound to help. Also, there was another woman in the commune who had been raped: she would understand.

Val hid the letter. That day, while Chris was napping, she went out for a walk. When she returned, Chris was white, panicked.

'Where *were* you!'

'I have to go out alone sometimes, Chris,' was all she said. That night she insisted Chris sleep in her own bed. She heard Chris pacing, all night long, but she held to it, the next night and the next. Chris gave up the pacing, but it was obvious from her face that she was not sleeping. After a week, Val went out one night. She told the incredulous Chris that she could not come. Chris was breathless, aghast, and when her mother returned after twelve – she'd gone to a movie, seen none of it – Chris glared at her with numb and silent hatred.

Finally, Val suggested to Chris that she go away for a while. There was this place in the Berkshires. Chris looked at her mother with a twisted mouth, with eyes in black sockets with a face that said it would never trust again.

'I take it you want me to go.'

'Yes. You can't spend your life glued to my side.'

'I'm sure I must be in your way. I suppose there's somebody you're dying to shack up with and I'm cramping your style.'

'No,' Val said quietly, dropping her eyes. Chris's

hatred was the most painful thing she had ever experienced.

'If you want to get rid of me, I'll go live with Bart.'

'Bart works. You couldn't go to work with him every day. You'd have to stay alone. His neighborhood is dangerous.'

'STOP, STOP, STOP!' Chris shrieked, jumping up. 'Do you have to do this to me? Stop! I can't stand it! I can't stand anymore.' She ran into her room and slammed the door. Val got drunk and sloshed to bed.

The next morning, Chris gazed at her mother coolly over the coffee cups. 'All right, I'll go.'

Val gasped, flushed, smiled, reached out for Chris's hand. But Chris pulled away. She looked at her mother with a cold face.

'I said I'll go. But I'll never forgive you for wanting to be rid of me at the time I needed you most. I'll go. But don't expect to see me again, or hear from me again – ever.'

A few days later, Val drove Chris out to the farm. She walked into the farmhouse like a prisoner being delivered to jail, and did not kiss her mother or say good-bye when Val left.

19

Stella Dallas she had said. Yes. But not quite. Her daughter was not inside a brightly lighted mansion with music pouring out of it, marrying a society heir. And Val may have been standing out in the rain, but she was not crying.

If only she had been Stella Dallas. If only she could have cried. I think to this day that would have softened everything, that would have made everything pliable enough to recover. I think. But that's afterthought.

The truth is, she wrote Chris off. She hardened herself against the pain and decided they would not be close for a while, but would be again in a few years. She felt that betrayal was inevitable in a relationship as close as theirs had been. Chris was too dependent on her. It

580

is essential to a child's growth that their parents fail them, through inadequacy or malice; and since Val was strong and intelligent, her failure seemed malicious. Of course, she could have let Chris creep back inside her. She ruled that out. The rest followed as things will follow. There was nothing she could do for Chris, 'except die,' she told Mira, 'and I have no intention of doing that.'

She wrote to Chris occasionally, but Chris did not answer. And Val did not write true letters. Because Val had gone over the line. No one knew it but she.

Morality is fine, but it is limited. Morality is a set of rules for people to live together; it presumes the being together and it presumes the main chance. It has no hold over and no relevance to people who have passed over the edge. For instance, a few years ago a plane crashed in the Andes, and the survivors finally reached a point where they ate human flesh. That produced a so-called moral question. Except it didn't really, because who could answer it? You can bring one dogma or another, one citation or another, one authority or another to bear on it; you can talk until you die. But you can't say whether that was right or wrong. You are a Jew and your husband and your children have been turned to ashes by the Nazis (you were saved because your body appealed to some of them) and you are walking down a street in Argentina and you see the man who was the commandant of the concentration camp where you were held, and you have a gun in your pocket, a gun you carry everywhere you go, your finger always near its trigger as it lies nestled in your pocket, and you see this man . . . Oh, why go on? Some things cannot be categorized, judged, they can only be lived out by those who are willing to live them out, or perhaps, those who have to live them out. And such people do not worry about consequences.

I wonder if that is true. It is nice to sit here with the sun pouring through the window, a glass of iced tea on the desk, a walk on the beach in the offing, and write about people who don't worry about consequences. Are there such people? Doesn't even the most committed militant, his soul too scarred to live well, his hopes blasted, even as he heads his tank for the wall, his plane for the aircraft carrier, think fleetingly about the possibility that it is really just a nightmare that will end, that somehow he will be saved, will go back home and sit by the fire and pick up the cup of tea, the knitting, and laugh about stories of the old times and wipe a tear or two? . . . .

Oh, God. What's the use? Everything I write is lies. I am trying to tell the truth, but how can I tell the truth? I have been thinking for a long time now that extraordinary circumstances place one outside the human race, outside usual human concerns, and the rest of us cannot judge people who find themselves in such a condition. But even as I write it, a cold nervous germ attacks my spine, creeps up, all the way to my brain, and suggests that all life is like that, all lives.

But if that is so, how can one tell even the simplest story? I give up. I can't think anymore. All I can do is talk, talk, talk. Well, I will do what I can. I will talk, talk, talk. I will tell you the rest of what I know, take it to as much of an end as it has. It is not over. It will never be over. But I am finite. That is the only reason this account will end.

Val acted so strange and distant and cool after her return from Chicago that the women, caught up in their own lives anyway, did not stop in very often. Chris acted sullen and impossible, and they were hurt. They did not know the whole story of the rape, but because sex had never been a tabooed subject in Val's household, they assumed that Chris's shock was merely that and would soon be assuaged. Val herself never called any of them, and they felt some breach coming from her.

Mira, who was probably closest to her, felt guilty about it, and kept meaning to stop in. But something in her dreaded seeing Val. She felt as she had when she first knew Val, that Val could tell her something she did not know, and wasn't sure she wanted to know: but she felt this more intensely now. She felt almost as if Val had a contagious fatal disease. But one day she forced herself; she called, and Val said, rather halfheartedly, that she would be home.

Val was wearing jeans and a shirt; she had lost weight. Her face had lost its fullness, it was harder, firmer, older. Her hair was full of gray. The changes were slight, but she did not look the same person.

They talked small talk for a while. Kyla and Harley had gone to Aspen; Clarissa and Duke were having troubles; Iso was deeply into the research for her thesis; the boys were with Norm and would be going with Mira and Ben to Maine in August.

'How's Chris?'

Val's voice was thin, emotionless. 'She's in the Berkshires, on a farm. They seem to think she's getting better.'

'She was really upset,' Mira said, half-questioning, half making a statement, but she heard the edge of prim judgment in her voice. Chris was excessively upset was what she was really saying.

Val heard it too. She merely nodded.

'I'm sorry, Val. I don't understand, I guess. I've never been raped.'

'No. But almost, as I recall.'

Mira's eyebrows rose. 'The night in Kelley's; God!' She shivered. 'I had forgotten, I wanted to forget. Why is that?'

'Sanity, I suppose. Most women don't want to know much about rape. It's men who are interested in it. Women try to ignore it, try to pretend the victims asked for it. They don't want to face the truth.'

Mira felt her insides begin to shake, as if every blood cell in her body had suddenly become wary. But she had gone too far. 'The truth . . . ?' her voice asked tremulously.

Val sat back in her chair and lighted a cigarette. She had the same authority in posture and movement that she had always had, but it was heightened by her new leanness, and a lack, something gone, an ease, a fluidity, an expansiveness of movement. She was more intense, more focused, and narrower, like a light beam that finds its object and concentrates all force on it. She told Mira the story of the rape then, all of it. When she finished, Mira was tightly gripping the arms of her chair. Val sat back, and her voice eased a little.

'Last fall – at some meeting or other held out in Concord or Lexington, I don't recall – one of the participants asked me for a ride back to Cambridge. He was a young guy, a little stiff and pompous, a minister, in fact. He wanted to talk. He talked all the way back, and since we got stuck in traffic at one point, that took quite awhile.

'He was a gentle little fellow, the kind who is always careful about other people's feelings, or so it seems, the kind who can't say *shit* naturally and can't bring themselves to say *screw*. Needless to say, my language shocked him.'

Mira laughed a little, but Val did not even smile.

'What he wanted to talk about was this dream he'd been having for months on and off. He was, he said, happily married – he was in his mid-twenties, I imagine – and they had a little boy. He was having problems with the little boy, arguments with his wife. She thought he was too authoritarian and perfectionistic with the child. But his dream was not about that. It was about a girl he'd known in college, years before. He dreamt abut her all the time, but could not remember the dream. What did that mean?

'I asked him how he had felt about the girl. He had loved her, adored her, but she was a bit of a flirt, she flitted from man to man, and came back to him when she needed him. He always waited for her with open arms. I asked him if he'd screwed her. He answered, no, no, he had never' – and here Val did grin – 'engaged in the act of sexual intercourse with her, and neither, he imagined, had anyone else. They would have felt too sinful: it was a small religious college in the middle of farm country.

'I asked him how he felt about her now. He thought of her as ultimately desirable, but his memory of her was

584

singed with anger. He had loved her, he had wanted her, and he had done nothing. He was angry with her but angrier with himself. "What could you have done?" "I could have raped her."

'I wasn't even surprised. This guy was unbearably stiff and boring, impossibly correct, Christian, mild, meek, all that. But at heart, a rapist.'

'I know all this, I've known it always,' Mira said faintly.

'That story – and God knows how many others, how many pieces of history, laws, traditions, customs – everything congealed for me while I walked the streets of Chicago with Chris, watching the men looking at her. And it became an absolute truth for me. Whatever they may be in public life, whatever their relations with men, in their relations with women, all men are rapists, and that's all they are. They rape us with their eyes, their laws and their codes.'

Mira's head lay in her hand. 'I have two sons,' she said softly.

'Yes. That's one way they keep their power. We love our sons. Thank God I don't have one. It would hold me back.' Her face was fierce.

Mira sat up. 'Hold you back?'

'Everything came together. That guy – the minister – and the way Tad treated Chris, the kid who raped her, the lawyers who raped her soul, the courts and the way they treated her, the cops with their guns hanging down and the way they looked at her, and the men on the streets, one after another, looking at her, making remarks. There was no way I could protect her from it, and the way she's feeling now, no way I can help her to bear it.

'And my mind was wandering, I wasn't able to control it. I thought about marriage and its laws, about fear of going out at night, fear of traveling, about the conspiracy among men to treat women as inconsequential – there are more ways to rape than one. Women are invisible, trivial, or demons, castraters; they are servants or cunt, and sometimes both at once. And gay men can

585

be as bad as straight ones – some gay men hate women even more than straight ones do. All these years, these centuries, these millennia, and all that hate – look at the books – and under it all, the same threat, the same act: rape.

'And I thought: Christ! For years I worked in the civil rights movement, in the peace movement, to free political prisoners. I worked with the committee on Somerville schools, with the committee on Cambridge schools. All this while, I'd been thinking – people, or children. But half the people I was trying to help were males, males who would as soon rape me or my daughter as look at us. They'd take your body if they could, your soul if they can, get you in control and then abuse you or discard you. I have been spending my precious life helping them! A bunch of rapists! Because there is no turning back once you've faced this. All men are the enemy!'

Her eyes were fiery, and her voice passionate, but controlled.

Mira could not breathe. No, no, let it not be so, she kept repeating in her mind.

'You are expected to enjoy your own eradication! "What should a girl do if she's raped?" "Lie back and enjoy it." "What should a pacifist do if his wife is raped?" "Get between them." It's not possible for a husband to rape his wife: the word has no legal standing in context because rape is his right.

'I tell you,' Val's voice dropped low and full, and full of fury, 'I am sick of it. Shit, I used to pick up male hitchhikers! No more. Let them use their own feet, fight their own fucking battles, no man, ever again, in any way, will get any help from me. Never again will I treat a man as anything other than the enemy. I imagine Fetor, the state's attorney who browbeat Chris, has a daughter, and I'll lay you ten to one if she ever got raped, he'd treat her the way he treated Chris. I'm sorry.' Val glanced at Mira's face. 'I know you have sons. That's good. That will keep you able to live in the world, keep you,' she drawled the word sarcastically, 'sane.'

586

Mira's face was drenched with pain. Val's was clear, firm, she looked like a tough old soldier raising a standard. 'As for me, I'm glad I don't because he would interfere with my vision, I'd have to think about him and that would deflect me from the truth. A son would make me want not to see this, not to feel it, want to push it back down into my innards where it's lain for so long, slowly poisoning me.'

'But how can you live without men? I mean, you know, men are the bosses if you want to get a job, they control the foundations if you want to get a grant, a man is your dissertation adviser. . . .'

'I've dropped out of that world. I belong to all women's groups now. I shop at a feminist market, bank in a women's bank. I've joined a militant feminist organization, and in the future I will work only in that. Fuck the dissertation, the degree, Harvard. They're all part of the male world. You can't compromise with it. It eats you alive, rapes your body and soul. . . .'

'But, Val, how will you live?'

She shrugged. 'I'm willing to live any way at all. There's a bunch of women living in an old house in North Cambridge. They get by. I'll join them soon. I don't look for pleasure any more in life. It's a luxury I can't afford. For forty-odd years I've been a member of an oppressed people consorting with the enemy, advancing the enemy's cause. In some places that's called slavery. I'm through with it. I want to work with these women, those who give their lives up for our cause.'

'Give their lives up!'

'Give their lives to. However you people in English want to put it.'

'Sacrifice.'

'It's not sacrifice. It's realization. Sacrifice is giving up something you value for something you value more. That's not my state. Once I valued it – pleasure, joy, fun – but no matter what I did now, where I went, that is gone for me. There's no way I could go back to it, don't you see?'

She looked gravely at Mira. 'You look agonized.'

587

Mira's voice mourned, 'But you were so great. The way you were.'

'A great compromiser. What you see as my deformity, I see as my purification. Hate is a great definer. You lose something, but develop something else to fullness. Like blind people learning to hear with exquisite acuteness, or deaf people learning to read lips, eyebrows, faces. Hate has made me able to act as I should have been acting all along. My fucking love of mankind kept me from being a friend to womankind.'

Mira sighed. She wanted to cry, to turn Val back to what she had been, like a reel of film you could rerun and stop where you chose. She couldn't bear what she saw, heard: she was exhausted. She leaned toward Val. 'Let's have a glass of wine. For old times' sake,' and her voice cracked.

Val really smiled for the first time. She got the bottle and poured out two glasses.

'I feel as if this – all this new life of yours – will take you completely away from us – me,' Mira said sadly.

'Well,' Val sighed, 'not because I've stopped caring about you. But it would be hard. You wouldn't want to listen to me much, I suspect. And we wouldn't see things the same way anymore. You have two sons, Ben – you have to compromise. I'm serious, I'm not being patronizing. I'd seem fanatic to you, and you'd seem cowardly to me. I'm part of the lunatic fringe now,' she laughed, 'the lunatic fringe that gets the middle to move over a bit. It feels right to me.'

It was good-bye she was saying, Mira thought. Tears streamed down her face all the long walk home.

20

That summer seemed a period of renunciation for many of us. Was everybody playing Stella Dallas?

Kyla had been persuaded by Harley's arguments into giving their marriage one more chance. She returned to him, and promised not to see Iso at all anymore. He was very angry about Iso this time. She was puzzled. 'You were so understanding before.'

'I didn't take it seriously before.'

'Why not? I told you I loved her.'

'Kyla, she's a woman, for God's sake.'

'So?'

'Well, I don't mind having a complement. But I don't want to be supplanted.' He made his anger sound like jealousy, and she was more pleased than not. He couldn't be jealous if he didn't love her, could he? She arranged to sublet the apartment, and began the packing. Harley helped her more than usual, but still, life began to feel empty. She took to stopping at Iso's in the afternoons, full of guilt, but unable to help herself. She did not tell Harley about these visits. She told herself that in Aspen she would not be able to see Iso at all. Somehow that justified the deception.

She was searching for a dissertation subject, but half-heartedly. She sat in Child leafing through books. She sat at home, rereading the Romantic poets. Suddenly Romantic poetry seemed everything Harley said it was: self-indulgent embroidery on the real business of life. She could not muster her old excited reactions to Wordsworth's peculiar value-structures, or Keats's language. Coleridge had come to seem a bore, Byron a spoiled child in a tantrum, Shelley an adolescent in a continual wet dream. She read more and more, but the more she read and reread, the more she saw all of them as adolescents, exalting their own sensuality or declaiming pretentious self-aggrandizing wisdom. She wondered how she had ever been able to take them seriously. Every day, she closed her book in disgust. When it was time to pack their books for Aspen, she added to Harley's stacks only a complete Shakespeare. She decided she would spend the summer baking bread and growing flowers, and perhaps getting pregnant. She did not think of this as an abandonment but as a rest, a hiatus. Nevertheless, as they set off in the car for their first stop, Ohio and her parents' house, she did not feel light and free, like a person starting on a vacation. She glanced at Harley's profile, feeling the same rush of love she always felt when she looked at him without his knowing it, the

589

some distant admiration for his excellence, yet she felt also diminished, even abject. She had a vague sense she was driving off to prison. But she brushed it away, and her spirits lightened as soon as Harley needed navigational help. Kyla loved to read maps.

After Kyla left, Iso languished for a few days, but with her spectacular flexibility had within a week made new friends and was as busy as ever. And instead of daily visits from Kyla, she had daily visits from Clarissa.

Clarissa and Duke were having continual squabbles. She did not want to talk about them. 'It's the same old shit, you know, who's going to do the dishes. The trouble is, I guess, I don't ever want to do them. I hate all that, cooking, cleaning. I can't stand it. When Duke was away, I heated up TV dinners and threw the tray in the garbage. The silverware would pile up and I wouldn't wash that until there wasn't anymore. And I only cleaned up when he was coming home – if then. I don't care about food. Why should I have to cook?'

'Yeah. How about a housekeeper? I don't mind cleaning, Clarissa,' Iso grinned. 'And I need money. I'll do it for you for – let's see – three bucks an hour.'

Clarissa did not smile. 'That would just mask the problem.'

'It sounds serious,' Mira said.

'Oh, I guess it's manageable.' She would brush it off and return to other subjects. But the next time the women were together, it would come up again, and be brushed off again.

These days, Grete was often part of the group at Iso's. She would show up around four carrying a bottle of wine, wearing some outlandish costume or other and looking like the princess in a fairy-tale book. She found oddly embroidered blouses, used sari fabric to make something flowing, found strange beads and jewelry with great heavy stones, and wore them all as if they were her native dress. She tied her dark hair in kerchiefs and put heavy elaborate earrings on. Iso said Grete raised dress into a fine art. Grete was interested in art, and was planning a dissertation on the relations between a set of late eighteenth-century sketches and poetic images of the same period. She revitalized the group, and all summer the talk was wonderful.

Clarissa's problem continued. One day, when they were talking about reciprocity in politics, she broke in: 'That's what Duke's doing! I just realized it.'

'I guess from General Motors to Duke isn't such a leap,' Grete said. Grete had come from a poor family, and was prejudiced – her own word – against anybody with money.

'Okay. I see it now. Every time Duke goes to a Harvard party – and he hates them – or if he listens to a new album, and admits a rock group I like is good, or if he buys a particularly fancy shirt, he acts afterward as if he has the right to expect something in return, as if I owe him something. He'll sit on the couch while I clean up the dinner dishes alone, and when I complain, he gets really irritated, he says he never even has time to read the papers. And I've been getting angry at this, but you know you hate to turn into a continual nagger. And I haven't understood what was going on.'

'It's his idea of compromise,' Mira laughed.

'Yes. Quid pro quo. There's something wrong with it, logically. I can't put my finger on it, though.'

'He's expecting you to adopt the traditional role,' Grete began, 'while he . . .'

'Yes. While he what?'

'Dabbles in your values?'

Clarissa raised her chin and began clicking off points. 'Okay. So a proper quid pro quo would be my dabbling in his values. But I do. I went to a party given by his fellow officers and never once criticized Nixon. I visited his Rhinebeck relatives and drank after-dinner coffee with the women in the living room while the men sat drinking brandy in the dining room and talking politics.'

'People still *do* that!' Grete gasped.

'I don't know about people: *they* do. Okay. I was looking for a line of attack: got it. Thanks.'

That was the end of Duke for that day.

Another time Clarissa was discussing the effect of

social structures on the nineteenth-century English novel, which was her dissertation subject. 'It starts early, of course it's there in the eighteenth-century – in Defoe, say – in a subliminal way, but in people like Crabbe and Austen it becomes a full-blown subject: money, money, money. It's at the root of everything else. Just like Duke these days,' she added, then stopped short. Her head was bent forward, her hair hanging down almost covering her face, but Mira could see the little frown on her forehead, almost see the mind ticking away the realization that she never made these discoveries alone, only when she was with the women, talking about something else, as if they could come into her mind only unbidden, and as if that bothered her. She said nothing about it, however.

'Money! I love money!' Grete cried, waving her braceleted arms in air. 'But not too much money.'

Clarissa raised her head soberly. 'Yes, I like it too. But not like Duke. He talks about it all the time, he's obsessed with it. Ever since he has been living here. We go out and he looks in all the shops and he wants everything. He wants to buy some pictures from David, not because he likes them so much, but because he thinks David's going to be famous someday, and he wants an investment. He's talking about leaving the army – although he really loves it – and joining up with some guys at MIT whom he met through Harley. They're talking about using computers to do urban planning. It's a lucrative field these days, apparently. They want to set up a consulting firm even though they're still in school.'

'A consulting firm to do what?' Iso was sitting under the window, the light shining on her hair, one long leg dangling over the chair arm, one slender hand holding the small cigar she had recently taken to.

'You look just like Katharine Ross.'

'I don't!'

'You do.'

'Do you like Katharine Ross?'

'Ummmm,' Clarissa grinned and licked her lips.

'Then it's okay,' Iso laughed. 'I'll look like her.'

'They want to solve problems. They think cities and institutions would come to them and they would get together all the relevant data and feed it into the computer and tell the city what to do about pollution, say, or school systems, or cross-country migrations, or the birthrate. They think they can plan our future. They believe the reason things are such a mess is because they are never planned, they always happen haphazardly.'

Grete groaned. Mira said, 'Ugh.' Iso giggled: 'Thank heaven for the failure of human planning.'

'Duke thinks he'll make a fortune. I don't care whether he does it or not – that's his decision. But all this emphasis on money. I don't understand it. He used to be so idealistic.'

'It's true,' Iso said thoughtfully. 'Like last night at dinner, when he got on the subject, it was a little scary. As if he feels he's against a wall and only money is going to keep those soldiers out there from shooting their rifles at him. There's a desperateness about him, you can't call it greed, although it sounds like greed. But I always think of greed as an avidity for something you don't need just for the sake of possession. Duke acts as if he needs money horribly, as if he were being hounded by duns.' She turned to Clarissa. 'Maybe he's taken up secret gambling.'

'Maybe,' Mira said remembering Norm, 'that's how men feel.'

'What I find appalling,' Grete waved her arm, 'is that the very people who understand nothing about living are the ones who are presumptuous enough to imagine they can plan our lives.'

Mira glanced swiftly at Clarissa. She knew that Clarissa was a little edgy about Duke, that one could not say too much about him without offending her. But Clarissa smiled at Grete. 'Yeah. I told them if they were going to do this, they'd better get a few poets, preferably women, to join them.'

Mira decided then that the situation between Duke and Clarissa was really serious. Clarissa stopped talking about Duke, though, after that. It was only through Iso, in whom Clarissa had begun confiding, that Mira and Grete learned that things were bad indeed. Iso did not go into detail, but apparently Clarissa had shown up several nights in July with a tear-swollen face and eyes. Clarissa did not mention these things when the women were together. Mira felt hurt: she felt the whole point of the group was to be a group, to provide a community for each other. She sensed that Clarissa's withdrawal from the group, after Val's and Kyla's, would in time lead to its disintegration.

Clarissa's withdrawal, however, had less to do with a reluctance to share her experiences with them all than with her feelings about Iso. She felt in close rapport with her friend; she felt utter trust in her, and utter comfort with her. It was easier when she was alone with Iso, easier and somehow better. Many nights she would storm out after an argument with Duke and walk the five blocks to Iso's. Sometimes she would sleep there on Iso's lumpy couch. Duke was bewildered, he did not understand what was happening to them. He kept trying to grab Clarissa back. The conviction had grown in his mind that it was those women who were somehow taking her away from him, and he sought for any way to discredit them, to snipe at them. His hate and fear of the group expanded to include what he called women's lib; in time his remarks were directed just at women, period. Clarissa would flare up: 'I'm a woman'; he would rage, 'But you're different!' And Clarissa would storm out again. The harder he pulled, the harder she pulled. Duke was frantic, but there was no one he could talk to. Twice he went out himself, late, and picked up prostitutes and went to their rooms. Both times, he was unable to perform sexually. What he really wanted was to talk. His sense of potency was undermined, and one night he tried to force himself on Clarissa. She fought him off; he slapped her; she socked him in the jaw, hard, and he sat there a little stunned, wondering how this could be happening, happening to them who loved each other, she gazed coldly at him and turned away and walked out. She closed the door softly, instead of slamming it as she usually did after an argument. Duke sat there, rubbing his jaw, blinking at the door, sensing that something final had happened.

Clarissa's evenings with Iso had grown more and more intimate. They would kiss hello; they would frequently put an arm about each other. When Clarissa was especially tense, Iso would rub her back. Clarissa let herself relax into her friend, and ramble on, giving up the need she had always had to remain in control and to make logical sense out of things. She felt she did not have to worry about boring Iso, and she rambled about the trivialities that express the dissolution of a marriage. When she was especially upset, Iso would make her a drink, and stroke her head as she spoke, sitting on a chair beside the couch where Clarissa lay.

Clarissa did not know what was happening to Duke and her, or why. She tried to get past the surface irritations to the real issue, but every time she thought she saw it, she would draw back in horror, sure that couldn't be it. It couldn't be, not with Duke and her, it couldn't be the same trite fucking shit everybody else talked about. Surely they were better than that, larger, smarter. But over and over again, in these terrific arguments about dishes and cooking and her work – 'He says reading all day is not work. It was when he was finishing up at the Point, of course' – the same pattern emerged. 'He's trying to make a housewife out of me!' she gasped to Iso. 'Why? Why? I thought one of the things he loved about me was my mind, my independence, my personality. Why is he trying to turn me into the thing he claims, always claimed, bores him? Why?'

It did not make sense. It was beyond answer.

Clarissa sat up. She sipped her drink soberly. 'Something just came into my head. Val – I remember disliking her that night – talking about how the institutions get you in the end. No matter how you struggle.'

Iso nodded. 'I was angry with her for that too, not because what she said isn't true, but because she was being insensitive to you and Kyla and Mira. I mean there are times you shouldn't tell the truth.'

Clarissa looked at her and they both laughed. 'Not even to your best friend?' Clarissa glinted.

'If you tell the truth all the time, you won't have any best friends.'

There was a silence. 'Do you tell me the truth?'

Iso paused. 'Yes. As far as I can claim to know it.'

Clarissa looked deep into Iso's face. 'I tell you the truth.'

'I know,' Iso smiled tenderly at her, stroking her face.

'I had a horrible dream last night. Horrible.'

'Tell.'

'Duke and I are sitting in our living room when Kevin Callahan knocks and enters. Kevin is a real person. In the dream he's a young man about three years older than I am, but in real life I haven't seen him since I was a kid, maybe eight or nine. Last time I was home, my mother told me that he and his wife had adopted a child. I didn't ask her about it but I think I just assumed at the time that the reason they adopted a child was that Kevin was impotent. I don't know why I thought that. Maybe because when he was a kid, Kevin was very feminine. Anyway, Kevin notices that the house is a mess and tells Duke he should demand that I do a better job as a housewife. I get furious, I tell Kevin to go to hell, and I stomp off to the bedroom thinking that only an impotent male would insist on rigid sex roles.

'But once I'm in the bedroom, I begin to feel sorry about my outburst. I ask Duke to explain to Kevin that I have taken a pill which is altering my behavior. I have taken this pill because Duke and I are to be married in forty-eight hours. This pill will eventually put me in a comatose state almost identical to death. When the pill has its full effect, I will be shipped to some distant place where the wedding ceremony will take place.

'The time for shipping arrives. Drugged I am placed in a boxcar where I lay down on a laser beam. I'm in a deathlike trance. Eventually – I don't know if I've forgotten anything there – we arrive at the place for the wedding. A friend of my parents, who happens in real life to be an undertaker, takes over the arrangements for the ceremony. He is modeling a manikin/corpse of me, paying much attention to small details – the texture of my skin, the different colors of my hair. The doll he creates can walk, blink her eyelashes, and do whatever is demanded of a bride in a wedding. Somehow, it is decided that the bride/corpse/manikin will go through the ceremony instead of me. The audience will think it is me, and I will be able to escape the ceremony. The undertaker is also making an intricately carved bed/coffin which is to be placed on the altar. At the end of the ceremony, the couple will lie down on the bed/coffin as the audience watches.

'The whole thing happens – the wedding, the lying down. But meantime, Duke and I run off to New York together. We aren't even missed.'

' "It can sew, it can cook, it can talk, talk, talk," ' Iso quoted. 'But you do escape, you and Duke.'

'I feel as if I've been sleepwalking through my life. As if I'm Sleeping Beauty and still haven't wakened up.'

Iso gazed at Clarissa's round, child's face, still sweet despite new darkenings, the beginnings of lines. 'Well, it was such a nice dream there in the rose abor. Mummy and Daddy loved their little princess, and she never needed to need anything because before she could even ask, the good fairy whisked it in with her magic wand. And school was the same way. And Duke. And look at you, a bright, handsome young couple, well-connected, sure to have marvelous children, a marvelous future. An apartment full of gorgeous prints, rugs, vases, all picked up for peanuts on the Vietnamese black market—'

'Iso!'

'Related to a former muckamuck and another former muckamuck, families with places in Rhinebeck and Newport, apartments in the Dakota—'

'Iso!'

'You wanted me to tell you the truth. You thought you could get away from your values by burying yourself in Roxbury, but you always knew you'd come back and that you could come back.'

Clarissa jumped up and flung herself out of Iso's

apartment. She didn't even close the door. She ran all the way down the stairs.

Iso sat there until Clarissa's footsteps had vanished. She didn't even get up and close the door. She felt pounded on, abused, used. She finished her cigar, then slowly, like an old person, walked to the door and shut it and locked it, all three bolts. For over a year now, she had been feeling good about herself, had felt she could be herself. And herself felt like a pair of open arms. And all that had happened was that people had treated her house like a restaurant, had drunk her drinks and eaten her food and basked in her kindness and sometimes, her love, and then, when they were healed, restored to self-respect, they had left. There were always more where they came from, of course. There would always be more, as long as she left her heart and door open, kept her re-frigerator full.

She remembered a day she had spent with Kyla, a day they had planned, saved up for emotionally. Kyla had the car and they drove out to Concord, parked, got out and walked. They walked far beyond the public places, invading fenced meadows and fields. Kyla was nervous and jerky, she was biting her lip again, she tripped over branches. Finally, she ducked through a wire fence and got her hair caught. Iso ran to her and tried to unsnag her, and Kyla began to shriek, scream, curse at her.

'Leave me alone, fuck it! Leave me alone! I can do it myself!'

Iso dropped her hair and retreated a few feet and sat down in the grass with her back to Kyla. There were tears in her eyes. Kyla got free in time, she marched up to Iso, faced her, and when she saw her, plopped down opposite her and sobbed. Her face broke out in blotches. 'I don't need you! I don't want to need you!'

Iso's eyes dried. She looked at Kyla sadly. She knew that Kyla was crying because she was being cruel to her, Iso, and because she didn't want to be cruel and she couldn't help it. It was her own round robin, a circle of emotions only tangentially related to Iso. It was Kyla's trip.

'But what about me?' she asked quietly after a while. 'I am a person who has learned to demand nothing. Don't I count at all?'

'You! You! What about you! It's all pure pleasure with you, it's love, I owe you nothing!'

She leaned back and lighted another cigar, and watched the smoke circle around her. She felt utterly empty. She had poured herself out for them and they had drunk her. They would go on drinking her up as long as she poured herself out. But if she stopped, who would come to her, why would they come? She, with her strangeness. Men came because they wanted to screw her; women, because she offered them love. It never occurred to anyone that she wanted something too. But then she had not acted as if she wanted something too.

She stood up and began to pace, walking around the shabby room that had held so much dramatic life, straightening pictures, books, emptying ashtrays that had lain there for a week.

She felt completely isolated. She was a loving mother whose children had all grown up healthy and left. She thought: I am just as alone as if they had never existed, as if I had never poured them glasses of love and sympathy, spent myself on them. She sat down, her back erect, her head at attention. This was the nature of things. She was the woman for everyone; she played the woman to women's men. And suffered the way women suffered from men. Illegitimate of illegitimates, servant of servants. It was good; it was better than it had been; but it was not good enough. She would have to find a little man in her, whatever that meant. It did not mean being a champion sailor, or canoeing in white water, or being able to fence, all of which she did very well. It meant insisting on self, not the way they did, God forbid, but a little. Otherwise you were the tramping ground of the world. A little. But how did one do that?

She sat up late, thinking about it. She would have liked to talk to Val, and dialed her number several times, but there was no answer. Val had the secret, she really had things knocked. Tomorrow.

She went to bed with her mouth firmly set. But she could not decide anything about how to live. All she had decided was to close her door. From now on, she was going to spend more time with her work. She loved it, it was always a wrench for her to stop, but a wrench she had not minded for their sakes, her friends. No more. Let them knock.

But it was only a few nights later that Clarissa knocked, late, around ten, and without thinking, Iso went to open the door, glancing back at the last sentence she had written.

She stood at the door looking coolly at her friend. Clarissa stood there with intense eyes. 'I came to apologize,' she said. Iso opened the door. 'I'm working,' she said coldly. Clarissa stopped. 'Iso. I'm so sorry,' she said fervently. 'You've been true to me and a friend to me and I – it was just that I couldn't stand it, it was too painful, and I blamed you, I know that's ridiculous ...'

Iso tried not to smile, but she was delighted, and ended by returning Clarissa's embrace.

'Oh, well, I was tired anyway. It's about time to quit. How about a drink?'

Clarissa handed her a paper bag. 'I stopped and bought us some Scotch.'

They settled themselves in the living room with their drinks. The old rapport was there, the old comfort, but something subtle had changed. Iso was less affectionate, less demonstrative. She seemed to keep back part of herself.

'I came back to ask you if I can sleep here. I'm not going back to Duke. I'd be glad to pay the expenses if you'll let me stay here until I find a new apartment.'

'Sure.' She almost said, 'You don't have to pay anything,' but stopped herself.

'What I don't understand, what I can't forgive myself for, is having been blind for so long.'

Iso smiled. 'Shall I call Mira? She has you beat by some ten or so years. You can sing the lament chorus.'

'But it undermines your confidence in your own intellect, your own perceptions.'

'And we all go through it.'

Clarissa leaned forward grinning. 'Shit!' she said and reached for Iso's hand. 'Can I sleep with you tonight?'

Clarissa settled in with Iso very contentedly. Duke was wild. He threw himself into work with the MIT group every evening and weekends. He did not suspect that Clarissa and Iso were lovers; but he felt that 'the women' had won. He could not bear that; he felt emasculated. He told that to anyone who would listen. He never probed what lay beneath his words, what 'emasculated' meant to him. It was a term calculated to gain him sympathy, and with his male friends, and an occasional prostitute, it did. In fact, he was still not able to have an erection, but it never occurred to him that this had anything to do with him. It was all because of the bitch, Clarissa. His male friends shook their heads sympathetically: they knew how it was. They told their wives about this poor guy done in by his bitch of a wife who wouldn't even wash a dish. But behind his back, they joked about him.

Mira and Ben, however, were still fine. The summer seemed an idyll to them, broken only by the unhappiness of their friends, and Mira's shakenness for a few days after she visited Val. She had begun research for her thesis the day after her orals, and she found she loved the whole process. She was one of those odd people who enjoys compiling bibliographies, and takes pleasure in reading schoolarly books and articles. She was as painstaking in this work as she had been in running a house; she bought special file cards which enabled her to cross-reference by a set of ingenious little holes. She worked methodically from nine thirty every morning to three thirty every afternoon, and at home in the evenings. Yet it did not seem slavery to her but freedom. For the first time, she understood what graduate school had been about: it was all designed to free her for this. She did not have to worry over every detail; she had enough knowledge to make certain statements, and enough awareness of how to get knowledge to find out how to make others. That was liberating. She was free to be as methodical as she chose, in a work that seemed significant. What more could she ask?

She felt she was doing the work she had been born to do. She charged into her stack of books and articles with the exultation she imagined an explorer feels, starting off before the sun is fully risen, breathing the chilly, clean morning air, listening to bird noises and the tramp of her own feet in the dry brush as she choose a path into the wilderness. Each day she opened the volumes with a fast pulse: would she discover her own hard-won points spread out gracefully and easily in the pages of someone who wrote before she was born? Or a sharp word or sentence that would jab the seed in her mind into sudden fruitfulness? Would she reach the Indies, that place where literature, logic, and life came together in one beautiful whole, a crystal oval one could hold in one's palm? Or an interpretation so searching and so strongly argued that it demolished her fragments before they ever cohered?

She felt strongly, but confided only to Ben, that what she was doing required courage. It seemed ludicrous: courage, to sit in a library day by day reading, writing? Courage of the backside, perhaps. But so she felt it. She crowed to Ben, glowed to him, full of joy and the sense of discovery, of fury at the outrageous comments of A, awed love for poor B, dead so many years and smart so long ago, intense involvement with C, who was both brilliant and prejudiced. Ben glowed back and listened and grabbed her just a moment or two before she was through, always cutting her off in midsentence, but always at the right time, to kiss her. It was, she felt, love's hardest test, and his score went off the scale.

Ben's cartons had finally all been exposed, their contents arranged in careful piles in both rooms, and the hallway of his small apartment. He had begun to write, but it was wretched labor to him, and he would not show Mira his pages. He concerned himself most, he told her, with the state of his pencil points, sharpening them all many times each day. 'A pencil lasts me five days, tops. I guess I feel if they're sharp, I might be.'

Occasionally they took a day off; sometimes they drove to the coast with Iso and Clarissa and Grete, or with Ben's friends David and Armand, and Armand's wife Lee. But often, because they were apart most of the time, they went off alone, feeling a little treacherous toward those friends who were carless and suffering in the Cambridge heat, but with the same delicious delight kids feel sneaking out of school. And in August, Mira, Ben, and the boys went to Maine. They had rented a little cottage on a lake; it came with a rowboat, a canoe, and a barbecue grill. All of them threw off their work completely and rollicked for two weeks. Ben threw his work off with particular zest. He tore around the beach like a wild man, threw softballs and Frisbees with the boys, swam, rode, and took them out in the boats as if his body had been let out of a cage. Mira played with them sometimes, but sometimes sat with a book, wearing giant sunglasses, watching them, a smile of complete contentment on her face.

They all cooked together, and did what little cleaning they did together. They all experimented. Norm made chili (Mira's recipe) and Clark spaghetti sauce (Ben's recipe) and were applauded. Ben tried to make pecan pie, and Mira tried to put live lobsters in a pot: these experiments were not successful. At night they sat up talking, playing cards, teaching the boys to play bridge. There was poor TV reception on the lake, but no one seemed to notice. And late, tired, Mira and Ben sank into bed in each other's arms, and as often as not, turned over to go to sleep. When they did make love, it was quietly: the boy's room was contiguous to theirs. But if there was less passion, there was tenderness and complete security. No belch nor fart could dismay them. They might as well, Mira thought, have been married.

21

Kyla and Harley had planned to leave Aspen in mid-August to go to Wisconsin and visit Harley's parents, and return to Boston early in September. But one night in August, Iso's phone rang late, after midnight, and a nervous voice blurted, 'Iso, I've left Harley. For good.' She was at the MTA station; her apartment was sublet, and she had no place to stay.

It is at moments like this that a lifetime's formation is revealed. People write plays or movies about agonized decisions, but I think our important decisions are made instantly, and all the talk is simply later rationalization. Iso's life had been made up of concealment and that was her first impulse now.

'Take a cab to Mira's and wait for me there. She's away. I have her key. I'll meet you there in a half hour.'

Clarissa was in the living room watching a baseball game on a TV rebroadcast, but Iso was whispering. She stood in the bedroom with racing heart, feeling her hot cheeks, preparing a story. When Mira asked her later why she had not simply invited Kyla to stay with her and Clarissa, she had no answer. She knew only that it was necessary to lie. She and Clarissa had an acquaintance who was known as a gossip and a prude, a young graduate student named Peggy. Clarissa was not eager to have the truth about their relationship known. These facts came instantly into Iso's mind.

'That was Peggy,' she told Clarissa with an irritated frown.

'Peggy!'

'Yeah, she sounded very upset. I couldn't ask her to come here—' She let that hang.

'But why would she call you? You aren't a friend of hers.'

'Well, I guess she doesn't have many friends. And I was talking to her in Lehman Hall the other day. Maybe she thinks I'm her friend. She sounded almost hysterical. I told her I'd come over.'

Iso knew that Clarissa would not argue, would not question why Iso had to go there, and would not call Peggy or ever speak to her about the thing.

Iso raced to Mira's, but Kyla was already there, her small figure standing alone on the sidewalk in front of

Mira's house, a suitcase beside her, looking somehow battered. Iso spotted her under the streetlight. She could have been a worn-out prostitute, waiting for business, or a shopgirl who had worked ten hours and was waiting for a bus to take her to her cold room and a supper of bread and cheese. She looked like that, and Iso's heart turned over. Why did she look like that? Kyla saw her and ran toward her, and they embraced each other, laughing, nearly crying, Kyla babbling nonstop about planes and buses and Wisconsin and Ohio, and Iso had to grab her arm and drag her inside, and sit her down and make her start at the beginning while she searched Mira's closets for something to drink. All she could find was brandy.

Aspen had been deadly. They lived in a condominium where there was no possibility of growing flowers and no equipment for baking bread and she had no books but Shakespeare and the library there was terrible and Harley was unsympathetic because she had not had enough foresight to pack her books. He was at the conference every day; at night, as often as not, they had to attend stuffy dinners with visiting celebrities and other physicists – 'not notable for their conversational grace,' Kyla said dryly. After two weeks she decided to leave, to take the car and drive to New Mexico, Arizona, any-place. Harley didn't mind if she left, but he wanted the car. Harley was very happy there : he was in his element. She took to hanging around in the afternoons in the pretty bars and cafés that line the town, gardens in which you could sit all afternoon and drink beer. She met people, kids traveling who had come to see Aspen. She decided to go on the road with a bunch of them. They were heading for Santa Fe. Harley exploded, but she packed the little clothing, the one book she had brought out in a canvas backpack, and went. They hiked, camped, hitched, bussed all the way to Arizona. She shacked up with a couple of the guys. She was try-ing to have a 'real' experience, but, she laughed, 'Shabby as they looked, one was a Ph.D. candidate at Berkeley and one had his degree from Colorado. Another one was a geologist. The women were all students too, but young, undergraduates at Colorado and Utah. It was a pretty safe adventure.'

Last week she went back to Aspen; Harley wouldn't speak to her. 'I don't know, I suddenly *saw*. You know, you were the person who showed me what love could be.' She touched Iso's hand lightly. 'With you, every day was so rich. I felt good about myself, about life. But I guess I kept thinking that was because you were a woman and only women knew how to love. And I guess I couldn't see my future that way – I'm sorry, Iso.' Iso was gazing at her intently; she did not look wounded. 'You know, I still had the traditional picture – marriage, kids, the good life – especially after I visited my folks.' She bit her lip. Iso noticed it was almost healed, and she tapped Kyla's cheek lightly.

'Stop it! It's almost healed.'

Kyla stopped. 'Yes! My hands too!' She held them up. 'It was that time on the road. Not that it was good, you see. Oh, it was wonderful to travel and to travel that way, and I loved seeing those places. But the people I was traveling with, well they were okay, but they were a little disconnected too, you know, and not all that interesting. The women seemed terribly young to me. But I never felt the way I feel around Harley. Sex wasn't great, but it wasn't bad. It made me see that the difference wasn't between you and Harley, but Harley and most people. And that difference is exactly what I loved about Harley, his superiority, his excellence, his cold intelligence that keeps him from getting deflated by little things like emotions or sensations,' she laughed. 'With these people on the road, I felt comfortable, and I have to admit, for once in my life I felt superintelligent! I didn't feel squashed, the way I always do around Harley. I didn't feel that the best I could do in life would be to bake bread and grow flowers. I felt smart, and full of energy. I wanted to *do* something. So I went back to Aspen to tell Harley. But he wouldn't speak to me. He spat coldly at me the night I arrived that I'd humiliated him in front of his colleagues by going off like that with a bunch of bums. I'd humiliated him *again*. It was Kontarsky all over again. But this time I didn't feel guilty, and this time I understood what my problem was. Because I did love Harley, I do love Harley: I think he's great. But he crushes me. He's great for himself, but he's bad for me. I don't know why, I don't think he means to be.'

'Kyla, he's selfish and cold and unloving,' Iso burst out. She had never said a bad word about Harley before.

'No, he's just totally involved in his work. As he should be.'

Iso shrugged.

'Whatever,' Kyla said, brushing hair out of her face. In the past two years, she had let her bangs grow out, and her hair now hung down straight from the part. It looked straggly and dirty. She looked as if she hadn't changed her clothes in a month. And if her hands were healed, her fingernails were bitten to the skinline. 'I told Harley I'd come back to tell him why I was leaving him, and he turned pale. It's funny. He gets so mad, he seems to hate my guts, sometimes he looks at me with that icy glare of his and I think he wants to kill me. But he doesn't want me to leave. He wants me to hang around so he can hate me,' she giggled. 'So he can pick and carp and tell me how rotten I am. Isn't that strange?' But she was smiling, which seemed to Iso even stranger. 'He immediately assumed that I was going back to you, and he began to attack you. It was really strange. You know what he's mad at? He was interested – he wanted to have an affair with you! He felt you liked him—'

'I did.'

'But he thought you liked him sexually.'

'Some people can't tell an avocado from an acorn squash.'

'He isn't emotionally educated. He's emotionally ignorant, is what he is.' Kyla sounded bitter now, angry: this too was new. 'He was furious because, he said, "She came to *my* house, she acted friendly to *me*, she ate *my* food, she drank *my* liquor, and all to seduce *my* wife!" I said it was as much *my* house, food, liquor as his. My

607

fellowship paid as much as his, and that I was not just his wife, and that it was my choice. He said, "I refuse to talk about it. I refuse to be drawn into the pollution of that Cambridge cesspool. It's disgusting. And don't tell me you're going to her out of choice. You're just going to try to get at me, to try to prove something. Go, go ahead to your dyke friend! But when you get starved for real lovemaking, don't knock at my door!"'

Kyla smiled a cruel cold smile. 'I sat there very calmly through all that. I did not let myself think how much I loved him. When he was finished, I said, very coolly, "You don't need to worry about that, Harley. When I want real lovemaking, I go to Iso."

'He just sat there. You could see under his inexpressive exterior that he was stunned, but he said nothing, he sat there for a few minutes, then he got up and left the house. I called the airline, and got the first flight out. I left before he returned, so we never said good-bye formally. I'm sorry I hurt him. But he was so ugly, so stupidly assured. I can't tolerate stupidity in Harley.'

'We don't, in our idols.'

Kyla was playing with Iso's fingers. 'Do you think I was cruel?'

'Yes. I also think it was about time.'

Kyla rested her head on Iso's shoulder. Iso put her arm around Kyla, 'And where have you been since then?'

'At my brother's. I visited with them for a few days. That was good too, really good. You know, they have it all – the big house, the successful husband, the bright, handsome wife who does everything right, the three kids. God, it was deadly. The things they talk about, the things they're concerned with! Ugh! I could never stand it. If that's what baking bread turns into, I'll skip it. The kids were wonderful, though,' she said a little wistfully, as though she had already put such things behind. She sat up suddenly. 'How come I couldn't come to your place?'

Iso told her about the trouble between Clarissa and Duke. 'She's staying with me for a while, until she finds a place. I wanted to be alone with you, and I couldn't very well ask her to leave. She hasn't any other place to go. You know, Clarissa's so quiet, she doesn't have many friends.'

'Ummm. You're a sweetheart, Iso, you're so good.' Kyla nestled in Iso's arms. Iso spent the night there with her, sleepless long after Kyla had given in to her exhaustion, preparing tomorrow's lies.

For, having begun that way, there was no choice but to continue. She had to get Kyla back to Cambridge, she had to create stories to explain why Clarissa stayed on and on, and why Kyla could not show her feelings for Iso in front of Clarissa, and tales of explanation for Clarissa, as to where she was, day after day. She was aided in her fictions by Clarissa's desire for secrecy, by Duke's suspicion, and by Mira's empty apartment. For the next two weeks, she spent all her time either with Kyla or with Clarissa or plotting. Her work fell apart. She felt weary and trapped, but she kept going.

Mira returned to Cambridge; Kyla's apartment was free, but Harley was in it. Kyla did not want to stay there, and she demanded that it was time Clarissa found a place of her own. Iso became adept at the instant lie as she wove explanations: Clarissa was in love with Iso, Iso did not return the affection, but did not want to hurt Clarissa, who was in bad shape after the breakup with Duke. Clarissa did not seem to Kyla to be in a bad shape, in fact, she seemed happier than ever, if also, somehow, older. Clarissa did not understand why Iso was absent so much of the time, and when she stopped at Child, Iso was not there. Iso ran, more and more panicked. She did not stop to think where she was going. She was in a flying cage at an amusement park, being tossed so dizzyingly she had no leisure to consider what position she would be in when the motor slowed, the ride ended.

Frantic and pressured, one day she told Mira about it.

'The French would make a farce out of it,' Mira grinned.

'I know, I know,' Iso said, twisting her hands.

'Why don't you just tell them the truth?'

'I can't. I can't hurt them that way.'

Mira gazed at her. 'Hurt *them*?'

'You're right,' Iso said without looking up. 'I can't choose.'

Eventually, Iso lost control. Kyla, in a hassle with Harley about who would keep their apartment, although neither could afford to keep it alone, got disgusted with what she saw as Iso's weak kindheartedness to Clarissa, and went to see Clarissa herself. She understood that Clarissa was still shaky from the breakup of her marriage, but everything was shaky, and it was necessary now that Iso move in with Kyla, and that Clarissa either take over Iso's apartment or find another. Clarissa blinked: What? But it was Kyla who was shattered by the breakup of her marriage, which was why Iso had to spend so much time with her, listening to her grief. Kyla blinked. Both turned to Iso.

It was the worst moment in Iso's life. She sat there, on a wooden chair, under their interrogation, their accusation, and admitted it all. She had no excuse. Her fingers twisted, her mouth pursed, her eyes were moist, but she did not cry. She said only, 'I love you both. I couldn't choose.'

'I had given up all notion of living a normal life,' Kyla stormed. 'I was willing to live openly with you, to renounce marriage, to forget having children!'

'So was I!' Clarissa agreed.

'You weren't! You wanted secrecy.'

'Yes,' Clarissa said sadly. 'But I've been doing a lot of thinking. I decided some weeks ago that as soon as the divorce goes through, I would do it, make that leap, give up that life entirely, those aspirations.'

Things were probably still resolvable at that moment, Mira thought – for she had stumbled into the scene that afternoon. If Iso had even then been able to say, 'But you, you I can't live without!' to either of them, there would have been wounds and tears and attacks, but that one would have stuck. But she didn't. She looked up at them with dancing eyes and a wicked smile and said:

'Okay! How about we all live openly together, then?'
She giggled with delight at their love, and her pleasure
in them.

Clarissa leaped up, picked up the wooden chair she
had been sitting on, and smashed it to the floor and ran
out into the bathroom. Kyla leaped across the room and
hit Iso, pounding her around the head. Iso put her hands
over her head and cried out, 'Hey, stop! Stop, man, this
is crazy!' but she was giggling at the same time.

Mira tried to calm things down, but she was a bit like
a woman trying to give a tea party in the middle of the
London blitz. The cries, the tears, the accusations, the
stormings in and out of rooms went on for over an hour.
Mira sat back in an armchair, a glass of sharp bourbon
– someone had left it there – in her hand. Iso sat in the
middle, patiently, looking like a martyr being attacked
by Romans.

Eventually, Kyla fell on a chair exhausted, and Clarissa, startled at the silence, sat down across the room,
her arms folded across her chest, looking at no one. Iso
got up, went into the kitchen, and came back with four
glasses of gin and tonic. They all took one without looking at each other. Finally Clarissa said, still looking at
the wall, 'You don't take us seriously. That's the real
sin.'

Iso gazed at her with love. Clarissa turned and saw it,
and turned away again quickly. 'You're right,' Iso said
quietly, and they all turned to look at her. She was still
sitting on a wooden chair in the middle of the room which
was littered with a smashed chair, spilled ashtrays that
had been thrown across the room, spilled coffee from
cups that had been tipped over. She was looking down
at her hands, calm, but with the tremendous inner power
that comes when someone is digging inside themselves as
deeply as they can, and pulling up whatever old boots
and rusty cans and chipped axes they find.

'I won't ask you to forgive me; I don't really feel in
need of forgiveness. I am sorry I hurt you, but I'm not
sorry I was able to love you both all this while, or that
you loved me. And if hurt is the price for that, well, I'm

611

willing to pay it, and you must know I'm not feeling too good right now.'

'You paid it knowingly,' Clarissa said. 'We were never given a choice.'

Iso nodded. 'True, true. Look, I'm not trying to say what I did was right, or that you should think it was, or that you shouldn't hate me, or whatever you feel. I just want to tell you how I feel. I *don't* take you seriously. That isn't because of you, isn't because I don't respect you or your feelings. It's hard to explain. I don't take anything seriously, you see? It isn't you, it's me. I guess maybe I took Ava as seriously as I ever took anyone, but even then . . . there was always a part of me that didn't. I mean, think about it. What makes you take something seriously? It isn't ardor, or affection, or friendship – because we had those, and they were good, and they aren't the reason you're angry with me now. The thing that makes you take a thing seriously is the belief that it will endure. You were both planning futures – and I went along with that, I can't deny it – but I forget, you know, I'm inclined to slide over the fact that other people aren't like me. You felt you had sacrificed something – the proper, the respectable life, the husband, kids, career, house, whatever – a place in the world that you would not have to fight too hard to get, that was waiting for you because you are what you are and because you were doing things the usual way.

'But that has never existed for me. Well, once I tried to do it, I got myself engaged to a man, but that didn't last long, it was hopeless. So I've spent my life, sort of a beggar, standing outside the restaurant, waiting for table scraps . . .'

'Oooooooh!' Kyla brayed.

'No, now let me finish. I'm not, you should be able to see I'm not sitting here feeling sorry for myself. Not too sorry, anyway,' she laughed deprecatorily, and they all found themselves smiling at her.

'The image is true to my sense of my own ability to fit into the mainstream of life, to be like everybody else, to be accepted like other people, to be one of the people the minister talks to when he comes out of church, one of the people who invites him back for Sunday dinner, to try my baked beans and potato salad and banana cream pie. You know?'

'Would you want that?'

'That's not the point. I don't know if I'd want it or not. All I know is I can't ever have it. I couldn't bear to sleep with a man, but a normal life, husband, kids, house, all that, what is considered the good life, the right life, the fulfilling life – that's always been out of the question for me. Don't you see? It's a major difference, it changes the way you see everything.'

The women did not speak, but there was a change in the room. They were moving, crossing legs, sipping drinks, lighting cigarettes, and all of them heard a murmur, deep in the throat, inaudible but sensed, of assent.

'So I learned to take what I could get. Joy on the wing, or something like that. I don't think in terms of forever because forever is not something I can hope for. That I love you – you can't doubt that, can you? You don't?' she turned to them, almost desperately.

'No,' Kyla said fervently, softly, leaning forward.

'No,' Clarissa said, sitting back with crossed arms, her face looking like a tragic mask.

'Oh!' She sighed. 'Good.' She sighed again. 'You know, in a way, I'm glad it's over. I was getting really weary, really uptight: the deceit game is not fun.' She stopped, as if she felt it were over, and she smiled around the room, radiantly, like a child who feels the approval of the entire family.

'You're not quite off the hook, though,' Clarissa said.

Iso glanced swiftly at her.

'One thing we can't forgive you for is not taking us seriously. I guess we can understand that. But the basic thing we can't forgive you for is for not loving one of us more than the other.'

Iso threw herself back against the chair and hit her forehead with her hand. 'I can't! I can't! Why can't I?' she asked Mira wildly.

They all turned to Mira as if she would know, and she

613

gasped a laugh in embarrassment. She had to say something. She wished desperately that Val were there. Val would know. How should *she* know? 'It seems to me,' she heard herself say gropingly, 'that what Iso was saying is that she long ago gave up the hope that she would ever find the grail. You know – you must love God because He is the only one you can love for Eternity. The love that fills all need, assuages all hurt, excites and stimulates when boredom falls, and is absolute, I mean absolute, that never fails no matter what you do or don't do, what you are or fail to be. I think we all spend our lives searching for that, and obviously we never find it. Even if we do find it – like some people's mothers love them that way, you know? – it's not enough, it doesn't fulfill, it is too smothering or too submissively accepting, not exciting enough. So we go on searching, feeling discontent, sensing that the world or what it promised us has failed us, or even worse,' she glanced quickly at Kyla, 'that we have failed it. And some of us learn, late, I'm afraid, that that isn't possible. And we give up the hope. Once that happens, we are in a different place from other people; we can't communicate it easily, but we have different standards. We are more easily contented, more easily pleased. Love, rare thing, when it happens, is a wonderful gift, a toy, a miracle, but we don't count on it to protect us from future days when it rains and the typewriter breaks and it's just as well because the words won't come anyway, and the article has to be written by Monday and mailed, or there won't be enough money for next month's rent – you know. Love is a golden rain that comes down when it will, and as it spatters in your open palm you exclaim over its brightness, its wonderful moistening of your dry life, its glitter its warmth. But that's all. You can't hold on to it. It can't fill all of you. If there were five Bens out there in Cambridge, I could love all of them as much as I love him. But there are few Bens anywhere. But the two of you – and some others too – Grete, Val, my old friend Martha – my God! You are a cornucopia of wonders. Iso can't choose between you because she doesn't need

614

you, because neither of you can fill her up but both of you nourish her, and she doesn't imagine, delude herself that either of you can do for her what her mother's womb did.'

They all turned to Iso, who did have tears in her eyes now, and was gazing with love at Mira. 'You left one out,' she said. 'Yourself.'

Their parting that night was as graceful as a ballet, and as formal. The formality did not arise from stiffness or anger, but from the sense that all of them had that something had ended, some way of relating, and nothing new had yet arisen to supplant it. Until it did, a certain graciousness of manner, a deep courtesy, was all that could express their profound intimacy and their impassible distances. One could understand and understand; but one still needed what one needed. They remained friends; but the almost necessary visit to Iso's every afternoon turned into an occasional Friday or Saturday night. Clarissa found a room somewhere else; Kyla found someone to share her apartment. Iso's apartment still held afternoon visitors, but not as frequently, and it was a new group.

Dissertations proceeded, or snagged, Kyla still spent her days leafing through books, unable to find anything that touched her deepest places. She regretted she had not specialized in the Renaissance, with its moral categories, or had not gone into ethics. Clarissa read hard, but went further and further afield. The connection between social structures and novel form was a tenuous area, but the structures themselves grew more and more fascinating to her. Iso's work absorbed her totally, and she applied for a grant to go to England and France to study manuscripts not available in this country. Grete was working well but slowly. She and Avery were spending much time together, and even when she was not with him, she was thinking about him. Grete had been a prodigy, and was very young still, only twenty-four. 'I think,' she told her friends, 'that perhaps it is necessary to get some solidity, some *security* in one's emotional life before one can really sit down to work.'

'Have a baby,' Mira cracked, sounding like Val.

Mira's work went as well as ever; Ben had written fifty pages. They both expected to be finished within a year. Then in November, Ben got a letter from Lianu, an offer of a job as consultant from the president of the country. The Africans had difficulty in understanding the peculiar American mind. Ben soared. The job could not be counted on, at any moment Lianu might throw out all whites, but oh, it was so beautiful there, the people were so interesting, so wonderful, oh, Mira wait until you see the waterfalls, the volcanic craters, the jungles, the deserts, his friends . . .

Mira agreed it was wonderful, yes, you should go and stay until they kick you out, as they inevitably will, your career will nevertheless be made, you will be The Africa Expert, what all the white countries wanted, a White Man Who Really Knows Africa. She could not keep a sarcastic note out of her voice, and Ben felt it. He would retreat, and then, next time they were with people, start in all over again, with the same excitement, the same eagerness. It took Mira two weeks to isolate the source of her irritation.

Ben had never asked her if she wanted to go to Africa, he had just assumed that she would.

That alone was enough to distort her thinking about the thing. She remembered Normie saying he didn't know if he didn't want to be a doctor because he didn't want to be a doctor or because his father wanted him to be a doctor and her saying that by the time he found the answer, it would be too late. Norm was presently enrolled at Amherst, which was, he said, 'full of kids like me, privileged and pretending we're not.'

She had to get drunk to tell Ben, which she did, not consciously, one Friday night, feeling afterwards like Kyla, seeing in hindsight that it had been intentional if not conscious. Got drunk and nasty and picked on Ben until they got back to her place, he shouted at her, and then she felt justified in shouting back, and blasted him with his complacency, his arrogance, his selfishness, and other assorted sins.

He defended himself at first; he even lied. He insisted that he had asked her about it and that she had agreed. He insisted this for two hours. She argued that if this had happened, she would have known it, but he did not give it up. He moved from the expectation of compliance to flattery. It would be so painful to him without her that he could not even consider going without her and so had imagined this conversation she claimed they never had – although he remembered it distinctly – and had simply taken it for granted that she would go with him.

She shrieked. *'Fuck off, Ben!'*

One advantage to not using indecorous language is that when you do use it, it carries quite a wallop. Mira had, in the last year, uttered words that had been foreign to her tongue, but she had done this mainly with her women friends, rarely in front of Ben. Like her mother, she had categories.

He stopped dead in the middle of a sentence. He looked at her. He lowered his eyes. He said: 'You're right. I'm sorry. I don't know why I did that. But I think – Mira, I mean it – that the last thing I said was true. I can't imagine going without you. It would be too painful. I couldn't stand it.'

He looked up at her again. She was looking at him with a twisted mouth, and tears were streaming down her cheeks.

'Yes, I believe that, Ben,' she said in a hushed voice. 'You wanted to go, and it would hurt you to go without me, and so you simply assumed I would go with you because that was the simplest solution to the problem. And you never, never once,' she rose, and her voice rose, 'never thought about me! About my needs, my life, my desires! You *eradicated* me, me as a person apart from you, as successfully as Norm did!'

She ran from the room and into the toilet and locked the door. She sat there weeping. Ben sat for a long time, smoking his little foul-smelling cigarettes down to the last half inch. Eventually the bathroom door opened, and Mira came out and went into the kitchen and poured a drink. Ben sat, his mouth pursing and unpursing. He put out his cigarette and lighted another. Mira returned and sat down across from him. She crossed her legs lotus-fashion. Her eyes were puffy, but her face looked bony, austere, and her back was very straight.

'Okay,' he said. 'Okay. Your needs, your life, your desires. What are they?'

Mira seemed almost to squirm. 'I don't know exactly . . .'

He leaped forward, pointing one finger. 'Aha!'

'Shut up, Ben,' she said coldly. 'I don't know exactly, because I haven't had enough room in my life to think about what I wanted. But I know I love what I'm doing now, and that I'd like to go on doing it. I want to finish my dissertation. Beyond that, I can't want, because I don't know what I can get. I learned long ago, before I was twenty,' she said bitterly, 'not to want what I could not get. It hurts too much. Anyway, I think I'd like to teach. I know I want to do literary criticism, and I *will* finish my dissertation. And,' she turned her head aside and said, with a phlegmy throat, 'I also love you and would not like to separate from you. I want you too.'

He was across the room in two bounds, was kneeling on the floor before her chair, and had her in his arms, his head in her lap.

'I love you too, don't you see? Mira, don't you see? I can't bear the thought of separating from you!'

'Yes,' she said coldly. 'I see that. I also see that you were willing to eradicate me in order to keep me. Ironic. That's what Val says. The paradox of what gets called love.'

He sat back on the floor and crossed his legs. He sipped her drink. 'Okay. What can we do then? Mira, will you come to Lianu with me?'

'And what should I do in Il-lianu?' she lilted, but he did not catch her allusion.

'I don't know. I really don't. Look, I'll do everything I can . . . I don't know what will be available. But we'll buy all the books you need, we'll Xerox every article – I'll help you. We'll take it all down there with us. We'll subscribe to every journal that you think is important.

618

And you can write your dissertation there. There's no real problem. You can mail your copy to Everts. And after that . . .'

'And after that?' Her voice surprised her. It was so low, so cold, so controlled. It was not the self she had known.

He sighed. He took her hand. 'Look, sweetheart, I can't say there's much down there for you. Surely I can get you a secretarial job in a government office, possibly even a job as a transla – no, you can't speak Lianish. But something.'

'I want to teach.'

He sighed and slumped. 'Ten years ago,' he waved his arms around, 'that would have been possible. Now? I just don't think so. There are still a few white teachers there, but they're being phased out, and mostly they're in sectarian schools.' He looked directly at her. 'I don't think that will be possible.'

'Yet,' her mouth twisted as if she were about to cry again, 'you simply assumed I would go. Knowing I've spent the last five years of my life preparing to teach.'

His head drooped. 'I'm sorry,' he said, with pain in his voice.

They sat silent for a while. 'I won't be down there forever,' he said finally. 'The days of whites in Africa are numbered. We'll come back.' He looked up at her again.

She looked at him thoughtfully. 'Yes. That's true.' Her heart rose. The thing could be worked out. With rising excitement, she said, 'And if you don't get thrown out in a couple of years, and I feel stultified, I could always come back. My dissertation should be finished. Of course it will be difficult to do it so far from a library. It will take much longer than it needs to. But I could spend the time waiting for books . . . gardening,' she smiled, for the first time.

His brow was clouded. 'But, Mira, sweetheart, you couldn't just go off and abandon your child.'

'My child?'

He started. 'Well, sure. Isn't that what this is all about? Our kid. The one we're going to have.'

She froze. Her entire body felt freezing cold. She felt as if she had taken a drug, or were dying, and was pressed against some terrible wall where only basic truths could be uttered, and had found hers, and it horrified her, it was *I am, I am, I am.* And the second basic truth came right after the first, the way the lower part of a wave follows the upper: *I want, I want, I want.* And in the next second she realized that these were two statements she had never felt permitted to utter, or even to think. Cold, in a white frigid corner, she opened her blue lips:

'I don't want to have another child, Ben.'

It all fell apart then. Ben was hurt, shocked, whatever. He could understand her not wanting to have another child with Norm, or anyone else, perhaps, but not with him. They argued, he passionately, she desperately, for she was arguing against herself. She loved Ben, she would have loved (once, long ago) to have his child, it would have been joy (once, long ago) to go with him to a new place and grow flowers and bake bread and talk to a little one pattering around learning to say, 'Hot! Mats hot!' and have him come home at night and explain to her the subtleties of Marcusan theory while she explained to him the subtleties of Wallace Stevens' versification. Assuming he still had the leisure to be interested in such discussions. But now (after forty years) she wanted to do her own work, she wanted to pursue this stuff, this scholarship that she loved so much. It would be a sacrifice to go to Africa – it would hurt her career, would slow her work. But she was willing to do it, she would take the books with her, she would have things sent out. But she could not, no, she could not have another child. Enough, she said. Enough.

There would be plenty of help in Africa, Ben said. And when we come back? Or suppose I need something here and have to come back for a few months? That could be arranged, he said reluctantly. She had enough experience to be able to translate what was reluctance now to furious refusal later. And what about when they came back? The child would still be hers, although he was the one who wanted it. It would be her responsibility. There was not plenty of help here. He would do what he could, he said, but he was too honest to promise more.

She sat alone with her brandy, late. She and Ben did not break up, they simply did not see each other very often. There was little impulse for it, because every time they did see each other, they had an argument. She felt that Ben was regarding her from a height, that with part of his mind he was looking down coldly at this woman he had loved for almost two years whom he had just discovered to be selfish and egotistical. When they slept together, their sex life was poor : he was mechanical and she uninspired. She felt terribly squashed at his manner; she felt an intense need to protest, to justify, to vindicate herself from his unspoken charge. But she was too proud to do that, she understood that his superiority, her abasement, had nothing to do with them, were cultural accretions, that humanly he was not superior, she not beneath, but still . . .

She felt utterly alone. Val did not answer the phone. Iso and Kyla and Clarissa could not help, they listened to her, but they did not understand what it was like to be forty and alone, what did they know about aloneness? She tried to tot things up in columns. Column one – last chance for happy love; column two – what? Myself. Myself. She remembered sitting alone on the porch of her mother's house, insisting on *myself*. How horribly selfish! Maybe she was what Ben seemed to think she was.

She pulled at her hair, hurting her scalp, trying to think it through. All she had to do was pick up the phone, say, Ben, I'll go, Ben, I love you. He'd be there in a moment, he'd love her the way he used to love her. Her hand stopped in midair. The way he used to love her. Then he didn't love her anymore? No, not when she insisted on her own desires. But if he didn't love her insisting on her own desires, how did he love her? When her desires were the same as his. She poured another brandy. She felt herself getting drunk, but she didn't care. Truths were discovered in drunkenness sometimes. If he only loved her when her desires were the same as his, and stopped loving her when her desires were different from his, then that meant he didn't love her but only a reflection of himself, a complement who could comprehend and appreciate, but who was smaller and flattering.

But that was how it had been at the beginning. She felt smaller than he, she flattered him, sincerely, because she found him more important, larger, better than herself.

That was what he had been led to expect.

She put her glass down.

That was what she had led him to expect. And now she was reneging.

But she was different now.

She was different partly because of him.

That didn't count. He was different partly because of her too.

She leaned her head against the chair back. Suppose she went to him passionately, the way she loved it when he came to her, and grabbed him, the way she loved it when he grabbed her, and demanded, insisted, 'I love you! I want you! Stay here in Cambridge with me. Let us go on as we have. You can make a career here too!'

She smiled grimly and picked up the brandy. 'Hah!' she heard. It was Val's voice.

She pulled her feet up onto the seat of the chair and wrapped the blanket around them and her legs. She was sipping her brandy, and rocking in the chair, rocking her body back and forth, wrapped in the blanket from neck down. It will get you in the end: wasn't that what she had said? Mira was smiling, but it was a grim hard smile, it had no mirth. The phone rang. She jumped up, checking her watch. Past one. One of the boys, probably. But it was Iso.

'Mira. I just heard. Val's dead.'

CHAPTER SIX

1

Yes. That was what happened: everything opened up, anything seemed possible, and then everything closed up, dilation, constriction. It will get you in the end. But she also said: Why does every order have to be a permanent order? It was all that that led me to this beach. I see I have dandelion greens in my hand. How did they get there, do you suppose?

If there is dilation and constriction, then there has to be dilation again. Either that or death. Law of nature. If it isn't it ought to be.

Val was dead. It happened right under our eyes, but we didn't even notice it. Mira thought about Val only when she needed to talk to her. No, that's not fair. Val mattered to her, to all of them. Just not as much as she would perhaps have liked to matter, not as much as any of us would like to matter.

What happened took some piecing together. Roughly, it ran like this. A young black woman, Anita Morrow, who worked as a domestic during the day, attended classes at Northeastern at night. She wanted to be an English teacher. (The prosecutor held this up to ridicule during her trial, claiming Anita was nearly illiterate.) Anita had been walking from her class to the MTA one night when a man attacked her. He came up behind her and put his arm across her throat and dragged her into an alley. He threw her down and pulled her skirt up, but Anita had grown up on the streets and she had a knife in her pocket. She kicked him in the chin, and got up fast, and when he grabbed her again, she stabbed him. She kept stabbing him, blood and fear pounding in her ears, but the noises, her cries and his, had attracted some people. They saw her stabbing him after he had fallen, and they ran to stop her. They held on to her until the police arrived.

She was charged with murder. The man was from a respectable white family, he had a wife and six kids. The knife was Anita's. The prosecutor claimed she was a prostitute, she had lured him into the alley, and when he backed out, stabbed him in order to rob him. The major issue in the trial was whether or not Anita was educable. If she was attending school simply to find more trade, then she was a prostitute, and prostitutes can't be raped. These things were not stated, but implied.

Anita was interviewed by the Boston *Phoenix*. Claims were made that in the *Phoenix* interview, her grammar and syntax were cleaned up to make her look literate. The *Phoenix* quoted her: 'I want to go back to where I went to school. They couldn't help it, the teachers there – we was wild, we wouldn't listen. But we didn't learn, you know? But I know I could talk to them kids because I know them, I am one of them, and I know I could make them see what I see. Like there's this Blake poem, it goes "My mother groan'd! my father wept. / Into the dangerous world I leapt." Now you know babies don't leap. That man was telling us about it, he was saying life springs out, leaps out, even into danger, even into what's terrible like it was terrible there, in my neighborhood. Then it says: "Helpless, naked, piping loud" – just as if a baby's crying was a kind of music, like whistling down a dark street. I know the feeling, but I carry my knife too. And then "Like a fiend hid in a cloud." Wow! He's saying a baby's a fiend! Well you know as well as me that's true. That's true!' She laughed, her eyes glowing, the reporter claimed, and went on talking about poetry.

The state brought expert witnesses to judge Anita's grammar, syntax, and spelling. She was found sadly wanting; she would never, they insisted, be able to achieve teacher certification. Anita Morrow was found guilty of murder on grounds of illiteracy. Her trial had been attended, all the way through, by a group of militant feminists. The day of her sentencing, they picketed the courthouse. Only the *Phoenix* covered that, but they had a picture of the women shouting and waving their signs. Val was among them. Anita was sentenced to twenty years to life for first-degree murder. There was a picture of her being led from the courthouse, her face a child's, full of bewilderment and terror. 'He tried to rape me, so I stabbed him,' she said incredulously to the group of women before they led her back into the armed car.

Val's group was small and did not have many resources, but apparently they were large enough to warrant federal attention, because an FBI informant infiltrated them. It was only because of her that anyone found out anything afterward. The group was outraged by what had happened to Morrow, and they planned to rescue her. They had elaborate arrangements for after the rescue. She would be sent from group to group of sympathetic women until the case died down, then shipped to Cuba or Mexico, until they could find contacts who would forge the papers for her to teach school someplace. It was a crazy plan, born out of utter desperation. Perhaps they did not expect it to work. Perhaps subconsciously they foresaw what would happen, and were willing for it to happen to bring the thing to public notice.

On the day when Anita was to be transferred to the state prison (because she was deemed unreliable and dangerous to society, she was not released pending her appeal), the women arrived singly, dressed in jeans or skirts, disguised as just women, and hung around the street until Morrow was brought out to the van. Then suddenly, they mobilized in a circle, pulling guns out of skirts and coats.

But the authorities expected them. Behind the brick wall was a policeman, two, three: they stepped out with machine guns – the women had only handguns – and mowed them down. Four, five, six, seven, eight policemen came out with machine guns. Two pedestrians were wounded, the six women were all dead. Morrow was thrust into the van, and it sped off. That was all. But the police had sent so many bullets into two of the bodies that as they were lying there dead, they exploded, wounding some of the approaching cops. Later it was claimed the women had been carrying grenades that did not, for some odd reason, explode before. Val's was one of the exploded bodies. One of the cops died, and was given a ceremonial funeral: the mayor even attended. The other lived, but his face and his thighs were scarred.

There were a lot of people at Val's funeral. Iso said probably half of them were FBI agents, but I don't think so, I think Val had a lot of secret friends, people she'd spoken to once and said something real to. I'll bet that minister who was a rapist at heart was there. Howard Perkins was there, and Neil Truax, Val's onetime husband. Chris brought him over and introduced him to us. Chris looked pale and blank and helpless. Her father was handsome and elegant, nicely gray at the temples, nicely tanned for December, nicely tight across the stomach (tennis or squash). He shook his head as he shook our hands, kept shaking his head, glancing at Chris, put his hand on her head and smiled at her and touseled her hair. She just looked at him.

'It was irresponsible, simply irresponsible! She had a daughter to care for . . . she was always irresponsible . . .' He gazed off into the clouds. We looked at him. He turned back to Chris and put his arm around her shoulders. 'Come on, honey, you come home with Daddy,' he smiled, and said good-bye, gracefully, to us.

Chris glanced at us with blank eyes. Mira started, she put out her hand, but they had turned, they were walking away. Chris looked tiny and helpless, weighed down by a large hand on her shoulder.

Howard Perkins came up to us blinking. 'She was great, you know, really great. Once. My theory is she went nuts in menopause. Women do, you know? She was getting old, she was no longer attractive to men, and her basic hostility to them took over . . .'

'Fuck off, Howard,' Mira said, and everyone turned and looked at her. Howard looked at her offended, then his ectoplasm drifted off into the crowd.

The friends waited until the crowd had left. Ben was

there, with his arm around Mira, and Harley was there and Iso and Clarissa and Kyla, and Tad, looking gangly and lost, and Grant, looking fierce, and Bart, who watched as Chris went off with her father. He turned to Mira, he shrugged, he spread his arms. 'Nothing really changes,' he said with a full throat. She took his hand. 'It does, it does. It just takes longer than we do.'

The group walked slowly toward their cars. They did not speak. Then Ben and Tad and Grant got into Harley's car, and Iso and Kyla and Clarissa got into Mira's car, and the two cars drove back, dropping people at their homes, each of them returning alone, separate.

Mira got out her brandy and sat by the telephone, her head in her hands. The phone didn't ring. Ben's arm around her at the funeral had brought it all back, the warmth of love, the consolation that love brought to the terribleness of life. She picked up the receiver and dialed Ben's number. It rang and rang. She put it down. She felt frantic. She tried to remember all the arguments, the reasoning she had brought to bear on their split, the words, words, words she had said to herself to explain, to break, to cut it in half. They seemed ridiculous now, with that mass of exploded flesh piled into a grave and labeled Val. Val of the dashiki and the glass of wine lifted in air, the sudden loud laugh, the lifted eyebrow, Val who could not be put down but who was now put out, and that was in store for her too, for Mira, and for Ben, Ben who was so vivid, his thick dark-haired arms, his hair streaming uncontrollably out of his scalp like grass, his eyes, brown and alive, his laughter. . . . She picked up the phone and dialed again. No answer. Life was too short and too cold to give up love. Even if it meant giving up everything else. She poured another brandy and dialed again. No answer.

So what if it ended the same way her first marriage had? So what if she had a child at forty-one or -two and never wrote her dissertation, or wrote it and got the degree but then sat in Africa fanning herself, watching her child play with the strange flowers that grew in the compound? And it might not end. It might stay vital and

627

warm, their love, they might continue to excite each other forever, they might get in bed every night for the next thirty years and reach out to each other with the same desire, they might wait to see each other every day for the next thirty years with the same interest and eagerness. . . .

That was ridiculous. Ridiculous. That was the thing of all things most unlikely. That was why it had been turned into the ideal. From the ideal it got turned into a norm that somehow never materialized. She felt unbearably alone. She got up, put on her coat, picked up her brandy bottle, and drove to Iso's. Kyla and Clarissa were already there. They were all sitting in silence. She passed the bottle around. They poured brandy into glasses and held them up: 'To Val,' they said, and drank.

'There's just nothing to say. There are no words,' someone said.

No words to wrap her body in like a shroud, like clean white sanitized bandages, around and around and around until she was all clean and white and santized and pure, her blood dried, her mass of exploded flesh covered, her stink deodorized, and she sanitary, polite, acceptable for public notice, a mummy propped on a table for public ceremony, its very presence a promise, a guarantee that she will no longer disturb or threaten, that she will not rise up in rage with hair wild on her head, a knife in her hand, screaming, 'No! No! Kill before you accept!'

'Yes. But did she accept. She consented to her eradication just as if she had been Stella Dallas.'

'But there's no way not to do that, is there? I mean, whether you fight or submit, climb on a crag or creep in a cave, you're participating in it, in your destiny, you're creating it, you're responsible, aren't you?'

'But shit, man, we don't have to contribute to that, we don't have to help slide her into the deep freeze by labeling her, by defining her, she was this, she was that – neat as an obituary.'

Words soaking up her juices like the brown paper the

fishmonger wraps around an eviscerated, decapitated, scaled fish.

'But saying nothing obliterates her too. You know, the Greek word for truth – *alētheia* – doesn't mean the opposite of falsehood. It means tthe opposite of *lēthē*, oblivion. Truth is what is remembered.'

'All right. Then let's say: she died for truth, and she died of it. Some truths are mortal illnesses.'

'All truths are mortal illnesses.'

They clinked their glasses again, and drank them down.

2

The rest of us survived.

Kyla grew disgusted with her search for a topic. She went over to the law school and asked the professors if she could sit in on their classes. After a month, she was bouncing again. She was furious – 'All law cares about is property!' – but full of life. Law was something that worked the way she thought, something she could get into, something that might help. She applied to law schools for the fall, a late application, but she was accepted at Stanford, and went out there immediately and got a job to save the money and pay her tuition.

I had a letter from her last month. She's graduated from law school now and is cramming for her bar exams. She has a 'little job' for a judge as law clerk. That doesn't sound like a little job to me. I expect to see her come flying through my window like Batwoman, bearing in her hand the new ten commandments.

Clarissa stayed out the semester, reading documents more and literature less; in June, she went to visit a cousin of hers in Chicago, and walked into a Chicago TV station, with suggestions for some new, historical, lively programming. They hired her on the spot. She came back to Cambridge for her possessions, her new, older face glowing. She claimed TV was the most potent force for social change in the history of humankind. I said I though it was the most conservative force in existence, except for the Catholic Church. As usual with Clarissa and me, we agreed in our disagreement.

These days she is the producer of a Chicago program that is being touted as the most interesting and spectacular new program in the decade, and there is talk of putting it on national TV. Clarissa, though, doesn't get flapped by such things. She goes through her days efficiently, intelligently, with her eyes firmly fixed on ideas and people at once. She proves it can be done. It can be done. Someday, I expect to see her come flying through my TV screen like Superwoman, holding in her hand a list of candidates for President, all women.

Grete married Avery. They both finished their degrees. They seemed to be settling down to a quiet, culturally rich Cambridge life, but suddenly they took off for California. Grete got a job in a film. I don't know how. How do people do such things? She had only a small part, but she was very good and very beautiful, and she kept getting jobs. She finally landed a major role in a major film with an all-male cast except for her. She wrote that she's going to change the Hollywood biases after she has enough money and fame. She wants to direct movies, maybe even write them, or get the old group together to write them, movies with strong women's parts, movies with people in them like Val and Iso and Kyla and Clarissa and herself.

Avery is in southern California, teaching in an alternative school. He has no money, but Grete has lots. They spend every other weekend together, and are trying to keep their marriage intact. They sound as though they're rather enjoying this pain.

Ava is also married. I had a letter about her from Iso recently. Ava went to New York with only tremulous hopes, but did well. She did actually perform on the stage a couple of times, in the corps de ballet of an opera company, in a rear line. She kept dancing and practising. But then she fell one day. Everyone was solicitous; they didn't laugh. That bothered her. She knew they would have laughed if she'd been young. She fell again, and this time bruised her leg a little. Everyone ran to help

630

her. She thought a lot about that. She was weary. She had a job as a secretary in a public relations office, and had been dating a young man, younger than herself, and very much in love with her. He had asked her to marry him, and she had told him, with her uncompromising honesty, that she did not love him. But it was wearing her out, working five days a week, dancing four nights a week and Saturdays, and occasionally giving performances, keeping her apartment up to whatever degree she kept it, having, at the very least, to come home at night and fix some toast and tea. The third time she fell, she agreed to marry the young man if he did not object to a wife who did not love him. He did not. And now she is living in Pittsburgh, I guess she must be living as a housewife. I can't conceive of it. Ava, cooking and cleaning? There is no way I can see it. Only tense and surrendering over the piano, her thin shoulders hunched up, her fingers in command, as she communicates with it, this music, this instrument, her face hovering over it as tender and yielding as the face of love, as sad as that most tragic of mothers, Hecuba, and as strict and severe as the worst martinet. Or on her *pointes*, for I saw her dance once, lifted totally out of herself, in the music, become the music, translated into music.

But Iso swears she is married and living in Pittsburgh. It must be. Iso says she goes to see the ballet companies that visit that city, whenever they do. She wrote Iso: 'I keep falling. I am old. There is no hope.'

Iso herself is splendid. There is something to be said for lowered expectations. She finished her dissertation within another year and almost immediately it was accepted for publication. She's on a grant now, working on another book, living in England and working at the Bodleian and the British Museum. She is currently living with a marvelous woman she met in a pub who is divorced and has two young children and drives a cab. Iso writes about the children as if they were her own, and signs her name Isolde, but she also says she does not for a moment expect this to last. I don't expect her to come flying through anything except the air, and she will hover lightly and drop little fragments of Middle English down upon us like a blessing, before she moves on to deserts new.

She is still the center of us. There were bad feelings for a while, but in time Kyla wrote her a letter, then Clarissa. Mira and Grete had never stopped. We all write each other too, but it is Iso we all care most about. In my mind I will always see her striding jauntily down the street the way she looked when she first came out of disguise. She will bend to talk to a child with a dog; suddenly the child's mother appears. She has streaming hair and black boots, and a frightened look. Iso will talk to her for a few minutes and wham! Mother and child and dog and Iso will go off for a walk in the park, a cup of coffee, a nice home-cooked meal.

Ben went to Africa. Mira discovered later that Harley had driven Ben straight to the airport; he left right after the funeral, in fact, had delayed his flight so he could be there. Mira never heard from him again, but she heard about him through the grapevine. He stayed in Africa for a year and a half before they asked him to leave, and came back to a cushioned chair at a large state university. He is a consultant to a number of foundations and to the federal government, and is considered the world's expert on Lianu. At thirty-eight, he is a high success. He married the woman who was his secretary in Lianu, and they have two babies. She takes care of the babies and the house and him because he is very busy, very successful. They live in a large house in a good neighborhood, and people think they are a model couple. They are invited everywhere and women everywhere are attracted to him. His wife shows signs of whiny clingingness. Yes.

So, you see, the story has no ending. They go on, and who knows what they will make of their world in ten years, or twenty. Tad, I've heard, entered a Zen monastery. But that may be only a rumor. Grant is teaching in some little college in Oregon or Washington, where he is considered a firebrand, but is uncertain of tenure. And Chris. My heart hurts when I think of her. I don't know what happened to Chris.

And that's all, I guess, except for Mira. She finished her dissertation, and when it was accepted, took her divorce money and went to Europe and traveled around alone for eight months, breathing it in, sucking it up. Then she came back and tried to get a job, but the market had dried up and nobody wanted to hire a woman over forty even if she had a Harvard degree, and so she ended up at this little community college near the coast of Maine, and she walks the beach every day, and drinks brandy every night, and wonders if she's going mad.

Clark called me the other night at two o'clock in the morning. I was sitting as usual, with a brandy and a cigarette. He said 'Hi! I had nothing better to do and I wanted to talk to somebody and I thought – who else would be awake at two o'clock in the morning? So I called you.' He laughed when I cursed him out, and he talked for an hour about this girl in his math class and general horniness, and his vagueness about a thing he was supposed to have, namely, a career, and his wish that he could just marry some rich girl and cook and take care of her house. I talked about the lack of men in my world – not being in any math class – and general horniness, and my vagueness about a thing I was supposed to have, namely, a career. We laughed a lot. Only I won, because in addition to all my other problems, I'm forty-four, which is a far cry from twenty-one.

There are things I can do, I guess. But I have bad dreams. They are much more real to me than what is outside me, out there in that dinky town with its one lunch counter and its library that doubles as historical monument because it is actually a tiny eighteenth-century house, its one church that few people attend, and its one supermarket.

I have these dreams every night. Last night I dreamed that I am living alone in an apartment very like the one I had in Cambridge. I am lying in bed and a man appears in the room. I am a little frightened, but I look at him with curiosity. He is white, taller than I am, and he has a scar on his lip. But the thing that I notice most

633

is his eyes. They are empty. The threat he poses by being there does not frighten me, but the mindlessness in his eyes does. It is terrifying and repulsive: He has things in his hands – a pipe and a penknife. It is his mindlessness, though, not his tools, that makes him physically threatening. But I sit up, I act unfrightened, I act even agreeable. I say, 'It's cold, don't you think? Do you mind if I turn up the heat?' He nods, and I leave the room, and as soon as I do, I run down the stairs and out the door, and down another flight to the front door, and then I have to decide what to do. I hear his steps on the flight above. I decide to take my chances outside.

Suddenly, I come a little closer to consciousness. This often happens to me in dreams. I come to, just a little, although at the time I think I am totally awake, and I decide to change something in the dream. Later, when I am really awake, I can look back and see I never was awake, I only dreamed that I was awake. Anyway, that is what happens in this dream. I come to enough to realize that downstairs from my apartment in Cambridge, there are only houses which at this time of night will be dark and silent. So I decide to put a little store next door to my house, a store that is conveniently open. I run into the store and ask them to hide me and to call the police. They do. That is good. I have done this in other dreams, and they have refused, been frightened themselves and refused.

There is a series of scenes I don't recall. Then I am in town, I am in a police station, I am in a police car. I give directions, they find my house, they go in to clear it out. But now there are five of them, all brutal in their mindlessness, sitting cross-legged in a circle on my living room floor. I know that it is not their bodies which threaten me, but the vacancy in their eyes. The police take them out, and I see but do not remark that the apartment is empty, utterly empty. The police remove them and I walk away feeling that that at least is that; then I return to the living room and see them still there. I run out to call back the police, but the stairs have been removed. I don't know what to do. I hold on to the curving banister and slide down.

Later, I go back up. The men are gone. So is everything else. The apartment is bare, cold. The police come up to check on me, they tell me to keep my front door closed. I go to lock it, but the inner doorknob is missing. I cry out: : 'He's taken off the handle.' I don't any longer know who is standing outside the door. I don't any longer care. I am confronting my predicament. If I close the door it will lock and I will never be able to open it from the inside. It can be opened from the outside, but I do not believe in the tale of Sleeping Beauty. Even if I did, I could hardly qualify. What prince is going to cut through brambles to reach *me*? Besides they are mostly spurious princes, from ahistoric European duchies. I stand there in terror. If I close the door I will be trapped; if I do not, I may wake up again to face a set of mindless eyes, a vacant, unthinking threat. I wake up.

August is nearly over. School will open in two weeks and I have done nothing, I have not read Chomsky, or any new fairy tales, or found a better composition text. It doesn't matter.

I am a good scholar, and in a different market. I could have done decent work, but in this one, it seems hopeless. Maybe I'll do it anyway, just for myself. What else do I have to do? as Norm used to ask me.

I guess I keep expecting that there should be something out there that would make it easier to be in here. Like the snails, you know? They don't do anything except exist. This is not the world I would have wished.

I have done one thing: I have laid them to rest, my dear, dear ghosts. 'No!' one screams. Maybe I have let you live, my dear ghosts. She settles down, but she's watching me. I can feel her eyes.

It is over. It is time to begin something new, if I can find the energy, if I can find the heart.

The beach grows emptier every day. I can walk for a long time without anyone turning to stare at the mad-woman. In fact, people haven't been staring much lately. They seems to have grown used to me. Sometimes someone even nods and says 'Mornin'' as they pass, as if I were one of them.

The sand is beginning to turn amber. The sky is very pale. It grows paler day by day, and toward the north it is white, moving to stark immaculate whiteness.

Life is very short.

The sky grows icier day by day; it is large and vacant and mindless.

Some days I feel dead, I feel like a robot, treading out time. Some days I feel alive, terribly alive, with hair like wires and a knife in my hand. Once in a while my mind slips and I think I am back in my dream and that I have shut the door, the one without a handle on the inside. I imagine that tomorrow I will be pounding and screaming to be let out, but no one will hear, no one will come. Other times I think I have gone over the line, like Lily, like Val, and can no longer speak anything but truth. An elderly man stopped me the other day as I was walking along the beach, a white-haired man with a nasty face, but he smiled and said, 'Nice day, isn't it?' and I glared and snapped at him, 'Of course you have to say that, it's the only day you have!'

He considered that, nodded, and moved on.

Maybe I need a keeper. I don't want them to lock me up and give me electric shock until I forget. Forget: lēthē: the opposite of truth.

I have opened all the doors in my head.

I have opened all the pores in my body.

But only the tide rolls in.

ABOUT THE AUTHOR

Marilyn French was born in New York City, grew up on Long Island and attended Hofstra College and Harvard University, where she received her doctorate. She has taught at Hofstra, Harvard and Holy Cross College, and was most recently a Mellon Fellow at Harvard. She is the author of *The Book as World: James Joyce's Ulysses*, short stories, and numerous scholarly articles. *The Women's Room* is her first novel. She now lives in the Boston area.

3.50

All Sphere Books are available at your bookshop or
newsagent, or can be ordered from the following address:
Sphere Books, Cash Sales Department,
P.O. Box 11, Falmouth, Cornwall.

Please send cheque or postal order (no currency), and allow
19p for postage and packing for the first book plus 9p
per copy for each additional book ordered up to a
maximum charge of 73p in U.K.

Customers in Eire and B.F.P.O. please allow 19p for
postage and packing for the first book plus 9p per copy
for the next 6 books, thereafter 3p per book.

Overseas customers please allow 20p for postage and
packing for the first book and 10p per copy for each
additional book.